Don't Open This Book!

Don't Open This Book!

Selected and Edited by
Marvin Kaye

Doubleday Direct, Inc.
Garden City, New York

Published by GuildAmerica® Books,
an imprint and registered trademark of
Doubleday Direct, Inc., Department GB,
401 Franklin Avenue,
Garden City, New York 11530

Acknowledgments on page 590

The author and publisher have made a thorough effort to locate all persons
having any rights or interests in the material presented in this book and to
secure all necessary reprint permissions. If any required acknowledgments have
been omitted inadvertently or any rights overlooked, we regret the error and
will correct the oversight in future editions of the book.

Book design by Paul Randall Mize

To Mary Stuart
and Our Fellow Bookpals at P.S. 128, Manhattan—
Mary Bacon
Beth Dixon
Joanne Dorian
Taina Elg
Anita Flanagan
Leila Holiday
Connie Roderick
Ann Russell
Harry Shaw
Sherrie Villano
Billie Lou Watt
Judi West
and especially to
Jennie Delaney, Librarian at P.S. 128
and
Blanca Battino, Principal at P.S. 128

Contents

A Word of Warning

SINCE LANGUAGE is the most effective tool our species possesses for communicating ideas, stirring emotion and effecting change, it is no surprise that the free flow and potency of language is always under attack . . . with predictable non-results.

When governments, sects and self-appointed "moralists" try to legislate what they want you to—pick one—Read/Think/Worship, they fail to reckon with the healthy perversity of human nature as epitomized by the precept: "If they give you ruled paper, write the other way."* To brand a book unsuitable is an important step toward making it required reading. It is a variety of censorship as ridiculous as telling people to count to ten without thinking of polka-dotted elephants.

So when you ignored the titular warning and opened this book, you exercised your right to read whatever you damn well please—and good for you!

Or maybe not.

There is, after all, another side to censorship: the common sense variety that forbids the wanton cry of "Fire!" in a crowded theatre. Brains, like computers, are capable of freezing up and refusing to function. Some minds know how to—pick one—Ad-

---

* Attributed in Ray Bradbury's anti-censorship novel, *Fahrenheit 451*, to the Spanish Nobel Prize poet Juan Ramón Jiménez.

just/Learn/Synthesize. Some don't. For them, perhaps the caveat is relevant, and a little knowledge is indeed a dangerous thing.

So the book you hold in your hands has a warning label. By cracking its pages, you run the risk of reading some very potent fiction. Some of it is merely cautionary, echoing the conservative endings of several 1940's horror movies, "He tampered with knowledge Man is not meant to know." Other selections echo comedienne Anna Russell's declaration that if you don't do what you're supposed to, you just might end up "teddibly interesting!"

But reader, beware . . . some of the stories in *Don't Open This Book!* afford truly dreadful glimpses into the dark side of—pick one—Life/Death/Human Nature, or what Joseph Conrad called "the formidable Work of the Seven Days, into which mankind seems to have blundered unbidden."

This is neither "hype" nor hyperbolic. *Don't Open This Book!* is a Pandora's box chock-full of old and new tales of weird fantasy, taboo science, and harrowing revelations of souls in torment.

There is still time to close its covers. If not—well, don't say you *weren't* warned . . .

—MARVIN KAYE
New York City
December 1997

The
Pandora
Principle

Eve and Pandora are mythic sisters.

When Eve ate the prohibited fruit, she gained knowledge both precious and dreadful, for as Lord Byron observed, "They who know the most must mourn the deepest o'er the fatal truth, the Tree of Knowledge is not that of Life."

Pandora's action is an equally powerful metaphor. Her insistence on learning what was under the cover of the taboo jar—or box, in another version of the fable—loosed humanity's troubles upon the world. When she slammed the lid back on, the only thing she managed to keep in the container was Hope, a commodity whose sole cosmic purpose, according to Elmer Rice, is to keep us from totally going to pieces.

The eight tales in this opening section—half of them never published before—demonstrate the dire effects of dipping into dangerous tomes and other sources of forbidden lore.

Edward D. Hoch

The Problem
of the Country Mailbox

Books literally can be dangerous to open, as Dr. Sam Hawthorne discovers in this story from the pages of Ellery Queen's Mystery Magazine. *Former Mystery Writers of America president* EDWARD D. HOCH *is one of the most prolific writers in the history of mystery fiction. His bibliography numbers more short stories than Ed can remember; the current tally is somewhere over eight hundred, of which fifty-plus tales feature the sage New England physician you are about to meet. Dr. Sam also played detective in "The Problem of the Pilgrims Windmill," featured in my 1990 Doubleday anthology,* Haunted America.

THE AUTUMN of '38 (Dr. Sam Hawthorne told his visitor) was a time when the national press was full of Chamberlain and the Munich Pact with Hitler. War was on the horizon, and if it retreated for a time, most people realized that was only temporary. It would come, sooner or later, and the streets of Europe would run with blood.

Back home in Northmont, I was concerned with more prosaic matters that autumn. There were vaccinations to give and allergies to treat. We had more doctors practicing in town and there was a steadily growing population. We had not yet seen the boom that would come in the postwar years, but there were signs of change everywhere. A small private college was being built in a neighboring town, with plans to open its doors for the fall semester of 1939. Though that was still a year away, it had encouraged a man named Josh Vernon to open a bookstore in our town.

Josh's Books was a small store just off the town square. The previous tenant had been a shop selling penny candy out of large glass jars, and I imagined I could still smell the chocolate and licorice when I entered. Josh Vernon was a slender man with a graying moustache and pince-nez glasses that gave him a scholarly demeanor. I couldn't have imagined him as a butcher or baker, but he looked right at home among the bookshelves.

Though he carried a large stock of used books, Vernon also stocked the newest titles from New York and Boston publishers. If he had little space for Faulkner's *The Unvanquished* or Dinesen's *Out of Africa*, it was a place where one could find *Gone with the Wind, The Late George Apley,* and *The Yearling.* He knew what the market wanted and he supplied it.

"It'll be different next year when the college kids start coming around," he told me one day, puffing on his pipe. "If business goes well, I might be able to enlarge the place and carry more literary titles."

I took down a copy of Cronin's *The Citadel* and thumbed through it. I was naturally intrigued by novels about small-town doctors, even if the towns were an ocean away. "Is this any good?" I asked Josh.

"It's popular. I've sold three or four copies."

"I'll take it." I put down a few dollar bills and he wrapped it in his distinctive green paper and twine.

"I been hearing you're pretty good at solving mysteries, Doc. Some say you're better than Sheriff Lens."

"I've been lucky a few times," I admitted.

"I have a mystery that would baffle even you." He tapped his pipe on the ashtray to empty it, then opened his pouch of tobacco. "One of my regular customers is Aaron DeVille out on the Old Ridge Road. You know him, don't you?"

"Slightly. He's not a patient and he rarely comes to town."

The bookseller relit his pipe. "That's certainly true since his wife died. But he loves books. He subscribes to the *Saturday*

Review of Literature and every week he phones to order something he's seen in there. I've been open two months and I've probably sold him a dozen books. Says he used to order them from Boston, but I'm a lot closer. Of course, sometimes I don't have the books he wants and I have to order them myself, but quite often I can stop by on my way home and drop them in his mailbox."

"That's what I call service."

"But here is where the mystery comes in, Doc. Three times now I have left books in his mailbox and they disappeared!"

"Perhaps the postman takes them," I suggested. "They get fussy when mailboxes are used for things other than mail."

"That was my first thought, but the mail is always delivered on that route around one in the afternoon. Kenny Diggins drives along the Old Ridge right after lunch and fills the boxes from his car. I don't close the store till six and it's usually closer to six-thirty when I drop off the books. DeVille is sometimes watching for me. One time he even waved from the front porch. Then he walked out to the box and it was empty."

"Are there any mischievous children who might be sneaking up and stealing the books?" DeVille had a twelve-year-old son.

"I can't see how, at least not in the most recent instance where he was watching the box all the time."

"Maybe you'd better start pulling into the driveway and handing him the books."

"Isn't this the sort of puzzle you like to solve?"

"Well, yes," I admitted. "But I don't see where a serious crime has been committed. If someone is stealing the books—"

"They certainly are!" he insisted. "Could I call you the next time I make a delivery out there? I'd appreciate it if you could figure out what's happening."

"Sure, you can call me. If I'm not involved with a patient I'll try to help."

That seemed to satisfy him and I departed with my book. In the evening when I left the office I detoured on my way home and drove out the Old Ridge Road past Aaron DeVille's house. The mailbox sat on a raised wooden board with three others, inches apart. Each family's name was painted in small neat letters on the side of the box. DeVille's, one of the middle boxes, looked just like all the others.

Sylvia Grant was a bright young woman who worked part-time in Vernon's bookstore. She was in her twenties, with curly blond hair and eyeglasses with thin black frames that gave her face the appealing look of a studious pixie. Two days after my conversation with Josh Vernon I saw her crossing the town square near the bandstand.

"On your way to the bookstore?" I asked.

"Sure am! Want anything today, Dr. Sam?"

"I might walk over with you." I fell in beside her, though until that moment I hadn't thought about going there. "How's business at the store?"

"Fair. Josh thinks Christmas will be good, if we're not in a war by then."

"We won't be," I said with an assurance I didn't really feel. "Josh was telling me the other day that he's been having trouble delivering books out to Aaron DeVille's place. They keep disappearing out of the mailbox."

"That's what he says. Hard to believe, isn't it?"

"You mean you don't believe it?"

Sylvia shrugged. "DeVille's son is probably taking them somehow."

"Damon?"

"He's a bit precocious. He loves to baffle his dad with some sort of mystery."

"Whatever happened certainly seems to have bothered Josh."

"Well, he's the one who's had to replace the missing books. It's costing him money, a few dollars anyway."

"Do you think Aaron DeVille is lying about the books disappearing from his mailbox?"

"What would be his motive? To get a second copy? That doesn't seem likely."

barn on the DeVille property had been torn down long ago, and a storage shed was now used as a garage. The house itself, some two hundred feet back from the road, was in need of painting, but otherwise it seemed in good shape.

Josh Vernon pulled up by the line of mailboxes. As I'd observed before, each name was painted on the side of a box: Chesnut, Millars, DeVille, Breen. "Put it right in the box, Doc. This is your show."

I opened the mailbox and slid the book in. "Shall I put up the little red flag?"

"Better not. The post office could get really upset about that."

I turned to watch the boxes out the rear window as we drove on about fifty feet. Then Vernon stopped the car just beyond a clump of bushes. "Get out and watch. I'll drive on."

"Do you think I'll see someone?"

"DeVille will be out in a minute. I'm sure he saw us."

I got out quickly, still keeping an eye on the mailboxes. No one had approached them. Then, crouching down so I was partly hidden, I waited.

It didn't take long. A stocky man in his late thirties, whom I recognized as Aaron DeVille, came ambling down the driveway from the direction of the house. As he approached the mailbox I had to admit that I would be the most surprised man in the country if that book wasn't still inside.

DeVille paused before his box and opened it. From my viewing angle down the road I saw him pull the green-wrapped book out of the box and slip it into the pocket of his leather jacket. I almost sighed with relief. Josh Vernon had been wrong. This time, at least, the book hadn't vanished.

As he started back up the driveway DeVille seemed to have second thoughts about the book. He removed it from his pocket, untied the string, and ripped off the paper. I saw him start to open the cover. There was a terrible flash and a sound like a clap of thunder.

I broke from the cover of the bush and ran toward him, knowing even as I ran that Aaron DeVille was beyond the help of a doctor.

Sheriff Lens had been trying to lose weight that autumn, and it hadn't improved his disposition. He left it to his deputies to clean up what was left of Aaron DeVille while he questioned Josh Vernon and me. "You're telling me, Doc, that you were watchin' that mailbox the whole time and nobody came near it?"

"That's what I'm telling you, Sheriff."

He turned to Vernon, who was standing there pale and shaken. "There was a bomb inside that book you delivered, Josh. Looks to me like you're the only one who coulda put it there."

"But I couldn't have, Sheriff! Dr. Sam was with me when I wrapped it. I think he even flipped through the pages."

"That's right," I confirmed with some reluctance.

"He even held the book on his lap during the ride out here. It was never out of his sight."

Sheriff Lens looked at me with a sour expression. "That right, Doc?"

"I'm afraid so."

A few neighbors had been attracted by the explosion, and it was Marta Chesnut from across the road who said suddenly, "What about young Damon? He must still be at his piano lessons!"

Sheriff Lens scowled at her. "Could you go pick him up, Marta? I'll have my deputy drive you."

"Of course," she replied without hesitation.

While we waited for Damon's return the sheriff questioned the other neighbors, Millars and Breen, without learning anything. The three families occupied a trio of small cottage-type houses across the road from the DeVille home. The plots of land had been carved out of another piece of the DeVille farm when it was sold off by Aaron's father. They'd been having dinner when they heard the sound of the explosion and came running.

Sheriff Lens finished with them and came back to me. "What do you think, Doc?"

"I don't want to say, not quite yet."

"There was that case a few years back, the Fourth of July murder, when a firecracker had a stick of dynamite in it—"

"A different thing entirely. In that case the killer was nearby. No one was anywhere near Aaron DeVille. No one but me."

Our conversation was interrupted by the return of the sheriff's car carrying Mrs. Chesnut and the DeVille boy. It was obvious that she'd broken the news to him en route. He emerged crying from the car, clinging to her as she hurried him across the road to her house. "I think it's better if he stays with us tonight," Marta Chesnut explained to the sheriff. "He says there's an aunt in Hartford who should be contacted."

"We'll take care of it," Sheriff Lens assured her. "Could I just have a few words with him?"

"I think later would be better. He's had a terrible shock." Her husband had taken young Damon inside and she followed him.

"We'd better have a look inside the house," the sheriff said. "DeVille left the door open when he came out for the book."

I glanced at Josh Vernon, who'd been standing off to one side without speaking through all of this. "If you want to go along home, I'm sure the sheriff would give me a ride back."

He seemed reluctant to leave without permission from Sheriff Lens, who quickly gave it. "I know where to find you, Josh. Get along now and I'll drop by the store in the morning."

"Thanks, Sheriff." He trotted off to where he'd left the car, down the road.

"What do you think, Doc?" Lens asked again, patting his belly as if gauging the success of his weight reduction.

"Honestly?" I watched Josh's car drive away. "I think he suckered me somehow into delivering a book with a bomb in it, but for the life of me I can't figure out how he could have done it."

The inside of the house had the look of a bachelor's quarters. There was a bottle of bourbon on the coffee table along with a half-empty glass. A wall rack held three hunting rifles. And on either side of the stone fireplace were shelves of books, filled to overflowing. A pair of reading glasses was on the table next to the whiskey glass. The shelves were dusty and the windows dirty. The grass in the yard had been recently cut, but that only proved DeVille had a son to cut it. My eyes ranged over fiction, poetry, and books on building, hunting, guns, and explosives.

"What did DeVille do for a living?" I asked.

"Construction work, but lately he's been off. He got a settlement from the trucking company that killed his wife. He's been living off that."

I could see evidence of Rachel DeVille still present in the framed picture of smiling mother, father, and son on the mantel, and books like *Little Women* that still found a place on the shelves. I took it down and found her maiden name still on the leaflet—Rachel March. No wonder she was attracted to the Alcott novel, sharing the same last name as the book's family.

The kitchen showed signs of meal preparation, and the beds upstairs were unmade. The basement had the typical dirt floor of most farmhouses, with shelves holding a few jars of peaches and tomatoes no doubt left over from Rachel's time. Aaron had a work table in one corner with equipment for loading his own hunting cartridges. Sheriff Lens ran his finger over a container of gunpowder. "Everything's dusty. He hasn't been down here in a long time."

"Two years," I suggested, pointing out the hunting licenses tacked to the wall above the table. "The last one's thirty-six, the year his wife was killed. Looks like he lost interest in hunting after that." There were some old newspapers at the bottom of the stairs, dating back just a few months, that he or the boy must have brought down. A mousetrap sat under the steps, its bait moldy and its trap unsprung. I wondered if anyone, even a mouse, had spent time down there in the last two years.

We went back outside where the deputies were cleaning away the last evidence of the explosion. "We want to have it decent before the kid comes back," the sheriff said.

"What about the book and the wrapping?" I asked.

"All burned up except for a few charred pieces for the lab to check."

I bent to retrieve a piece of burned newspaper. *". . . sevelt Nominated by Acclaim . . ."* The rest of it was gone, blown away like Aaron DeVille.

"Before I can take you home, Doc, I'd like you to come with me and see if we can speak with young Damon."

"Of course."

It was starting to get dark as we crossed the road to the Chesnut house. Marta Chesnut answered the door. She glanced over her shoulder and said, "Come in. He's pretty good now."

Damon was a sandy-haired boy who seemed a bit thin and short for his age. Not surprisingly, his eyes were red from crying and he faced us now with a trembling lip. Sheriff Lens said a few words to relax him and then asked, "When did you last see your father, Damon?"

"This—this afternoon. I left for school at my usual time, about eight-thirty. I came home around three-thirty to pick up my music, and later my dad drove me to the piano lesson. He was supposed to pick me up at six-thirty but he never came. Mrs. Chesnut—"

"We know, son. That's all right."

I sat down next to him. "Damon, you know me, don't you? I'm Dr. Hawthorne. I know these questions are difficult, but we're just trying to learn what happened to your dad." He'd lost both his mother and father within two years and in his eyes I could see a desperate plea for help.

"Did someone kill him?" Damon asked.

"We think so. Was anyone at the house this afternoon when you came home? Anyone who might have fooled with the books?"

"No. When Mom was alive I could never touch the books, and Dad was still fussy about people handling them."

"Were there any recent visitors?"

He glanced away. "Not while I was there."

I wondered what that meant but decided not to pursue it at the moment. "What about the mail?" I asked instead. "Did your dad bring it in every day?"

"I guess so, yeah. I always looked in the box when I got home but it was usually empty."

"You looked even if the flag wasn't up?"

"Sure," he said with a shrug.

I looked up at Marta Chesnut. "You can take care of him overnight?"

"Of course." Her blue eyes sparkled. "We're planning to."

"I'll be out again in the morning," I promised.

Riding back to town with Sheriff Lens, I pondered the mailbox problem. "I think I should talk with Kenny Diggins tomorrow."

"The postman?"

"Yeah. There was a bomb in that book. Either Vernon switched packages on me somehow or it was done in the mailbox."

"You told me you were watching it the whole time."

"I was. Right now I don't know which of my alternatives is the more impossible."

I went out to the Chesnut house in the morning and talked to Damon again. He was doing pretty well and Marta told me his aunt and uncle would be arriving later that afternoon. They would stay for the funeral and then take the boy back to Hartford with them.

"Did he sleep all right?" I asked Marta when we were alone.

"I don't know. He was up roaming around some. I heard him go outside once, over to his house, but he wasn't gone long. I suppose he wanted to convince himself it wasn't all a terrible dream."

I went outside and crossed the road myself, stopping to examine the mailboxes closely for the first time. All four had been bolted to the stout board that supported them. The boxes on either end, for Chesnut and Breen, were beginning to work loose, but the middle two, for DeVille and Millars, were tightly bolted in place. Since three of the boxes were for houses across the road

I wondered why DeVille's box was the second in line rather than being at one end or the other. It was already afternoon, so I decided to wait for Kenny to bring the day's mail.

Just before one I spotted his Chevy coming over the hill, stopping at each roadside mailbox to make a delivery and lift the flag. I walked out and hailed him as he reached the boxes in front of the DeVille house. "Hi, Doc," he greeted me. "What's this I heard about Aaron DeVille?"

"Someone put a bomb in his mailbox."

The postman stared at the box as if unable to believe such a thing, then gradually opened it to peer carefully inside. "It's against the law to put anything but mail into these boxes."

"Especially bombs," I pointed out.

"Yeah." He scratched his head. "I heard Josh Vernon was delivering a book to him. You know, that Vernon is always putting things in the mailboxes that he's not supposed to."

"Ever see anyone else doing it?"

He thought about it. "Just kids once in a while. If I catch them I give 'em a good scolding." As he spoke he was slipping mail into the boxes. He put a few bills and the *Saturday Review of Literature* in DeVille's box.

"He's dead," I reminded him.

"I go by the book, Doc. Nobody's notified the post office to stop delivery."

"Tell me something, Kenny. How come the DeVille mailbox is second in the row instead of at the end? The other houses are all across the street."

"That's easy. DeVille was always here. Then they built the Chesnut house and their box went next to his. When the other two families moved in a few years later, their boxes went on the other side of DeVille. I guess they just put 'em there for no special reason."

As he drove on I noticed another car coming over the hill. It was traveling fast, raising a cloud of dust behind it. When the driver saw me he pulled to a stop. "You Sheriff Lens?" he asked.

He was in his mid-thirties, dressed for the city in suit and tie and hat. The woman next to him wore a plain black dress and hat.

"No, I'm Dr. Sam Hawthorne. You'd be the DeVille family from Hartford?"

"That's correct. They phoned about my brother—"

"A terrible tragedy. I can't tell you how sorry I am."

"The boy—Damon?"

"Staying with neighbors across the street. Pull into the driveway and we'll walk over."

It was the woman, Florence, who hurried to the boy. Zach DeVille hung back as if unsure of himself. "We'll give him a good home, of course," he tried to reassure me.

"Were you close to your brother?"

"Not really. He was five years older: the first, as you probably gathered from his name. I was the last. Our folks did things like that."

He said a few words to his nephew and then left him in his wife's care. "Would you like to see the house?" I asked.

"I suppose I should. Florence and I will get the job of cleaning it out and selling it. And we'll be staying there till the funeral."

"Aaron had no other relatives?"

"None."

I went back to the Chesnut house and got the key from Marta. Then Zach DeVille and I went in. "Sorry about the liquor bottle. The deputies didn't bother cleaning up."

"I've seen plenty of them before around Aaron."

"What was he like when he drank?"

"Miserable to Rachel when she was alive. Gave her a black eye once. She called me long distance that night and I had to talk to him."

"What about the night she died?"

"I think she was running away from him, but what difference does it make? Her death was clearly an accident. There was nothing anyone could do to Aaron."

"Somebody did something to him. They blew him away."

Zach DeVille glanced around the room and shrugged. "Maybe

he found another woman, one who didn't like being pushed around."

I thought about that as we walked back over to the Chesnut house. When Zach and Florence took Damon back home I asked Marta if I could have a word with her outside. "What is it?" she asked.

"Your front window is right across the road from the DeVille house. You must have noticed his comings and goings, things like visitors."

"He didn't have many visitors."

"Young Damon hinted there might have been someone."

"Oh, there was that woman from town. She came out occasionally. Damon probably didn't like her."

"What woman from town?"

"The one who works at Vernon's bookstore. I think her name is Sylvia."

I had no patients scheduled the following morning so I dropped by the sheriff's office early. Sheriff Lens was pondering the report from the state police laboratory, where he'd sent the charred remains of the bomb. "You might find this interesting, Doc," he said as he passed the report to me. "It's only preliminary. They got more tests to run."

I glanced over the pages. "A mousetrap?"

"A mousetrap set to go off when the book's cover was opened. That in turn set off a detonator and exploded a charge of gunpowder. The whole thing was packed in with newspaper to keep the gunpowder from spilling out."

I remembered finding a piece of charred newspaper. But the most interesting part of the report proved to be about the book itself. The center had been hollowed out to make room for the mousetrap and gunpowder, but it was not a copy of *War and Peace*. It was Pearl Buck's *The Good Earth*. "Josh couldn't have switched books on me," I insisted.

"Someone did, and you claim no one else approached the

mailbox until Aaron DeVille removed the book. He sure didn't kill himself."

"Maybe he did." I was grasping at straws now. "He slipped the book into the pocket of his jacket and then took it out again and unwrapped it. Maybe he switched packages."

But Sheriff Lens shook his head. "He had three rifles hanging over the fireplace, and it's not as awkward as you might think to kill yourself with one. A lot easier than buildin' a bomb and hollowing out a book to put it in. Besides, what happened to *War and Peace?*"

I had to agree he was right. "Did the wrapping match the paper Josh uses?"

"Identical, though I suppose anyone could have gotten it by simply buying a book."

I shook my head. I still came back to Josh. And now I thought I might have his motive. I left the sheriff's office and walked down the street to Josh's Books.

Sylvia Grant was working behind the counter. There was no sign of Josh. "He's gone over to the funeral parlor to pay his respects. It's a closed coffin, of course. Mr. DeVille is being buried tomorrow."

"Did you know him well?" I asked casually, thumbing through Van Doren's impressive biography of Benjamin Franklin.

"Hardly at all, just as a voice on the telephone."

"That's odd, because one of the neighbors told me you used to go out to his house occasionally."

Sylvia took off her glasses and stared at me. Maybe she could see me better without them. "I might have gone there once or twice to deliver books."

"No, I got the impression these visits were more personal. They were usually when Damon was away, but he knew about them."

Her pretty face froze into a noncommittal mask. "What are you trying to do to me, Dr. Sam?"

"Just get at the truth."

"My God, do you think I killed him?"

"No, but you might have supplied the motive. I'm sorry to ask you these personal questions, Sylvia, but they've become important. I need to know about your relations with Josh—and with Aaron DeVille."

She shook her head, laughing now. "My relations with Josh are strictly employee-employer. I've never even had a drink with the man. Frankly, I doubt if he cares too much about women."

"All right. What about DeVille?"

"He was almost twice my age but we liked each other. I won't deny it. I think it had pretty much run its course, though. He was looking for a wife and I didn't see him as a husband for me."

"Thank you for being honest with me," I said. "I was thinking Josh might be jealous about—"

The door opened and he walked in, cutting short our conversation. "I'm glad you stopped by, Doc. I have another book here that might interest you."

I winked at Sylvia and turned my attention to Josh. "Were you over at the funeral parlor?"

"Yes. A terrible thing, really. The more I think about it the more it seems he must have killed himself. How else could it have happened?"

"I've been talking to Sheriff Lens. The bomb was in a copy of *The Good Earth*. If he killed himself, Josh, what happened to *War and Peace?*"

He thought about that. "Damned if I know."

Sylvia had moved away, tactfully, to arrange the window display.

"It's a mighty thick book to just disappear," I said, and even as I spoke the words I knew how it was done, and who had done it.

The funeral was scheduled for the following morning, and I needed to consult with Sheriff Lens about how to proceed. It was going to be difficult, either way. When I told him my suspicions, and went over it all bit by bit, he could only shake his head.

"You're bringing this to me, Doc?"

"I'm just asking, would it be better to make an arrest now, or wait till after the funeral in the morning?"

"After the funeral," he decided grimly. "I'll do it then."

There was a typical autumn chill in the air the following morning as the mourners gathered about the grave site. Aaron DeVille was buried alongside his wife Rachel as the minister intoned words of final rest. I heard a few murmurs about the shortness of the wake, but most people seemed glad to have it over with. All of DeVille's neighbors were present, along with his brother and sister-in-law and Damon. Josh Vernon and Sylvia Grant had come too, apparently locking the bookstore for a few hours. Even Kenny Diggins was there, watching from the road where he'd parked his car before resuming his mail route.

Most everyone went back to the DeVille house afterwards. The neighbors had brought food, a country custom, and most people sat outside eating despite the chilly breeze. Sheriff Lens and I walked around the back of the house, where I spotted young Damon attacking some dead flowers with a stick.

"Come here, boy," I said kindly. "I want to talk to you." The sheriff stood off to one side as I put my arm around his shoulders. "I know it's a bum day when they bury your dad."

He muttered something, head down. I went on, gripping his shoulders just tightly enough so he couldn't break away. "It's an especially bad day when you know it was you who caused his death."

"Me? I didn't—" He tried to jerk away but I held him fast.

"Sylvia Grant told me you liked to baffle your dad with mysteries. This was just the sort of thing to appeal to you, making books disappear out of mailboxes. Then you decided to carry it one step further, causing a copy of *War and Peace* to turn into *The Good Earth,* all while the mailbox was being watched. It took me a while to figure out how you did it, but I should have guessed it a lot sooner. I put a thick copy of *War and Peace* in that box, but a moment later your dad removed a book slim enough to slip into his jacket pocket, slim enough that even he must have realized it was a mistake. He unwrapped it on the spot, there in the yard, setting off the bomb you'd carefully planted."

"No!" the boy screamed. "I didn't mean to kill him. I didn't mean to! I didn't—"

"It took me the longest time to realize that you switched the books, Damon, in the same way that you caused the earlier ones to vanish. You did it simply by switching mailboxes."

He was breathing heavily, trying to break away, and Sheriff Lens moved in on his other side. "Just calm down, son. We'll let you make a statement after we talk to your aunt and uncle."

"I noticed yesterday that the boxes for your house and the Millars's place were tightly bolted down while the end ones were loose. That told me something when I thought about it later. It told me they'd been tampered with, loosened, removed—and transposed. Kenny delivered the mail around one. You got home at three-thirty and simply switched your mailbox with the Millars's, putting them back in their correct positions after dark. Josh Vernon would drive up, look at the names, and deliver his books to the third box from the left, just as I did the day your father died. Naturally your dad, used to the position of the box, second from the left, opened it without bothering with the names. He came out that day without his reading glasses, so the names on the boxes were probably a blur to him anyway. The first three times the Millars's box—the one he opened by mistake—was empty. The last time, the bomb was in it, made from material you found around your own basement—a mousetrap, gunpowder from your father's cartridge reloading. When you put the boxes back in position the other night—Marta Chesnut heard you go across to your house—you made the mistake of tightening the nuts and bolts too much. They were different from the others."

Sheriff Lens had one question. "Why didn't any of the neighbors see him making the switch in the afternoons, Doc?"

"He probably loosened the bolts earlier, so he only had to give them a quick turn and lift the boxes. His body would have shielded the action from across the street. They'd think he was just checking for mail, if they noticed it at all."

Damon was crying now, heavy gasping sobs that seemed to shake his entire body. "I didn't do it, I didn't kill him!"

"You had the paper from Josh's store because you'd stolen the earlier books. Why'd you pick *The Good Earth?* Just because it was the right size to fit the wrapping for one of the earlier books?"

"That's enough, Doc," Sheriff Lens decided. He took the sobbing boy and led him away.

I was breathing hard myself, trying to calm my emotions. It was a terrible thing to accuse a twelve-year-old boy of killing his father. Had he done it because of the cruelty to his mother years earlier, or because he felt that Sylvia Grant was gradually taking his mother's place? I walked away from the DeVille house, through the tall weeds, because I hadn't really come to grips with the motive yet. If he resented the beating of his mother he would have acted much earlier than this, wouldn't he? Sylvia had said he liked to baffle his dad. That implied trickery. Any one of the tricks could have been deadly before this. And if he resented Sylvia he would have acted against her and not his father.

I went over the reasoning again in my own mind, remembering the position of the mailboxes clearly. I'd placed the book in the third box in line, the one with DeVille's name on it. Later the second box had carried his name. The boxes had been switched, and only Damon DeVille could have done it. He was trying to baffle his father with another mystery. Everything fit. The material for the bomb had come from the DeVille basement, where the killer must have had access to it. Therefore the killer had to live in the house. Certainly DeVille wouldn't have left Sylvia alone in the house long enough for her to fashion a bomb, even if she'd had a motive. No, it had to be a member of the household. There were only the two of them, Aaron and Damon. I'd shown it couldn't be suicide, so that only left Damon—

"Damon!"

How could I have been so wrong?

I ran through the grass and weeds, calling his name as I reached the house. It was Sheriff Lens who told me he was in the sheriff's car with his Uncle Zach. He'd admitted switching the mailboxes and the books, but denied any knowledge of the bomb.

I ran out to the car and yanked open the rear door where the boy sat with his uncle. "Damon, you'll have to forgive me. I had it all wrong. Because it had to be you who switched the boxes, I jumped to the conclusion you assembled the bomb. It wasn't you. It was never you."

"Then who was it?" Zach DeVille demanded.

"Rachel DeVille killed her husband, even though she's been dead nearly two years."

Sheriff Lens was shaking his head sadly. "You almost made a terrible mistake, Doc. We all did."

I was staring out the window of his car as we drove back to town. "The motive didn't work out for Damon, but it did for his mother, who'd been beaten and abused by Aaron DeVille. I said the makings of the bomb were in the basement, but there were no detonators there. A detonator isn't the sort of thing a boy comes up with. And what about the other things? I saw a mousetrap in the DeVille basement that probably hadn't been touched in a couple of years. And there was a thick layer of dust on the containers of gunpowder. More than that, a charred bit of newspaper used as packing for the bomb had a headline about Roosevelt's renomination, dating it from late June of 1936—more than two years ago. Yet the old newspapers in the basement only went back a few months."

"She made the bomb back then?" Sheriff Lens asked. "Before she died in that accident? How'd she even know how to assemble it?"

"Probably from one of her husband's books. I saw one there on guns and explosives. She probably did it in a moment of controlled rage, then put *The Good Earth* back on the shelf and waited. The ten-year-old Damon was forbidden to touch the books, so she knew only her husband would be likely to open it. If he didn't, I'm sure she had another scheme. She might phone him and say, 'I'm leaving you. There's a letter in *The Good Earth* explaining everything.' As fate would have it, she died before she could complete her plan."

"How do you know Damon didn't find the bomb in the book and follow through with his mother's plan?"

"Because if he'd opened that book he'd be dead now instead of Aaron."

As we drove back to town I remembered that photograph of the happy family at the DeVille house. I remembered Rachel's smiling face—a woman already punished for a crime she'd only now committed.

A. M. Burrage

The Bargain

Used-book stores are magical places. I don't mean those ginger-bread emporiums with pompous clerks that collectors merely visit in hopes of finding long-sought, unsuspected (i.e., under-priced) treasures; I mean meccas like the Gryphon Bookshop on upper Broadway, where bibliophiles congregate for fervent con-versation about books, films, music, theatre—anything other than the garish ephemeral world on the other side of the door. Some-times, during a rare lull in conversation, one might be tempted to explore the shop's dark inner reaches, and there's the risk. You never know what strange tome rests forgotten on some dusty shelf, such as the "bargain" in this chilly tale by A. M. BURRAGE (1889–1956), one of England's forgotten masters of supernatural fiction, and author of several classic weird stories, such as "Be-tween the Minute and the Hour," "Smee" and "The Waxwork."

WALTON WENT to the sale because Mrs. Walton had seen a carpet, in quite good condition, which would do for one of the spare rooms if it could be had cheap enough. It was one of the early lots, so he arrived in good time, before the auctioneer mounted the rostrum with the air of a judge ascending his throne. Walton said that he always felt that everybody ought to stand up when the auctioneer came in.

With a few minutes to spare he did a little prospecting on his own and noticed a bundle of books. There were about fourteen of them carelessly tied together with string, with the number of the lot—21—stuck on the cover of the uppermost volume. The bundle was rendered more untidy than it would otherwise have been by one book in the middle which was about twice the length and breadth of the largest of the others. There was nothing on the back of the binding to give any indication of its contents.

The books were shabby and not at all interesting on the whole. *The Collected Sermons of Dean Widgeon, A Child's Guide to Trigonometry, Half Hours with the Cannibals* by a Missionary, *Mother Gruesome's Cookery Book,* and so forth. But there was a *Wanley's Wonders* which Walton coveted.

The book is rare without being valuable. Copies may be had for a few shillings when found, but they are difficult to find. There were no other books in the catalogue and therefore no book dealers present. He decided to wait a few minutes after the carpet had been put up and see if he could buy *Wanley* at a reasonable price.

The lots were not the effects of any particular person, but consisted of the unwanted "junk" of a dozen households. Hideous Victorian furniture, still more hideous Victorian engravings, incomplete sets of chinaware, fishing rods, ornaments, clocks, garden implements, they stood in dingy disorder around the room, each waiting for a new home.

The carpet which Walton had been commissioned to buy was Lot No. 8, or, as he preferred to phrase it, "it went in sixth wicket down." He was able to buy it at a price at which even Mrs. Walton could not complain. About a quarter of an hour later Lot 21 was held aloft by a man in a green baize apron for the bored inspection of the assembly.

Everybody seemed too shy to speak for a few moments, and then a voice tentatively muttered, "Two shillings."

"Three," said Walton crisply.

This advance scared away the opposition. The auctioneer looked around, gave the rostrum a crack with his hammer, and proceeded to become lyrical over the value and beauty of Lot 22—two horsehair armchairs of the 1860 period, one designed for a lady and the other for a gentleman. The bundle of books was Walton's for three shillings.

In due time Walton, the carpet, and the books arrived at the Waltons' house in a taxi. Walton carried the carpet upstairs and left Mrs. Walton and one of the maids to play with it. Then he went down to examine his books.

The *Wanley* was a fifteenth edition, printed at the close of the eighteenth century. Still he had not expected to find a first, and it was the book itself he wanted, not merely its value. All but that and the big flat book he put outside his study door to go down to the kitchen. The maids had a taste in literature which he considered execrable. They liked tales about sheiks who did not suffer from a trouble common to their kind—namely fleas—and who behaved with all the decorum of the nonconformist ministry towards the white girls who fell into their hands; also stories about he-babies who, having been lost in the jungle and reared by apes, grew up to be perfect gentlemen.

Walton reflected that the sermons of Dean Widgeon might do a lot of good below stairs, where the only gleam of religion came by way of the wireless until one of the maids had the presence of mind to turn it off. He liked to think of the cook wrestling with trigonometry—which probably she had hitherto believed to be a difficult and dangerous surgical operation.

Then he sat down and opened the big flat book, and uttered a muffled cry. It was an ordinary scrap-book such as children once used for pasting in the "scraps" off a Christmas cracker—and probably do so to this day. And the first page he looked at assured Walton that he had a "find." He had not collected stamps for many years, and there were few old stamps on which he could have put an approximate value without consulting an up-to-date catalogue, but he had a *flair* which those once addicted to the vice of philately never quite lose.

The turning of every page revealed a fresh discovery. He passed eagerly from page to page and became more and more assured that the contents of the scrap-book were worth many hundreds of pounds, and he soon noticed that no stamp had been issued after 1870.

Obviously the collection had not been made by a boy. Sprightly boyhood would have used gum, mounted the stamps awry, and cut off the corners of some of them to make them look pretty. They were neatly arranged and if they were not all good specimens they were at least clean. The name of each country was written at the head of each page in beautiful old English characters. Walton estimated that the collection numbered some six or seven hundred.

Of course there was a proportion of rubbish; stamps which, despite their antiquity, were still catalogued at from a penny to a shilling, but there were some colonials which would make Redlake's mouth water when he saw them.

Redlake was stamp mad. He had one of the finest collections of British colonials in the country. He had spent tens of thousands of pounds on the contents of the twelve large volumes which he kept locked in a safe. He belonged to the most exclusive stamp clubs; he could smell a forgery as the witch-finder was once supposed to be able to smell out a witch; he could "sense" the most skillfully mended stamp by touching it with a pair of tweezers. At the mention of stamps he was always liable to start gabbling in the jargon of philately and talk about "mint" and "errors" and "part-worn plate."

Well, here was something that would interest Redlake. Walton decided that he would show his find to Redlake on the morrow and get the expert to estimate its value.

That night he brought the album into his bedroom for safety's sake. The table beside his bed was already littered with books. Beside the fireplace was another table—a small round one—on which his breakfast tray was placed on those mornings when he was in a lazy mood. His mind was full of stamps when he fell asleep.

He woke—or seemed to wake—suddenly and found himself staring in the direction of the table. With a cold tingle of fear and astonishment he observed that the album was moving, or rather its pages were, as if somebody were slowly turning them. And then that "somebody" sprang suddenly into the focus of his vision.

It was a very old man who bent gloating over Walton's bargain. He was bald-headed and wore a long white beard. Some kind of dark stuff robe, like a monk's habit, enveloped him from neck to heels. It might have been a dressing-gown. He looked a little like Father Time without his scythe.

But although none of us have any reason for loving Father Time an incarnation of him would not be vile as this visitant was vile. There was something indescribably repulsive about him which dried the saliva in Walton's mouth and set the flesh shrinking back upon his bones. He groped for the hanging switch above his bed and flooded the room with light.

He looked again. The album lay closed upon the table and there was no old man. Mrs. Walton, in her twin bed, stirred, moaned plaintively, and slowly woke, demanding to know what was the matter. Walton, in a shaken voice, told her that he had had a bad dream. He always kept brandy in the room and he got out and helped himself to three stiff "fingers" in a tooth-glass. Then he went back to bed and ventured to turn out the light.

"It must have been a dream . . . I suppose," he assured himself before he fell asleep.

Next morning he took the album round to Redlake. Redlake turned several pages perfunctorily but gave a little start when he came to a page headed "Ceylon." He spent five minutes poring over it, and another five minutes over another page headed "British Guiana." But it was over the Australasian stamps that he showed most interest. He spent half an hour examining them.

"Well," he said at last, "you've got something here! How did you get hold of them?"

Walton explained and Redlake swore, just as Walton had expected.

"Damn it!" Redlake continued. "Some people have all the luck! I've had a few good bargains in my time, but I've never had something for nothing, like this."

"What do you think they're worth?"

"My dear chap, how can I say now? I'm not a walking catalogue, and even if I were, you know as well as I do that you can't trust catalogues. It would take me a month to vet this lot properly. I daresay a lot of them are thinned at the back. As usual the best stamps are bad copies. Look at that Victoria. It would be worth a hundred pounds if some fool of a postmaster nearly ninety years ago hadn't let his scissors run from the margin. Now you'd be lucky to get a tenner for it."

"Give me a rough estimate."

"Oh, I daresay the combined catalogue prices would come to about £2,000. Want to sell?"

"We-ell, I don't mind."

Truth to tell Walton had been out of love with those stamps since the preceding night. He had toyed with the thought of making them the nucleus of a new collection. He had no such intention now.

"I'll give you £200 for them."

It was a poor offer but not a scandalously bad one. Walton knew that it would take years to sell the stamps piecemeal, and stamps do not bring in interest while they are being kept. Besides, between the buying and the selling thereof there is a great gulf fixed.

"Have a heart!" he urged. "Make it £300."

Redlake slowly shook his head.

"I tell you what," he said presently. "I haven't had time to examine them, as you can see, but I'll take a chance and offer you £250. Afterwards, if I find I've stumbled on some great rarity, I'll make it right with you."

Walton considered. He knew that collectors are generally rather less conscientious than race-course thugs, but Redlake was something of an exception. Also Walton had his own reasons for wanting to get rid of the stamps as soon as possible. Another factor was that he had some small but pressing accounts to meet and those grasping gentlemen of the Inland Revenue were keeping up a brisk correspondence with him.

"All right," he said. "Done!"

Redlake unlocked a drawer and took out his check-book . . .

Two days later Walton and Redlake met in the street.

"Had another look at those stamps?" Walton asked.

Redlake eyed him coldly.

"No," he said briefly, "I've sold them."

Walton's heart sank. Redlake's superior knowledge, he thought, had earned him a quick dividend.

"Make much on the deal?" he asked casually.

"I lost £70. I took them to Flake and Thorpe's. The dogs saw that I wanted to get rid of them. I suppose they thought I was hard up. Couldn't get 'em to offer me more than £180."

"But my dear fellow, I don't understand."

"Don't you! Well, come and have a drink and I'll tell you. I spent the whole of yesterday pickling my liver, and I'll have to have another spot now before I can bring myself to talk about it."

At the back of an adjacent tavern, said once to have been a resort of the poet Swinburne, there was a small discreet room, where young men with golf clubs are generally to be found sitting on the table and swinging stockinged legs. But the room was empty when they entered, and Redlake began the proceedings by lowering a large dark-complexioned whisky as if it were water. Walton noticed that his hand shook.

"Now I can tell you," Redlake said in a steadier voice. "I wouldn't have those damned stamps in my house another night even if they were all Post Office Mauritius.

"Before turning in that night I locked 'em in the safe with my collection. Of course you won't believe what I'm going to tell you, but I think you'll give me credit for believing it myself. I'm not the man to lose £70 on a deal in a few hours.

"Well, I went to bed and woke up some time during the night. I couldn't say what time it was. My room's always light unless I draw the blinds, for a street lamp shines right in. I woke up lying on my right side within hand's reach of the table beside the bed. As I became more and more conscious I thought what a queer thing it was that that album I had just bought of you should be there when I distinctly remembered locking it in the safe. Moreover it was open. Then I opened my eyes wider and wished I hadn't."

A fit of trembling seized Walton.

"There was an old man—"

"Yes," said Walton, "bald-headed and with a long white beard, something like Father Time—a degraded and repulsive Father Time."

Redlake jumped like a stranded fish. His eyes bulged.

"How did you know?" he demanded.

"Because I saw him myself. That's why I sold you the stamps, or one of the reasons."

"Thanks," said Redlake laconically, "then I can spare myself the misery of describing the abomination to you. He was sitting on the edge of my bed, if you please, and dabbing his forefinger on a Ceylon stamp in a way no philatelist would touch it. I couldn't see which one it was, but I could see Ceylon written at the top of the page. I'd never believed in things like—like *him* before, and I think I must have felt just as a murderer feels when the procession enters his cell on the morning of his execution.

"This ghastly thing mumbled at me as if he were trying to tell me something, while he went on tapping the stamp. But he didn't make a sound and—he hadn't any teeth. I tumbled out of bed on the other side and rushed into my wife's room, where I spent the rest of the night. Next morning I found the album locked up in the safe where I had put it."

There was a pause.

"Who is he?" Redlake asked in a shaken voice. "Or, rather, who *was* he?"

"How should I know?" Walton returned.

"I'd like to find out. I'd like to know whether it was he who made the collection or whether that particular Ceylon stamp—whichever it was—is associated with something damnable he once did. I suppose it's impossible to find out now."

"Over sixty years ago," Walton commented.

"I know. I dreamed of the old horror three times last night, and

I suppose I shall go on dreaming of him for the rest of my life. Walton, I wish he'd had some teeth!"

Walton nodded sympathetically.

"He was on the other side of the room when I saw him, and I turned the light on pretty quick. Have another drink?"

"Not here. Let's go back to my place. Did you notice that barman's mouth? Damn people who haven't any teeth!"

A week passed before the two men met again. They encountered in the tube. Redlake looked shaken and ill and his face was a greenish white. He changed his seat and went to sit beside Walton.

"I've just been up to Flake and Thorpe's," he said.

"Oh?"

"They've just got a New Zealand I wanted. I asked them to try to get it for me three months ago. It's a very fine copy, so they lumped fifty per cent on their catalogue price."

Walton smiled.

"Well," he said, "I suppose it's worth it to you if you wanted it enough."

"That wasn't what I meant to tell you. Can you stand a shock?"

"What do you mean?"

"They've had some trouble at Flake and Thorpe's. Their night watchman died."

"Didn't know they'd got a night watchman."

"My dear fellow, but of course. They've got thousands and thousands of pounds' worth of stamps locked up in safes. It was three mornings ago. The manager let himself in and found the poor old chap lying on the floor unconscious. Evidently he'd had some kind of fit, for there was froth on his lips.

"They bundled him to hospital, but he died on the way. Just before the end he became semi-conscious and muttered something about 'the old man,' and 'Ceylon.' "

Walton drew a quick, cold breath, and found himself staring

straight across the compartment at the comfortable sight of a girl with a well-powdered face, who was reading a book from a circulating library.

"Let's talk about something else," he said.

Carole Buggé

The Sins of the Father

CAROLE BUGGÉ *has written several nigh-perfect Sherlock Holmes pastiches for St. Martin's Press, which soon will publish her first Holmesian novel,* The Star of India. *She wears many hats well: improvisational comedy teacher and performer, playwright-composer, poet, and writing instructor. She has written several excellent fantasy stories, including "A Day in the Life of Comrade Lenin," "Laura," "Miracle at Chimayo" and this strange tale of secrets that should have stayed that way.*

I AM A MAN of science. Having spent my life in the quiet pursuit of scientific truth, I have neither sought out nor wished for the kind of adventure that presented itself to me on a rainy night in September of 1898 at my club in the person of Richard Moore. I had been at Oxford with Moore but knew him only slightly then and had not seen him for years. I am not particularly sociable by nature, but Moore was a cheerful, handsome fellow with a strong Celtic chin and high cheekbones; his wavy, rust-colored hair was rather longer than the current fashion, and fell over his forehead when he talked.

"I understand you're engaged in scientific research?" Moore said, sipping his brandy as we sat in front of a roaring fire in the club lounge while the rain pelted the streets outside.

"Yes," I replied; "I am engaged as a Research Fellow by London Hospital."

"Have you ever done any research into the nature of dreams?"

"No, I can't say that I have."

"I have," he continued, leaning back in his chair and staring at the ceiling. "Oh, I should tell you that I am in the fortunate position of not having to earn a living; shortly after leaving Oxford I inherited my father's considerable estate. After Oxford I spent some years in India, then I went to Tibet with my father, and that's where it began."

"Where what began?"

He did not reply, but stood up and poked at the logs in the fireplace, sending yellow sparks shooting up the chimney. He stood with his back to the fire, which crackled and sputtered behind him; his faraway gaze seemed to transport him beyond the Thalladium Club, with its hunting prints, soft leather armchairs, and Persian carpets thick with cigar smoke.

"When I was at Oxford I specialized in the study of ancient manuscripts, and that was where I first came across what the Tibetans call the 'Dream Travelers.' "

"The what?"

"The Dream Travelers," he repeated softly. "Are you familiar at all with Tibetan culture?"

"No, not really . . . look, I should tell you right off that as a scientist I don't believe in anything, no matter how intriguing, unless it can be repeated in rigorously scientific experimental conditions."

"Capital!" he said, practically leaping from his chair and pacing back and forth upon the burgundy Persian rug that covered the floor. "That's exactly what I intend to do!"

"What exactly *is* it you intend to do?" I repeated, still confused.

Moore stopped pacing. "Why, become a Dream Traveler." He sat down again, and I saw that his hands were gripping his brandy glass tightly. "You see, these Tibetan holy men—or so they are considered, and rightly so—have developed the ability to move at will in and out of other people's dreams."

"Do you expect me to believe that—"

"No, no; I don't expect you to *believe* it; that's just it, don't you see? I don't expect anybody to believe it until they experience it firsthand as I did!"

"Wait a minute," I interrupted, "people 'appear' in dreams all the time, but it doesn't mean they're actually *there;* the slumbering mind simply creates the *image* of that person—"

"Yes, yes," he said impatiently; "I have been through the same line of reasoning as yourself a thousand times, and yet I tell you it *happened!* You see, not only did he appear in my dream, but he *described it in perfect detail afterwards, without my telling him anything whatsoever!* He described it to me so flawlessly that I could hardly believe it; I even thought that he had somehow hypnotized me and tricked me into revealing the dream to him, but I had to reject that as a possibility; there was a witness in the room at the time, a man whom I trusted implicitly. No," he said, rubbing his forehead with a long, nervous hand; "it happened just as I tell you, I swear on my mother's grave. He even revealed events which I dreamed but had forgotten myself, and remembered only as he told them to me."

I was impressed in spite of myself, though I tried not to show it. "What is it that you want from me?"

"I need someone to help establish, as you said before, the 'rigorous scientific conditions' necessary to a true experiment. Oh, don't worry," he added quickly; "I am prepared to pay for your services—as I said before, I am very well off. I shouldn't worry about it interfering with your normal working hours, by the way—my research will naturally be done at night."

I said I would think about it.

"Capital, Lawrence!" His hearty manner had returned. "And now I shall leave you to your brandy and your books," he said, indicating the small volume of fiction that protruded from my jacket pocket. "Poe, eh? I am fond of him myself. 'As I wandered weak and weary, on a midnight dark and dreary'—good stuff, that . . . well, I'll leave you now; here's my card," he added, producing from his pocket an ivory-colored embossed business card; the elegant printing said simply *Richard Moore,* followed by his address in Kensington.

We agreed to meet at his flat in two days' time.

The next two days were unexpectedly busy ones at the laboratory, and I stayed late two nights in a row going over some data. I was so engrossed in my work that I hardly gave Moore a thought until the laboratory clock struck eight on the second evening. I looked up from my desk and suddenly realized that I had agreed to meet Moore that very hour; I tore off my lab coat, threw on my jacket, and dashed outside to find a cab in a pouring rainstorm.

I arrived some twenty minutes later soaking wet. Moore answered the door himself, and seeing my sodden figure, burst out laughing.

"My dear fellow, what happened to you?"

"I had trouble finding a cab," I replied sullenly.

"Well, good heavens, you must get into some dry clothes or you will catch your death of cold! Roper will find you something to wear."

Twenty minutes later I was seated before a blazing fire in Moore's sitting room, clad in a dark red dressing gown a bit too long in the sleeves.

"It suits you, really it does," said Moore as he handed me a glass of port. "Well, what do you think of my little nest—rather cozy, isn't it?"

Cozy was hardly the word I would have chosen: the walls of the foyer and sitting room were adorned with flamboyantly painted murals of peacocks. As I sat there, surrounded by bright pinks and blues, I had the impression that we were in the South Sea Islands somewhere; I expected any moment to hear the crashing of surf against the reefs.

"It's quite extraordinary," I said, looking around.

"Oh, do you mean the paintings? They were done by Whistler—"

"*James McNeill* Whistler?"

"The same," Moore answered, grinning widely. "You see, this flat belonged to a chum of his, and he asked Whistler to decorate the walls—and this, as you can see, was the result. When I saw the place I was taken with it, and even though my tastes are naturally somewhat more subdued, I thought it would make a conversation piece."

"You were right," I said, laughing. There was a childlike ingenuousness about Moore which made it impossible not to like him.

"Well, Lawrence, are you as hungry as I am?" Moore asked, rising from his armchair. At that moment, as if on cue, his butler Roper entered the room.

"Dinner is served, sir," he said, then turned and withdrew from the room with an economy of movement so fluid that it barely appeared to disturb a single molecule of air around him. He was dark of complexion, almost as tall as Moore, and so excessively lean that I had the impulse to invite him to join us to dine.

"Good man, Roper—I'll bet you can't guess his age within ten years," said Moore with a wink as we made our way to the dining room.

I considered it. I had noticed that Roper's hair was black as jet, and though his dark, lean face showed some wear, his jawline was razor-sharp and his back was straight as a rod.

"I suppose he could be as old as forty-five," I said.

Moore laughed—a hearty, ringing sound which was so unaffected that I had to smile myself. "He's sixty-five!" he cried triumphantly.

"I don't believe you!" I exclaimed. "I can't believe that—"

"Ask him yourself," Moore replied airily, seating himself at the polished mahogany table lit only by the light of a brass candelabrum; "here he is."

Again Roper entered, a bottle of red wine in the crook of his capable arm.

"Ask me what, sir?"

"Lawrence here couldn't believe your age when I told him. I said he should ask you himself."

"I shall be sixty-six next month, sir," Roper said gravely, pouring us each a glass of Merlot. I noticed his eyes were strikingly green under their dark lashes. I didn't know what to say; his manner was so dignified that I felt transfixed, caught up in his quiet efficiency, and I just nodded.

Moore's cook had prepared us a feast: there was an exquisite soup flavored with exotic spices, a fish course, a stately roast duck with orange slices, and numerous side dishes, all with unusual flavorings, delicate yet distinctive. It was clear there was a foreign influence in the cuisine, and when I asked Moore about it he raised his eyebrows and smiled.

"My cook is Roper's sister, Tieba; she came over from Tibet with Roper and myself. Would you like to meet her?"

I said I would, and Moore asked Roper to send his sister out to the dining room. Moments later she appeared—she was tall like her brother, her lustrous skin several shades darker than his. She appeared to be in her late twenties. She stood with her eyes cast down to the ground and answered my questions in monosyllables, though in perfect English.

When she had gone, leaving behind a faint scent of jasmine, Moore turned to me. "She's lovely, isn't she?"

I agreed that she was.

"Is she upset about something?" I added after a moment.

"Why?"

"Well, she seemed . . . remote, I suppose."

Moore shrugged. "I don't know . . . I'll ask Roper," he added, but I felt he was hiding something.

Moore picked up his glass. "I propose a toast," he said, lifting the goblet so that it sparkled in the warm glow of the candelabrum. "To science!"

I raised my glass and lightly touched the rim to his, releasing a delicate bell tone. "To science."

He smiled, and again I was struck by the warmth of his green eyes in the gleam of candlelight. A silence fell between us. I could hear the crackle of the fire in the next room and the clop of horses' hooves on the cobblestone streets outside. I looked around the room and noticed a handsomely framed oil portrait of a ginger-haired man seated on a splendid white horse. His resemblance to Moore was startling.

"Is that a relative?" I asked, indicating the painting.

"My father."

"The resemblance is uncanny."

Moore smiled. "Yes, isn't it?" He looked up at the painting. The expression on his father's face was proud, almost defiant, and his pose on the huge white horse was that of a conquering *conquistador*.

"It was done shortly after he returned from Tibet for the first time. He was—an energetic man, my father. He made many friends in his travels, and some would say just as many enemies."

As Moore spoke, Roper entered noiselessly and poured us each some more wine. As he stood over me, I felt oddly uncomfortable, as though a cold breeze had swept into the room. I was relieved when he withdrew into the kitchen.

Moore rose from the table and stretched his long frame.

"Well, Lawrence, you must be tired; I know I am."

The hall clock struck midnight. I realized all at once that I was completely drained; a wave of fatigue swept over my body, filling my limbs with sand.

"Would you like to stay the night? I have plenty of spare rooms."

"That's very kind, if you don't mind—"

"Oh, not at all; I'll get Roper to make up the bed and air it out a bit."

Once again Roper appeared at the door almost on the very second his name was mentioned, and in my drowsy state I found myself wondering if he also had the power to materialize at will.

"Ah, Roper—Mr. Lawrence is going to stay here tonight. If you wouldn't mind readying his room—oh, and would you lay out a spare set of my nightclothes for him?"

"Very good, sir," Roper said smoothly, but something in his voice made me stiffen. I looked at him, but his face was as bland as pudding, impossible to read.

"Will there be anything else, sir?" Perhaps it was just my imagination, but I thought I detected a sharp edge in his voice, a barely concealed hostility. Moore didn't seem to notice anything, though.

"That's all; thank you, Roper," he replied.

Roper bowed stiffly and left the room, and I immediately began to feel more cheerful.

"I think I'll sit up for a while; I'm not sleepy yet," said Moore. Indeed, his face was flushed and animated, and his hands fidgeted nervously on the linen tablecloth. "I think you'll be quite comfortable," he continued; "the room is in the back, away from the street, and is very quiet."

"Thank you."

The room was as comfortable as he had promised, and the bed even more so; upon lying down I immediately sank into a deep slumber . . . and found myself walking through an unfamiliar mountainous landscape. It was a glorious spring day, so unlike the foggy London weather I was accustomed to that I spread my arms out in pure enjoyment, letting the warmth of the sun caress my bare arms. I heard the song of a dozen exotic birds, and up ahead I saw a shimmering lake. As I walked along the mountain path toward the beckoning blue water, suddenly I was aware of a voice at my ear.

"Hello, Lawrence."

Startled, I spun around, expecting to find someone behind me. I saw no one. I looked in all directions, but the path was in an open meadow, and it would have been impossible for anyone to sneak up on me.

"It's me, Lawrence; don't be alarmed."

The voice was as clear as if its owner were standing next to me.

"Moore—where are you?"

"In your dream, Lawrence. Not entirely, though—this is only the beginning."

"The beginning?"

"The preliminary to appearing physically—the first step, as it were."

"Oh. So where *are* you?"

"In my sitting room, just as you are in your bed."

I stopped to ponder this concept.

"Now I want to try something. Let's see if you can change this scene. Go somewhere else; see if you can make it happen by just willing it."

"Where should I go?"

"Oh, I don't know—wherever you like."

For some reason I thought of my grandmother's house in Surrey—and instantly I was there, standing in the foyer, the smell of my grandmother's lemon cake coming from the kitchen.

"My God, Moore—it worked!" I cried.

"Yes, it did," he replied, or rather his voice did, for I still could not see him. I took a step toward the kitchen, but before I could go any further the scene changed again, and I was seated upon a cold stone floor, surrounded by chanting Tibetan monks.

"Moore?" I whispered. "Where am I?"

But he did not answer. A tall man entered the room, and although he was dressed in the same robes as the seated chanting men, his face was hidden behind a grotesque painted mask. It resembled the head of a bull, and the painted hair rose sharply from the head in the shape of flames. The frozen grimace of its blood red lips was frightening, and as the man advanced I instinctively shrank away.

"Moore!" I whispered fiercely; "Moore! Get me out of here!"

But there was no response; as the man in the mask continued to walk toward me I closed my eyes . . . and awoke to sunlight streaming through white lace curtains and the smell of toast and orange juice. Dazed, I turned my head upon the pillow and saw a tray on my bedside table: orange juice, toast, jam, and a hard-boiled egg. There was a knock on my door.

"Come in."

Roper entered with a pot of coffee.

"I took the liberty of setting out your breakfast, sir; I hope you don't mind." He poured coffee into a thin Blue Willow china cup.

"Mr. Moore was concerned that you should not be late to your work at the hospital."

London Hospital felt like another world to me right now, and I blinked and rubbed my eyes, thick with sleep.

"That's very kind of him," I replied, sipping the coffee Roper handed me. He hesitated, and I thought he was going to say something, but then he just bowed his stiff little bow and slipped out quietly.

I looked around the room I had barely noticed the night before. The bed I found so comfortable was a canopy—and old, by the look of it. Everything in the room had been carefully chosen to provide both the feeling of luxury and comfort, from the intricately carved oak wardrobe to the brass bed warmer.

With a start, I saw hanging upon the wall above the dressing table the mask from my dream. It was made of wood and, bathed in the hazy morning sunshine, not as frightening as it had been in my dream. Still, it made me uncomfortable—and yet, oddly, drew me to it. I was gazing at it when there was another knock on the door.

"Come in."

Moore entered. He looked tired; his eyes were rimmed by bluish circles, and I wondered if he had slept. His voice was cheerful enough, though, and he greeted me warmly.

"I hope you slept well."

"Oh, yes, indeed."

"Did anything unusual happen last night?"

My jaw dropped open. I must have looked rather silly, because he laughed.

"Ah, I can see that it did—excellent! You *are* a good subject, as I suspected!" He proceeded to relate every last detail of my first dream, including the conversation I had with his disembodied voice. He elaborated upon what he had said in the dream: that the first manifestation is rarely corporeal; that was the next stage.

When I mentioned the second part of the dream, though, he looked puzzled.

"It sounds as though you were in a Tibetan monastery," he said. "Have you ever been in one?"

"No; I've never even seen pictures of one."

"That *is* curious."

I told him about the strange man wearing the mask which hung upon the wall.

"Ah—I forgot that was in here," he said, walking over to study it. "No doubt you saw the mask before falling asleep, and your mind quite naturally retained the image, inserting it into your dream."

"What is it?"

"It's a Tibetan god—Yama, king and judge of the dead. He is said to sit in the centre of Hell, and the wicked are brought before him to be judged before demons escort them to their fate."

I shuddered.

"Where did you get it?"

"It belonged to Roper's father. Roper took it with him when he left Tibet, though I can't imagine why he wanted the horrible thing. I suppose I should take it down so it doesn't frighten any more guests." He reached for the mask.

"No—don't!" I cried with a vehemence that surprised me.

Moore paused and looked at me, incredulous. "You *like* it?"

"No, no—I just don't think you should move it . . . oh, I don't know what I mean; I just think it shouldn't be disturbed."

Moore shrugged. "Very well," he said, then smiled. "You sound like Roper; he was convinced that if he left it in Tibet, terrible things would happen to him. Superstitious people, the Tibetans . . . Oh, but I see I interrupted your breakfast; I beg your pardon! Roper has dried and ironed all your clothing; I will send him up with some towels for your bath, and then when you are dressed we will talk some more."

It was Saturday and so I was not expected at the laboratory, but I was in the middle of an experiment and anxious to get to work. When Moore suggested we continue our experiments again that night, I agreed.

I said good-bye and made my way to London Hospital. The rain of the night before had cleared, though a few sullen clouds still hung over the city, casting their shadow on the puddles I carefully stepped over as I made my way towards Hyde Park.

The day was mild, and I strolled along caught up in my thoughts. Purple and white crocuses and yellow daffodils lined the path, stretching their petals toward the sun as it began to break through the clouds. I had just reached Round Pond, when suddenly I heard quick footsteps behind me. I turned, and when I saw who it was I stopped: it was Moore's cook, Tieba, running along without a coat, her long skirt whipping in the wind.

"Begging your pardon, sir," she said, quite out of breath, "but I just had to speak to you."

"What is it, Tieba?"

"Well, sir, you have to believe me when I say that I didn't listen on purpose, but I couldn't help overhearing part of your conversation with Mr. Moore—"

"This morning, you mean?"

"Yes, sir. You may think it's none of my business, but I beg you to listen to me—"

"Go ahead; I'm listening."

"Well . . ." She paused, and I noticed the black sheen of her hair in the late morning light. I inhaled the same faint aroma of jasmine as the night before. "Did he tell you who I am?"

"You are Roper's sister—"

"Did he tell you anything else?"

"Why, no; what do you mean?"

"Never mind," she replied with some bitterness, and I detected the slightest accent in her otherwise impeccable English. She looked at me, her deep-set black eyes round with fear. "No non-Tibetan has ever become a Dream Traveler, you see; virtually no one outside our country has even heard of it. Did you notice the strange mask in your room, Mr. Lawrence?"

"Why, yes—Moore said it belonged to your father."

She looked earnestly into my face, and once again I was struck by the resemblance to her brother. "There are many things you do not know, Mr. Lawrence; things you would do better to leave alone. . . ."

She paused, and we both watched as a flock of mallards landed upon the pond, green feathers flashing in the bright sunlight, their webbed feet kicking up a white spray of water behind them.

"The circumstances surrounding my father's death are much more complicated than you know," she continued, digging a toe of her polished shoe into the soft black mud at the side of the path we were on. "You would do better to stay out of matters you know nothing about. My brother . . . he can be a very dangerous man."

"But—"

"Mr. Lawrence, please believe me: *the prize isn't worth the price!*" She suddenly looked over her shoulder as if she were afraid of being followed. "I must go now, before they notice I am missing—I beg you to say nothing of this conversation to my brother."

"Don't worry, I won't—" I said, but before I had finished she turned quickly and walked rapidly back in the direction from which she came. I wanted to call after her, but the park was beginning to fill up with people enjoying a stroll among the flowers. I stood looking after her for a few moments and then continued on my way.

All the way to the laboratory I thought about Tieba's words, but as the day wore on I became increasingly involved in my work and gradually forgot about the incident. I passed the rest of the morning and the entire afternoon engaged in rapt contemplation of peptides and enzymes, and it was not until my laboratory partner McGee left for the day that I looked up at the clock and saw that it was half past seven. I threw off my lab coat and put on my jacket, which was still a little stiff from its soaking the evening before. I stepped outside into the mild night and hailed a cab.

I arrived at Moore's at about a quarter past eight, paid the driver and disembarked rather stiffly from the cab. My back muscles were cramped from bending over a microscope all day long, and I stretched my arms as I walked to the front gate. I had not taken a good look at the town house earlier, but noticed now that it was a handsome place, with its sturdy wrought iron gate and gleaming whitewashed exterior. Moore himself came to the door when I rang.

"Ah, Lawrence—come in, come in! I was just pouring myself an aperitif, and I trust you'll join me."

"Yes, thank you."

I followed him into the sitting room. I had forgotten all about the peacocks, and the impression they made the second time was even stronger than the first: they were so gaudy, so whimsical that they made me want to laugh. I contented myself with a smile.

"Ah, yes," Moore said, handing me a glass of amontillado, "one never does get used to the birds; that's one of the splendid things about them!" I commented on his choice of beverage, and he smiled. "Under the circumstances, I thought it might be appropriate . . . put us in the mood, so to speak."

As I observed the glass of golden liquid in my hand, I thought of the final horrifying image in Poe's story, "The Cask of Amontillado": the pitiful jingling of bells from the jester's cap that the ironically named Fortunato is wearing as his vengeful enemy walls him up forever in a cold stone vault. But then I looked at my host's cheerful face and rosy English cheeks and, reassured, held up my glass to the light.

"To adventure," I said with an enthusiasm that I did not quite feel. As we touched glasses, Roper entered the room to say that dinner was ready.

As we made our way to the dining room, Moore said, "I forgot that tonight is Tieba's night off. Don't worry, though; there's some cold beef and I'm sure Roper managed to put something together; he's endlessly resourceful."

The thought struck me that it wasn't Tieba's night off at all, but that—for some reason—her brother wanted her out of the way. I remembered Tieba's words: *My brother can be a very dangerous man.* I had an impulse to tell Moore about her warning, but I had promised Tieba to say nothing.

We entered the dining room just as Roper carried in a gleaming silver tray upon which sat a mouthwatering slab of rare roast beef, a loaf of bread and salad. I was starving, having worked straight through luncheon, so I attacked the food with relish. I ate rather more than I should have, and drank more amontillado than was good for me. As we ate, I glanced from time to time at the portrait of Moore's father, glowering down at us from its heavy gilt frame.

Over coffee and cognac in front of the fire, Moore said, "There's something else I should tell you before we proceed any further with this business." He leaned toward me, his green eyes dark in the dim light. "You yourself noted that Roper appears to be a man of forty-five, when he is in fact well over sixty. Do you know why this is so?"

"No, of course not."

"It is because he was once a Dream Traveler."

I tried to digest this information while Moore went on.

"I haven't told you the *most* extraordinary thing about dream traveling: that while one is inside the dream, one does not age! *Now* do you see why I became so excited by the prospect? Think what it could mean to mankind, to expand one's life span by one third!"

My head began to spin with the possibilities. I saw my name on the front page of every London newspaper and scientific journal. I thought of the grant money that would come pouring in . . .

Moore broke my reverie. "There is, however, another thing that I must tell you. The process is not entirely without risk."

"What kind of risk?"

"The barrier between life and dreaming is erased. To the Dream Traveler, food eaten is digested, knives really cut. This is equally true for the dreamer. He, too, is at risk. This is why so few people in Tibet are Dream Travelers. The danger is enormous. Roper was a Dream Traveler—but he gave it up."

"Why?"

"Because Roper's father was a respected Tibetan Dream Traveler, but he met an enemy of his in another person's dream, and could not control the dreamer."

"Control the dreamer? What do you mean?"

"Dream Travelers learn how to influence dreamers to change the dream if danger presents itself. But sometimes the dreamer cannot be controlled and if that happens, then the Traveler is caught and must confront the danger as though it were real life."

"What happened to Roper's father?"

"His enemy in the dream killed him."

"But who was the dreamer? His enemy?"

"No," Moore said softly. "His son."

At his words, a tingle went up my spine. Tieba's words rang in my ears: "The circumstances surrounding my father's death are much more complicated than you know." Now I understood what she meant when she said *the prize isn't worth the price* . . .

"Roper blamed himself for his father's death," Moore continued, "and so did a lot of the people in his village. It was one of the reasons he left Tibet. I helped him to get out."

"Why were you in Tibet in the first place?"

"I went with my father. He'd been there before I was born and always wanted to return. I suppose I feel a certain kinship to Roper because soon after his father met his end, my father also died in his sleep. It makes me feel that our destinies are somehow—how shall I say?—linked. You see, I did not bring Roper over here just to be my butler; that was his idea. I brought him here to be my tutor. He's taught me well—and now I'm ready for tonight's experiment."

I set down my coffee and stood up in front of the fire. "Are you sure this is worth the risk? What if I can't control what I'm dreaming? Hasn't that fellow in Vienna been telling us that dreaming is a—what does he call it?—a 'subconscious' process?"

"But I will be right there with you. I will tell you what to do."

"But Roper's father was an experienced Dream Traveler, and yet he couldn't control his own son!"

Moore stared into the glowing embers of the fire. "If you want to back out, I will not hold it against you."

I had an impulse to do just that. Tieba's warning niggled at me, and yet I could not imagine what motive Roper might have for harming either of us. My curiosity got the better of my caution, and I nodded.

"I'm willing."

"Capital!"

The nightclothes were on the bed as Moore had promised, and I no sooner slipped under the covers than I felt sleep pressing down gently upon me like a soft hand. The last thing I noticed was that the Tibetan mask upon the wall was missing . . .

I found myself walking through an underground cavern, damp, dark and dank. The passage was dimly lit by gas lamps set into its stone walls. Its corridors twisted and wound ahead of me. The only sound I heard beside my own footsteps was the steady drip of water upon stone, and the walls gave off the familiar musty smell of mouldy basements.

"Lawrence."

I turned, but saw no one.

"Lawrence!"

This time the voice seemed to be coming from behind me. Again I turned, and this time I saw, ever so faintly, the shadowy white outline of a man.

"Moore?"

Gradually the outline began to fill in, gaining in substance, until Moore himself stood in front of me. He was dressed as a jester, in orange and blue motley, complete with cap and bells.

"Moore! Is it—are you—?"

"Yes, Lawrence, I have done it: I am a Traveler!"

"But why the costume?"

"I don't know."

Then I remembered that just before I fell asleep, Poe's story had been running through my head, and I mentioned this to Moore.

He nodded. "Perhaps that explains it. There are many things I don't understand yet." He looked at the damp, water-stained walls that surrounded us. "Do you recognize this place?"

"No, but it reminds me of the underground cavern in Poe's story."

Just then, another voice came booming out of the half-darkness.

"Your deduction is correct."

We both turned and saw Roper in a long black cloak with a red silk lining, and a broad-brimmed hat shadowing his face so we could not see his expression.

"Roper, what are you doing here?" Moore asked.

"I have waited patiently for this day," Roper replied, his voice a snarl. "The time has come at last for you to atone for the sins of the father—brother."

Moore turned pale.

"*B-brother?* How can that be?"

Roper clenched his fists and the muscles in his jaw stood out. "My mother was hardly more than a girl when *your* father had his way with her. Without even bothering to see whether his actions had any consequences, he returned to England and married a respectable *white* English woman. When he finally returned to see what had become of the woman he abandoned so carelessly, he met my sister—and lecherous old man that he was, he tried to force himself upon her! My stepfather found out and was going to reveal his crimes, but *your* father murdered him!" Roper's voice was harsh, steel against steel. "*I* was the helpless dreamer who watched him kill the man who raised me as his own child, but I am no longer helpless . . . and I shall not allow you to corrupt my sister as your father corrupted my mother!"

"You're insane!" Moore gasped, his voice shaking.

"I have seen the way you look at her." As Roper approached, his form cast a ghastly shadow upon the wall behind us.

"Lawrence! Change the dream, quickly!" Moore cried frantically.

"*He* can do nothing," Roper sneered, his green eyes hard as flint. "My powers are much greater than his." He stretched out an arm towards me and suddenly my limbs grew rigid as stone.

"Help me, Lawrence!" Moore's voice was barely a whisper above the steady tattoo of water upon smooth stone.

I tried to move, but I was frozen as stiff as a statue. I could not even lift my hand.

Roper took something out of his cloak and placed it over his face. I saw with horror what it was: the Tibetan mask of Yama, king and judge of the dead.

"Wake up, Lawrence—try to wake up!" cried Moore, but I could not even shake my head or speak. I watched helplessly as Roper advanced upon my friend, the slow, steady *drop drop drop* of water upon rock in my ears. He drew a long curved knife from his belt and, raising it high above his head, moved slowly and inexorably toward his cowering prey.

"Well, brother, say your prayers."

"No, Roper, *no!*" Moore retreated back through the corridor, the bells on his ridiculous cap jingling with a mocking hollow sound. He turned to run, but found himself in a cul-de-sac. He stood with his back to the wall.

A flash of steel in the dim yellow light. Moore's scream mingled with the tinkling bells on his cap.

My own cry welled up in my throat, but I could make no sound. Helplessly, I watched Roper deposit Moore's limp body in a shallow alcove within one of the walls. Then he bent over a pile of loose bricks and slowly began piling them up, one by one, till they reached the ceiling. My blood froze at the implacable ritual; I made one last supreme effort to move—and suddenly woke.

My eyes gradually focused in the darkness. I was in the same bed in the same room of Moore's flat as before. I sat up and listened, but the house was silent as a tomb.

Climbing out of bed, I hurried down the corridor to Moore's room. I knocked on the door, but, receiving no answer, pushed the door open. The bedside lamp was lit. Moore lay upon the bed fully clothed, his eyes open, staring up at the ceiling. I saw no mark upon his body, but knew instantly that he was dead.

As I backed out of the room, trembling, I collided with someone. I spun around, a cry caught in my throat. It was Tieba. Her hair was disheveled; she was barefoot and clad only in a night-gown.

"Go at once!" she whispered, her hands frantically clawing at me. "Go from this house and don't look back!"

"But—" I pointed vaguely in the direction of Moore's lifeless form.

"You can do nothing more for him! Go before my brother comes for you!"

"What about you?"

"I am in no danger; he loves me and would do anything to protect me!"

I needed no further urging. Without bothering to collect my clothes, I ran down the stairs and out the front door in my bare feet, heading for Hyde Park. The streets were deserted. Running along the sidewalk, I reached the park within minutes, stopping only to catch my breath and listen for the sound of a pursuer. I heard nothing but the clicking of crickets and the cooing of mourning doves.

I was relieved to see pale yellow dawn lighting up the sky in the East. Wearily, I set off for my own house, my bare feet digging into the soft spring soil.

The next day, I searched the paper for any mention of Moore's death, but not until a day later did I find a small piece in the back section: *Kensington Heir Dies in Sleep; Sole Occupant of Whistler's "Peacock House."* The article explained that Moore left no heir to his estate, so the proceeds would go to charity. There was no suggestion of foul play; his death had been ruled a heart attack. Nor was there any mention of Roper or his sister.

I considered going to the police, but I was certain they would think I was mad, and perhaps even charge me with murder; there may have been someone who saw me emerge wild-eyed and bare-foot from Moore's town house the night he died. So with a heavy heart I kept quiet about the whole affair. I took to sleeping with the lights on at night; I got a spaniel and trained him to sleep at the foot of my bed.

The incident haunted me for some time. I read volumes on

Tibetan culture, but could find no reference in any book to Dream Travelers. Sometimes I awoke at night with the sound of Moore's screams in my ears, but as the years passed it gradually faded in my memory, receding into the blurry, half-remembered quality of a fevered dream.

Henry Slesar

The Moving Finger Types

HENRY SLESAR *is the author of more than five hundred novels and stories, approximately one-third of them science-fantasy. He won the Mystery Writers of America's Edgar Award for* The Grey Flannel Shroud *and another one of his novels was filmed as the cult favorite* Twenty Million Miles to Earth. *Slesar, for many years the head writer of* The Edge of Night *and a regular contributor to the once-popular TV series* The Man from U.N.C.L.E., *knows plenty about screenwriting, but hopefully "The Moving Finger Types" isn't based on firsthand knowledge. . . .*

LEGGET KNEW that Mitch Cohen had been ducking him, but in his vegetative condition of the last few weeks, Legget hadn't cared. Now things were different, and he cared enough to have figuratively backed Mitch up against the non-figurative wall of Thomajon's, a small bistro on Sunset Strip. They had been friends since meeting at a studio party and discovering that they were fellow Chicagoans, transplanted like the palm trees. Both had been dutifully nostalgic about the Loop, critical of L.A., and cynical about the movie business. Now, three years later, Mitch was working steadily behind a camera, pulling in large, satisfying paychecks, and Legget, a man with producing aspirations, had drifted, bobbed, sunk, floated, and somehow survived the Hollywood waters.

There was no doubt in Legget's mind about why Mitch had

been reluctant to see him, not after their last psyched-up luncheon at Tail o' the Cock. "Look, let's not even talk about that," Mitch said generously, waving his blunt fingers in a wipe across the past. "You were pretty low, Norman; this town had you talking to yourself. Uh, by the way, you working?"

"Yes," Legget said, staring into his drink. "Got a job this morning. Assistant to Marty Lang at Universal."

"Great! You're moving again."

"Yes," Legget said. "That's the word, Mitch, I'm *moving*. I'm not stuck on dead center any more; that's what I wanted to tell you." He let Mitch see his eyes, even though he knew his friend might be jolted by their intensity. "I found my place, Mitch," he said. "Just like I told you. I lost my place and then I found it again . . ."

"Norman, Norman," Mitch groaned. "Not that again, not that *idea* of yours . . ."

"But it's not just an idea. It's a *fact*. I know I sounded like a nutcase the last time, I didn't have any proof. But now I've got it, Mitch. I can prove it to you, to anybody. If you'll just *listen*.

"I told you about that office in Chicago. I was working in this old building on Michigan, writing a lot of junk for a trade publisher, about dry cleaning and poultry farming and God knows what else. You know those office buildings, a million frosted glass doors with all kinds of weirdo names painted on them, people who make gold fillings and corrugated boxes and who knows what, and one day, I noticed a door with the words: DESTINY PRODUCTIONS. It could have been fourteen million things, of course, but I got curious enough to go in and ask. There was a girl out in front with a face like a blank sheet of paper, and she gave me a lot of vague answers, and all I could see from the anteroom was a million filing cabinets and all I could hear was a lot of clattering typewriters. She offered to have me talk to one of the executives, but by this time I didn't want to bother, so I walked out.

"Well, that would have been the end of it, except for that day I was looking for Willie Hyam's Theatre West building; he had an acting class going, and he wanted me to talk to his kids. It was someplace way out on Ventura, and I got lost and saw this white stucco building tucked behind the telephone poles, so small maybe nobody else would have noticed it. But I did, because there was a little white sign outside that said: DESTINY PRODUCTIONS, and I got curious all over again. Whatever those guys in Chicago were doing with their file cabinets and typewriters, they had a West Coast branch.

"So I tried the same routine. I went into the office, and I got an ice-water reception from the girl out front, who wanted to know my business, but *exactly*. I faked being a freelance reporter, curious about the name of the company, and that got me nowhere, especially since I wasn't carrying any press identification. This time, though, I stuck it out long enough to have some guy come out of the main section to talk to me. His name was Ankim, and he was a tall, thin man in an undertaker's Sunday suit, and all I can remember about his looks was a head of waxy white hair, probably a falsie. In fact, that was a funny thing I thought about later, the *nothingness* of Ankim's face, and the nothingness of that *girl's* face, too. Anyway, he was polite enough, in a non-oily, non-informative way, and when I asked him if his company had something to do with movie production, hinting around that maybe I was a biggie who could *do* things for him, he smiled and said, in a way, in a *limited* kind of way. And the next thing I remember—pay attention to this part, it's crazy—the very next thing I remember is being back behind the wheel of my Volks. I wasn't drinking, I didn't have any blackout, I was just *there*, driving along the Hollywood Freeway, heading back for Westwood. I never saw Willie Hyam's theatre or anything, and all I could remember about Destiny Productions was a feeling, a visceral kind of thing, a cold, twitchy sensation right down to the bone. I felt as if I had touched something outside of any kind of *realness*—I don't mean ghostly or freakish—the closest thing to it was my one and only, thank God, trip, you remember that, when I felt as if my eyes were in my fingertips? . . . No, you're wrong,

Mitch, I can see what you're thinking. I wasn't drunk, I wasn't coked, I wasn't anything but shook up.

"Anyway, I didn't think about Destiny Productions again, not until a good year and a half later, when that damned fog settled over me.

"I don't know how to describe what happened to me. It was a kind of lethargy, an inertia, but it was more than that. It happened about the time I got my divorce from Phyllis; at first, I thought that had something to do with it, the change of my marital status, but it couldn't have been the answer. Divorcing Phyllis was like chopping off a limb that had been dead for years; I didn't even feel the cut of the axe. I was moving around like an automaton, eating, drinking and sleeping only because my instincts were still operating, pushing me between the dining table and bathroom and bedroom. I didn't want to see anyone, talk to anyone, go anywhere, do anything I didn't absolutely have to do. I finally got up enough energy to mention my plight to Fiedler—that's my shrink—and he called it an *Oblomov* syndrome. It's some freaky Russian novel, where the hero gives up on life, just wants to stay in bed all the time. Only I didn't want to do that, either; I was indifferent, but I was restless.

"Of course, this attitude didn't do me much good on the job. I was working for Dmitri at Warners at the time, and you know what happened; he canned me. I didn't give a damn; I didn't even try to make another connection. I spent all my mornings lying around the house, and all my afternoons at the movies. That was one thing I didn't lose; maybe it was part of my problem. Ever since I was a kid, I used to take myself to the movies, just cop out in the balcony, jaws agape, and let other people live my life for me. It suited my mood perfectly, so that's what I did. I saw every movie in town, some of them twice. And that's when I remembered about Destiny Productions.

"Mitch, stop looking around, I'm not going to get violent. I know my theory sounded nuts to you the last time, but you didn't know the whole story then. I mean, it's not just *my* theory, about predestination and stuff, whole civilizations and cultures have believed in it, for centuries. Millions of people believe in it right now. *It is Written.* You've heard that, Mitch. Everything is written down, beforehand, our whole lives, all put down on some kind of—celestial paper. Karma. Fate. Kismet. Destiny. *Destiny,* Mitch, you see?

"That's when I got the idea that maybe this outfit, this Destiny Productions, maybe they were the ones that did the Writing. After all, if it's *Written,* really *Written,* then somebody's got to put it all down, maybe literally, I mean. You take a movie; maybe it's only a simulation of reality, of life, but it has to be *Written* first, somebody's got to put words into those mouths, somebody's got to tell the actors what to *do.* And it seemed to me that if *my* life was written down, maybe all that had happened to me was—*I'd lost my place.* That's all it could have been, Mitch, maybe it's what happens to millions of people, they just lost their place in the manuscript of their lives . . .

"Well, I had to go and find out. So I went looking for Destiny Productions, and it was only after days of trying that I located that white stucco building, only now I saw it really wasn't that small; its architecture was deceptive. This time, I was more deceptive, too; I even took an old press identification card with me, and I wouldn't budge out of that anteroom until the receptionist with the nothing face got Mr. Ankim out to see me.

"I told Ankim straight out what I thought, about the kind of work they did at Destiny Productions, and he looked at me with a forced sort of smile, pretending that I was some kind of religious nut that had wandered in off the Freeway, only I wouldn't let him play that game. I kept up my 'reporter' pose and dropped a lot of hints about exposing his company to a large, nosy Southern California public, and he looked even whiter and waxier when he heard that, and asked me into his private office.

"And then they told me the truth, Mitch. That this was it. This was the place where *It Was Written.* The whole thing. Your life. Mine. Everybody's.

"Now you're looking at me funny again. Okay, I can't blame you. But just hear the rest and see how it adds up. Because I was shown the evidence, Mitch, the proof that this was where all the *Writing* was done. No, not *all* of it, this was just the L.A. branch office; they had thousands all over the world, Ankim told me, looking sort of harried. With the way the population was exploding, they'd had to establish more and more offices all the time, and that meant finding all kinds of new ways of disguising their activities. And of course, they kept up with the times. Ankim said they used to write down a man's life like an old-fashioned Victorian novel, only now they used faster, modern techniques, the scenario format . . . Don't grin at me like that, Mitch; I actually *saw* one of these scripts, I actually saw my *own* . . .

"Yeah, that's right. I told Ankim what had happened to me, how I was *stuck* in some kind of groove. I told him I'd lost the place in my life scenario, and I wanted to find it again, find out what I was supposed to do next. Well, he didn't like that idea at all; he said I was mistaken, that people often felt undecided about what to do, but nobody actually lost their *place*. He even recommended psychoanalysis, can you feature that? But I told him no dice, that I wanted to *know*. I wanted advice, guidance, *direction*. And he said no, absolutely not, nobody could *ever* see the scenario of their own lives, it was strictly against Regulations. And I said to him, look, I don't want to see the whole thing, I don't *want* to know everything that's coming, it would give me the shakes to know that. All I wanted to learn was my next move, my next *scene*. And if he didn't help me—well, I won't kid you, Mitch, I threatened the guy; I said I'd tell the whole damned world about what went on there, and in all those Destiny Productions offices on earth—and *then* he'd be sorry he didn't bend the rules just a little bit . . .

"So that's when he gave in. He pushed a button on his desk, and told his nothing-faced secretary what to do, and she let out a little gasp. But she went out obediently, and a little while later, she came back with a script. Yes, a *script*, Mitch, thicker than the Los Angeles Telephone Directory, thank God—it looked like a nice, long, fat story for me—and then Ankim himself found my *place* in the scenario. It wasn't even halfway through the script, and he wouldn't let me see more than a couple of pages, and guess what it said? It was Scene 13490, and it took place *at the offices of Destiny Productions.* Do you see, Mitch? Even my visit there. It was all *Written.* Typed, anyway.

"Then he let me see the next page of the script, and it was Scene 13491. And the heading was:

INTERIOR—MARTY LANG'S OFFICE—DAY.

"It was the whole scene, Mitch, I swear to you. It was me and Lang, talking about the picture he had just signed to do at Universal. And after we shot the breeze awhile, Lang made me an offer, and I took it. That was where the scene ended, and that was where Ankim took the book out of my hands.

"Well, I didn't make any protest; Ankim was looking pretty distressed by now, and I decided I'd gotten enough out of him anyway. He walked me out of this office, relieved that it was all over, I guess, because he even put his arm on my shoulder real friendly-like. He showed me a little bit of the operation, the long rows of filing cabinets, maybe a hundred blank-faced girls hammering away at IBMs. He didn't see me all the way out; he said he had to return my scenario to the proper place, and I said goodbye to him at the door of an office at the end of the hallway; it said something on the door, but I didn't take much notice of it. I was too excited, thinking about tomorrow, wondering if it was really going to happen the way it was put down . . .

"The next morning—no, *this* morning, Mitch—I went out to Universal and made a cold call on Marty Lang. No appointment, nothing, I just told the guard at the gate I wanted to see him, and Lang okayed it. Nine times out of ten, I would have gotten turned away, but this time Lang saw me. And you know what happened, Mitch? We played the scene. The same scene. *The way it was Written.* I knew every one of my lines, and he seemed to know his—like he'd been memorizing them all night. And like the script said, I got the job."

Mitch Cohen didn't talk for a while. Then he smiled weakly, and said, "Hey, aren't you supposed to be keeping all this a secret? I mean, isn't that what you promised what's-his-name in return for looking at your—script?"

"Yes," Legget said, pushing his glass around in a circle. "That was what I promised. But it's hard to keep quiet about a thing like this. I think even Ankim realized that, and that's why I'm worried, Mitch, that's why I'm scared stiff . . ."

Mitch was looking at his watch. "Gee, I didn't realize it was so late, Norman. There's something I've got to do tonight—"

Legget put a hand over his friend's extended wrist. "You see, I remember now, Mitch, what it said on that office door. The office where Ankim took my scenario, when I was leaving—"

"I'm not snowing you, Norman, no kidding, I really have to go. There's this screening tonight—"

"Mitch, please *listen*. What it said on that door was—REWRITE ROOM."

"What?"

"It said Rewrite Room," Legget said. But there was no reaction from his friend. He looked into Mitch Cohen's no-longer-involved eyes, and saw that he had lost his audience. Instead of trying to recapture it, Legget gave Mitch a sagging smile, and clapped his drinking arm.

"Sure, pal," he said. "You go to your screening. I didn't mean to keep you so long."

"We'll get together soon," Mitch said. "Maybe you and Phyllis—I mean, maybe you can come up to the Canyon for a weekend sometime."

"Sure," Legget said. "I'd like that."

He ordered another drink after Mitch left. The bar was getting more crowded. A young couple, the girl smartly dressed and coolly indifferent to what was obviously a sales pitch, sat two stools away from Legget. He listened to the familiar rhythm of their argument, and then watched with interest when the young man tightened his jaw and walked away angrily. The girl didn't seem to mind losing him. She gave Legget a sideways glance. He thought how satisfying it would be to slide over the vacant stools between them, say hello, and start talking to her, telling her, with properly amused expressions, the story that Mitch Cohen didn't believe. She wouldn't believe it either, of course, but Legget wanted to tell it again, about Destiny, and Ankim, and the script, and that chilling Rewrite Room. He had just decided to make his move when he realized that the girl, the bar, and the room were beginning to Fade Out.

Darrell Schweitzer

The Story of Obbok

"The Story of Obbok" is a cautionary tale that warns of knowledge so potent that you can't even hear about it secondhand. DARRELL SCHWEITZER is a prolific fantasist and editor whose stories appear regularly in my anthologies. His most recent contributions were two Sherlock Holmes tales, "The Adventure of the Death-Fetch" in The Game Is Afoot *and "Sherlock Holmes, Dragon-Slayer" in* The Resurrected Holmes.

THERE ONCE was a poet named Obbok who lived in the court of the King of Rhoon. He had written thirteen books and was a poet in good standing, and on the third day of every week he would recite his poems before the King and his vassals and the ladies of the court. Each time his audience would applaud politely when he finished, and at banquets he was given a place of honor, as befitted a person of his high calling.

Now, by the time Obbok was entering into old age his son began to show great promise at poetry also, and it was sure that he would succeed Obbok in the position. The young man's verses showed a proper regard for meter and rhyme, and treated those subjects poets usually write about in the manner they traditionally treat them. Thus he was exactly like his father in all matters of literature and content to travel the sure path that lay before him.

But Obbok was not satisfied, and between his appearances in

court he dreamed. He dreamed of what it would be like to be a great poet, to have the power to move men with his words, to evoke laughter and sorrow and awe, to carry them to the very ends of the universe, to traverse eternity itself, from the Days Before Time to the Ending of All, to wrench the hearts and souls of his listeners with his songs.

He knew that the respect given him was borne more of ritual than appreciation. Often he would see the King's eyes wander as he recited, and the ladies would whisper among themselves, and the nobles tended to sneak out before he was finished. He wanted to put an end to this, to mean something to the people, to uplift them and contribute something to their lives.

So he sat down one day and considered the things that great poets write about, these being gods, nature, and wars, and he composed verses about them in his usual style, and delivered the verses at the appointed hour on the appointed day, and the King was as polite as ever. He thanked Obbok and praised his poetry in the customary manner, and when the poet left the throne room the men went on with their gaming and arguing, and the women continued their chatter, and servants were reminded of urgent tasks left undone. All was as before.

Sorrow came to the heart of Obbok, for he knew he would die soon and his body would be laid in the Hall of Bards along with his ancestors, and no one would remember him, and when his son died the same thing would happen, and the process would continue until the ending of his line.

He resolved then to pray to the gods, and thrice daily and thrice nightly he climbed to the top of the Tower of Stillness and communed with them, yet nothing came of it and his next performance was like the one before, like all the ones of his lifetime and the lifetimes of his father and grandfather, no doubt also like all the times his son would read until he too passed from the lands of the living.

Many months passed and Obbok was greatly unhappy, until one day it was mentioned to him by a scribe that south of Rhoon and Lan and east and south of Dzim there was a mountain called

Cloudcap, whereon dwelled a holy prophet named Amayar who spoke with the gods as if they were his kin, and was thus the possessor of great wisdom.

This news lifted the heart of Obbok and he arranged for an absence from court, and three days later he set out on his horse for Cloudcap, and the King and his nobles scarcely noticed that the poet was gone.

For three days and three nights Obbok rode southeast from the capital at Klor, and on the morning of the fourth day he crossed the river Xrum and entered into Lan. Two days later he was at the feet of the mountains which divided Lan from Dzim. He had to wait six days there until a caravan came along, for the mountains were infested with robbers, but finally one did come, and in the company of twenty Rhoonish tea merchants, he made the crossing. Four more days brought him to the southern frontiers of Dzim, again to mountains similarly haunted. This time there was no caravan, for no traders went into the seven wastes beyond, and Obbok crossed alone. He was not molested and he reached the Last Hall by evening, and early the next morning traded his horse for a camel and set out across the desert.

Five more days and nights passed and he stopped only briefly to rest and draw water from one of the few oases to be found in that region. He guided himself by the sun and stars, till finally he espied Cloudcap on the morning of the sixth day, standing tall above the world, caressed by the light of dawn.

Of the prophet Amayar he found no trace save for an old abandoned hovel which could have as easily belonged to a beggar or a thief. It was all but buried in the sand, its roof blown away, obviously uninhabited for many years. So it was that Obbok himself ascended the mountain to speak to the gods.

All that day he struggled up the precarious trail, till by evening there was no trail at all, and he inched his way over seamless rocks and up all but vertical cliffs. This was not work suited to an old man's muscles, and many times he was tempted to lie down and rest where he was, but he did not, for this was a sacred mountain from which blessings flowed and the lands spread out, and on its slopes no man could sleep. Such a thing would be a horrible sin in the face of the gods. Does a slave dare doze before a great king?

Dawn was just lighting the east when he reached the summit, and as the sun rose Obbok performed the proper rituals with earth and air and fire and metal, and he invoked the gods, that they might aid him in this hour of need. All that day and into the next night he called out to them, never pausing, his voice never silent.

Now Gheeznu, the god of poets, is a small and insignificant god in the eyes of the Great Ones, and he is not often involved in the important affairs of the universe. Thus it happened that he had nothing to do at the time that Obbok addressed him, and he decided to hear the old man's prayers. He peered down from his ivory seat in the Land Behind the Sky, looked down through the clouds and corporeal airs, and saw there on the summit of Cloud-cap the tiny figure of Obbok the poet. And for reasons not known to theologians he granted Obbok's wish. Some say that he was moved by pity, while others claim he meant what came after as a moral lesson to make men content with their stations in life, although another school of thought holds the whole affair to be one of the mischievous pranks the gods often play upon men. But regardless of the motivations of the gods, which are only speculation, the results were definite and obvious.

Obbok's fire rose until it touched the sky and the tops of the flames vanished into the clouds overhanging the peak, and when it again receded and burned low and extinguished itself, lo! there was before the aging poet a wondrous scroll not even hot from the fire, engraved in nine and ninety languages, none of which could ever be deciphered by men. Obbok took up this scroll with great reverence. He wrapped it in his cloak lest his hands soil it, and hastily departed from that holy place, shouting thanks aloud to the gods as he did.

On his way back across the Seven Wastes he pondered over the writings, and as he rested in the Last Hall he gazed at the scroll often. Men saw it and recognized its nature and source, and Obbok was treated with great respect, as one touched by the divine.

In truth, though, nothing happened to Obbok until he returned to Klor and laid the scroll on a special stand which he commanded his apprentices to build. Exhausted then he retired to bed without trying any more to learn the meaning of the thing. And that night, as Time strode across the world and his hounds drove the day fleeing before them, the spirits of the gods came down between the stairs masked in dreams, and to them the scroll in Obbok's chamber shone like a bright beacon. They clustered about it and read thereon the instructions of Gheeznu. And thus wondrous things entered into the head of Obbok that night.

He saw all eternity as a continuous strip, past, present, future and end molding into one. He saw the primal screaming chaos which spawned the gods, and against which they battled in the days before Time. Revealed to him was the shaping of the world in the hands of the various deities, and the reigns of the Kings Before Men, the driving into the sky of the immortal dragon which threatened to devour the world and still nibbles at the sun. He saw also the coming of Time from the mists of chaos, and he knew then how the brothers Time and Fate drove the world before them with sword and hammer and toppled Throramna, the Father of Cities, and smote also the ancient lords of Earth, toppling their corpses into the jaws of the jackal Death. The coming of man Obbok saw, and before the eyes of his dream, kingdoms rose and melted away like seasons before the onslaught of years. And from the Farthest East he saw the hounds of time come, unleashed by their master, howling after the lives of men. Gnath and Belhimra came and went. Even his own country died before a flood of savages from the south. He saw new continents arising, only to sink again beneath the seas, and he caught a glimpse of the war the gods fought over Aduil; he gazed in horror at the coming of the Lizard Earls, the return of chaos and the dimming of days, the final death of the world and the gods. And yet more was revealed, all the secret thoughts of men laid bare. He saw into their minds and hearts, discerned nobility, self-sacrifice, stupidity and cowardice, love of country, greed, treason, murder and love—all the things which make men what they are. The veils were drawn back yet further and he saw into the hearts of the gods, and in them he saw the same things again, plus their contempt for all creatures lesser, their conceit and contempt for one another, and finally their fear of the One who is greater than the gods and keeps the universe in a bottle in his pocket.

At this point the gods cried out and the world trembled, for the spirits had shown too much, and the gods recalled them at once and sent the Sisters of Forgetting into Obbok's sleep. But it was too late, for Fate and Time, who are impervious to the gods, again strode over the world scattering the night before them, and the dreams of Obbok left him with the coming of morning.

And the gods were very much afraid, save for Gheeznu, who seemed rather pleased with himself.

Great was the wonderment that seized the awakened Obbok. He roused his servants even though it was before the accustomed hour, and sent them scurrying to fetch all the pens, ink and writing parchments they could find. There was fire in his face that made them all fearful, and they went off at once. Soon a great pile of writing materials was in Obbok's chamber. Night and day he wrote, and wore out pens, and higher and higher grew the pile of pages. Cautiously his apprentices and servants approached him and laid out a meal before him, only to remove it again when they saw it was cold. They muttered among themselves, saying, "Surely the Master is possessed by a demon or devil," for Obbok had never previously taken writing too seriously and had only composed verses out of necessity or boredom. Now, of course, the heat of inspiration was in him, but the others did not understand, for they knew nothing of the true meaning of the mysterious scroll.

One day the King sent a messenger into the room of Obbok to summon the poet so that he might hear some of this new poetry that the whole castle was talking about. Yet the poet did not come, and the messenger spoke as if to one deaf, for Obbok did not speak or even slow his hand, and the messenger was moved with fear when he saw the look on the old man's face.

At this point the King grew angry and sent his guards to seize Obbok and bring him to the courtroom at once, for never before had anyone dared to ignore a royal command, and the King would have an explanation. The guards went, but when they came to lay their hands on the bard, Obbok *did* look up, although he paused not an instant from his writing, and the terrible glare frightened the guards, for they saw something in those eyes that was not of mortal Earth. They too turned and fled.

Then the King himself came to Obbok and the poet paused for the briefest of seconds and spoke a single word which gave reason for everything and caused the King to fall down on his knees and beg forgiveness for the interruption. That word was a god word, and it had come at the very end of the dream. It was never intended to be uttered by the mouths of men or heard by their ears.

The King withdrew, and all the castle was moved with fear and bewilderment at this new thing. All activities stopped. Everyone waited for Obbok to finish his work as they would await the sentence of a harsh judge, and the court soothsayer proclaimed a miracle of the first order, bidding all to go and purify themselves in the temple, then return and hear the wondrous revelation of Obbok.

And after fifteen days Obbok called out from his room and bade his servants lift him into bed. With failing voice he commanded them to bring food and water, and medicines, for he was exceedingly weary. These things were done and Obbok slept for two days after he had eaten, and none dared enter and read the manuscript while he slumbered.

Finally the poet roused himself and sent word to the King, informing him that he was ready. Nearly all the people of the castle came to hear him this time, every lord, every general, even the guards from the walls and the cooks from the kitchen. All stood in silence and complete attention was on Obbok, and the ladies did not whisper among themselves, and no one *dared* slip out.

Obbok came and recited his poem before them, and it was four thousand and nine stanzas in length.

There is some confusion as to what happened after that. No books tell of it, and the whole affair and especially the ending of it has been shrouded in great secrecy. The King died shortly afterwards, and it is only by piecing together the accounts of the various servants and courtiers who were *not* present at the recital that the tale is known at all. And yet no two of them have ever been able to agree on certain parts of it.

According to some, so terrible was the content of Obbok's poem that its words drove all who heard it mad, and for this reason none who heard it could tell any of it, and if asked they would only roll their eyes up to heaven and mutter something obscure, or else not respond at all. Great were the secrets revealed that day, all the things beyond the knowing of philosophers, and no one had the courage to understand it let alone repeat it. Fervently they begged the Sisters of Forgetting to slay them, but there was no relief. Many went out and slew themselves afterward.

And others claim that the King declared Obbok to be possessed by a devil, and he had him hanged from the highest tower. The poem was cast into the fire, according to this version, for none dared leave it around. It had the power to corrupt.

Yet others will tell you that it was Obbok who went mad, and after speaking the final verse he collapsed to the floor and whimpered like a child, begging gods and men to forgive him for what he had done. He was carried away and locked in a remote tower in a distant castle, for it would have been bad luck and poor form to allow a madman to wander about one's court.

And still others insist that while all were dazed by the effect of the poem, Obbok grabbed the manuscript and fled from the court, and not able to destroy his work, he hid it in a place from which it will issue forth on the last day, rendering men helpless with its words and bringing back Chaos, causing the final death of the universe. And those who tell the tale this way believe that Obbok still walks the world in the guise of a minstrel, and he sings only of simple things and pleasant happenings, of the birds of the air and the bees of the flowers and the coming of spring. Those that behold him see a sorrow beneath his calm and do not ask of it.

And finally there are some who swear by all that is holy that as soon as Obbok finished his poem, the floor was rent apart and a demon sprang up into the throne room, devouring Obbok and the manuscript in a single gulp, and thus the blasphemy and horror of it were removed from the lands of mortal man.

No one can be sure of any of these things now, for there is a new king in Klor, and Rhoon is troubled by wars and no one has time to bother with the past. Furthermore the King has been cautious and has decreed that anyone prying into the matter will be tortured to death by devices unimaginable, learned by wicked sorcerers from demons conjured for that purpose alone.

The son of Obbok dwells in the court now, and once every week he recites his new poems, all of which deal with the subject matter common to courtly verses and written in the classical manner. They are applauded out of courtesy, and the ladies whisper and giggle during the performances, and some of the men slip away unnoticed, and the poet is given a place of high esteem and privilege in the court, as befits one of his noble calling.

Kathleen C. Szaj

Revised Expectations

Many consider Great Expectations *to be Charles Dickens's greatest novel, and that includes* KATHLEEN C. SZAJ, *educator, director of the* Growing A Story *literacy enrichment program, and author of* I Hate Goodbyes *and* Elizabeth, Who Is Not a Saint, *acclaimed children's books published by Paulist Press. "Revised Expectations" requires no foreknowledge of its Dickensian source, but will hold special resonance for those who know and love Boz's tale of Pip and his ill-starred love. (For a brief synopsis of the plot of* Great Expectations, *see Note, p. 588.)*

"PROPPED UP on my bed, with my book next to me ready to be opened again, I have completed two steps of my nightly ritual. The third rests in a napkin on my lap, waiting for my attention: a miniature orange. I peel it, circling round and round the fruit, dropping little clumps of rind into my napkin. I carefully approach the tiny green star that marks the spot where the stem originally connected the fruit to the orange, gently prying out the pulpy membrane attached to the star. I hold my breath: will I find the stubby trunk of an ordinary orange, or the exciting magic of a full ghost tree?

"Eureka! A ghost tree: a lovely blanched, empty-branched, tiny ghost tree in tonight's orange. I know what I must do now. I hold up my ghost tree in front of my eyes, gripping my book—precisely marked at pages 218–219—in my other hand. Once again,

I am about to be transported—ghost tree and me—into the land of Mr. Dickens, where I will join Pip, Estella and Miss Havisham in *Great Expectations*. Unlike my last faulty attempt, this time I will not fail to restore them to their rightful destiny."

Those were my words, triumphantly scribbled in my journal some seventy-five years ago. Oh, yes, I succeeded in penetrating what most people regard as mere words to enter Mr. Dickens's story itself. Perhaps if I tell you the details of those long-ago events, I can finally put the story to rest before *I* am laid to rest. But, before I begin, I must issue a word of caution. Never fool with a ghost tree. Never tamper with an author's final revision. And never underestimate the truth of a story.

Mind you, I was a silly girl of fifteen when all this happened. With the death of my grandfather—an event that left me bereft in ways I still feel today—I inherited all fifteen of his personal journals. Knowing me for the precocious girl and avid reader that I was, and acknowledging the exceptionally close relationship I had maintained with my paternal grandfather, my parents handed me my voluminous inheritance with only a cursory review of the books' seemingly safe contents.

I read feverishly, entry after entry, page after page, book after book, like someone pursued, or maybe possessed. As I read, I took it into my head that I must investigate two extraordinary entries. One contained the fantastical story of the "ghost tree"; the other described a dramatic alteration in Mr. Dickens's original manuscript of *Great Expectations*.

I remember memorizing Grandfather's passages describing how to find a "ghost tree." If one were to obtain a certain kind of orange, he wrote, and if one were to peel that orange in a way that saved the rind around the stem until last, and if one pulled out the pulp connected to that stem in a single precise motion, one might find what he called a "ghost tree." And the right ghost tree, he explained, was a key to the door between the world of literature and the world of flesh. The right ghost tree could send the beholder hurtling through countless layers of reality to the other side where phantom and fantasy ruled. Poring over every page thereafter, I desperately searched for the source of Grandfather's information, or signs that he himself undertook ghost-tree travel. To my great disappointment, I found none. Instead, I found dozens of pages of notes about Charles Dickens.

As he read each of Mr. Dickens's works volume by volume, my grandfather wrote in his journal, probing the author's likeliest intentions, phrasing, and word choices, filling pages with descriptions, suppositions and deductions. In the middle of journal number thirteen, I found his commentary about *Great Expectations*. My heartbeat quickened with anticipation. I pored over his passages, which emphatically proclaimed that Mr. Dickens's final draft of this novel had undergone serious and astonishing metamorphosis from the original version—a change that few scholars traced and none proved.

Both manuscripts, wrote Grandfather, recalled the history of how a poor boy named Pip was hired by the wealthy, scheming Miss Havisham to play with Estella, her adopted daughter, whom she bred to be heartless; how Pip suffered as a young man from Estella's ongoing ridicule and rejection of his declarations of love; and, how Miss Havisham—herself once an abandoned bride-to-be—derived an ugly avenging pleasure from Estella's cruel exercise of power over men. Both accounts also described the last-minute repentance and anguished guilt of Miss Havisham. But the two drafts diverged sharply afterward. In the latter, published version—the one I consumed when I was twelve—Miss Havisham's remorse did not change Estella's disdainful treatment of men. Estella's subsequent manipulation of a titled and wealthy brute into a loveless and abusive marriage yields her years of considerable misery. In the earlier draft uncovered by my grandfather, Estella comprehends the damage unleashed by Miss Havisham's vindictive teachings and, in one excruciatingly poignant scene, repudiates that upbringing, forgives her adoptive mother, and promises to marry Pip.

I fell madly, utterly in love with this lost redemptive version.* Each time I reread *Great Expectations* as published, I passionately denounced Mr. Dickens's sentencing of the protagonist Pip and his beloved Estella to their long separation and painful end-of-story reunion. How my adolescent adrenaline raced upon reading my grandfather's notes. How vindicated I felt! Two years before receiving the journals, while attending Miss Hogarth's Seminary for Young Ladies, I wrote a theme for my English literature class in which I stubbornly maintained the very premise my grandfather's writings supported. An assignment, I might add, that earned me a humiliating C– and the immortal words, "An inventive thesis, but where is your evidence?"

The point *is* that I, a girl of unfettered imagination and abundant willfulness, fancied myself a true-life heroine entrusted with an exalted rescue mission. I would find a ghost tree, enter Mr. Dickens's narrative, and repair the story's climax to the version that the author abandoned more than fifty years before I was born. Such was my misguided resolve that led to the next catastrophic events—and my inevitable collision with humbling reality.

If challenged to discover the correct species and exact specimen of orange that confers rumoured magical powers, I believe that most sensible people would laugh, or at least question the sanity of this proposition. But a self-confessed unrepentant creature of unremitting fantasies like me was not sensible. No. Instead, for one entire year I patiently undertook the task of procuring, peeling and eating (I was not a wasteful romantic) oranges of every classification and size in pursuit of the ghost tree. Consequently, my parents and the kitchen staff at my school were puzzled yet pleased by this extraordinary conversion to healthy eating. I

---

* The origin of this specific revision is solely my imagination, and not Charles Dickens's actual writings. However, at the urging of a novelist friend, Dickens *did* rewrite his original unhappy ending of *G.E.*—in which Pip and Estella are permanently separated—to include a moderately hopeful reunion scene.—K.S.

saved my near-daily acquisition of two or three oranges until just before bedtime, waiting until I was in the privacy of my room to develop and refine my rind-peeling and core-pulling techniques. Some peelings bore pulp membranes more closely resembling tree stumps or squat bushes than trees. These I promptly discarded. Gradually, I collected an assortment of pulp sculptures that simulated exquisitely carved ivory trees with a profusion of spindly, leafless "branches" and white "roots" planted in scraggly bits of reversed-orange-peel terrain. I ardently believed that at least one of these was a ghost tree. However, I didn't have a single clue as to what I should do next to release their singular powers.

One night, during my examination of one particularly well-formed and notably eerie-looking ghost tree, my obsessive tenacity was rewarded. I balanced this latest, most perfectly shaped ghost tree on my tattered, repeatedly read copy of *Great Expectations,* eagerly imagining this miniature as part of the spooky, dramatic literary landscape of nineteenth-century English moors and marshes. Intuitively, I raised the ghost tree eye-level, about six inches in front of my forehead. I shivered with a sudden chill of desolation, then succumbed to a vortex of wind.

I opened my tightly shut eyes and saw a desolate cemetery in a forbidding land at dusk. I heard the clanking of heavy chains accompanied by low curses. I froze, my mutinous body rejecting my command to flee. . . .

Oh, yes, I succeeded. This was my *Great Expectations.* But this was the cemetery where Pip, as a poor little boy, first encountered and aided the escaped convict, Abel Magwitch. This was only chapter one! As zealous as I was, I knew I could never fix a 450-page story from its beginning.

The convict's sudden growl and crash behind me sent me leaping in fright, dropping and stepping on the ghost tree. The scene evaporated and a rush of air pushed at my face, overwhelming me, making me flail my arms and cough as I struggled to breathe. A knock on my dormitory room door and a proctor's inquiring voice interrupted my involuntary shouts and forced my quick recovery.

* * * *

You might think that these results would dampen my ardour towards further experimentation with the ghost tree. Not so. I replayed my first brief journey, labouring to understand why, of all chapters and all locales, I found myself in chapter one's cemetery. I opened my book, discovering a connection that I seized as *the* answer. I had arbitrarily stuck my bookmark in chapter one, between pages two and three. And I "landed" in chapter one, precisely within the events of pages two and three. If I changed the location of my bookmark, I reasoned, I would also change my landing geography. I was determined to test my hypothesis by randomly plunging my bookmark between any two pages of the novel. Which is when I remembered that the ghost tree that took me into *Great Expectations* remained in that literary world. My reaction, I recall, included a few expressions considered unbecoming to a refined young lady at Miss Hogarth's Seminary.

Four additional, agonizingly slow months of orange procurement, peeling, and pulling passed before I found another fully intact ghost tree that evoked that same chilling feeling in me when I held it before my eyes. I seized the ever-present copy of *Great Expectations,* which I kept in readiness on my bedside table at school or home, flipped open the book, and wedged the bookmark between the two exposed pages. I still can recite the exact page numerals: chapter twenty-nine, pages 218–219. I can envision the adult Pip perfectly, dressed in the finery of an affluent gentleman of great expectations, thanks to an anonymous benefactor's generosity. Pip is summoned by Miss Havisham, who taunts the young man with the beauty and brutal indifference of Estella. I could hardly contain my fervor. What a perfect moment to bestow my tender ministrations. I imagined myself earnestly addressing Miss Havisham, warning her of the impending tragic consequences to herself and Estella. I heard myself persuading the old woman to cast off the decomposing wedding gown that enshrouded her deteriorating body. I saw myself helping her sweep out the smothering cobwebs she hoarded in home and heart. Yes, I would save Miss Havisham, Estella and Pip from

Mr. Dickens's final revision with its disheartening closing chapters. The story would conclude as I knew Mr. Dickens meant it to be.

I opened my eyes and rejoiced to find myself in a dreary dressing room lit with a multitude of candles. On my right sat an elderly, gaunt and desiccated woman wearing a mouldy, yellowed wedding gown and one bridal shoe. A nervous, fidgeting Pip stood before me.

I opened my mouth, ready to identify myself and my rescue mission, but the old woman, whom I instantly recognized as Miss Havisham, stared at me with a strange, possessive look that strangled me like a noose around my neck. I could not speak. Her eyes bound me to my chair.

She interrogated Pip: did he find me much changed? The hopelessly enamoured young man blushed and stammered a confused reply. And I? demanded Miss Havisham. Did I notice changes in Pip?

The hair on my arms and the back of my scalp rose in alarm. I swung my head toward a mirror on Miss Havisham's dressing table for verification. My familiar eyes, now imprisoned within the body of Estella, accurately reflected my abundant panic.

I slammed the open book I still held in my lap, squashing the ghost tree between the pages. I hastily exited the nineteenth century, returning abruptly to my twentieth-century bed.

For two weeks I pondered the outcome of my unexpected convergence with Estella. A single conclusion dominated my thoughts and stoked my desire: the power of the ghost tree was not mere literary travel, but merger with an actual story character. What better way to change a particular character's development than by *becoming* that character at a pivotal narrative moment?

I felt undaunted by the enormity of my self-appointed task. I excelled in passionate obstinacy. Let this explain the six additional months of countless oranges in pursuit of yet another travel-ready ghost tree. Finally, success. I greedily clutched the orange peeling anchoring my new ghost tree with one hand, using my other hand to turn the pages of my book in search of the perfect landing site. *There it was:* the climactic moment in which Miss Havisham is overwhelmed by the ugly results of her manipulations.

I vowed that I, in the guise of Estella, would save Miss Havisham before she set herself on fire, before she was consumed by endless and piteous remorse for her deeds. I trembled with excitement as I located chapter forty-nine, pages 370–371, marked the precise passages in which Miss Havisham pleads with Pip for his forgiveness, and quickly transported myself to her room with the huge decayed wedding cake bloated with spiders and mice.

Inexplicably, I found myself prostrate and sobbing on the floor next to the lit fireplace. I raised my head and saw the booted feet of a man who was trying to console me. What had I done? I hadn't rescued Miss Havisham. Instead, I *became* this devastasted, wasted Miss Havisham—a woman without a future because she/I felt devoured by the past.

I struggled to regain *my* separate consciousness, *my* superior understanding, *my* unquestioned right to change the destinies of Miss Havisham, Estella and Pip. I could only cry in frustration and helplessness. I willed myself to believe that what I did, I could undo. I grasped blindly around me, searching for the ghost tree, spying it at the edge of the blazing hearth . . .

I dove toward the flames, seized the tiny tree and crumpled it in my hand just as the rotted layers of my decrepit wedding dress caught fire.

Maddening obstinacy is one thing; unsurpassed stupidity is quite another. That same day I renounced membership in both. I surrendered my crusade to rescue characters within their stories.

Mind you, I haven't stopped imagining what might have been; I'm simply not eager to insist that what could be must be better than whatever already is. Characters—whether bound within books or bound for cemeteries—choose from whomever they are and what they know within their stories, not what the reader or spectator knows or wants. Mr. Dickens knew that. That's why he abandoned his first draft intentions, allowing Pip, Estella and Miss Havisham to dictate their own true, difficult endings.

That's why my author abandoned this story's original ending, allowing me to disclose two final pertinent details: I am named for my grandmother, Estella; and, to honour the wishes of Abel Magwitch, whom he discovered to be his late benefactor, my grandfather always retained his nickname, "Pip."

Tanith Lee

The Pandora Heart

The award-winning British writer TANITH LEE *is the author of*
The Birthgrave, Companions on the Road, Dark Dance, East of
Midnight, Drinking Sapphire Wine, Red As Blood *and many
other acclaimed works of fantasy, including her unique ghost (?)
story,* "A Room with a Vie," *which appears in my 1995
GuildAmerica collection,* Angels of Darkness. *"The Pandora
Heart," a new story specially commissioned for* Don't Open This
Book!, *is a wonderful "riff" on the Pandora theme, with its lova-
bly imprudent heroine dabbling with powers she doesn't under-
stand.*

I WAS BORN the daughter of a king, and my nurse told me early
that a princess carries her head high, and is proud. But when you
learn early, too, that you are only the child of a palace woman,
who anyway has died, that you are plain of face, that your sisters
are full-royal, (all but one) fierce and fiery, and wear red-gold
necklets to match their hair (and that anyway, to be a woman is
to be an afterthought of the gods), there comes a little droop to
the neck, and any pride is very humble. Or so it was with me.

But then this story, naturally, is not really about myself, but
about the strange and mystical fruit so many do not even believe
in. I had heard the tale long before Akris, my brother, brought his
trophy home. I remember it as one of the first tales, told in the
warm light of the brazier, one winter, in my small room. The

slave girl sat weaving a dress length for me by the cold shine of the darkening window, and the lamps were not yet lit because, being who I was, we were careful with our allowance of oil. I must have been about four. I had wanted to look into my nurse's private chest, which stood in a corner. I do not know why—maybe only a child's curiosity about all things adult. Or perhaps she had promised me a surprise. She told me it was not always wise to look into a chest, or to open up a sealed jar. I, of course, asked why.

"Araegne," said my nurse, "I'll tell you the story of Pandora."

My nurse looked old to me, with grey in her long fair hair, but also oldness did not matter. To a child the grown ones are difficult, godlike, and so tall, with carved faces.

"Pandora was not born, but *made* by the gods. She was given every gift—beauty, wit, grace—and guile. She never had a childhood, because she was fashioned as a woman. And so there was always something childlike to her—which seemed at first very charming."

I saw from the corner of my eye, the slave was listening too, her fingers slowing. She liked the tales of my nurse as much as I.

My nurse told us then how fire had been stolen from the gods to assist mankind, and Zeus, the king god, was angry. He meant Pandora to work out a punishment on men. And so he gave her in marriage to the brother of the hero who stole the fire. This man—who was partly mortal and partly divine—wanted Pandora from the second he set eyes on her, and was overjoyed.

But Pandora brought with her a dowry from the gods, a black jar sealed fast. Cunning tricky Hermes, the god of messengers, thieves and whores, told Pandora she must on no account allow it ever to be opened, since what was inside was so precious.

Her husband had no interest in the jar—he would have taken the gorgeous Pandora gladly without any dowry. He forgot it. But Pandora, curious and always asking Why?, like all children, could not rest. And one day, when no one else was in the house, she broke the seal and opened the jar.

I held my breath—so did the slave, although surely she at least had heard the history of Pandora before. Even old Ebony, my cat Owl's mother, seemed to be listening. And they say cats know all stories.

"Every evil of the world was in the jar," said the nurse, "and they escaped to plague mankind. Illness and sadness, bad luck and old age. But, too, the very best things were in the jar as well, true love, glory, genius. And they also escaped, and now men only come on them by chance, or the will of the gods."

"What did Pandora do then?" I asked. Always a question.

"She wept," said the nurse. "But soon she dried her eyes. When her husband came home she was all smiles. She said she had cleaned the house and wiped out the old jar—which had nothing in it. She hoped he didn't mind she had peeped inside."

After this, Pandora and her husband lived together a long while, but in the end he died, for now there was death on the earth. Pandora, being a creature created rather than born, existed far longer. But in the end even her perfect mechanisms wore out. She too fell into the sleep of death, and was buried. It was her children who survived the Great Flood.

By now it was so dark in my room, the slave left her loom, and dipping a taper to the brazier, touched two lamps alight.

"A tree grew from Pandora's tomb," said my nurse, "out of the side of it. It was nourished by her beauty even in death. Such a tree had never been seen in the world. The leaves were so deep a green they were almost the black of her hair, and in spring there were amber flowers, the colour of her peachy skin. Last, in the fall of the year, came fruits, a deep, glowing red—her uncanny blood. Out of awe, no one harvested these fruits, and one by one they fell to the earth. Here, they never rotted, but remained like smooth rubies, lying round the tomb of Pandora."

After the Flood, however, my nurse went on to say, the nature of the tree was forgotten. Long, long after the waters receded, a new race of men came upon it and found it still blooming and fruiting. Then they tried the fruits, but so terrible and impossible was their effect, if eaten, that in the end humanity was mostly afraid to touch them. The gods at last sent a great serpent with orichalc scales to guard the tree, so few would be tempted. And finally, after the earth had changed her shape two or three more times, the situation of the tree was lost.

I asked for a more detailed description of the fruit.

My nurse said that they were roughly heart-shaped. I shuddered. I had seen the hot, still-vibrating hearts of oxen and rams offered to the gods by priests. My nurse guessed, and said, "No, no, not like that. The poetic shape seen only in jewels—look." And she drew with a charcoaled stick on the floor the shape we associate, wrongly, with the form of the human heart.

What did the fruit *taste* like, then, I asked, was it *meat?*

My nurse and the slave both laughed. My nurse said, "No one knows except those who tasted it. But they say the fruits had a lovely smell, and inside there were seeds, as there are in pomegranates."

I asked what happened to those who ate the fruits, something which she had seemed to gloss over.

She frowned and said, "Fate dealt them what was theirs."

I could get nothing more helpful from her.

When I was older, then, I heard the other story of the fruit, which was that still, even in our age, it might be found. For, after all, a scatter of heroes had, by drugging or distracting or fighting the serpent, robbed the tree. Some of the fruits were then eaten, but others, since they never decayed, even when cut in two, had passed into various lands, as curiosities and treasures. They were known as Pandora Hearts, and worth a king's ransom. I had heard a harper sing, too, a tale of one of them, one night when I was old enough to sit in the women's place in my father's hall. I was twelve years old then, but did not ever forget the song. It was of a hero who tricked the serpent that guarded the tree, and took a fruit away, and cutting it open. ate one half with all its rosy seeds.

"Then came on him such madness," the harper sang,/"That the very rocks made themselves small./But he ran up the hills, and baying like a dog,/He raised his sword against the sun,/Shouting and crying out,/Till merciful and merciless,/The sun god struck him down."

Curious yet, I asked my sister Pyrrha, so called for her fiery gold-red hair, (but the name was also that of Pandora's daughter), what the song meant. Did the flesh and seeds of the fruit drive a man insane?

Pyrrha struck me lightly. I should not have spoken to her directly, she told me so, and that I had been corrected. Then she said the Pandora Heart Fruit brought out of men their best or their worst, depending on which was the strongest in them. I protested—"But he was a hero." And was slapped harder. My sister said, "Don't do it a third time, or I shall tell the king. He will get a slave to give you three lashes from the whip. Do you want to be whipped by a slave?" Then she added, "Only the gods know what's truly deep inside us. We may be brave and wonderful in all eyes, but have a secret flaw. Or most wretched, and have a true heart. The fruit finds it, whatever it is."

I had the sense, nursing my slaps, not to ask her anything else. By then I no longer had my old nurse, but only my slave, who was a mere five years older than I. Therefore I told my cat, Owl— his mother had passed on the summer before.

Owl is striped and spotted in such a way that, from a short distance, he seems to have feathers not fur. His eyes are large, round and yellow, and his ears extend sideways rather than up. The nurse said, when she saw him—he was Ebony's last child— that some god, probably tricky, cranky Hermes, had taken cat form to mate with her. But I think it may have been Dionysos, who likes cats, especially spotted ones.

Owl sat quietly while I spoke of the fruit of Pandora's tree. Then he lay down on his right side, which signifies that what has been said is true. So Pyrrha had been right, even though she had made me pay for telling me.

At that time I never, of course, thought I would see such a fruit, for my father Rhexenor's kingdom lies below the Towering Gates, and above us were the great snows. On our other side was the Green Sea. Though travellers came, they came rarely. But then there was the war.

Up the coast King Labron had his kingdom. Our people traded with his, and my father was in alliance with him. Suddenly a prince from across the sea, staying in the Golden Palace as Labron's guest, hatched a plot to steal the Luck of the City, a famous statue of the goddess Artem-Qirri. Soon the princely thief was gone, and the statue with him. Labron sent battle galleys after him, and next was at war. Into this war, as allies of Labron, many smaller kingdoms were drawn, Rhexenor's with them.

A band of our warriors was sent, and a levy of male citizens. My full-royal brothers Pallos and Akris went as war-leaders, because my father, having no intention of fighting, pointed out his grey head. Pallos and Akris were eager to go in any case. They were at the ages thought perfect for war, twenty and eighteen, the ideal of young manhood, bronzed and athletic, Pallos all golden, and Akris, the younger, with more red than gold in his hair.

The war itself was short, less than three months. The thief gave way, the statue was brought back in triumph to Labron's city. Akris said it was made of cedar, coated four inches thick all over with silver, and ornamented with gold, the robes decorated with gold crescents and silver bees, the eyes being two sapphires. But the autumn weather had set in, and some of the returning ships were lost. Pallos sailed home within two months, but there was no news of Akris. The queen, Rhetis, went into a shadow phase of grief, which angered my father. Pyrrha said it did not matter if Akris were lost, because the heir had survived. There were sacrifices in scores, the morning air thick with smokes and the stink of cooked blood.

Eventually we had news that Akris lived after all.

His vessel had foundered, and he and his men had been picked up by a captain, Udyzeus, who knew the sea route well, and the islands. But then again Fate befell them, and a storm forced the ship to put in at one island even Udyzeus, who claimed also to be a king, did not know.

Akris and his band, when they arrived home, were not the poorer for their adventures. They were burnt almost black by the sun, dressed in the finest of leathers, and with wonderful foreign jewelry. Akris claimed the island, a large one, had never been mapped. The women there went veiled, and only the lowest of them was ever seen. In the centre of the marketplace was a well that spoke oracles in a human voice. They worshipped Zeus, but also a mother goddess they named Herakte. The king of the city entertained them for three nights with feasts, and shows of extraordinary skill, one of which was a girl who danced with a huge gilded snake. As a parting guest-gift, the king had taken Akris to a treasure-chamber and loaded him with presents. Then came a slave as black as night, who knelt and held out a tray of beaten gold.

"On this tray," said Akris, "was a single fruit. It was a bright dark red, firm-fleshed and smooth of skin, with a deep central division, and two swelling sides. The stalk was also red. Even from where I stood, the perfume overwhelmed me." Akris looked about the hall, where he was telling the story to everyone, evidently with Rhexenor's permission.

I recollect to this hour the hush, greater than the respectful but broken quiet in which they had heard the tale so far, now and then bursting into laughter or applause.

Behind Akris, where the two king-pillars of indigo blue went up to hold the roof, my father sat on his carved chair, listening, his face very still. Akris turned and bowed to the king.

"At first I didn't think what it could be. So I asked the island king if this was a local refreshment. His face went pale, although he was a dark man."

The island king had told Akris that the fruit was a treasure of the island, one of several that had been brought there long ago. All were kept hidden, and guarded by strong men and savage beasts together. But this one was to be a gift, a token of friendship between himself and Prince Akris.

The fruit was, of course, a Pandora Heart.

When Akris, thanking the king profoundly, took the Heart in

his hand, it felt warm and living, like an animal. He had put it swiftly away, and presently brought it home to his father.

One of the old lords, who were accorded special privileges, spoke straight out, "Were you tempted, prince, to eat some of the fruit, for glory's sake?"

"Yes," said Akris simply. His eyes blazed pale as diamonds in his sunburned face. "But I had a warning dream. I saw Fate herself, standing with her knife, and her sisters behind her, one of whom kept her finger to her lips, and one of whom shook her head slowly at me."

The hall sighed. My father said, "You did very well, my son."

The old lord spoke intransigently again. "But will the king eat the fruit?"

My father scowled. Then he said, "It never rots. Its perfume, I promise you, is delicious. If eaten, it's gone. Though it might make one man into a god, we are many. It is better, sir, to keep our treasure, as does the king on his island."

At this the old lord bowed. It could not be, demonstrably, Rhexenor was afraid of some flaw in himself that might, should he eat, rather than deify him, send him mad, or otherwise destroy him. No, it was for the good of all that he took thought, putting us before his own desires.

Soon, the Pandora Heart was set out where it might be seen, in an antechamber of the king's apartment. It rested on an amber dish, on a stand with claw-feet of gold.

All those of any position, however slight—even I—were permitted to go and look.

The king was there, and Akris, and my father called me up to him.

"Your hair is fine and brown, and of a good length. Araegne, is it? You may buy gold wires to have plaited in. You've not done badly, and you walk well." He turned to my brother. "No beauty, but tidy and meek. In a woman, two solid virtues." Akris nodded, not even glancing at me.

I should not have been humiliated by this, perhaps pleased,

relieved not to have offended. But that night I cried into my pillow. So the first view of the magical fruit, and the smell of its sweet perfume, were mixed with the salt of tears.

Of what, then, did the fruit smell? I have heard some people say it smells of Pandora herself, like a lovely woman freshly bathed and anointed with sweet unguents. But the fruit of Pandora's tree smells of fruit, as really perhaps is reasonable. Yet, though, it is no aroma we recognize. Soft yet acidulous—a grape? an apple?—but with something of flowers, the asphodel, the purple hyacinth that grew from blood. It is a clear scent that comes and goes in waves.

In shape it is the form of my nurse's drawn, spiritual heart, not the lump of offal pulled reeking out of carcasses to read omens.

The colour is lush, dark, ripe crimson, with that glow of a paler redder light inside. One longs to cut or bite, moisture fills your mouth. But this is so terrible, too, knowing that, if unworthy, it may ruin you, and you tremble more the more hungry for it you become.

I turned away in fear at last, and saw others do so. But Rhexenor ignored the fruit, chatting to his men, calling up Pyrrha to pinch her slim waist and laugh. A king must be easy with supernatural, valuable things. But the frown lines were between his eyes, the sort that came, not when he was angry, but when he had a slight difficulty, as say with a parchment he was unable to read, and tossed to his scribe with a "You do it. Why else are you here?"

After the Pandora Heart had been among us for some twenty days, attention turned rather from it. Akris went away hunting with his friends, and there was rumour of a marriage between Pyrrha and one of the younger sons of King Labron, a reward for work in the war. Pyrrha tossed her fiery head. At fifteen, she knew, here was her chance. No man could fail to want her, and she thought she could manage men. Besides, king's heirs died, and a younger son might one day become a king after all. (This was in fact how it happened with her. There was some strange talk. I know nothing about it.) For myself, I was just then fourteen, and had sandals now with little heels, and the gold wires for my hair. It was my old nurse who taught me to walk "well." I only stooped and drooped when I stood or sat, and then, apparently, this was virtuous. I would besides no more think I could manage a man than call the mile-distant Sea to my window. There is still only one male I would trust, Owl, my cat. Who at that time had already sired several families around the palace. His sons would tend to have one or two unusual spots or stripes about them.

On the twenty-third day after the fruit was shown, I woke to uproar. My slave came flying in to tell me that during the night, someone had struck unconscious the guard who stood in the antechamber, and stolen the Pandora Heart.

Rhexenor's palace was in pandemonium. Slaves ran in all directions with enormous staring eyes. The men stood rigid and warlike. It was as if we were about to be sacked. There was too the smell of heavy smoke in the air, an extra sacrifice and divination was taking place at the altar on the sunside terrace.

No clue was found, however. Nor did we need one for very long.

To my last days I shall carry the image of that scene.

I saw first the queen, Rhetis, staggering down the passage like one of the slaves. Her hair was coming undone from its ornate dressing, and her eye-paint had run.

Against the wall, I flattened myself, but she seized me with her hand. "This way, girl." She had no idea who I was, and probably thought me one of the lesser handmaidens, exactly what my mother had been. But she forced me along with her, leaning on me, and after her rushed her slaves and women, all squeaking and crying out.

The king was coming from the sacrifice. His face was slightly smudged with the soot. Behind him were the three priests, and his lords and warriors.

"What is it now?" he said sharply.

Rhetis put back her head and let out a scream of terror and despair. Then she sank over in her women's arms.

It was one of these who crouched before my father. "Oh, king—your son—your son has gone mad—"

"Akris is in the hills," said Rhexenor.

The woman made a little mewing sound. "Pallos," she whispered.

It was then that Pallos, the king's heir, came.

He strode through the women, and his passage was like a hot and burning wind from some land on fire. I fell to my knees in utter horror. Because I had glimpsed his eyes, his mouth—

His face was stern, not mad, drained pale behind his bronze. His mouth was stained red, and for a moment I thought he had been drinking blood—but then I knew what he had taken.

"See me," he said loudly, without inflection. "Down on your face, my father. I am a god."

"What is this—" said Rhexenor. He too had gone sallow.

"A god, a god," boomed Pallos. And then he swung around at us, the women fallen at his back. And again I saw the mouth stained from eating the Pandora Heart. And again, I saw his eyes. They were *scarlet*. The white, the iris, the black centre—all blood red. His eyes were pools of ichor.

"I can see the stars through the earth," said Pallos, almost carelessly now, "and the Encircling Ocean. I can see the bones in your bodies. Yes, worship me."

Rhexenor said, "He has eaten—"

And Pallos said, "Only seven seeds. Seven seeds of the Pandora. The taste was holy. Look now—I'm invulnerable, immortal. I will climb the White Mountain and be received among the gods. Give me your sword."

"Pallos," said Rhexenor, "wait a moment—"

"Shall I take it? Don't anger me, it will rock the world."

Pallos leaned and took the king's sword by its golden-bound hilt. This was treasonable, but no one moved.

"Now watch me, and know my power," said Pallos, and he ran the sword straight through his belly, as if his body were made of butter. "See, I am immortal and take no hurt," he said. Then he crashed headlong. His appalling eyes shut, and the blood poured instead and in fact out of his mouth.

The funeral of Pallos was an awesome occasion. Maidens walked behind the bier, singing in lament. I was one of them. We rent our hair and scratched our faces, with red paint under our nails so we did not have to score the skin. A white bull, ten white sheep were sacrificed, and a red dove. Pallos's band of warriors watched all night about the tomb. In the morning, piled with vessels of gold, and swords set with jewels, like the one that killed him, it was closed. Rhexenor had wanted to slaughter the two hunting dogs of Pallos and send them with him, but Akris pleaded for them. Under his care they recovered from their grief.

Alone in my room, I held Owl in my arms. I told him, if I died, I would only wish him to live, faithless and happy without me.

But anyway, I made an offering to Hera, and to Persephone, to care for him above, or below, Pallos who had never spoken to me one word, and probably, like the rest, did not know I existed.

In the days which followed, the fruit of Pandora's tree, what was left—most of it—was put into a chest, and the chest sealed with the seal of the king. A slave known for his massive strength and utter stupidity, was set to guard the storeroom where the chest was set. Magic rituals took place also, closing the corners with blood.

It was put about that Pallos had died of a sudden fit. But I believe the story flew, how he had eaten of the Heart, and it had found the imperfection in him, and so he lost his mind and died.

There were few legends of those who had eaten the fruit and become great. Yet they existed. One heard them spoken of, behind hands, curtains. My father's house had been spoiled, for the king did not want the fruit, and even wondrous Akris had been warned from it in a dream.

Once, in his cups, my drunken father was supposed to have said, "It's our curse. I wish we might be rid of the thing."

Akris, they said, wept for shame at bringing it home, and the king comforted him.

• • • •

When I was just turned fifteen, I was informed the queen had sent for me.

I knew at once what this meant, and I felt a shiver of distress, and, partly, fear. My slave, Onopi, was watching me with big eyes, so I told her that probably they had made a marriage for me. At once Onopi burst into tears. She dropped down and clasped my ankles and begged me not to leave her behind when I went away. I was astonished. From her cries I came to understand I was a kind mistress, that she liked me, that, in fact, we had become friends. I lifted her up and hugged her close. "Of course I shan't leave you. I'd be lost without you. And Owl would never forgive me."

Actually, it was unlikely they would deprive me of her, because I mattered so little, she mattered even less. I determined, however, to ask my father, as a parting favour to me, to free her, so she might become my handmaiden, which had more kudos in it.

Warmed by the exchange, I went into the apartment of Rhetis. There were paintings of doves and dancers on the walls, a bed of walnut with gold rings, sunlight and women everywhere. One could have fit my own room inside four or five times over.

Rhetis was sitting in her gilded chair, while her hair was dressed carefully for the day. She had recovered from her anguish at Pallos's death, yet it had left its mark. Strands of grey in her hair now were being twined with sea pearls to hide them.

I kneeled and obeised myself. Rhetis said I might get up.

"Tell me your name again." I said my name. "And you are fifteen?" I said I was. "I think," she said, "you know. Araegne, why I've sent for you." Then, not waiting for my irrelevant comments, she told me I was to marry one of twelve part-royal princes in a neighbouring kingdom. The alliance was obviously helpful to Rhexenor, but not of vast importance. It plastered up the family ties between allies, but in the smallest and least costly way.

When she had given me the news, she asked if there were any questions I might have. I inquired the prince's age, and was reassured he had twenty years—sometimes, in such concoctions, the man may be as young as eleven or twelve, or as old as fifty. There was nothing else that could be of any use to me. If he were ugly or handsome, cruel or easygoing, were things I had maybe better not know until I met him before the altar. (In fact, he is a good man, not ugly, nor so good-looking my plainness can offend him unduly. Although he has many other women, he accords me always absolute respect as his wife. I am not unhappy.)

I asked Rhetis if she would speak to the king on my behalf, in the matter of freeing Onopi. She said she would, but of course forgot. I was able to have a letter written to him, and so see to it myself, later.

After all this, Rhetis had me poured a courtesy drink, sweet wine with butter and honey.

Then the tokens of my dowry were brought. I had expected very little, but the king had been quite generous to such a lesser, part-royal daughter. There were some vessels of silver, a whole tiring set, with copper paring knives and dishes of alabaster for cosmetics, and bronze tongs for the hair. And a necklace of amber, with eight silver disks and three golden sunflowers.

When the last thing was brought, I was already amazed, and had thanked Rhetis, bowing low. Then I checked. Even after so many months, even though the dark smoke of the funeral sacrifice had come between, I knew at once that perfume.

My mouth fell open, and I stared, suddenly numb as if with terrible cold, at the little black, painted chest the slave was setting down on the table by the jewels.

"Yes, you're right in your thought," said Rhetis in a light, metallic voice. "Your father does you very great honour."

"But—" I gasped, "but is it—it is—the fruit—"

"The Pandora Heart," said Rhetis. The words slid from her lips as if she had oiled her mouth to get them out quickly and without harm. Then she said, "Oh, naturally you are surprised. In the general way of things, such a rarity would never fall to you. But—here, I will be honest—the king believes you were meant to have this treasure. You have had very little in this house, and now must go far away. It will remind you of his care for you."

I collected my scattered wits, bowed again, and again thanked her. Her own slaves carried my dowry after me to my room, and put everything on a table, and left me. Onopi was elsewhere, and Owl up in his usual morning place on the sunlit roof. The scent of the Pandora Heart swiftly filled the chamber. And as I stared and stared at the painted black box, which was closed with the king's seal, I seemed to see through it to a core of gleaming crimson.

The horror on me was very great. I knew, obviously, my father had not given me the fruit out of kindness. Since the death of his eldest son he had been oppressed, and had sought an oracle from Hera's Oak, that stands just below the Towering Gates. No one else knew what the oracle had said, but perhaps it was exactly this, that the Heart had brought a curse on us, and must be given away, sent out of the kingdom.

He could have sent it with Pyrrha, in *her* dowry, when she married Labron's son. But Rhexenor loved Pyrrha, and there were rumours he had wept in private after she was gone. I did not matter much, and might take the curse with me. To the neighbouring kingdom it would seem a marvellous gift. Let them, then, deal with it.

While I was thinking all this, someone scratched on my door. As I opened it, I found the slave of my half sister Kleia, with Kleia at her back, all ruffled and startled, saying she wanted to come and bid me good-bye, though I had otherwise spoken with her that year perhaps twice, and when we were children she had pulled my hair—she said, to make it grow.

Kleia's own hair was the colour of lemons, and shiny as water. But despite her pretty face, she was sour.

"Oh, how lucky you are to be wedded. To have a man soon, and all those *delights*. I wonder if Father will ever remember *me?*" She was the daughter of a dancing girl, and not yet fifteen, but mature for her years.

Then she pretended to become aware of the black box.

"Can it be true? I heard it whispered—he gave you *that*. *Is* it?"

"Yes."

"Aren't you afraid?"

"Yes."

Kleia, who had sent her slave out and shut the door, now prowled about the box, sniffing the scented air.

"Don't you want to look at it again? I'd have to see. Oh, open it, Araegne. Let's see if it looks the same. Pallos cut it in two pieces, and ate seven seeds. But it never rots. Shall I break the seal?"

"No!" I cried.

Kleia laughed. "But the king means you to eat it. Surely even you can see that he does."

Such a possibility had not occurred to me. Kleia was a maker of mischief, and I tried to keep my head.

"It's a present for my husband, and his father the king, through me."

"No. Oh, Araegne, what a fool you are. Our father knows that, inside yourself, you are all the things a woman is meant to be. The Pandora Heart can harm, but also it can render wonderful. If you ate the fruit—just think—it might make you beautiful, and powerful as a goddess. Just *think*, Araegne. Wouldn't you like that? Even if you ate *just one seed*."

The door flew open, and there stood Onopi. "Lady," she said, bowing to Kleia, "someone said the queen wants you."

Kleia made a vast flurry and was gone without farewell.

Onopi shut the door and lowered her eyes.

I said, "You lied."

"Yes. But I knew she meant no good."

I thanked Onopi. Next day, when she was doing my hair, I saw a welt on her arm. Kleia had done it. I sent a message to Kleia that if she hurt my slave again, I would ask our father to make her pay me restitution. It was the boldest thing I ever attempted, and certainly Rhexenor would have paid no attention, but Kleia was always careful where the king was concerned, and so we lived in peace.

By that next day, too, I had put my dowry into a chest and the

Pandora Heart with it. The scent still hung about the room, however. Even in the passage outside it was faintly to be smelled.

Did all the palace know it had been given to me? I shrank, and made excuses to leave my room. At night I slept poorly, dreaming of gardens where the crimson Hearts hung on every tree, beating softly, exuding perfume, and all about lay the tangled skeletons of men and women who had eaten them, gone mad, slain each other or themselves, or been struck down by the just and pitiless gods.

Indeed, along with the harper's song, which had prefigured the death of Pallos, there were the stories of how a Pandora Heart was eaten by old men, who grew young and mighty, and by crippled children, who then ran fleet as deer. And there was one story of a hideous woman, so foul she dared not show her face, who was given a little sliver of the flesh of the fruit, at which her beauty became so flame-like, it burned off the veil from her face.

It was not often that I looked long into my mirror, but now I came to do so. I was young enough, and my secret dreams, kept even from myself, uneasily began to surface. Surely I was not wicked. Surely I had done no wrong to anyone, or slighted the gods. If I were to taste the fruit, could it be that I would change— my hair into gold, my eyes into the sapphires of the lucky Artem-Qirri? And I would be not only beautiful, but have the powers the goddesses have, of healing and wisdom and love. To be a woman, even a fair woman, counted for little. But to be a goddess among men—

However much I chided myself for these thoughts, I could not help them. Who has never yearned for something they may not have? To see, even once, a handsome man gaze at me, as I had seen them do always at Pyrrha. To see them gaze, not in that way alone, but as they must at the loveliness of a goddess. To command my own destiny. To say, I will not marry here, but where I choose. To have the power to say this and not to be denied.

Over and again I wrestled with these ideas. Then would come the other notion. Pallos had not seemed flawed. And yet, eating the fruit, it had found him unworthy. I, too, no doubt, was worthless, and if I risked the fruit, it would kill me, perhaps even outright. And did my death matter? No, for I did not. Would it be better if I died?

Otherwise, living, I should take with me, to the new kingdom, the Pandora Heart, sealed in its box. And would they not find it irresistible? Would they not remove it from its cover, stand before it, charmed and mesmerized and full of fear, as we had done? Would there be dreams of warning such as Akris had and heeded, and would at last some man, perhaps even a man to whom they would wed me, take up the fruit already cut for him by my brother, eat it, eat it all—and be plunged into the horror that had taken Pallos, besmirching forever the king's house, as our house had been besmirched, with the shadow of untimely death?

And how then would they look at me, my second kindred? I, the woman who had carried the misery to them all as a gift. Maybe, worse, it would bring on a war.

With all these thoughts, I, at fifteen, struggled, day by day, and night after night. Until at last I dreamed Akris's own dream.

I was in some starry place, and the three Women stood before me, Fate in her grey mist, with the knife in her pale hand that cuts the thread of life. And behind her the others, their spinning set aside. And one shook her head at me, but the other nodded solemnly. And when I woke up I wept in dismay, and only Owl, coming in at my window from his nightly hunting, where he kills like the gods, pitiless and swift, brought me any comfort.

My wedding garments were almost done, the borders of colours almost woven, when at last I gave in. I took the box from the chest, broke the seal with one of the paring knives of copper, and tipped out the fruit of life, glory and awful death, into a dish.

At once the scent of it flooded the room, making me dizzy, and from the plate seemed to rise a ruby glow, as if from a lamp.

It lay in two almost circular halves now, the flesh moist and succulent as it must have been in the moment of cutting. The seeds, like tiny drops of fire, nestled in the centre of each circle, and it was just possible to see that a few had been daintily picked out by the tip of a knife.

Apart from myself, the room was empty, and dusk powdered over the window.

I leaned to the fruit, and it was as if I hung above a great abyss. Had Pallos felt this, too? No, for he was, and thought himself, a hero. He had not hesitated.

I had meant only to look, and then to replace the fruit in its box. Or had I meant only that?

The gods know our inner minds, not we.

Breathing in the aroma of beauty, I could guess the deliciousness of the taste. It would be easy to gobble every part of it, the ever-ripe flesh and thin silky skin, the crackling little seeds with their bursts of bright juice. Could I? Would I?

Onopi was gone on a long errand that would keep her busy until late after supper in my father's hall. I had devised it with care. And if I did not go to supper, who would miss me? If I lay dead, who would mourn, save only poor gentle Onopi? But she and Owl would soon forget. She was free now, and skilled, and might even leave the palace if she wished.

And I would move between them all and Fate. Perhaps they would remember that.

Or, I would become a goddess.

Oh the scent. I smell it still. There is truly no fruit like it, and no flower. What must the gods be, if this came from them?

So near I was to the fruit that when my door was knocked upon, I started almost out of my body—or back into it, more probably.

For a moment I did not know what to do. But in my father's palace, someone like myself might not ignore a summons. I took up a light shawl that had been lying on the chair, and flung it over the dish and the fruit. Then I went to the door.

There was no one outside, but looking along the corridor I seemed to see the flit of a skirt, the flash of a bangled heel turning the corner. As I left my room, the door closed on the latch.

At the corner there was no one, but a little further on a guard stood, to keep the entrance to the women's apartments. I went up to him.

"Did some slave pass along here just now?"

"No, lady. No one passed. I'd certainly have seen."

I wondered if it were another trick of Kleia's, and the guard had been bribed to be in on it. But I would never get it from him without a larger bribe, so I had better pretend I did not mind.

Beyond the corridor, I saw the evening on the palace courts. Doves, gold-lit by a now-invisible sun, fluttered over the roofs. It was supper-time. After all, I was here, finally. I would go and sit with the women, and eat some food, and hear the harper play or the princes strum some song of war or male cunning.

I felt lighter. I had escaped the tyranny of the fruit. And tonight I would drink a little extra wine, and when I went back to my room, I would put it away, the Pandora Heart. This was too vast a thing for Araegne to tackle. How could I ever have thought otherwise?

I had no fear, being gone, that anyone would go in to steal the Heart. They were all afraid of it. As for Onopi, she would be busy. She would not have to suffer the temptation I had done.

Yes, I felt light. As if reprieved, let off some ghastly duty to the living—or the dead.

To this hour I do not know who knocked upon the door, to save me. But Hermes is the god of messengers, and tricks . . .

The harper sang a long history of two lovers that the gods parted, and I was late returning, and hurried, concerned that Onopi might get back before me. Then I glimpsed her down at the Little Fountain under the torch, gossiping with a kitchen girl, and knew all was well.

When I reached my door, I opened it, and saw the one lamp burning I had wastefully left, and everything in its place, except for the shawl I had put over the Pandora Heart. And on the dish, a dark red smear, like blood, and nothing else.

My heart gave such a jolt, I almost fainted. I leaned on the upright of the door, gasping, and then I saw lying under the table, my cat, Owl, on his left side, the lamp limning his stripes with gold, still as a stone.

At once I was in tears. This, of all things, I had not thought of. But he was adept at jumping, clever at finding, always hungry. The desperate beauty of the fruit must have lured even him. (I had known him lick flowers before.) And so simple it had been for him to come in at the window, jump to the table, eat the Pandora Heart, skin and flesh and seeds, till everything was gone but that one smear of juice, almost licked clean.

I ran to him and took him up, and only as I held him weeping on my breast did I feel that he was warm, and flexible as a snake. And waking up, he yawned smiling in my face.

His tongue was stained red, and his carnivore's breath had on it the faintest, most unusual, most marvellous perfume.

"Oh, Owl—what have you done?"

Owl yawned again, and let out a rippling bead-string of purrs. In my arms he stretched, then rested his head, as he does, on my shoulder.

"Owl—Owl—"

It was true, he had devoured every shred. Every seed. Nothing was left but the smear of juice I wiped up now with the shawl. I then put by the shawl for burning in the morning.

He stayed all this while, purring and praising me, for to Owl I am a goddess, if also an idiot, being omnipotent in some things, and otherwise not always able to do what he demands or guess what he wishes.

I puzzled over him and his deed. Until at length, he desired to go out again, and I placed him at the window, and watched him run off along the roofs, a black shape glimmering on the night.

What had happened to him? Was it that the fruit could not change him, since he was already perfect, beautiful, and partly a god—was it that he *had* been changed, yet I could not see it, being myself human and mortal?

His eyes had shone, their normal, exquisite lamps. His paws

were fleet. He sprang like a lion. But this was as it had always
been.

I could ask him nothing—how he felt, what now he could see
and hear—for perhaps he saw the Ocean under the world, the
bones in my body, the faces of the stars, and the goddess standing
on the moon; perhaps he heard the language of the birds and the
wind. Or perhaps, being a cat, he was impervious, the same,
immutable as the purest metal and the purest heart.

At the hour Onopi returned, the box was shut and sealed and put
away. Sealed and shut, it went with me to my new home, and
sealed and shut it remains. I think they have forgotten all talk, by
now, of what it might be the plain, foreign princess brought with
her in the black-painted little casket. (Its lingering perfume was
faded and gone by the time my journey ended.) They do not
credit every legend they hear, and Onopi has even told me that
she once slapped a slave girl who announced that Owl had not
been fathered by a god. My husband asked me only one question,
"That fruit, did your brother Pallos die of it?" I shook my head
and replied as they had said I must, that he died of a sudden fit.
My husband expressed no desire to see the Pandora Heart. If he
had, or his father, the king, I should have had to confess. The
gods know what would have happened. I suppose it may one day
happen yet. But I think really they believe we are all liars, and
that the box is as empty as, in fact, it is.

Owl is growing old now, but as with his race, shows little sign
of it. He has sired new families about this palace in the mountains. In the winter, when the snows come, he is sometimes gone
a day or a night, at his hunting. Perhaps I will find he is immortal
now, but I think not. I discovered some grey hairs in his spotted
coat not three evenings back. He sleeps more than he did. And
though he talks to me often, it is still in the language of cats.

My father by now has died, and Akris is king in my birthland. I
wonder if he thinks of me sometimes, seeing that I took the curse
away from his kingdom. Otherwise, they have forgotten my
name. I do foretell that in the end they will forget other names

than mine. For men go back to dust and cities crumble, and even the earth changes her shape. At last our world will be gone, and with it, its mysteries and its essential terrors. Let me say softly, I have heard that even the gods may one day die.

Patricia Mullen

Don't Open That Book!

The hallmark of a good book is its ability to absorb the reader in the world its author has "subcreated," to use a verb coined in an essay by J.R.R. Tolkien. Still, there ought to be limits, as the narrator learns in the ensuing story by PATRICIA MULLEN, *a New York University theatre teacher and author of* The Stone Movers *(Warner Aspect Novels). Her earlier stories, "Lydia's Season" and "The Curse of the Wandering Gypsy" appeared, respectively, in my anthologies* Angels of Darkness *and* Witches and Warlocks.

FROM THE BEGINNING I was afraid that Stella would be precocious, that if she were to inherit any curse from her father, it would be that one. She is my niece, he was my brother. Colleagues and mutual friends tell me that in his last years he recovered a little, mellowing enough to marry and become a father. I doubt that. I think that he made a final, desperate attempt to live a normal life and simply failed.

When I was born, my brother Sam was an established prodigy of five years old. Our parents were tenured academics, too prosaic to be called intellectuals, but with an obsessive dedication to their children's education. Their theories of learning were as effective and direct as clubs. They pushed my brother, as they later pushed me, to be nothing less than brilliant. He complied. With his bad example before me, I did not.

It was my mother who tutored us to read before we could

walk, who drove us to understand calculus before our peers could spell the word. Although we were not a close family, my parents rarely let us out of their sight. Sam and I competed against each other endlessly, striving to win our parents' affection by mastering theorems and equations, by battling for the right to study late and gain an advantage. We had no time to play.

My brother entered Harvard when he was twelve, already the author of half a dozen groundbreaking papers in three different disciplines. When he was twenty, he was sought by heads of state and leaders of technology, the subject of the type of popular scrutiny that some think of as fame. When he was thirty, someone dared ask him how it felt to have done his best work at nine. At forty he was bitter, depressed and unemployable. At fifty he found a teaching position at a small college, married a bright student not unlike our mother, fathered Stella and drove his secondhand car into a tree.

His wasted life saved mine. Mother had educated me as she had him, but in the beginning he was so brilliant—and a boy—that I was able to win some growing room. I cried the first time they put me on television with him. I sulked whenever I was exposed to the reporters who were periodically called in to challenge our genius. When I was eight, I began resisting the endless study of math and physics, and at night I read science-fiction novels under the covers by flashlight. "Trash," my mother called them, and threw them out when she caught me. I entered college when I was thirteen, and like my older fellow undergraduates, feasted on fiction. *The Lords,* as we called them, were popular with certain freshmen, and I read *Lord of the Flies* twice and *The Lord of the Rings* often enough to be able to quote obscure passages at parties. "Insane drivel," Mother called it.

My brother was eighteen when he earned his doctorate in physics, but for some time he had been showing signs of strain. I believe that he was truly brilliant, that he would have accomplished much had he been allowed to grow up naturally. But my parents were obsessed with him, they would not let him rest, driving him on as though their lives depended on his success. The media was just as bad, and Sam lived in a spotlight. I was able to slip away quietly to take my own doctorate at Oxford, out of their reach. I never went home again.

I am an archaeologist, I dig to understand the past. Mother told me that archaeology was not a science at all, merely the discipline of interpretation. "An art at best," she once said, her voice heavy with scorn. "You're going to waste your mind digging in dirt!"

For thirty years I have dug in all manner of dirt and I have often been happy, sometimes almost fulfilled. Occasionally I have moments of brilliance, but I've learned to control them. I am nearly fifty, tenured, already postmenopausal and loving it. I am well liked by my students and respected by colleagues. Although I suspect my late brother thought of me as his old maid sister, my life has been a wonderful adventure and I have sampled too much of it to qualify for spinsterhood.

I'd never sampled children, however. I didn't have the time, didn't want to inflict on anyone the kind of childhood I'd experienced. So Stella came as a shock. My brother's fatal encounter with that tree took not only his life, but his wife's as well. As Stella's only surviving relative, I found myself guardian of a three-year-old girl. I had no idea that I could love another human being that much, or that loving could bring me such joy.

I went to get her in San Francisco, where Sam and Darcy had died. Stella was trapped in a bureaucratic web that took days to untangle, but by rush hour on the third day she was mine. We sat in a hotel room with a view of the fog and got to know each other.

"Poor baby," I said. She had been crying and her nose had run. "Poor Sweetheart." I had brought her toys. It's wonderful, this modern age, for children's toys are labeled with the age range of the child they're intended for. I had learned from these labels that she was too old for either the plain yellow rubber duck, which I had liked best, or a splendid green caterpillar that could be pulled by a string. Instead, the labels revealed a hateful assortment of toys designed to teach three-year-olds letters and numbers. I loathed them and bought her both the duck *and* the caterpillar. The caterpillar rolled on red wheels and made a loud noise. "See what I've brought you." I pulled the toy's string. "Clackity-clack," it blared.

Stella ignored it, watching me with large brown eyes made larger with apprehension. "Mama?" she said.

I tugged the caterpillar again, hoping to distract her. This child, this *baby*, couldn't understand death, I thought, the concept of coming and going was hard enough. "Mommy and Daddy aren't here right now, Stella," I said as gently as I could. "I'm your Aunt Phoebe. You're going to stay with me for a while." I was struggling with my own sense of loss, but if I'd spent more time with babies and less with broken pots and crochety old men, I might have known immediately that something was different about this child.

"Aunt Phoebe," Stella said, and reached out to me. "Mommy's gone." I picked her up and held her while she cried. I had expected her to be squalling and shrill, but she wept softly. "Mommy's gone, Daddy's gone," she repeated with simple finality, her arms around my neck, dampening my collar with her tears until I, too, wept, grieving my brother Sam and the rich entanglements of my past.

So from the beginning it was not what I expected or had avoided so assiduously all those fertile years. I loved her immediately, as if my maternal instincts had only lain fallow while I wrote papers, dug up ancient cities and lectured in large, cold classrooms.

Dr. Rafael Peterson, a crochety colleague who has been my mentor and nemesis over the years, had gotten us a grant to continue a dig in Turkey that summer. I bowed out to stay with Stella. Peterson was glad. It was a good site that we'd found and he's always hated sharing the limelight with a woman. We agreed that I should stay in Massachusetts with Stella and catalog the relics in my basement.

My home is a three-bedroom ranch house set on a half-acre semiwooded lot twelve miles from Amherst campus. Semiwooded because I gave up mowing and pruning years ago. Ornamental shrubs and white birch saplings have taken over the back of the lot, leaving only a tiny front yard that I mow only when I can't find the porch steps.

I moved the books out of the bedroom adjoining mine and moved in Stella with her toys, training pants, and child's paraphernalia. I repapered the place with swans and balloons and slept with my door ajar so to hear her slightest nocturnal whimper.

During the day she preferred my study to all the rooms in the house. Crammed floor to ceiling with books on three walls, the fourth is covered with drawers and shelves that hold some of the more interesting pieces from past excavations. It might seem foolish to allow a three-year-old to wander freely around the reconstructed shards of thousand-year-old pots, but from the beginning Stella was careful.

"This was the chalice of a great king," I told her one day only a few months after she had come to me. I was working over a handful of fragments as she crawled into my lap. "Careful, Honey, it's very fragile."

"Don't breathe," she said, repeating what I had told her earlier that afternoon.

"You can breathe, just don't bounce," I said.

With sticky fingers—at that age she always had sticky fingers— she picked up a fragment and placed it against the larger piece I was examining. "Jigsaw," she said triumphantly. It fit.

"Very good!" I told her. She reached for another. "No, Honey, Aunt Phoebe's working." I extracted the piece from her hand and set her down on the floor, pulling the caterpillar's string to make him bang.

"Don't breathe," she said again sadly.

"Holler your head off, if you want," I told her. "Just give me an hour with this thing, then we'll go back in the woods and watch the squirrels."

Stella was content with my promise. I found that the shard I had taken from her matched exactly the first piece she had fitted.

Along with what I'd already assembled, it formed almost one quarter of one side of a cup. At my feet, Stella crawled across the floor toward the bookcase, happy to entertain herself.

I spent an hour deep in the twin puzzles of fitting the fragments together and deciphering the inscription. I found only one more fragment that fit, but already I could see that the cup was poly-chromatic, a lovely piece. There was part of an inscription, and an edge of figures along the lip which might be satyrs. Stella had found the bookshelves and now sat surrounded by volumes she had pulled from the lower shelf. That's where I keep the encyclo-pedia. She shrieked when I scooped her up, squirming until I set her down again beside an open volume. It was open at "Greece: History and Origins; The Doric Invasion."

"Read me," she pleaded, pointing at a picture of a polychro-matic amphora, c. 400 B.C.

Shortly after she came to me, I took her to the doctor to be sure she was all right. He pronounced her healthy, though small for her age. I also called my old therapist to be sure *I* was all right. I was, Dr. Stein said, awash with maternal instincts. He also said to be alert. Small children often seem to shrug off the most severe trauma fairly quickly. "Consciously she will seem to forget her parents and in the years to come may not be able to remember anything about them," he said. "But unconsciously she may feel abandoned by those she depended on. That's where you must help her—be a bridge to her origins."

I did not want to do that. I wanted a normal, happy childhood for Stella, and any reminder of her father would spoil that. There had been so little happiness in our parents' home, so little room to be children, what could I tell Stella? That her father had knuckled under and been driven by others' goals all his life? Al-most all. Just before he was accepted to Harvard, when he had just turned thirteen, I think he briefly rebelled.

Harvard was reluctant to grant admission to a child, and had demanded proof of Sam's brilliance. Nothing stimulated my par-ents as much as a challenge to their children's genius, and my parents worked in tandem to extract from Sam the papers that later led to his theories on time and chaos. They worked day and night, driving him, grilling him. I knew even then that it took no knowledge or education on their part to make us learn. It was a routine of endless questions. Our problem-solving had become as instinctive as that of a slave who obeys to escape the lash.

One night late, while my father questioned him, ignoring Sam's tears and protests of "I can't," a book fell from the bookcase. I was in the room, and saw a heavy volume suddenly emerge from between the other books on the shelf and fall with a crash on the desk. Father was startled. I felt a rush of blood in my head, for there was no way the book could have fallen by itself. For the next few days, other books fell from shelves, some even seemed to fly across the room. A lamp was broken. My mother grilled Sam until late one night, and the next morning screamed when she found all the dinner dishes broken into shards in the kitchen sink. Walls shook. Carpets glided across the floor, dragging furniture with them. Then Sam was accepted to Harvard, and everything returned to normal.

Years later I mentioned it to Sam and he scoffed at me. "Poltergeists? Are you crazy?"

"No, you are," I challenged him. "Poltergeists occur around angry adolescents."

"I was never an angry adolescent," he retorted, out of touch to the end. "That was your specialty." And I never stopped being angry at my brother for denying the only moments when he was himself. But Dr. Stein was right, and I would try to heal those old feelings for Stella's sake. I preserved Sam's dry, fact-filled journals for her. I learned from his wife's careful diary that Stella had been physically advanced. She sat up when she was four months old. She talked early, and Darcy's journal was full of the vanity of a parent who finds her own pride in her child's accomplishments. "Whole sentences!" she had gushed when Stella was only nine months old.

I let Stella talk baby talk. She chattered incessantly, full of questions, and I explained everything I knew about the world to her in my own whimsical terms. When I ran out of things to say, I read to her. I went out and bought scores of children's books. Of course Sam and I were never allowed children's books, so I read *The Wizard of Oz* for the first time and loved it. Stella loved it, too, and asked me to read it to her again. Then again. For variety, I was amazed by the wonders of Pooh Corner and enjoyed the zaniness of Dr. Seuss.

Because of my work, there are many things that I *must* read: bulletins to the faculty, correspondence, colleagues' papers. "Read me!" Stella would command, and as I read out loud she would climb into my lap, her sweet brow furrowing with concentration as she scanned the pages. Because I read so rapidly, I traced the margin with my finger to keep track of my place. That probably helped her.

In September, just before I returned to a full-time teaching schedule, I looked up from working on a pot. Stella was often surrounded with ducks and toys, but this time she had pulled volumes of the *Encyclopaedia Britannica* from the shelf. "What are you up to, Stella?" I asked my frowning three-year-old. I meant what was she doing.

"Catamount," she said. "See Panther, American mountain lion, volume fourteen, page 246d."

I felt my ears frizzle. It's the same peculiar sensation that I first felt that night the book fell from the bookcase. I felt it again the moment I knew I had to escape to England or become Mother's remaining resident genius. I fell it sometimes when I get the gist of a tricky translation. Peterson says it's the sound of realisation when the realised is a deep and simple truth that until now has been obscure. Frizzle. "Stella, are you reading?"

She was reading. Everything. The encyclopedia, phone bills, junk mail, books. Stella was wonderful with books. She seemed to be born knowing not to lay them face down or bend pages to keep her place. When she finished a book, she put it back where she found it, so that often I didn't even know that she'd read a volume until she mentioned it later. But the peculiar poignancy of the situation was that, while she understood everything she read, she was emotionally and physically just a three-year-old girl.

Baby-proofing in my house was different than what many people experience. It was torturous deciding which books to leave within reach, which to relegate to the higher shelves. It was a form of censorship that I was not used to. It forced me to view the world with a mother's eyes for the first time. Cold-edged, manipulative Mother's Eyes. I had to protect my child.

But not from science, surely. The piles of books and papers by my colleagues and me, the stacks of painstakingly shot videos of excavations and reconstructions, all those stayed down on the bottom shelves. And I didn't feel I had to protect her from sex. I have never felt inhibited about that topic and share a sense with many of my generation that openness of expression is healthier than lurid secrets. Although, quite honestly, I had little that is graphic in video or literature.

No, I was deeply shocked at what I censored. Hatred. Violence. Dark impulses of the soul. Which is much of history, most fiction and almost all of literature. I have always read constantly, extensively, and now I was forced to go back over my life of books and reexamine them.

Shakespeare, for instance. I knew immediately that all the Histories with their sadistic killings and ruthless intrigue had to go up to the top shelf. But what about Lear and the terrible loss that he suffers because he mistakes love for flattery? What of Hamlet, who is everything a human should be, thoughtful and prudent and strong, but who finally resorts to murder? I was appalled when I reread *Twelfth Night* and *As You Like It*, while I agonized over *The Taming of the Shrew* and *The Tempest*.

I have never been able to part with a favorite book, but now the worn, brown, flaking paperbacks of my youth had to be reexamined. Bradbury, Heinlein and Leiber all went into the trash. Of my hardcovers, Tolstoi and Dostoyevski clearly had to be bumped to the upper shelves, and with them went D. H. Lawrence, Joseph Conrad, Henry Miller and a host of other writers who had given my adult life much of its pleasure. On Stella's fourth birthday, I filled the lower shelves with her children's books. I knew that when she grew up, my books would come down again. But not before she was ready.

Something about Oz resonated for her—probably the tale of a little girl lost in a strange place, separated by a terrible storm from those she loved, yet aided by strangers. I saw the parallel, although I tried not to feed into it even when, echoing Dorothy's "Auntie Em," Stella called me "Auntie Phoebe." She read the book and reread it until the pages were falling off. I finally found *The Scarecrow of Oz*. And then *Ozma of Oz*, *The Emerald City of Oz* and all the rest of the sequels. Stella was reading voraciously at that point, of course, so I didn't read them all. Who has the time to read all their child's books, to see all their films?

I did my best, but with no practical experience in mothering, I didn't recognize the truth when it happened. That first year, my teaching schedule was light. A nice woman named Amber MacPhillip came up from town to babysit on the days I had class. Mrs. MacPhillip (who despite her name is half Italian, half Jewish) is the perfect nanny because her three grandchildren live out of state and she is often overwhelmed by the desire to hug somebody small. One afternoon she was upset as she met me in the driveway when I got home. "Nothing to worry about, she's fine now, but Stella went into the woods today."

"What do you mean, went into the woods? Is she all right?"

She understood a working mother's panic and repeated her first message carefully. "Stella's fine, Dr. D'Amato. She's upstairs resting. Or at least she's upstairs. I told her she couldn't come down until you came home because she'd done a bad thing. But it gave me a scare. And she lied."

It seemed that after lunch, Mrs. MacPhillip installed Stella in her room for a nap. Half an hour later, Stella was gone. Mrs. MacPhillip searched the house and basement, the yard, called the neighbors, explored the woods behind the house and up and down the road. "I was out of my mind, Doctor! Forty-five minutes I'm searching like a crazy person, not a trace of her and I'm out of my mind. I decide I've got to call you and maybe the cops. I go back to the house and there she is, in bed where I left her!"

"Thank God," I said.

"She's never lied to me before. She's a good child, but when I told her never to go into the woods again, she says she didn't. When I told her don't hide from me, she says she didn't."

I had regained my calm, and it was Mrs. MacPhillip who was quite indignant at this point. I assured her that I didn't blame her, paid her for the day and got her out of the house. Stella was in her room, cranky and pouting. "You shouldn't leave your room when you're supposed to be napping," I chided her.

"I didn't!" She had a four-year-old's sense of justice and was clearly outraged. "I didn't! I didn't go anywhere!" Her voice was hoarse with exasperation.

"Mrs. MacP. said she couldn't find you."

"I didn't leave my room!"

She seemed genuinely upset, so I didn't argue. Mrs. MacPhillip had yelled at her, I suspected. I made Stella promise never to leave the house without telling someone and then let it go.

It happened again about a month later, when I was alone with her. We had shared a lovely morning, culminating in a wrestling match on the living room floor. She had her juice and graham crackers, then held my hand as we climbed the stairs. She giggled as I tossed her on her bed, and yawned as I took off her shoes. I hugged her more tightly than I should have and she squirmed away from me. "Read me?" she asked, holding up her shopworn *Wizard of Oz*.

"No, you read it yourself, I've got work to do. See you in half an hour." I kissed the top of her head, her delicious little-girl-smell delighting my nostrils.

Usually I hear her restless stirring. Forty-five minutes later, I investigated and she was gone. The imprint of her tiny body was still on the bed, her book fallen open on her pillow. There was no way she could have gone downstairs without passing me.

I remembered Mrs. MacPhillip's experience, so I didn't panic right away. I searched the room—the closet, beneath the bed. I searched the other bedrooms. I searched her room again. I called her name. I searched the attic, the basement, every place in between. That's when the panic began. I called the state police. While I waited for them, I searched the road and the woods out back. The state trooper was calm, methodical, and called me "Ma'am." When he had collected a description of both child and event, he demanded to see the place where she was last seen.

And there she was, sitting up in bed, looking warm and alive, feeling very cranky. "Can I get up now?" she demanded in the voice of one who has waited for too long.

The trooper was not amused. "Just a moment, ma'am." He crossed the room and squatted down beside Stella's bed, the muzzle of his gun holster burying itself in her shell-pink comforter. "Now, honey, I'm Officer Daniels. Your aunt said she couldn't find you after your nap. Did you go somewhere?"

Stella regarded him suspiciously. "No," she said.

"Did you maybe play a game or hide under the bed?"

"No," she repeated stonily. "I was reading."

He lifted his eyebrows at me. "Maybe she was in the closet."

I pretended I thought he was right, even to myself.

The next day I found a strange object among her toys, where it clearly didn't belong. It was metal, about six inches high, conical, with a crooked copper tube emerging from its top. I took it to Ethan's Antiques the next time I was in town.

"Oil can. American. Not an antique, but close. Probably 1912–1915. Before The War." Ann Ethan, a former student of mine, is the only person I know who says "The War" and means World War I. "Where'd you get it?"

"It was in Stella's toy box. She must have found it out in the woodshed."

"Want to sell it?"

"How much?"

"Ten dollars."

"No, thanks. I'll keep it until it's an antique." I put it on a shelf in the garage and forgot about it. Or at least put it in the back of my mind and didn't take it out for a while.

. . . .

Not long afterward, Mark and Nancy Marsten rented the house next door. Mark was an instructor in the psychology department at Hampshire College. Nancy was a pretty girl in a fragile, frantic sort of way, who tended to preface everything with "Mark says . . ." They had a son, David, who was two months older than Stella.

One day Nancy asked me to watch David while she ran an errand. A little later she invited me to bring Stella over to her house. For Stella and David it was baby-love at first sight. They celebrated David's fourth birthday at his house, where I video-taped them covered with frosting and crumbs.

For me, having Mark and Nancy right next door seemed ideal. If Mrs. MacP. was busy, I could drop Stella over there on my way to classes, pick her up on the way home. David stayed with me when his mother went shopping and on the occasional evenings when Mark and Nancy went to the movies or some function at the college.

The only problem was Mark and Nancy. They were fascinated with accelerated learning. When Mark learned of my back-ground, he wanted to talk of nothing else, and his intensity was repulsive. Nancy was envious that Stella could already read. She cheerfully informed me that Mark was teaching David, setting goals for the boy, punishing him when he failed to meet his fa-ther's expectations. David was a sweet little boy, and I felt sorry for him.

When David spent an afternoon with us, I would often read to Stella and him before their nap, but Stella loved to read so much that I sometimes let her read for the two of them. I should never have allowed it. From my study I would hear Stella's voice rise and fall, clear and astonishingly articulate. Then it would sud-denly cease and the children would nap. Or so I thought.

They did nap at first. I know, because I would peek in at them. Minutes at a time I was entranced by the rise and fall of their breaths. My passion had always been the distant past, but I began to see these children as little arrows aimed at the future. I would think of my brother, all past now, and pity him. I felt nothing for him now but gratitude for this brilliant spark he had thrown.

And then, one day I peeked in and they were gone. Their beds were empty, the bedspreads crumpled where they had lain. I touched Stella's pillow and it was still warm from her body heat. I knew they could not have left the room, but I searched the house anyway.

There is something to be said for logic, particularly when one is in a state of panic. My urge to call for help was offset by my fear of telling Nancy that I had lost her child as well as my own. Stella had disappeared before and returned. In the end, I sat on the floor between the twin beds and waited.

It didn't take long. There was a sound as though someone were rubbing their fingers on an overinflated balloon, and I heard my name being called. I had a momentary impression of the room's dimensions being stretched, or squeezed, or snapped like a table-cloth being shaken out. Suddenly both children lay on their beds again. David was crying and Stella was shouting my name, her arm was scratched and bleeding from wrist to elbow.

"Auntie Phoebe! Auntie Phoebe!" Stella shrieked, and even as I leapt to snatch her up, her flailing foot caught me with a direct blow to the solar plexus. I fell beside her on the bed, momentarily speechless. As I regained my breath with a painful gasp, I felt Stella hugging me fiercely, saying, "Auntie Phoebe, I knew you'd save us."

I reached out, grateful for the feel of her. I freed one arm and groped out to David, who joined us on Stella's bed. They clung to me like a life raft and I squeezed them both as tightly as I could without breaking them. Then I went to get Betadine and ban-dages.

"All right, both of you," I said sternly as I cleaned Stella's wound. It was not deep, but ragged like a cat scratch. "Where did you go?"

"Oz," they both said at once. *Frizzle.*

Stella told me that the first time it happened by accident. She had been restless when she should have been resting, and picked up a book. *Wizard,* of course. Her favorite part was where the companions, the Scarecrow and Dorothy, begin at the beginning of the Yellow Brick Road. Toto scampers ahead. "It's how you hold the book," Stella said, showing me how her short, pink fingers curled loosely around the frayed edges of the thick book.

"What else?" I prompted. It was clearly a lot more than how she held the book, but it's hard for a four-year-old, even a terribly bright four-year-old, to describe the workings of her mind. But she described her thoughts as pictures, and that helped me to understand.

Some of it is time. When I think of time, I think of it as though it were a line that extends from past, through present, to future. Stella saw it as a globe, and imagined herself on the surface of that globe. And she *saw* the Yellow Brick Road as well. Not dimly, the way I see what I read most of the time, but with a sharp, reflective inner vision. That first time it happened, she wondered if the bricks were glazed on only one side, like the bricks in the mall walkway, or whether the glaze went all the way around. And in her mind's eye—she used that phrase constantly—she imagined bending down to look at a loose one, and yes, she saw that they were glazed on all sides. At that moment the book was gone and she was *there.*

Dorothy and the Scarecrow were just disappearing from sight around a corner. Toto looked back at Stella and barked. Stella froze for a moment, then ran after them, shouting, "Dorothy! Wait!" But Dorothy and the Scarecrow were out of sight and the Yellow Brick Road stretched out empty before her. She pursued them for a while before she became tired and then frightened. Thinking she wanted to go home, she thought of her bedroom. And when she remembered the pattern of her bedspread, the swans and balloons and baby ducks, she was back. As easy as that.

It got easier with each nap. Eventually she caught up with and made friends with Dorothy. The Scarecrow was her special protector. The Tin Woodsman asked her to oil his ankles because they were hard for him to reach. Each time she joined them, she traveled a little further on their journey. Then one day she was reading to David, and he came along, too.

As Stella told this, David was sniffling, watching me carefully, trying to stifle his tears. I reached over and gave him a hug. "It's okay, David. All right, Stella. So, what happened?" But she began crying again and it was David who finished the story. Stella lost the Tin Woodsman's oil can, so he was getting rusty. When the Flying Monkeys attacked, he was too slow to escape and the others stayed by him. Fighting off the monkeys, Stella panicked and called my name.

The three of us recovered over milk and cookies while I tried to explain to them about the danger. I had been worried for some time about her reading, and now it wasn't flying monkeys in Oz that concerned me as much as what happens to children with gifts. I made her promise to tell no one. I think Stella understood as much as a child could. I wasn't worried about David. Nancy had told him never to leave the yard, and he was terrified that his father would find out that he had done something wrong.

I had already purged my shelves of all literature, now I got rid of the Oz books. With them went all of Stella's other books in tightly sealed boxes to a rented storage space in Springfield. Stella swore that she would never go "away" again, but she was upset, for she loved to read. In fairness to her, I don't know if she could control it. But over the next few years she became very good at concealing everything that made her different. I had to insist that Mrs. MacP. and Nancy keep story books away from her. They thought I was a little "off," but things have gotten progressively calmer.

Her first-grade teacher never guessed that Stella read at a college sophomore's level, and sent home complaints that she was easily distracted and needed special classes to help her concentrate. I agreed and Stella went to special reading classes for a year, forced to read and reread first-grade-level stories. Mark was ungraciously delighted. Stella's educators were pleased and self-congratulatory when her schoolwork improved in the second grade.

When she was in the third grade, I found a remarkable coin—a gold head of Trajan, looking freshly minted—on the floor of her room. She said she had found it in my study. Perhaps she did, although I don't remember seeing it before. The only reason I wondered was that I had brought home a student's particularly brilliant thesis about Trajan's Rome. I preferred to believe Stella, but I knew that it was possible that she was learning to conceal her abilities, even from me.

But I had to fight for her, I could not let talent destroy her as it had her father. I gave her a childhood. She had a bunny we kept in a hutch in the backyard, ballet lessons once a week, friends, birthday parties, summer trips to Tanglewood. I even got her a television and let her watch cartoons on Saturday mornings. Everything was fiction. I thought she was growing out of it, that everything was going to be all right.

So last night was a shock. It was Friday, a long day for me. When classes were finished, Peterson called a last-minute department meeting to complain, basically, about the rest of us. It was late by the time I drove home. I could see the flashing lights of the police cars in Mark and Nancy's yard even before I turned down the street.

Nancy was having hysterics in the bedroom, Mark was glowering intensely in the kitchen by the phone. A state trooper explained the situation to me. While his training showed in his perfect monotone and stern face, his consistent *"He* says," referring to Mark, starkly underlined that he didn't believe much of what he was telling me. But I believed what I heard.

Apparently, when Stella learned from my phone call that I would be late, she went home with David after school. It was cold out, threatening to snow. Nancy forbids watching television on weekdays and recommended that the children read, ignoring my one rule. They went to David's room and had been there for almost an hour when Nancy went to check them. They were gone, of course. Their coats and boots are still by the door.

The police have searched Mark and Nancy's house and mine. It's been snowing through the night and the yards are a pattern of boot tracks and paw prints from the search dogs—one a German shepherd, the other a lugubrious hound that Stella would love. They have searched the woods and the other side of the road, but the dogs only whine and run in circles. In the past few hours, it's clear the police have developed a theory.

They have isolated Mark and Nancy, questioning Nancy repeatedly. Their tone is no longer reassuring. Not an hour ago Mark raged at them, "Are we under suspicion? Are you crazy? My son has disappeared!" He called his lawyer and wept. While he covered his face, the troopers shared knowing glances.

They have verified that I was at Peterson's interminable meeting, so they are kind to me. They let me see David's room. It is a boy's room, wallpapered in a manly plaid, clashing with the childlike rumpled quilt decorated with bears. "They were reading," I observed, seeing the worn paperback lying on the bed.

"I read that book," the older cop said. "Back when I was in college, everybody read that." He didn't seem to mind when I picked it up. The pages were well worn, but the spine was still sturdy and the page corners unbent. The appendix had the used look of a textbook that has been studied and committed to memory. "I saw the movie," the younger cop said. "It was dumb."

"The book was better," observed the first.

I slipped *The Fellowship of the Ring* into my pocket.

It's now thirty-six hours since the children disappeared. It's possible that the reporters gathered out on the road with their television cameras, extra telephone lines and ever-present car phones may have distorted some delicate balance and made it impossible for Stella to get back. But I know this book. It was among the first to catch my own imagination when I was an undergraduate, only a little older than Stella is now. I know why a little girl who loved *The Wizard of Oz* would love it. I know this book and I know that the children are in trouble. I have to find them. I have to try.

So I have filled my backpack with food, water and warm clothes for the three of us. I have packed my only weapon, an old geologist's pick. I am curled up on Stella's bed, covered by her quilt. I imagine the crystal of my watch bulging, becoming a globe. I pick a spot upon which to stand. I hold the book loosely in my hand, as she told me. I turn to the first page.

The
Eden
Syndrome

The obverse of *The Pandora Principle* is that curiosity just might benefit more cats than it kills. Every quest for knowledge, whether scientific, spiritual or some combination of both, is fraught with danger in direct proportion to the magnitude of the reward.

The next six stories (half of them never before published) pose problems that yield varyingly satisfactory results for the characters who dare to solve them, but be warned: one story's solution will appeal only to existentialists and solipsists . . .

Patrick LoBrutto

Genesis for Dummies

Reading is such a seductive activity . . . ever wonder why? Here's very possibly the first and the ultimate word on the subject! PATRICK LoBRUTTO *is cofounder of the Foundation science-fiction imprint, and was for many years the editorial director of the Doubleday trade science-fiction department. One of the most popular editors in the fantasy and science-fiction genre, he has been named Best Editor in the prestigious World Fantasy Awards. His comic story, "Vision Quest," appeared in my 1993 anthology,* Masterpieces of Terror and the Unknown.

. . . AND the LORD God formed a man of the dust of the ground, and touched the man's finger with his outstretched forefinger; and the man became a living soul.

And the LORD God planted a garden eastward in Eden; and there He put the man that He had created. And out of the ground made the LORD God to grow every tree that is pleasant to the sight, and good for food; the tree of Life also in the midst of the garden and close by the tree of the knowledge of Good and Evil. And the LORD God put the man into the garden of Eden to dress it and to keep it as the LORD God had made it perfect.

And the LORD God commanded the man, saying, "Of every tree of the garden thou mayest freely take: But of the tree of the knowledge of Good and Evil, thou shalt not pick of it; for the day that thou takest thereof thou shalt surely know death." And the

LORD God said, "It is not good that the man should be alone; I will make him an help meet for him."

And out of the ground the LORD God imagined every beast of the field, and every fowl of the air and it became as thus. And the LORD God brought them unto Adam to see what he would call them: and whatsoever Adam called every thing, that was the name thereof. And Adam gave names to all the cattle, and to every fowl of the air, and to every beast of the field; and to all that the LORD God had formed; but for Adam there was not found for him an help meet for him.

And the LORD God caused a deep sleep to fall upon Adam, and he slept and dreamed: and He took one of his ribs, and closed up the flesh instead thereof; and the rib, which the LORD God had taken from the man, made He a woman. And the LORD God waked her from her dream and brought her to the man. And Adam said, "This is now bones of my bones and flesh of my flesh: she shall be called woman because she was taken out of man. And Eve because she will be the mother of all the living." Therefore shall a man leave his father and mother, and shall cleave unto his wife: and they shall be one flesh.

Now the serpent was more *subtil* than any beast of the field which the LORD God had made. And he said unto the woman, "Yea, hath God said ye shall not choose from every tree of the garden?" And Eve said unto the serpent, "We may eat of the fruit of the trees of the garden: But of the fruit of the tree which is in the midst of the garden, God hath commanded, 'Ye shall not devour it, nor touch it, lest ye know death.' "

And the serpent said unto the woman, "Ye shall not die: For God doth know that in the day that ye choose a fruit thereof and devour it ye shall be as God, knowing Good and Evil."

And the serpent led the woman with him unto the tree of Life which is in the midst of the garden. Then, in the dust of the ground under that tree, he put his face. "Here," saith the serpent, in his subtilty, "is a letter." And then more letters made he in the dust thereon. Forming the noise of them for the woman to hear.

And Eve bent to the serpent and made the letters also, as so did the serpent. And the woman went to her husband saying, "There under the tree of Life is a sound in the dust you shall see with thine eyes." Thus did Adam holding his help meet's hand that had dust all over it, walk with her even unto the tree of Life, and he looked down upon the letters in the dust of the ground.

Now the serpent saith, "It is not from the LORD God that these come." And with a serpent's persuasion he showed them in the dust to take the letters and form them into a word. And the man and the woman both together knew the word. And Adam and Eve knew the spirit in the word. And they began with this word. They knew, then, a choice in their heart of hearts. And they both together desired a new word.

Then did the serpent with his face make a new word in the dust. So the man, Adam, and his help meet, Eve, did write the words in the dust thereon; of all the names of all the beasts of the fields, and every fowl in the air above, and every creeping thing they did write. And they remembered them of their dreams when they came into the garden, beginning to form the words of them also in the dust of the ground.

And many evenings and mornings passed for the man and the woman to write these things of heaven and earth. It was then that the serpent returned to Adam and Eve and said unto them, "Come with me that your eyes shall be opened knowing Good and Evil as I promised."

With hands covered in dust, the man and the woman walked with the serpent; and he brought them to the tree of the knowledge of Good and Evil that was a tree of many books that were of many words. And the words in the books were the fruit of the tree of the knowledge of Good and Evil.

The man, Adam, and the woman, Eve, exclaimed in wonder and fear at the books bound in the skin of the beasts of the field and the fowl of the air; of the pages of words therein formed of the trees that yielded seed and bore fruit they were troubled with joy.

They touched them with their outstretched fingers, then, the books of the tree. And Adam and Eve did together choose a fruit of the tree of the knowledge of Good and Evil.

And the serpent saith unto them, "That book is a good book. Read to me its story . . .."

Zenna Henderson

Turn the Page

The late ZENNA HENDERSON *was an Arizona writer and school teacher best known for her warm and moving science-fiction stories of "the People," a race of gentle aliens trying to live quietly in our midst. She also wrote the chilling, unexpectedly poignant "Walking Aunt Daid," which appears in the closing spot of* Angels of Darkness. *Ms. Henderson's characteristic love and compassion for humanity glows brightly in "Turn the Page."*

WHEN I WAS in the first grade, my teacher was magic. Oh, I know! Everyone thinks that his first teacher is something special. It's practically a convention that all little boys fall in love with her and that all little girls imitate her and that both believe her the Alpha and Omega of wisdom—but *my* teacher was really magic.

We all felt it the first day when finally the last anxious parent was shooed reluctantly out the door and we sat stiff and uneasy in our hard, unfriendly chairs and stared across our tightly clasped hands at Miss Ebo, feeling truly that we were on the edge of something strange and wonderful, but more wonderful than strange. Tears dried on the face of our weeper as we waited in that moment that trembled like a raindrop before it splinters into rainbows.

"Let's *be* something!" Miss Ebo whispered. "Let's be birds."

And we were! We were! *Real birds!* We fluttered and sang and flitted from chair to chair all around the room. We prinked and preened and smoothed our heads along the brightness of feathers and learned in those moments the fierce throbbing restlessness of birds, the feathery hushing quietness of sleeping wings. *And there was one of us that beat endlessly at the closed windows, scattering feathers, shaking the glass, straining for the open sky.*

Then we were children again, wiggling with remembered delight, exchanging pleased smiles, feeling that maybe school wasn't all fright and strangeness after all. And with a precocious sort of knowledge, we wordlessly pledged our mutual silence about our miracle.

This first day set the pace for us. We were, at different times, almost every creature imaginable, learning of them, and how they fitted into the world and how they touched onto our segment of the world, until we saw fellow creatures wherever we looked. *But there was one of us who set himself against the lessons* and ground his heel viciously down on the iridescence of a green June-bug that blundered into our room one afternoon. The rest of us looked at Miss Ebo, hoping in our horror for some sort of cosmic blast from her. Her eyes were big and knowing—and a little sad. We turned back to our work, tasting for the first time a little of the sorrow for those who stubbornly shut their eyes against the sun and still curse the darkness.

And soon the stories started. Other children *heard* about Red Riding Hood and the Wolf and maybe played the parts, but we took turns at *being* Red Riding Hood and the Wolf. Individually we tasted the terror of the pursued—the sometimes delightfully delicious terror of the pursued—and we knew the blood lust and endless drive of the pursuer—the hot pulses leaping in our veins, the irresistible compulsion of hunger-never-satiated that pulled us along the shadowy forest trails.

And when we were Red Riding Hood, we knew under our terror and despair that help would come—*had* to come when we turned the page, *because it was written that way.* If we were the wolf, we knew that death waited at the end of our hunger; we leaped as compulsively to that death as we did to our feeding. As the mother and grandmother, we knew the sorrow of letting our children go, and the helpless waiting for them to find the dangers and die of them or live through them, but always, always, were we the pursuer or the pursued, the waiter or the active one, we knew we had only to turn the page and finally live happily ever after, *because it was written that way!* And we found out that after you have once been the pursuer, the pursued and the watcher, you can never again be only the pursuer or the pursued or the watcher. Ever after you are a little of each of them.

We learned and learned in our first grade, but sometimes we had to stop our real learning and learn what was expected of us. Those were the shallow days.

We knew the shallow days when they arrived because Miss Ebo met us at the door, brightly smiling, cheerily speaking, but with her lovely dark eyes quiet and uncommunicative. We left the door ajar and set ourselves to routine tasks. We read and wrote and worked with our numbers, covering all we had slighted in the magic days before—a model class, learning neat little lessons, carefully catching up with the other first grades. Sometimes we even had visitors to smile at our industry, or the supervisor to come in and sharply twitch a picture to more exact line on the bulletin board, fold her lips in frustration and make some short-tempered note in her little green book before she left us, turning her stiff white smile on briefly for our benefit. And, at day's end, we sighed with weariness of soul and burst out of class with all the unused enthusiasm of the day, hoping that tomorrow would be magic again. And it usually was.

The door would swing shut with a pleased little chuckling cluck and we would lift our questioning faces to Miss Ebo—or the Witch or the Princess or the Fairy Godmother—and plunge into another story as into a sparkling sea.

As Cinderella, we labored in the ashes of the fireplace and of lonely isolation and of labor without love. We wept tears of hopeless longing as we watched the semblance of joy and happiness leave us behind, weeping for it even though we knew too well the ugliness straining under it—the sharp bones of hatefulness jabbing at scarlet satin and misty tulle. Cinderella's miracle came to us and we made our loveliness from commonplace things and learned that happiness often has a midnight chiming so that it won't leak bleakly into a watery dawn and, finally, that no matter how fast we run, we leave a part of us behind, and by that part of us, joy comes when we turn the page and we finally live happily ever after, *because it is written that way.*

With Chicken Little, we cowered under the falling of our sky. We believed implicitly in our own little eye and our own little ear and the aching of our own little tail where the sky had bruised us. Not content with panicking ourselves with the small falling, we told the whole world repeatedly and at great length that the sky was falling for everyone because it fell for us. And when the Fox promised help and hope and strength, we followed him and let our bones be splintered in the noisome darkness of fear and ignorance.

And, as the Fox, we crunched with unholy glee the bones of little fools who shut themselves in their own tiny prisons and followed fear into death rather than take a larger look at the sky. And we found them delicious and insidious.

Mrs. Thompson came down to see Miss Ebo after Chicken Little. There must be some reason why Jackie was having nightmares—maybe something at school? And Miss Ebo had to soothe her with all sorts of little Educational Psychology platitudes because she couldn't tell her that Jackie just wouldn't come out of the Fox's den even after his bones were scrunched to powder. He was afraid of a wide sky and always would be.

So the next day we all went into the darkness of caves and were little blind fish. We were bats that used their ears for eyes. We were small shining things that seemed to have no life but grew into beauty and had the wisdom to stop when they reached the angles of perfection. So Jackie chose to be one of those and he didn't learn with us anymore except on our shallow days. He loved shallow days. The other times he grew to limited perfection in his darkness.

And there was one of us who longed to follow the Fox forever. Every day his eyes would hesitate on Miss Ebo's face, but every day the quietness of her mouth told him that the Fox should not come back into our learning. And his eyes would drop and his fingers would pluck anxiously at one another.

The year went on and we were princesses leaning from towers, drawing love to us on shining extensions of ourselves, feeling the weight and pain of love along with its shiningness as the prince climbed Rapunzel's golden hair. We, as Rapunzel, betrayed ourselves to evil. We were cast into the wilderness, we bought our way back into happiness by our tears of mingled joy and sorrow. And—as the witch—we were evil, hoarding treasures to ourselves, trying to hold unchanged things that had to change. We were the one who destroyed loveliness when it had to be shared, who blinded maliciously, only to find that all loveliness, all delight, went with the sight we destroyed.

And then we learned more. We were the greedy woman. We wanted a house, a castle, a palace—power beyond power, beyond power, until we wanted to meddle with the workings of the universe. And then we had to huddle back on the dilapidated steps of the old shack with nothing again, nothing in our lax hands, because we reached for too much.

But then we were her husband, too, who gave in and gave in against his better judgment, against his desires, but always backing away from a *no* until he sat there, too, with empty hands, staring at the nothing he must share. And he had never had anything at all because he had never asked for it. It was a strange, hard lesson and we studied it again and again until one of us was stranded in greed, another in apathy and one of us almost knew the right answer.

But magic can't last. That was our final, and my hardest, bitterest, lesson. One day Miss Ebo wasn't there. She'd gone away, they said. She wouldn't be back. I remember how my heart tightened and burned coldly inside me when I heard. And shallow day followed shallow day and I watched, terrified, the memory of Miss Ebo dying out of the other kids' eyes.

Then one afternoon I saw her again, thin and white, blown

against the playground fence like a forgotten leaf of last autumn. Her russetty dress fluttered in the cold wind and the flick of her pale fingers called me from clear across the playground. I pressed my face close against the wire mesh, trying to cry against her waist, my fingers reaching hungrily through to her.

My voice was hardly louder than the whisper of dry leaves across a path. "Miss Ebo! Miss Ebo! Come back!"

"You haven't forgotten." Her answer lost itself on the wind. "Remember. Always remember. Remember the whole of the truth. Truth has so many sides, evil and good, that if you cling to just one, it may make it a lie." The wind freshened and she fluttered with it, clinging to the wire. "Remember, turn the page. Everyone *will* finally live happily ever after, *because that's the way it's written!*"

My eyes blurred with tears and before I could knuckle them dry, she was gone.

"Crybaby!" The taunt stung me as we lined up to go back indoors.

"I saw her!" I cried. "I saw Miss Ebo!"

"Miss Ebo?" Blank eyes stared into mine. There was a sudden flicker way back behind seeing, but it died. "Crybaby!"

Oh, I know that no one believes in fairy tales any more. They're for children. Well, who better to teach than children that good must ultimately triumph? Fairy-tale ending—they lived happily ever after! *But it is written that way!* The marriage of bravery and beauty—tasks accomplished, peril surmounted, evil put down, captives freed, enchantments broken, humanity emerging from the forms of beasts, giants slain, wrongs righted, joy coming in the morning after the night of weeping. The lessons are all there. They're told over and over and over, but we let them slip and we sigh for our childhood days, not seeing that we shed the truth as we shed our deciduous teeth.

I never saw Miss Ebo again, but I saw my first grade again, those who survived to our twenty-fifth anniversary. At first I thought I wouldn't go, but most sorrow can be set aside for an evening, even the sorrow attendant on finding how easily happiness is lost when it depends on a single factor. I looked around at those who had come, but I saw in them only the tattered remnants of Miss Ebo's teachings.

Here was the girl who so delighted in the terror of being pursued that she still fled along dark paths, though no danger followed. Here was our winged one still beating his wings against the invisible glass. Here was our pursuer, the blood lust in his eyes altered to a lust for power that was just as compulsive, just as inevitably fatal as the old pursuing evil.

Here was our terror-stricken Chicken Little, his drawn face, his restless, bitten nails, betraying his eternal running away from the terror he sowed behind himself, looking for the Fox, any Fox, with glib, comforting promises. And there, serene, was the one who learned to balance between asking too much and too little—who controlled his desires instead of letting them control him. There was the one, too, who had sorrowed and wept but who was now coming into her kingdom of children.

But these last two were strangers—as I was—in this wistful gathering of people who were trying to turn back twenty-five years. I sat through the evening, trying to trace in the masks around me the bright spirits that had run with me into Miss Ebo's enchantment. I looked for Jackie. I asked for Jackie. He was hidden away in some protected place, eternally being his dark shining things, afraid—too afraid—of even shallowness ever to walk in the light again.

There were speeches. There was laughter. There was clowning. But always the underlying strain, the rebellion, the silent crying out, the fear and mistrust.

They asked me to talk.

I stood, leaning against the teacher's desk, and looked down into the carefully empty faces.

"You have forgotten," I said. "You have all forgotten Miss Ebo."

"Miss Ebo?" The name was a pursing on all the lips, a furrow

on the brows. Only one or two smiled even tentatively. *"Remember Miss Ebo?"*

"If you have forgotten," I said, "it's a long time ago. If you remember, it was only yesterday. But even if you have forgotten her, I can see that you haven't forgotten the lessons she taught you. Only you have remembered the wrong part. You only half learned the lessons. You've eaten the husks and thrown the grain away. She tried to tell you. She tried to teach you. But you've all forgotten. Not a one of you remembers that if you turn the page everyone will live happily ever after, *because it was written that way.* You're all stranded in the introduction to the story. You work yourselves all up to the climax of terror or fear or imminent disaster, but you never turn the page. You go back and live it again and again and again.

"Turn the page! Believe again! You have forgotten how to believe in anything beyond your chosen treadmill. You have grown out of the fairy-tale age, you say. But what have you grown into? Do you like it?" I leaned forward and tried to catch evasive eyes. "With your hopeless, scalding tears at night and your dry-eyed misery when you waken. Do you like it?

"What would you give to be able to walk once more into a morning that is a-tiptoe with expectancy, magical with possibilities, bright with a sure delight? Miss Ebo taught us how. She gave us the promise and hope. She taught us all that everyone will finally live happily ever after *because it is written that way.* All we have to do is let loose long enough to turn the page. Why don't you?"

They laughed politely when I finished. I was always the turner of phrases. Wasn't that clever? Fairy tales! Well—

The last car drove away from the school. I stood by the fence in the dark school yard and let the night wash over me.

Then I was a child again, crying against the cold mesh fence—hopeless, scalding tears in the night.

"Miss Ebo. Miss Ebo!" My words were only a twisted shaping of my mouth. "They have forgotten. Let me forget too. Surely it must be easier to forget that there is a page to be turned than to know it's there and not be able to turn it! How long? How long must I remember?"

A sudden little wind scooted a paper sibilantly across the sidewalk . . . *forever* . . . *after* . . . *forever after* . . .

Chelsea Quinn Yarbro

Become So Shining That We Cease to Be

CHELSEA QUINN YARBRO *is an award-winning fantasist perhaps best known for* The Saint-Germain Chronicles *and other vampire stories, one of which, "Advocates," was co-winner of the prestigious World Horror Award for Best Novelette. The following story will be new to most of her readers; before now it was only published in the program book of the first World Horror Convention in Nashville in 1991.*

WHEN ERIC first moved into the flat above Fanchon, she considered him nothing more than a noisy intruder. He played music every hour of the day and night, he spent the greater part of his afternoons doing something—she could only imagine what—that made her living room sound like the inside of a drum, and he was surly to her on those rare occasions when they actually met. She was too daunted to approach him.

"He's driving me crazy!" she complained to her old friend Naomi at the end of an especially loud two hours. "He's the most obnoxious creep Peterson's ever let into this building, and that *includes* the idiot with the saxophone. This guy's never quiet."

"Have you told Peterson?" asked Naomi in her most reasonable and irritating tone, the one she reserved for undergrads. "Haven't any of the other neighbors complained?"

"Once, I called him once, but so what? All he did was say he'd talk to him, and what good will that do?" She sighed. "Listen, I'd invite you over for a drink tonight, but I don't know what the place is going to sound like."

"I'll meet you somewhere," Naomi suggested much too promptly for Fanchon's current mood. "What about the Gryphon? Say ten, fifteen minutes?"

Fanchon knew she could not afford the time, the money, or the calories, but she liked the restaurant tucked into the side of a multishop building; she let herself be persuaded, assuaging her guilt with the promise that she would not touch the smorgasbord offered at five in the afternoon—the salmon pâté on black bread had been her undoing more than once. "All right. The Gryphon. Four-thirty."

"And tell that bastard he'll have the place to himself for an hour or so, and to get it out of his system while you're gone." Naomi didn't sound as sympathetic as Fanchon would have liked, but her humor was welcome.

"I hardly ever see him, let alone speak."

"Small wonder, but . . . See you in a bit." Naomi hung up.

Since it was sunny, Fanchon decided to walk in spite of the nip in the air. She pulled on a bulky sweater over her silk shirt and changed into low-heeled shoes. She examined her grey slacks in the mirror, thinking that she really ought to take them to the cleaners. Above her, sound rained down, engulfing as a storm at sea. She made a rude gesture to the ceiling as she picked up her purse and went out the door, taking care to lock the deadbolt. It was senseless to take chances.

Naomi was waiting for her, leaning back in one of the comfortable, caterpillar-shaped love seats away from the window. "You made good time," she called out, waving so Fanchon could locate her.

"You're looking very smart," said Fanchon as she sat down opposite Naomi.

Naomi brushed the lapel of her cobalt-blue wool suit. "It's supposed to be impressive. I like it. I never used to wear blue." In her right hand she held a very small glass of something clear. "How's the noise front?"

"You heard it, didn't you?" Fanchon asked.

"Not over the phone," said Naomi. "Just a kind of rattle. It didn't seem very bad. But that's phones for you."

"That's more or less what Peterson said when I called him." Fanchon leaned back and tucked her purse into the curve of the chair.

"You ought to talk to him again, get him to understand what's happening. You ought to insist he come over and listen for himself. He's the landlord. He's responsible for keeping the building in good order, isn't he? The Rent Board could probably make him put in better insulation or—" She made a sweeping swipe with her arm.

A waitress appeared behind the love seat. "Want another aquavit?"

"Sure," said Naomi, glancing at Fanchon. "You?"

"Coffee," said Fanchon. Then forgot her stern resolution. "And a small brandy, in a snifter."

The waitress nodded and went away.

"So how's everything with you?" Naomi asked. "Other than the neighbor, I mean? Any luck with the class load, or are you still stuck with that eight A.M. thing? I forget what it's called."

"Working Women of the Nineteenth Century," said Fanchon. "I've got it and eleven sleepy sophomores." She looked around. "When I set this up, I thought doing all my teaching in the morning would leave me lots of time for research, but it isn't working out, and not just because of the noise."

"Does it really go on all the time? Nighttime, too?" The aquavit was almost gone.

"Day, night. Afternoons are probably the worst, but it happens any time. Loud heavy metal banging and noise." She saw the waitress returning and dug out her purse.

"Three dollars for the brandy, one-fifty for the coffee. Three-fifty for the aquavit." She took the offered money and made change. "If you want refills, try to order in the next fifteen minutes, okay? We get swamped after five."

Fanchon made a point of giving the waitress a two-dollar tip. Then she looked at Naomi. "How about your schedule?"

"Busy, busy, busy. We're seeing more faculty—not the top guys, they have their own shrinks—but midlevel. I had a mathematician in the other day, in a real state. He's so worried about the ozone he can't sleep."

"What do you think is causing it?" Fanchon asked, thinking she wasn't being fair to impose on her friend when so many other demands were being made of her.

"I don't know," said Naomi, taking her second glass of aquavit. "There is a hole in the ozone, and it probably will get bigger, and that will cause problems. He's right about that. I can't say anything to dismiss his fear. Some of the others are upset about the world economy, the air quality, the crowding. They're all real things." She took a long sip. "I probably shouldn't drink this stuff, but it's good."

Fanchon picked up the small brandy snifter and held it between her palms, warming it. "Is it any worse than pills?"

"Depends on who you're talking to," said Naomi. "Well, you're the historian. What compares to our ecological worries?"

"People are always afraid of catastrophe. If it isn't the ozone layer, it's plague or famine. If it isn't that, there are barbarians or the Inquisition or Lady Wu." She lifted the snifter and let the brandy fire her tongue.

"But what in the past has had the potential to obliterate the whole planet? Aside from nuclear war. That was what I heard five years ago." She looked away toward the frosted windows and the autumn afternoon beyond. "You ever stop to think how many people in this town are in the destruction business? The guys in math and physics are calculating the end of the world every day. They come to me with horrible things on their minds, and they can't talk about them. I tell you, Fanchon, there are times I think it's easier to go crazy."

"Better than become impervious to it all, I guess," said Fanchon.

"I guess," echoed Naomi. She glanced at the door as a group of men came in. "Ah, the sociologists have arrived."

"Is that good?" asked Fanchon, noticing how animated Naomi had become.

"Well, Bill's with them." Her blush was very out of character, and Fanchon could not resist mentioning it.

"What's special about Bill?" Now she felt like an intruder, a duenna at an assignation.

"I'll let you know when I'm sure." She waved. "There he is: tall, moustache, tweed jacket, jeans."

"Well, that describes most of them," said Fanchon, taking the rest of her brandy in a single gulp.

"Red-brown hair going grey. It looks a little like cinnamon and sugar on toast." Her laughter was self-conscious. She snuggled more deeply into the love seat. "He's spotted me. I'll introduce you."

"Thanks," said Fanchon, not at all certain what she meant. "I hope things work out the way you want."

"Yeah." Naomi laughed uncertainly. "It's not always easy to figure out what that is, you know?"

"Oh, yeah," said Fanchon. "If you ever learn the trick, you teach it to me."

Naomi drained her aquavit. "Well, that's my limit." She frowned. "You want another?"

Ordinarily Fanchon would have refused, but this time she decided she might as well have another. Perhaps more brandy and coffee would warm her up, for she was still very chilly. "Sure. Why not." Impulsively she reached for her purse. "I'll buy. We'll celebrate something—things working out for you, me getting some peace and quiet—something."

"You don't have to," said Naomi.

"Let me," said Fanchon.

Naomi considered it and accepted with a quick nod. "God, it is a world of despair sometimes, isn't it?"

"General malaise?" Fanchon suggested. "It comes with fall, or the new semester, or taking chances with Bill?"

"It's worse than that, I think," Naomi said, gesturing to the waitress for the same again. "It's getting so that there's very few ways to feel good about who you are and what you do. And that is not midlife crisis talking, it's a very scared psychologist."

Fanchon sat still, staring at her empty snifter and half-full coffee cup. "I don't have any answers. It's all I can do to try to explain to my students why Victorian women were so savagely exploited by employers. The present and the future are beyond me."

The waitress brought their drinks. "The smorgasbord is out." It was part of the same pitch she delivered at this time every evening. "Five-fifty for all you want."

"Thanks," said Naomi as Fanchon handed the waitress a ten-dollar bill. "We'll get something in a couple of minutes." She straightened up. "So. What are you going to do about that neighbor of yours?"

"I suppose I'll have to talk to Peterson again. But to tell you the truth, I wish it would just go away. The noise." She sipped her coffee and found it too hot. "I don't want it to come down to one of us moving. I'm not prepared to move, and I've got a pretty good idea that the guy doesn't want to move, either. He just got there."

"Maybe if you approached the neighbor again, talked to him about the problem as a way not to go to the landlord, maybe he'd be more cooperative."

"Are you practicing shrinkery on me?" Fanchon asked, doing her best to avoid the discussion completely.

"Habit," said Naomi. She looked up as a tall, moustached man approached her. "Oh, shit. My hair's a mess."

"You look fine," said Fanchon in the same tone she used with her older sister when she claimed to be poorly groomed.

The man reached down, putting his hand on Naomi's shoulder. "I don't want to interrupt, but I've got a table reserved for us in twenty minutes." He smiled vaguely in Fanchon's direction. "Excuse the interruption."

"No problem," said Fanchon. "I'm not staying long."

Naomi beamed at him. "Twenty minutes is fine." She patted his hand before he removed it and moved away. "Well, what do you think?"

"Seems pleasant enough. But ten seconds probably isn't long enough for good judgment."

"Thanks a bunch. You're supposed to be bolstering me up," Naomi protested.

"Hey, with my track record, I'm the last person you ought to be asking for bolstering. Two failed live-ins in eight years isn't a recommendation." Fanchon drank her coffee quickly. Then she tossed off the brandy, feeling its jolt with certain pleasure. "It's getting pretty dark. I better head for home." She picked up her purse. "I really hope it turns out okay for you, Naomi." She almost meant it.

"So do I," said Naomi. "But what about upstairs?"

"I guess I'll try your way—I'll talk to him. It can't hurt. If that doesn't work, I suppose I'll have to call Peterson." She smiled crookedly. "I'll call you."

"Good," said Naomi, her attention already on Bill.

It was colder and Fanchon realized her sweater wasn't enough to keep her warm. She hugged her arms across her chest and walked faster.

Evenings were always the hardest for her, the time when the noise was more intrusive. It made her feel isolated, empty. "Maybe I should get a dog," she said aloud. She had got into the habit of talking to herself in the last two years, and occasionally it troubled her. "Peterson doesn't allow pets." Maybe she would get a tank of fish. She doubted the landlord would object to fish.

The house seemed fairly silent as she approached it, but as soon as she went in through the kitchen door, the steady, thumping, screeching wail shuddered down the walls from above. Fanchon gripped the edge of the sink and gave up on eating dinner. She hated scenes. Angry voices made her stomach hurt.

She went out the rear door and climbed to the upper flat. "Hey!" she shouted, pounding on the door. There was the sound of banging pots in the kitchen. "Hey! In there!"

Loud, hurried footsteps sounded and a moment later the door was jerked open. "What is it?" her upstairs neighbor demanded.

Now that they were face-to-face, it was difficult for Fanchon to speak. "I . . . I have to talk to you. It's about the music you play."

"Again?" He folded his arms. "I had a call from the landlord about it. I said I'd turn it down and I did."

"Turned it down?" Fanchon forced herself to be calm. "Look, I'm sorry to disturb you this way, but it doesn't sound like you've turned it down to me. I can't get any work done because of the racket. I can't sleep. I don't know what kind of sound system you have, but it's—"

Her neighbor scowled at her. "What are you talking about? You're the one with the system that takes the roof off." He sizzled with resentment. "You aren't the only one with work to do."

"Mister . . ." Fanchon began, forgetting his name.

"Muir. Doctor, actually," he corrected her. "Like the woods. No relation."

"Okay. Dr. Muir. It might seem like a lot of noise to you, but maybe the floor does something. In my flat, it's really awful."

Eric Muir rubbed his chin. "What about your system?"

"I hardly ever play it. Most of what I have is Mozart and Bach. I don't have any modern music. You and that heavy metal—"

"You're kidding, right?" He favored her with a tight, uncordial smile. "You don't expect me to believe all you ever listen to is 'Eine Kleine NachtMusik,' do you?"

"Well, not all. But I don't play rock, not any kind of rock." She screwed up her courage. "Maybe you ought to come down right now and listen to what it sounds like."

"Now? I don't have the system on right now." He braced one arm across the door. "But you tell me you have noise?"

Fanchon stared at him. He was either the most accomplished liar she had ever met, or he had not been paying attention. "Come down and listen," she said at last. Then she turned on her heel and started down the wooden stairs, hoping he would be curious enough to follow her.

As they stepped into her kitchen the sound rose up around them, battering them invisibly. Fanchon winced as she held the door for Eric, then put her hands on her hips, watching him.

"This is incredible." He had to shout to be heard. "Worse than I've had it."

"My system's off. Go into the front room and look," Fanchon yelled back. She pointed down the hall, although this was not necessary since the floor plan of both flats was the same.

He lifted a skeptical eyebrow, but did as she told him. When he returned a few minutes later, he was mollified. He started to speak, then motioned her to join him on the back steps. As soon as the door was closed, he said, "God, that's terrible."

"It's not quite so loud most of the time," she admitted, not wanting to turn him from her side now that he appeared to be on it. "Whatever is doing it, please, you can understand why I want it stopped. I really can't ignore it."

"How long does it go on?" he asked. "A couple of hours or what?"

"That's about all it *doesn't* go on." She heard the exhaustion in her voice and wondered if he did, too. "Sometimes at night it's worse."

"All night?" He didn't wait for an answer. "I never play my system after ten, and I keep the TV down after then."

"The TV doesn't bother me," she said quickly. "It's just that awful music."

"Well, I don't play the music," he said firmly. "And I think if someone else in the building next door were making so much noise, I'd hear it upstairs, and so would the Dovers downstairs. Sometimes I do hear . . . but it isn't your system, and it's nothing like the noise you have." He stared hard at the back door to her flat. "This makes me very curious."

"Curious?" she repeated. "How can it?"

"You're not a theoretical physicist, are you? I am." His expression just missed being smug. "There's got to be a reason why this happens. And there's got to be a reason why it's loudest in your flat. How long has it been going on?"

"Since shortly after you moved in, maybe three weeks now. I thought you'd bought new speakers." She did her best not to sound as irritated as she felt. "I only complained when it had been over a week."

"I can't blame you, not with that going on." He opened the door and sound rushed out like a tidal bore.

"What can you do about it?" She hated asking the question; she dreaded the answer.

"I don't know. I don't know what I'm up against." He listened for a moment. "It's hard to hear if there are any words to it, or just some kind of howling. I'll want to bring a tape recorder down and hook it up, if you don't mind."

"Fine with me," she said wearily. "I tried it once, but all I got was static."

"Probably overloaded," Eric said. "I'll check this out with acoustics first, so we can make sure we get it all on tape. We'll be improvising, but there should be an answer somewhere." He smiled once. "I'm glad you told me about this."

"I wish I didn't have to," she responded at once. "I hope you can do something. I can't wait around forever, waiting for a lull in the storm."

He chuckled because it was expected of him. "I'd feel the same way in your position." With the suggestion of a wave he left her on the back porch and climbed up to his flat.

Fanchon had a loud evening; by ten she was seriously considering breaking her lease without notice. Sacrificing the various deposits seemed like a small price to pay for sleeping through the night. She set aside her tables of salaries of domestic servants in London in 1870–1880 and turned on her television, hoping to find a late, late movie to distract her.

The pounding on her door at last broke through the relentless moaning of the walls.

"What is it?" she shouted as she fumbled her way to the back door. It was early morning, the sun not strong enough to break through the haze.

Eric Muir held out a tape recorder as she pulled the door open.

"Sorry to stop by at this hour, but I thought you'd want this set up as soon as possible." He strode into her kitchen without invitation. "Where's the noise the worst? I want to put this as near the epicenter as possible."

"In the front. The main room or the bedroom, it's all about the same." She rubbed her fingers through her hair.

"There's a sound-activated switch on it, and it's an extended reel of tape. It'll pick up sound for six hours." He went about his self-imposed task, ignoring her as he worked.

"Some coffee?" She had to bellow it twice before he refused.

"It's all ready to go," he told her a little later as she sat in the kitchen, unable to eat the light breakfast she had made for herself. "It ought to pick up all fluctuations pretty well. That thumping part must be the hardest to take."

"It's pretty bad," she agreed.

"There's half a dozen guys in the department who're interested in what's going on here. We'll probably come up with some kind of answer in a day or two."

A spattering kind of rattle joined the twanging beat. Fanchon winced. "Any idea what it is?"

"Perturbed spirits?" Eric ventured enthusiastically. "Demon CBers? Dish antenna misfocus? Underground water carrying sounds through the plumbing? A misfunction of a cable? They're all possibilities."

"How delightful." Fanchon got up from the table. "What am I supposed to do while you figure it out?"

"You might want to find somewhere to stay while I work this out," he said.

"Any recommendations?" she inquired, knowing already that her sister lived too far away and her stepfather preferred she keep her visits to a minimum.

"Call a friend. You must know someone who can let you have a spare room for a few days." He was unconcerned. "Leave me a number where I can reach you."

That night the noise was endless, a crooning, moaning, wordless scream over steady banging and deep sobs. Fanchon went to bed at two, trying to recall everything she had read about sleep deprivation and hallucinations. It was disappointing to see the windows lighten with approaching dawn. She dragged herself into the bathroom and dressed for running, selecting her warmest sweats against the gelid fog.

By the time she got back, the sound was less oppressive. While Fanchon showered and dressed, the noise was no more distressing than recess in a schoolyard might be. She gathered her materials and hiked to campus, doing her best to convince herself that in a day or so her ordeal would be over.

The plight of working-class women a century ago seemed as remote as the extinction of the dinosaurs. She could not concentrate on her lecture, and when she opened the class to questions, she gave arbitrary answers that left her students more puzzled than before.

When she got back to her flat she found Eric Muir waiting for her. "How was last night?"

"Terrible. What about you?"

"Bearable but not pleasant. If you don't mind, I want to change tapes." He let her open the door, then hesitated as a series of deep, clashing chords shook her entry hall. "Nothing that bad, certainly."

"Want to trade flats?" she inquired weakly.

"No," he answered. He checked the microphone to be certain it was functioning properly, then switched one cassette for another. "I'll talk to you later."

The noise was not as ferocious as it had been, but Fanchon could hardly bear it. She felt as if her skin had been made tender by the noise. When four aspirin made no dent in her headache, she picked up the phone and did what she had vowed not to do. "Hello?" she said when Naomi answered the phone.

"What's the matter?" Naomi asked, her tone distant.

"It's Fanchon. I wondered if I could sleep on your couch a couple of nights?"

"Your neighbor's being a prick about the music?"

"It's not him. At least, it doesn't seem to be. He wants to check it out for me." She let her breath out slowly, hearing Naomi's hesitation.

"Does he have to do it now?" Naomi asked.

"Well, something has to be done, and he's the only person who's interested in finding out what it is." She wanted to bite her tongue.

"You mean you don't know if he's doing it, after all? That sounds a little ooo-eeee-ooooo-eeeeee to me. Maybe we'd better send over some of those flakes from the parapsych division to have a look around." She tried to laugh. "They really like poltergeists, and this one sure has the polter part down."

"Naomi, please," said Fanchon, doing her best not to beg.

"Oh, Fanchon, I don't want to let you down. I know I'm being a pain about this but, it's just that . . . well, the way things are right now with Bill and me, it would be . . . touchy to have someone else in the house. You know how it is. Maybe Gail or Phyllis would have room if you asked them." She paused. "Any other time, I'd love to have you here. I don't like to say no, but . . . Fanchon, it's important to me not to fuck this up. I'm sorry."

Fanchon sighed. "Never mind. I'll buy some earplugs."

"Call Phyllis," Naomi urged her again.

"Phyllis doesn't like history, and we're not close enough to make up for that." What was the point in feeling sorry for herself, she wondered. It wouldn't do her any good.

"Then take a couple days off. Go somewhere. Tell Bassinton that you have a family emergency, and get away." Now that she was off the hook, Naomi was doing her best to provide an alternative. "What about your sister?"

"No chance there. She's moving to Boston next month. And I've got two papers assigned in my classes, I can't miss them. The students are depending on them for a third of their grades." She stared at the window, seeing the plants growing on the far side of it. "I'll call you later, okay?"

"Go to a hotel," said Naomi, determined to make some contribution. "There's places around here that don't cost an arm and a leg, and they aren't awful. What about that place down from campus that does bed and breakfast, the old Victorian place? This time of year they must have a lot of space. And it's a great building, all that gingerbread. And quiet room service, too, so they tell me." This last was embarrassed.

"Yeah," said Fanchon. "Well, thanks anyway." She was ready to hang up; there was nothing else to say.

"Give me a call when you decide what you're going to do, Fanchon, will you? We can get together for coffee or lunch or . . . we can talk over everything. Okay?"

"Sure," said Fanchon, hanging up. So she was trapped in the house, and there was nothing she could do to change it. No matter where she went, the road would bring her back here.

She found an excuse to go back to campus for a good part of the day and into the evening. So much research, so many appointments with students—it took time, and time was what she wanted to have away from her flat. She hated to think of Eric as an insensitive clod, but she could not avoid such a conclusion, not after everything that had happened to her. He wanted more statistics and he didn't much care where they came from, except downstairs was convenient. It was easier to resent Muir than to think about what might be happening to her. There was too much mystery, too much of the unknown for her to dismiss it as a freak or an accident. Somehow that made the whole thing worse.

By the time she had been back in her flat for twenty minutes, Eric Muir was knocking on her back door. Reluctantly she let him in, not bothering to apologize for her bathrobe and ratty slippers.

"It's been worse," she said, indicating the low level of throbbing that echoed through her rooms.

"You could put it that way," said Muir, leaning back against the old-fashioned kitchen counter and crossing his arms. "We listened to the tape today."

"And?" She had started to make some soup, and offered him a bowl with a gesture instead of words. She was pretty sure she could keep soup down.

"Let's go out for some fish instead. I'll give you fifteen minutes to change. There's a lot to tell you. This whole thing is damned weird. And that's a rare admission for a theoretical physicist to make." He looked at her more closely, as if seeing her for the first time. "You're exhausted, aren't you?"

"I suppose so. I haven't been sleeping much." She might have laughed if he hadn't been so worried.

"It's more than that. You're . . . drained. Get changed. Find your coat. It's starting to rain and you shouldn't get wet." He did not wait for her to refuse but turned off the fire under her pan of soup. "You can eat that tomorrow, if you want to."

"I can't afford another dinner out," she warned him, recalling the twelve dollars in her purse that was supposed to last her until Friday. "I don't have enough for anything fancy."

"Then I'll buy. I think I owe you something. You've been through a lot, and you haven't anything but circles under your eyes to show for it." He rested his hands on the back of one of her two kitchen chairs.

"Yeah," she said, trying to remember the last time she had had dinner out with a man for any reason other than professional.

"Good."

She changed and ran a brush through her hair. As an afterthought she put a little lipstick on, then took her four-year-old trenchcoat from the closet before joining him at the front door.

They drove in silence, and when they reached the restaurant they were told that it would be a twenty-minute wait until they could be seated. Eric accepted this with a shrug and left his name with the hostess. "No smoking."

"It might be a little longer for that," the hostess warned.

Muir found a table as far from the large-screen TV as possible and held the chair for Fanchon. "I've spent the afternoon going over the tape we made in your flat. It's almost completely silent," he said as they were waiting for his name to be called. "There are sounds of you moving about the flat, talking to yourself occasionally, and muttering about the noise, but for the rest, there's a few whispers and something that could be the sound of traffic in the street. We took more than four hours to go over the tape. We can make out a little rhythmic pattern, but that's all there is."

"Oh, come off it," she said, not willing to fight about it.

He looked directly at her, as if eye contact would convince her where explanations would not. "I'm telling you the truth, Fanchon. I listened to it first, and we checked out the equipment, to make sure it was working right. It's delicate and sophisticated, and if there were any sounds there that were real sounds, that machine would pick them up. I guarantee it. No question. It didn't fail. We checked it for that."

"Then there has to be noise on the tape," Fanchon said reasonably. "Lots of noise."

"As I've already told you, only a few whispers and the hint of rhythm. Nothing else. Nothing like what I heard in your flat. I know what I heard in your flat, and it isn't on the tape."

"Oh." She realized her appetite was gone. No matter what they were serving tonight, she could not eat it.

"I don't know what's going on there yet, but I want to put my graduate students on it." He looked over at her. "I know it isn't convenient for you, but all that noise has to be less convenient than a couple of students monitoring the noise. Can't you stick out a couple days more?"

"And then it'll be over?" she said wistfully.

"I don't know. I damn well hope so. You don't want any more of the noise, and neither do I. But we'll have a better understanding about it than we have now, that much is certain." He paused as the waitress approached. "I think our table is ready."

"Fine," she said, rising and following him so automatically that she might have been mechanical instead of human. "Lead the way."

"Come on," said Eric. "Let's get some food into you."

She couldn't eat much at dinner, no matter how she tried. She was embarrassed that Eric had to pay when she wasn't able to eat anything. By the time he drove them back to the house, she was so tired that all she wanted was a chance to sleep the clock around. Maybe, she thought as she opened her front door, I should give up and move out. Maybe I should call Peterson and tell him I can't deal with this any longer.

The noise pressed on her like thick blankets when she went to bed. All attempts at sleep were useless.

For three more days there was no news from Eric Muir. Fanchon saw him only once, and he had nothing to say to her then. She made herself go to her classes, did extra research to keep away from her flat, and tried to catch naps at her office when her partner was off doing other things. She wasn't certain if the noise were getting worse or if she were losing her ability to cope.

When she met Naomi for lunch, Naomi said that it was probably nerves, since she—Fanchon—had gone so long without real sleep. Going without sleep was an invitation to disaster. She wanted Fanchon to know that at any other time she would have taken her into her house. But Bill had just moved in, and there was less time for things outside their relationship.

Her own depression deepened as Fanchon once again wished Naomi the best of luck.

The next morning when she returned from running fifteen minutes early, she saw Eric Muir was waiting for her.

"We've been over the tapes and over them," he said without any greeting. "It's still a mystery, but we've been able to add a few more wrinkles to the mystery. That might or might not help you out." He indicated the stairs to his flat. "I've got some fresh coffee brewing."

"I ought to shower," said Fanchon, but followed him up the stairs.

"There really are some words in that noise, did you realize that?" he said when he offered her a white mug filled with hot coffee.

"Really?" She didn't care about the words, just the noise. She had nothing to contribute to his revelations.

"And they're recognizable with a little fiddling with the tape." He sat down opposite her. "They're from a song that was popular back in the early seventies, done by a local group called The

Spectres. They never got very far, and apparently they broke up in seventy-four or -five. Their lead guitarist went to a better band, their main songwriter went to L.A. to write lyrics for commercials—they tell me he's been very successful—but the others just . . . disappeared."

"Okay." Fanchon tugged at her fleece pullover. "So they disappeared. What has that to do with the noise in my flat. If anything?" She thought about the many times she had used the present to make a bridge to the past, for she did it often in her classes. But what could a rock band have to do with a history instructor?

"I said disappeared," Eric repeated.

"College towns are like that," Fanchon reminded him. "Take any five-year period and about a third of the town will change."

Eric ignored her. "And no one knows what became of them. We called the two we could locate and they haven't heard from the other four since they broke up, and that was years and years ago. They don't know what became of the others."

"What's all this leading up to?" Fanchon asked, drinking the coffee he offered her. It was strong and bitter; she found it very satisfying.

"People disappear. They disappear all the time and no one really notices, especially in a place like this. Students move and transfer and drop out. No one expects them to stick around, so they don't pay much attention when they go." He held up his hand. "Bear with me."

"Go ahead." There was some noise in his flat, but not very much, nothing like what she endured downstairs.

He gathered his thoughts. "People disappear. We always assume they go somewhere else. And in a certain sense, they do. Everyone goes somewhere; into a grave or . . . away."

"Is this physics or mysticism?" Fanchon asked, looking past him to the window where tree branches waved.

"It's something between the two, probably," he answered without a trace of embarrassment. "Consider this: a person disappears *sideways,* to use a metaphor. This person goes somewhere else not spatially but dimensionally."

"More spooks," said Fanchon. "Naomi suggested poltergeists."

Eric would not be distracted. "And when there is someone who is also slipping away—"

"Now, wait a minute—"

He went on. "When someone is slipping toward the same dimension, they become sensitized, like an electric eye, and . . . and that person, it's as if they're being drawn to that *sideways* place. Do you follow this at all?"

"Not really, no," she lied.

"You're triggering this because—"

"You mean it's my fault? I'm going *sideways* and all this noise is the result?" She put down the mug. "A few unsuccessful rock musicians disappear fifteen or twenty years ago, and this noise is the result? And it's my fault?" She started to leave, but he took hold of her wrist.

"You live alone, you do most of your work alone. You have no close friends here, and your family is scattered. That makes you—"

"Makes me what, Dr. Muir?" She pulled away from him; she slammed the door as she left.

"Fanchon!"

Outside, she paused long enough to shout, "Just do something about the noise, that's all!"

Back in her own flat, she listened for the words that Eric claimed could be heard in the sounds, but she could make no sense of it. She went to the bathroom and filled the tub, hoping that a warm soak would help her to sleep. She felt sweaty and sticky, and solid as granite. She wanted to be free of Eric Muir's absurd notions. "He's ridiculous," she remarked to the walls as she peeled off her clothes. It would serve him right if she used all the hot water and he had to shave with cold. "He doesn't want to tell Peterson to fix the wiring, or whatever's wrong. He's making it up." She stared into the full-length mirror on the back of the bathroom door, examining herself. In the cream-colored, steamy bathroom, her pallor made her appear transparent.

She leaned back in the bath, letting the pulse of the music blend with the movement of the water and the blood in her veins. It wasn't as bad as she used to think, that music. Once you accepted it, it could be fairly pleasant. The music wasn't as disruptive as Muir's ludicrous theories. Her life, she thought, was not so empty as Muir had made it sound. It was not awful or painful or degrading; it was not pleasant or fulfilling or challenging. It was just . . . ordinary, she supposed.

Perhaps it was nothing, and she was nothing, too. She laughed, but could not hear herself laugh over the welling music.

"Do you hear something?" Sandra asked Paul as they stopped at the top of the stairs, a bookcase balanced between them.

"Just my joints cracking," said Paul. "Where do you think this ought to go?"

"In the living room, I guess," she said.

"It'd probably make more sense to put it in the hall," he said.

She nodded at once. "Sure. In the hall's fine." She got into position to drag the bookcase a few feet further.

"We were lucky to get this place on such short notice," he said for the third time that morning.

"Great," she said. "We didn't have a lot of time to pick and choose."

"All the more reason to be glad this place was available." He shoved at the bookcase, cursing.

"The upstairs neighbor said it was haunted." She hadn't intended to tell him that, but she was getting tired of his insistence at their luck.

"Hey, he's a theoretical physicist. Peterson told me about him. You know what those guys are like. Give me engineering any day." He stood up. "Why don't you bring up a couple of boxes? I can manage the sofa cushions on my own."

"Fine," she said, glad to escape. As she came back up the stairs, she paused once more. "He said—the man upstairs—that she just disappeared. The woman who used to live here."

"Come on, Sandra," Paul protested. "What's in the box?"

"Kitchen things," she said, squeezing by him. As she passed the bathroom door, she paused again. "Do you hear something?"

"Not again." He rounded on her. "This is an old house. It makes noise. We're not used to it. Okay?"

She continued to listen, a distant, distracted frown blighting her face. "I could swear I heard . . ."

"There's a lot to unload," he warned her.

She made herself go to the kitchen and put the box down. She stood listening a few minutes.

"Sandra!"

She shook her head. "Never mind," she said. "It's nothing."

Christine Jacobsen

The Resurrection

A chance figure glimpsed in the lamplight, a few words in a prayerbook, the savory scent of a mother's kitchen . . . from these modest materials CHRISTINE JACOBSEN *fashions a heart-warming tale of a rabbi's spiritual rebirth. A resident of Queens, New York, Ms. Jacobsen is both a professional storyteller and schoolteacher.*

RABBI HOWARD SCHECHTER lived with his loving mother until he was forty years old. When it was raining, she'd bring his galoshes to shul so his feet wouldn't get wet. Her feet might get wet, but what did it matter? Her son, Howard, her only son, was a rabbi. He was good to his mother. He shined her shoes! What rabbi would shine his own and his mother's shoes, too? On Shabbas, she lit the candles and blessed the bread, then sang the prayer for her angel. Her son, the angel, Rabbi Howard Schechter. He made his mother so happy. Every time she made gefilte fish, Rabbi Schechter would somehow talk about it in his sermon. Everyone who came to shul in Kew Gardens Hills knew how good Rabbi Schechter's mother's gefilte fish tasted. For weeks afterward, she'd get requests for the recipe, and would make gefilte fish for the entire neighborhood! Her son, Rabbi Howard Schechter, made her very happy. Then one day, the expected happened. She was eighty years old, exactly forty years older than Rabbi Schechter when she died. She had just made another batch of gefilte fish, felt a little tired, and went upstairs to her bed to rest. The rabbi was out, making house calls to the sick and elderly. When he came home, he found his dear mother in her bed, dead. Some say it was the gefilte fish that killed her!

Rabbi Howard Schechter was such a good son. He sat shiva for two weeks instead of one. His mother was most probably happy, but he was not. He was lonely, especially in the house. He stayed away from it whenever he could. His sermons lost their special shine and sense of humor. He could hardly eat. He lost weight. Rabbi Schechter was definitely in mourning.

The rabbi went to the synagogue twice a day and stayed long after the evening service. When he could no longer justify to himself the reason for being there, he slowly prepared for his departure. Rabbi Schechter first went through the ritual of closing up the arc where the sacred scrolls were kept. Next, he removed his prayer shawl, being careful to fold it so that no wrinkles would be visible. In smoothing over the folds, the rabbi could feel the softness of the silk on his hand. He remembered the very first time his mother taught him how to fold a blanket. He was just a boy, about five years old. She didn't want to show him how to do it, but because he insisted on learning and helping so much, she gave in. He could remember the words he said at that time which caused his mother to change her mind. "Mother, if I don't learn how to fold this wool blanket now, how will I ever learn to fold my tallis when I'm a rabbi one day?"

He remembered the look on his mother's face. Her brown eyes widened and the wrinkles on her face softened. Rabbi Schechter saw her mouth form a little smile; that smile swelled with a pride larger than the waves on the sea. She simply told him, "Howard, you are a good boy."

The rabbi felt very sad and very lonely tonight. An inexpressible longing for his mother filled his being. Of course, he thought about her every day of his life, several times a day, but tonight, he seemed to see her face and hear her voice so clearly. Tonight was different from other nights, and he began to cry. The sound of Rabbi Schechter's crying echoed throughout the synagogue. So engrossed was he in his grief that when he heard the echo, he became frightened—he thought someone else was in the synagogue with him! The rabbi looked out into the rows of pews but saw no one. He reached into his pocket for his white handkerchief to wipe his eyes, but instead took out an ochre-colored cloth. The cloth reminded Rabbi Schechter that he was not finished with his nightly routine. He slowly walked through the synagogue, stopping at each pew to wipe it off with the cloth. Even though the shamus kept the shul clean, this holy place was Rabbi Schechter's life. He wanted it to be meticulous.

Yes, the services for the day were over. Rabbi Schechter had led the mourning prayer, the kaddish, this morning, and with his minyan of ten men conducted the evening's service. No women had attended the service this evening. Yet, when he had finished wiping the last pew downstairs, he felt a strange pulling towards the balcony, where the women usually sat and prayed. He felt a need to wipe down their pews, too; Rabbi Schechter climbed the stairs to the balcony, deep in thought. He envied the women, for he believed that they were closer to God being up there. His mother used to sit up in the balcony, and she certainly knew more about God than he did. The longing for her was growing with each step he took. Life was so lonely without his mother. Rabbi Schechter could remember standing at the bimah, nearly a year ago, reading from the torah, and speaking the words of the prophet Isaiah. He directed the words of the prophet up, up to his mother who loved him and who listened to every word he spoke:

The Lord God has given me the tongue of one who has been instructed to console the weary with a timely word; he made my hearing sharp every morning, that I might listen like one under instruction.

Tonight, he felt his mother's presence was everywhere, downstairs, upstairs. The need for her love was powerful. There was more to the verse of Isaiah, but the rabbi could not remember it, his sorrow was so great. His eyes filled up with tears once more, and fell over his eyelashes when he blinked. When he blinked again, it was for a different reason; Rabbi Schechter saw the corner of a black siddur lying open on the pew directly across from him! No man or woman ever left a prayer book open on a pew. Could this be a sign from God? The rabbi walked slowly over to the empty pew and picked up the thick leather siddur. He lifted it up, putting the open page close to his eyes, and read:

The Lord God opened my ears and I did not disobey or turn back in defiance.

The words, they too came from Isaiah, and they were the very ones he was trying to remember! Rabbi Schechter was frightened. He didn't understand what this meant. His head began to hurt, his heart was already hurting, it was time to go home.

Rabbi Howard Schechter closed the siddur carefully and put it back in its holder behind the pew. He went down the stairs, feeling the wind blow cold air through the cracks in the windows, and under the door, persistently pushing its way into the shul. The emptiness in the rabbi's heart was like that air, cold and persistent; he walked slowly along the tile floor, to the closet where he kept his coat and hat. Once dressed, he pushed open the thick wooden door and went out of the synagogue. Tonight, even the door felt especially heavy.

As he was locking up, Rabbi Schechter thought he saw a woman some distance away. She was standing under a streetlight. Rabbi Schechter was intrigued by the woman because her outline looked very much like his own mother's. He felt a little afraid, too. Did he feel his mother's presence so powerfully in the synagogue tonight for a reason? Rabbi Schechter was a spiritual man. His love for God was very strong. He believed God spoke to him through signs, and he thought he had received one tonight. Whenever the rabbi saw a sign, he was as much ready to receive it as to be frightened enough to want to run away. Being the good and religious man he was, he usually tried to understand it with all his being. But the sign he received in the synagogue tonight frightened him. God was such a mysterious fellow—He could quickly appear then disappear, and Rabbi Schechter never knew when this would happen. He didn't know if the woman under the streetlight was his mother, or another sign from God. Fear filled him once more, the rabbi didn't want to know tonight. He needed time to think. Rabbi Schechter tried to take his time in locking up the synagogue. He turned the key in the lock several times, click, click, lock-unlock; but no matter how long he stood there trying to focus on this familiar task, his head, as if on its own, kept turning towards the streetlight where the mysterious woman still stood. *Why doesn't she move? Is she hurt? Is she lost? Is she waiting for someone? Is she waiting for me?* thought the rabbi. He could not control the impulse to look towards her again and again, and knew that he had to go and find out who she was. Rabbi Schechter let the lock lock for the final time, and walked towards the streetlight. His legs were shaking so rapidly that he could only take a few steps at a time. Maybe she was his mother.

Rabbi Howard Schechter kept his eyes focused forward as he walked. It was as if an imaginary string pulled him along, towards the light. He walked onwards, slowly but surely, as if for hours, and as if in a trance. Rabbi Schechter walked right past the streetlight, right past the large trunk of the old oak tree he went by every day, and walked straight to the front door of his house. Once he was there, he realized what he had done. He didn't understand how he could have missed the streetlight. He wondered if God was sending another sign. Should he go back to the synagogue and start over again? Should he go inside his house? What was going on inside his brain? Was he being hypnotized? Rabbi Schechter didn't know the answers to these questions, so he went back. How could he not? The power of the sign beckoned him. He hurriedly walked past the oak tree, and to the synagogue. He positioned himself in front of the door of the shul and turned around. She wasn't there. He couldn't remember which streetlight it was. They all looked the same. Rabbi Schechter just couldn't remember. He picked a streetlight and walked towards it. He didn't feel the same way inside this time as he did just a little while ago. The rabbi counted the streetlights, there were six of them on this block. How was it that he never noticed that before? No matter, there was no one under any of them now. Whoever or whatever it was that was there was gone! Maybe there never was a woman standing under the streetlight. Sadly, the rabbi walked home.

Every night after the streetlight experience, Rabbi Schechter looked forward to leaving the synagogue. He left at different hours, he went home and came back; he felt a need to see the mysterious woman again under one of those six ordinary streetlights. But never, ever, did the rabbi find that woman under the light again. He was finally coming to believe that he had imagined the whole thing. He examined the experience over and over, and tried to accept that there was no sign. Maybe it was at forty, not fifty, that one's brain cells started dying off. Was he mad or intensely lonely? Sitting shiva for two weeks didn't end the mourning for his mother. His grief was stronger than his life. Rabbi Schechter's mother and Rabbi Schechter's shul were his whole world. His mother was truly gone, and the empty space inside was hard to fill. Perhaps he had been trying to fill it through his imagination. He couldn't do it. He didn't know how to make himself happy. He didn't even know how.

One night, the rabbi sat at his small wooden kitchen table with head in hand. His mind traveled back to his ancestors. His grandfather and his great-grandfather were both rabbis. They came from Russia, Russian Jews they were referred to, Ashkenazis. All humans had a biological clock ticking away inside, and all humans had some sort of routine that helped them organize their lives. Rabbi Schechter certainly had his routine, and it kept him going. It didn't matter if it was colorless. He had a reason to get up in the morning. Rabbi Howard Schechter began to travel back in time. He truly wondered if we changed at all in two thousand years. In the spaces of his mind, he pictured the first humans competing for a piece of food. His mind was traveling backwards, but his nose stayed in the present. There was a very strong smell in the room that forced the rabbi back into the moment. Where was that smell coming from? It was such a familiar odor. Memories of the past, not the ancient past, arose in him, and Rabbi Howard Schechter finally recognized the smell as that of herring and eggs. In this lonely, quiet, dimly lit kitchen, he could see his mother at the stove, wearing the apron she always wore. With one hand, she was holding the handle of a stainless steel pot with a dishtowel. In the other hand was the cover of the pot. His mother took the pot off the stove, and was pouring the boiling water from the eggs into the sink. "Mother," he found himself saying. "Mother, I see you." Rabbi Schechter looked up and into the air. "Mother, was that you under the streetlight near shul? I thought I was going crazy, but now I know, it was a sign from God. I don't know what it means, Mother, but I'm now sure it *was* you standing there. God never tries to trick me. Where did you go, Mother? Why didn't you come back? I miss you so much, Mother." In the warmth of the quiet room, the rabbi could go on, tears streaming down his cheeks. "Mother, I'm lonely. I don't know what will become of me. I'm afraid. God loves me, you love me, but you are all spirits. Mother, don't be angry, please, but I think I didn't want the woman under the streetlight to be you! Mother, I'm forty years old. I never had a woman, if you know what I mean. You gave me the love inside that I need, but Mother, even a rabbi needs . . ." The smell of herring and eggs was getting stronger, and the rabbi stopped. He was definitely getting another sign. It was some time before he could speak again, and when he did, it was in a whisper. "Mother, you were the best mother in the whole world. You were my best friend, too. You made me feel proud of myself. I was proud of you. You were an angel to me. God sent me His angel, my mother! My dear mother! I miss you. I miss your cooking, too. I'm hungry, Mother, I'm hungry for your herring and eggs, your famous gefilte fish even, but I'm hungry for something else, Mother. I'm hungry for love. I have always been so honest with you, Mother, so why should it be any different now that you're in some other place? Mother, I want a woman! There, I said it!" Rabbi Howard

Schechter waited for the smell of herring and eggs to knock him over, to kill him maybe, but it didn't. The smell was still there, but fainter. Still there, but like a good friend and a happy memory.

Jane Yolen

The Confession of Brother Blaise

JANE YOLEN *has written well over seventy superb works of fantasy, folklore, and children's literature, including* Dove Isabeau, The Princess Who Couldn't Sleep, Tales of Wonder, The Witch Who Wasn't, The Wizard of Washington Square, *and "Angelica," which appeared in* Angels of Darkness. *"The Confession of Brother Blaise" may stretch one's notion of Eden, but its secrets are undeniably both profane and divine.*

Osney Monastery, January 13, 1125

THE SLAP of sandals along the stone floor was the abbot's first warning.

"It is Brother Blaise." The breathless news preceded the monk's entrance as well. When he finally appeared, his beardless cheeks were pink both from the run and the January chill. "Brother Geoffrey says that Brother Blaise's time has come." The novice breathed deeply of the wood scent in the abbot's parlor and then, because of the importance of his message, he added the unthinkable. *"Hurry!"*

It was to the abbot's everlasting glory that he did not scold the novice for issuing an order to the monastery's head as a cruder man might have done. Rather, he nodded and turned to gather up what he would need: the cruse of oil, his stole, the book of prayers. He had kept them near him all through the day, just in case. But he marked the boy's offense in the great register of his mind. It was said at Osney that Abbot Walter never forgot a thing. And that he never smiled.

They walked quickly across the snow-dusted courtyard. In the summer those same whitened borders blossomed with herbs and berry bushes, adding a minor touch of beauty to the ugly stone building squatting in the path before them.

The abbot bit his lower lip. So many of the brothers with whom he had shared the past fifty years were housed there now, in the stark infirmary. Brother Stephen, once his prior, had lain all winter with a terrible wasting cough. Brother Homily, who had been the gentlest master of boys and novices imaginable, sat in a cushioned chair blind and going deaf. And dear, simple Brother Peter-Paul, whose natural goodness had often put the abbot to shame, no longer recognized any of them and sometimes ran out into the snow without so much as a light summer cassock between his skin and the winter wind. Three others had died just within the year gone by, each a lasting and horrible death. He missed every one of them dreadfully. The worst, he guessed, was at prime.

The younger monks seemed almost foreign to him, untutored somehow, though by that he did not mean they lacked vocation. And the infant oblates—there were five of them ranging in ages from eight to fourteen, given to the abbey by their parents—he loved them as a father should. He did not stint in his affection. But why did he feel this terrible impatience, this lack of charity toward the young? God may have written that a child would lead, but to Abbot Walter's certain knowledge none had led *him*. The ones he truly loved were the men of his own age with whom he had shared so much, from whom he had learned so much. And it was those men who were all so ill and languishing, as if God wanted to punish him by punishing them. Only how could he believe in a God who would do such a thing?

Until yesterday only he and Brother Blaise of the older monks still held on to any measure of health. He discounted the aching in his bones that presaged any winter storms. And then suddenly, before compline, Blaise had collapsed. Hard work and prayer, whatever the conventional wisdom, broke more good men than it healed.

The abbot suddenly remembered a painting he had seen in a French monastery the one time he had visited the Continent. He had not thought of it in years. It represented a dead woman wrapped in her shroud, her head elaborately dressed. Great white worms gnawed at her bowels. The inscription had shocked him at the time: *Une fois sur toute femme belle . . .* Once I was beautiful above all women. But by death I became like this. My flesh was very beautiful, fresh and soft. Now it is altogether turned to ashes. . . . It was not the ashes that had appalled him but the worms, gnawing the private part he had only then come to love. He had not touched a woman since. And that Blaise, the patrician of the abbey, would be gnawed soon by those same worms did not bear thinking about. God was very careless with his few treasures.

With a shudder, Abbot Walter pushed the apostasy from his mind. The Devil had been getting to him more and more of late. Cynicism was Satan's first line of offense. And then despair. *Despair.* He sighed.

"Open the door, my son," Abbot Walter said, putting it in his gentlest voice, "my hands are quite full."

Like the dortoir, the infirmary was a series of cells off a long, dark hall. Because it was January, all the buildings were cold, damp, and from late afternoon on, lit by small, flickering lamps. The shadows that danced along the wall when they passed seemed mocking. *The dance of death,* the abbot thought, *should be a solemn, stately measure, not this obscene capering Morris along the stones.*

They turned into the misericorde. There was a roaring fire in the hearth and lamps on each of the bedside tables. The hard bed, the stool beside it, the stark cross on the wall, each cast shadows. Only the man in the bed seemed shadowless. He was the stillest thing in the room.

Abbot Walter walked over to the bed and sat down heavily on the stool. He stared at Blaise and noticed, with a kind of relief crossed with dread, that the man's eyes moved restlessly under the lids.

"He is still alive," whispered the abbot.

"Yes, but not, I fear, for long. That is why I sent for you." The infirmarer, Brother Geoffrey, moved suddenly into the center of the room like a dancer on quiet, subtle feet. "My presence seems to disturb him, as if he were a messenger who has not yet delivered his charge. Only when I observe from a far corner is he quiet."

No sooner had Geoffrey spoken than the still body moved and, with a sudden jerk, a clawlike hand reached out for the abbot's sleeve.

"Walter." Brother Blaise's voice was ragged.

"I will get him water," said the novice, eager to be *doing* something.

"No, my son. He is merely addressing me by name," said the abbot. "But I would have you go into the hall now and wait upon us. Or visit with the others. Your company should cheer them, and a man's final confession and the viaticum is between himself and his priest." The abbot knew this particular boy was prone to homesickness and nightmares and had more than once wakened the monastery hours after midnight with his cries. Better he was absent at the moment of Blaise's death.

The novice left at once, closing the door softly. Geoffrey, too, started out.

"Let Geoffrey stay," Blaise cried out.

Abbot Walter put his hand to Blaise's forehead. "Hush, my dear friend, and husband your strength."

But Blaise shook the hand off. "The babe himself said to me that it should be writ down."

"The babe?" asked the abbot. "The Christ child?"

"He said, 'Many of those who shall read or shall hear of it will be the better for it, and will be on their guard against sin.'" Blaise stopped, then as if speaking lent him strength he otherwise did not have, he continued. "I was not sure if it was Satan speaking—or God. But *you* will know, Walter. You have an instinct for the Devil."

The abbot made a clicking sound with his tongue, but Blaise did not seem to notice. "Let Geoffrey stay. He is our finest scribe and it must be written down. His is the best hand and the sharpest ear, for all that you keep him laboring here amongst the infirm of mind and bowels."

The abbot set his mouth into a firm line. He was used to being scolded in private by Blaise. He relied on Blaise's judgments, for Blaise had been a black canon of great learning and a prelate in a noble house before suddenly, mysteriously, dedicating himself to the life of a monk. But it was mortifying that Blaise should scold in front of Geoffrey, who was a literary popinjay with nothing of a monk's quiet habits of thought. Besides, Geoffrey entertained all manner of heresies, and it was all the abbot could do to keep him from infecting the younger brothers. The assignment to the infirmary was to help him curb such apostatical tendencies. But despite his thoughts, the abbot said nothing. One does not argue with a dying man. Instead he turned and instructed Geoffrey quietly.

"Get you a quill and however much vellum you think you might need from the scriptorium. While you are gone, Brother Blaise and I will start this business of preparing for death." He regretted the cynical tone instantly though it brought a small chuckle from Blaise.

Geoffrey bowed his head meekly, which was the best answer, and was gone.

"And now," Abbot Walter said, turning back to the man on the narrow bed. But Blaise was stiller than before and the pallor of his face was the green-white of a corpse. "Oh, my dear Blaise, and have you left me before I could bless you?" The abbot knelt down by the bedside and took the cold hand in his.

At the touch, Brother Blaise opened his eyes once again. "I am not so easily got rid of, Walter." His lips scarcely moved.

The abbot crossed himself, then sat back on the stool. But he did not loose Blaise's hand. For a moment the hand seemed to warm in his. *Or was it,* the abbot thought suddenly, *that his own hand was losing its life?*

"If you will start, father," Blaise said formally. Then, as if he had lost the thread of his thought for a moment, he stopped. He began again. "Start. And I shall be ready for confession by the time Brother Geoffrey is back." He paused and smiled, and so thin had his face become overnight, it was as if a skull grinned. "Geoffrey will have a retrimmed quill and full folio with him, enough for an epic, at least. He has talent, Walter."

"But not for the monastic life," said the abbot as he kissed the stole and put it around his neck. "Or even for the priesthood."

"Perhaps he will surprise you," said Blaise.

"Nothing Geoffrey does surprises me. Everything he does is informed by wit instead of wisdom, by facility instead of faith."

"Then perhaps you will surprise him." Blaise brought his hands together in prayer and, for a moment, looked like one of the stone *gisant* carved on a tomb cover. "I am ready, father."

The opening words of the ritual were a comfort to them both, a reminder of all they had shared. The sound of Geoffrey opening the door startled the abbot, but Blaise, without further assurances, began his confession. His voice grew stronger as he talked.

"If this be a sin, I do heartily repent of it. It happened over thirty years ago, but not a day goes by that I do not think on it and wonder if what I did then was right or wrong.

"I was confessor to the King of Dayfed and his family, a living given to me as I was a child of that same king, though born on the wrong side of the blanket, my mother being a lesser woman of the queen's.

"I was contented at the king's court, for he was kind to all of his bastards, and we were legion. Of his own legal children, he had but two, a whining whey-faced son who even now sits on the throne no better man than he was a child, and a daughter of surpassing grace."

Blaise began to cough a bit and the abbot slipped a hand under his back to raise him to a more comfortable position. The sick man noticed Geoffrey at the desk in the far corner. "Are you writing all of this down?"

"Yes, brother."

"Read it to me. The last part of it."

". . . and a daughter of surprising grace."

"Surpassing. But never mind, it was surprising, too, given that her mother was such a shrew. No wonder the king, my father, turned to other women. But write it as you will, Geoffrey. The words can change as long as alteration does not alter the sense of it."

"You may trust me, Brother Blaise."

"He may—but I do not," said the abbot. "Bring the desk closer to the bed. You will hear better—and have better light as well—and Blaise will not have to strain."

Geoffrey pushed the oak desk into the center of the room where he might closer attend the sick man's words.

When Geoffrey was ready, Blaise began again.

"She was his favorite, little Ellyne, with a slow smile and a mild disposition. Mild disposition? Yes, that was her outer face to the world. But she was also infernally stubborn about those things she held dear.

"She had been promised before birth to the Convent of St. Peter by her mother, who had longed for a daughter after bearing the king an heir. All his by-blows had been boys, which made the queen's desire for a daughter even greater.

"When Ellyne was born, the queen repented of her promise at once, for the child was bright and fair. Rings and silver candlesticks and seven cups of beaten gold were sent to the church in her stead. The good sisters were well pleased and did not press for the child.

"But when Ellyne was old enough to speak her own mind, she determined that she would honor her mother's promise. Despite the entreaties of her mother and father and the assurances of the abbess that she need not come, she would not be turned aside from her decision.

"I was, at that time, her confessor as well as the king's. At his request I added my pleas to theirs. I loved her as I loved no other, for she was a beautiful little thing, with a quick mind I feared would be dulled behind the convent walls. It was thought that she would listen to me, her 'Bobba,' as she called me, sooner than to another. But the child shamed me, saying, 'Can you, who has turned his life entirely toward God, ask me not to do the same?' It was that question that convinced me that she was right, for, you see, I was a priest by convenience and not conviction. Yet when she said it, she set me on the path by her side.

"She entered the convent the very next day."

Blaise paused, and the abbot moistened his mouth with a cloth dipped in a bowl of scented water that stood on the table. The *scratch, scratch, scratch* of Geoffrey's pen continued into the silence.

"She was eight when she entered and eighteen when the thing came to pass that led me to Osney—and eventually to this room."

Abbot Walter moved closer to the bed.

"I was in my study when the mother superior herself came bursting into the room. Ordinarily she would have sent a messenger for me, but such was her agitation, she came herself, sailing into my study like a great prowed ship under full sail.

" 'Father Blaise,' she said, 'you must come to my parlor at once, and alone. Without asking a single question of me yet.'

"I rose, picked up a breviary, and followed her. We used the back stair that was behind a door hidden by an arras. It was not so much secret as unused. But Mother Agnes knew of it and insisted we go that way. As we raced down the steps, dodging skeins of cobwebs, I tried to puzzle out the need for such secrecy and her agitation and fear. Was there a plague amongst the sisters? Had two been found in the occasion of sin? Or had something happened to little Ellyne, now called Sister Martha? Somehow the last was my greatest fear.

"When we arrived in her spare, sweet-scented parlor, there was a sister kneeling in front of the hearth, her back to us, her face uplifted to the crucifix above.

" 'Stand, sister,' commanded Mother Agnes.

"The nun stood and turned to face us and my greatest fear was realized. It was Sister Martha, her face shining with tears. There was a flush on her cheeks that could not be explained by the hearth, for it was summer and there was no fire in the grate."

Blaise's voice was becoming ragged again, and the abbot offered him a sip of barley water, holding the cup to his mouth. Geoffrey's pen finished the last line and he looked up expectantly.

"When she saw me, Sister Martha began to cry again and ran to me, flinging her arms around me the way she had done as a child.

" 'Oh, Bobba,' she cried out, 'I swear I have done nothing, unless sleeping is more than nothing.'

"Mother Agnes raised her head and thrust her chin forward. 'Tell Father Blaise what you told me, child.'

" 'On my faith, father, I was asleep in a room several months ago, surrounded by my sisters. Sisters Agatha and Armory were on my right, Sisters Adolfa and Marie on my left. Marie snores. And the door was locked.'

" 'From the outside!' said Mother Agnes, nodding her head sharply, like a sword in its downward thrust. 'All the sisters sleep under lock, and I and my prioress hold the only keys.' "

"A barbaric custom," muttered Abbot Walter. "It shows a lack of trust. And, should there be a fire, disastrous."

Blaise coughed violently, but after a few more sips of barley water, he was able to go on.

"Ellyne folded her hands before her and continued. 'In my deepest sleep,' she said, looking down as if embarrassed by the memory, 'I dreamed that a young man, clothed in light and as beautiful as the sun, came to my bed and embraced me. His cheeks were rough on mine and he kissed my breasts hard enough to leave marks. Then he pierced me and filled me until I cried out with fear. And delight. But it was only a dream.'

" 'Such dreams are disgusting and violate your vows,' spat out Mother Agnes.

" 'Now, now, mother,' I interrupted, 'all girls have such

dreams, even when they are nuns. Just as the novice monks, before they are purged of the old Adam, often have similar dreams. But surely you did not call me here to confront Ellyne . . . ah, Sister Martha . . . about a bad dream which is, at worst, a minor venial sin.'

" 'A bad dream?' Mother Agnes was trembling. 'Then, Father Blaise, what call you *this*?'

"She stripped away the girl's black robe, and Sister Martha stood there in a white shift in which the mark of her pregnancy was unmistakable."

Geoffrey's quill punctuated the sentence with such vehemence that the ink splattered across the page. It took him several minutes to blot the vellum, and the abbot bathed Blaise's brow with water and smoothed down the brychan around his legs until Geoffrey was ready again.

" 'I do not understand, Ellsie,' I said to her, in my anger returning to her childhood name.

" 'I do not understand either, Father Blaise,' she answered, her voice not quite breaking. 'When I awoke I was in the room still surrounded by my sisters, all of whom slept as soundly as before. And that was how I knew it had been but a dream. On my faith in God, more than this there was never between a man and myself.' She stopped and then added, as if the admission proved her innocence, 'I have dreamed of him every night since, but he has not again touched me. He just stands at my bed foot and watches.'

"I put my hands behind me and clasped them to keep them from shaking. 'This sort of thing I have heard of, mother. The girl is blameless. She has been set upon by an incubus, the devil who comes in dreams to seduce the innocent.'

" 'Well, she carries the other marks she spoke of,' said Mother Agnes. 'The burns on her cheeks you can see for yourself. I will vouch for the rest.' She draped the cloak again over the girl's shoulders almost tenderly, then turned to glare at me. 'An incubus—not a human—you are sure?'

" 'I am sure,' I said, though I was not sure at all. Ellyne had been headstrong about certain things, though how a young man might have trysted with her with Mother Agnes her abbess, I could not imagine. 'But in her condition she cannot remain in the convent. Leave her here in your parlor, and I will go at once and speak to the king.' "

Blaise's last word faded and he closed his eyes. The abbot leaned over and, dipping his finger into the oil, made the sign of the cross on Blaise's forehead. *"In nomine Patris, et Filii, et Spiritus sancti, exstinguatur in te omnis virtus diaboli per . . ."*

Opening his eyes Blaise cried out, "I am not done. I swear to you I will not die before I have told it all."

"Then be done with it," said the abbot. He said it quickly but gently.

"Speaking to the king was easy. Speaking to his shrewish wife was not. She screamed and blamed me for letting the girl go into the convent, and her husband for permitting Ellyne to stay. She ranted against men and devils indiscriminately. But when I suggested it would be best for Ellyne to return to the palace, the queen refused, declaring her dead.

"And so it was that I fostered her to a couple in Carmarthen who were known to me as a closemouthed, devoted, and childless pair. They were of yeoman stock, but as Ellyne had spent the last ten years of her life on the bread, cheese, and prayers of a convent, she would not find their simple farm life a burden. And the farm ran on its own canonical hours: cock's crow, feed time, milking.

"So for the last months of her strange pregnancy, she was—if not exactly happy—at least content. Whether she still dreamed of the devil clothed in sunlight, she did not say. She worked alongside the couple and they loved her as their own."

Blaise struggled to sit upright in bed.

"Do not fuss," the abbot said. "Geoffrey and I will help you." He signaled to the infirmarer, who stood, quickly blotting the smudges on his hands along the edges of his robe. Together they helped settle Blaise into a more comfortable position.

"I am fine now," he said. Then, when Geoffrey was once more

standing at the desk, Blaise began again. "In the ninth month, for the first time, Ellyne became afraid.

" 'Father,' she questioned me day after day, 'will the child be human? Will it have a heart? Will it bear a soul?'

"And to keep her from sorrow before time, I answered as deviously as I could without actually telling a lie. 'What else should it be but human?' I would say. 'You are God's own; should not your child be the same?' But the truth was that I did not know. What I read was not reassuring. The child might be a demon or a barbary ape or anything in between.

"Then on the night before All Hallow's, unpropitious eve, Ellyne's labor began. The water flooded down her legs and the child's passage rippled across her belly. The farmer came to my door and said simply, 'It is her time.'

"I took my stole, the oil, a Testament, candles, a crucifix, and an extra rosary. I vowed I would be prepared for any eventuality.

"She was well into labor when I arrived. The farm wife was firm with her but gentle as well, having survived the birth of every calf and kitten on the place. She allowed Ellyne to yell but not to scream, to call out but not to cry. She kept her busy panting like a beast so that the pains of the birth would pass by. It seemed to work, and I learned that there was a rhythm to this, God's greatest mystery: pain, not-pain, over and over and over again.

"Before long the farm wife said, 'Father Blaise, the child, whatever it be, comes.' She pointed—and I looked.

"From between Ellyne's legs, as if climbing out of a blood-filled cave, crawled a child, part human and part imp. It had the most beautiful face, like an ivory carving of an angel, and eyes the blue of Our Lady's robe. The body was perfectly formed. Up over one shoulder lay a strange cord, the tip nestling into the little hollow at its neck. At first I thought the cord was the umbilicus, but when the farm wife went to touch it, the cord uncoiled from the child's neck and slashed at her hand. Then I knew it was a tail.

"The farm wife screamed. The farmer also. I grabbed the babe firmly with my left hand and, dipping my right finger into the holy oil, made the sign of the cross on its forehead, on its belly, on its genitals, and on its feet. Then I turned it over and pinned it with my left forearm, and with my right hand anointed the tail where it joined the buttocks.

"The imp screamed as if in terrible pain and its tail burst into flames, turning in an instant to ash. All that was left was a scar at the top of the buttocks, above the crack.

"I lifted up my left arm and the child rolled over, reaching up with its hands. It was then I saw that it had claws instead of fingers and it scratched me on the top of both my hands, from the mid finger straight down to the line of the wrist. I shouted God's name and almost dropped the holy oil, but miraculously held on. And though I was now bleeding profusely from the wounds, I managed somehow to capture both those sharp claws in my left hand and with my right anoint the imp's hands. The child screamed again and, as I watched, the imp aspect disappeared completely, the claws fell off to reveal two perfectly formed hands, and the child was suddenly and wholly human."

Blaise had become so agitated during this recitation that the bed itself began to shake. Geoffrey had to leave off writing and come over to help the abbot calm him. They soothed his head and the abbot whispered, "Where is the sin in all this, Blaise?"

The monk's eyes blinked and with an effort Blaise calmed himself. "The sin?" His voice cracked. Tears began to course down his cheeks. "The sin was not in baptizing the babe. That was godly work. But what came after—was it a sin or not? I do not know, for the child spoke to me. *Spoke.*"

"A newborn cannot speak," said Geoffrey.

"*Jesu!* Do you think I do not know that? But this one did. He said, 'Holy, holy, holy,' and the words shot from his mouth in gouts of flame. 'You shall write this down, my uncle,' he said, 'write down that my mother, your half sister, was sinless. That her son shall save a small part of the world. That I shall be prophet and mage, lawgiver and lawbreaker, king of the unseen worlds and counselor to those seen. I shall die and I shall live, in the past and in the future also. Many of those who shall read what you write or who shall hear it read will be the better for it and will be on their guard against sin.' And then the flames died down and the babe put its finger in its mouth to suck on it like any newborn and did not speak again. But the sin of it is that I did *not* write it down, nor even speak of it save to you now in this last hour, for I thought it the devil tempting me."

Abbot Walter was silent for a moment. *It was so much easier,* he thought, *for a man to believe in the Devil than in God.* Then he reached over and smoothed the covers across Brother Blaise's chest. "Did the farmer or his wife hear the child speak?"

"No," whispered Blaise hoarsely, "for when the tail struck the woman's hand, they both bolted from the room in fear."

"And Ellyne?"

"She was near to death from blood loss and heard nothing." Blaise closed his eyes.

Abbot Walter cleared his throat. "You have done only what you believed right, Blaise. I shall think more on this. But as for you, you may let go of your earthly life knowing that you shall have absolution, that you have done nothing sinful to keep you from God's Heaven." He anointed the paper-thin eyelids. *"Per sitam sanctam Unctionem, et suam piissimam misericordiam, indulgeat tibi Dominus quid quid per visum deliquisti. Amen."*

"Amen," echoed Geoffrey.

The abbot added the signs over the nose and mouth, and Blaise murmured in Latin along with him. Then, as the abbot dipped his fingers once more into the jar of oil, Geoffrey took Blaise's hands in his and lay them with great gentleness side by side on top of the covers, and gasped.

"Look, father."

Abbot Walter followed Geoffrey's pointing finger. On the back of each of Blaise's hands was a single, long, ridged scar starting at the middle finger and running down to the wrist. The abbot crossed himself hastily, getting oil on the front of his habit. *"Jesu!"* he breathed out. Until that moment he had not quite believed Blaise's story. Over the years he had discovered that old men and dying men sometimes make merry with the truth.

Geoffrey backed away to the safety of his desk and crossed himself twice, just to be sure.

With deliberate slowness, the abbot put his fingers back into the oil and with great care anointed Blaise's hands along the line of the scar, then slashed across, careful to enunciate every syllable of the prayer. When he reached the end, ". . . *quid quid per tactum deliquisiti. Amen,*" the oil on Blaise's skin burst into flames, bright orange with a blue arrow at the heart. As quickly, the flames were gone and a brilliant red wound the shape of a cross opened on each hand. Then, as the abbot and Geoffrey watched, each wound healed to a scab, the scab to a scar, and the scar faded until the skin was clean and whole. With a sigh that seemed a combination of joy and relief, Blaise died.

"*In nomine Patris, et Filii, et Spiritus sancti . . .*" intoned the abbot. He removed the covers from the corpse and completed the anointing. He felt better than he had all winter, than he had in years, filled with a kind of spiritual buoyancy, like a child's kite that had been suddenly set free into the wind. If there was a Devil, there was also a God. Blaise had died to show him that. He finished the prayers for absolution, but they were only for the form of it. He knew in his inmost heart that the absolution had taken place already and that Blaise's sinless spirit was fast winging its way to Heaven. Now it was time to forgive himself his own sins. He turned to Geoffrey, who was standing at the desk.

"Geoffrey, my dear son, you *shall* write this down and in your own way. Then we will all be the better for it. The babe, imp or angel, magician or king, was right about that. Only, perhaps, you should not say just *when* all this happened, for the sake of the Princess Ellyne. Set it in the past, at such a time when miracles happened with *surprising* regularity. It is much easier to accept a miracle that has been approved by time. But you and I shall know when it took place. You and I—*and God*—will remember."

Surprised, Geoffrey nodded. He wondered what it was that had so changed the abbot, for he was actually smiling. And it was said at Osney that Abbot Walter never smiled. That such a thing had happened would be miracle enough for the brothers in the monastery. The other miracle, the one he would write about, *that* one was for the rest of the world.

L. Jagi Lamplighter

Never Again the Same

Quite some time ago, L. JAGI LAMPLIGHTER introduced herself to me at the annual science-fiction convention I attend in Philadelphia. I invited her to submit a story for possible inclusion in a future anthology. After waiting several years, she sent me "Never Again the Same," which happily fits this book—and was well worth waiting for!

MIST WAS RISING about the old house. Its gabled peaks, overgrown with moss, jutted out of the swirling gloom. Behind them, the tall oaks and maples were barely visible.

Patrick stepped slowly from the back door of his parents' car, gazing apprehensively at the spooky old mansion. He had never been away from home before. Sleeping over at his friend Jason's house did not count, as Jason only lived two blocks down the street. The thought of spending the summer here, with no one for company except his creepy old great-grandfather who could hardly speak English, was too much to bear. Patrick burst into tears.

His mother came and wrapped her arms about him.

"Be brave, Paddy, you're a big boy now. You're nearly seven."

Patrick nodded and sniffled and wiped his eyes on his sleeve. As he did so, he noticed a strange little cottage to the left of the main house, barely visible through the mist. It stood by the curve of a little stream and had an oddly peaked roof which slanted downwards and then rose with a curve. Curious, he left his mother's arms and went cautiously forward across the lawn to investigate.

As Patrick drew near the tiny Japanese temple, the door opened and out stepped a bent old man in a black quilted robe. His snow-white hair was drawn back into a strange bun. In his gnarled hands he held a large iron key. Seeing Patrick, he quickly inserted the key into the small door and turned it, locking the temple.

Patrick halted, frightened. Then, he realized that this apparition was his great-grandfather.

"You no go inside. Forbidden!" his grandfather announced in his crackly old voice, glaring at Patrick from under unbelievably bushy white eyebrows. Patrick shrank back. He almost turned and ran to his mother and the car. However, the mystery of the forbidden little house won over his fear.

"What's in there?" asked Patrick.

"Very evil book," said his great-grandfather sternly. "Not for little boys."

A book? Patrick could not believe such an intriguing little house could hold anything so dull.

"That's okay," Patrick said, disappointed, "I hate reading anyway."

As the two of them walked back to the car, however, Patrick could not help glancing back at the forbidden temple one more time.

Later, as he sat on the dark blue mat, hardly six inches off the floor, which his mother had explained was to be his bed for the summer, Patrick recalled the conversation he had with his parents on the long drive to his great-grandfather's house.

"But why do I have to stay with Great-grandfather? It's his fault I can't go to summer school with Jason!" Patrick asked.

His mother had been sitting in the front passenger seat. She reached her hand back to take his, frowning sadly. "It is not your great-grandfather's fault that he is Japanese, Patrick."

"But why does that make me Asian?" Patrick complained, his

voice growing louder. "Why can't Asian boys go to Blackcourt summer school?"

His mother had taken a deep breath; something she did when she wanted to yell, but thought she should not. "It's not that Asian boys can't go to Blackcourt, honey. It's just that your school, Great Mills, doesn't have enough Asian boys. So, they would not agree to letting you transfer over to Blackcourt for the summer. They said that they would be accused of being unfair if they had too few Asian children."

"But now I'm not going to either summer school! And I can't stay at Jason's house while you go away, because *he's* going to Blackcourt Summer Reading School. And it's all because I have Great-grandfather's eyes. It's not fair!" Patrick cried.

"You can say that again," Patrick's father muttered from the driver's seat.

"Now, Gregory, don't . . ." Patrick's mother began, but Patrick interrupted her.

"I'll show them! I'll never learn to read!" he announced.

Seated on the futon in the bleak room on the second floor of his great-grandfather's eerie mansion, Patrick repeated his vow.

"Never!" he declared fiercely.

That evening Patrick dined with his great-grandfather in the grown-up dining room. Everything was wrong. They sat cross-legged on cushions at a table hardly as high as Patrick's knee. The food was weird flat noodles and cooked vegetables. Patrick hated vegetables. There was not even a knife and fork—though Patrick rather liked that part. However, when he expressed his opinion of vegetables, his great-grandfather did not even offer him a peanut butter sandwich. Instead, he merely glowered from beneath his huge eyebrows and gestured at the table.

"All there is. Eat or no eat."

Glumly, Patrick picked at the unfamiliar food, while gazing around him at the many photographs that plastered two walls of the dining room. Most of them were old black and white photos in dark frames. A few smaller color photos in standing frames rested on the mantelpiece to either side of the large rusty key that his great-grandfather used to lock the forbidden temple. Patrick wondered if any of the girls in those pictures were his mother.

One large color picuture, however, caught his eye. It showed a smiling young Japanese man dressed in a Yankees uniform. Patrick loved baseball. He had never heard that anyone in his family knew someone who had played for the Yankees. When he stood up to leave the table, his great-grandfather did not object. So Patrick wandered over to the picture and examined it more closely.

His great-grandfather's voice startled Patrick.

"That your great-uncle Eddie. Good baseball player! Train very many years. Wanted to play major league. Once chosen for Yankees B team."

"My great-uncle was going to be a Yankee!" Patrick asked, amazed. "What happened? Did he ever get to play?"

His great-grandfather slowly lowered his head. He was silent for a moment. When he finally spoke, he did so very slowly.

"He read book," he said.

"Book? What book? . . . You mean the one out in that little house?" Patrick asked, his voice growing squeaky from his surprise. "How'd that stop him?"

"Once you read that book—you are never the same," said his great-grandfather, choosing his words with great care.

"What happened?"

"Eddie left team. He enlisted in army. Shot down in airplane," said his grandfather. He nodded towards another picture of the same man, now grim and humorless, dressed in an air force uniform.

"Oh, wow," whispered Patrick, awed.

His great-grandfather rose suddenly to his feet. His scowl caused pure terror to run in Patrick's veins.

"Not wow!" he commanded. "Book destroyed my son. Great-grandson, you are an idiot!"

Patrick bolted from the dining room.

. . . .

For two days, it rained. Lonely and bored, Patrick stayed in his room playing with his Sega Saturn. He would have liked to go downstairs and watch TV or perhaps explore the house. However, he did not want to meet his great-grandfather. The old man's glowering eyes frightened Patrick, and his broken English caused Patrick to blush with shame. No, it was better to stay in his room on his hard mat of a bed, bored to tears, than wander out over the creaking floor boards of the old house and risk another scolding.

On the third day, the sky was clear, and Patrick ventured outside. He spent a magical day playing in the old cherry orchard and wading through the stream. Just behind the little temple, a wide shallow area formed a little pool just perfect for the stamping of bare feet. Patrick remained there until his great-grandfather struck the gong, summoning him for dinner.

As Patrick came running back towards the house, his bare feet slapping against the grass, his shoes in his hand, his great-grandfather appeared on the front porch. He saw the direction Patrick was coming from, and his face darkened.

"You try to go into temple! You went to see book! Very bad!" he shouted angrily, brandishing his fist. Patrick stopped in his tracks, shocked.

"No! No, I was playing in the river. Look at my feet!" Patrick yelled back. He balanced on one leg and held out his wet, muddy foot.

"Naughty boys get no dinner. You go near temple again, I smack your bottom!" his great-grandfather announced, and he stepped into the house and slammed the door.

"It's not as if I could read your stupid old book, anyway!" shouted Patrick. Then he sat down on the lawn and burst into tears.

Patrick cried late into the night. He wished he could have stayed with Jason and gone to summer reading school, like they had originally planned. He wished that he could have gone with his parents on their business trip. He wished that he could be anywhere but where he was: alone in an eerie old house with a crazy old man who was afraid of a book.

"I wish I could read that old book!" Patrick whispered, sniffling. "I wouldn't let it scare me!"

He was imagining doing just that when the door to his room opened. In the doorway stood his great-grandfather. Patrick shrieked and hid under his Winnie-the-Pooh blanket. His great-grandfather had known that he was thinking about the evil book. His great-grandfather could read minds!

However, no scolding came. Instead, his great-grandfather shuffled slowly into the room. Patrick could hear him placing something on the floor and leaning it against the wall. Curious, he peeked out.

The moonlight coming in the room's only window bathed his great-grandfather in dappled light. In his hands, his great-grandfather held two large posterboards. A third poster already rested against the wall.

Seeing Patrick emerge, his great-grandfather said gruffly, "Walls very plain. Perhaps Great-grandson want poster to hang on walls?"

Patrick slithered across his futon to get a better look at the posters. They were movie posters. Nothing so cool as the posters he had at home, but after four nights in this dreadful, bleak room, Patrick was delighted with anything that broke the monotony. He peered closer, examining the closest picture. It showed a man swinging on a cable and a pretty oriental girl in a fancy dress aiming a gun.

"That's Aunt Lily!" he cried, delighted. "Mommy told me that she was a famous actress!"

"Lily was very sweet girl, but very weak and sickly. Spent much time in bed. Doctor did not believe she would live to be woman."

"What happened? How did she get better?" Patrick asked, looking up. His great-grandfather did not answer. Patrick could not make out his expression. "What happened to her?" he asked again.

"She read book," his great-grandfather answered reluctantly.

Patrick was thunderstruck. "You mean the book cured her? But I thought it was a force for evil!"

"Evil wear many faces," his great-grandfather said.

"How can getting healthy and becoming a famous actress be bad?" asked Patrick.

"Very sweet girl—grow up. Chose bad husband. Drink too much. Die young," he said.

"Very tragic," Patrick finished seriously.

In the dappled light, it was hard to make out his great-grandfather's face, but Patrick thought he saw the old man smile. Patrick peered up at him, thinking. There was a question he wanted to ask, but he was afraid his great-grandfather would just yell at him and call him an idiot again. Screwing up his courage, he asked.

"Great-grandfather?" he began. His great-grandfather cut him off.

"Great-grandfather no proper name. Better you call me Papa-san," he said. Patrick nodded.

"Papa-san," he asked, trying again, "where did the book come from?"

"Hmmphf," said his great-grandfather. He shifted his shoulders beneath his robes. Then he sat down on the thick straw mat that covered the floor, upon which the futon rested, and tucked his white-socked feet into his robe, so that he was sitting in a position his mother called Lotus. Patrick sat down and tried to sit that way too. It took some effort, but he did it. His great-grandfather nodded in approval.

"Story take place many years ago—nineteen forty-two. Book come to me while at war camp," his great-grandfather said.

"Like a concentration camp?" Patrick asked. He had read about concentration camps in school. "I didn't know you were in Germany."

"Yes, like concentration camp, but here, in America. Camp for

Japanese people," he said stiffly. "We put in camp because we were 'Yellow Peril.' "

Comprehension dawned on Patrick's face.

"You mean because you were Asian?" he asked.

His great-grandfather harrumphed again. "Asian? Gandhi was Asian. I am Japanese!"

"But you weren't helping the enemy, were you?" asked Patrick.

"No," said Papa-san.

"So it was like me—at school?" Patrick asked. "When they won't let me go to Jason's summer school 'cause I'm Asian?"

He considered and nodded. "Yes, you and I both treated unfairly because of our heritage. But you're unhappy because of overzealous people, not hateful people. After war camp, people passed laws—said 'no do that again.' 'Must be very nice to Japanese.' " He scowled. "Law cannot make people very nice. Laws only punish. So when your school have too few 'Asians,' " he scowled as he spoke the word, "they fear American government will come punish them. When good American boy wants to change schools, they say no. Very bad!" He was silent a time.

Patrick sat quietly too. He had been so angry at his great-grandfather for being "Asian" and making him miss summer school with Jason. It had never occurred to him that it could have been hard on his great-grandfather as well.

The old man looked up, frowning, "What was it you ask?"

"About how you got the book," prompted Patrick.

"Oh, yes! Book! Old man come to me in camp—very old, older than I am now. He ask, 'Can you read English?' I told him no. He said, 'Good, then you will be safe. Take this book. It very old and very dangerous. To read it changes whole life.'

"So," his great-grandfather continued, "I asked, 'If book so very bad, why not burn it?' Old man shook head, weeping, and begged me not to harm book." Here his great-grandfather paused and took a deep breath, then continued. "He told me, 'one man out of thousands who read book is changed for good. Becomes very great man.' "

With this, Papa-san unfolded his feet, rose, and began to leave.

"Papa-san!" Patrick called, jumping up after him and pulling on his robes. "What about you? Did you ever read the book?"

Papa-san turned on Patrick, glowering from under his immense eyebrows. Patrick let go of his robes and cowered. But then the fire drained from the old man's face. He shook his head sadly.

"Never found courage to learn to read English," he said.

Alone in the moonlit room, Patrick lay on his futon, kept awake by wonder. Who would have thought that something as uninteresting as a book could have such power? Whole members of his family had had their lives ruined by just reading a book. Even more intriguing, however, was the promise—the hope—that that very same evil book might, just once, produce greatness instead of sorrow.

Patrick could not say exactly when the idea came to him, but after that he could not sleep at all. He absolutely had to see the book—just to look at it. After all, he could not read it, so he had nothing to fear. But what did an evil book look like? He had to know!

Very quietly, Patrick stole out of his bed. He put on a pair of sports socks, the best for sneaking across creaking floors, and made his way softly and silently down to the dining room where his great-grandfather kept the key to the forbidden temple. Carefully, one step at a time, he crept up to the mantelpiece. Sure enough, there was the key.

Upstairs, a floorboard creaked.

Patrick stood stock-still, frozen with fear. He remembered the terrible glower on his great-grandfather's face the day he had been playing in the stream. The sadness with which Papa-san talked of Lily and Great-Uncle Eddie. If his great-grandfather caught him now . . .

But time passed, and his great-grandfather did not appear. Eventually, Patrick began to breathe more easily. He considered running back upstairs to the safety of his bed, but he did not. He absolutely had to see that book! Carrying a chair quietly over to the fireplace, he took the cold heavy key from the mantel.

Slipping out the front door, Patrick ran across the lawn as quickly as his socked feet could carry him. The door of the tiny Japanese temple opened without trouble. Patrick crept inside, shutting the door behind him. A round table stood in the center of the tiny chamber, lit by moonlight from the two side windows. On the table sat a single old lamp, with a red glass base and paper shade, and . . . the *book*.

The book was bigger than any dictionary and bound in real black leather. Patrick could smell the musky scent of leather as he fumbled with the light. Once it came on, Patrick examined the book more carefully. The book looked exactly as an evil book should—large, black, and very old. The gilded title letters had chipped off over the years and were now too faded for Patrick to read, but he stared in fascination at the intricate knotwork on the cover. It seemed to form a hedge and an arbor surrounding a swing, or maybe it was a sword.

Patrick was so excited, it was hard for him to breathe. He opened the cover with trembling fingers. Inside, an etched plate showed a knight on horseback facing a mounted skeleton. His mouth wide with awe, Patrick turned to the opening page.

The words were written in ordinary print. Patrick felt a slight pang of disappointment. He had been hoping for something glorious, like dried blood. But perhaps it was what the book said that mattered, not its ink. He peered curiously at the words written there.

They did not seem too hard. In fact, he recognized most of them. He really did know all the parts of reading, he thought with surprise. After all, he could understand the instructions in his video games, and the sentences that his teacher wrote on the board. It was just that when it came to books . . . well, everyone made such a fuss about them.

Peering closer, he began to puzzle out the first line.

Many hours later, Mr. Ishizuka put down the binoculars he had been using to look across the yard into the window of the tiny temple. He lifted the receiver of his phone and made a call. When he reached his party, he said:

"Trisha? This is your grandfather. I call about Patrick. You can bake me cake anytime now—I win bet," he said, grinning broadly. He was silent a moment, listening, then continued.

"Yes, he reading right now. Doing very good job! You have not more trouble with him at school."

Silence again, then, "No, no need thank me. But I must warn you"—the old man glanced back across the lawn towards the temple, a glint in his eye and a subtle smile on his lips—"Great-grandson may never again be the same."

Sinister Science and Frankensteinian Formulae

Science-fiction buffs may dislike the media stereotype of mad doctors "tampering with laws that Man was not meant to know," but the metaphor is inescapable. The line of demarcation that separates Victor Frankenstein and Henry Jekyll from Linus Pauling is indeed fine; more than a chemical bond holds them together.

New discoveries in science often have their negative side, as Charles Dickens demonstrated when exposing the horrors of the Industrial Revolution. Still, it took the Twentieth Century and the advent of atomic power to show just how dangerous a little knowledge can be.

Strange gadgets, wicked elixirs and sinister discoveries abound in the next ten stories. Some of them are serious, some are humorous. All are science-fictional.

H. P. Lovecraft

The Temple

H. P. LOVECRAFT *(1890–1937) is generally considered the most important American horror writer since Edgar Allan Poe, but though his tales are generally crafted as exercises in fear, many are also interdimensional science-fantasy—"The Call of Cthulhu," "The Colour Out of Space," "The Dreams in the Witch-House" (in my 1993 collection,* Masterpieces of Terror and the Unknown), *"The Music of Erich Zann" and others.*

(Manuscript found on the coast of Yucatan.)

ON AUGUST 20, 1917, I, Karl Heinrich, Graf von Altberg-Ehrenstein, Lieutenant-Commander in the Imperial German Navy and in charge of the submarine U-29, deposit this bottle and record in the Atlantic Ocean at a point to me unknown but probably about N. Latitude 20 degrees, W. Longitude 35 degrees, where my ship lies disabled on the ocean floor. I do so because of my desire to set certain unusual facts before the public; a thing I shall not in all probability survive to accomplish in person, since the circumstances surrounding me are as menacing as they are extraordinary, and involve not only the hopeless crippling of the U-29, but the impairment of my iron German will in a manner most disastrous.

On the afternoon of June 18, as reported by wireless to the U-61, bound for Kiel, we torpedoed the British freighter *Victory,*

New York to Liverpool, in N. Latitude 45 degrees 16 minutes, W. Longitude 28 degrees 34 minutes; permitting the crew to leave in boats in order to obtain a good cinema view for the admiralty records. The ship sank quite picturesquely, bow first, the stern rising high out of the water whilst the hull shot down perpendicularly to the bottom of the sea. Our camera missed nothing, and I regret that so fine a reel of film should never reach Berlin. After that we sank the lifeboats with our guns and submerged.

When we rose to the surface about sunset a seaman's body was found on the deck, hands gripping the railing in curious fashion. The poor fellow was young, rather dark, and very handsome; probably an Italian or Greek, and undoubtedly of the *Victory*'s crew. He had evidently sought refuge on the very ship which had been forced to destroy his own—one more victim of the unjust war of aggression which the English pig-dogs are waging upon the Fatherland. Our men searched him for souvenirs, and found in his coat pocket a very odd bit of ivory carved to represent a youth's head crowned with laurel. My fellow-officer, Lieutenant Klenze, believed that the thing was of great age and artistic value, so took it from the men for himself. How it had ever come into the possession of a common sailor neither he nor I could imagine.

As the dead man was thrown overboard there occurred two incidents which created much disturbance amongst the crew. The fellow's eyes had been closed; but in the dragging of his body to the rail they were jarred open, and many seemed to entertain a queer delusion that they gazed steadily and mockingly at Schmidt and Zimmer, who were bent over the corpse. The Boatswain Müller, an elderly man who would have known better had he not been a superstitious Alsatian swine, became so excited by this impression that he watched the body in the water; and swore that after it sank a little it drew its limbs into a swimming position and sped away to the south under the waves. Klenze and I did not like these displays of peasant ignorance, and severely reprimanded the men, particularly Müller.

The next day a very troublesome situation was created by the indisposition of some of the crew. They were evidently suffering from the nervous strain of our long voyage, and had had bad dreams. Several seemed quite dazed and stupid; and after satisfying myself that they were not feigning their weakness, I excused them from their duties. The sea was rather rough, so we descended to a depth where the waves were less troublesome. Here we were comparatively calm, despite a somewhat puzzling southward current which we could not identify from our oceanographic charts. The moans of the sick men were decidedly annoying; but since they did not appear to demoralize the rest of the crew, we did not resort to extreme measures. It was our plan to remain where we were and intercept the liner *Dacia*, mentioned in information from agents in New York.

In the early evening we rose to the surface, and found the sea less heavy. The smoke of a battleship was on the northern horizon, but our distance and ability to submerge made us safe. What worried us more was the talk of Boatswain Müller, which grew wilder as night came on. He was in a detestably childish state, and babbled of some illusion of dead bodies drifting past the undersea portholes; bodies which looked at him intensely, and which he recognized in spite of bloating as having seen dying during some of our victorious German exploits. And he said that the young man we had found and tossed overboard was their leader. This was very gruesome and abnormal, so we confined Müller in irons and had him soundly whipped. The men were not pleased at his punishment, but discipline was necessary. We also denied the request of a delegation headed by Seaman Zimmer, that the curious carved ivory head be cast into the sea.

On June 20, Seaman Bohm and Schmidt, who had been ill the day before, became violently insane. I regretted that no physician was included in our complement of officers, since German lives are precious; but the constant ravings of the two concerning a terrible curse were most subversive of discipline, so drastic steps were taken. The crew accepted the event in a sullen fashion, but it seemed to quiet Müller; who thereafter gave us no trouble. In the evening we released him, and he went about his duties silently.

In the week that followed we were all very nervous, watching for the *Dacia*. The tension was aggravated by the disappearance of Müller and Zimmer, who undoubtedly committed suicide as a result of the fears which had seemed to harass them, though they were not observed in the act of jumping overboard. I was rather glad to be rid of Müller, for even his silence had unfavorably affected the crew. Everyone seemed inclined to be silent now, as though holding a secret fear. Many were ill, but none made a disturbance. Lieutenant Klenze chafed under the strain, and was annoyed by the merest trifles—such as the school of dolphins which gathered about the U-29 in increasing numbers, and the growing intensity of that southward current which was not on our chart.

It at length became apparent that we had missed the *Dacia* altogether. Such failures are not uncommon, and we were more pleased than disappointed; since our return to Wilhelmshaven was now in order. At noon June 28 we turned northeastward, and despite some rather comical entanglements with the unusual masses of dolphins were soon under way.

The explosion in the engine room at 2 A.M. was wholly a surprise. No defect in the machinery or carelessness in the men had been noticed, yet without warning the ship was racked from end to end with a colossal shock. Lieutenant Klenze hurried to the engine room, finding the fuel-tank and most of the mechanism shattered, and Engineers Raabe and Schneider instantly killed. Our situation had suddenly become grave indeed; for though the chemical air regenerators were intact, and though we could use the devices for raising and submerging the ship and opening the hatches as long as compressed air and storage batteries might hold out, we were powerless to propel or guide the submarine. To seek rescue in the life-boats would be to deliver ourselves into the hands of enemies unreasonably embittered against our great German nation, and our wireless had failed ever since the *Victory* affair to put us in touch with a fellow U-boat of the Imperial Navy.

From the hour of the accident till July 2 we drifted constantly to the south, almost without plans and encountering no vessel.

Dolphins still encircled the U-29, a somewhat remarkable circumstance considering the distance we had covered. On the morning of July 2 we sighted a warship flying American colors, and the men became very restless in their desire to surrender. Finally Lieutenant Klenze had to shoot a seaman named Traube, who urged this un-German act with especial violence. This quieted the crew for the time, and we submerged unseen.

The next afternoon a dense flock of sea-birds appeared from the south, and the ocean began to heave ominously. Closing our hatches, we awaited developments until we realized that we must either submerge or be swamped in the mounting waves. Our air pressure and electricity were diminishing, and we wished to avoid all unnecessary use of our slender mechanical resources; but in this case there was no choice. We did not descend far, and when after several hours the sea was calmer, we decided to return to the surface. Here, however, a new trouble developed; for the ship failed to respond to our direction in spite of all that the mechanics could do. As the men grew more frightened at this undersea imprisonment, some of them began to mutter again about Lieutenant Klenze's ivory image, but the sight of an automatic pistol calmed them. We kept the poor devils as busy as we could, tinkering at the machinery even when we knew it was useless.

Klenze and I usually slept at different times; and it was during my sleep, about 5 A.M., July 4, that the general mutiny broke loose. The six remaining pigs of seamen, suspecting that we were lost, had suddenly burst into a mad fury at our refusal to surrender to the Yankee battleship two days before; and were in a delirium of cursing and destruction. They roared like the animals they were, and broke instruments and furniture indiscriminately; screaming about such nonsense as the curse of the ivory image and the dark dead youth who looked at them and swam away. Lieutenant Klenze seemed paralyzed and inefficient, as one might expect of a soft, womanish Rhinelander. I shot all six men, for it was necessary, and made sure that none remained alive.

We expelled the bodies through the double hatches and were alone in the U-29. Klenze seemed very nervous, and drank heavily. It was decided that we remain alive as long as possible, using the large stock of provisions and chemical supply of oxygen, none of which had suffered from the crazy antics of those swine-hound seamen. Our compasses, depth gauges, and other delicate instruments were ruined; so that henceforth our only reckoning would be guess work, based on our watches, the calendar, and our apparent drift as judged by any objects we might spy through the portholes or from the conning tower. Fortunately we had storage batteries still capable of long use, both for interior lighting and for the searchlight. We often cast a beam around the ship, but saw only dolphins, swimming parallel to our own drifting course. I was scientifically interested in those dolphins; for though the ordinary *Delphinus delphis* is a cetacean mammal, unable to subsist without air, I watched one of the swimmers closely for two hours, and did not see him alter his submerged condition.

With the passage of time Klenze and I decided that we were still drifting south, meanwhile sinking deeper and deeper. We noted the marine fauna and flora, and read much on the subject in the books I had carried with me for spare moments. I could not help observing, however, the inferior scientific knowledge of my companion. His mind was not Prussian, but given to imaginings and speculations which have no value. The fact of our coming death affected him curiously, and he would frequently pray in remorse over the men, women, and children we had sent to the bottom; forgetting that all things are noble which serve the German state. After a time he became noticeably unbalanced, gazing for hours at his ivory image and weaving fanciful stories of the lost and forgotten things under the sea. Sometimes, as a psychological experiment, I would lead him on in the wanderings, and listen to his endless poetical quotations and tales of sunken ships. I was very sorry for him, for I dislike to see a German suffer; but he was not a good man to die with. For myself I was proud, knowing how the Fatherland would revere my memory and how my sons would be taught to be men like me.

On August 9, we espied the ocean floor, and sent a powerful beam from the searchlight over it. It was a vast undulating plain, mostly covered with seaweed, and strown with the shells of small mollusks. Here and there were slimy objects of puzzling contour, draped with weeds and encrusted with barnacles, which Klenze declared must be ancient ships lying in their graves. He was puzzled by one thing, a peak of solid matter, protruding above the ocean bed nearly four feet at its apex; about two feet thick, with flat sides and smooth upper surfaces which met at a very obtuse angle. I called the peak a bit of outcropping rock, but Klenze thought he saw carvings on it. After a while he began to shudder, and turned away from the scene as if frightened; yet could give no explanation save that he was overcome with the vastness, darkness, remoteness, antiquity, and mystery of the oceanic abysses. His mind was tired, but I am always a German, and was quick to notice two things: that the U-29 was standing the deep-sea pressure splendidly, and that the peculiar dolphins were still about us, even at a depth where the existence of high organisms is considered impossible by most naturalists. That I had previously overestimated our depth, I was sure; but none the less we must still be deep enough to make these phenomena remarkable. Our southward speed, as gauged by the ocean floor, was about as I had estimated from the organisms passed at higher levels.

It was at 3:15 P.M., August 12, that poor Klenze went wholly mad. He had been in the conning tower using the searchlight, when I saw him bound into the library compartment where I sat reading, and his face at once betrayed him. I will repeat here what he said, underlining the words he emphasized: "*He* is calling! *He* is calling! I hear him! We must go!" As he spoke he took his ivory image from the table, pocketed it, and seized my arm in an effort to drag me up the companionway to the deck. In a moment I understood that he meant to open the hatch and plunge with me into the water outside, a vagary of suicidal and homicidal mania for which I was scarcely prepared. As I hung back and attempted to soothe him, he grew more violent, saying: "Come *now*—do not wait until later; it is better to repent and be forgiven than to defy and be condemned." Then I tried the opposite of the soothing plan, and told him he was mad—pitifully demented. But he was unmoved, and cried: "If I am mad, it is mercy! May the gods pity the man who in his callousness can remain sane to the hideous end! Come and be mad whilst *he* still calls with mercy!"

This outburst seemed to relieve a pressure in his brain; for as he finished he grew much milder, asking me to let him depart alone if I would not accompany him. My course at once became clear. He was a German, but only a Rhinelander and a commoner; and he was now a potentially dangerous madman. By complying with his suicidal request I could immediately free myself from one who was no longer a companion but a menace. I asked him to give me the ivory image before he went, but this request brought from him such uncanny laughter that I did not repeat it. Then I asked him if he wished to leave any keepsake or lock of hair for his family in Germany in case I should be rescued, but again he gave me that strange laugh. So as he climbed the ladder I went to the levers and allowing proper time-intervals operated the machinery which sent him to his death. After I saw that he was no longer in the boat I threw the searchlight around the water in an effort to obtain a last glimpse of him; since I wished to ascertain whether the water-pressure would flatten him as it theoretically should, or whether the body would be unaffected, like those extraordinary dolphins. I did not, however, succeed in finding my late companion, for the dolphins were massed thickly and obscuringly about the conning tower.

That evening I regretted that I had not taken the ivory image surreptitiously from poor Klenze's pocket as he left, for the memory of it fascinated me. I could not forget the youthful, beautiful head with its leafy crown, though I am not by nature an artist. I was also sorry that I had no one with whom to converse. Klenze, though not my mental equal, was much better than no one. I did not sleep well that night, and wondered exactly when the end would come. Surely, I had little enough chance of rescue.

The next day I ascended to the conning tower and commenced the customary searchlight explorations. Northward the view was much the same as it had been all the four days since we had sighted the bottom, but I perceived that the drifting of the U-29 was less rapid. As I swung the beam around to the south, I noticed that the ocean floor ahead fell away in a marked declivity, and bore curiously regular blocks of stone in certain places, disposed as if in accordance with definite patterns. The boat did not at once descend to match the greater ocean depth, so I was soon forced to adjust the searchlight to cast a sharply downward beam. Owing to the abruptness of the change a wire was disconnected, which necessitated a delay of many minutes for repairs; but at length the light streamed on again, flooding the marine valley below me.

I am not given to emotion of any kind, but my amazement was very great when I saw what lay revealed in that electrical glow. And yet as one reared in the best *Kultur* of Prussia, I should not have been amazed, for geology and tradition alike tell us of great transpositions in oceanic and continental areas. What I saw was an extended and elaborate array of ruined edifices; all of magnificent though unclassified architecture, and in various stages of preservation. Most appeared to be of marble, gleaming whitely in the rays of the searchlight, and the general plan was of a large city at the bottom of a narrow valley, with numerous isolated temples and villas on the steep slopes above. Roofs were fallen and columns were broken, but there still remained an air of immemorially ancient splendor which nothing could efface.

Confronted at last with the Atlantis I had formerly deemed largely a myth, I was the most eager of explorers. At the bottom of that valley a river once had flowed; for as I examined the scene more closely I beheld the remains of stone and marble bridges and sea-walls, and terraces and embankments once verdant and beautiful. In my enthusiasm I became nearly as idiotic and sentimental as poor Klenze, and was very tardy in noticing that the southward current had ceased at last, allowing the U-29 to settle slowly down upon the sunken city as an airplane settles upon a town of the upper earth. I was slow, too, in realizing that the school of unusual dolphins had vanished.

In about two hours the boat rested in a paved plaza close to the rocky wall of the valley. On one side I could view the entire city as it sloped from the plaza down to the old river-bank; on the other side, in startling proximity, I was confronted by the richly ornate and perfectly preserved façade of a great building, evidently a temple, hollowed from the solid rock. Of the original workmanship of this titanic thing I can only make conjectures. The façade, of immense magnitude, apparently covers a continuous hollow recess; for its windows are many and widely distributed. In the center yawns a great open door, reached by an impressive flight of steps, and surrounded by exquisite carvings like the figures of Bacchanals in relief. Foremost of all are the great columns and frieze, both decorated with sculptures of inexpressible beauty; obviously portraying idealized pastoral scenes and processions of priests and priestesses bearing strange ceremonial devices in adoration of a radiant god. The art is of the most phenomenal perfection, largely Hellenic in idea, yet strangely individual. It imparts an impression of terrible antiquity, as though it were the remotest rather than the immediate ancestor of Greek art. Nor can I doubt that every detail of this massive product was fashioned from the virgin hillside rock of our planet. It is palpably a part of the valley wall, though how the vast interior was ever excavated I cannot imagine. Perhaps a cavern or series of caverns furnished the nucleus. Neither age nor submersion has corroded the pristine grandeur of this awful fane—for fane indeed it must be—and today after thousands of years it rests untarnished and inviolate in the endless night and silence of an ocean chasm.

I cannot reckon the number of hours I spent in gazing at the sunken city with its buildings, arches, statues, and bridges, and the colossal temple with its beauty and mystery. Though I knew that death was near, my curiosity was consuming; and I threw the searchlight's beam about in eager quest. The shaft of light permitted me to learn many details, but refused to show anything within the gaping door of the rock-hewn temple; and after a time I turned off the current, conscious of the need of conserving power. The rays were now perceptibly dimmer than they had been during the weeks of drifting. And as if sharpened by the coming deprivation of light, my desire to explore the watery secrets grew. I, a German, should be the first to tread those eon-forgotten ways!

I produced and examined a deep-sea diving suit of jointed metal, and experimented with the portable light and air regenerator. Though I should have trouble in managing the double hatches alone, I believed I could overcome all obstacles with my scientific skill and actually walk about the dead city in person.

On August 16 I effected an exit from the U-29, and laboriously made my way through the ruined and mud-choked streets to the ancient river. I found no skeletons or other human remains, but gleaned a wealth of archeological lore from sculptures and coins. Of this I cannot now speak save to utter my awe at a culture in the full noon of glory when cave-dwellers roamed Europe and the Nile flowed unwatched to the sea. Others, guided by this manuscript if it shall ever be found, must unfold the mysteries at which I can only hint. I returned to the boat as my electric batteries grew feeble, resolved to explore the rock temple on the following day.

On the 17th, as my impulse to search out the mystery of the temple waxed still more insistent, a great disappointment befell me; for I found that the materials needed to replenish the portable light had perished in the mutiny of those pigs in July. My rage was unbounded, yet my German sense forbade me to venture unprepared into an utterly black interior which might prove the lair of some indescribable marine monster or a labyrinth of passages from whose windings I could never extricate myself. All I could do was to turn on the waning searchlight of the U-29, and with its aid walk up the temple steps and study the exterior carvings. The shaft of light entered the door at an upward angle, and I peered in to see if I could glimpse anything, but all in vain. Not even the roof was visible; and though I took a step or two inside after testing the floor with a staff, I dared not go farther. Moreover, for the first time in my life I experienced the emotion of dread. I began to realize how some of poor Klenze's moods had arisen, for as the temple drew me more and more, I feared its aqueous abysses with a blind and mounting terror. Returning to the submarine, I turned off the lights and sat thinking in the dark. Electricity must now be saved for emergencies.

Saturday the 18th I spent in total darkness, tormented by thoughts and memories that threatened to overcome my German will. Klenze had gone mad and perished before reaching this sinister remnant of a past unwholesomely remote, and had advised me to go with him. Was, indeed, Fate preserving my reason only to draw me irresistibly to an end more horrible and unthinkable than any man has dreamed of? Clearly, my nerves were sorely taxed, and I must cast off these impressions of weaker men.

I could not sleep Saturday night, and turned on the lights regardless of the future. It was annoying that the electricity should not last out the air and provisions. I revived my thoughts of euthanasia, and examined my automatic pistol. Toward morning I must have dropped asleep with the lights on, for I awoke in darkness yesterday afternoon to find the batteries dead. I struck several matches in succession, and desperately regretted the improvidence which had caused us long ago to use up the few candles we carried.

After the fading of the last match I dared to waste, I sat very quietly without a light. As I considered the inevitable end my mind ran over preceding events, and developed a hitherto dormant impression which would have caused a weaker and more superstitious man to shudder. *The head of the radiant god in the sculptures on the rock temple is the same as that carven bit of ivory which the dead sailor brought from the sea and which poor Klenze carried back into the sea.*

I was a little dazed by this coincidence, but did not become terrified. It is only the inferior thinker who hastens to explain the singular and the complex by the primitive short cut of supernaturalism. The coincidence was strange, but I was too sound a reasoner to connect circumstances which admit of no logical connection, or to associate in any uncanny fashion the disastrous events which had led from the *Victory* affair to my present plight. Feeling the need of more rest, I took a sedative and secured some more sleep. My nervous condition was reflected in my dreams, for I seemed to hear the cries of drowning persons, and to see dead faces pressing against the portholes of the boat. And among the dead faces was the living, mocking face of the youth with the ivory image.

I must be careful how I record my awakening today, for I am unstrung, and much hallucination is necessarily mixed with fact. Psychologically my case is most interesting, and I regret that it cannot be observed scientifically by a competent German authority. Upon opening my eyes my first sensation was an overmastering desire to visit the rock temple; a desire which grew every instant, yet which I automatically sought to resist through some emotion of fear which operated in the reverse direction. Next there came to me the impression of *light* amidst the darkness of dead batteries, and I seemed to see a sort of phosphorescent glow in the water through the porthole which opened toward the temple. This aroused my curiosity, for I knew of no deep-sea organism capable of emitting such luminosity. But before I could investigate there came a third impression which because of its irrationality caused me to doubt the objectivity of anything my senses might record. It was an aural delusion; a sensation of rhythmic, melodic sound as of some wild yet beautiful chant or choral hymn, coming from the outside through the absolutely sound-proof hull of the U-29. Convinced of my psychological and nervous abnormality, I lighted some matches and poured a stiff dose of sodium bromide solution, which seemed to calm me to the extent of dispelling the illusion of sound. But the phosphorescence remained, and I had difficulty in repressing a childish impulse to go to the porthole and seek its source. It was horribly realistic, and I could soon distinguish by its aid the familiar objects around me, as well as the empty sodium bromide glass of which I had had no former visual impression in its present location. This last circumstance made me ponder, and I crossed the room and touched the glass. It was indeed in the place where I had seemed to see it. Now I knew that the light was either real or part of an hallucination so fixed and consistent that I could not hope to dispel it, so abandoning all resistance I ascended to the conning tower to look for the luminous agency. Might it not actually be another U-boat, offering possibilities of rescue?

It is well that the reader accept nothing which follows as objective truth, for since the events transcend natural law, they are necessarily the subjective and unreal creations of my overtaxed mind. When I attained the conning tower I found the sea in general far less luminous than I had expected. There was no animal or vegetable phosphorescence about, and the city that sloped down to the river was invisible in blackness. What I did see was not spectacular, not grotesque or terrifying, yet it removed my last vestige of trust in my consciousness. *For the door and windows of the undersea temple hewn from the rocky hill were vividly aglow with a flickering radiance, as from a mighty altar-flame far within.*

Later incidents are chaotic. As I stared at the uncannily lighted door and windows, I became subject to the most extravagant visions—visions so extravagant that I cannot even relate them. I fancied that I discerned objects in the temple; objects both stationary and moving; and seemed to hear again the unreal chant that had floated to me when first I awakened. And over all rose thoughts and fears which centered in the youth from the sea and the ivory image whose carving was duplicated on the frieze and columns of the temple before me. I thought of poor Klenze, and wondered where his body rested with the image he had carried back into the sea. He had warned me of something, and I had not heeded—but he was a soft-headed Rhinelander who went mad at troubles a Prussian could bear with ease.

The rest is very simple. My impulse to visit and enter the temple has now become an inexplicable and imperious command which ultimately cannot be denied. My own German will no longer controls my acts, and volition is henceforward possible only in minor matters. Such madness it was which drove Klenze to his death, bareheaded and unprotected in the ocean; but I am a Prussian and a man of sense, and will use to the last what little will I have. When first I saw that I must go, I prepared my diving suit, helmet, and air regenerator for instant donning; and immediately commenced to write this hurried chronicle in the hope that it may some day reach the world. I shall seal the manuscript in a bottle and entrust it to the sea as I leave the U-29 forever.

I have no fear, not even from the prophecies of the madman Klenze. What I have seen cannot be true, and I know that this madness of my own will at most lead only to suffocation when my air is gone. The light in the temple is a sheer delusion, and I shall die calmly, like a German, in the black and forgotten depths. This demoniac laughter which I hear as I write comes only from my own weakening brain. So I will carefully don my suit and walk boldly up the steps into that primal shrine, that silent secret of unfathomed waters and uncounted years.

John Gregory Betancourt

The Green Thumb

You wouldn't think a packet of seeds could hold enough reading matter to be dangerous, yet botany always seems to have a dark side when science-fiction writers delve into its possibilities. JOHN BETANCOURT *is head of Wildside Press and has written many short stories and novels, including* Johnny Zed, The Blind Archer *and* Rememory.

THE SLEIGH BELLS on the front door jangled when I went into Debarre's Rare Books. Old Edward Debarre looked up over his half-moon reading glasses and frowned at me. He always did that whenever anyone came into his bookstore, I knew. Definitely *creepy.* That helped explain why he seldom had customers. That, and the fact that rare as his books purported to be, nobody really wanted them. He didn't specialize in mysteries or Americana or even great literature. No, he specialized in the odd and unpopular. A first edition (1890) of *Birds Shown to the Children* had been my only purchase in three years of occasional visits to his shop. That particular book was unremarkable in any way, except that it had a mediocre color plate illustrating sedge-warblers, and I'd been involved in a dispute with my neighbor, June Akoras, over the local existence of those particular birds. I had been right, as the illustration clearly proved. Well worth the $10.60 (including tax) I'd invested in that volume.

Behind me, Debarre cleared his throat. That was the first sound

I'd ever heard him utter, except for the price of the bird book I'd bought last year. I felt a chill go down my back. *Don't look,* something inside me said. *Whatever you do, don't look.*

"You like plants?" he asked. His voice was high and wheezy, like an asthmatic's.

I glanced up at the small hand-printed sign thumbtacked over the section I was browsing: HORTICULTURE it said. He had me.

"Yes," I said. With a mental sigh, I turned around.

Debarre was rummaging under the counter. Finally he pulled out a thin book—perhaps thirty or forty pages long—bound in drab olive-green cloth. He set it gingerly on the glass display case, facing it toward me. Then he frowned again.

"What's that?" I asked, peering at it, intrigued despite myself. The book didn't seem to have any lettering stamped on the spine or cover.

"About plants."

"Oh?" I picked it up and carefully opened to the first page. There were a number of dried flowers pressed inside, but that didn't surprise me; lots of old books had them. I'd found roses, baby's breath, even daisies pressed flat in books over the years.

As I leafed forward, the beautiful hand-drawn watercolor illustrations of flowers took my breath away. I recognized Myrtle and Hogswort in the first two-page spread, but the rest—some half a dozen—I didn't know.

The text at the bottom had been hand set in blocky old type, small but legible. Unfortunately, it wasn't in English . . . German, maybe? Or Dutch? Something with far too many consonants.

I flipped in a few more pages. The beautiful illustrations continued. This was, I thought, more a work of art than a book. It belonged in a museum. Whoever this long-ago artist had been, his talent was impressive.

Hands trembling, I closed the book and set it down. I wanted it. I wanted it very badly. But I knew I would never be able to afford it. If Debarre charged ten bucks for a beat-up bird book, what would he charge for *this* one? Hundreds, said a little voice inside me. It might as well be thousands, with the meager book-buying budget I allowed myself.

"How much?" I asked. I heard a slight tremor in my voice. Great, I thought, a killer bargaining move. Now he'd *know* I loved the book.

"Twelve dollars, plus tax," he said, still frowning.

"Twelve?" I swallowed. Had I misheard? "Twelve *dollars?*"

He nodded once, almost imperceptibly.

I fumbled my purse open and pulled out a twenty. He plucked it from my fingers, made change from his ancient register, then wrapped my book in brown paper like a fish from the market. I accepted the parcel and hurried out before he could change his mind.

All the way home, I kept expecting to hear footsteps behind me and his wheezing old voice calling, "Hey lady, I made a mistake!"

But by then it would be too late, I thought. The book was mine, and I had no intention of giving it back, mistake or not. I hugged it to my chest. *Mine.*

Nobody chased me. The ten-minute walk home proved entirely uneventful. Once I left Main Street, I saw not a living soul, not even June Akoras, my next-door neighbor, who could usually be found working among her prize-winning flowers every Saturday afternoon.

"I hope you get aphids," I told her rose beds as I hurried past.

I took June's absence as a good sign. She beat me every year in the Springfield Gardening Club's Town Beautiful Awards, and she liked to gloat and rub my nose in it when she collected her blue ribbons. Invariably, I came in second or third. Worst of all, she always hung her ribbons where I could see them from my kitchen window.

Her wins were a deliberately calculated maneuver. Whatever I planted, she made sure she planted the same thing. She bought the most expensive, exotic, and beautiful varieties available, and as a result her flowers always outshone mine. I neither forgot nor forgave her for it.

This year we had both planted rosebushes and peonies. With the flower judging coming up in just a few days, I expected her to be out around the clock, puttering, pruning, and fussing over her flowers. And truly they *were* beautiful, the roses huge and heavy, all reds and blushes, the peonies white and red in elegant stripes and swirls.

When I looked at my own peony beds to either side of my front door, they paled in comparison, weak and spindly, with many small buds and only a scattering of open flowers. My roses, though—there we would have a real competition. This year I had watered and fertilized and pruned and mulched with especial fervor, and my efforts had been rewarded with a luxuriant thatch of roses, a veritable garden hedge between our properties, done all in pink and yellow blossoms. I gave a low but satisfied chuckle. *This* year we would be evenly matched, I thought.

I carried my slender new book inside my pink and white Cape Cod house, where I set it on the kitchen table and unwrapped it carefully.

"I can't believe you're mine," I whispered.

My hands trembled as I opened the first page, spilling pressed flowers out. As with the illustrations, some I recognized and some I did not. All were dried to the point of brittleness. I could have crumbled them all to dust.

Something stopped me from throwing them out, though. They *were* pretty, in an odd sort of way. Perhaps I could make a dried flower arrangement out of them . . .

Again I paged through that slender book, admiring the watercolors. Mistletoe, I recognized, and holly, and wolfbane. It struck me, suddenly, that all the plants I could identify had some sort of mystic connection. I chuckled. Was this a horticulture book, or a witch's guide?

I examined the binding material more closely.

"Odd . . ." I murmured to myself.

The book wasn't bound in cloth, I realized, but something fibrous, like a huge leaf. Running my fingers along the covers, I felt natural ridges and bumps. Not a leaf, exactly, I decided, but something like corn husks. I sniffed it, but it just smelled musty, like it had been stored in somebody's attic too long.

It was nearly five o'clock. I'd better start dinner; Jim would be back from the golf club any time now.

Sighing, I pulled an old mixing bowl from the pantry, gathered up all the loose bits and pieces of dried flowers, put them inside, and set the bowl on a high shelf. Tomorrow would be soon enough to deal with *them,* I decided.

Jim didn't understand or particularly like my book-collecting habit, so I took my new trophy into the living room, opened the top shelf of my four-shelf barrister's bookcase, and slipped it neatly inside. He'd never notice.

Sunday morning, after breakfast, Jim headed off to the golf course again. I got the usual peck on the cheek, the usual mumbled "Back soon, Hon." I heard the front door slam and the crunch of car wheels on our driveway, and then he was gone.

Sighing, feeling like a perpetual golf widow, I pulled down my old mixing bowl and looked at the dried flowers—what was left of them, anyway. Most of them hadn't survived the night, crumbling to dust while I slept.

I shook my head. Well, you get what you pay for. I hadn't much liked them after all, I told myself.

I was about to dump the whole batch into the garbage when I noticed something small, black, and shiny off to one side of the bowl. It was a seed, I realized, as I peered down at it.

Using my thumb and forefinger, I plucked it out and studied it. A seed, but like none I had ever seen before . . . black, shiny like a beetle, and perfectly round except for the tiniest nub on one end. It must have been pressed in the book, too, I thought.

I'd heard of some seeds lasting years. I wondered if this one might sprout.

With a growing sense of excitement, I fetched my new book, opened it, and began searching among the pictures, trying to identify which plant it came from.

An hour later, I had to give up; I just couldn't tell. There were too many pictures, too many unfamiliar plants, and no real illustrations of seeds.

I paused for a second, wondering where to put it. I had a small spot next to the peonies, I finally decided, where it might well grow. There it would get plenty of sun, and I could water it when I watered the rest of the garden.

Nodding, I fetched my gardening fork, gloves, and trowel, then went outside to plant it.

The moment I stepped out my door, I heard a long, loud *sssss* sound. It was a spray can, I realized, and the sound came from June Akoras's yard.

I peered at her—her, with the orange-frizz hair and that neon-orange fingernail polish, looking more like a refugee from clown college than a filthy-rich widow—and suddenly I recognized the bright yellow can whose contents she was spraying in the air. And then I realized the wind was carrying that spray over the fence and straight toward my roses.

"Stop that!" I screeched, dropping everything and running over.

She stopped spraying and looked at me, a perfect semblance of puzzlement on her face. Oh, but she knew what she was doing, all right. My hatred boiled over.

"You—you—" I began.

"What on *earth* are you stammering about?" she asked almost sweetly.

I pointed at the spray can. "That! How could you? *How could you?*"

She looked at the can of wasp spray. "I didn't know you like the little monsters," she said. "They were buzzing all around the fence, so I thought I'd take care of them."

"You know perfectly well you can't spray that stuff around plants! It kills them!"

"I'm spraying in my own yard," she said.

"But it's blowing into *mine*!"

"I'm very sorry," she said, half turning and pretending to read the label. One bright orange fingernail tapped with satisfaction on the can. "I'll be more careful."

I stood there and fumed as she retreated toward her house. I had a funny feeling that tomorrow all my roses would be covered with little black dead spots where the mist had landed on them. But what hurt more than that was the look of supreme satisfaction I glimpsed on her face as she slipped inside.

Turning, I looked hopelessly at my roses. All the delicate pinks, the pastel yellows . . . there was no telling how much damage she'd done. Hopefully I'd caught her in time. But I had a distinct feeling I hadn't.

Shaking my head, I headed back toward my house. Only then did I realize I'd dropped that tiny black seed somewhere near my front door. I sighed. So much for that. June had beaten me again.

It probably wouldn't have grown anyway, I told myself. It probably died fifty years ago. Besides, I didn't even know if it *was* a flower seed.

Somehow, that didn't comfort me one bit. I tried to bury my anger and frustration in weeding and troweling in my peony bed, but I only managed to scare worms and sal bugs, and then I stabbed myself in the finger with my gardening fork.

Yelping, dripping blood, I hurried into the house. June Akoras had certainly ruined this day for me, I told myself.

After bandaging my finger—luckily, it felt worse than it looked after I rinsed it off and put antiseptic cream on it—I retreated to my kitchen and put the kettle on to boil. A cup of chamomile tea, that's what I needed.

As I waited for the water to boil, I opened that old picture book and again gazed down at the flowers. They were beautiful enough, I thought, that any of them would have beaten June Akoras's garden. Try as I might, I just didn't have the green thumb she did.

Or the spraying index-finger, a dark part of my mind added.

My vision blurred with tears. I would have given anything to beat her this year. *Anything.*

. . . .

The next morning, after Jim left for the office, I hurried out to check on my roses.

As I expected, half of them were covered with tiny black spots: leaves, flowers, stems. The wasp spray had burned them wherever it landed. They were ruined. Nobody would give me an award this year.

Head down, close to tears, I started back inside. Only then did I notice the change in the peony bed to the left of my front door.

All the peonies had vanished. In the space of a night, every single round red-and-white flower had disappeared, replaced by a luxuriant growth of some splendid russet-leafed plant. Roots spilled out from the flower bed, twining this way and that in the lawn, and leafy runners headed off across my yard in all directions. I even saw one pressed against the basement window almost as though it were peering inside.

"What *are* you?" I asked, bending down to touch one leaf gently.

Something pinched me, and I jerked my hand back. A single drop of blood beaded on my right index finger. Had something stung me? No, I realized, I'd missed the thorns on these strange new plants. Needle-sharp and an inch long, they stuck out all over the stems.

More gently, I parted the leaves.

Then I spotted my peonies. They hung, brown and shriveled, mostly dead, from the thorns. They had been neatly skewered by these new plants. It seemed as though the life had been sucked out of them, but of course that was ridiculous. Plants didn't cannibalize each other, did they?

I sat on my front stoop. As I stared, I noticed small dark buds all over the new thorn plants. Had those buds been there five minutes ago? I hesitated. Nothing grew that fast, I told myself, not even kudzu. No, I'd missed them, like I'd missed the thorns when I'd first looked at the plant. I shook my head. June Akoras had me more rattled than I'd thought.

I studied the runners, heading in every different direction.

"That's where you need to go," I told them, pointing to June's house. "Go suck the life out of her and her rosebushes." I chuckled. It would serve her right, too.

My finger began to throb, so I went back inside. More Band-Aids, more antiseptic cream, and more chamomile tea. This year would be a write-off for the garden club. I'd had a good shot with the roses, but with them gone . . .

I remembered a Desirée Diamond film festival on TV that afternoon, and I decided to make myself comfortable, curl up with a bowl of popcorn, and try to while away the hours till I had to make dinner for Jim.

The garden club toured on Tuesday, inspecting members' gardens before giving out ribbons. I hadn't a chance in the world this year. But next year . . . yes, next year, I vowed, I'd win once and for all.

That night, as Jim and I lay spooned together in bed, I dreamed of flowers. I dreamed of that strange plant coming alive, entering the house all over, sending out feelers to investigate. I dreamed that it tickled my nose as it curled protectively about me, about its mistress, about the one who had freed it, the one who had showered blood on it and brought it to life, and we laughed together, my voice melodic, the plant's like the tinkle of wind chimes on a breezy day.

We were one, it and I, of one mind, one body, one voice, and one thought. It became part of me, and together we planned and dreamed. We *would* win that blue ribbon, my familiar and I. It would be easy.

Together we stole into June's garden and sucked the life from her roses. Together we pushed under her back door, sent tendrils into her bedroom, and lifted her—Gently, gently! Don't wake her!—from her sheets. Together we bore her out and away.

All about my house and garden all the plants danced and sang, and I danced with them, a wild Disneyfied frenzy of green and white and pink and red, and I knew true happiness for the first time in many years.

• • • •

When I awakened, I felt curiously refreshed. I no longer cared that June Akoras has maimed my roses. It was a wonderful day, and nothing could spoil it.

After I sent Jim off to work with a huge breakfast of blueberry pancakes under his belt, I ventured outside to check on my thorn bed. To my surprise, I found it beautifully in bloom. Huge pink flowers, some the size of dinner plates, some the size of teacups, and all splashed with deep blood red at the centers, had opened everywhere.

The five judges from the garden club were all standing around, *ooh*ing and *aah*ing.

"What is it?" one of them asked me. "It's beautiful—I've never seen anything like it. Does it belong to the hibiscus family?"

"Uh, yes, I believe so," I said. The plant looked familiar now that I saw it in bloom; there were several pictures of it in that strange old plant book. "I'm not sure what its common name is. If you'll wait a minute, I can look up its scientific name—"

"We can get to that later," she said. "We just have one more house to look at, but I think I can say with all confidence that you're going to have a ribbon this year."

"A . . . ribbon?" I stared at her, shocked. It was all happening so fast.

"Come, ladies," she said, and she turned and headed for June Akoras's garden.

I trailed them as far as my fence, almost stumbling over a large runner, as big around as a garden hose, from my strange little thorn plants. This runner went to the edge of my property, then vanished underground. But on the other side of the fence I could see its effects.

Every one of June's beautiful rosebushes lay dead or hopelessly withered. Blackened flowers dropped like dead fruit from thin brown stalks. I had never seen anything so pathetic.

Neither, it seemed, had the garden club. *Tsk-tsk*ing, they checked a few boxes on their clipboards.

I was amazed June hadn't come outside to protest that I'd done something to her roses. She probably didn't have the nerve after what I caught her doing yesterday, I told myself. She was sneakier than that. I was more likely to find her digging up my garden at midnight than trying to persuade the judges I'd bushwhacked her garden.

I went back to my strange new flower bed, gazing down at all the beautiful flowers. As I stood there, half numb with pleasant shock, I glimpsed a bright neon-orange something lying on the ground.

No, I thought, bending down to look, it wasn't *on* the ground, it was poking up *through* the ground. It was a pale, bloodless, two-inch length of finger. Its nail had been painted bright orange. From the tip of the finger emerged a plant stalk, one leading to an exceptionally bright and beautiful flower.

I did *not* scream. Instead, I coolly moved my toe, subtly scuffing mulch up to cover that telltale digit.

After all, I couldn't have June ruining my chances to win a ribbon now, I told myself. What would the judges think of a plant growing from a human finger? No, they would not be happy.

I would bury it more deeply later, I decided. And I'd search my garden for any more fingers or toes that might be poking up too conspicuously.

Sighing happily, I knelt by my beautiful thorn plant. As I reached down to touch it, I sensed its thorns drawing back to protect me. Gently, I began to stroke its russet-colored leaves.

"Good girl," I whispered to it, a proud mother now. "Good, good girl."

Later that afternoon, when the garden club presented me with my first blue ribbon—Best Flower Garden—I blushed and stammered.

"I couldn't have done it without June Akoras," I said. "She has always been a source of inspiration."

Secretly, I smiled.

Harry Harrison

Famous First Words

Here's an amusing tale of Pandora-like curiosity by a prolific American writer now living in Ireland. HARRY HARRISON *began his career as a comic-book artist, but began selling science-fiction stories in the early 1950s to* Astounding Science Fiction *(later* Analog) *and other magazines, and later wrote many SF novels, including* The Dalek Effect, *the* Deathworld *trilogy,* Make Room! Make Room! *(filmed as* Soylent Green), The Technicolor Time Machine, War with the Robots, *and the wild adventures of Slippery Jim DiGriz, "the Stainless Steel Rat."*

MILLIONS OF WORDS of hatred, vitriol and polemic have been written denigrating, berating and castigating the late Professor Ephraim Hakachinik, and I feel that the time has come when the record must be put straight. I realize that I too am risking the wrath of the so-called authorities by speaking out like this, but I have been silent too long. I must explain the truth as my mentor explained it to me because only the truth, lunatic as it may sound, can correct the false impressions that have become accepted coin in reference to the professor.

Let me be frank; early in our relationship I too felt that the professor was—how shall we call it—eccentric even beyond the accepted norm for the faculty of backwater universities. In appearance he was a most untidy man almost hidden behind a vast mattress of tangled beard that he affected for the dual purpose of saving the trouble and the expense of shaving and to dispense with the necessity of wearing a necktie. This duality of purpose was common in most everything he did; I am sure that simultaneous professorships in both the arts and in the sciences is so rare as to be almost unique, yet he occupied two chairs at Miskatonic University, those of Quantum Physics and Conversational Indo-European. This juxtaposition of abilities undoubtedly led to the perfection of his invention and the discovery of the techniques needed to develop its possibilities.

As a graduate student I was very close to Prof. Hakachinik and was present at the very moment when the germ of an idea was planted that was to eventually flower into the tremendous growth of invention that was to be his contribution to the sum of knowledge of mankind. It was a sunny June afternoon and I am forced to admit that I was dozing over a repetitious (begat, begat, begat) fragment of Dead Sea Scroll when a hoarse shout echoed from the paneled walls of the library and shocked me awake.

"Neobican!" the professor exclaimed again, he has a tendency to break into Serbo-Croatian when excited, and a third time, "Neobican!"

"What is wonderful, professor?" I asked.

"Listen to this quotation, it is inspirational, by Edward Gibbon, he was visiting Rome, and this is what he wrote:

" 'As I sat musing amidst the ruins of the Capitol, while the barefooted friars were singing vespers in the Temple of Jupiter . . . the idea of writing the decline and fall of the city first started to my mind.'

"Isn't that wonderful, my boy, simply breath-taking, a real historical beginning if I ever heard one. It all started there and twelve years and 500,000 words later, wracked by writer's cramp, Gibbon scribbled The End and dropped his pen. Decline and Fall of the Roman Empire was finished. Inspiring!"

"Inspiring?" I asked dimly, head still rattling with begats.

"Dolt!" he snarled, and added a few imprecations in Babylonian that will not bear translation in a modern journal. "Have you no sense of perspective? Do you not see that every great event in this universe must have had some tiny beginning?"

"That's rather an obvious observation," I remarked.

"Imbecile!" he muttered through clenched teeth. "Do you not understand the grandeur of the concept! The mighty Redwood piercing the sky and so wide in the trunk it is pierced with a tunnel for motor vehicles to be driven through, this goliath of the forests was once a struggling, single-leafed shrub incapable of exercising a tree's peculiar attractions for even the most minuscule of dogs. Do you not find this concept a fascinating one?"

I mumbled something incoherent to cover up the fact that I did not, and as soon as Prof. Hakachinik had turned away I resumed my nap and study of the scroll and forgot the matter completely for a number of days, until I received a message summoning me to the professor's chambers.

"Look at that," he said, pointing to what appeared to be a normal radio housed in a crackle-grey cabinet and faced with a splendid display of knobs and dials.

"Bully!" I said with enthusiasm. "We will listen to the final game of the World Series together."

"Stumpfsinnig Schwein!" he growled. "That is no ordinary radio, it is an invention of mine embodying a new concept, my Temporal Audio Psychogenetic detector, TAP for short, and 'tap' is what it does. By utilizing a theory and technique that are so far beyond your rudimentary powers of comprehension that I will make no attempt to explain them, I have constructed my TAP to detect and amplify the voices of the past so that they can be recorded. Listen and be amazed!"

The professor switched on the device and after a few minutes of fiddling with the dials exacted from the loudspeaker what might be described as a human voice mouthing harsh animal sounds.

"What was that?" I asked.

"Proto-mandarin of the latter part of the thirteenth century B.C., obviously," he mumbled, hard at work again on the dials, "but just idle chatter about the rice crop, the barbarians from the south and such. That is the difficulty, I have to listen to volumes of that sort of thing before I can chance on an authentic beginning and record it. But I have been doing just that—and succeeding!" He slapped his hand on a loose pile of scrawled pages that stood upon the desk. "Here are my first successes, fragmentary as yet, but I'm on the way. I have traced a number of important events back to their sources and recorded the very words of their originators at the precise moment of inception. Of course the translations are rough—and quite colloquial—but that can be corrected later. My study of beginnings has begun."

I'm afraid I left the professor's company then, I did want to hear the ball game, and regret to say that it was the last time that I—or anyone—ever saw him alive. The sheets of paper he so valued were taken to be the ravings of an unwell mind, their true worth misunderstood and they were discarded. I have salvaged some of them and now present them to the public who can truly judge their real worth. Fragmentary as they are, they cast the strong light of knowledge into many a darkened corner of history that has been obscured in the past.

". . . even though it is a palace it is still my home, and it is too small by far with my new stepmother who is a *bitz*.* I had hoped to continue in my philosophy studies, but it is impossible here. Guess I better run the army down to the border, there may be trouble there . . ."

Alexander of Macedonia—336 B.C.

". . . hot is not Ye words for it, and alle of VIRGINIA is like an Oven this summer. When Opportunity arose to earn a little l.s.d. running a Survey line through the hills I grabbed it before M.F. could change his Minde. That is how I met ———— today (forgot his name, must ask him tomorrow) in the Taverne. We did have an Ale together and did both complain mightily upon the Heat. With one thing leading to Another as they are wont to do, we had

---

* Thought to refer to the *peetz*, a small desert bird, but the reference is obscure.

more Ales and he did confide in me. He is a member of a secret club named, I *think* since Memory is hazy here, The Sons of Liberty, or some such . . ."

George Washington—1765

"France has lost its greatness when an honest inventor gains no profit from his onerous toil. I have neglected my practice for months now, perfecting my Handy Hacker Supreme Salami Slicer. I should have earned a fortune selling the small models to every butcher in France. But no!—the Convention uses the large model without paying a sou to me, and the butchers are naturally reluctant now to purchase . . ."

J. I. Guillotin, M.D.—1791

"My head doth ache as though I suffereth an ague, and if I ever chance on the slippery-fingered soddish son of an ill-tempered whore who dropped that night-vessel in Fetter Lane, I will roundly thrash him to within an inch of his life, and perhaps a bit beyond. Since arrival in London I have learned the neatness of step and dexterity of motion needed to avoid the contents of the many vessels emptied into the street, but this is the first time there was need to dodge the container itself. Had I moved a trifle quicker this body of the crockery in motion would have continued in motion. But my head at rest brought it to rest and there was a reaction . . . My head doth ache. As soon as it is better I must think on this, there is the shade of an idea here."

Sir Isaac Newton—1682

"I. is afraid that F. knows! If he does I have had it. If I. was not so seductively attractive I would find someone else's bed, but she does lead me on so. She says she can sell some of her jewelry and buy those three ships she was looking at. The last place I want to go is the damn spice islands, right now at the height of the Madrid season. But F. *is* king, and if he finds out . . . !"

(Attributed to Cristoforo Colombo of Genoa, 1492,
but derivation is obscure.)

. . . .

"Am I glad I got little Pierre the Erector Set. As soon as he is asleep I'll grab the funny tower he just made. I know the Exposition committee won't use anything like this, but it will keep them quiet for a while."

Alexandre-Gustave Eiffel—1888

"Woe unto China! Crop failures continue this year and the Depression is getting worse. Millions unemployed. The only plan that seems at all workable is this construction project that Wah Ping-Ah is so hot about. He says it will give a shot in the arm to the economy and get the cash circulating again. But what a screwball idea! Build a wall 1,500 miles long! He wants to use his own initials and call it the W.P.A. project, but I'm going to call it something different and tell the people it's to keep the barbarians out, as you can always sell them on defense appropriations if you scare them enough."

Emperor Shih Hwang-ti—252 B.C.

"There will be a full moon tonight so I'll have enough light to find that balcony. I hate to take a chance going near that crazy family, but Maria is the hottest piece of baggage in town! She made her kid sister Julie—the buck-toothed wonder!—promise to have the window unlocked."

Romeus Montague—1562

(Extract from the ship's log.) "Made a landfall today on a hunk of rock. What navigation! We head for Virginia and end up in Massachusetts! If I ever catch the Quaker brat who stole the compass . . . ! ! !"

Brig *Mayflower*—1620

There are many more like this, but these samples will suffice to prove that Prof. Hakachinik was a genius far ahead of his time, and a man to whom the students of history owe an immeasurable debt.

Since there have been many rumors about the professor's death I wish to go on record now and state the entire truth. I was the one who discovered the professor's body so I know whereof I speak. It is a lie and a canard that the good man committed suicide, indeed he was in love with life and was cut off in his prime, and I'm sure he looked forward to many more productive years. Nor was he electrocuted, though his TAP machine was close by and fused and melted as though a singularly large electrical current had flowed through it. The official records read heart failure and for wont of a better word this description will have to stand, though in all truth the cause of death was never determined. The professor appeared to be in fine health and in the pink of condition, though of course he was dead. Since his heart was no longer beating, heart failure seemed to be a satisfactory cause of death to enter into the records.

In closing let me state that when I discovered the professor he was seated at his desk his head cocked towards the loudspeaker and his pen clutched in his fingers. Under his hand was a writing pad with an incomplete entry, what he appeared to be writing when death struck. I make no conclusions about this, but merely record it as a statement of fact.

The writing is in Old Norse which, for the benefit of those not acquainted with this interesting language, I have translated into modern English.

". . . this meeting will come to order and if you don't put those mead horns away there'll be a few cracked skulls around here, I tell you. Now, order of business. There have been some reports of tent caterpillars in Yggdrasill and some dead branches, but we'll get onto that later. Of more pressing interest is the sandy concrete that has been found cracking in the foundations of Bifrost Bridge. I want to—just one moment—this is supposed to be a closed meeting and I notice that there is someone listening in. Thor, will you please take care of that eavesdropper . . ."

Jack Snow

The Super Alkaloid

JACK SNOW *(1907–1956) was a broadcasting executive at NBC who spent his spare time writing excellent fantasy tales, as well as two of the best Oz pastiches since L. Frank Baum died,* The Shaggy Man of Oz *and* The Magical Mimics of Oz. *He also prepared the indispensable bibliophilic guidebook,* Who's Who in Oz. *"The Super Alkaloid" involves a formula that might not have interested Frankenstein, but I'll bet H. G. Wells's island-dwelling Dr. Moreau might have checked it out.*

OLMSTED PHONED shortly after dinner, inquiring if I would be at leisure during the evening. I assured him that it was my intention to remain at home the entire evening, unless, of course, I should be summoned on an urgent case—a possibility that confronts physicians twenty-four hours a day. That was excellent, Olmsted announced, adding that he would call on me not later than nine for the purpose of discussing a subject which he averred would be of intense interest.

Olmsted was in the habit of these impromptu visits and it was my custom just as often and informally to invade the seclusion of his home. We had attended the same medical college ten years ago; we later practised our profession together in this city, and we had neither of us married nor mingled to any great extent in society. Outside of these casual similitudes there were others that joined our natures. Olmsted was a fervent researcher in a certain realm of chemistry. He studied diligently the various effects of chemicals upon the nerve cells and divisions of the brain. I conducted a series of similar experiments and research, but very modestly since I was forced to devote my efforts toward building a substantial medical practice. Olmsted with his wealth could readily overlook such matters. He lived absolutely alone, eating at a club and making of himself a mysterious, flitting figure.

One more likeness we had in common—we were moderately addicted to the use of opium.

He came that night at 8:45. At 9:10 he departed. He was exceedingly nervous, he paced the floor never ceasing an instant. In a torrent of locution verging upon incoherency he made me promise that I would come to his home the next evening sharply at 8:30. He said further that he had produced a substance possessing delights far beyond anything offered by opium and that he would divulge the whole affair the next evening. He was resolute, he turned his back upon me and departed; nothing more would he tell me now.

The following day passed in an ecstasy of expectation. By the discreet use of opium I had come to know its horrible, forbidden joys. And now Olmsted offered—I wondered.

That night Olmsted appeared at the door in summons to my ring. There were tense, suppressed lines about his long, wanly thin face and I readily perceived by his sharp movements that his nerves were drawn to a point beyond tautness. He said not a word as he stood there in the doorway, his slight form diminished even more by the encroachment of the night shadows. Thinking that I had offended him in some strange manner by arriving before the pre-mentioned time (it was now only 8 o'clock), I ventured, "I am early, Olmsted, a half hour, but you were so devilishly excited last night that I have thought of little else all day long."

He smiled quickly and murmured that a few moments in either balance could bear but little significance. Immediately he led the way to the second floor of the building and thence through a darkened corridor to a long, narrow room which housed his laboratory. The room was excessively spacious, extending more than a hundred feet in length and fifty feet in width. It was very lofty, and along one of its lengthy sides far up almost to the ceiling was a tier of transoms that served as ventilators while closer to the floor in this same wall were arranged numbers of huge, wide windows, now very carefully obscured with translucent blinds.

There was the usual chemist's equipment, only with a luxurious repleteness seldom accosted in even the most lavish laboratories. The center table was strewn with a confusion of test tubes, drying tubes, thistle tubes, numerous other fantastically curved tubes employed in the conduction of gases, Ehrlenmeyer and Florence flasks, watch glasses, beakers, microscopes, retorts, mortars, graduates in profusion and an array of delicate cylinders of crystalline glass. The side of the room opposite the windows was divided by partitions into small alcoves bearing triple rows of shelves. On these shelves was arranged an assemblage of valuable chemicals, rare compounds, ancient essences and tinctures such as I am positive was never before collected into one repository and placed at the command of a sole person. Olmsted's laboratory had always been a source of wonder for me, and as he was very secretive about it and his work therein, I would not hesitate to affirm that, save for Olmsted himself, I was the only man, to whom the shimmering glass forms conveyed an intelligible impression, to roam at will the confines of that lengthy chamber.

Olmsted returned directly to the task which my arrival had undoubtedly interrupted. He hovered over a small tripod supporting a two-ounce porcelain crucible. The lowered flame of a Bunsen burner was applied nakedly to the crucible and produced a curling, gaseous vapor that rose vigorously from the simmering liquid. At times he stirred this purple fluid with a slender glass rod; at other times he pressed into the crucible a drop or two of a greenish substance from a small syringe; and all the time he talked excitedly, nervously.

"As I disclosed to you last evening," he was saying, "I have formed a compound which produces stupor and the resultant sensations and dreams—visions, much the same as does opium. This substance may be used unrestrainedly, however, with no habit formation as accompanies the addiction of opium."

"You are informed in elementary chemistry," he went on, acquiring prolixity as his actions grew more abbreviated, "of the existence of a related group of compounds designated as the alkaloids because of their basic properties. Each of these members is found in some part of a certain plant. Thus caffeine is present in the coffee berry, opium in the unripe capsules of the poppy, quinine in the bark of certain tropical trees, nicotine in the leaves of the tobacco plant, atropine in the berry of the deadly nightshade, while strychnine is present in the seeds of the members of the Strychnos family. Opium itself contains morphine and a number of lesser alkaloids. Nicotine is unusual in that it is practically the only liquid alkaloid."

Olmsted paused for a moment to maneuver a difficult adjustment of the burner flame. All these trivial facts he was giving out so ponderously I had learned by heart years ago and could repeat as readily as he. But his chatter seemed to relieve the strain he was under, so I said nothing as he hurried on again.

"My procedure included a close study of the chemical changes and reactions wrought by the habit-forming alkaloids upon the nervous tissue of the human body. I have disregarded all present theories and concluded for myself that the alkaloid when introduced into the blood flow either by inhalation or injection travels inertly with the blood until it eventually reaches the brain. There it acts subtly and by means of involved processes upon the brain cells, first inducing unconsciousness and then conjuring or awakening visions or scenes which have been previously in either a conscious or subconscious state consigned to those certain cells to which the blood stream carried the alkaloid. Of course the drug usually varies in intensity of its strength and this accounts for the varied scenes that haunt the opium dream. The weaker the alkaloid the farther the blood carries it into the brain before it begins to react, and thus with each differing strength a new set of cells and a new group of visions is excited. The alkaloid also has the effect of stimulating the blood supply to these cells, serving to agitate them even more in this manner."

"You believe, then," I broke in, "that the theory asserting that the brain retains a record of every sensation, event and scene experienced by the individual is tenable?"

"Precisely," Olmsted answered sharply, "nothing, not even the stamp of a foot in childish anger is left unnoted. From that theory I have derived a fluid that I shall call The Super Alkaloid. It is merely a concentrated alkaloid divested of its objectionable properties and furnished with others which will, I feel safe in stating, create a world of romance into which the mortal may relapse at will with no attending fear whatever."

I became enthused, accepting Olmsted's statements completely since I well understood his nature and realized that he would more likely diminish the properties of his discovery than amplify them. "Think," I dreamed aloud, "what an escape from drudgery such a thing would offer. It would surpass any of the present forms of entertainment; reading would pale before its vividness and the moving pictures would not be able to compete. We, ourselves, would be the heroes of daring adventures into fanciful realms; we would transcend the burden of reality and dwell in gorgeous, regal splendor, in sensuous luxury or in truth in whatever lavish surroundings we may be carried."

"Ah, there you are wrong." Olmsted spoke slowly and for the first time ceased his attention to the crucible. He turned the bright gaze of his black eyes upon me. "You are wrong," he repeated, staring queerly, "wrong, it will not be wherever we *may* be carried, but wherever we *will*."

I gasped and protested incredulously. "What—what do you mean?"

Olmsted was again the scientist not to be astounded, and his own period of contemplation forgotten, he spat out in staccato. "Simply this"—and now he turned again to the stirring of the liquid in the crucible as he talked—"after the alkaloid is swallowed, there follows a brief space of normal consciousness enduring perhaps for three minutes. In this period the whole force of the mind must be exerted in concentration upon a scene or location in which it is desired to spend the period of fantasy. The blood flow to those cells of the brain which embrace the impression of the suggested vision is increased and the nature of The Super Alkaloid is such that it finds its course with the strongest flow of blood. The alkaloid also differs from common drugs in that it is uniform in strength and does not move on with the blood stream but lodges itself in the cells which have been agitated. Naturally it reacts within these definite cells and formulates in the ensuing stupor the location which was decided upon."

I was aghast. I glanced sharply at Olmsted, he was stirring as complacently as though he had uttered only the merest platitudes.

"Do you realize what you are saying?" I cried. "Have you considered that you will be able to recall the past, and picture it as vividly as the present? Your discovery will have powers far beyond that of mere personal solace and pleasure."

"I have thought of that," Olmsted answered quietly. "The slightest details of an event half a century old will be obtainable, and obtainable in all their clarity since I have succeeded in removing from The Super Alkaloid the impurities which cause the confusion and wild disorder usually existent in an opium debauch."

My brain whirled as I conjectured and silently contemplated the possibilities of this grotesque drug. The vistas of the past would swing open. We could be youths romancing, children playing; the dead would return in all their beloved sentience; the changed scenes of long ago would exist again; the sprawling city would revert for a time to a swaddling elm-shaded village; the machinery, the noise and clamor would hush and the dusty country lanes be filled with shining rigs and prancing horses. Then, too, what mighty value would the drug possess for the historian and data seeker. Full and detailed accounts of battles and momentous occasions could be salvaged from fading memories.

My reverie was shattered when Olmsted required my assistance in cooling the crucible which he was about to remove from the tripod. I drew a beaker partially full of cold water and into it Olmsted plunged the crucible. The receptacle rested on the surface of the water, a thin, wisp-like steam arising from its surface, accompanied by a most disagreeable odor.

"While the fluid is cooling," Olmsted declared, "I will tell you something more of its properties. Yesterday morning I submitted it to the final test, one which was the culmination of two years work. I swallowed exactly ten cubic centimeters of the alkaloid. Immediately I concentrated on my recollections of New York City and particularly on the endless mob of people that flowed through the streets. For a minute or two nothing happened, and then like a flash, with marvelous abruptness I was hovering over a certain street that I remembered well. I mingled with the throng, I listened and understood their remarks, I felt them brush past me, I felt the chilly breeze and the coolness of the day, in fact everything was just as if I had been there with all my active perceptions—save for one inconsistency." Olmsted paused and smiled slightly as he continued. "Floating through the air, and scattered upon the pavement were test tubes, beakers, graduates and numerous other laboratory apparatus. These were present as naturally as were the people and, strangest of all, the people seemed to notice them, for they dodged the beakers that were suspended in their path, stepped over the graduates that strewed the walk, and one young chap evidently on his way to his office had the temerity to impatiently kick my best microscope into the gutter."

"I concluded when I regained my senses a half hour later," continued Olmsted, "that the liquor was not sufficiently potent to banish all traces of reality from the dreamer's mind. So today I have prepared a concentrated solution that has ten times the power of that to which I subjected myself yesterday."

I was amazed at this recital and not altogether without apprehension. "Do you think," I stammered, "that it is safe to use it in so highly concentrated a form?"

Olmsted fairly shouted. "If you have any doubts," he said, "you may leave immediately and I will test the stuff alone."

His tone left me a little ashamed of my distrust and I affirmed stoutly. "No, I will stay, I am quite as interested as you."

He trembled slightly as he watched the mercury of the delicate thermometer, which he had suspended in the liquid, falling rapidly. It was now slightly below thirty degrees centigrade.

Olmsted now placed on the table before me two small beakers, saying, "I will pour the requisite amount of alkaloid into each of the beakers. You will drink the fluid from one, I from the other. As soon as you have swallowed the draught, immediately close your eyes and concentrate with all your will upon a scene which it would please you to visit. Do not be alarmed at anything you see or hear regardless of the reality it may seem to possess."

He withdrew the crucible from the beaker of water and measured perhaps a teaspoonful of its contents into each beaker. His eyes glistening into mine, and with no further word, Olmsted raised the nearer beaker to his parted lips. In like manner I grasped the remaining beaker and gulped the contents. It was very sweet, and seemed to coat my tongue with a viscous film. Olmsted had drawn up two straight-back chairs and into these we sank. As I relaxed I felt a surging vibrating sensation seizing me. Suddenly I recalled Olmsted's instructions and I quickly closed my eyes and began frantically to concentrate upon the first fanciful vision that occurred to me. I set deeply to reviewing all the wild pictures I had ever formed of the fantastic land of China.

I can only fail in attempting to put down the utterly unreal sensations that ensued, that rolled and billowed upon me from an endless space. First, the crystal aerial expanse that seemed to exist before my eyes was broken by the appearance of glowing, greenish and bluish globules of light. One by one these little bubbles burst inward, flooding the air with an infinity of flat disc-like splotches of color. My body seemed to be very light, very evanescent, as though I had transcended material weight.

I was rushing headlong on a horizontal plane, my face down, directly through the midst of those curious disc lights. Inevitably I collided with some of them, and as their substance touched my body they broke, shattered, and pervaded my flesh. Whenever this occurred I endured the most supreme, most incomparable sensation imaginable. Suffice it to say that there is positively no earthly balm as highly delightful as the touch of those glowing discs.

Completely the air cleared, I was moving no more, the discs had vanished. About me were the streets of Shanghai, of Canton; the wilderness of Manchuria and a motley realm of guttural-tongued, yellow-hued men who moved without animation and wore as a mask their fixed countenances. It was the weird China-land of my dreams, far removed from the Orient of reality but nevertheless very real, very vivid. Grotesque? Yes. Whimsical? Yes. But like a powerful dream startlingly defined. There I roamed, shrinking in terror from villainous mandarins; thrilling at the subtle allure of beautiful high-caste women; and spying on the demons of surpassing intellect who sought to subject the white race with their forgotten lore of mysticism.

It was quite a common dream of oriental adventure such as might be disclosed in many an adventure novel, yet it was real, amazingly real; the sounds, the stenches, the rare perfumes, it was like a heavy intoxicant.

There was no time. I seemed to exist for a moment—for an eternity, and then I felt myself coming back. I did not, however, encounter the discs. Instead there was about me an oppressive sense that somehow I had failed to leave, entirely, the scene of my dream, that its effluvia was still clinging to me as is sometimes the case in the return from a dream encountered in normal slumber.

Then I awoke. I *was* awake; I sensed it perfectly, yet there was something amiss. About me was Olmsted's laboratory and there stood Olmsted himself, he too had awakened and had risen from his chair. I knew it was Olmsted but how changed he was, the features were grotesquely his yet his skin was yellow! His eyes were almond-shaped and a thin sliverous moustache drooped from his lips. In place of his rubber apron Olmsted stood there wrapped in a silken robe embroidered with dragons with flaming mouths. And the room, only the laboratory equipment remained unchanged. Where there had been a calcimined ceiling now appeared a magnificent inlaid marble dome and the floor on which I stood was tiled fancifully with gorgeous patterns. Numerous colored lanterns hung from the top of the dome, suffusing the room with a roseate glow; and scattered about the floor were delicately woven rugs of the most fragile texture.

Was I mad? I glanced in a sudden apprehension at my person. I was draped in a resplendent, omni-hued kimono and crowned with an octagon-shaped hat; sandals were strapped to my bare feet and the sleeves of my garb hung a foot's length from my arms.

Olmsted was smiling stonily and brandishing an absurd fan. "Sit down and be quiet for a moment," he said with perfect calmness. Speech was, indeed, beyond me, and I sank weakly into a chair. Olmsted crossed the room and removed two of the bottles from the shelves. Carefully he measured out a portion of the contents of each and mixed them in a beaker. A noxious vapor arose with a boiling hissing sound. When the reaction had ceased, Olmsted swallowed a few drops of the liquid and advanced to me, extending the beaker and commanding me to drink likewise. I did so unhesitatingly. I felt as though I had been struck a terrific blow; I was stunned, shocked. Dizzily I reeled and slowly opened my eyes.

Olmsted appeared clad in a rubber apron, I wore my plain black suit and the floor was laid with simple figured linoleum. I sighed. "What in heaven's name was it?" Olmsted was greatly amused.

"I neglected to warn you," he said, "that the effect of the alkaloid might extend into consciousness. Obviously it did in your case as well as mine. Exactly how long the condition would have endured I have no way of determining. But when the alkaloid is taken in the strength which we used it, its influence might extend over a period of months, possibly years. What The Super Alkaloid did was merely to set a certain group of thought cells functioning in precedence over all others. That is the actual reason why humans become accustomed to surroundings and grow fond of the homes in which they pass their lives, the cells that retain those scenes and impressions are activated oftener than the others."

"So it was that when I swallowed the alkaloid and thought of my childhood days, I passed a pleasant half hour with my mother and father and brother on our old farm in Virginia. But when the soporific influence of the drug diminished, those cells, which had been aroused, retained their ascendency under the various other effects of the alkaloid and as I returned to consciousness and actual surroundings, I must admit that you made a charming dirty-faced youngster." Olmsted was now openly smiling at my bewilderment. He went on more sensibly. "The latter fluid we drank was the counteraction and was, of course, of acid properties. It immediately destroyed the basic alkaloid, neutralizing it and converting it into a harmless complex salt."

My mind was in a mad whirl as I endeavored to reason with some degree of intelligence. Olmsted talked on.

"Our physical aspects and conditions are, as would be supposed, governed by the group of cells which have the greatest authority over the brain as a whole." And now for some unaccountable reason I fancied that his voice grew tremulous. "That," he concluded "is the cause of my reversion tonight to my childhood."

With these words Olmsted seized a small mirror from the table and gazed fixedly into it. The next instant he dropped the glass and shouted wildly.

"Do you see? I was right! The scar from the burn I received two years ago has disappeared!"

I stared amazedly at his face; surely he was right. The scar *was* gone, and gone, too, were numerous tiny lines and wrinkles, while in their stead had come a light flush and bright vivacity. Olmsted was chortling.

"I have found it—found it—the eternal youth! Why, man," he cried gleefully, "if I had not drunk the antidote when I did, I would by now be a knee-high freckle-faced boy."

But I was not listening to him. Trembling, I picked up the mirror and turned my eyes toward it. My skin was faintly, delicately, yellow, and my eyes slanted at an unmistakable angle—upward.

Roberta Rogow

"I Am a Fine Musician . . ."

ROBERTA ROGOW *is a New Jersey children's librarian who contributes to science-fantasy periodicals, the Merovingen Nights anthologies, and at least three collections of new Sherlock Holmes tales published by St. Martin's Press, which is also slated to publish her first mystery novel. Paragon published her study,* Futurespeak: A Fan's Guide to the Language of Science Fiction. *"I Am a Fine Musician . . ." tells of a time machine that, well, goes flat . . .*

JOHANN SEBASTIAN BACH stepped out of my front hall closet. He looked just like the cover of my copy of "The Passion According to St. Matthew": middle-height, stocky build, full wig, plum-colored coat, dark vest, blue knee britches, buckle shoes, the works. He looked around and asked, *"Wo ist das?"*

My German is strictly from Berlitz. I stepped aside and let him out of the closet, trying to figure out how to ask a Baroque musician how the hell he got into my front hall.

He stepped gingerly into the hall. The first shock he got was the sight of my legs. I don't wear pants in May, and this was the hottest Decoration Day weekend on record. And I had only opened the closet to get my umbrella out, in case those reports of thunderstorms were true.

So here he is, the Great Bach, and what was I supposed to do with him? All I wanted to do was get out to the deli for some dinner food, and get back in time to see the Channel Thirteen Gala. Yes, I know it was a repeat, but Arthur and I were sitting in the second row, and every so often the camera picked us up, me grinning madly away, him looking as if he'd prefer to be at one of his science-fiction conventions. (In case you happen to see it, I'm the large woman in the red silk, with the blonde bun and the beads, and he's the skinny guy with the billy-goat beard and homemade knitted vest under his tux.)

I smiled at Bach. He looked puzzled. I tried some of my Grandma's Yiddish on him: *"Essen, Herr Bach?"*

That he understood. I led him through the front hall into the kitchen, which takes up most of the back end of our house. Thanks to Arthur's great-grand-something, who knew a good thing when he saw it, we actually own a whole brownstone on West Fifth Street, almost in the Hudson River. And thanks to Arthur's inventions, we can afford to keep all of it for ourselves instead of renting bits of it out. Between his patents and his consultancy fees, he can support me and the kids very nicely, and have plenty left over for opera and concert tickets. I have a subscription to the Met and another to the Philharmonic, and we make a sizable contribution to PBS at pledge time. Which explains why I really wanted to relive last year's annual gala. But how could I, with Bach in the house?

The kitchen seemed to puzzle him more than ever. I would have thought with all those kids in his house he'd be familiar with kitchens, but I guess our stove, refrigerator, and sink were more than he could handle. I used up some more of my Yiddish with *"Setzen, bitte,"* and a gesture at the nearest chair, while I thought furiously.

The most obvious question was, what was he doing here? The second question was, what *was* he? I knew Arthur had been working on some new hologram stunt for one of the gaming companies, but if Bach was a hologram, he was the solidest one I'd ever seen.

"Wait here," I told him. "I go get wurst."

He brightened up immediately. "Wurst" is something all Germans understand.

I headed for the deli on the corner, and picked up a dozen hot dogs and a pound of sauerkraut, some dill pickles and a strudel. After all that spice and sour, a little sweet wouldn't hurt.

I tiptoed into the kitchen gingerly. Bach was still there. He'd been joined by someone else, much better dressed, more elaborate wig, and bigger buckles on higher-heeled shoes. He looked at me expectantly.

"Was gibts?" I asked.

He let out a stream of German that went over my head by a mile. Suddenly I figured it out. "Herr Handel? You speak English!" I was saved!

He looked me over, assessing the short skirt vs. the paper bag of groceries, and tried to place me in his social scale.

"I'm the, er, landlady," I said.

"Ah. I wondered where we were. What is this place, and why are we here?" He did speak English, sort of. Imagine a stage-Irish brogue overlaid with a heavy stage-German accent and you get some idea.

I started cooking up the hot dogs. I must admit, this nearly finished my culinary expertise. Usually I tell Angelica what I want and leave it to her, but I'd given her and Monique the whole weekend to go visit their families in the Islands. Never let it be said that I refuse my help anything! Besides, I had just gotten the newest in the Lincoln Center video series, and I had planned to spend the entire weekend working my way through the Ring . . . but here were Bach and Handel, and I have always been known as a Patroness of Music.

As far as I could make out, they were as puzzled at their sudden appearance in my front closet as I was. They didn't seem to be ghosts (although with those accents, it was hard to explain religious concepts), and they couldn't give me any clues as to their whereabouts before they appeared in my front closet. I dished out the wurst and the sauerkraut, and tried to join the conversation, but it was pretty difficult since I couldn't follow their German.

Meanwhile, Bach and Handel were getting along pretty well, considering. They'd never met in their lifetimes, of course, and Handel knew Bach mostly as the slightly old-fashioned father of one of his musical acquaintances in England. They sat swapping stories in Plattdeutsch and eating hot dogs and kraut, while I tried to remember what Arthur had tried to tell me last week about the hologram idea.

That's when we heard the weird humming coming from the front hall. Bach looked startled, Handel frowned.

"I heard that sound when I arrived," he announced. "Another comes."

Another did come, in embroidered satin and pigtail wig: Haydn, as it turned out. I began to see where this thing was coming from. There seemed to be some kind of music-appreciation logic to this phenomenon, if I could only work out the source.

Haydn made an elaborate bow. Handel told him not to bother, since I wasn't anybody important, just the landlady, and there was a pot of wurst in the kitchen. At least that's what I think he said.

Haydn's accent was less impenetrable than Handel's, and he was used to eating in the kitchen. He also knew how to make himself useful as a majordomo (he'd always been regarded as a kind of upper servant at the Esterhazy estate anyway). He and Handel started one-upping each other on patrons, in English for my benefit and in German for Bach's. Bach could only boast of a Margrave or two. Handel had a king, but before George Louis had been king of England he'd been a mere elector, and a jumped-up family at that. Haydn's Esterhazys, of course, were not only noble but ancient, and thought themselves much, much better than the mere Hapsburgs who happened to be running the empire at the moment.

I wondered if the closet was going to disgorge anyone before I could get to bed. Sure enough, just about three A.M., out popped Wolfgang Amadeus Mozart.

I'd had enough. I left Mozart and Haydn to their reunion, and went to bed, thinking I'd better get to the deli for more hot dogs early tomorrow. If I had my music history right, I was about to have a houseful of Germans.

I had my music history wrong. I woke up to find a Napoleonic war going on in the front hall. I also realized that there was a distinct odor in the kitchen. I promptly demonstrated the flush toilets to Bach, Handel, Haydn and Mozart, and instructed Gluck, Vivaldi and Corelli to have baths!

This meant that they had to leave the kitchen and explore the rest of the house. They were polite about the living room, with its abstracts on the walls and the square furniture Arthur likes, but when they got upstairs to the second floor they stared at the practice room, where I keep the Steinway and the kids' old violins and guitars. The "company bathroom" had Bach mumbling about *"hexen,"* but I assured him (via Handel and Haydn) that there was no witchcraft in plumbing. Mozart went into ecstasies when he discovered Arthur's collection of outmoded clothes. Arthur never throws anything away, and Wolfie (as he insisted I call him, after he pinched my bottom) tried on all the leisure suits and bell-bottom pants before settling on a Nehru jacket in pink brocade that Arthur once wore to a peace concert somewhere when we were first married.

I had a pretty good idea who would step out next, and sure enough, there he was, yelling fit to wake the dead (in this case, not very funny). I mentally added a hearing aid to my shopping list. Ludwig van Beethoven had arrived.

I hustled down with Haydn and Mozart (after all, they had known him, and might be able to calm him down), and pointed the Baroque contingent up one more flight of stairs to my son's studio apartment, the one he uses when he's in town with his band. With all these people in the house, some kind of sleeping and eating arrangements were going to have to be made. They had already demonstrated that they were undeniably *there*. They ate . . . about a pound of hot dogs per composer. They eliminated (I wasn't too keen about washing out the improvised pot-ties). And what was I supposed to do if Mozart decided he wanted to go on the town? I decided that I'd cross that one when I came to it. Sufficient to the day is the evil thereof, or something like that. Right now, I thought. I'd better get some more food in.

By the time I got back, there had been another arrival. Franz Schubert was blinking his way out of the closet, looking shy and confused. Beethoven was rampaging around the living room, yell-ing about the furniture. I dumped the groceries in the kitchen, fetched Haydn, and told him to tell his old student that I had a cure for deafness.

I was guessing that Beethoven's problem wasn't nerves, it was bones; he might have had arthritis that fused his ear apparatus, so to speak. The man at the drugstore told me that the hearing aid would amplify the sound for my "eccentric relative." I sat Bee-thoven down with Haydn and drew weird pictures of ear trum-pets and sound waves, and the Great One reluctantly permitted me to adjust the gadget on one ear. The result was miraculous. My hand got kissed, my cheeks got kissed.

Haydn, ever the conciliator, smiled and said, "Good. We now have a fourth for cello. Do you know there is a full set of strings upstairs? I want to go over some of those quartets with you. Whatever were you thinking of when you wrote them? Those harmonies do not exist!"

"They must exist. I wrote them!" Beethoven and Haydn headed up to the practice floor.

I could hear music all the way through the house. From the sounds drifting down, I could tell that Schubert was strumming the guitar, Haydn had formed his string quartet, Bach must have figured out how to turn on the Moog, and Handel had Vivaldi and Corelli working on a motet (or maybe the Italians were working with Handel). My next shopping expedition had better be to the stationery store for music paper and pencils.

The place was getting fuller all the time. A trio of Italians popped through at the same time, all arguing about prima donnas and box office receipts: Donizetti, Rossini and Bellini. I added spaghetti and meat sauce to my shopping list. After one taste of my attempts, Rossini wrote out a recipe and sent me back out to the nearest specialty store for extra garlic, oregano, fennel, and thyme. I remembered (belatedly) that having shot his bolt as a musician, he had spent thirty years wining and dining the fashionable world. My cooking was a terrible shock to his palate.

When Robert Schumann came through, I wondered if I should add lithium tablets to my list (I couldn't remember if he'd been a manic-depressive or a schizophrenic). I counted the minutes until the two hours were up, and Clara Schumann came through. At last, another woman!

You might well ask, with all this music in the house, wasn't I in ecstasy? Hadn't I always said that I wished I had been around when Beethoven and Schubert and Schumann were jamming, just to pick up their improvisations? Hadn't I always wanted to listen to their discourse on music and musicians? Unfortunately, I was spending all my time running between the kitchen, the deli, and the stationery store. So much for music!

It took Clara Schumann to set me straight. Dear Clara! She took a lot of the mother-henning off my hands. For one thing, she knew a lot of the people who were crowding my house, and she was able to help me with the menus. (Even Bach was getting tired of hot dogs and kraut.) For another, she had a certain status. I, after all, was still the landlady, and most of these characters had a very low opinion of landladies.

"You see, my dear woman," she told me, "we must consider ourselves the handmaidens of Genius."

"Frau Schumann," I said firmly. "I live with a genius. I do not consider myself his handmaiden!"

"How odd," Clara said. "And where are your servants?"

"I gave them the weekend off," I explained. "I really wasn't expecting all this company."

Clara gave me the look she must have given hundreds of incompetent slaveys, and took over the Salon. I was banished to the kitchen with the hot dogs and the spaghetti.

I'd been keeping the boys oiled with beer and wine from the liquor store and the deli. Arthur and I don't drink much, but we do have a nice selection for our guests. I guess the next development was inevitable. Haydn found the wine cellar.

He'd sort of appointed himself my butler, and he went into the basement to see if we had anything that he considered drinkable (he didn't think much of the Gallo Chianti that fueled the Italian opera contingent). He came bursting into the kitchen with his eyes popping.

"Madame!" He pointed to the open cellar door with a trembling finger. "There is a device down there that is clearly the work of the Devil!"

"There is?" I didn't want to admit it, but I was terrified. Arthur has his workshop down there, and it's strictly off limits. He has ways of making sure no one messes around with his stuff. The whole place is set up with electric eyes and burglar alarms. I wondered if Haydn had set any of them off, and how was I going to explain all of this to the cops if they came to investigate?

"I'd better take a look," I said finally. Maybe Arthur had left something running while he went off to his convention. It would be just like him! Unless . . . but I couldn't believe my sweet, uncomplaining Arthur would be so devious. I know he's not as musically inclined as the rest of the family, but deliberately planting all these people on me, just to test his device . . . or to teach me a lesson . . . ?

I edged my way down the steep stairs that hide behind an inconspicuous door in the kitchen. Haydn tiptoed after me, eager to demonstrate his find. I approached the door to Arthur's lab cautiously. He'd rigged up an electric buzzer that gave you a nasty shock if you touched the knob. The door was unlocked, and it swung open as I tapped it.

There it was. It was a tangle of wires and neon-glow tubing, shimmering gently and humming. Leading out of the center of the tangle was a sort of tube. I made a few mental calculations. The tube must be directly under the front closet. Well, that explained how they all got there . . . but it didn't solve the problem of getting them all back. The machine was surrounded by Arthur's electric eyes, lasers, and zappers, all ready to fire if anyone so much as approached the contraption.

"What is it, Madame?" Haydn asked.

"I believe it is what brought you here," I told him.

"And will it send us back?" he asked.

"I assume so," I said, circling it. "Do you want to go back?"

Haydn sighed. "Madame, I led a long and generally happy life. I made music, and I loved it. But to spend eternity in this place, with all these people . . . no. I have heard what passes for music in future eras. There is no harmony, no logic in it."

"Wait till the Russians get here," I muttered, and I started towards the machine.

It responded with an ominous rumble. Clearly, Arthur was going to give me a large enough dose of music and musicians to keep us out of concerts and operas for the next year or so.

I went back upstairs, where Clara Schumann was greeting Felix Mendelssohn (who spoke English, thank goodness!) and explaining that Chopin and Liszt were fighting over custody of the piano. Schubert and Schumann had found my library and were selecting poems for possible lieder. Bach and Handel were still at the Moog. And could I please get some more cigars? Brahms should be along any minute and Clara knew just the brand he smoked.

This was getting expensive! I found acceptable cigars for Brahms (Schumann was astonished to see the beard he'd grown since their parting). I ordered several chickens for cacciatore, hoping that Rossini would approve of the sauce.

Wagner arrived with the dawn on Sunday morning. By that time I was getting so fed up with these guzzling freeloaders that I left Clara Schumann in charge, with Haydn as majordomo, to accept the groceries, and holed up in my own bedroom, thinking furiously. I *had* to turn that damned machine off before my food budget for the year went blooey!

I went downstairs, to find that Verdi had arrived. So had the aforementioned Russians: Mussorgsky, Tchaikovsky, and Borodin. Puccini had joined the other Italians in the living room. I demonstrated the VCR (cries of witchcraft, then delight at the idea of seeing an opera in one's home) and they were roundly lambasting the performers for murdering the music.

The pianists on the second floor were banging away. Liszt and Wagner were pointedly not speaking to each other. That was my fault. I had remarked that while Clara Schumann had made it through, Cosima Wagner hadn't.

"And that is grossly unfair," I added, as I was clearing off another round of wineglasses, beer bottles, and dirty tableware. "Wagner would probably be totally unknown today if she hadn't kept the flame going, running the Bayreuth Festival for fifty years . . ."

"Cosima was always the best of wives," Wagner gloated.

"The woman was considerably more than that, and you were too dense to realize it," Liszt said. "The girl was, after all, my daughter . . ."

"But the genius was mine!" Wagner shouted. "She could do no less than keep it alive!"

That did it! They arued over the Place of Woman in Society, over the Place of Genius in Society, and the Place of Wagner and Liszt in the Musical Pantheon. By the time they were finished, no one was speaking to anyone else! The best Clara and I could do was to place them at opposite ends of the table when we served up dinner.

The closet never stopped. Midway through the evening we started into the twentieth century. Stravinsky turned up around nine P.M., and I wondered if Gershwin qualified. (He did; he shared Brahms's taste in cigars, and Mozart's love of limelight.) Around eleven Kurt Weill came through, and I began to get worried. At this rate, things would get weird . . . and maybe dangerous. Would the machine stop when it ran out of composers?

I knew the answer to that one when Leonard Bernstein came through on Monday morning. This was getting serious! I began to wonder how Gian-Carlo Menotti was feeling, and what was the news on John Williams's health? Something had to be done, and fast!

"Judy?" Lenny said when he saw me. Of course I was flattered that he'd remember me. We'd been introduced at a few cocktail parties, but I never thought he would remember my name. "What's going on?"

"Don't ask!" I said. I led him to the cellar, showed him the machine and shrugged. "I can't even get near the dreadful thing without setting off all kinds of lasers and Arthur's at one of those weird conventions of his. He gets into discussions and he's impossible to locate."

Bernstein looked the contraption over from a safe distance. "Fascinating. And you say it's brought back all the great composers of Western music?"

"Yes, and you were the last one through."

"How very flattering," he said with the famous Bernstein smile, "but I was sort of looking forward to a rest, you know. Harps, and things, but no conducting, no piano."

"You'll have to fight Chopin, Beethoven and Liszt for it," I told him. "Bach's taken over the Moog, Puccini and Verdi have the VCR and the operatic crowd's got the TV set. Haydn and Handel refuse to work unless they get paid, but Mozart and Beethoven have filled about ten notebooks, and I'm running out of music paper."

"Judy, darling, I'm sure we will all find a way to get back to our proper places. In the meanwhile, do you mind introducing me? I've only had a passing acquaintance with some of your guests, but Copeland should be here, and Charles Ives. If they're not great musicians, who is?"

Oh, grand. I was now being lectured for my lack of musical taste by a dead composer. I heard the front doorbell, and ran with dread in my heart. The cops had heard the noise and were complaining, although compared with some of the other doings on that block, my houseful of deceased musicians was nothing. The maids were back, with their exorcist? I wondered if anything could get worse.

It could. My son had arrived with that gang of biker-outlaw rejects that he calls a band.

You'd think with an upbringing like his, instruction in the best music, Young People's Concerts at Carnegie Hall, Juilliard School training, he'd be at least a concert pianist. Concert yes . . . pianist? That's not my opinion! Not even good jazz! He's lead vocals and keyboard with a rock group that changes its name and personnel every so often. Right now they call themselves Whips'n'chains, and their bus was taking up most of the space in front of my house.

Fred's a nice boy, under the tattoos and the leather pants. He kissed me on the cheek and stomped into the hall. That's when he saw Bernstein and stopped dead.

"Mom?" he asked uncertainly.

"There are more of them," I said. The gang traipsed in, and Old met New with a resounding thud.

"Hey, man, there's an old dude up here laying out charts like no one's business!" came trickling down from the fifth floor.

"Bach," I said, in answer to Fred's look.

A frenzied thumping on the bathroom door. "Richard, get the hell out of that bathtub! The rest of us want to piss!"

"I get my best ideas in the tub!"

"My best ideas will soon be watering your best ideas if you don't get out of there!"

"Liszt and Wagner," I explained.

"Chère Madame, the bread has not arrived, and we are out of coffee again."

"Herr Haydn, my son, Fred."

Haydn looked at the leather pants, bare chest and tattoos. "You have my sincere sympathy, Madame."

"Uh . . . I was going to ask if I could dump the guys here for the night, but I see you've got a full house," Fred said. His eyes bugged out as Mozart and Chopin swished past, decked out in his father's early-seventies finery. Close after came Tchaikovsky (I had to keep an eye on him all the time whenever Chopin was near).

"Fred, isn't it?" Trust Lenny to remember a name. "Do you happen to have your equipment with you?"

"Sure. It's in the bus. You're Leonard Bernstein. I thought you were dead."

"I am supposed to be. However, there seems to be a problem about that."

"You know," I said slowly, "I've been thinking about this thing in the basement. All of you have appeared as you were at the height of your powers, when you wrote your greatest master-pieces. This machine must be manufacturing these images using some kind of hologrammatic projector."

"Like on *Star Trek*," Fred put in.

"Exactly," I said. "Your father was working on something that would approximate that holodeck thing."

Fred tugged at his earring. "I suppose it plugs in somewhere. Maybe we could get close enough to it to unplug it?"

"Unplug it? I can't get near it!" I told him. "I tried, and one of the fail-safes went off. No way will I touch that thing until Arthur gets back."

Fred dragged his band out of their conferences with the other musicians and hauled the lot of them back to the cellar, where everyone stared at the machine, while it glittered, sparkled and blinked.

"So that is what brought us here," Borodin said. He'd been a chemist, after all.

"And it won't let us go back," complained Vivaldi. "I don't like it here."

"The cigars aren't bad, but the beer stinks," contributed Brahms.

"And they have no idea how to play the piano properly." This from Chopin. "The touch of bull elephants."

"It's not so bad," from Puccini. "At least the sopranos look like women."

"So do the tenors," said Rossini snidely.

"Gentlemen . . . and Madame Schumann . . ." Bernstein

said. "I may have a way to get us back to wherever we were when we came here."

"If we can't unplug it, and we can't shake it . . ." I suddenly realized what he had in mind. "You don't mean . . . ?"

"I certainly do," Bernstein said.

"What about the neighbors? And the police?" I had horrible visions of blowing every fuse in lower Manhattan with what he had in mind.

"Desperate times call for desperate measures," he said grandly. "Fred, get your crew together."

"Lenny Bernstein, yes?" Kurt Weill recognized him. "Did you ever write that Romeo and Juliet thing?"

"Yes, but we can discuss that later, when we're back . . . wherever we are. Right now I think we must go to the front hall. Fred, you and the band set up right here in the basement. Amps, woofers, subwoofers, the lot."

"It'll take some time," Fred said. He looked at his techies. They shrugged.

"We can't go beyond the door," Brahms complained.

"Then at least we can help with the equipment once it's inside," Bernstein said. "According to Judy, someone's due in two hours, and I don't want it to be anyone I know."

So we all schlepped (even Chopin, who claimed to be too aristocratic, and Wagner, who insisted that a genius should be above all this manual labor) and set up the band in record time.

Whips'n'chains got set for the concert of their lives. I flipped madly through every *Music News* I had to see who was doing what, and if anyone who would qualify for the front closet was in danger. Would Arthur be guilty of murder if his machine took someone out?

The music (if that's your taste) started. Fred whanged out his latest hit, "Eggs on the Planet," which he insists is a protest against the destruction of the rain forest. I still think it sounds like cats and crocodiles mating in a boiler factory. I could feel the vibrations inside my eardrums as the amps amped and the woofers woofed. Beethoven took off his hearing aid, but he still looked uncomfortable as the lead guitarist zipped up and down the scales.

"Louder!" Bernstein yelled over the wail of the guitars. The drummer started his riffs. The bass guitar did a solo. The whole house started to vibrate. I wondered if the bedrock on which the house stood would crack with the strain.

And then I was alone, except for Fred and Whips'n'chains. The machine was dark. The band stopped. There was silence. Blessed, blessed silence. And in the silence, I heard Arthur's voice: "Hey, is anyone home?"

Fred, the boys and I climbed out of the cellar. Arthur met us in the kitchen.

"Aw, you spoiled my surprise. I was going to show it to you when I got back. It works on videotapes and I programmed it with that *History of Music* . . ." He looked at the kitchen, with its mountains of chicken bones and empty beer and wine bottles and piles of dishes. "Have some company over while I was away?"

I took a deep breath, counted to ten, and let it out. "Arthur," I said, "did you deliberately leave that . . . that *thing* turned on all weekend?"

Arthur looked both sheepish and gleeful. "I wasn't even sure it would work," he admitted.

"Oh, it works," I told him.

Arthur said, "There's a lot of money in that machine."

I led him out of the kitchen. "Arthur, maybe you'd better think it through again. There's more to a genius than his or her creations, you know. And geniuses aren't all that easy to live with."

"Oh. I could rework the program." He brightened up and looked at his paintings. Arthur may not know much about music, but his taste in art is impeccable, if you run to abstract. We have an original Klee drawing, a couple of numbered Picasso prints, and some early paintings by people who later got to hang in the Museum of Modern Art. "Musicians might have been too hard. Maybe artists . . ."

He wandered through the kitchen and down to the workroom. I sincerely hoped that Fred's concert had fused every fuse in that thing. If not . . . perhaps I could persuade Whips'n'chains to make our house their permanent headquarters.

Isaac Asimov

Obituary

The scientist in this little-known tale by the late, very great ISAAC
ASIMOV *may not be mad, but he's certainly irascible. Isaac (everyone in the business was welcome to call him by his first name)
wrote hundreds of works of science-fact, but he is likely to be
best known for his series of Foundation science-fiction novels, as
well as* The Caves of Steel, The Naked Sun *and his other remarkable "robot" novels and short stories.*

MY HUSBAND, Lancelot, always reads the paper at breakfast.
What I see of him, when he first appears, is his lean, abstracted
face, carrying its perpetual look of angry and slightly puzzled
frustration. He doesn't greet me, and the newspaper, carefully
unfolded in readiness for him, goes up before his face.

Thereafter, there is only his arm, emerging from behind the
paper for a second cup of coffee into which I have carefully
placed the necessary level teaspoonful of sugar—neither heaping
nor deficient, under pain of a stinging glare.

I am no longer sorry for this. It makes for a quiet meal, at least.

However, on this morning, the quiet was broken when Lancelot barked out abruptly, "Good Lord! That fool, Paul Farber is
dead. Stroke!"

I just barely recognized the name. Lancelot had mentioned him
on occasion, so I knew him as a colleague; as another theoretical
physicist. From my husband's exasperated epithet, I felt reason-

ably sure he was a moderately famous one who had achieved the success that had eluded Lancelot.

He put down the paper and stared at me angrily. "Why do they fill obituaries with such lying trash?" he demanded. "They make him out to be a second Einstein for no better reason than that he died of a stroke."

If there was one subject I had learned to avoid, it was that of obituaries. I dared not even nod agreement.

He threw down the paper and walked away and out the room, leaving his eggs half-finished and his second cup of coffee untouched.

I sighed. What else could I do? What else could I ever do?

Of course, my husband's name isn't really Lancelot Stebbins, because I am changing names and circumstances, as far as I can, to protect the guilty. However, the point is that even if I used real names you would not recognize my husband.

Lancelot had a talent in that respect; a talent for being passed over, for going unnoticed. His discoveries are invariably anticipated, or blurred by a greater discovery made simultaneously. At scientific conventions, his papers are poorly attended because another paper of greater importance is being given in another section.

Naturally, this has had its effect on him. It has changed him.

When I first married him, twenty-five years ago, he was a sparkling catch. He was well-to-do through inheritance and already a trained physicist with intense ambition and great promise. As for myself, I believe I was pretty then, but that did not last. What did last was my introversion and my failure to be the kind of social success an ambitious young faculty-member needs for a wife.

Perhaps that was part of Lancelot's talent for going unnoticed. Had he married another kind of wife, she might have made him visible in her radiation.

Did he realize that himself after a while? Was that why he grew away from me after the first two or three reasonably happy years? Sometimes I believed this and bitterly blamed myself.

But then I would think it was only his thirst for fame, which grew for being unslaked. He left his position on the faculty and built a laboratory of his own far outside town, for the sake, he said, of cheap land and of isolation.

Money was no problem. In his field, the government was generous with its grants and those he could always get. On top of that, he used our own money without limit.

I tried to withstand him. I said, "But it's not necessary, Lancelot. It's not as though we have financial worries. It's not as though they're not willing to let you remain on the university staff. All I want are children and a normal life."

But there was a burning inside him that blinded him to everything else. He turned angrily on me. "There is something that must come first. The world of science must recognize me for what I am; for a—a—great investigator."

At that time, he still hesitated to apply the term, genius, to himself.

It didn't help. The fall of chance remained always and perpetually against him. His laboratory hummed with work; he hired assistants at excellent salaries; he drove himself roughly and pitilessly. Nothing came of it.

I kept hoping he would give up someday; return to the city; allow us to lead a normal, quiet life. I waited, but always when he might have admitted defeat, some new battle would be taken up, some new attempt to storm the bastions of fame. Each time he charged with such hope and fell back in such despair.

And always he turned on me; for if he was ground down by the world, he could always grind me in return. I am not a brave person, but I was coming to believe I must leave him.

And yet—

In this last year he had obviously been girding himself for another battle. A last one, I thought. There was something about him more intense, more a-quiver than I had ever seen before. There was the way he murmured to himself and laughed briefly at nothing. There were the times he went for days without food and nights without sleep. He even took to keeping laboratory notebooks in a bedroom safe as though he feared his own assistants.

Of course I was fatalistically certain that this attempt of his would fail, also. But surely, if it failed, then at his age, he would have to recognize that his last chance had gone. Surely he would have to give up.

So I decided to wait, as patiently as I could.

But the affair of the obituary at breakfast came as something of a jolt. Once, on an earlier occasion of the sort, I had remarked that at least he could count on a certain amount of recognition in his own obituary.

I suppose it wasn't a very clever remark, but then my remarks never are. I had meant it to be lighthearted, to pull him out of a gathering depression during which I knew, from experience, he would be most intolerable.

And perhaps there had been a little unconscious spite in it, too. I cannot honestly say.

At any rate, he turned full on me. His lean body shook and his dark eyebrows pulled down over his deep-set eyes as he shrieked at me in falsetto, "But I'll never read my obituary. I'll be deprived even of that."

And he spat at me. He deliberately spat at me.

I ran to my bedroom.

He never apologized, but after a few days in which I avoided him completely, we carried on our frigid life as before. Neither of us ever referred to the incident during that time.

Now there was another obituary.

Somehow, as I sat there alone at the breakfast table, I felt it to be the last straw for him; the climax of his long-drawn-out failure.

I could sense a crisis coming and didn't know whether to fear or welcome it. Perhaps, on the whole, I would welcome it. Any change could not fail to be a change for the better . . .

Shortly before lunch, he came upon me in the living room, where a basket of unimportant sewing gave my hands something to do and a bit of television occupied my mind.

He said, abruptly, "I will need your help."

It had been twenty years or more since he had said anything

like that and, involuntarily, I thawed toward him. He looked unhealthily excited. There was a flush on his ordinarily pale cheeks.

I said, "Gladly, if there's something I can do."

"There is. I have given my assistants a month's vacation. They will leave Saturday and after that you and I will work alone in the laboratory. I tell you now so that you refrain from making any other arrangements for the coming week."

I shrivelled a bit. "But Lancelot, you know I can't help you with your work. I don't understand—"

"I know that," he said, with complete contempt. "But you don't have to understand my work. You need only follow a few simple instructions and follow them carefully. The point is that I have discovered something, finally, which will put me where I belong—"

"Oh, Lancelot," I said, involuntarily, for I had heard this before a number of times.

"Listen to me, you fool, and for once try to behave like an adult. This time I have done it. No one can anticipate me this time because my discovery is based on such an unorthodox concept that no physicist alive but myself is genius enough to think of it—not for a generation at least. And when my work bursts on the world, I could be recognized as the greatest name of all time in science."

"I'm sure I'm very glad for you, Lancelot."

"I said I *could* be recognized. I could not be, also. There is a great deal of injustice in the assignment of scientific credit. I've learned that often enough. So it will not be enough merely to announce the discovery. If I do, everyone will crowd into the field and after a while, I'll just be a name in the history books, with glory spread out over a number of Johnny-come-latelies."

I think the only reason he was talking to me then, three days before he could get to work on whatever it was he planned to do was that he could no longer contain himself. He bubbled over and I was the only one who was nonentity enough to be witness to that.

He said, "I intend my discovery to be so dramatized, to break on mankind with so thunderous a clap, that there will be no room for anyone else to be mentioned in the same breath with me, ever."

He was going too far, and I was afraid of the effect of another disappointment on him. Might it not drive him mad? I said, "But Lancelot, why need we bother? Why don't we leave all this? Why not take a long vacation? You have worked hard enough and long enough, Lancelot. Perhaps we can take a trip to Europe. I've always wanted to—"

He stamped his foot. "*Will* you stop your foolish meowing? Saturday, you will come into my laboratory with me."

I slept poorly for the next three nights. He had never been quite like this before, I thought; never quite as bad. Might he not be mad already, perhaps?

It could be madness now, I thought, a madness born of disappointment no longer endurable, and sparked by the obituary. He had never allowed me in the laboratory before. Surely he meant to do something to me, to make me the subject of some insane experiment, or to kill me outright.

They were miserable, frightened nights.

But then morning would come and I would think, surely, he wasn't mad; surely, he wouldn't offer me violence. Even the spitting incident was not truly violent and he had never actually tried to hurt me physically.

So in the end I waited, and on Saturday I walked to what might be my death as meekly as a chicken. Together, silently, we walked down the path that led from our dwelling to the laboratory.

The laboratory was frightening just in itself, and I stepped about gingerly, but Lancelot only said, "Oh, stop staring about you as though something were going to hurt you. You just do as I say and look where I tell you."

"Yes, Lancelot." He had led me into a small room, the door of which had been padlocked. It was almost choked with objects of very strange appearance and with a great deal of wiring.

Lancelot said, "To begin with, do you see this iron crucible?"

"Yes, Lancelot." It was a small but deep container made out of thick metal and rusted in spots on the outside. It was covered by a coarse wire netting.

He urged me toward it and I saw that inside it was a white mouse with its front paws up on the inner side of the crucible and its small snout at the wire netting in quivering curiosity, or perhaps in anxiety. I am afraid I jumped, for to see a mouse without expecting to is startling, at least to me.

Lancelot growled, "It won't hurt you. Now just back against the wall and watch me."

My fears returned most forcefully. I grew horribly certain that from somewhere a lightning bolt would shoot out and incinerate me or some monstrous thing of metal might emerge and crush me; or—or—

I closed my eyes.

But nothing happened; to me, at least. I heard only a *ph-f-ft*, as though a small firecracker had misfired, and Lancelot said to me, "Well?"

I opened my eyes. He was looking at me, fairly shining with pride. I stared blankly.

He said, "Here, don't you see it, you idiot? Right here."

A foot to one side of the crucible was a second one. I hadn't seen him put it there.

"Do you mean this second crucible?" I asked.

"It isn't quite a second crucible, but a duplicate of the first crucible. For all ordinary purposes, they are the same crucible, atom for atom. Compare them. You'll find the rust marks identical."

"You made the second one out of the first?"

"Yes, but in a special way. To create matter would require a prohibitive amount of energy, ordinarily. It would take the complete fission of a hundred grams of uranium to create one gram of duplicate matter, even granting perfect efficiency. The great secret I have stumbled on is that the duplication of an object at a point in future time requires very little energy if that energy is applied correctly. The essence of the feat, my—my dear, in my creating such a duplicate and bringing it back, is that I have accomplished the equivalent of time travel."

It was the measure of his triumph and happiness that he actually used an affectionate term in speaking to me.

"Isn't that remarkable?" I said, for to tell the truth, I *was* impressed. "Did the mouse come, too?"

I looked inside the second crucible as I asked that and got another nasty shock. It contained a white mouse; a dead white mouse.

Lancelot turned faintly pink. "That is a shortcoming. I can bring back living matter, but not as living matter. It comes back dead."

"Oh, what a shame. Why?"

"I don't know yet. I imagine the duplications are completely perfect on the atomic scale. Certainly, there is no visible damage. Dissections show nothing wrong."

"You might ask—" I stopped myself quickly as he glanced at me. I decided I had better not suggest a collaboration of any sort, for I knew from experience that in that case the collaborator would invariably get all the credit for the discovery.

Lancelot said, with sour amusement, "I *have* asked. A trained biologist has performed autopsies on some of my animals and found nothing. Of course, they didn't know where the animal came from and I took care to take it back before anything would happen to give it away. Lord, even my assistants don't know what I've been doing."

"But why must you keep it so secret?"

"Just because I can't bring objects back alive. Some subtle molecular derangement. If I published my results, someone else might learn the method of preventing such derangement, add his slight improvement to my basic discovery, and achieve a greater fame, because he would bring back a living man who might give information about the future."

I saw that quite well. Nor need he say it "might" be done. It would be done. Inevitably. In fact, no matter what he did, he would lose the credit. I was sure of it.

"However," he went on, more to himself than to me, "I can wait no longer. I must announce this, but in such a way that it will be indelibly and permanently associated with me. There must be a drama about it so effective that thereafter there will be no way of mentioning time travel without mentioning me, no matter what other men may do in the future. I am going to prepare that drama and you will play a part in it."

"But what do you want me to do, Lancelot?"

"You'll be my widow."

I clutched at his arm. "Lancelot, do you mean—" I cannot quite analyze the conflicting feelings that upset me at that moment.

He disengaged himself roughly. "Only temporarily. I am not committing suicide. I am simply going to bring myself back from three days in the future."

"But you'll be dead, then."

"Only the 'me' that is brought back. The real 'me' will be as alive as ever. Like that mouse." His eyes shifted to a dial and he said, "Ah. Zero time in a few seconds. Watch the second crucible and the dead mouse."

Before my eyes, it disappeared and there was a *ph-f-ft* sound again.

"Where did it go?"

"Nowhere," said Lancelot. "It was only a duplicate. The moment we passed that instant in time at which the duplicate was formed, it naturally disappeared. It was the first mouse that was the original, and it remains, alive and well. The same will be true of me. A duplicate 'me' will come back dead. The original 'me' will be alive. After three days, we will come to the instant at which the duplicate 'me' was formed, using the real 'me' as a model, and sent back dead. Once we pass that instant, the dead duplicate 'me' will disappear and the live 'me' will remain. Is that clear?"

"It sounds dangerous."

"It isn't. Once my dead body appears, the doctor will pronounce me dead, the newspapers will report me dead, the undertaker will prepare to bury the dead. I will then return to life and announce how I did it. When that happens, I will be more than the discoverer of time travel; I will be the man who came back from the dead. Time travel and Lancelot Stebbins will be publicized so thoroughly and so intermingled, that nothing will extricate my name from the thought of time travel ever again."

"Lancelot," I said softly, "Why can't we just announce your discovery? This is too elaborate a plan. A simple announcement will make you famous enough and then we can move to the city perhaps—"

"*Quiet!* You will do what I say."

I don't know how long Lancelot was thinking of all this before the obituary actually brought matters to a head. Of course, I don't minimize his intelligence. Despite his phenomenally bad luck, there is no questioning his brilliance.

He had informed his assistants before they had left of the experiments he intended to conduct while they were gone. Once they testified, it would seem quite natural that he should be bent over a particular set of reacting chemicals and that he should be dead of cyanide poisoning.

"So you see to it that the police get in touch with my assistants at once. You know where they can be reached. I want no hint of murder or suicide, or anything but accident, natural and logical accident. I want a quick death certificate from the doctor, a quick notification to the newspapers."

I said, "But Lancelot, what if they find the real you?"

"Why should they?" he snapped. "If you find a corpse, do you start searching for the living replica, also? No one will look for me and I will stay quietly in the temporal chamber for the interval. There are toilet facilities and I can bring in enough sandwich fixings to keep me."

He added regretfully, "I'll have to make do without coffee, though, till it's over. I can't have anyone smelling unexplained coffee here while I'm supposed to be dead . . . Well, there's plenty of water and it's only three days."

I clasped my hands nervously and said, "Even if they do find you, won't it be the same thing anyway? There'll be a dead 'you' and a living 'you'—" It was myself I was trying to console; myself I was trying to prepare for the inevitable disappointment.

But he turned on me, shouting. "No, it won't be the same thing at all. It will all become a hoax that failed. I'll be famous, but only as a fool."

"But, Lancelot," I said, cautiously, "something always goes wrong."

"Not this time."

"But you always say 'not this time,' and yet something *always*—"

He was white with rage and his irises showed clear all about their circle. He caught my elbow and hurt it terribly but I dared not cry out. He said, "Only one thing can go wrong, and that is *you*. If you give it away, if you don't play your part perfectly, if you don't follow the instructions exactly, I—I—" He seemed to cast about for a punishment. "I'll *kill* you."

I turned my head away in sheer terror and tried to break loose, but he held on grimly. It was remarkable how strong he could be when he was in a passion. He said, "Listen to me! You have done me a great deal of harm by being you, but I have blamed myself for marrying you in the first place and for never finding the time to divorce you in the second. But now I have my chance, despite you, to turn my life into a vast success. If you spoil even that chance, I will kill you. I mean that literally."

I was sure he did. "I'll do everything you say," I whispered, and he let me go.

He spent a day on his machinery. "I've never transported more than a hundred grams before," he said, calmly thoughtful.

I thought: *It won't work. How can it?*

The next day, he adjusted the device to the point where I needed only to close one switch. He made me practice that particular switch on a dead circuit for what seemed an interminable time.

"Do you understand now? Do you see exactly how it is done?"

"Yes."

"Then do it, when this light flashes and not a moment before." *It won't work,* I thought. "Yes," I said.

He took his position and remained in stolid silence. He was wearing a rubber apron over a laboratory jacket.

The light flashed, and the practice turned out to be worthwhile, for I pulled the switch automatically before thought could stop me or even make me waver.

For an instant, there were two Lancelots before me, side by side, the new one dressed as the old one, but more rumpled. And then the new one collapsed and lay still.

"All right," cried the living Lancelot, stepping off the carefully marked spot. "Help me. Grab his legs."

I marvelled at Lancelot. How, without wincing or showing any uneasiness, could he carry his own dead body, his own body of three days in the future? Yet he held it under its arms without showing any more emotion than if it had been a sack of wheat.

I held it by the ankles, my stomach turning at the touch. It was still blood-warm to the touch; freshly dead. Together we carried it through a corridor and up a flight of stairs, down another corridor and into a room. Lancelot had it already arranged. A solution was bubbling in a queer all-glass contraption inside a closed section, with a movable glass door partitioning it off.

Other chemical equipment was scattered about, calculated, no doubt, to show an experiment in progress. A bottle, boldly labelled "Potassium cyanide" was on the desk, prominent among the others. There was a small scattering of crystals on the desk near it; cyanide, I presumed.

Carefully, Lancelot crumpled the dead body as though it had fallen off the stool. He placed crystals on the body's left hand and more on the rubber apron; finally, a few on the body's chin.

"They'll get the idea," he muttered.

A last look-around and he said, "All right. Go back to the

house now and call the doctor. Your story is that you came here
to bring me a sandwich because I was working through lunch.
There it is." And he showed me a broken dish and a scattered
sandwich where, presumably, I had dropped it. "Do a little
screaming, but don't overdo it."

It was not difficult for me to scream when the time came, or to
weep. I had felt like doing both for days, and now it was a relief
to let the hysteria out.

The doctor behaved precisely as Lancelot had said he would.
The bottle of cyanide was virtually the first thing he saw. He
frowned. "Dear me, Mrs. Stebbins, he was a careless chemist."

"I suppose so," I said, sobbing. "He shouldn't have been working himself, but both his assistants are on vacation."

"When a man treats cyanide as though it were salt, it's bad."
The doctor shook his head in grave moralistic fashion. "Now,
Mrs. Stebbins, I will have to call the police. It's accidental cyanide
poisoning, but it's a violent death and the police—"

"Oh, yes, yes, call them." And then I could almost have beaten
myself for having sounded suspiciously eager.

The police came, and along with them a police surgeon, who
grunted in disgust at the cyanide crystals on hand, apron, and
chin. The police were thoroughly disinterested, asked only statis-
tical questions concerning names and ages. They asked if I could
manage the funeral arrangments. I said yes, and they left.

I then called the newspapers, and two of the press associations.
I said I thought they would be picking up news of the death from
the police records and I hoped they would not stress the fact that
my husband was a careless chemist, with the tone of one who
hoped nothing ill would be said of the dead. After all, I went on,
he was a nuclear physicist rather than a chemist, and I had a
feeling lately he might be in some sort of trouble.

I followed Lancelot's line exactly in this, and it worked. A
nuclear physicist in trouble? Spies? Soviet agents?

The reporters began to come eagerly. I gave them a youthful
portrait of Lancelot and a photographer took pictures of the lab-

oratory building. I took them through a few rooms of the main laboratory for more pictures. No one, neither the police nor the reporters, asked questions about the bolted room or even seemed to notice it.

I gave them a mass of professional and biographical material that Lancelot had made ready for me, and told several anecdotes designed to show a combination of humanity and brilliance. In everything I tried to be letter-perfect and yet I could feel no confidence. Something would go wrong; *something* would go wrong.

And when it did, I knew he would blame me. And this time, he had promised to kill me.

The next day I brought him the newspapers. Over and over again, he read them, eyes glittering. He had made a full box on the lower left of *The New York Times*'s front page. The *Times* played down the mystery of his death and so did the A.P., but one of the tabloids had a front-page headline: ATOM SAVANT IN MYSTERY DEATH.

He laughed aloud as he read that, and when he completed all of them, he turned back to the first.

He looked up at me sharply. "Don't go. Listen to what they say."

"I've read them already, Lancelot."

"Listen, I tell you."

He read every one aloud to me, lingering on their praises of the dead, then said to me, aglow with self-satisfaction, "Do you still think something will go wrong?"

I said hesitantly, "If the police come back to ask why I thought you were in trouble—"

"You were vague enough. Tell them you had had bad dreams. By the time they decide to push investigations further, if they do, it will be too late."

To be sure, everything was working, but I could not hope that all would continue so. And yet the human mind is odd; it will persist in hoping even when it cannot hope.

I said, "Lancelot, when this is all over and you are famous, really famous—then after that, surely you can retire. We can go back to the city and live quietly."

"You are an imbecile. Don't you see that once I am recognized, I *must* continue. Young men will flock to me. This laboratory will become a great Institution of Temporal Investigation. I'll become a legend in my lifetime. I will pile my greatness so high that no one afterward will ever be able to be anything but an intellectual dwarf compared to me—" He raised himself on tip-toes, eyes shining, as though he already saw the pedestal onto which he would be raised.

It had been my last hope of some personal shreds of happiness, and a small one. I sighed.

I asked the undertaker that the body be allowed to remain in its coffin in the laboratories before burial in the Stebbins family plot on Long Island. I asked that it remain unembalmed, offering to keep it in a large refrigerated room with the temperature set at 40. I asked that it not be removed to the funeral home.

The undertaker brought the coffin to the laboratory in frigid disapproval. No doubt this was reflected in the eventual bill. My offered explanation that I wanted him near me for a last period of time and that I wanted his assistants given a chance to view the body was lame and sounded lame.

Still, Lancelot had been most specific in what I was to say.

Once the dead body was laid out, with the coffin lid still open, I went to see Lancelot.

"Lancelot," I said, "the undertaker was quite displeased. I think he suspects that something odd is going on."

"Good," said Lancelot, with satisfaction.

"But—"

"We need wait only one more day. Nothing will be brought to a head out of mere suspicion before then. Tomorrow morning the body will disappear. Or should."

"You mean it might not?" *I knew it; I knew it.*

"There could be some delay, or some prematurity. I have never transported anything this heavy and I'm not certain how exactly my equations hold. To make the necessary observation is one reason I want the body here and not in a funeral parlor."

"But in the funeral parlor it would disappear before witnesses."

"And here you think they will suspect trickery?"

"Of course."

He seemed amused. "They will say: Why did he send his assistants away? Why did he run experiments himself that any child could perform and yet manage to kill himself running them? Why did the dead body happen to disappear without witnesses? They will say: There is nothing to this absurd story of time travel. He took drugs to throw himself in a cataleptic trance and doctors were hoodwinked."

"Yes," I said faintly. How did he come to understand all that?

"And," he went on, "when I continue to insist I have solved time travel and that I was indisputably pronounced dead and am now indisputably alive, orthodox scientists will heatedly denounce me as a fraud. Why, in one week, I will have become a household name to every man on Earth. They will talk of nothing else. I will offer to make a demonstration of time travel before any group of scientists who wish to see it. I will offer to make the demonstration on an intercontinental TV circuit. Public pressure will force scientists to attend, and the networks to give permission. It doesn't matter whether people will watch hoping for a miracle or for a lynching. They will watch! And *then* I will succeed, and who in science will ever have had a more transcendent climax to his life?"

I was dazzled for a moment, but something was unmoved within me, something said: Too long, too complicated; something will go wrong.

That evening, his assistants arrived, and tried to be respectfully grieving in the presence of the corpse. Two more witnesses to swear they had seen Lancelot dead; two more witnesses to confuse the issue and help build events to their stratospheric peak.

By four the next morning, we were in the cold-room, bundled in overcoats and waiting for zero moment.

Lancelot, in high excitement, kept checking his instruments and doing I-know-not-what with them. His desk computer was working constantly, though how he could make his cold fingers jiggle the keys so nimbly, I am at a loss to say.

I, myself, was quite miserable. There was the cold, the dead body in the coffin, the uncertainty of the future.

We had been there for what seemed an eternity, and finally Lancelot said, "It will work. It will work as predicted. At the most, disappearance will be five minutes late, and this when seventy kilograms of mass are involved. My analysis of chronous forces is masterly indeed." He smiled at me, but he also smiled at his own corpse with equal warmth.

I noticed that his lab jacket, which he had been wearing constantly for three days now, sleeping in it I am certain, had become wrinkled and shabby. It was about as it had seemed upon the second Lancelot, the dead one, when it had appeared.

Lancelot seemed to be aware of my thoughts, or perhaps only of my gaze, for he looked down at his jacket and said, "Ah, yes, I had better put on the rubber apron. My second self was wearing it when it appeared."

"What if you didn't put it on?" I asked tonelessly.

"I would have to. It would be a necessity. Something would have reminded me. Else *it* would not have appeared in one." His eyes narrowed as he tied the apron strings. "Do you still think something will go wrong?"

"I don't know," I mumbled.

"Do you think the body won't disappear or that I'll disappear instead?"

When I didn't answer at all, he said in a half-scream, "Can't you see my luck has changed at last? Can't you see how smoothly and according to plan it is all working out? I will be the greatest man who ever lived . . . Come, heat up the water for the coffee." He was suddenly calm again. "It will serve as celebration when my double leaves us and I return to life. I haven't had any coffee for three days."

It was only instant coffee he pushed in my direction, but after three days that, too, would serve. I fumbled at the laboratory hotplate with my cold fingers until Lancelot pushed me roughly to one side and set a beaker of water upon it.

"It'll take a while," he said, turning the control to high. He looked at his watch then at various dials on the wall. "My double will be gone before the water boils. Come here and watch." He stepped to the side of the coffin.

I hesitated. "Come," he said, peremptorily.

I came.

He looked down at himself with infinite pleasure and waited. We both waited, staring at a corpse.

There was the *ph-f-ft* sound and Lancelot cried out, "Less than two minutes off."

Without a blur or a wink, the dead body was gone.

The open coffin contained an empty set of clothes. The clothes, of course, had not been those in which the dead body had been brought back. They were real clothes and they stayed in reality. There they now were: underwear within shirt and pants; shirt within tie; tie within jacket. Shoes had turned over, dangling socks from within them. The body was gone.

I could hear water boiling.

"Coffee," said Lancelot. "Coffee first. Then we call the police and the newspapers."

I made the coffee for him and myself. I gave him the usual level teaspoon from the sugar bowl, neither heaping nor deficient. Even under these conditions, when I was sure that for once it wouldn't matter to him, habit was strong.

I sipped at my coffee, which I drank without cream or sugar, as was my habit. Its warmth was most welcome.

He stirred his coffee. "All," he said softly. "All I have waited for." He put the cup to his grimly triumphant lips and drank.

Those were his last words.

Now that it was over, there was a kind of frenzy in me. I managed to strip him and dress him in the clothing from the coffin.

Somehow I was able to heave his weight upward and place him in the coffin. I folded his arms across his chest as they had been.

I then washed out every trace of coffee in the sink in the room outside, and the sugar-bowl, too. Over and over again I rinsed, until all the cyanide, which I had substituted for the sugar, was gone.

I carried his laboratory jacket and other clothes to the hamper where I had stored those the double had brought back. The second set had disappeared, of course, and I put the first set there.

Next I waited.

By that evening, I was sure the corpse was cold enough, and called the undertakers. Why should they wonder? They expected a dead body and there was the dead body. The same dead body. Really the same body. It even had cyanide in it as the first was supposed to have.

I suppose they might still be able to tell the difference between a body dead twelve hours and one dead three and a half days, even under refrigeration—but why should they dream of looking?

They didn't. They nailed down the coffin, took him away and buried him. It was the perfect murder.

As a matter of fact, since Lancelot was legally dead at the time I killed him, I wonder if, strictly speaking, it was murder at all. Of course, I don't intend to ask a lawyer about this.

Life is quiet for me now; peaceful and contented. I have money enough. I attend the theatre. I have made friends.

And I live without remorse. To be sure, Lancelot will never receive credit for time travel. Someday when time travel is discovered again, the name of Lancelot Stebbins will rest in Stygian unrecognized darkness. But then, I told him that whatever his plans, he would end without the credit. If I hadn't killed him, something else would have spoiled things, and then he would have killed me.

No, I live without remorse.

In fact, I have forgiven Lancelot everything; everything but that moment when he spat at me. So it is rather ironic that he did have one happy moment before he died, for he was given a gift few could have, and he, above all men, savored it.

Despite his bitter words that time he spat at me, Lancelot did manage to read his own obituary.

Jay Sheckley

One-Shot Beamish
and His Wonderful Feminals

JAY SHECKLEY *has worked as a newspaper editor, mistletoe distributor, writing instructor, hot-tub (women only) hypnotherapist, book publicist, artist and designer of humorous bumper stickers ("Gefilte" and forty other fish); was top earner at the 1992 San Francisco AIDS Dance-a-Thon and is co-owner of the Dark Carnival Bookstore in Berkeley, California. Her work has appeared in* Gallery, Heavy Metal, National Lampoon, Night Cry, Pulpsmith, Twilight Zone, Weird Tales *and the anthologies,* Devils and Demons, Fantasy and Terror *and* Total Abandon.

CAUTION: "One-Shot Beamish and His Wonderful Feminals" combines science-fiction with humorous erotica. The latter element, though mild, is sexually explicit.

IN THE LABORATORY'S LAVATORY stood Dr. Donald Beamish, 30. He was a man in trouble, trying to comb his hair. Yesterday it had looked good; now he could not reproduce the style. "One-Shot" Beamish, they'd called him at Stanford. For his thesis he'd synthesized a Denver omelet from sewage. But the publicity-minded dean wanted to see it done—on TV. Live, Beamish failed to cook up the project. He was expelled for fraud until a witness to the first experiment testified that "the sewage changed, but it needed more green peppers." Even now, Beamish was known for the great work he could do—once and only once.

Giving up on his hair, Beamish tried to saunter casually down the hall. He loped like a trained panda. *Why bother?* he thought miserably. *Why not crawl into Grey's office?* Dr. Talbot Grey, Dynamic Laboratories' director of research, had called Beamish to his office to "discuss breach of contract." Beamish could only guess how much Grey knew.

He passed identical doors made cheery by red and yellow signs which said CAUTION: RADIOACTIVE MATERIALS. Eyes almost shut, he was trying to perceive some small grace in the hall-walking process when he bumped into something soft and firm. "Miss Lüstgren!" Beamish declaimed. "Sorry!"

Allison Lüstgren, an excellent lab technician, was an even better distraction. A geneticist once whispered that Allison was Italian, Japanese, and Swedish. That's when Beamish resolved to get an epithelial cell sample from her cheek lining.

"Tsk, tsk, Don," Allison said, waggling a forefinger in mock anger. "You'll get in trouble the way you stumble onto things."

Does she know? Beamish thought.

Allison smiled playfully. "How are my little clones today, Doctor?"

Beamish blanched white as a lab rat.

"You must be doing *something* with my cheek cells," she laughed. "Take care of them." With marvelous attenuation, she walked away down the hall. Beamish turned to watch her departure. Coyly, Allison looked back at him and called, "I loved your hair yesterday!"

Dr. Grey brought the steaming half-liter mug to his lips with one hand while the other pressed the "Brew" button on his desk-side Sir Cafeen machine. The pleasure and pain of administrative duty danced a mad jig in his eyes. "Donald Beamish," Grey announced, "you're in a shaky position."

Beamish nodded. A chrome-framed print caught his eye: magenta swirls did endless innocuous battle with an orange bow tie. Beamish's eyes could not rest there; he looked at his gleeful captor. "Yes, Dr. Grey."

"Don, my boy," Grey countered. "Such formality after three years! Call me Talbot."

"Thank you, Dr. Grey," Beamish said absently.

"All right then, Donald." Grey's smile disappeared into the sinister recesses of his face. "Let's discuss your career." Talking to underlings, Grey pronounced "career" slowly, so it rhymed with "diarrhea." He went on in the same vein. "You, Beamish, are a failure, a flake, and what's worse, a weirdo. Yeah, we can still get grants with you on staff; but what other lab would deal with you? Eh, One-Shot? Two years ago, seven hundred rats were cured of cancer, and we're *still* trying to piece together what you did right. You don't know yet, *do* you?"

Beamish shrugged. "The electricity and the oatmeal—" he began.

"We've been *over* that," Grey said. "It's not a cure until we can make it happen twice. You give me an ulcer!" Grey poured a fresh pint of coffee and started sipping. Above the cup, his eyes grew rounder. "Your contract, Beamish, provides that your work here is the property of Dynamic Labs. All patents bear the Dynamic name. All projects remain on premises. I'm not one to claim that two plus two is four. Not until the facts are in. But when you left the lab yesterday, didn't you drop something?"

Beamish stared at his wing tips.

"I have it on good authority," Grey said, "that your parcel screamed."

Donald Beamish was being followed. From the lab he went to House of Miniatures. At 5:47 he emerged into the rain carrying six identical giftwrapped packages. Then a man in a brown polyester suit tailed him to his apartment complex, but did not go in.

Wilbur Scoggins, 45, was a private investigator. Essentially, he was on a modeling job. It required a simplified sense of justice, a minimal sense of humor, and a face so boring that a suspect sighting him ten times in a day wouldn't be sure. Scoggins was the common man. Thrift-shop clothes fit him. He reminded clerks of a brother or a cousin. He could pass a check anywhere, then fade into the crowd. But Scoggins was on the side of Corporate Order.

Beamish whistled the song "Short People" while he fumbled outside his door. He'd already unlocked the tumblers, and then by error locked them again. For "One-Shot" Beamish, the second time was never the charm. Now, he turned the key precisely, but one of the six parcels slipped from his arms, hitting the floor. He grabbed it up, rushed into his apartment, and bolted the door behind him.

Ah, the sanctuary of his living room! The shelves held pairs of model ships; the first of each pair was beautiful, imaginatively painted and detailed. The second of each set was overworked, ugly, or broken. The TV was on, singing a tampon jingle. From below the TV, delighted squeaks could be heard. This was his finest moment. Until tonight, Beamish never had anything or anyone to come home to. After seeing countless lab tests on cats, dogs—you name it—he found pet animals depressing. And with girls, "One-Shot" invariably made a terminal second impression. But now they ran to him. His six feminals.

They were six inches tall and slim as a thumb. They were feminals—female animals. They were friendly, high-strung, healthy, and completely, voluptuously human. They were a mix of Italian, Japanese, and Swedish. And they loved him.

Like the feminals she had innocently engendered, Allison Lüstgren, 25, had long hair the color of butter. Further, she sported plush full lips, an oval face, and improbable Japanese eyes. Each evening, while Donald Beamish grated cheese for his miniature sextet, his mental Betamax slowly replayed his one time alone with Allison.

They did it in the supply room one drizzly Tuesday in February. Among canisters of disposable lancets he told his lie: "The cells are merely for comparison." But Allison was incomparable. She wore, he'd noted, a hint of maddening perfume. The dull wooden "scraper" had felt like a large Popsicle stick in his nervous hand. "Miss Lüstgren," Beamish remembered whispering, "this will involve opening your mouth." Then her mouth opened, revealing perfect teeth. When he put two fingers on her cheek, he began shaking, physically startled. He hadn't touched anyone, he'd recalled, since Bridget Rackner drank too much and wouldn't let go of his hand at a Christmas party. That same hand held the instrument to Allison now; on it he felt her soft breath. Within, against her resilient fuchsia lining, he dabbed his stick. Three times he tracked across an inch, his hand ionized by her living energy. They both knew only one sample was needed. "That's it, I guess," he'd mumbled afterward, running the tool through a shallow specimen jar. He'd capped it, looked up, and Allison was staring into his eyes. Beamish felt himself falling; he felt his hair follicles attempt a mad dash for the door. She was transcendentally beautiful, and to speak to her again could only spoil things. For "One-Shot," there was no next time. He turned away, letting her cells drop into the pocket over his heart . . .

In the weeks that followed, Beamish worked every spare minute with the cells. As yet another inspiration that Beamish could not repeat, he photoreduced Allison's living genetic pattern, so the tiny female animal itself would have to be patented, rather than the process. Dynamic Labs would not like this. To ensure survival of at least one miniature, the doctor secretly cloned a half-dozen "feminals." In the lab, they flourished and grew; their metabolisms ran like blenders on "Whip." Feminals soon scampered about the steel tables and glass-fronted cabinets while Beamish played them educational tapes. One day, while Beamish was attempting to relearn the photoreduction of living cells, the feminals went swimming in his photographic chemicals. Before he could scold them, the developer solution had aged the feminals. No longer children, they were postadolescent—sexually mature. As a detached, sophisticated biochemist, Beamish was intrigued. They were gorgeous.

Their development was the good news. But the fixative, too, had affected them. They didn't feel good, they said. Beamish filled his desk drawer with cotton balls, and there the feminals rested all June and July, hardly moving. Each night Beamish slept at the lab beneath the desk. *What if they die?* he thought. He could picture his colleagues giddily autopsying the perfect little ladies— fodder for the medical journals. Drowsy under the desk, Beamish would clench his fists. His whole lopsidedly lucky career had led him to these lovelies. He had to keep at least one; he could not give them up.

Then he realized he might not have to. The feminals were re- covering. By mid-August, they'd resumed relay races to the door- jamb. Beamish examined them, one by one, and he learned some- thing: The fixative that almost killed them had stopped all cellular deterioration. Since the accident months before, the feminals had not aged one hour. Now, not only were these the world's only feminals; with proper care they just might be im- mortal.

Beamish waited one week. The feminals seemed completely re- covered and indelible. Then, without excuse, without rationaliza- tion, and certainly without permission, Beamish took them home.

The first three (Cynthia Allison, Donna Allison, and Theresa Allison) he took secretly from the lab. But he slipped up, natu- rally, with the second three. Poor Beamish. He was a clumsy, half-lucky chemist in love—and Grey was on to him.

Beamish wasn't worried about Grey tonight. Oh, he had cause to worry. He had cause to apply for a passport under a false name. But tonight, how could he care? They ran to him—his feminals! Four were naked, two were gussied up in toilet-tissue sarongs. They were tanned from sunbathing on the windowsill.

Beamish sat on the carpet and began unwrapping their gifts: six tiny rocking chairs. All the while they leapt on him, squirming into his pockets, hugging his wrists, his earlobes, and the graying locks of his hair.

One of the rocking chairs was broken; it had fallen in the hall. But the feminals delightedly greeted the five new chairs. In cele- bration, Beamish mixed a rum and Coke. He took a sip, then tipped the glass. The feminals cupped their tiny, slender hands and slurped, giggling at the feel of fizz and syrup and firewater. In the midst of this merriment came a knock at the door.

The feminals scattered. One jumped into Beamish's shirt pocket; the rest ran for the bedroom. Wilbur Scoggins, rain-soaked private eye, was about to peer into Beamish's living room window from the fire escape when he too heard the knock. Scoggins froze in place.

Beamish turned off the TV, crushed the broken rocker, and ran it down the DispozAll. He gathered the other little chairs and hid them in the sink cupboard. His heart pounded louder than the DispozAll. He felt like a madman. Did he remember how to answer a door? He opened it. "Good morning," he said.

"Good evening," said the elderly woman. It was Mrs. Glottle, from 13-Q. He stared at her, half-expecting her body to part like clouds and reveal his fate. There was an itchy silence.

Beamish ventured, "Think it will rain?"

"It's raining now," Mrs. Glottle said. She tilted her head, reexamined him, shrugged, and thrust something into his hands. "This is for you," she said.

Beamish now held a plastic box, six and a half inches by one inch by one inch. One of the long sides was grooved so it could be pried off and reattached. The item was embossed with a wood-grain pattern. Beamish began to shake. This was obviously a miniature cadaver file—a feminal coffin. The lab had it in for them all. Clearly, Mrs. Glottle was planted by Dynamic: cameras, secret sound systems . . .

"You know what it is," she was saying, "don't you, Doctor?" The seconds were of great duration. "Of course you do!" she cried. "It's a waterproof, bugproof, boilable butter dish. A free gift. I'm having a Succorware party at eight. Chips, dips, and a new cookie made with my favorite breakfast cereal. You'll come?"

"I—don't feel well," Beamish said. Sweat was running off his temples into his ears.

"You look terrible," Mrs. Glottle opined. "Yesterday even your hair looked healthier."

After Beamish shut the door, he leaned back against it, feeling weak. Had his knees softened? He stared unseeing at the window. At the same time, Investigator Wilbur Scoggins crept farther along the fire escape, peeked in, and saw the staring man. Scoggins was certain he'd been caught; adrenaline rushed through his body, simulating electrocution.

Then Beamish looked down and smiled. This didn't help Scoggins's nerves. How could he know that Beamish was returning a small smile that began with his breast pocket? "Cynthia Allison," Beamish whispered. Slowly (and to Scoggins, mysteriously), Beamish walked into the bedroom and shut the door.

That night and the next night and the next, Beamish was sexually besieged by the trial-size beauties. The feminals had joy. They had spirit. Arms about each other's waists, they wrapped themselves around his shaft—because they wanted to, and because he liked it.

They licked with tiny tongues, all the while running round and round this nerve center. The special perfume Allison wore in the supply room—a fine perspiration—oiled their smooth torsos with the very scent of girlflesh. When they clutched their slim, strong, tiny legs around him, the feminals were irresistible.

That first time, Beamish imagined that he should stop them. Why, it was almost incestuous, his inventions behaving this way. But when he put on his glasses and reached to extricate the tiny limbs from his person, the sight was too much. Six lovely faces excited and anticipant, the perfect uplift of a dozen breasts against him—these visual stimuli conspired with the teasing pressure until it was all over, all over him; he was awash in his own delight . . .

Dr. Donald Beamish, a sometimes-lucky biochem researcher, lay back on his pillows. The pillows—and each detail of his circumstance—seemed impossibly deluxe. *I'm going bonkers,* he thought, giggling to himself.

The feminals positioned themselves in an oval across his belly and chest; they lay mouth to cunt to mouth to cunt to mouth, etc.

They used pools of semen as lubricant for fingers, and to shine one another's breasts, and to playfully slick back their long, wild hair. They busied themselves happily, while the rain fell and fell, and then they slept.

Beamish would not have believed it, but that week did not go well for him. Friday, Scoggins found something. It was more suggestive than a hair, more conclusive than a footprint, and almost as incriminating as a signed confession. It was the rough draft of a BO application—the patent for bio-organisms.

"It fell out of his pocket," Wilbur Scoggins said. He hovered around Dr. Grey, waiting for the Medal of Honor.

"You're in my light," Grey said.

"Beamish had just crossed Main Street midblock during Don't Walk," Scoggins reported. "Then he went into the Minibigmart."

"This is his handwriting," Grey said. "Awful."

"I chased it for blocks," Scoggins enthused. "Crazy wind. If it hadn't stuck on that dog turd—"

"Dog *dropping?*" Grey's face pruned at the thought. He removed his hand from the pages, separated them with two fingers, then smelled the fingers.

"All in a day's work," Scoggins said humbly.

"Will you pipe down!" Grey shouted. "Don't you know what this *is?*"

Scoggins retracted into professionalism. He pressed his lips together and directed his best clue-seeking eyes at the administrator.

Grey's fist slammed the desk. Coffee spilled, flowing across the papers, while the radio gushed a Muzak version of "You Light Up My Life." "You've been tricked!" Grey yelled over the mood music. The inoffensive art print rattled against the wall.

Then, impressed with the density of the man he addressed, Grey explained, "Since the decision to allow organism patents, it's a standing gag: To make a million, all you have to do is patent *the girl.* This patent is based, it claims, on the molecular particulars of one Allison Lüstgren, a frequently *studied* lab tech here—if you get what I'm saying." Grey frowned in acid response to base frivolity. With one motion, he swilled down his coffee dregs and assembled a new gallon. "If you can keep one thing in mind, Scoggins," he said, "let it be this: *You can't patent a girl!*"

"No, no!" Donna Allison laughed. "Give me ten minutes. We're making a surprise. Come on, Donny, close the door!"

"Ten minutes," Beamish allowed. "Then I'm coming in."

"Yeah! Yeah!" the feminals cried. "It's a surprise." Slowly, Beamish shut the bedroom door.

Ever since the advent of feminals in his life, Beamish was at the gates of terminal anxiety. *Six of them,* he often thought, *six.* Who could keep track? He feared crushing little bodies in the door or locking one in the refrigerator. At night he kept waking, terrified he'd rolled over and killed someone. What if he broke a tiny leg? He imagined bringing a feminal to the emergency room—there'd be riots.

In crazy daydreams he imagined himself atop a sturdy full-sized girl. Just yesterday, in Dynamic's infamous "Cafeteria Employees Only," he had watched Allison Lüstgren in line ahead of him. She bought a cheese sandwich and Coke: the feminals' favorite meal! At this, it occurred more to his body than to his mind that he knew every centimeter of lovely Ms. Lüstgren's topography. He gave her a thorough once-over that made them both blush. She was just the size to—*mustn't think about that.* He, after all, had the *six* most beautiful—er, roommates. Not that he dared consummate the bigamy. Trigamy? Sexamy? Late last night he had considered taking feminal virginity with a new glass thermometer. But no, the idea was monstrous. Instead, he banned them from his bed, pleading exhaustion. The resultant tears were too much for worn-out One-Shot. Finally, he had sworn he didn't mean any of it. If only he could give them away like kittens. In love though he was, Beamish felt irrevocably married by circumstance.

From behind the door, feminal shouts were almost decipherable. They never had to whisper; their normal tone was like the distant hush of the sea. Now, Beamish tried to listen to the traffic, or the building's mysterious hums. But like a new mother, his ears were cued to his little ones' breaths. He heard them shouting. But shouting what?

Something didn't seem cricket. Beamish's first impulse was to fling open the door. Certainly his first impulses were his redeeming feature. But Donald Beamish had promised little Donna Allison that he would wait.

At 5:30 A.M., five feminals stood on the kitchen table, hands clasped. They appeared to stare at their unshod feet. At the head of the table stood Beamish. A naked bulb glared yellow above the group and shone its merciless light on the corpse of Donna Allison.

Donna Allison was laid out in the upper portion of a Succorware butter dish. It fit her perfectly. The first rays of sun infiltrated floral drapes and hit Beamish square in the cornea. This was his first eulogy, and so it wouldn't sound like a paper on pancreatic function, Beamish had to work at it.

"Donna Allison was one of you," Beamish said. The clones nodded in unison. Eulogists can count on a sympathetic audience. "Donna Allison was generous," he continued. "She lost her life making a present; she drowned in the milk of her own kindness—an attempted mixture of Coca-Cola and 151 rum.

"Contrary to rumor, 151 rum is only seventy-five point five percent alcohol. But I digress. Donna Allison was an individual." The five clones nodded. "We loved her; she loved us. Now we are six. We are mortal. One by one we will be knocked off. Like the hundred bottles of beer, we wait on our wall."

The feminals smiled briefly through their tears, recalling early counting lessons. "We have plenty to be proud of," Beamish said. "Cynthia Allison and Elizabeth Allison did a commendable job learning artificial respiration. Theresa Allison and Sarah Allison are to be thanked for rinsing the Coca-Cola off the cadav—uh, off Donna Allison's body. Starting today, we're going to take better care of each other. This afternoon, I'll pay my debt to

Dynamic Labs. Then we go to Mexico. Objections? No? Let us raise our voices in song!"

After an emotional round of "100 Bottles of Beer," Barbara Allison, Elizabeth Allison, Theresa Allison, and Sarah Allison rocked mournfully in four of the five remaining chairs. Cynthia Allison climbed into a pile of dirty laundry. There, she cried herself to sleep in her favorite place: Donald Beamish's shirt pocket.

"Wilbur?" the phone said. "Grey here. There's been a break."

"Fneh," said Wilbur Scoggins.

"For chrissake!" Grey said. "It's past nine. I'm on my third pot. Wilbur? Scoggins!"

"Uh," said Scoggins. Between his temples the idea of 9:00 A.M. painted a red stripe of pain.

"Beamish was just in my office," Grey said. "He dropped off a waterproof, bugproof, boilable Succorware butter dish containing a six-inch-tall woman. Dead."

"Murder?" Scoggins was waking up.

"Don't give him too much credit," Grey said. "Beamish couldn't kill an endangered species of cholera. Sure, if Dynamic held the patent now, we *could* charge murder . . . That's *my* notion of fun. Cops, legal definition of 'human,' page one of the *Times.* But we've got to handle this quietly. Did I tell you I found a patent draft? Sick handwriting. Coffee and dog manure all over it."

At this, Scoggins would have contradicted Grey. That is, if Scoggins were another man. "Gotcha," he said.

"Beamish quit," said Grey, "contract or no. Says he's going to Mexico. He's cleaning out his office now. I want you to search his place before he gets back home. Look for what he calls feminals."

"Feminals?" asked Scoggins. "What's feminals?"

"One hint," Grey said, "a novel by Louisa May Alcott."

"I'm looking for a *book?*" Scoggins asked.

"Dolt!" Grey snapped. "Look for *Little Women!*"

• • • •

It looked like a dollhouse stirred up with a spatula. But it was full-size, Beamish size. It was Beamish's apartment. The sock drawer was emptied to match the laundry pile; the fridge was open; the freezer had drained into a puddle. Full boxes of Cocoa Puffs and Minute Rice had been emptied into the sink. The pairs of model boats were in bits. On the rug, where tiny rocking chairs had been, there were now five chalk circles. Tissue-paper sarongs and yellow film boxes littered the floor. Beamish heard no little voices.

He felt alone—in his fingertips, which were numb, and in his throat, where a walnut of sadness was growing. He felt alone in the unlovable hollows of his cheeks, alone to the roots of his unstylable hair. In his living room, in the exact dead center of household gravity, in the mess of personal effects and garbage, Beamish sat down. For the first time in years, and without knowing that he could, Dr. "One-Shot" Beamish cried.

When the numbness from his fingertips had spread throughout his skull, he was through crying. He looked up. There on the carpet in front of him was Cynthia Allison, shouting through cupped hands, "They didn't get *me!*"

Later, in bed, Cynthia Allison curled up beside his ear to tell him the story. A four-man goon squad led by a standard-looking fellow had come rushing through the unlatched window by the fire escape. They knew of one corpse and saw five rocking chairs, so they concluded that only four feminals lived there. The chase had gone on and on. "The others were rocking when they came in," Cynthia Allison said. "I was in the nice smell of your shirts. Nobody even looked for me. Thank God I was off my rocker."

Despite the day, or maybe as consolation, Cynthia Allison and Donald Beamish made love. Oh, it wasn't easy. Cynthia wasn't used to trying to please with only one set of arms and legs. She wore herself out, snuggling, clasping, and pumping. Afterwards, Beamish took a wisp of goose down from the comforter and passed it close over a sensitive spot on Cynthia's microcircuitry. She squealed.

"I know what," Cynthia said when she came back to herself.

"We'll get you another girl friend. A full-size one. You'll see." She curled up engagingly beside his pillow.

"Easy for you to say," Beamish told her. "The only girls who ever went for me were you little Allisons. Cynthia, you're all I have."

This was so. "One-Shot" Beamish was out of a job and on the run. He foresaw a lifetime of hiding Cynthia Allison in run-down haciendas. Dr. Beamish closed his eyes; she was worth it. They fell into a dreamless sleep.

The phone was ringing. Grey's Sir Cafeen machine wasn't brewing. "Want me to get that fixed?" Allison Lüstgren asked.

"Put all my calls on hold!" Grey shouted into his intercom. Then to Allison he said, "I've had it with coffee. This whole thing is making me a mass of nerves." He rolled up an issue of *Research Today* and hurled it at the offending appliance. "Scoggins just called," he raved. "Beamish bought a ticket for the seven A.M. flight to Guadalajara."

"Mexico?" said Allison. "Too bad."

"Bad?" Grey repeated. "It's impossible. I'm getting big offers. Big. Offers for grants. Offers of outright donations—Mobil Oil public relations, and of course the Xerox Corporation . . . But to get any of this money, I need Beamish!"

"I never heard you say *that,*" Allison said.

"I never thought I would," Grey mourned. "But this is bigger than all of us. This is *Money.* I want you to talk to Beamish tonight."

"Me?"

"Just listen!" Grey said. "For one thing, I haven't got the temper for this. For another thing, Miss Lüstgren, *you* can blackmail him. Did he have the legal right to duplicate you? Did you sign anything?"

"Well, I—no." Allison Lüstgren didn't mention that she couldn't consider threatening old "One-Shot." That went against her sense of loyalty. But why?

"Aha!" Grey declared. "You'll be a plaintiff. Considering the fix he's in, Dynamic is being quite generous. Here's what we're prepared to offer . . ."

Allison half-listened, disturbed. Something in her believed that if Beamish knew how, he had a right to make pets of her. But, no! Anyway, she *could* drop by.

When the doorbell rang, Beamish was hunched over his desk. He had never found the feminal patent draft, and although he was singularly ungifted at recreating, he wanted to try before his self-imposed exile. Above Beamish, on the bookshelf, Cynthia Allison had been drawing with a charcoal sliver. The doorbell rang. They looked at each other.

"I hope that's your girl friend," Cynthia said.

"You know I don't have a girl friend," Beamish said.

Cynthia pouted. "I need someone to play with."

Beamish slipped the feminal into his desk drawer and glanced about the room. The model ships were gone. Aside from that, no one could guess the room had been trashed. Beside the TV stood two suitcases.

Whatever was at the door, Beamish's first impulse was not to resist it. Through the burglar scope, thoughtfully provided in his custom-paranoiac door, Beamish saw a big eye staring back at him. The eye was somehow familiar. It was the full-size eye of Allison Lüstgren.

Beamish managed the door. After a pregnant pause, Allison invited herself in. She wasn't wearing a lab coat; she wore a tight red cashmere blouse, silk slacks, and a marvelous smile. "Grey sent me," Allison explained. Shyly she gestured for Beamish to sit beside her on the couch. "He's going crazy," she went on. "He's giving up coffee."

"Why?" Beamish said. A scientist is the perfect straight man.

"His phone rings all day," Allison said. "It's become a Clone Hotline. Everybody's asking about you—foundations, labs, the government, and the press. None of the four top researchers is coming into the lab anymore. Each has a feminal now. They claim that home atmosphere is most conducive to feminal study."

Allison's smile was getting caught in her dimples. "So, Don," she said, "your feminals got wonderful homes."

"You talk about them as if they're stray cats," Beamish protested. Really, he was as pleased as if he'd won the Nobel prize. His grin was a one-of-a-kind inspiration.

"I'm supposed to make it clear," Allison told him. "The lab wants you back. They'll give you a new contract, 'research time' in Mexico, custody of the feminals—anything to have you on staff."

"Really?" asked Beamish. "Well, sure, I'll—I'll consider that." He was squirming; there were no textbooks about looking at ease on a sofa beside your dream girl. He blurted out, "Can you forgive me for secretly messing with your DNA? The ethics of this are beyond me, but—"

"Forgive you?" Allison ran her long fingers through her hair. "I've decided, Don, that I don't mind that you got into my genes. Lots of girls get roses, but isn't imitation the sincerest form of flattery?"

Beamish watched Allison Lüstgren. Her pants sincerely traced her life-sized form as she walked slowly toward his bedroom. This was the *second time* that "One-Shot" Beamish was alone with her; a new chance to research that perfect walk.

And this time—this golden, lucky time—she wasn't walking away.

Arthur C. Clarke

Patent Pending

2001 brought media fame to ARTHUR C. CLARKE, *but the British author and Sri Lanka resident had already distinguished himself as one of the giants of science fiction with novels and essays both factual and poetically philosophical, including* Childhood's End, Earthlight, Prelude to Space, Rendezvous with Rama, The Sands of Mars *and one of the seminal SF novels of the 1950s,* The City and the Stars. *Clarke's series of amusing "bar stories,"* Tales from the White Hart, *includes "Patent Pending," which seemed far-fetched in 1954, but with virtual reality and 3D computer graphics already established fact, yesterday's science fiction might be tomorrow's, uh, software . . .*

THERE ARE no subjects that have not been discussed, at some time or other, in the saloon bar of the "White Hart"—and whether or not there are ladies present makes no difference whatsoever. After all, they came in at their own risk. Three of them, now I come to think of it, have eventually gone out again with husbands. So perhaps the risk isn't on their side at all . . .

I mention this because I would not like you to think that all our conversations are highly erudite and scientific, and our activities purely cerebral. Though chess is rampant, darts and shove-ha'penny also flourish. The *Times Literary Supplement,* the *Saturday Review,* the *New Statesman* and the *Atlantic Monthly* may be brought in by some of the customers, but the same people are quite likely to leave with the latest issue of *Staggering Stories of Pseudoscience.*

A great deal of business also goes on in the obscurer corners of the pub. Copies of antique books and magazines frequently change hands at astronomical prices, and on almost any Wednesday at least three well-known dealers may be seen smoking large cigars as they lean over the bar, swapping stories with Drew. From time to time a vast guffaw announces the *dénouement* of some anecdote and provokes a flood of anxious enquiries from patrons who are afraid they may have missed something. But, alas, delicacy forbids that I should repeat any of these interesting tales here. Unlike most things in this island, they are not for export . . .

Luckily, no such restrictions apply to the tales of Mr. Harry Purvis, B.Sc. (at least), Ph.D. (probably) F.R.S. (personally I don't think so, though it *has* been rumoured). None of them would bring a blush to the cheeks of the most delicately nurtured maiden aunts, should any still survive in these days.

I must apologise. This is too sweeping a statement. There was one story which might, in some circles, be regarded as a little daring. Yet I do not hesitate to repeat it, for I know that you, dear reader, will be sufficiently broad-minded to take no offence.

It started in this fashion. A celebrated Fleet Street reviewer had been pinned into a corner by a persuasive publisher, who was about to bring out a book of which he had high hopes. It was one of the riper productions of the deep and decadent South—a prime example of the "and-then-the-house-gave-another-lurch-as-the-termites-finished-the-east-wing" school of fiction. Eire had already banned it, but that is an honour which few books escape nowadays, and certainly could not be considered a distinction. However, if a leading British newspaper could be induced to make a stern call for its suppression, it would become a best-seller overnight . . .

Such was the logic of its publisher, and he was using all his wiles to induce co-operation. I heard him remark, apparently to allay any scruples his reviewer friend might have, "Of course not!

If they can understand it, they *can't* be corrupted any further!" And then Harry Purvis, who has an uncanny knack of following half a dozen conversations simultaneously, so that he can insert himself in the right one at the right time, said in his peculiarly penetrating and non-interruptable voice: "Censorship does raise some very difficult problems, doesn't it? I've always argued that there's an inverse correlation between a country's degree of civilisation and the restraints it puts on its press."

A New England voice from the back of the room cut in: "On *that* argument, Paris is a more civilised place than Boston."

"Precisely," answered Purvis. For once, he waited for a reply.

"O.K." said the New England voice mildly. "I'm not arguing. I just wanted to check."

"To continue," said Purvis, wasting no more time in doing so, "I'm reminded of a matter which has not yet concerned the censor, but which will certainly do so before long. It began in France, and so far has remained there. When it *does* come out into the open, it may have a greater impact on our civilisation than the atom bomb.

"Like the atom bomb, it arose out of equally academic research. *Never*, gentlemen, underestimate science. I doubt if there is a single field of study so theoretical, so remote from what is laughingly called everyday life, that it may not one day produce something that will shake the world.

"You will appreciate that the story I am telling you is, for once in a while, second-hand. I got it from a colleague at the Sorbonne last year while I was over there at a scientific conference. So the names are all fictitious: I was told them at the time, but I can't remember them now.

"Professor—ah—Julian was an experimental physiologist at one of the smaller, but less impecunious, French universities. Some of you may remember that rather unlikely tale we heard here the other week from that fellow Hinckelberg, about his colleague who'd learned how to control the behaviour of animals through feeding the correct currents into their nervous systems. Well, if there *was* any truth in that story—and frankly I doubt it—the whole project was probably inspired by Julian's papers in *Comptes Rendus.*

"Professor Julian, however, never published his most remarkable results. When you stumble on something which is really terrific, you don't rush into print. You wait until you have overwhelming evidence—unless you're afraid that someone else is hot on the track. Then you may issue an ambiguous report that will establish your priority at a later date, without giving too much away at the moment—like the famous cryptogram that Huygens put out when he detected the rings of Saturn.

"You may well wonder what Julian's discovery was, so I won't keep you in suspense. It was simply the natural extension of what man has been doing for the last hundred years. First the camera gave us the power to capture scenes. Then Edison invented the phonograph, and sound was mastered. Today, in the talking film, we have a kind of mechanical memory which would be inconceivable to our forefathers. But surely the matter cannot rest there. Eventually science must be able to catch and store thoughts and sensations themselves, and feed them back into the mind so that, whenever it wishes, it can repeat any experience in life, down to its minutest detail."

"That's an old idea!" snorted someone. "See the 'feelies' in *Brave New World.*"

"All good ideas have been thought of by somebody before they are realised," said Purvis severely. "The point is that what Huxley and others had talked about, Julian actually did. My goodness, there's a pun there! Aldous—Julian—oh, let it pass!

"It was done electronically, of course. You all know how the encephalograph can record the minute electrical impulses in the living brain—the so-called 'brain waves,' as the popular press calls them. Julian's device was a much subtler elaboration of this well-known instrument. And, having recorded cerebral impulses, he could play them back again. It sounds simple, doesn't it? So was the phonograph, but it took the genius of Edison to think of it.

"And now, enter the villain. Well, perhaps that's too strong a

word, for Professor Julian's assistant Georges—Georges Dupin—
is really quite a sympathetic character. It was just that, being a
Frenchman of a more practical turn of mind than the Professor,
he saw at once that there were some milliards of francs involved
in this laboratory toy.

"The first thing was to get it out of the laboratory. The French
have an undoubted flair for elegant engineering, and after some
weeks of work—with the full co-operation of the Professor—
Georges had managed to pack the 'playback' side of the apparatus into a cabinet no larger than a television set, and containing
not very many more parts.

"Then Georges was ready to make his first experiment. It
would involve considerable expense, but as someone so rightly
remarked, you cannot make omelettes without breaking eggs.
And the analogy is, if I may say so, an exceedingly apt one.

"For Georges went to see the most famous *gourmet* in France,
and made an interesting proposition. It was one that the great
man could not refuse, because it was so unique a tribute to his
eminence. Georges explained patiently that he had invented a
device for registering (he said nothing about storing) sensations.
In the cause of science, and for the honour of the French *cuisine,*
could he be privileged to analyse the emotions, the subtle nuances
of gustatory discrimination, that took place in Monsieur le
Baron's mind when he employed his unsurpassed talents? Monsieur could name the restaurant, the *chef* and the menu—everything would be arranged for his convenience. Of course, if he was
too busy, no doubt that well-known epicure, Le Compte de—

"The Baron, who was in some respects a surprisingly coarse
man, uttered a word not to be found in most French dictionaries.
'*That* cretin!' he exploded. 'He would be happy on English cooking! No, *I* shall do it.' And forthwith he sat down to compose the
menu, while Georges anxiously estimated the cost of the items
and wondered if his bank balance would stand the strain . . .

"It would be interesting to know what the chef and the waiters
thought about the whole business. There was the Baron, seated at
his favourite table and doing full justice to his favourite dishes,

not in the least inconvenienced by the tangle of wires that trailed from his head to that diabolical-looking machine in the corner. The restaurant was empty of all other occupants, for the last thing Georges wanted was premature publicity. This had added very considerably to the already distressing cost of the experiment. He could only hope that the results would be worth it.

"They were. The only way of *proving* that, of course, would be to play back Georges' 'recording.' We have to take his word for it, since the utter inadequacy of words in such matters is all too well-known. The Baron *was* a genuine connoisseur, not one of those who merely pretend to powers of discrimination they do not possess. You know Thurber's 'Only a naive domestic Burgundy, but I think you'll admire its presumption.' The Baron would have known at the first sniff whether it was domestic or not—and if it had been presumptuous he'd have smacked it down.

"I gather that Georges had his money's worth out of that recording, even though he had not intended it merely for personal use. It opened up new worlds to him, and clarified the ideas that had been forming in his ingenious brain. There was no doubt about it: all the exquisite sensations that had passed through the Baron's mind during the consumption of that Lucullan repast had been captured, so that anyone else, however untrained they might be in such matters, could savour them to the full. For, you see, the recording dealt purely with emotions: intelligence did not come into the picture at all. The Baron needed a lifetime of knowledge and training before he could *experience* these sensations. But once they were down on tape, anyone, even if in real life they had no sense of taste at all, could take over from there.

"Think of the glowing vistas that opened up before Georges' eyes! There were other meals, other gourmets. There were the collected impressions of all the vintages of Europe—what would connoisseurs not pay for them? When the last bottle of a rare wine had been broached, its incorporeal essence could be preserved, as the voice of Melba can travel down the centuries. For, after all, it was not the wine itself that mattered, but the sensations it evoked . . .

"So mused Georges. But this, he knew, was only a beginning. The French claim to logic I have often disputed, but in Georges's case it cannot be denied. He thought the matter over for a few days: then he went to see his *petite dame*.

" 'Yvonne, *ma chérie,*' he said, 'I have a somewhat unusual request to make of you . . .' "

Harry Purvis knew when to break off in a story. He turned to the bar and called, "Another Scotch, Drew." No-one said a word while it was provided.

"To continue," said Purvis at length, "the experiment, unusual though it was, even in France, was successfully carried out. As both discretion and custom demanded, all was arranged in the lonely hours of the night. You will have gathered already that Georges was a persuasive person, though I doubt if Mam'selle needed much persuading.

"Stiffling her curiosity with a sincere but hasty kiss, Georges saw Yvonne out of the lab and rushed back to his apparatus. Breathlessly, he ran through the playback. It worked—not that he had ever had any real doubts. Moreover—do please remember I have only my informant's word for this—it was indistinguishable from the real thing. At that moment something approaching religious awe overcame Georges. This was, without a doubt, the greatest invention in history. He would be immortal as well as wealthy, for he had achieved something of which all men had dreamed, and had robbed old age of one of its terrors . . .

"He also realised that he could now dispense with Yvonne, if he so wished. This raised implications that would require further thought. *Much* further thought.

"You will, of course, appreciate that I am giving you a highly condensed account of events. While all this was going on, Georges was still working as a loyal employee of the Professor, who suspected nothing. As yet, indeed, Georges had done little more than any research worker might have in similar circumstances. His performances had been somewhat beyond the call of duty, but could all be explained away if need be.

"The next step would involve some very delicate negotiations and the expenditure of further hard-won francs. Georges now had all the material he needed to prove, beyond a shadow of doubt, that he was handling a very valuable commercial property. There were shrewd businessmen in Paris who would jump at the opportunity. Yet a certain delicacy, for which we must give him full credit, restrained Georges from using his second—er—recording as a sample of the wares his machine could purvey. There was no way of disguising the personalities involved, and Georges was a modest man. 'Besides,' he argued, again with great good sense, 'when the gramophone company wishes to make a *disque,* it does not enregister the performance of some amateur musician. *That* is a matter for professionals. And so, *ma foi,* is *this.'* Whereupon, after a further call at his bank, he set forth again for Paris.

"He did not go anywhere near the Place Pigalle, because that was full of Americans and prices were accordingly exorbitant. Instead, a few discreet enquiries and some understanding cabdrivers took him to an almost oppressively respectable suburb, where he presently found himself in a pleasant waiting room, by no means as exotic as might have been supposed.

"And there, somewhat embarrassed, Georges explained his mission to a formidable lady whose age one could have no more guessed than her profession. Used though she was to unorthodox requests, *this* was something she had never encountered in all her considerable experience. But the customer was always right, as long as he had the cash, and so in due course everything was arranged. One of the young ladies and her boy friend, an *apache* of somewhat overwhelming masculinity, travelled back with Georges to the provinces. At first they were, naturally, somewhat suspicious, but as Georges had already found, no expert can ever resist flattery. Soon they were all on excellent terms. Hercule and Susette promised Georges that they would give him every cause for satisfaction.

"No doubt some of you would be glad to have further details, but you can scarcely expect me to supply them. All I can say is that Georges—or rather his instrument—was kept very busy, and that by the morning little of the recording material was left unused. For it seems that Hercule was indeed appropriately named . . .

"When this piquant episode was finished, Georges had very little money left, but he did possess two recordings that were quite beyond price. Once more he set off to Paris, where, with practically no trouble, he came to terms with some businessmen who were so astonished that they gave him a very generous contract before coming to their senses. I am pleased to report this, because so often the scientist emerges second best in his dealings with the world of finance. I'm equally pleased to record that Georges had made provision for Professor Julian in the contract. You may say cynically that it was, after all, the Professor's invention, and that sooner or later Georges would have had to square him. But I like to think that there was more to it than that.

"The full details of the scheme for exploiting the device are, of course, unknown to me. I gather that Georges had been expansively eloquent—not that much eloquence was needed to convince anyone who had once experienced one or both of his playbacks. The market would be enormous, unlimited. The export trade alone could put France on her feet again and would wipe out her dollar deficit overnight—once certain snags had been overcome. Everything would have to be managed through somewhat clandestine channels, for think of the hub-bub from the hypocritical Anglo-Saxons when they discovered just what was being imported into their countries. The Mother's Union, The Daughters of the American Revolution, The Housewives League, and *all* the religious organisations would rise as one. The lawyers were looking into the matter very carefully, and as far as could be seen the regulations that still excluded *Tropic of Capricorn* from the mails of the English-speaking countries could not be applied to this case—for the simple reason that no-one had thought of it. But there would be such a shout for new laws that Parliament and Congress would have to do something, so it was best to keep under cover as long as possible.

"In fact, as one of the directors pointed out, if the recordings were banned, so much the better. They could make much more money on a smaller output, because the price would promptly soar and all the vigilance of the Customs Officials couldn't block every leak. It would be Prohibition all over again.

"You will scarcely be surprised to hear that by this time Georges had somewhat lost interest in the gastronomical angle. It was an interesting but definitely minor possibility of the invention. Indeed, this had been tacitly admitted by the directors as they drew up the articles of association, for they had included the pleasures of the *cuisine* among 'subsidiary rights.'

"Georges returned home with his head in the clouds, and a substantial check in his pocket. A charming fancy had struck his imagination. He thought of all the trouble to which the gramophone companies had gone so that the world might have the complete recordings of the Forty-eight Preludes and Fugues or the Nine Symphonies. Well, *his* new company would put out a complete and definite set of recordings, performed by experts versed in the most esoteric knowledge of East and West. How many *opus* numbers would be required? That, of course, had been a subject of profound debate for some thousands of years. The Hindu text-books, Georges had heard, got well into three figures. It would be a most interesting research, combining profit with pleasure in an unexampled manner. . . . He had already begun some preliminary studies, using treatises which even in Paris were none too easy to obtain.

"If you think that while all this was going on, Georges had neglected his usual interests, you are all too right. He was working literally night and day, for he had not yet revealed his plans to the Professor and almost everything had to be done when the lab was closed. And one of the interests he had had to neglect was Yvonne.

"Her curiosity had already been aroused, as any girl's would have been. But now she was more than intrigued—she was distracted. For Georges had become so remote and cold. He was no longer in love with her.

"It was a result that might have been anticipated. Publicans have to guard against the danger of sampling their own wares too often—I'm sure *you* don't, Drew—and Georges had fallen into this seductive trap. He had been through that recording too many times, with somewhat debilitating results. Moreover, poor Yvonne was not to be compared with the experienced and talented Susette. It was the old story of the professional versus the amateur.

"All that Yvonne knew was that Georges was in love with someone else. That was true enough. She suspected that he had been unfaithful to her. And *that* raises profound philosophical questions we can hardly go into here.

"This being France, in case you had forgotten, the outcome was inevitable. Poor Georges! He was working late one night at the lab, as usual, when Yvonne finished him off with one of those ridiculous ornamental pistols which are *de rigueur* for such occasions. Let us drink to his memory."

"That's the trouble with all your stories," said John Beynon. "You tell us about wonderful inventions, and then at the end it turns out that the discoverer was killed, so no-one can do anything about it. For I suppose, as usual, the apparatus was destroyed?"

"But no," replied Purvis. "Apart from Georges, this is one of the stories that has a happy ending. There was no trouble at all about Yvonne, of course. Georges's grieving sponsors arrived on the scene with great speed and prevented any adverse publicity. Being men of sentiment as well as men of business, they realised that they would have to secure Yvonne's freedom. They promptly did this by playing the recording to *le Maire* and *le Préfet,* thus convincing them that the poor girl had experienced irresistible provocation. A few shares in the new company clinched the deal, with expressions of the utmost cordiality on both sides. Yvonne even got her gun back."

"Then, when—" began someone else.

"Ah, these things take time. There's the question of mass production, you know. It's quite possible that distribution has already commenced through private—*very* private—channels. Some of those dubious little shops and notice boards around Leicester Square may soon start giving hints."

"Of course," said the New England voice disrespectfully, "you wouldn't know the *name* of the company."

You can't help admiring Purvis at times like this. He scarcely hesitated.

"*Le Société Anonyme d'Aphrodite,*" he replied. "And I've just remembered something that will cheer *you* up. They hope to get round your sticky mails regulations and establish themselves before the inevitable congressional enquiry starts. They're opening up a branch in Nevada: apparently you can still get away with anything there." He raised his glass.

"To Georges Dupin," he said solemnly. "Martyr to science. Remember him when the fireworks start. And one other thing—"

"Yes?" we all asked.

"Better start saving now. And sell your TV sets before the bottom drops out of the market."

William C. Morrow

The Monster-Maker

Aficionados of the gothic tradition rank WILLIAM CHAMBERS MOR-
ROW *(1854–1923) on a par with Ambrose Bierce, Fitz-James
O'Brien and Edgar Allan Poe. In this forgotten masterpiece of
American weird fiction, Morrow's characteristic gruesomeness
mingles with uncommon pathos to produce a work of genuine
tragic force.*

A YOUNG MAN of refined appearance, but evidently suffering
great mental distress, presented himself one morning at the residence of a singular old man, who was known as a surgeon of
remarkable skill. The house was a queer and primitive brick affair, entirely out of date, and tolerable only in the decayed part of
the city in which it stood. It was large, gloomy, and dark, and had
long corridors and dismal rooms; and it was absurdly large for
the small family—man and wife—that occupied it. The house
described, the man is portrayed—but not the woman. He could
be agreeable on occasion, but, for all that, he was but animated
mystery. His wife was weak, wan, reticent, evidently miserable,
and possibly living a life of dread or horror—perhaps witness of
repulsive things, subject of anxieties, and victim of fear and tyranny; but there is a great deal of guessing in these assumptions.
He was about sixty-five years of age and she about forty. He was
lean, tall, and bald, with thin, smooth-shaven face, and very keen

eyes; kept always at home, and was slovenly. The man was strong, the woman weak; he dominated, she suffered.

Although he was a surgeon of rare skill, his practice was almost nothing, for it was a rare occurrence that the few who knew of his great ability were brave enough to penetrate the gloom of his house, and when they did so it was with deaf ear turned to sundry ghoulish stories that were whispered concerning him. These were, in great part, but exaggerations of his experiments in vivisection; he was devoted to the science of surgery.

The young man who presented himself on the morning just mentioned was a handsome fellow, yet of evident weak character and unhealthy temperament—sensitive, and easily exalted or depressed. A single glance convinced the surgeon that his visitor was seriously affected in mind, for there was never a bolder skull-grin of melancholia, fixed and irremediable.

A stranger would not have suspected any occupancy of the house. The street door—old, warped, and blistered by the sun—was locked, and the small, faded-green window-blinds were closed. The young man rapped at the door. No answer. He rapped again. Still no sign. He examined a slip of paper, glanced at the number on the house, and then, with the impatience of a child, he furiously kicked the door. There were signs of numerous other such kicks. A response came in the shape of a shuffling footstep in the hall, a turning of the rusty key, and a sharp face that peered through a cautious opening in the door.

"Are you the doctor?" asked the young man.

"Yes, yes! Come in," briskly replied the master of the house.

The young man entered. The old surgeon closed the door and carefully locked it. "This way," he said, advancing to a rickety flight of stairs. The young man followed. The surgeon led the way up the stairs, turned into a narrow, musty-smelling corridor at the left, traversed it, rattling the loose boards under his feet, at the farther end opened a door at the right, and beckoned his visitor to enter. The young man found himself in a pleasant room, furnished in antique fashion and with hard simplicity.

"Sit down," said the old man, placing a chair so that its occupant should face a window that looked out upon a dead wall about six feet from the house. He threw open the blind, and a pale light entered. He then seated himself near his visitor and directly facing him, and with a searching look that had all the power of a microscope, he proceeded to diagnosticate the case.

"Well?" he presently asked.

The young man shifted uneasily in his seat.

"I—I have come to see you," he finally stammered, "because I'm in trouble."

"Ah!"

"Yes; you see, I—that is—I have given it up."

"Ah!" There was pity added to sympathy in the ejaculation.

"That's it. Given it up," added the visitor. He took from his pocket a roll of banknotes, and with the utmost deliberation he counted them out upon his knee. "Five thousand dollars," he calmly remarked. "That is for you. It's all I have; but I presume— I imagine—no; that is not the word—*assume*—yes; that's the word—assume that five thousand—is it really that much? Let me count." He counted again. "That five thousand dollars is a sufficient fee for what I want you to do."

The surgeon's lips curled pityingly—perhaps disdainfully also. "What do you want me to do?" he carelessly inquired.

The young man rose, looked around with a mysterious air, approached the surgeon, and laid the money across his knee. Then he stooped and whispered two words in the surgeon's ear.

These words produced an electric effect. The old man started violently; then, springing to his feet, he caught his visitor angrily, and transfixed him with a look that was as sharp as a knife. His eyes flashed, and he opened his mouth to give utterance to some harsh imprecation, when he suddenly checked himself. The anger left his face, and only pity remained. He relinquished his grasp, picked up the scattered notes, and, offering them to the visitor, slowly said:

"I do not want your money. You are simply foolish. You think you are in trouble. Well, you do not know what trouble is. Your only trouble is that you have not a trace of manhood in your nature. You are merely insane—I shall not say pusillanimous. You should surrender yourself to the authorities, and be sent to a lunatic asylum for proper treatment."

The young man keenly felt the intended insult, and his eyes flashed dangerously.

"You old dog—you insult me thus!" he cried. "Grand airs, these, you give yourself! Virtuously indignant, old murderer, you! Don't want my money, eh? When a man comes to you himself and wants it done, you fly into a passion and spurn his money; but let an enemy of his come and pay you, and you are only too willing. How many such jobs have you done in this miserable old hole? It is a good thing for you that the police have not run you down, and brought spade and shovel with them. Do you know what is said of you? Do you think you have kept your windows so closely shut that no sound has ever penetrated beyond them? Where do you keep your infernal implements?"

He had worked himself into a high passion. His voice was hoarse, loud, and rasping. His eyes, bloodshot, started from their sockets. His whole frame twitched, and his fingers writhed. But he was in the presence of a man infinitely his superior. Two eyes, like those of a snake, burned two holes through him. An over-mastering, inflexible presence confronted one weak and passion-ate. The result came.

"Sit down," commanded the stern voice of the surgeon.

It was the voice of father to child, of master to slave. The fury left the visitor, who, weak and overcome, fell upon a chair.

Meanwhile, a peculiar light had appeared in the old surgeon's face, the dawn of a strange idea; a gloomy ray, strayed from the fires of the bottomless pit; the baleful light that illumines the way of the enthusiast. The old man remained a moment in profound abstraction, gleams of eager intelligence bursting momentarily through the cloud of sombre meditation that covered his face. Then broke the broad light of a deep, impenetrable determina-tion. There was something sinister in it, suggesting the sacrifice of something held sacred. After a struggle, mind had vanquished conscience.

Taking a piece of paper and a pencil, the surgeon carefully wrote answers to questions which he peremptorily addressed to his visitor, such as his name, age, place of residence, occupation, and the like, and the same inquiries concerning his parents, together with other particular matters.

"Does anyone know you came to this house?" he asked.

"No."

"You swear it?"

"Yes."

"But your prolonged absence will cause alarm and lead to search."

"I have provided against that."

"How?"

"By depositing a note in the post, as I came along, announcing my intention to drown myself."

"The river will be dragged."

"What then?" asked the young man, shrugging his shoulders with careless indifference. "Rapid undercurrent, you know. A good many are never found."

There was a pause.

"Are you ready?" finally asked the surgeon.

"Perfectly." The answer was cool and determined.

The manner of the surgeon, however, showed much perturbation. The pallor that had come into his face at the moment his decision was formed became intense. A nervous tremulousness came over his frame. Above it all shone the light of enthusiasm.

"Have you a choice in the method?" he asked.

"Yes; extreme anæsthesia."

"With what agent?"

"The surest and quickest."

"Do you desire any—any subsequent disposition?"

"No; only nullification; simply a blowing out, as of a candle in the wind; a puff—then darkness, without a trace. A sense of your own safety may suggest the method. I leave it to you."

"No delivery to your friends?"

"None whatever."

Another pause.

"Did you say you are quite ready?" asked the surgeon.

"Quite ready."

"And perfectly willing?"

"Anxious."

"Then wait a moment."

With this request the old surgeon rose to his feet and stretched himself. Then with the stealthiness of a cat he opened the door and peered into the hall, listening intently. There was no sound. He softly closed the door and locked it. Then he closed the window-blinds and locked them. This done, he opened a door leading into an adjoining room, which, though it had no window, was lighted by means of a small skylight. The young man watched closely. A strange change had come over him. While his determination had not one whit lessened, a look of great relief came into his face, displacing the haggard, despairing look of a half-hour before. Melancholic then, he was ecstatic now.

The opening of the second door disclosed a curious sight. In the centre of the room, directly under the skylight, was an operating-table, such as is used by demonstrators of anatomy. A glass case against the wall held surgical instruments of every kind. Hanging in another case were human skeletons of various sizes. In sealed jars, arranged on shelves, were monstrosities of divers kinds preserved in alcohol. There were also, among innumerable other articles scattered about the room, a manikin, a stuffed cat, a desiccated human heart, plaster casts of various parts of the body, numerous charts, and a large assortment of drugs and chemicals. There was also a lounge, which could be opened to form a couch. The surgeon opened it and moved the operating-table aside, giving its place to the lounge.

"Come in," he called to his visitor.

The young man obeyed without the least hesitation.

"Take off your coat."

He complied.

"Lie down on that lounge."

In a moment the young man was stretched at full length, eyeing the surgeon. The latter undoubtedly was suffering under great excitement, but he did not waver; his movements were sure and quick. Selecting a bottle containing a liquid, he carefully measured out a certain quantity. While doing this he asked: "Have you ever had any irregularity of the heart?"

"No."

The answer was prompt, but it was immediately followed by a quizzical look in the speaker's face.

"I presume," he added, "you mean by your question that it might be dangerous to give me a certain drug. Under the circumstances, however, I fail to see any relevancy in your question."

This took the surgeon aback; but he hastened to explain that he did not wish to inflict unnecessary pain, and hence his question.

He placed the glass on a stand, approached his visitor, and carefully examined his pulse.

"Wonderful!" he exclaimed.

"Why?"

"It is perfectly normal."

"Because I am wholly resigned. Indeed, it has been long since I knew such happiness. It is not active, but infinitely sweet."

"You have no lingering desire to retract?"

"None whatever."

The surgeon went to the stand and returned with the draught.

"Take this," he said, kindly.

The young man partially raised himself and took the glass in his hand. He did not show the vibration of a single nerve. He drank the liquid, draining the last drop. Then he returned the glass with a smile.

"Thank you," he said; "you are the noblest man that lives. May you always prosper and be happy! You are my benefactor, my liberator. Bless you, bless you! You reach down from your seat with the gods and lift me up into glorious peace and rest. I love you—I love you with all my heart!"

These words, spoken earnestly in a musical, low voice, and accompanied with a smile of ineffable tenderness, pierced the old man's heart. A suppressed convulsion swept over him; intense anguish wrung his vitals; perspiration trickled down his face. The young man continued to smile.

"Ah, it does me good!" said he.

The surgeon, with a strong effort to control himself, sat down upon the edge of the lounge and took his visitor's wrist, counting the pulse.

"How long will it take?" the young man asked.

"Ten minutes. Two have passed." The voice was hoarse.

"Ah, only eight minutes more! . . . Delicious, delicious! I feel it coming . . . What was that? . . . Ah, I understand. Music . . . Beautiful! . . . Coming, coming . . . Is that—that water? . . . Trickling? Dripping? Doctor!"

"Well?"

"Thank you . . . thank you . . . Noble man . . . my savior . . . my bene . . . bene . . . factor . . . Trickling . . . trickling . . . Dripping, dripping . . . Doctor!"

"Well?"

"Doctor!"

"Past hearing," muttered the surgeon.

"Doctor!"

"And blind."

Response was made by a firm grasp of the hand.

"Doctor!"

"And numb."

"Doctor!"

The old man watched and waited.

"Dripping . . . dripping."

The last drop had run. There was a sigh, and nothing more. The surgeon laid down the hand.

"The first step," he groaned, rising to his feet; then his whole frame dilated. "The first step—the most difficult, yet the simplest. A providential delivery into my hands of that for which I have hungered for forty years. No withdrawal now! It is possible, because scientific; rational, but perilous. If I succeed—*if*? I *shall* succeed. I *will* succeed . . . And after success—what? . . . Yes; what? Publish the plan and the result? The gallows . . . So long as *it* shall exist . . . and *I exist,* the gallows. That much . . . But how account for its presence? Ah, that pinches hard! I must trust to the future."

He tore himself from the reverie and started.

"I wonder if *she* heard or saw anything."

With that reflection he cast a glance upon the form on the lounge, and then left the room, locked the door, locked also the door of the outer room, walked down two or three corridors, penetrated to a remote part of the house, and rapped at a door. It was opened by his wife. He, by this time, had regained complete mastery over himself.

"I thought I heard someone in the house just now," he said, "but I can find no one."

"I heard nothing."

He was greatly relieved.

"I did hear someone knock at the door less than an hour ago," she resumed, "and heard you speak, I think. Did he come in?"

"No."

The woman glanced at his feet and seemed perplexed.

"I am almost certain," she said, "that I heard foot-falls in the house, and yet I see that you are wearing slippers."

"Oh, I had on my shoes then!"

"That explains it," said the woman, satisfied; "I think the sound you heard must have been caused by rats."

"Ah, that was it!" exclaimed the surgeon. Leaving, he closed the door, reopened it, and said, "I do not wish to be disturbed to-day." He said to himself, as he went down the hall, "All is clear there."

He returned to the room in which his visitor lay, and made a careful examination.

"Splendid specimen!" he softly exclaimed; "every organ sound, every function perfect; fine, large frame; well-shaped muscles, strong and sinewy; capable of wonderful development—if given opportunity . . . I have no doubt it can be done. Already I have succeeded with a dog—a task less difficult than this, for in a man the cerebrum overlaps the cerebellum, which is not the case with a dog. This gives a wide range for accident, with but one opportunity in a lifetime! In the cerebrum, the intellect and the affections; in the cerebellum, the senses and the motor forces; in the medulla oblongata, control of the diaphragm. In these two latter lie all the essentials of simple existence. The cerebrum is merely an adornment; that is to say, reason and the affections are almost purely ornamental. I have already proved it. My dog, with its cerebrum removed, was idiotic, but it retained its physical senses to a certain degree."

While thus ruminating, he made careful preparations. He moved the couch, replaced the operating-table under the skylight, selected a number of surgical instruments, prepared certain drug-mixtures, and arranged water, towels, and all the accessories of a tedious surgical operation. Suddenly he burst into laughter.

"Poor fool!" he exclaimed. "Paid me five thousand dollars to kill him! Didn't have the courage to snuff his own candle! Singular, singular, the queer freaks these madmen have! You thought you were dying, poor idiot! Allow me to inform you, sir, that you are as much alive at this moment as ever you were in your life. But it will be all the same to you. You shall never be more conscious than you are now; and for all practical purposes, so far as they concern you, you are dead henceforth, though you shall live. By the way, how should you feel *without a head?* Ha, ha, ha! . . . But that's a sorry joke."

He lifted the unconscious form from the lounge and laid it upon the operating-table.

About three years afterwards the following conversation was held between a captain of police and a detective:

"She may be insane," suggested the captain.

"I think she is."

"And yet you credit her story!"

"I do."

"Singular!"

"Not at all. I myself have learned something."

"What!"

"Much, in one sense; little, in another. You have heard those queer stories of her husband. Well, they are all nonsensical—probably with one exception. He is generally a harmless old fellow, but peculiar. He has performed some wonderful surgical operations. The people in his neighborhood are ignorant, and they fear him and wish to be rid of him; hence they tell a great many lies about him, and they come to believe their own stories. The one important thing that I have learned is that he is almost insanely enthusiastic on the subject of surgery—especially experimental surgery; and with an enthusiast there is hardly such a thing as a scruple. It is this that gives me confidence in the woman's story."

"You say she appeared to be frightened?"

"Doubly so—first, she feared that her husband would learn of her betrayal of him; second, the discovery itself had terrified her."

"But her report of this discovery is very vague," argued the captain. "He conceals everything from her. She is merely guessing."

"In part—yes; in other part—no. She heard the sounds distinctly, though she did not see clearly. Horror closed her eyes. What she thinks she saw is, I admit, preposterous; but she undoubtedly saw something extremely frightful. There are many peculiar little circumstances. He has eaten with her but few times during the last three years, and nearly always carries his food to his private rooms. She says that he either consumes an enormous quantity, throws much away, or is feeding something that eats prodigiously. He explains this to her by saying that he has animals with which he experiments. This is not true. Again, he always keeps the door to these rooms carefully locked; and not only that, but he has had the doors doubled and otherwise strengthened, and has heavily barred a window that looks from one of the rooms upon a dead wall a few feet distant."

"What does it mean?" asked the captain.

"A prison."

"For animals, perhaps."

"Certainly not."

"Why!"

"Because, in the first place, cages would have been better; in the second place, the security that he has provided is infinitely greater than that required for the confinement of ordinary animals."

"All this is easily explained: he has a violent lunatic under treatment."

"I had thought of that, but such is not the fact."

"How do you know?"

"By reasoning thus: He has always refused to treat cases of lunacy; he confines himself to surgery; the walls are not padded, for the woman has heard sharp blows upon them; no human strength, however morbid, could possibly require such resisting strength as has been provided; he would not be likely to conceal a lunatic's confinement from the woman; no lunatic could consume all the food that he provides; so extremely violent mania as these precautions indicate could not continue three years; if there is a lunatic in the case it is very probable that there should have been communication with someone outside concerning the patient, and there has been none; the woman has listened at the keyhole and has heard no human voice within; and last, we have heard the woman's vague description of what she saw."

"You have destroyed every possible theory," said the captain, deeply interested, "and have suggested nothing new."

"Unfortunately, I cannot; but the truth may be very simple, after all. The old surgeon is so peculiar that I am prepared to discover something remarkable."

"Have you suspicions?"

"I have."

"Of what?"

"A crime. The woman suspects it."

"And betrays it?"

"Certainly, because it is so horrible that her humanity revolts; so terrible that her whole nature demands of her that she hand over the criminal to the law; so frightful that she is in mortal terror; so awful that it has shaken her mind."

"What do you propose to do?" asked the captain.

"Secure evidence. I may need help."

"You shall have all the men you require. Go ahead, but be careful. You are on dangerous ground. You would be a mere plaything in the hands of that man."

Two days afterwards the detective again sought the captain.

"I have a queer document," he said, exhibiting torn fragments of paper on which there was writing. "The woman stole it and brought it to me. She snatched a handful out of a book, getting only a part of each of a few leaves."

These fragments, which the men arranged as best they could, were (the detective explained) torn by the surgeon's wife from the first volume of a number of manuscript books which her husband had written on one subject—the very one that was the cause of her excitement. "About the time that he began a certain experiment three years ago," continued the detective, "he removed everything from the suite of two rooms containing his study and his operating-room. In one of the bookcases that he removed to a room across the passage was a drawer, which he kept locked, but which he opened from time to time. As is quite common with such pieces of furniture, the lock of the drawer is a very poor one; and so the woman, while making a thorough search yesterday, found a key on her bunch that fitted this lock. She opened the drawer, drew out the bottom book of a pile (so that its mutilation would more likely escape discovery), saw that it might contain a clew, and tore out a handful of the leaves. She had barely replaced the book, locked the drawer, and made her escape when her husband appeared. He hardly ever allows her to be out of his sight when she is in that part of the house."

The fragments read as follows: ". . . the motory nerves. I had hardly dared to hope for such a result, although inductive reasoning had convinced me of its possibility, my only doubt having been on the score of my lack of skill. Their operation has been only slightly impaired, and even this would not have been the case had the operation been performed in infancy, before the intellect had sought and obtained recognition as an essential part of the whole. Therefore I state, as a proven fact, that the cells of the motory nerves have inherent forces sufficient to the purposes of those nerves. But hardly so with the sensory nerves. These latter are, in fact, an offshoot of the former, evolved from them by natural (though not essential) heterogeneity, and to a certain extent are dependent on the evolution and expansion of a contemporaneous tendency, that developed into mentality, or mental function. Both of these latter tendencies, these evolvements, are merely refinements of the motory system, and not independent entities; that is to say, they are the blossoms of a plant that propagates from its roots. The motory system is the first . . . nor am I surprised that such prodigious muscular energy is developing. It promises yet to surpass the wildest dreams of human strength. I account for it thus: The powers of assimilation had reached their full development. They had formed the habit of doing a certain amount of work. They sent their products to all parts of the system. As a result of my operation the consumption of these products was reduced fully one-half; that is to say, about one-half of the demand for them was withdrawn. But force of habit required the production to proceed. This production was strength, vitality, energy. Thus double the usual quantity of this strength, this energy, was stored in the remaining . . . developed a tendency that did surprise me. Nature, no longer suffering the distraction of extraneous interferences, and at the same time being cut in two (as it were), with reference to this case, did not fully adjust herself to the new situation, as does a magnet, which, when divided at the point of equilibrium, renews itself in its two fragments by investing each with opposite poles; but, on the contrary, being severed from laws that theretofore had controlled her, and possessing still that mysterious tendency to develop into something more potential and complex, she blindly (having lost her lantern) pushed her demands for material that would secure this development, and as blindly used it when it was given her. Hence this marvellous voracity, this insatiable hunger, this wonderful ravenousness; and hence also (there being nothing but the physical part to receive this vast storing of energy) this strength that is becoming almost hourly herculean, almost daily appalling. It is becoming serious . . . narrow escape to-day. By some means, while I was absent, it unscrewed the stopper of the silver feeding-pipe (which I have already herein termed 'the artificial mouth'), and, in one of its curious antics, allowed all the chyle to escape from its stomach through the tube. Its hunger then became intense—I may say furious. I placed my hands upon it to push it into a chair, when, feeling my touch, it caught me, clasped me around the neck, and would have crushed me to death instantly had I not slipped from its powerful grasp. Thus I always had to be on my guard. I have provided the screw stopper with a spring catch, and . . . usually docile when not hungry; slow and heavy in its movements, which are, of course, purely unconscious; any apparent excitement in movement being due to local irregularities in the blood-supply of the cerebellum, which, if I did not have it enclosed in a silver case that is immovable, I should expose and . . ."

The captain looked at the detective with a puzzled air.

"I don't understand it at all," said he.

"Nor I," agreed the detective.

"What do you propose to do?"

"Make a raid."

"Do you want a man?"

"Three. The strongest men in your district."

"Why, the surgeon is old and weak!"

"Nevertheless, I want three strong men; and for that matter, prudence really advises me to take twenty."

At one o'clock the next morning a cautious, scratching sound might have been heard in the ceiling of the surgeon's operating-room. Shortly afterwards the skylight sash was carefully raised and laid aside. A man peered into the opening. Nothing could be heard.

"That is singular," thought the detective.

He cautiously lowered himself to the floor by a rope, and then stood for some moments listening intently. There was a dead silence. He shot the slide of a dark-lantern, and rapidly swept the room with the light. It was bare, with the exception of a strong iron staple and ring, screwed to the floor in the centre of the room, with a heavy chain attached. The detective then turned his attention to the outer room; it was perfectly bare. He was deeply perplexed. Returning to the inner room, he called softly to the men to descend. While they were thus occupied he re-entered the outer room and examined the door. A glance sufficed. It was kept closed by a spring attachment, and was locked with a strong spring-lock that could be drawn from the inside.

"The bird has just flown," mused the detective. "A singular accident! The discovery and proper use of this thumb-bolt might not have happened once in fifty years, if my theory is correct."

By this time the men were behind him. He noiselessly drew the spring-bolt, opened the door, and looked out into the hall. He heard a peculiar sound. It was as though a gigantic lobster was floundering and scrambling in some distant part of the old house. Accompanying this sound was a loud, whistling breathing, and frequent rasping gasps.

These sounds were heard by still another person—the surgeon's wife; for they originated very near her rooms, which were a considerable distance from her husband's. She had been sleeping lightly, tortured by fear and harassed by frightful dreams. The conspiracy into which she had recently entered for the destruction of her husband was a source of great anxiety. She constantly suffered from the most gloomy forebodings, and lived in an atmosphere of terror. Added to the natural horror of her situation were those countless sources of fear which a fright-shaken mind creates and then magnifies. She was, indeed, in a pitiable state, having been driven first by terror to desperation, and then to madness.

Startled thus out of fitful slumber by the noise at her door, she sprang from her bed to the floor, every terror that lurked in her acutely tense mind and diseased imagination starting up and almost overwhelming her. The idea of flight—one of the strongest of all instincts—seized upon her, and she ran to the door, beyond all control of reason. She drew the bolt and flung the door wide open, and then fled wildly down the passage, the appalling hissing and rasping gurgle ringing in her ears apparently with a thousandfold intensity. But the passage was in absolute darkness, and she had not taken a half-dozen steps when she tripped upon an unseen object on the floor. She fell headlong upon it, encountering in it a large, soft, warm substance that writhed and squirmed, and from which came the sounds that had awakened her. Instantly realizing her situation, she uttered a shriek such as only an unnameable terror can inspire. But hardly had her cry started the echoes in the empty corridor, when it was suddenly stifled. Two prodigious arms had closed upon her and crushed the life out of her.

The cry performed the office of directing the detective and his assistants, and it also aroused the old surgeon, who occupied rooms between the officers and the object of their search. The cry of agony pierced him to the marrow, and a realization of the cause of it burst upon him with frightful force.

"It has come at last!" he gasped, springing from his bed.

Snatching from a table a dimly-burning lamp and a long knife which he had kept at hand for three years, he dashed into the corridor. The four officers had already started forward, but when they saw him emerge they halted in silence. In that moment of stillness the surgeon paused to listen. He heard the hissing sound and the clumsy floundering of a bulky, living object in the direction of his wife's apartments. It evidently was advancing towards him. A turn in the corridor shut out the view. He turned up the light, which revealed a ghastly pallor in his face.

"Wife!" he called.

There was no response. He hurriedly advanced, the four men following quietly. He turned the angle of the corridor, and ran so rapidly that by the time the officers had come in sight of him again he was twenty steps away. He ran past a huge, shapeless object, sprawling, crawling, and floundering along, and arrived at the body of his wife.

He gave one horrified glance at her face, and staggered away.

Then a fury seized him. Clutching the knife firmly, and holding the lamp aloft, he sprang toward the ungainly object in the corridor. It was then that the officers, still advancing cautiously, saw a little more clearly, though still indistinctly, the object of the surgeon's fury, and the cause of the look of unutterable anguish in his face. The hideous sight caused them to pause. They saw what appeared to be a man, yet evidently was not a man; huge, awkward, shapeless; a squirming, lurching, stumbling mass, completely naked. It raised its broad shoulders. *It had no head,* but instead of it a small metallic ball surmounting its massive neck.

"Devil!" exclaimed the surgeon, raising the knife.

"Hold, there!" commanded a stern voice.

The surgeon quickly raised his eyes and saw the four officers, and for a moment fear paralyzed his arm.

"The police!" he gasped.

Then, with a look of redoubled fury, he sent the knife to the hilt into the squirming mass before him. The wounded monster sprang to its feet and wildly threw its arms about, meanwhile emitting fearful sounds from a silver tube through which it breathed. The surgeon aimed another blow, but never gave it. In his blind fury he lost his caution, and was caught in an iron grasp. The struggling threw the lamp some feet toward the officers, and it fell to the floor, shattered to pieces. Simultaneously with the crash the oil took fire, and the corridor was filled with flame. The officers could not approach. Before them was the spreading blaze, and secure behind it were two forms struggling in a fearful embrace. They heard cries and gasps, and saw the gleaming of a knife.

The wood in the house was old and dry. It took fire at once, and the flames spread with great rapidity. The four officers turned and fled, barely escaping with their lives. In an hour nothing remained of the mysterious old house and its inmates but a blackened ruin.

H. Nearing, Jr.

The Maladjusted Classroom

Professor Cleanth Penn Ransom is alive and well! His chronicler, H. NEARING, JR., is a resident of Swarthmore, Pennsylvania, a veteran English professor and author of scholarly essays that include a doctoral dissertation on seventeenth-century historical poetry. Between 1950 and 1963, Professor Nearing composed a delightful series of science-fictional spoofs about mathematics professor Ransom and his long-suffering philosophical colleague, Professor Archibald MacTate. Doubleday collected many of them in 1954 as The Sinister Researches of C. P. Ransom, *but "The Maladjusted Classroom" was not included. Hopefully its reappearance after nearly forty years of undeserved neglect will lead to a resurgence of interest in the risible schemes of the liveliest math teacher in academic history!*

"GIVE ME a place to sit," said Professor Cleanth Penn Ransom, of the Mathematics Faculty, "and I will move the world." He leaned back in his swivel chair, stuck out his little belly, and looked at his wristwatch.

Professor Archibald MacTate, of Philosophy, lit a cigarette and regarded him poignantly. "Really, old boy, isn't the world in a bad enough fix without your—"

"No, no, MacTate." Ransom laughed. "I just wanted to see if you'd catch me. It ought to be 'stand.' *You* know." He folded his arms behind his head and began to swing back and forth. "And the world is just a figure of speech, because I'm only going to transpose the United States Army. Part of it. But of course since I'll probably be sitting down—"

"You're going to what?" MacTate pulled the icosahedral ashtray across the desk, purging his memory for any possible connection between Ransom and the military.

"I'm going to transpose Colonel Flowerbottom's ROTC class." Ransom looked at his wristwatch again. "We got scheduled in the same classroom at the same time. By mistake. So we've got to make some adjustments to fit into it."

"We?" MacTate looked up suspiciously.

"The Colonel and me. I've got a class in analysis situs, and he—"

"Analysis what?"

"Situs. Geometry of position. Suppose you want to make a tube with no inside and no outside—"

"But does anybody actually want to study that?"

"Sure." Ransom blinked with dignity. "Five men signed up for it."

"And you're displacing a big ROTC class for the sake of five people?" MacTate eyed his colleague reprovingly.

"Not displacing," said Ransom. "Transposing. Into another dimension. The only other room open at that hour is over next to the new hydroponics building they're putting up. Too much racket to hold a class there. So we agreed to both stay upstairs in 417 where we were assigned. The Colonel and me."

"And what dimension are you going to transpose them into?" said MacTate. "As if I didn't know."

Ransom grinned. "Look. Here's a two-dimensional classroom." He took a tablet and a pencil out of his top desk drawer and drew a large rectangle on it. "With two-dimensional students in it." He sketched in a series of circles, putting a smaller circle on top of each one for a head and two sticks underneath for legs. "Suppose you want to get another two-dimensional class in at the same time. All you've got to do is swing each student out at right angles to the plane of the room, and the other class can come into the vacated spaces. Right? Of course the transposed students have to leave one foot in the room so they can pivot back again. But the other class won't be disturbed by a bunch of shoes."

MacTate studied the sketch. "And the teacher?"

"Swings right out with them." Ransom drew a two-dimensional teacher at the front of the classroom. "If he doesn't twist out at the same angle as they do, he might look at them broadside and see a cross-section of their insides." He pointed at the center of one of the circles. "See, these outlines represent their skins, and the bounded regions are their insides. But that shouldn't bother the Colonel."

MacTate smiled. "So now all you have to do is discover a method for swinging the students out of their continuum."

"Oh, that's easy." Ransom looked up. "The tough part was talking the Colonel into trying it out." He reached into his top drawer again and tossed a thick packet of memorandums over to MacTate. "That's his correspondence on the subject."

MacTate read the first and last memorandums. The first said:

"Dear Ransom: In re the bi-occupancy of room 417 by your class of 5 and ROTC section 2C. This is to advise you that the Fifth Army does not tolerate bi-occupancy of this nature in the administration of the ROTC program. As of this date you will evacuate your class of 5 from the room indicated in order to immediately make it available to the ROTC section. It is hoped that it will not be necessary to report this matter to the Fifth Army. J. R. Flowerbottom, P.M.S. & T."

The last said:

"Professor Ransom: Due to the fact that the Dean has not seen fit to concern himself in the matter of the bi-occupancy of room 417, and it is wished to delay reporting this situation to the Fifth Army until all available solutions have been investigated, you may proceed with plan B at 1400 on 7 October only. It is understood that your class of 5 will be de-activated for the testing period. Be advised that the decision of the Fifth Army as to subsequent procedure will depend on the success of this demonstration. J.R.F., P.M.S. & T."

MacTate looked up. "What was plan A?"

Ransom grinned. "That he should move over next to the hydroponics thing. He decided right off that the Fifth Army wouldn't tolerate that either."

"And so you're going to try plan B on"—MacTate glanced at the date in the memorandum—"why, that's today. See here, Ransom, you don't mean you actually have a method for—"

"Transposing them." Ransom nodded. He drew two concentric circles inside the two-dimensional classroom on his tablet. "See, you take a two-dimensional ring like this, cut through it at one place, and put a magnet on each side of the cut with similar poles facing each other. What will happen? The magnets will swing around so the opposite poles can come together, and you've got a Moebius strip. Two-dimensional thing that twists through the third dimension. So if a two-dimensional student sticks one hand up around the twist and then reaches out with the other hand to clasp them together, he can pull himself out into the third dimension."

MacTate frowned. "But if it's a three-dimensional student that aspires to the fourth dimension—I trust it *is* the fourth dimension you intend to put the Colonel in?"

"That's right." Ransom nodded. "You simply make a three-dimensional Moebius strip that twists through the fourth dimension. It's called a Klein bottle." He opened his bottom desk drawer. "Suppose you took a bicycle tire, cut through it, and stuck electromagnets in the two holes, positive poles out. Under certain conditions the magnets would twist around through the fourth dimension to join the ends of the tire together while they're facing in the same direction, like two hoses running into one nozzle, and you'd get this." He reached into the drawer and held up something that looked like a section of a bicycle tire, though the ends were indistinct, like a badly focused photograph.

"What's wrong with the ends?" MacTate crushed out his cigarette and leaned forward to peer closely at the curved cylinder. "What makes them shimmer like that?"

"They're not ends. They're intersectors of the fourth dimension." Ransom ran a finger along the tire. When his finger reached the end of the visible section, the tip disappeared. "See. It's a whole tire, only part of it's twisting through the fourth dimension so you can't see it. If I ran my hand on up around it and then reached out with the other one—"

"No, no." MacTate grabbed convulsively at Ransom's sleeve and pulled his hand away from the tire. "If you're going to float away into hyperspace, I want witnesses around to testify I had nothing to do with it."

Ransom grinned. "Look, MacTate. You don't float away into hyperspace. You keep one foot in this continuum, see? So you can always come back when you want to."

"How?"

"Well, take this fellow for instance." Ransom pointed at one of the two-dimensional students on the tablet. "Since a plane is determined by three points, all he has to do is grab his pivot foot with both hands, so three parts of him will be back in the continuum, and then three of his friends can pull him all the way back. Your three-dimensional student just has to add the other foot so you can stretch four points of him out."

MacTate stared at the tire. "How on earth did you make a thing like that?"

"Like I told you." Ransom leaned back and started to swing again. "I cut the tire and stuck magnets in the holes." He looked at the section with a hint of perplexity. "It was really sort of an accident, I guess. I was trying to work out an automobile tire you could change without twisting a lot of nuts. Like chains. You know. Just wrap it around the wheel and snap it shut. Only I was using a bicycle tire, because it's smaller and easier to experiment with. Well, I must have got one of the magnets in backwards by mistake, because all of a sudden there was a big bang and here was this thing."

"Why didn't you take it apart to see?"

Ransom shook his head. "Remember the story about the mechanical leg Benjamin Franklin made for Captain Dogbody? They took it apart to see how it worked, and couldn't ever get it back together again. See, I was experimenting in a cold box. Had it good and cold to simulate the worst possible weather you might have to change a tire in. The trouble is, I'm not sure just what the temperature was. At the time of the bang, I mean. Afterwards it was different, on account of the heat released by the thing twisting around like that. So when I tried it with another tire, it wouldn't work. The temperature that first time must have been just right for weakening the continuum enough to let the ends fly—"

He was interrupted by a knock on the door. "That must be him now." He looked at his wristwatch and then at the door. "Come in."

A young man dressed in an ROTC uniform opened the door and looked uncertainly at Ransom, as if wondering whether to salute him. Finally, with a nothing-to-lose expression, he did. "Sir, the Colonel said to tell you he's ready."

"Right." Ransom grinned. "You go on ahead and announce our entrance." He got up and grabbed the Klein bottle. "Come on, MacTate. It's zero hour."

"But, old boy. Do you think the Colonel—"

"Sure. You're an official observer. For our side."

The chair behind the teacher's desk in room 417 was occupied solidly by a person who had learned to live with suspicion. It was in his eyes. He had an apoplectic complexion and close-cropped gray hair.

Ransom and MacTate marched down the aisle between the rows of uniformed students. "All right, Colonel," said Ransom. "Ready for the big push?"

The Colonel eyed the Klein bottle in Ransom's hand. "Now get this, Ransom." He plunged a stubby finger at him. "If this idea of yours isn't completely satisfactory—"

"I know, I know." Ransom waved at him soothingly. "The Fifth Army and all that. But you'll be delighted with it. The arrangement." He looked around at the students. "Here, let's start with this man." He pointed to a student in the front row and went over to him. The student rose to attention. "Look." Ransom grabbed his right hand and put the Klein bottle into it. "Slide your hand up around this till you feel a twist in it, then let go and straighten your arm over your head."

The boy looked startled when his hand disappeared, but followed Ransom's instructions and turned to him, wide-eyed, with his whole arm invisible.

"That's it." Ransom pulled the Klein bottle away. "Now hold your right arm steady and reach up with your left hand till you can clasp your hands together."

The boy squeezed his lips together grimly, twisted his shoulders, and began to grope in the air with his left hand. "Can't find it," he grunted.

"Sure you can," Ransom said enthusiastically. "Keep trying."

The boy writhed and grimaced like a uniformed Laocoön. His forehead grew damp. "I can't do it," he said. "It's like trying to find a keyhole in the dark."

"Look." Ransom jabbed a finger at him. "Forget you're in a classroom. You're a boxer. Heavyweight. You're meeting the champion. For the title. Madison Square Garden, fifteenth round. Suddenly you see an opening. Out snakes your left. He staggers. This is it. You follow up mercilessly. Right left, right left. He's down. Neutral corner. Now the referee. Onetwothreefour—*ten*. He's out. You're champion. Champion. The crowd goes wild. You raise your arms in triumph, high over your head—" Ransom swung his arms up. His glassy-eyed auditor imitated his motion, and abruptly there was nothing left of the boy but a leg. Ransom lifted his foot and kicked the rigid extremity gently behind the knee. All of it disappeared but the shoe.

Ransom pinched his nose and regarded the shoe thoughtfully. "There must be some easier way to—"

"Now, see here, Ransom." The Colonel got up and walked stiffly over to face him. "If he's—out there, how can he see me?"

Ransom raised his eyebrows. "You go out with him."

"I go—? Now, see here, Ransom." The Colonel fixed him with his eye and shook his head ominously.

"Here. Try it." Ransom seized the Colonel's hand and put the

Klein bottle into it. "It may seem a little—odd. At first. But when you get used to it, you won't want any other arrangement. Makes cribbing in tests next to impossible."

The Colonel looked at the thing in his hand with open hostility.

"Slide your hand up. Like this." Ransom grabbed his elbow and pushed it up. The Colonel's arm disappeared. "That's it. Now clasp your hands together." Ransom pulled the Klein bottle away and stepped back. The Colonel lifted his other arm and groped spasmodically in the air, twisting like an eccentric dancer.

Ransom leaned toward MacTate and spoke without moving his lips. "Wonder if we could sort of startle him into swinging out."

MacTate frowned dubiously. "I don't know, old boy. I don't think I'd—"

"Well, we've got to figure out some efficient way to get them out there. It's an experiment. He'd understand."

"All the same, I don't think—no, Ransom. Don't—"

"*Achtung,* Colonel." Ransom swung his arm back and hurled the Klein bottle, like an oversize quoit, straight at the Colonel's diaphragm. There was a thud and an explosive "Oof," and the Colonel's arm reappeared. But his head was gone.

"Didn't work," said Ransom. "Here, MacTate. Help me pull him back and we'll start over." He grabbed the Colonel's arm and gave it a violent jerk. The head did not reappear, but both legs vanished up to the knees. "Come on, MacTate. I can't do it by myself." Ransom grasped the arm again, but it was snatched angrily away, and forthwith all of the Colonel disappeared except the hand.

"I thought you said it took four people, old boy." MacTate looked apprehensively at the Colonel's hand, which had doubled into an irate fist.

"My God, that's right." Ransom surveyed the students, some of whom had risen to watch the proceedings with macabre glee while their less scientific classmates sat in stunned horror. "Let's see. You"—he pointed to one of the more avid expressions—"and—"

"Look, Ransom. He's—churning about." MacTate pointed.

The Colonel's fist was replaced by a knee, a shoulder, and an unidentified portion of the anatomy, all in rapid succession. At last a patch of gray bristle appeared and rolled up to reveal his head. His eyes were popping.

"Ransom," he bellowed. "You lunatic! You butcher! You've murdered him. Blown him to bits."

"Him?" Ransom looked confused. "Who?"

The Colonel's hands appeared beside his cheeks, and he extended his arms back into the third dimension. "Him." He pointed at the patient shoe of Ransom's first victim. "Poor chap. And I let you do it. His organs, floating all over out there—it's horrible. It's—"

"Oh, my God!" Ransom turned to MacTate. "I forgot to tell him about looking through the insides of the class. Look, Colonel." He turned back to the head and arms. "The boy is all there, only—"

"Only in a hundred fragments. You criminal." The Colonel's arm shook an agitated finger at Ransom. "Mark my words, Ransom. This is not mere disrespect for the Fifth Army. This is an atrocity. You have a man's blood on your—"

"Look, Colonel. If you'll just let me explain—"

"Explain." The Colonel's head snorted. "I recall only too well your plausible explanation of plan B." Suddenly the cold fury in his eyes turned hot. "But you'll blow no more innocent men to bits." His arms reached down for the Klein bottle.

"No, look, Colonel. It didn't do anything to *you*, did it? This boy—No! Wait—"

The Colonel's hands had disappeared at the top of the Klein bottle. His red face showed signs of extreme muscular exertion. Suddenly there was a miniature thunderclap, and the space the Colonel had occupied was entirely empty.

"The Klein bottle. He broke it." Ransom picked up a severed bicycle tire with iron bars stuck in its ends. "Look at it. All three-dimensional." There was a hint of hysteria in his voice. "God knows how we'll ever get it together again. Benjamin Franklin's leg—"

MacTate was not listening. With a horrified glance at the place where the Colonel had been, he grabbed the experimental student's ankle and began to tug at it. Nothing happened. With a sorrowful shrug he took a pack of matches from his pocket, inserted a match, head out, just above the insole of the shoe, and lit it with another. As the flame approached the leather, the shoe shook violently and two hands materialized to slap at it. "Grab them." MacTate motioned two students to seize the hands. "Three points. Now let's—maneuver him." They began to worry the hands and foot this way and that. Suddenly a wisp of fuzz appeared in the air. "There's his hair." MacTate motioned to another student to seize it. "Four points. Now stretch him out." The experimental student reappeared entirely and fell to the floor. "There." MacTate took out his handkerchief and wiped his brow. "The boy's intact. But the—" He turned to Ransom. "Good heavens, Ransom, what shall we do about the Colonel?"

"I don't care what you do about the Colonel." Ransom was still scowling at the tire. "Damned fathead, busting the bottle like that. This class"—he glanced angrily around at the students— "this class is dismissed. Plan B is all over." He strode down the aisle muttering over the tire.

"But, Ransom—" With another anxious look at the recent site of the Colonel, MacTate hastened after his departing colleague.

Ransom was back in his office before MacTate could catch up with him. He took a pair of pliers out of his desk drawer and began to fiddle with the ends of the tire. "Maybe if I put a bigger magnet in one end—"

"But, Ransom," said MacTate, "even if you do reconstruct it, how can you bring him back with it?"

"Him?" Ransom looked up. "Who?"

"The Colonel. Good heavens, man, don't you realize we're responsible for his—departure?"

Ransom looked at him for a moment, then put the pliers down

and sank into his swivel chair. "My God, that's right. I hadn't thought of that."

"What do you suppose they'll do to us? Can they court-martial civilians?"

"No." Ransom jabbed a finger at him. "Look. They can't do anything to us. What crime did we commit?"

"Defenestration. Into the fourth dimension."

"Where's the body to prove it?" Ransom began to swing back and forth.

"Very well. Abduction then. Whatever you like." MacTate wiped his brow. "The fact is, a roomful of students saw us do away with the Colonel. A keen prosecutor might even find a subversive motive in it."

Ransom stopped swinging and paled slightly. "You mean we attempted to undermine the armed might of—my God, MacTate, they could shoot us for that."

"Hang us, old boy. We were in civilian clothes at the time."

Ransom darted to his feet. "Let's get down to the cold box and try to fix the bottle before they find out. You can glue a rope to me, and I'll go out looking for him. We—"

The phone rang.

Ransom's pallor became tinged with green. "Already—"

MacTate sat down wearily. "Better answer it, old boy. Perhaps we can request clemency in the name of science."

The phone rang again. Ransom stared at it as if it were a cobra. It rang again. He gulped a deep breath and picked it up. "Hello."

The receiver began to crackle angrily. Ransom's mouth fell open. He sank back into his chair.

MacTate leaned forward and raised his eyebrows with interrogative apprehension.

Ransom put his hand over the mouthpiece and looked up. "It's the Colonel." He listened to the tirade for another moment, then looked up again. "He's calling from a filling station near Wheeling, West Virginia. Landed on a farm— No, no, Colonel. We had no intention—" He lifted his hand from the mouthpiece to interpose an objection. "Now listen, Colonel—" The crackling in the receiver continued without pause. He shrugged and looked at MacTate again. "He landed on a farm down there. About an hour ago."

"An hour—? But good heavens, Ransom, how—"

"Fourth dimension. Time factor. *You* know—" Ransom turned his attention back to the Colonel's voice. "No, look, Colonel. It wasn't my fault you—Now, wait a minute—What? Listen, you—"

"Old boy—" MacTate noticed his colleague's rising blood pressure. "Don't you think—"

"All right, Flowerbottom." Ransom made a visible effort to keep his blood pressure down. "I admit you have some justification for getting mad. But look, do you know what plane tickets cost? I—look. How about if I buy you a train ticket? It won't take that much longer. And I'll take your class tomorrow. Along with mine—All right. Give me your address there, and I'll wire the money down." He seized a pencil and scribbled on the tablet. "All right, I'll—What? Now listen, Flowerbottom, I said I'd— *What?* Listen, you fatheaded—" He sputtered for a moment, then put the receiver down and regarded it with contempt. "Hung up. That's the tactical mind—"

"But you *are* going to wire him the money and take his class?"

"Oh, I guess so." Ransom looked up. "But look, MacTate. You sit in on that class. As a witness. He's liable to accuse me of teaching the overthrow of the Fifth Army."

The next day MacTate fell into a state of semi-hypnosis filling in the o's in the *Journal of Aesthetics* with a pencil, and did not remember Ransom's class until it was more than half over. He trotted across the campus to Ransom's building, ran up the stairs to room 417, and sank out of breath into a seat in the back row.

Ransom had drawn an S-curve horizontally on the blackboard. "Here's the Tennessee River, with Chattanooga"—he put a dot in the upward bulge at the right—"in the bend. Over here's the Confederate left on Lookout Mountain." He drew a slender parabola, its nose almost touching the river, below the city and to its left. "And here's the Confederate right on Missionary Ridge."

He drew a line, parallel to the axis of the parabola, to the city's right. "While down here in Rossville, Georgia," he put a dot toward the bottom of the line, "sits Braxton Bragg, nervously chewing his big black beard." He turned to the class and flourished the chalk. "On account of he knows that his left is threatened by Fighting Joe Hooker, his right by William T. Sherman, and his center by George H. Thomas. While back here in Chattanooga, directing the whole show, is none other than Ulysses S. Grant. It's a predicament."

A student in the front row raised his hand. "Wheah's General Lee?"

"Well, he's up the road a piece taking care of George G. Meade. We'll get to him later." Ransom turned back to the blackboard and surveyed the battlefield. "Anyway, at 1330 hours on the 23rd of November, Grant sends Thomas flying at Bragg's center"—he drew a demonstrative arrow on the board—"which gets pushed down the valley until Thomas can occupy Orchard Knob, a big hill about here." He put an X between Chattanooga and Missionary Ridge. "But that's nothing. Next morning at 800, here comes Fighting Joe Hooker with nine thousand Blues to storm Lookout Mountain." He drew a large, aggressive arrow pointing at the left side of the parabola. "The Grays on the palisades at the top can't see Hooker at all, on account of the low clouds hanging over everything; while Edward C. Walthall, commanding the brigade on the west slope, isn't much better off. Fighting Joe hits his flank in the fog and chases him all the way around the mountain." Ransom turned and regarded the class portentously. "Well, you can just imagine how Braxton Bragg is taking all this. Defeat stares him in the face. Frantically he orders a general retreat to Missionary Ridge, while Ulysses S. Grant in person comes down to Orchard Knob to watch the fun."

"General Lee still not theah?" said a wistful voice in the front row.

"No." Ransom shook his head. "Bragg's in this all by himself. But wait." He shot out a dramatic finger. "Suddenly Bragg's got an idea. His boys have been retreating just about an hour. Out goes a general order to the brigades of the left and center to get out their bottles. The bugles scream the weird new call. Then at a signal of six cannon shots from Rossville, the left drops over to Lookout Valley, where Hooker came from; and the center drops up to Chattanooga, where Thomas started. You see what they've done. Traded places with the Union armies. This time Walthall comes up through the fog and chases Hooker around Lookout Mountain; while Bragg smacks down on Orchard Knob, where Ulysses S. Grant is still waiting for the fun. Bragg's right, you remember, is still at the upper end of Missionary Ridge playing who'll-flinch-first with Sherman. Now Bragg tells them to charge the other side of the Knob, and Grant is sandwiched in between. So with him captured, it's no trouble at all to rout the other Blues. Bragg . . ."

"I say, Ransom—" MacTate, in the back row, had a worried look on his face. But Ransom was too far absorbed in his narrative to notice.

". . . invests Chattanooga and then takes half his army up to help Robert E. Lee in the . . ."

"Heah's General Lee."

". . . Mine Run campaign. Between them they make short work of Meade, take Washington and Philadelphia, and besiege New York. After Bragg has made his terrible march to Boston, cutting a swath of devastation through the heart of New England, Chief of Staff Halleck meets Lee at Albany to surrender the Union armies." Ransom looked at his wristwatch. "And that's enough for today. Class dismissed." He marched down the aisle, waved to MacTate to follow him, and went down to his office.

"Wanted to get out of there before that professional Southerner could corner me." Ransom leaned back in his swivel chair. "I—"

"Ransom." MacTate's expression was somewhat severe. "Am I crazy, or did I just hear you teach that class that the South won the Civil War?"

"No, no." Ransom laughed. "You should have come on time and heard the whole thing. See, I took the first half of the period to explain the principle of the Klein bottle. For *my* class. Then I used the rest of the time to illustrate a hypothetical military application. What could have happened if the South had had calibrated Klein bottles at Chattanooga. It was all imaginary."

"You think that boy in the front row thought it was imaginary?"

"Oh, him. Well, who cares"—suddenly Ransom whipped a handkerchief from his pocket and sneezed violently—"whad he thigs." He blew his nose. "Damn it, MacTate, I'm coming down with something bad." A faraway look came into his eyes. "I wonder if I could have picked up a bunch of four-dimensional germs fooling with that Klein bottle."

Ransom's diagnosis proved accurate in effect if not in cause. The next two days he was kept at home with a severe cold. MacTate wondered if the Colonel was taking Ransom's class along with the ROTC students, but was diffident of investigating.

"You see, old boy," he told Ransom on his return, "I was afraid he might interrogate me as to the soundness of your military doctrine, and as Plato says, a lie—"

"What did I teach them wrong?" Ransom swung petulantly in his swivel chair. "Anyway, we'll soon know whether he took them." He looked at his wristwatch. "We've got another joint class this afternoon."

"Yes." MacTate pursed his lips. "I was just wondering how you're going to arrange it now that the Klein bottle—"

The door opened. Ransom and MacTate looked up. It was the Colonel.

"Well, Ransom, I see you're back." He strode past the desk as if he were reviewing troops, but there was a nasty glint in his eye.

Ransom closed his mouth and tried to look nonchalant. "Sure, I'm back. I see you're back, too."

"Yes." The Colonel sat down on the edge of a chair, leaning forward slightly, as if with eagerness. "I'm back." He took a paper from his breast pocket, unfolded it, and glanced at it with an expression of unmitigated malice. "I was interested in finding out what you had been teaching the ROTC class while I was—

away." He looked up at Ransom. "So I gave them a test yesterday."

MacTate had a sudden odd feeling in the pit of his stomach. "On the Battle of Chattanooga. That's what you—presented to them, wasn't it?"

"Sure." Ransom was swinging in his swivel chair with nervous twitches. He took a deep breath. "I trust everybody came away with a vivid impression."

"Yes." The Colonel looked at the paper in his hand with a peculiar smile. "One chap in particular wrote an extremely interesting account. Perhaps you'd like to hear it."

Ransom glowered. The Colonel began to read.

"General Bragg was in Rossville, Georgia, nervously chewing on his big black beard account of General Lee wasn't anywheres near the battlefield so at 1330 Grant captured Orchard Knob which made General Bragg feel mighty low account of he knew the north had pretty good generals without General Lee was there so next morning at 800 Hooker stormed Lookout Mountain in a fog and General Bragg he started to retreat to Missionary Ridge only he remembered his men had fourth-dimensional canteens and weird new bugles which they traded places with the northern armies with so Grant gave hisself up on Orchard Knob to our right so then General Bragg could go help General Lee march to Washington, Philadelphia and Boston and they finally surrendered at Albany the north."

The Colonel regarded the paper with malevolent satisfaction. "I've called several papers to send reporters out to see me." He looked up at Ransom again.

"Why?"

"Oh, I thought they might be interested in the way some university professors teach history. It might even get national coverage, since it's about American history. Of course"—the Colonel looked Ransom straight in the eye—"if room 417 were to be made available—"

"Flowerbottom. That's blackmail."

"A harsh word, Ransom. Let's say it's a proffered bargain.

Since you don't feel that you owe me anything after that das-
tardly trick you played with the Klein bottle—"

"The trick *I* played? How about you tearing it apart like that?
For no reason at all? To think what we could have done with it if
you—"

"By the way, Ransom," said MacTate. "Not to change the
subject, but do you think the Klein bottle might actually have an
application of the sort you described to the class?"

Ransom looked at him. "You mean in tactical maneuvers? I
don't know. How'll we ever know now that he's busted it?"

MacTate rubbed his nose. "But if you were planning to attempt
a reconstruction, wouldn't the Army be interested in it? Give you
a research subsidy or something like that?"

"Well, what if they would? What's that got to do with who
gets room—"

"Nothing really, I suppose. It just occurred to me that they
might like to know about the loss of a gadget that could transport
personnel to a place like Wheeling and gain an hour doing it."

"MacTate, what are you—" Suddenly Ransom's eyes brightened. "You mean in my application for a research grant I'd have
to tell them how the first one got broken?" He turned slowly and
looked at the Colonel. "And by whom?"

"Oh, well, of course you wouldn't want to do it in that case,"
said MacTate.

"No, of course not." Ransom grinned. "We wouldn't want the
Colonel to get in trouble for sabotaging developmental war gadgets. Would we?"

The Colonel looked uncomfortable.

"But on the other hand," said MacTate, "I'm sure the Colonel
was only joking about his intention of publishing the Southern
chap's test paper. It would simply be a matter of your blowing
each other up, so to speak. So that the matter of room 417 actually remains unsolved."

"What a big help *you* are." Ransom leaned back in his swivel
chair.

"Well, to take a constructive view of the matter," MacTate

went on unperturbed, "I would suggest that you take turns occupying 417, thus arriving at that equality of dissatisfaction which, as someone—Talleyrand I think—observed, is the nearest approach to happiness possible in the human state."

Both Ransom and the Colonel looked at him resentfully.

"Of course it's none of my business. Just a suggestion." MacTate shrugged.

The Colonel sighed. "In that case, who gets the room today?"

"Well, you've really had it only once, while Ransom's had it—" MacTate caught Ransom's glance and stopped abruptly.

"Then it's mine today." The Colonel got up. "After that I take turns. With a class of five." He turned his back on Ransom and walked stiffly to the door. As he opened it, he turned around. "Someday, Ransom, I'm going to catch you when your lawyer isn't with you. Then watch out." He slammed the door behind him.

"I say, Ransom, does he really think I'm your—" MacTate stopped again. Ransom was still staring at him.

"Don't worry about what he thinks." Ransom shook his head slowly. "You should hear what I'm thinking."

"But, old boy, I did get you out of some sort of mess, didn't I?"

"You got him out of one, too." Ransom laughed sardonically. "I don't know what we'd do without you. Either of us." He grinned. "Fighting Joe Flowerbottom and Braxton P. Ransom, having a nice quiet little battle, both get kicked in the rear by Benedict MacTate. And if that's the wrong war"—he sighed and swung back to his desk—"I'm glad."

Satan's Fine Print and Memoranda from Hell

Old Nick has been accused of many damnable faults, but I do not believe he was ever guilty of being called a bore. Satanic grimoires, devilish contracts and other diabolical printed matter make for lively, if daring, reading—risqué, perhaps, but not risky—unless you sign your name.

Four of the stories in this section, those by Robert Bloch, Laura J. Catanzariti, Ron Goulart and Nathaniel Hawthorne, are figuratively or literally concerned with Satanic printed matter. The other tales deal with characters already involved in a Hell of their own making.

Robert Bloch

Black Bargain

The late, beloved ROBERT BLOCH *(1917–1994), best known as the author of* Psycho, *was a prolific contributor of stories to* Weird Tales, *America's greatest fantasy periodical. Some of his stories were humorous, most were horrific, like "Enoch," "The Unspeakable Betrothal," "Yours Truly, Jack the Ripper" or "Black Bargain," with its literal aura of shadowy menace.*

IT WAS GETTING LATE when I switched off the neon and got busy behind the fountain with my silver polish. The fruit syrup came off easily, but the chocolate stuck and the hot fudge was greasy. I wish to the devil they wouldn't order hot fudge.

I began to get irritated as I scrubbed away. Five hours on my feet, every night, and what did I have to show for it? Varicose veins. Varicose veins, and the memory of a thousand foolish faces. The veins were easier to bear than the memories. They were so depressing, those customers of mine. I knew them all by heart.

In early evening all I got was "cokes." I could spot the "cokes" a mile away. Giggling high-school girls, with long shocks of uncombed brown hair, with their shapeless tan "fingertip" coats and the repulsively thick legs bulging over furry red ankle socks. They were all "cokes." For forty-five minutes they'd monopolize a booth, messing up the tile table-top with cigarette ashes, crushed napkins daubed in lipstick, and little puddles of spilled water. Whenever a high-school girl came in, I automatically reached for the cola pump.

A little later in the evening I got the "gimme two packs" crowd. Sports-shirts hanging limply over hairy arms meant the popular brands. Blue work-shirts with rolled sleeves disclosing tattooing meant the two-for-a-quarter cigarettes.

Once in a while I got a fat boy. He was always a "cigar." If he wore glasses he was a ten-center. If not, I merely had to indicate the box on the counter. Five cents straight. Mild Havana—all long filler.

Oh, it was monotonous. The "notions" family, who invariably departed with aspirin, Ex-Lax, candy bars, and a pint of ice-cream. The "public library" crowd—tall, skinny youths bending the pages of magazines on the rack and never buying. The "soda-waters" with their trousers wrinkled by the sofa of a one-room apartment, the "hairpins," always looking furtively toward the baby buggy outside. And around ten, the "pineapple sundaes"— fat women Bingo-players. Followed by the "chocolate sodas" when the show let out. More booth-parties, giggling girls and red-necked young men in sloppy play-suits.

In and out, all day long. The rushing "telephones," the doddering old "three-cent stamps," the bachelor "toothpastes" and "razor-blades."

I could spot them all at a glance. Night after night they dragged up to the counter. I don't know why they even bothered to tell me what they wanted. One look was all I needed to anticipate their slightest wishes. I could have given them what they needed without their asking.

Or, rather, I suppose I couldn't. Because what most of them really needed was a good long drink of arsenic, as far as I was concerned.

Arsenic! Good Lord, how long had it been since I'd been called upon to fill out a *prescription*! None of these stupid idiots wanted *drugs* from a drug-store. Why had I bothered to study pharmacy? All I really needed was a two-week course in pouring chocolate syrup over melting ice-cream, and a month's study of how to set up cardboard figures in the window so as to emphasize their enormous busts.

Well—

He came in then. I heard the slow footsteps without bothering to look up. For amusement I tried to guess before I glanced. A "gimme two packs"? A "toothpaste"? Well, the hell with him. I was closing up.

The male footsteps had shuffled up to the counter before I raised my head. They halted, timidly. I still refused to give any recognition of his presence. Then came a hesitant cough. That did it.

I found myself staring at Caspar Milquetoast, and nearly rags. A middle-aged, thin little fellow with sandy hair and rimless glasses perched on a snub nose. The crease of his froggish mouth underlined the despair of his face.

He wore a frayed $16.50 suit, a wrinkled white shirt, and a string tie—but humility was his real garment. It covered him completely, that aura of hopeless resignation.

To hell with psycho-analysis! I'm not the drug-store Dale Carnegie. What I saw added up to only one thing in my mind. A moocher.

"I beg your pardon, please, but have you any tincture of aconite?"

Well, miracles *do* happen. I was going to get a chance to sell drugs after all. Or was I? When despair walks in and asks for aconite, it means suicide.

I shrugged. "Aconite?" I echoed. "I don't know."

He smiled, a little. Or rather, that crease wrinkled back in a poor imitation of amusement. But on his face a smile had no more mirth in it than the grin you see on a skull.

"I know what you're thinking," he mumbled. "But you're wrong. I'm—I'm a chemist. I'm doing some experiments, and I must have four ounces of aconite at once. And some belladonna. Yes, and—wait a minute."

Then he dragged the book out of his pocket.

I craned my neck, and it was worth it.

The book had rusty metal covers, and was obviously very old. When the thick yellow pages fluttered open under his trembling thumb I saw flecks of dust rise from the binding. The heavy, black-lettered type was German, but I couldn't read anything at that distance.

"Let me see now," he murmured. "Aconite—belladonna—yes, and I have this—the cat, of course—nightshade—um-hum—oh, yes, I'll need some phosphorus, of course—have you any blue chalk?—good—and I guess that's all."

I was beginning to catch on. But what the devil did it matter to me? A screwball more or less was nothing new in my life. All I wanted to do was get out of here and soak my feet.

I went back and got the stuff for him, quickly. I peered through the slot above the prescription counter, but he wasn't doing anything—just paging through that black, iron-bound book and moving his lips.

Wrapping the parcel, I came out. "Anything else, sir?"

"Oh—yes. Could I have about a dozen candles? The large size?"

I opened a drawer and scrabbled for them under the dust.

"I'll have to melt them down and reblend them with the fat," he said.

"What?"

"Nothing. I was just figuring."

Sure. That's the kind of figuring you do best when you're counting the pads in your cell. But it wasn't my business, was it?

So I handed over the package, like a fool.

"Thank you. You've been very kind. I must ask you to be kinder—to charge this."

Oh, swell!

"You see I'm temporarily out of funds. But I can assure you, in a very short time, in fact within three days, I shall pay you in full. Yes."

A very convincing plea. I wouldn't give him a cup of coffee on it—and that's what bums usually ask for, instead of aconite and candles. But if his words didn't move me, his eyes did. They were so lonely behind his spectacles, so pitifully alone, those two little puddles of hope in the desert of despair that was his face.

All right. Let him have his dreams. Let him take his old iron-bound dream book home with him and make him crazy. Let him light his tapers and draw his phosphorescent circle and recite his spells to Little Wahoo the Indian Guide of the Spirit World, or whatever the hell he wanted to do.

No, I wouldn't give him coffee, but I'd give him a dream.

"That's okay, buddy," I said. "We're all down on our luck sometime, I guess."

That was wrong. I shouldn't have patronized. He stiffened at once and his mouth curled into a sneer—of superiority, if you please!

"I'm not asking charity," he said. "You'll get paid, never fear, my good man. In three days, mark my words. Now good evening. I have work to do."

Out he marched, leaving "my good man" with his mouth open. Eventually I closed my mouth but I couldn't clamp a lid on my curiosity.

That night, walking home, I looked down the dark street with new interest. The black houses bulked like a barrier behind which lurked fantastic mysteries. Row upon row, not houses any more, but dark dungeons of dreams. In what house did my stranger hide? In what room was he intoning to what strange gods?

Once again I sensed the presence of wonder in the world, of lurking strangeness behind the scenes of drug-store and apartment-house civilization. Black books still were read, and wild-eyed strangers walked and muttered, candles burned into the night, and a missing alley-cat might mean a chosen sacrifice.

But my feet hurt, so I went home.

II

Same old malted milks, cherry cokes, vaseline, Listerine, hairnets, bathing caps, cigarettes, and what have you?

Me, I had a headache. It was four days later, almost the same time of night, when I found myself scrubbing off the soda-taps again.

Sure enough, he walked in.

I kept telling myself all evening that I didn't expect him—but I *did* expect him, really. I had that crawling feeling when the door clicked. I waited for the shuffle of the Thom McAn shoes.

Instead there was a brisk tapping of Oxfords. English Oxfords. The $18.50 kind.

I looked up in a hurry this time.

It *was* my stranger.

At least he was there, someplace beneath the flashy blue pin-stripe of his suit, the immaculate shirt and foulard tie. He'd had a shave, a haircut, a manicure, and evidently a winning ticket in the Irish Sweepstakes.

"Hello, there." Nothing wrong with that voice—I've heard it in the ritzy hotel lobbies for years, brimming over with pep and confidence and authority.

"Well, well, well," was all I could say.

He chuckled. His mouth wasn't a crease any more. It was a trumpet of command. Out of that mouth could come orders, and directions. This wasn't a mouth shaped for hesitant excuses any longer. It was a mouth for requesting expensive dinners, choice vintage wines, heavy cigars; a mouth that barked at taxi-drivers and doormen.

"Surprised to see me, eh? Well, I told you it would take three days. Want to pay you your money, thank you for your kindness."

That was nice. Not the thanks, the money. I like money. The thought of getting some I didn't expect made me genial.

"So your prayers were answered, eh?" I said.

He frowned.

"Prayers—what prayers?"

"Why, I thought that—" I'd pulled a boner, and no mistake.

"I don't understand," he snapped, understanding perfectly well. "Did you perhaps harbor some misapprehension concerning my purchases of the other evening? A few necessary chemicals, that's all—to complete the experiment I spoke of. And the candles, I must confess, were to light my room. They shut my electricity off the day before."

Well, it *could* be.

"Might as well tell you the experiment was a howling success. Yes, sir. Went right down to Newsohm with the results and they put me on as assistant research director. Quite a break."

Newsohm was the biggest chemical supply house in our section of the country. And he went right down in his rags and was "put on" as assistant research director! Well, live and learn.

"So here's the money. $2.39, wasn't it? Can you change a twenty?"

I couldn't.

"That's all right, keep it."

I refused, I don't know why. Made me feel crawling again, somehow.

"Well then, tell you what let's do. You are closing up, aren't you? Why not step down the street to the tavern for a little drink? I'll get change there. Come on, I feel like celebrating."

So it was that five minutes later I walked down the street with Mr. Fritz Gulther.

We took a table in the tavern and ordered quickly. Neither he nor I was at ease. Somehow there was an unspoken secret between us. It seemed almost as though I harbored criminal knowledge against him—I, of all men, alone knowing that behind this immaculately-clad figure of success, there lurked a shabby specter just three days in the past. A specter that owed me $2.39.

We drank quickly, both of us. The specter got a little fainter. We had another. I insisted on paying for the third round.

"It's a celebration," I argued.

He laughed. "Certainly is. And let me tell you, this is only the beginning. Only the beginning! From now on I'm going to climb so fast it'll make your head swim. I'll be running that place within six months. Going to get a lot of new defense orders in from the government, and expand."

"Wait a minute," I cautioned, reserve gone. "You're way ahead of yourself. If I were in your shoes I'd still be dazed with what happened to me in the past three days."

Fritz Gulther smiled. "Oh, that? I expected *that*. Didn't I tell you so in the store? I've been working for over a year and I knew just what to expect. It was no surprise, I assure you. I had it all planned. I was willing to starve to carry out my necessary studies, and I did starve. Might as well admit it."

"Sure." I was on my fourth drink now, over the barriers. "When you came into the store I said to myself, 'Here's a guy who's been through hell!' "

"Truer words were never spoken," said Gulther. "I've been through hell all right, quite literally. But it's all over now, and I didn't get burned."

"Say, confidentially—what kind of magic did you use?"

"Magic? Magic? I don't know anything about magic."

"Oh, yes, you do, Gulther," I said. "What about that little black book with the iron covers you were mumbling around with in the store?"

"German inorganic chemistry text," he snapped. "Pretty old. Here, drink up and have another."

I had another. Gulther began to babble a bit. About his new clothes and his new apartment and the new car he was going to buy next week. About how he was going to have everything he wanted now, by God, he'd show the fools that laughed at him all these years, he'd pay back the nagging landladies and the cursing grocers, and the sneering rats who told him he was soft in the head for studying the way he did.

Then he got into the kindly stage.

"How'd you like a job at Newsohm?" he asked me. "You're a good pharmacist. You know your chemistry. You're a nice enough fellow, too—but you've got a terrible imagination. How about it? Be my secretary. Sure, that's it. Be my secretary. I'll put you on tomorrow."

"I'll drink on that," I declared. The prospect intoxicated me. The thought of escape from the damned store, escape from the "coke"-faces, the "ciggies"-voices, very definitely intoxicated me. So did the next drink.

I began to see something.

We were sitting against the wall and the tavern lights were low. Couples around us were babbling in monotone that was akin to silence. We sat in shadow against the wall. Now I looked at my shadow—an ungainly, flickering caricature of myself, hunched over the table. What a contrast it presented before *his* suddenly erect bulk!

His shadow, now—

His shadow, now—

I saw it. He was sitting up straight across the table from me. But his shadow on the wall was *standing*!

"No more Scotch for me," I said as the waiter came up.

But I continued to stare at his shadow. He was sitting and the shadow was standing. It was a larger shadow than mine, and a blacker shadow. For fun I moved my hands up and down, making heads and faces in silhouette. He wasn't watching me, he was gesturing to the waiter.

His shadow didn't gesture. It just stood there. I watched and stared and tried to look away. His hands moved but the black outline stood poised and silent, hands dangling at the sides. And yet I saw the familiar shape of his head and nose; unmistakably his.

"Say, Gulther," I said. "Your shadow—there on the wall—"

I slurred my words. My eyes were blurred.

But I felt his attitude pierce my consciousness below the alcohol.

Fritz Gulther rose to his feet and then shoved a dead-white face against mine. He didn't look at his shadow. He looked at me, through me, at some horror behind my face, my thoughts, my brain. He looked *at* me, and *into* some private hell of his own.

"Shadow," he said. "There's nothing wrong with my shadow. You're mistaken. Remember that, you're mistaken. And if you ever mention it again, I'll bash your skull in."

Then Fritz Gulther got up and walked away. I watched him

march across the room, moving swiftly but a little unsteadily. Behind him, moving very slowly and not a bit unsteadily, a tall black shadow followed him from the room.

III

If you can build a better mousetrap than your neighbor, you're liable to put your foot in it.

That's certainly what I had done with Gulther. Here I was, ready to accept his offer of a good job as his secretary, and I had to go and pull a drunken boner!

I was still cursing myself for a fool two days later. Shadows that don't follow body-movements, indeed! Who was that shadow I saw you with last night? That was no shadow, that was the Scotch I was drinking. Oh, fine!

So I stood in the drug-store and sprinkled my sundaes with curses as well as chopped nuts.

I nearly knocked the pecans off the counter that second night, when Fritz Gulther walked in again.

He hurried up to the counter and flashed me a tired smile.

"Got a minute to spare?"

"Sure—wait till I serve these people in the booth."

I dumped the sundaes and raced back. Gulther perched himself on a stool and took off his hat. He was sweating profusely.

"Say—I want to apologize for the way I blew up the other night."

"Why, that's all right, Mr. Gulther."

"I got a little too excited, that's all. Liquor and success went to my head. No hard feelings, I want you to understand that. It's just that I was nervous. Your ribbing me about my shadow, that stuff sounded too much like the way I was always kidded for sticking to my studies in my room. Landlady used to accuse me of all sorts of things. Claimed I dissected her cat, that I was burning incense, messing the floor up with chalk. Some damn fool college punks downstairs began to yap around that I was some kind of nut dabbling in witchcraft."

I wasn't asking for his autobiography, remember. All this

sounded a little hysterical. But then, Gulther looked the part. His sweating, the way his mouth wobbled and twitched as he got this out of me.

"But say, reason I stopped in was to see if you could fix me up a sedative. No, no bromo or aspirin. I've been taking plenty of that stuff ever since the other evening. My nerves are all shot. That job of mine down at Newsohm takes it all out of me."

"Wait a minute, I'll get something."

I made for the back room. As I compounded I sneaked a look at Gulther through the slot.

All right, I'll be honest. It wasn't Gulther I wanted to look at. It was his shadow.

When a customer sits at the counter stools, the storelights hit him so that his shadow is just a little black pool beneath his feet.

Gulther's shadow was a complete silhouette of his body, in outline. A black, deep shadow.

I blinked, but that didn't help.

Stranger still, the shadow seemed to be cast *parallel* with his body, instead of at an angle from it. It grew out from his chest instead of his legs. I don't know refraction, the laws of light, all that technical stuff. All I know is that Fritz Gulther had a big black shadow sitting beside him on the floor, and that the sight of it sent cold shivers along my spine.

I wasn't drunk. Neither was he. Neither was the shadow. All three of us existed.

Now Gulther was putting his hat back on.

But not the shadow. It just sat there. Crouched.

It was all wrong.

The shadow was no denser at one spot than at another. It was evenly dark, and—I noted this particularly—the outlines did not blur or fade. They were solid.

I stared and stared. I saw a lot now I'd never noticed. The shadow wore no clothes. Of course! Why should it put on a hat? It was naked, that shadow. But it belonged to Gulther—it wore spectacles. It was his shadow, all right. Which suited me fine, because *I* didn't want it.

Fiddling around compounding that sedative, I got in several more peeks.

Now Gulther was looking down over his shoulder. *He* was looking at his shadow now. Even from a distance I fancied I saw new beads of sweat string a rosary of fear across his forehead.

He knew, all right!

I came out, finally.

"Here it is," I said. I kept my eyes from his face.

"Good. Hope it works. Must get some sleep. And say—that job offer still goes. How about coming down tomorrow morning?"

I nodded, forcing a smile.

Gulther paid me, rose.

"See you then."

"Certainly." And why not? After all, what if you do work for a boss with an unnatural shadow? Most bosses have other faults, worse ones and more concrete. That shadow—whatever it was and whatever was wrong with it—wouldn't bite me. Though Gulther acted as though it might bite *him.*

As he turned away I looked at his departing back, and at the long, swooping black outline which followed it. The shadow rose and stalked after him. Stalked. Yes, it followed quite purposefully. To my now-bewildered eyes it seemed larger than it had in the tavern. Larger, and a bolder black.

Then the night swallowed Gulther and his non-existent companion.

I went back to the rear of the store and swallowed the other half of the sedative I'd made up for that purpose. After seeing that shadow, I needed it as much as he did.

IV

The girl in the ornate outer office smiled prettily. "Go right in," she warbled. "He's expecting you."

So it was true, then. Gulther was assistant research director, and I was to be his secretary.

I floated in. In the morning sunshine I forgot all about shadows.

The inner office was elaborately furnished—a huge place, with the elegant walnut panelling associated with business authority. There was a kidney-desk set before closed venetian blinds, and a variety of comfortable leather armchairs. Fluorescent lighting gleamed pleasantly.

But there was no Gulther. Probably on the other side of the little door at the back, talking to his chief.

I sat down, with the tight feeling of anticipation hugged somewhere within my stomach. I glanced around, taking in the room again. My gaze swept the glass-topped desk. It was bare. Except in the corner, where a small box of cigars rested.

No, wait a minute. That wasn't a cigar-box. It was metal. I'd seen it somewhere before.

Of course! It was Gulther's iron-bound book.

"German inorganic chemistry." Who was I to doubt his word? So naturally, I just had to sneak a look before he came in.

I opened the yellowed pages.

De Vermis Mysteriis.

"Mysteries of the Worm."

This was no inorganic chemistry text. It was something entirely different. Something that told you how you could compound aconite and belladonna and draw circles of phosphorescent fire on the floor when the stars were right. Something that spoke of melting tallow candles and blending them with corpse-fat, whispered of the uses to which animal sacrifice might be put.

It spoke of meetings that could be arranged with various parties most people don't either care to meet or even believe in.

The thick black letters crawled across the pages, and the detestable odor arising from the musty thing formed a background for the nastiness of the text. I won't say whether or not I believed what I was reading, but I will admit that there was an air, a suggestion about those cold, deliberate directions for traffic with alien evil, which made me shiver with repulsion. Such thoughts have no place in sanity, even as fantasy. And if *this* is what

Gulther had done with the materials, he'd bought himself for $2.39.

"Years of study," eh? "Experiments." What was Gulther trying to call up, what did he call up, and what bargain did he make?

The man who could answer these questions sidled out from behind the door. Gone was the Fritz Gulther of the pin-stripe suit personality. It was my original Caspar Milquetoast who creased his mouth at me in abject fear. He looked like a man—I had to say it—who was afraid of his own shadow.

The shadow trailed him through the doorway. To my eyes it had grown overnight. Its arms were slightly raised, though Gulther had both hands pressed against his sides. I saw it cross the wall as he walked toward me—and it moved more swiftly than he did.

Make no mistake. I saw the shadow. Since then I've talked to wise boys who assure me that under even fluorescence no shadow is cast. They're wise boys all right, but I saw that shadow.

Gulther saw that book in my hands.

"All right," he said, simply. "You know. And maybe it's just as well."

"Know?"

"Yes. Know that I made a bargain with—someone. I thought I was being smart. He promised me success, and wealth, anything I wanted, on only one condition. Those damned conditions; you always read about them and you always forget, because they sound so foolish! He told me that I'd have only one rival, and that this rival would be a part of myself. It would grow with my success."

I sat mute. Gulther was wound up for a long time.

"Silly, wasn't it? Of course I accepted. And then I found out what my rival was—what it would be. This shadow of mine. It's independent of me, you know that, and it keeps growing! Oh, not in size, but in *depth*, in intensity. It's becoming—maybe I *am* crazy but you see it too—more solid. Thicker. As though it had palpable substance." Crease-mouth wobbled violently, but the words choked on.

"The further I go the more it grows. Last night I took your sedative and it didn't work. Didn't work at all. I sat up in the darkness and watched my shadow."

"In darkness?"

"Yes. It doesn't need light. It really *exists* now. Permanently. In the dark it's just a blacker blur. But you can see it. It doesn't sleep, or rest. It just waits."

"And you're afraid of it? Why?"

"I don't know. It doesn't threaten me, or make gestures, or even take any notice of me. Shadows taking notice—sounds crazy, doesn't it? But you see it as I do. You can see it waiting. And that's why I'm afraid. What's it waiting for?"

The shadow crept closer over his shoulder. Eavesdropping.

"I don't need you for a secretary. I need a nurse."

"What you need is a good rest."

"Rest? How can I rest? I just came out of Newsohm's office. He doesn't notice anything—yet. Too stupid, I suppose. The girls in the office look at me when I pass, and I wonder if they see something peculiar. But Newsohm doesn't. He just made me head of research. Completely in charge."

"In five days? Marvelous!"

"Isn't it? Except for our bargain—whenever I succeed, my rival gains power with me. That will make the shadow stronger. How, I don't know. I'm waiting. And I can't find rest."

"I'll find it for you. Just lie down and wait—I'll be back."

I left him hastily—left him sitting at his desk, all alone. Not quite alone. The shadow was there, too.

Before I went I had the funniest temptation. I wanted to run my hand along the wall, through that shadow. And yet I didn't. It was too black, too solid. What if my hand should actually encounter *something*?

So I just left.

I was back in half an hour. I grabbed Gulther's arm, bared it, plunged the needle home.

"Morphine," I whispered. "You'll sleep now."

He did, resting on the leather sofa. I sat at his side, watching the shadow that didn't sleep.

It stood there towering above him unnaturally. I tried to ignore it, but it was a third party in the room. Once, when I turned my back, it moved. It began to pace up and down. I opened my mouth, trying to hold back a scream.

The phone buzzed. I answered mechanically, my eyes never leaving the black outline on the wall that swayed over Gulther's recumbent form.

"Yes? No—he's not in right now. This is Mr. Gulther's secretary speaking. Your message? Yes, I'll tell him. I certainly will. Thank you."

It had been a woman's voice—a deep, rich voice. Her message was to tell Mr. Gulther she'd changed her mind. She'd be happy to meet him that evening at dinner.

Another conquest for Fritz Gulther!

Conquest—two conquests in a row. That meant conquests for the shadow, too. But *how?*

I turned to the shadow on the wall, and got a shock. It was lighter! Grayer, thinner, wavering a little!

What was wrong?

I glanced down at Gulther's sleeping face. Then I got another shock. Gulther's face was dark. Not tanned, but dark. Blackish. Sooty. *Shadowy.*

Then I did scream, a little.

Gulther awoke.

I just pointed to his face and indicated the wall-mirror. He almost fainted. "It's combining with me," he whispered.

His skin was slate-colored. I turned my back because I couldn't look at him.

"We must do something," he mumbled. "Fast."

"Perhaps if you were to use—that book again, you could make another bargain."

It was a fantastic idea, but it popped out. I faced Gulther again and saw him smile.

"That's it! If you could get the materials now—you know what I need—go to the drug-store—but hurry up because—"

I shook my head. Gulther was nebulous, shimmery. I saw him through a mist.

Then I heard him yell.

"You damned fool! Look at *me*. That's my shadow you're staring at!"

I ran out of the room, and in less than ten minutes I was trying to fill a vial with belladonna with fingers that trembled like lumps of jelly.

V

I must have looked like a fool, carrying that armful of packages through the outer office. Candles, chalk, phosphorus, aconite, belladonna, and—blame it on my hysteria—the dead body of an alley-cat I decoyed behind the store.

Certainly I felt like a fool when Fritz Gulther met me at the door of his sanctum.

"Come on in," he snapped.

Yes, snapped.

It took only a glance to convince me that Gulther was himself again. Whatever the black change that frightened us so had been, he'd shook it off while I was gone.

Once again the trumpet-voice held authority. Once again the sneering smile replaced the apologetic crease in the mouth.

Gulther's skin was white, normal. His movements were brisk and no longer frightened. He didn't need any wild spells—or had he ever, really?

Suddenly I felt as though I'd been a victim of my own imagination. After all, men don't make bargains with demons, they don't change places with their shadows.

The moment Gulther closed the door his words corroborated my mood.

"Well, I've snapped out of it. Foolish nonsense, wasn't it?" He smiled easily. "Guess we won't need that junk after all. Right when you left I began to feel better. Here, sit down and take it easy."

I sat. Gulther rested on the desk nonchalantly swinging his legs.

"All that nervousness, that strain, has disappeared. But before I forget it, I'd like to apologize for telling you that crazy story about sorcery and my obsession. Matter of fact, I'd feel better about the whole thing in the future if you just forget that all this ever happened."

I nodded.

Gulther smiled again.

"That's right. Now we're ready to get down to business. I tell you, it's a real relief to realize the progress we're going to make. I'm head research director already, and if I play my cards right, I think I'll be running this place in another three months. Some of the things Newsohm told me today tipped me off. So just play ball with me and we'll go a long way. A long way. And I can promise you one thing—I'll never have any of these crazy spells again."

There was nothing wrong with what Gulther said here. Nothing wrong with any of it. There was nothing wrong with the way Gulther lolled and smiled at me, either.

Then why did I suddenly get that old crawling sensation along my spine?

For a moment I couldn't place it—and then I realized.

Fritz Gulther sat on his desk, before the wall *but now he cast no shadow.*

No shadow. No shadow at all. A shadow had tried to enter the body of Fritz Gulther when I left. Now there was no shadow.

Where had it gone?

There was only one place for it to go. And if it had gone there, then—*where was Fritz Gulther?*

He read it in my eyes.

I read it in his swift gesture.

Gulther's hand dipped into his pocket and re-emerged. As it rose, I rose, and sprang across the room.

I gripped the revolver, pressed it back and away, and stared into his convulsed countenance, into his eyes. Behind the glasses, behind the human pupils, there was only a blackness. The cold, grinning blackness of a shadow.

Then he snarled, arms clawing up as he tried to wrest the weapon free, aim it. His body was cold, curiously weightless, but filled with a slithering strength. I felt myself go limp under those icy, scrabbling talons, but as I gazed into those two dark pools of hate that were his eyes, fear and desperation lent me aid.

A single gesture, and I turned the muzzle in. The gun exploded, and Gulther slumped to the floor.

They crowded in then; they stood and stared down, too. We all stood and stared down at the body lying on the floor.

Body? There was Fritz Gulther's shoes, his shirt, his tie, his expensive blue pin-stripe suit. The toes of the shoes pointed up, the shirt and tie and suit were creased and filled out to support a body beneath.

But there was no body on the floor. There was only a shadow—a deep black shadow, encased in Fritz Gulther's clothes.

Nobody said a word for a long minute. Then one of the girls whispered, "Look—it's just a shadow."

I bent down quickly and shook the clothes. As I did so, the shadow seemed to move beneath my fingers, to move and to melt.

In an instant it slithered free from the garments. There was a flash—or a final retinal impression of blackness, and the shadow was gone. The clothing sagged down into an empty, huddled heap on the floor.

I rose and faced them. I couldn't say it loud, but I could say it gratefully, very gratefully.

"No," I said. "You're mistaken. There's no shadow there. There's nothing at all—absolutely nothing at all."

Nathaniel Hawthorne

The Devil in Manuscript

America's Puritan tradition attains its literary summit in the mas-
terpieces of NATHANIEL HAWTHORNE *(1804–1864), the Salem,*
Massachusetts, author of The Scarlet Letter, The House of the
Seven Gables, *"Rappacini's Daughter" and other novels and*
short stories, most of them somber and often tragic. "The Devil
in Manuscript" reminds us that Hawthorne, after all, did not
practice Art in an ivory tower. He was a working professional
who once declared, "The only sensible ends of literature are, first,
the pleasurable toil of writing; second, the gratification of one's
family and friends; and, lastly, the solid cash."

ON A BITTER EVENING of December I arrived by mail in a
large town, which was then the residence of an intimate friend,
one of those gifted youths who cultivate poetry and the belles-
lettres, and call themselves students at law. My first business,
after supper, was to visit him at the office of his distinguished
instructor. As I have said, it was a bitter night, clear starlight, but
cold as Nova Zembla—the shopwindows along the street being
frosted, so as almost to hide the lights, while the wheels of
coaches thundered equally loud over frozen earth and pavements
of stone. There was no snow, either on the ground or the roofs of
the houses. The wind blew so violently that I had but to spread
my cloak like a mainsail and scud along the street at the rate of
ten knots, greatly envied by other navigators, who were beating

slowly up, with the gale right in their teeth. One of these I capsized, but was gone on the wings of the wind before he could even vociferate an oath.

After this picture of an inclement night, behold us seated by a great blazing fire, which looked so comfortable and delicious that I felt inclined to lie down and roll among the hot coals. The usual furniture of a lawyer's office was around us—rows of volumes in sheepskin, and a multitude of writs, summonses, and other legal papers, scattered over the desks and tables. But there were certain objects which seemed to intimate that we had little dread of the intrusion of clients, or of the learned counselor himself, who, indeed, was attending court in a distant town. A tall, decanter-shaped bottle stood on the table, between two tumblers, and beside a pile of blotted manuscripts, altogether dissimilar to any law documents recognized in other courts. My friend, whom I shall call Oberon—it was a name of fancy and friendship between him and me—my friend Oberon looked at these papers with a peculiar expression of disquietude.

"I do believe," said he soberly, "or, at least, I could believe, if I chose, that there is a devil in this pile of blotted papers. You have read them and know what I mean—that conception in which I endeavored to embody the character of a fiend, as represented in our traditions and the written records of witchcraft. Oh, I have a horror of what was created in my own brain, and shudder at the manuscripts in which I gave that dark idea a sort of material existence! Would they were out of my sight!"

"And of mine too," thought I.

"You remember," continued Oberon, "how the hellish thing used to suck away the happiness of those who, by a simple concession that seemed almost innocent, subjected themselves to his power. Just so my peace is gone, and all by these accursed manuscripts. Have you felt nothing of the same influence?"

"Nothing," replied I, "unless the spell be hid in a desire to turn novelist, after reading your delightful tales."

"Novelist!" exclaimed Oberon half seriously. "Then, indeed, my devil has his claw on you! You are gone! You cannot even pray for deliverance! But we will be the last and only victims, for this night I mean to burn the manuscripts and commit the fiend to his retribution in the flames."

"Burn your tales!" repeated I, startled at the desperation of the idea.

"Even so," said the author despondingly. "You cannot conceive what an effect the composition of these tales has had on me. I have become ambitious of a bubble and careless of solid reputation. I am surrounding myself with shadows, which bewilder me, by aping the realities of life. They have drawn me aside from the beaten path of the world and led me into a strange sort of solitude—a solitude in the midst of men—where nobody wishes for what I do, nor thinks nor feels as I do. The tales have done all this. When they are ashes, perhaps I shall be as I was before they had existence. Moreover, the sacrifice is less than you may suppose, since nobody will publish them."

"That does make a difference, indeed," said I.

"They have been offered, by letter," continued Oberon, reddening with vexation, "to some seventeen booksellers. It would make you stare to read their answers; and read them you should, only that I burnt them as fast as they arrived. One man publishes nothing but schoolbooks; another has five novels already under examination."

"What a voluminous mass the unpublished literature of America must be!" cried I.

"Oh, the Alexandrian manuscripts were nothing to it!" said my friend. "Well, another gentleman is just giving up business, on purpose, I verily believe, to escape publishing my book. Several, however, would not absolutely decline the agency, on my advancing half the cost of an edition and giving bonds for the remainder, besides a high percentage to themselves, whether the book sells or not. Another advises a subscription."

"The villain!" exclaimed I.

"A fact!" said Oberon. "In short, of all the seventeen booksellers, only one has vouchsafed even to read my tales; and he—a literary dabbler himself, I should judge—has the impertinence to criticize them, proposing what he calls vast improvements, and concluding, after a general sentence of condemnation, with the definitive assurance that he will not be concerned on any terms."

"It might not be amiss to pull that fellow's nose," remarked I.

"If the whole 'trade' had one common nose, there would be some satisfaction in pulling it," answered the author. "But there does seem to be one honest man among these seventeen unrighteous ones, and he tells me fairly that no American publisher will meddle with an American work—seldom if by a known writer, and never if by a new one—unless at the writer's risk."

"The paltry rogues!" cried I. "Will they live by literature and yet risk nothing for its sake? But, after all, you might publish on your own account."

"And so I might," replied Oberon. "But the devil of the business is this. These people have put me so out of conceit with the tales that I loathe the very thought of them and actually experience a physical sickness of the stomach whenever I glance at them on the table. I tell you there is a demon in them! I anticipate a wild enjoyment in seeing them in the blaze, such as I should feel in taking vengeance on an enemy, or destroying something noxious."

I did not very strenuously oppose this determination, being privately of opinion, in spite of my partiality for the author, that his tales would make a more brilliant appearance in the fire than anywhere else. Before proceeding to execution, we broached the bottle of champagne, which Oberon had provided for keeping up his spirits in this doleful business. We swallowed each a tumblerful, in sparkling commotion; it went bubbling down our throats and brightened my eyes at once, but left my friend sad and heavy as before. He drew the tales toward him, with a mixture of natural affection and natural disgust, like a father taking a deformed infant into his arms.

"Pooh! Pish! Pshaw!" exclaimed he, holding them at arm's length. "It was Gray's idea of Heaven, to lounge on a sofa and read new novels. Now, what more appropriate torture would

Dante himself have contrived, for the sinner who perpetrates a bad book, than to be continually turning over the manuscript?"

"It would fail of effect," said I, "because a bad author is always his own great admirer."

"I lack that one characteristic of my tribe—the only desirable one," observed Oberon. "But how many recollections throng upon me as I turn over these leaves! This scene came into my fancy as I walked along a hilly road on a starlight October evening; in the pure and bracing air, I became all soul and felt as if I could climb the sky and run a race along the Milky Way. Here is another tale, in which I wrapt myself during a dark and dreary night ride in the month of March, till the rattling of the wheels and the voices of my companions seemed like faint sounds of a dream, and my visions a bright reality. That scribbled page describes shadows which I summoned to my bedside at midnight: they would not depart when I bade them; the gray dawn came and found me wide awake and feverish, the victim of my own enchantments!"

"There must have been a sort of happiness in all this," said I, smitten with a strange longing to make proof of it.

"There may be happiness in a fever fit," replied the author. "And then the various moods in which I wrote! Sometimes my ideas were like precious stones under the earth, requiring toil to dig them up and care to polish and brighten them, but often a delicious stream of thought would gush out upon the page at once, like water sparkling up suddenly in the desert; and when it had passed I gnawed my pen hopelessly, or blundered on with cold and miserable toil, as if there were a wall of ice between me and my subject."

"Do you now perceive a corresponding difference," inquired I, "between the passages which you wrote so coldly and those fervid flashes of the mind?"

"No," said Oberon, tossing the manuscripts on the table. "I find no traces of the golden pen with which I wrote in characters of fire. My treasure of fairy coin is changed to worthless dross. My picture, painted in what seemed the loveliest hues, presents nothing but a faded and indistinguishable surface. I have been eloquent and poetical and humorous in a dream—and behold! it is all nonsense, now that I am awake."

My friend now threw sticks of wood and dry chips upon the fire and, seeing it blaze like Nebuchadnezzar's furnace, seized the champagne bottle and drank two or three brimming bumpers successively. The heady liquor combined with his agitation to throw him into a species of rage. He laid violent hands on the tales. In one instant more their faults and beauties would alike have vanished in a glowing purgatory. But, all at once, I remembered passages of high imagination, deep pathos, original thoughts and points of such varied excellence that the vastness of the sacrifice struck me most forcibly. I caught his arm.

"Surely, you do not mean to burn them!" I exclaimed.

"Let me alone!" cried Oberon, his eyes flashing fire. "I will burn them! Not a scorched syllable shall escape! Would you have me a damned author? To undergo sneers, taunts, abuse, and cold neglect, and faint praise, bestowed, for pity's sake, against the giver's conscience! A hissing and laughingstock to my own traitorous thoughts! An outlaw from the protection of the grave— one whose ashes every careless foot might spurn, unhonored in life and remembered scornfully in death! Am I to bear all this, when yonder fire will insure me from the whole? No! There go the tales! May my hand wither when it would write another!"

The deed was done. He had thrown the manuscripts into the hottest of the fire, which at first seemed to shrink away, but soon curled around them and made them a part of its own fervent brightness. Oberon stood gazing at the conflagration and shortly began to soliloquize in the wildest strain, as if Fancy resisted and became riotous at the moment when he would have compelled her to ascend that funeral pile. His words described objects which he appeared to discern in the fire, fed by his own precious thoughts; perhaps the thousand visions which the writer's magic had incorporated with these pages became visible to him in the dissolving heat, brightening forth ere they vanished forever, while the smoke, the vivid sheets of flame, the ruddy and whitening coals caught the aspect of a varied scenery.

"They blaze," said he, "as if I had steeped them in the intensest spirit of genius. There I see my lovers clasped in each other's arms. How pure the flame that bursts from their glowing hearts! And yonder the features of a villain writhing in the fire that shall torment him to eternity. My holy men, my pious and angelic women stand like martyrs amid the flames, their mild eyes lifted heavenward. Ring out the bells! A city is on fire. See!—destruction roars through my dark forests, while the lakes boil up in steaming billows, and the mountains are volcanoes, and the sky kindles with a lurid brightness! All elements are but one pervading flame! Ha! The fiend!"

I was somewhat startled by this latter exclamation. The tales were almost consumed but just then threw forth a broad sheet of fire, which flickered as with laughter, making the whole room dance in its brightness, and then roared portentously up the chimney.

"You saw him? You must have seen him!" cried Oberon. "How he glared at me and laughed, in that last sheet of flame, with just the features that I imagined for him! Well! The tales are gone."

The papers were indeed reduced to a heap of black cinders, with a multitude of sparks hurrying confusedly among them, the traces of the pen being now represented by white lines, and the whole mass fluttering to and fro in the draughts of air. The destroyer knelt down to look at them.

"What is more potent than fire!" said he in his gloomiest tone. "Even thought, invisible and incorporeal as it is, cannot escape it. In this little time it has annihilated the creations of long nights and days, which I could no more reproduce, in their first glow and freshness, than cause ashes and whitened bones to rise up and live. There, too, I sacrificed the unborn children of my mind. All that I had accomplished—all that I planned for future years— has perished by one common ruin and left only this heap of embers! The deed has been my fate. And what remains? A weary and aimless life—a long repentance of this hour—and at last an obscure grave, where they will bury and forget me!"

As the author concluded his dolorous moan the extinguished embers arose and settled down and arose again, and finally flew up the chimney, like a demon with sable wings. Just as they disappeared there was a loud and solitary cry in the street below us. "Fire!" Fire! Other voices caught up that terrible word, and it speedily became the shout of a multitude. Oberon started to his feet in fresh excitement.

"A fire on such a night!" cried he. "The wind blows a gale, and wherever it whirls the flames the roofs will flash up like gunpowder. Every pump is frozen up, and boiling water would turn to ice the moment it was flung from the engine. In an hour this wooden town will be one great bonfire! What a glorious scene for my next—Pshaw!"

The street was now all alive with footsteps and the air full of voices. We heard one engine thundering round a corner and another rattling from a distance over the pavements. The bells of three steeples clanged out at once, spreading the alarm to many a neighboring town and expressing hurry, confusion, and terror, so inimitably that I could almost distinguish in their peal the burden of the universal cry, "Fire! Fire! Fire!"

"What is so eloquent as their iron tongues!" exclaimed Oberon. "My heart leaps and trembles, but not with fear. And that other sound, too—deep and awful as a mighty organ—the roar and thunder of the multitude on the pavement below! Come! We are losing time. I will cry out in the loudest of the uproar and mingle my spirit with the wildest of the confusion and be a bubble on the top of the ferment!"

From the first outcry my forebodings had warned me of the true object and center of alarm. There was nothing now but uproar, above, beneath, and around us; footsteps stumbling pell-mell up the public staircase, eager shouts and heavy thumps at the door, the whiz and dash of water from the engines, and the crash of furniture thrown upon the pavement. At once the truth flashed upon my friend. His frenzy took the hue of joy, and with a wild gesture of exultation he leaped almost to the ceiling of the chamber.

"My tales!" cried Oberon. "The chimney! The roof! The fiend has gone forth by night and startled thousands in fear and wonder from their beds! Here I stand—a triumphant author! Huzza! Huzza! My brain has set the town on fire! Huzza!"

Laura J. Catanzariti

Feeling Lucky

I met LAURA J. CATANZARITI *at a writing conference and encouraged her to send me some of her work. She promptly sent me "Feeling Lucky," a tale about a deal with the Devil so wonderfully sly that I kept waiting for a punchline that never seemed to happen . . . until I realized that that* is *the punchline!*

JACKSON FARWELL, Jack to his friends, of which there were few as of late, peeked his disheveled head out of his apartment door and carefully looked around the hallway. No one was around, so he crept out, his socks moving noiselessly as a ninja on the cheap industrial carpet. He leaned down and quickly snatched up his neighbor's paper. He looked in dismay as he saw he had stolen a tabloid rag and not a more erudite publication. He would have to get a better class of neighbors, but if he could afford to do that, he wouldn't have to resort to stealing their papers, would he? Anyway, he normally wouldn't be so fussy about his choice of reading materials, but this was important. Jackson Farwell was looking for a job.

Not just any job, either. He had strict requirements for the position he was searching for. They had to be willing to hire him.

He took the purloined paper back into his apartment and tore off the plastic bag, adding it to the other debris that had piled up behind his chair. He pushed away the remains of his ersatz breakfast, corn flakes au gratin (he hadn't been to the market as of late;

he couldn't afford not to be creative). Jack quickly skimmed the front pages, the usual melange of bludgeonings and political corruption. He stifled a cheesy belch as he perused the comics, pleased that Charlie Brown still had less hair than he did. And of course, he was still a loser. Jack felt a certain pang of sympathy for the head Peanut.

Here they are, Jack said to himself, folding back the page where the want ads began. He ran a dirty fingernail down the columns, pausing briefly at the personals in a burst of voyeuristic interest.

Jackson truly found the classified ads the low point of his already dismal day. He sat on his unemployed butt cataloguing all the jobs he was not qualified for: accountant, automotive sales, baker, banker, camp counselor, dentist, dog groomer, electrician, florist, greengrocer, handyman, insurance agent, jewelry salesman, kitchen help, lumberjack, mover, newspaper delivery (he paused here, but the thought of being beaten out by a ten-year-old was more than he could bear), ophthalmologist, piano teacher, radiologist—but then, what was this? Soul Coordinator. The advertisement jumped out at him; it was the only one printed in blood red ink. But why hadn't he seen it before? No matter, he saw it now.

As he read further, he had a sinking feeling he would be turned away, but he figured what the hell. "Wanted: Soul Coordinator for multinational concern. Good compensation, excellent benefits, fun working atmosphere. No experience, no education required. No calls, please. Apply in person. We are an equal opportunity employer."

Jackson looked at the address. He carefully tore the ad out of the paper and threw the rest away. He was going down there today, before they saw anyone else and raised their standards. He knew this was not going to be just tidying up for an interview, but some major reconstruction before he could present himself as employable meat.

He crawled into the tub and soaked the accumulated grunge from himself as he mapped out his plan of action. His appearance was somewhat of a concern, his hair slightly overlong and thinning, but would at least be clean; the crud exorcised from neglected fingernails, and the most respectable outfit he owned laid out neatly on his unmade bed. He would have to wear the shoes that pinched, but it was a short walk to the bus stop, and the building was close by it. Holey sneakers did not make a good impression on a potential employer. He was grateful there would be no underwear check.

Bathed, manicured, stubble scraped from chin and cheeks, he slapped on aftershave lotion from an unmarked bottle. He pulled his hair back into a skinny pigtail and tucked it into the slightly worn collar of his polyester shirt. He looked in the mirror. He wouldn't hire anyone that looked like him, but maybe if luck was with him it would be dark inside the office. He chewed a couple of breath mints that he found on his dresser and walked out the door, address in pocket.

Jackson was starting to rethink his position on the holey sneakers after standing for twenty-five minutes on a crowded bus. He stepped off the wheezing behemoth, wincing with every step. The driver would not let him out at his corner, and he had to double back three blocks. Three long blocks. It was hot out, something he had failed to check on when he had the newspaper. His polyester shirt felt like it was stuck to his skin, his too-wide tie forming an unstylish noose. Jack squinted into the bright sunlight. He found the right corner, but he could find no door to enter. He went to check the address on the scrap of paper, but the flaw in the plan was that the paper had escaped from his front pocket. He turned to see it skittering down the street in the breeze that had suddenly picked up just to inconvenience him.

"Oh, this couldn't get worse," Jack moaned.

"I wouldn't say that. It can always get worse." Jackson turned around to see who had spoken. A gorgeous redheaded woman, the sort that a less enlightened man would refer to as a "knockout," was holding open a large red door and beckoning him to come in.

Never one to argue with a lady, particularly not one that made his teeth sweat, he dumbly followed her inside. She put her small black purse into a drawer in the desk she gracefully slid her sleek form behind. "Now then, I believe you are here to apply for the job, Mr. . . . ?" she said, running her tongue nonchalantly over her gleaming crimson lips.

Jack took a moment to remember his name. This was hardly fair, was it? "Jackson Farwell," he finally got out.

"Why don't you have a seat, Mr. Jackson Farwell," she purred. Jack went to find a seat in the small and mercifully dim waiting room. "Oh, and would you be a dear and fill out this application?" She handed him a form with a graceful sweep of her hand.

"Certainly," Jack said, groping in his jacket for a pen.

She handed him a pen and asked, "By the way, do you have a résumé?"

"Um, no, I forgot to bring one," Jack lied.

"Oh, that's all right," she said soothingly. Jack couldn't help but notice that she was smoothing a hand over the waist of her black and red suit. "It was lucky I found you out there. I was just coming back from lunch, and I just knew that you were here to apply for the job."

"I once was lost, but now I am found," Jack said. The receptionist furrowed her creamy brow and became very busy filing her nails. Jack guessed that she didn't like his lame little joke and he went back to fabricating a tissue of lies for his application.

Easy-listening music was piped into the lobby. Jack tried very hard not to listen, but the words melodically hammered themselves into his unwilling brain:

> You fill up my senses/ like a dirty old sneaker
> Like a bag full of mucus/ like a kick in the groin . . .

He didn't remember those words, but the tune was hauntingly familiar. Were the Seventies really that bad? Jack peeked over at the receptionist from behind his clipboard. She appeared not to hear the music; she was far too busy filing her nails. I suppose, Jack thought, that if one listens to something long enough, one can become used to anything.

Jack signed his name with a flourish, the only entirely true part of the document. He handed it to the receptionist, who gave him a chilly look and a curt "Thank you." She tore it off of the clipboard and walked into the office in back of her. Jack could not see inside. He sighed deeply and looked at the worn and outdated magazines that lay in a fan on the table. He didn't recognize any of the titles, though there was something unsettling about the titles: *Damned People, McClaw's, Deadbook,* and a fashion magazine called *Morgue.* Jack picked the latter up and flipped idly through the pages, which seemed to be full of wraith-like young women made up to be ghastly pale and modeling designer shrouds.

"How is he?" Harry asked, taking the application from the receptionist.

"Shiny brown suit, white socks, black shoes . . . should I go on?"

"No need. Why don't you go wipe his drool off your shoes and let the fool know that I'll be with him shortly?"

"You got it, boss," she replied. She looked down at her shoes, letting out a *tsk*ing noise with such force it sounded like the *Hindenberg* with a slow leak. She strode out of the office with slinky cat steps. Her employer observed appreciatively, then put himself to the task of the application. Jackson Farwell could apparently read and write, so that was a good sign. He had all the necessary qualifications, then. Harry smiled. He could knock off early.

Jack looked up expectantly from his reading.

"Mr. Suede will be with you in just a few moments," the receptionist said, then returned to her manicuring.

"Thank you," Jack said meekly. He wondered what he had done or said to make her turn cold to him. He breathed against his hand to check his breath. Was cheese coming through the mints? Nah, it couldn't be that. He was just having his usual effect on the opposite sex, though this time the reaction was slightly delayed. Usually women hated him right from the start.

The office door opened. Jack hastily placed the magazine back on the table and wiped his sweaty palms on his pants, where the moisture left two trails across his thighs. Wet paws never made a good impression on a prospective employer. He remembered to make good eye contact and stand up and offer a firm handshake. No wet fish, he told himself. He finally screwed up enough courage to raise his eyes and meet his accuser—interviewer, he corrected himself.

"Jackson Farwell?"

"That's me," Jack said.

"Harry Suede. Pleased to meet you," Harry said, extending a cool, dry, well-manicured hand, which pumped Jack's own in effusive greeting. The hand was attached to the arm that was clothed, along with the rest of Harry Suede, in a creaseless white linen suit, impeccably tailored and set off by a hand-painted silk tie. His hair was thick and dark, with exactly the right amount of gray shot through the temples, and moussed to perfection. His smile offered Jack a good look at his large, white, bonded teeth. Jack felt Harry's pinkie ring rub against his finger, and when he looked at it he saw it sported a two-carat square-cut diamond.

"Likewise," Jack said. His hand retained the scent of Harry's powerful aftershave.

Harry smiled, a smile that made Jack squirm from the sheer brightness of it. His teeth were every bit as white as his suit.

"Pleased to meet you," Jack stammered. "I'm Jackson Farwell."

"Yes, we covered that territory. Why don't you come on in my office, where we can talk?" Harry flashed him another sunglasses-needed smile.

"Oh, right, of course." Jack wanted to slap himself. Suave moves on an interview, he chided. Way to impress the crowd.

He followed Harry meekly into his office. "Jack, have a seat, make yourself comfortable. Cup of coffee?" Harry asked, pointing to the elaborate brass cappuccino machine set up in the corner of the plush office.

"No thanks, I just had breakfast," Jack said. He looked around, trying not to gape at his surroundings.

But gape he did. The area he traveled through to get to the office was not the highest rent district in the city, though perhaps not the very worst. Jack was used to the neighborhood; he lived in one very much like it. Though the neighborhood could be charitably described as "dingy," and the outer office itself not much more than spartan, Harry's office was a vision in gilt and red crushed velvet that was opulent enough for any sultan or Mafia don. Behind the modest outer door the surroundings seemed to sprawl in all directions. Works of a most erotic nature, all nymphs and satyrs, graced the walls, proving to be quite the distraction for Jack. He was so lost in his visual tour that he was having trouble keeping up his end of the conversation.

"No coffee, eh?" Jack heard Harry saying. "How about a scotch or a painfully dry martini?"

"Oh, I'm not much for liquor," Jack said, hoping his tone was convincing.

"Of course you're not," Harry said too sweetly. "Just my little joke."

Jack chuckled weakly. What were they doing in that painting?

"Gorgeous out today, isn't it, Jack?"

"Oh, yes, lovely. Not a cloud in the sky." Jack could faintly hear a clap of thunder as the words escaped his mouth.

"Let's get down to it, Jack. What brings you down here to see me today?" Harry leaned back in his plush Italian leather chair, putting his fingertips together to form a steeple. This was Harry Suede's patented look-we're-equals-and-let's-level-the-playing-field-but-keep-in-mind-I'm-still-the-one-in-charge-of-this-situation maneuver.

His positioning was unmistakable, even to Jack. "I'm looking for a job," Jack said. He hoped he wasn't being too subtle.

"In response to our ad, I imagine," Harry said noncommittally.

"Yes."

"Pretty brave of you, still and all, to come here in response to an ad that essentially describes nothing about the situation offered."

"Actually, Mr. Suede—"

"Harry, please."

"Actually, Harry, that doesn't really matter to me. I think I could be happy in a variety of career positions."

"A variety of positions," Harry mused. "How intriguing. Opens up a lot of possibilities, if you know what I mean."

Jack didn't. He was oftentimes a man singularly without imagination. In this instance, this lack of imagination worked in his favor, for if he were able to grasp the full flavor of Jack's words, he would have been forced by his remaining shred of decency to walk out of the office, and remain jobless for yet more time. He continued to listen to what Harry had to say. Harry was a man with money in his voice.

"Let's review some of your previous experiences that you've written down here. What exactly did you do at Williams Publishing?"

"Oh, I did a specialized sort of editing," Jack said. "I kind of made sure that everything was clean at the end of the day. A lot of after-hours kind of work."

"Janitor," Harry noted.

"Custodial engineer," Jack said a bit testily.

"Forgive me. Now, at Adamson Machinery, you said you were a technical consultant."

"Oh, yes, at that position I handled all of the important paperwork. The president couldn't make a move without me."

"Possibly mailroom," Harry noted, both verbally and on the form. "More probably rest room attendant."

Jack sighed. This was not going well. "I've also had retail experience."

"Door-to-door, I imagine. Brushes or encyclopedias?"

"It's honest work."

"Ah, now, here's something. Cafe Braggadocio. Oh yes, I've had many a sumptuous meal at that fine establishment. Very exclusive, isn't it?" Harry asked.

"You have to know the right people, I suppose," Jack demurred.

"And as a busboy, I'm sure you knew them all. Not to denigrate your fine dish-clearing efforts, mind you." Harry leaned back in his chair. "You know what I think, Jack?" Harry said.

"What, Mr. Sued—Harry?"

"This form you filled out for me, sort of an acting résumé, as it were?"

The air hung heavy with anticipation and cologne.

"Yes?" Jack ventured.

"This is a thinly disguised tissue of lies that you have dared to present me with. No, strike that statement. It would improve the stench of this prevarication if you disguised it. You are trying to deceive me, aren't you, Jack? Trying to pull one over on old Harry? Do you think I'm stupid, Jack?" He said the name with much sharpness at the end.

"No," Jack mumbled, and tried to hide in the upholstery of his chair.

"Stop squirming, you," Harry said. "Admit that you fudged some of this information. Be a man."

Jack swallowed hard. "All of it," he said. He stood up to leave. This interview was over.

"Where are you going?" Harry asked.

"You caught me. What more do you want?" Jack asked. His dignity was rapidly failing him, having never been all that reliable to start with.

"Sit your dead butt down, you beanhead."

"But, but—"

"That's right, plant yours back down here. I'm not done talking to you." Jack dropped back in his chair, too stunned to do otherwise.

"You're quite a liar, Jack." Harry got up from his chair and began to pace behind the broad expanse of his desk.

"I can explain—"

"Of course you can," Harry said, waving his hand dismissively. "But that isn't the point, or at least not the main focus is. Jack, are you a 'people person'?"

"Oh, I like to think so."

"No, you're not, you hate them. You have no compunction

about lying to them, cheating them, or using them to serve your ends—"

"Now just you wait one minute—"

"See, you're going to make me think you're insulted, when I know you are secretly flattered."

Jack stared at Harry for a long moment. "You're spooky."

"You think?" Harry asked with a bleached white smile.

"Oh yeah," Jack said quickly. "So what are we doing?"

"Let's get down to it then, Jack. We could spend all day with me chasing you around the desk, or I can come right out with it. Jack, I like you. I think you'd be just right for our company. How would you like a lucrative position with all the bennies, and no selling?"

"Wow, I'd love it," Jack said. "No selling?"

"Of course there is selling. I was lying. I'm a demon, aren't I?"

"You are?"

Harry sighed. "Tell me you didn't know. Look around, man. We are in the absolute worst section of the city, yet my reception- ist feels free to strut around as if she owned the streets. Did you notice the late model luxury car parked directly outside?"

"I noticed it as I was getting off the bus, yes," Jack said.

"Would I dare park it on the street if I didn't have some pretty scary connections?" Harry paused to take a cigar out of the hu- midor, bit the tip neatly while offering the box to Jack. He lit the tip with a flick of his finger, the flame dancing on the tip.

"That's supposed to convince me?" Jack said. He knew better than to smoke on an interview, so he tucked three cigars into his pocket to enjoy later.

"Bit of a cliché, I'll admit. So c'mon already, you need a job or you don't. You think I've got all of eternity to wait for you? Oh, right, I do. Anyway, what color is your parachute—never mind, I'm sure it won't open for you. Why don't you 'Black Sky' me a job here?"

"Let's get back to the selling thing. What precisely is it that I will be selling?" Jack had now chosen to travel down a com- pletely different avenue for the moment.

"Actually, you will be doing more buying. Souls mostly. But don't sweat the details. If you will just sign at the X, we can get the ball rolling. The sooner you act, the sooner the money starts rolling in."

Jack realized that he had to get back to it, and sort of face what he was doing once and for all. "Why should I consign my soul to an eternity of damnation in your evil employ?" Jackson spluttered, tossing down the contract and jumping up to leave.

"Did I mention that we offer full dental coverage?" Harry asked.

"I'm listening," Jack said, sitting back down.

"Fabulous, you won't be sorry," Harry said.

"Really?" Jack asked, reaching for the gold pen Harry was holding out to him.

"Lying again," Harry said with a finger-as-a-gun gesture and a sly wink. "But seriously, what choice do you have?"

Jack shrugged and took up the fountain pen. "Do I have to sign in my own blood?"

"Nah," Harry said. "We're working for Hell. We got lawyers up the wazoo if you try to worm out of the deal."

"That figures," Jack said, and quickly scrawled his name across the bottom of the page before he could change his mind.

"Excellent," Suede said. The signed document disappeared into thin air. "Oh, where is my head today?" He snapped his fingers and the document reappeared. "I forgot, you need to initial here. And here. Here too. Press firmly, Jack. You're making three copies." Jack obliged, Harry beaming at him. "Good man, Jack. Now, I just have to make a phone call to our central office, so why don't you just get a jump on the rest of the paperwork."

"That will be fine," Jack said. Harry pushed a mountain of rainbow-hued paper that materialized on the desk. Jack sighed, and began writing.

"Remember to press hard," Harry reminded, dialing the phone. "Harry Suede here, calling for S. Lucifer Beelzebub—no, I will not hold! Thank you, I trust that wasn't so difficult." Harry put his hand over the mouthpiece. "You've got to be firm with these underlings, Jack. Always remember that." Jack nodded and went back to his paperwork. "Yes, I'm here, you imbecile—oh, I'm so sorry, sir, I thought it was your assistant." Harry sat up, straightening his tie with his free hand. "So, Scratch, how are you? Listen, I've got a live one. No, I mean a real live one. Oh, sorry, death impaired. Political correctness, it will be the life of me yet. I'm just having our Jack fill out the paperwork now, and then I thought he would be just right for the southeast territory of the city." Harry listened for a moment. "Good, good, that's settled, then. By the way, how's the wife and kid? He's quite a little imp, that one. Well, you take care of yourself, I'll see you at the meeting next week. Good-bye."

A total sleazebag is all in the details, Jack thought as he listened to him. Damn, how he admired him for that. "All finished, Harry," he said brightly. "Completely and accurately filled out." He tried his first dazzling smile, with mixed results. He still had a bit of cheese in his teeth.

"Really?" Harry asked. He seemed pleased.

"No, I'm lying. It's what I do," Jack said, looking at his fingernails.

"Welcome aboard, friend," Harry said, grabbing Jack's hand and pumping it enthusiastically. "I knew you had it in you."

"I didn't know until just today, actually. Lucky, lucky me."

"No. Lucky, lucky us." Again with the smile. "Let's get a photo for your ID badge." He pressed the intercom button. Almost at that instant, the receptionist sauntered in, snapped a photo with an instant camera, tossing the picture to be developed on Harry's desk. She left as quickly as she came in. Harry picked it up and examined it critically. "It's really bad. That proves it's an official identification." He reached into his desk drawer. "Here is everything you'll need. First, here is your handbook. This will tell you everything that you could want to know but had too much sense to ask before now. There are your territory maps, and here is your credit account." He handed Jack a gold card. "Do yourself a favor, Jack. Get yourself some new clothes

and a decent haircut. It looks like you've been cutting it yourself
with a dull knife."

"Will there be anything else?" Jack asked.

"Keys to your car. It's the red one next to mine. No more bus
for you. Oh, and here is your badge of office. Never conduct
business without it." He handed Jack a black velvet jewelry box.

Jack opened it. "My own pinkie ring. Well, this does make it
official." He placed the ring on his finger and admired the glint of
the diamond.

"Go get 'em, Tiger," Harry said, holding the office door open.

"See you soon, Jack," the receptionist said in a husky whisper.

"Thank you very much," Jack said. He hurried out the door
before it could all disappear.

Jack slid behind the wheel of his new Jaguar. He took out one
of the cigars and lit it with the tip of his finger and sat back,
savoring the smoke. It certainly was his lucky day.

Andrew Warren

Mendoza

ANDREW WARREN *of Croton-on-Hudson, New York, says that he was powerfully influenced by Guy de Maupassant's "Diary of a Madman" when he wrote the next tale, but "Mendoza" is not the least derivative; in its own deceptively quiet way, it is truly a diary entry from Hell.*

May 21. It's Saturday and what a glorious day it is. I woke up early this morning and as I opened my eyes I saw two bluejays in love sitting on my windowsill chirping an operatic duet. I could hardly contain my excitement, especially since I planned to spend the whole day in the woods. Mother stayed up late last night, carefully packing my picnic basket with all those tasty goodies which she knew I was so fond of. I saw her prepare that fleshy Mediterranean eggplant salad that when mixed with chopped red onions sends me into ecstasy. I also saw her sneak in a small jar of Beluga caviar and a bottle of red wine.

I don't think I've ever felt so good in my entire life. I took a hot shower, I shaved, without nicking my face even once, and put on the white cotton chinos and blue sweatshirt Mother laid out for me the night before. I picked three books out of our library. I knew that at least one of them would fit whatever mood I might be in during the day. One was Dostoyevsky's *Crime and Punishment*, the other de Maupassant's *Gil Blas* and the third, Kafka's

The Castle. I had read them all before, but on a day like today I wanted to visit old friends and leave nothing to surprise.

I fastened the picnic basket to my bicycle's rear rack, letting the long French bread jut out like a flag's mast, threw my books into my knapsack and started pedaling the mile and a half that separates our house from the woods.

I didn't get home till after dark. Mother seemed worried when I walked in and was about to reprimand me, but when she saw how happy I was, she just told me to wash up and go to bed.

I slept like a log.

May 23. Today is Memorial Day. The village of Chappin Hill where I live is the site of one of the biggest parades around. Our house is built on a hill overlooking the village and from the window of my den I can see all my neighbors and their families, dressed in their Sunday best, walking up and down Main Street.

I would normally be there myself, but I have a slight fever and an upset stomach. It must be the flu. I know it's going around. Our cleaning woman called in sick last Thursday, complaining of the same symptoms. Mother seems worried, though, and said that if it didn't go away in a couple of days I should go see Dr. Schecter.

May 25. My condition is getting worse. I still have a fever and my head is pounding. I am also feeling jumpy and depressed. It must be that my physical indisposition is affecting my mind. Mother is getting quite alarmed. She even called Dr. Schecter and demanded that he see me tomorrow, but, to her annoyance, he didn't have any time open before next Friday. I told her that I didn't think there was anything urgent, and that next Friday would be all right. She seemed mollified.

May 28. It's Saturday again. What a difference does a week make. Last week I was having the most glorious day of my life. I remember lying on the grass, serenely daydreaming, staring up at the sky with nothing else around me except for two majestic oak trees whose branches formed a canopy above my head filtering out the sun.

I am still feeling lousy. I haven't been to work since last Friday, but that's not worrying me. I work for my uncle in his office supply mail order house. I could keep this job even if I never showed up again. Mother even tells him how much to pay me.

June 1. I am spending a lot of time in bed. I haven't shaved in three days. Mother is in a state of frenzy. I keep telling her that there is a bug going around and I'll be fine.

But it doesn't feel like a bug. My skin feels very sensitive to the touch and I am very anxious. I hope Dr. Schecter can figure out what's wrong with me.

June 4. I went to see Dr. Schecter yesterday. He ran a whole battery of tests, but all he found was that my pulse was slightly elevated and so was my blood pressure. He told me to get a lot of rest, but he thought there was nothing else physically wrong with me. I am greatly relieved. I plan to go back to work on Monday.

As I was leaving his office, he took my arm and gently suggested that I may be suffering from some nervous condition and that I should consider seeing a psychiatrist. He gave me the name of a Dr. Tanenbaum, who happens to have an office right here in Chappin Hill. I told Mother, but she found his insinuation offensive and preposterous, so I decided to drop the whole idea.

June 10. I didn't go to work all week. My condition is worsening. I feel something terrible may happen to me. I am experiencing pangs of fear, as if something dangerous and ominous could strike me at any time. I try to find an explanation for all this. I feel very depressed.

June 12. I've been home for three weeks now with no reprieve in sight. I feel that I am losing the battle. Lately, I've been having fits of anxiety that leave me feeling paralyzed, unable to move, as if I am being held prisoner by some unseen force. I know it's all rubbish, but I believe that my mind is yielding its grip on reality.

I can't concentrate; I can't read; I can't watch television; I can't even eat. I know Mother, feeling out of control and not knowing what to do about it, is on the verge of a nervous breakdown. I feel terribly sorry, but I can't deal with her. I can't worry about her now.

I am spending most of my time in my den, lying on the couch in my pajamas, focusing on each object, first individually, then in concert with other objects around it. This task is painstaking and takes up a great deal of my time. Every few hours I return to the same object to see if there's been any change. I believe the answer to my condition lies somewhere in this room.

It's a beautiful room. I used to think that it had everything I ever needed to make me happy. I close my eyes and I see everything exactly where it is.

To the left of the door there is a large old-fashioned oak desk facing the wall, covered with papers, books, magazines, a porcelain cup filled with pens and pencils, a telephone, and a large picture of Mother in an elegant gold frame, taken many years ago, showing the face of a bewitchingly beautiful woman looking right at the camera lens. Mother gave me this picture when I was a child. She told me to always have it with me and whenever I feel lonely I should look at it. She was right. As I now gaze at the picture, I feel her loving presence.

When I first started my careful inventory, I thought how messy the desk was. Now I feel that everything is exactly where it should be, and I am afraid of touching anything for fear of moving it.

Next to the desk, against the far wall there is a matching oak table on which a computer, a printer, two boxes of diskettes and a stack of Xerox paper sit side by side. Right above the table there is a large bay window, facing south, that, were it not for the heavy dark brocade blinds now covering it, would allow a resplendent stream of sunshine to burst in. As I stare at it I realize that beyond it there is a world that's leaving me behind.

Next to the oak table there is a television set, or, as it was more accurately described by the salesman who sold it to us, an entertainment center. It does in fact contain, in addition to the TV, record and audiotape players, a couple of speakers and a VCR. The only time I've had it on, though, was to watch TV. Now I don't even do that.

To the left of the entertainment center is my pride and joy. Covering the entire wall there is a bookcase built right into the wall that houses all my books. It even contains several manuscripts of some obscure writers and one shelf is dedicated entirely to nineteenth-century first editions. I can't say I've read all of these books, but I've held every one in my hands and touched it, felt its texture and sniffed its pungent scent. As I look at them now, I feel that I could recognize each one of them blindfolded, simply by touch and smell. Seeing them all together, cover to cover, as if competing for my attention, like a child wanting to be picked up, fills my heart with agony, as I fear that I may soon not see them again. I look away to ease the pain.

On the near wall, to the right of the door there is a large overstuffed couch that has been my constant refuge since my body seems to have been invaded by this evil force.

The two side walls are adorned with several paintings and lithographs. My favorite is a reproduction of an oil canvas by Georgia O'Keeffe showing a bleak vision of the Brooklyn Bridge. The heavy reckless brush strokes of glistening black paint, conjuring the power of solid steel, reach out and grip my very soul.

The entire room is bathed in the light of a handsome brass and etched crystal fixture in the shape of a bowler hat, which is now constantly left on as the blinds remain permanently drawn.

Having once again completed my inspection of every item in the room, I begin the cycle anew. Nothing seems to have changed.

June 28. I am having great difficulty falling asleep at night. I think I am subconsciously afraid of sleep, since that's when my guard is down. When I finally do fall asleep, late into the night or sometimes even as I see the first rays of dawn piercing through the bedroom window shades, I have these horrifying nightmares. The plots are different, but the outcome is always the same: death— violent, bloody death. I wake up in a pool of sweat and have the sensation that I am drowning in it.

July 4. Independence Day. I decided to gain *my* independence, to shed all these debilitating feelings and sensations. I know it's all psychological. I can do it. I know I can do it.

I managed to get dressed today. I had breakfast downstairs with Mother. For the first time in weeks I had a full breakfast with Eggs Benedict, Mother's specialty, toasted challah and coffee. We even had a pleasant conversation. She seemed so happy to see me up and about. She wasn't at all angry with me for the way I have been shutting her out of my recent tormented existence.

Then I went out for a walk. I felt ecstatic. I started jumping and running. I felt the nightmare I had been living was all over. I looked up at the sky. It was a cloudless, windless hot summer day. Suddenly I felt as if someone were trying to catch up to me. I tried to run faster, but there was no use. Since I was so out of shape, I quickly began panting and feeling queasy.

The power was overcoming me. I felt helpless, paralyzed. It was pulling me back towards the house with an energy that swiftly overwhelmed my will to resist. I obediently turned around and listlessly began shuffling my way back into the house. I knew I could never escape again. A sense of deep terror consumed me.

July 18. I am a prisoner in my own house. I occasionally have periods when I feel completely at ease and, during those precious moments, the thought that somehow the evil power would leave me, never to return, fills me with boundless hope. But these moments are short-lived. I am no longer in control of my body.

August 2. Mother decided :o take me away on a short holiday to our summer place in the Hamptons. I think it would be just the thing that I need right now. We're planning to leave the day after tomorrow. Mother has been very busy all week making travel arrangements, packing our clothes and personal items and loading up the car. I wasn't up to helping her. I spent the whole time sitting motionless on the couch, knees crammed against my chest, worrying over whether he'll try to stop me. I feel highly agitated and tense.

August 14. We returned from the Hamptons yesterday. I had a wonderful time. I had no anxiety attacks, no problem sleeping. I felt great, as if I had been cured, completely and irrevocably cured. Mother was constantly hovering over me, not knowing what to do for me first. In my forty-three years, I've never seen her so cheerful and relaxed. It was as if she had finally reached her ultimate goal, to see me happy in her presence.

August 16. The anxieties are back. I can't eat, I can't sleep, I can't do anything. I am filled with fear.

August 23. He's back sucking the life out of me. I don't even have the energy to go to the bathroom. Mother got hysterical today seeing me in my condition. I yelled at her to leave me alone. I had never yelled at her before.

August 28. Someone has been through my den. I know it. Everything has been changed around. The papers on my desk were not in their proper place. Someone moved them. I screamed at Mother. I thought she had done it, but she swore to me that it wasn't her. I believe her. It must be him. He has taken over my life.

September 2. This morning when I came into the den I couldn't believe my eyes. The place looked like it had been burglarized. Pages from an old manuscript were strewn all over the rug. My desk was in total disarray, with torn papers and magazines scattered all over it. Most distressing, though, was finding Mother's picture tossed behind the table, its glass shattered and a large puncture hole right between her beautiful eyes. Now I know he's been here. I have to catch him and kill him.

September 12. When I entered the den this morning I felt as if under a spell. I walked right up to my bookcase and picked out a book I had never seen before. It was very old and in tatters. Where did it come from? He must have put it there. I compulsively began reading it. It described the doctrines of Shabbetai Tsevi, a false messiah of the Sixteenth Century who founded Lurianic Kabbalah, the mystical Jewish belief that the Divine world is flawed, and Evil, if allowed to flourish, will eventually conquer us. Shabbetai Tsevi ended up converting to Islam, continuing his messianic premonition that Evil will make itself known to man in human form and when that happens man will be doomed. After Shabbetai Tsevi's death, his disciples insisted that this personification of evil had a name. He was called Mendoza.

I closed the book. I now know my tormentor.

September 23. I am going to kill Mendoza. I know he often spends time in the den watching me. I can't see him, but I know he's there. I will trap him and I will kill him and I and the rest of the world will be free once and for all of his evil.

September 27. I meticulously drew up the entire plan. Mendoza cannot escape my trap.

I had Mother buy me three heavy bolt locks and two large metal window gates. I stashed them between the mattress and the box spring of my bed. He would never think of looking there. Besides, he never goes into my bedroom. Tomorrow around noon I'll install them. He's never around during the day.

October 5. The last few days have been hell. I think he suspects something. He's been watching me constantly, day and night. I don't know when I'll have my chance. I have to be very cautious.

• • • •

October 9. I have been trying to act very normal so as not to arouse his suspicion. When I know he's looking over my shoulder trying to see what book I'm reading I don't cover up the page anymore. I am trying to give him a sense of security. I want him to think that everything is all right.

October 11. It worked. I had him duped. He hasn't been around all morning. I'm going to put up the locks now.

October 12. I can hardly contain my enthusiasm. I installed the locks. I put up the gates and two of the locks on the windows and secured them to the windowsill. I mounted the third lock on the outside of the den door. Now I have to play it cool. He mustn't suspect anything. I am going for it tonight.

October 13. Just as I thought, he showed up around midnight. I was expecting him. I was sitting down on the couch reading a book and appearing very calm and collected. I didn't look up but I felt his hand squeezing my shoulder, letting me know that he would never leave me. Then, suddenly, as if by touching me he was able to sense my guilt, he nervously started pacing the room frantically. I tensed up when he came close to the window. I was afraid that he might look behind the heavy brocade blinds and see the gates, but he didn't.

After he had been there for about ten minutes and he seemed to calm down, I slowly got up and nonchalantly walked towards the door. I kept an indifferent smile on my face so as not to arouse suspicion. As I reached the door, I firmly grabbed the knob and sprung myself out, slamming the door behind me before he had a chance to realize what had happened. I then quickly bolted the lock, trapping him inside, ran downstairs, picked up a large gasoline canister from the basement and deliriously started to douse the entire house. I ran out the front door and when I got outside, I threw a match in the canister that still had enough gasoline to ignite and threw the fiery missile through one of the downstairs windows. The house instantly caught on fire, turning it into a monumental inferno. I knew I had him. There was no escape for him now.

Suddenly the quiet night air was pierced by the shrieking sound of a human voice. I looked up and saw, in chest-crushing horror and disbelief, Mother's body, enveloped in flames, staggering up to the blazing upper floor window, burning to death. I threw myself to the ground, overwhelmed by my hopelessness. There will never be an escape from Mendoza.

Ron Goulart

Satan's Home Page

RON GOULART *is one of the most likable chaps you're likely to meet in the world of science fiction, and his good spirits spill over into his charming, often hilarious prose. In addition to his* Vampirella *novels and works like* Star Hawks *and* Challengers of the Unknown, *based on comic strips/books, his works include* After Things Fell Apart, Clockwork's Pirates, Death Cell, Gadget Man, The Sword Swallower, The Tin Angel *and his twist on an H. G. Wells title,* When the Waker Sleeps. *He also wrote* Cheap Thrills: An Informal History of the Pulp Magazines *and* The Adventurous Decade: Comic Strips in the Thirties. *"Satan's Home Page" was written specially for* Don't Open This Book!

MOTION PICTURES, as you probably know, sometimes get financed in very unusual ways. The final movie that Roy Jason scripted was one such and the writer himself made an unusual, and unanticipated, contribution to its reaching the screen. Initially, when he began to suspect that something strange was going on, he was concerned chiefly with the activities of his current ladyfriend. He wasn't at all worried about his own fate.

Roy's suspicions were first aroused on a grey overcast afternoon in late autumn. He had returned earlier than he expected to the cottage in Santa Rita Beach that he'd been sharing with Danni Goff for the past year and four months. Crossing the threshold into the small, shadowy living room, he frowned. Halting, he started sniffing the air.

"Danni, what's that godawful smell?" he inquired loudly.

There was no reply.

Once, briefly, in the spring she'd had an affair with an out-of-work stuntman who smoked Cuban cigars. But this was a different smell.

Sulfur and brimstone maybe?

Or were sulfur and brimstone the same damn thing?

"Danni, why does our living room smell of sulfur and brimstone?"

No answer.

Frowning more deeply, Roy prowled the entire cottage. The actress wasn't there and she hadn't left him a note in any of the usual places.

His cat seemed to be missing, too. "Ambrose?" he called. "C'mon, boy."

No response from the cat, either.

Roy went into his den. "Maybe Ambrose—he's ten after all, which is old for a cat—had some sort of seizure and Danni had to rush him to the vet," he suggested to himself aloud. "Naw, she loathes Ambrose and he doesn't think much of her. She wouldn't rush him anywhere."

When he settled in at his computer, he noticed that it had been left on. "Shit, I keep telling her to turn it off after she uses the damned thing."

The screen saver in operation was the one with the dancing cockroaches. Danni's favorite.

Leaning back in his rickety chair, he poked the message button on his phone answering machine.

"Roy, old buddy," came the voice of Pontius Gaffney, the producer-director of his movie. "We're all extremely high on your latest rewrite of the *Satan's Home Page* script. We all—what's that, Mona honey? Okay, I'll tell him. Mona says she's especially high on the stuff in the cathedral and—"

"What stuff in the cathedral? What cathedral?"

". . . few more very minor changes, old buddy, and we'll be ready to go into production. Call me."

"This is the third damned rewrite. It's about time we were ready to go into production."

The rest of the messages, five more in all, were from people who claimed he owed them money.

It was while enduring the polite request for instant payment from someone representing the Santa Monica Debt Resolution Bureau that Roy noticed the sheet of paper lying on the floor near his wastebasket.

"I keep telling her to toss stuff *in* the damn basket and not *near* it."

". . . hope we can reach a swift resolution of the problem," continued the Santa Monica Debt Resolution Bureau. "Have a nice day, Mr. Jansen."

"Jason," he corrected as he picked up the sheet of paper.

It had been printed out on his own printer and was set in an odd, old-fashioned font. It seemed to be in Latin, a language in which he was not fluent.

"Why are you snooping in my mail?"

He looked up from the screed to see Danni leaning in the doorway. A slim red-haired young woman, tan and pretty, scowling his way. "I found it on *my* floor," he told her.

"We *share* this ramshackle office, love," she reminded him.

"What is this, anyway?" He rattled the paper.

"Nothing."

Folding it, he slipped it into his shirt pocket. "Where's Ambrose?"

"He was meowing oddly all afternoon. I imagine he went off into the woods to die."

"We live on the beach, Danni. The nearest woods are eight, nine miles inland."

She shrugged. "Maybe he walked into the sea to die."

"What makes you think Ambrose is dead?"

"You didn't hear the way he was meowing."

He eyed her. "You never liked my cat."

"On the contrary, love. I doted on the little prick. But he hated me." She came into the room, sat in the only other chair and crossed her long tan legs. "He tried to smother me while I slept on several occasions, as you'll recall."

"Where is he?"

"Haven't the faintest notion. How was your meeting with your agent?"

"Lovely. But she doesn't have anything lined up beyond *Satan's Home Page.*"

"You need an agent with balls. Wanda isn't anywhere near aggressive enough," Danni pointed out, uncrossing her long legs. "Of course, you can't expect much aggression from somebody named Wanda. Especially somebody named Wanda Tammerman."

"She did get me the *Satan's Home Page* scripting job."

"At Guild scale," she mentioned. "It's a dippy movie and shamefully low budget."

"How come you're going to be acting in it, then?"

"I happen to be on my way up. I'm young," reminded Danni, recrossing her legs. "For me a piece of garbage like *Satan's Home Page* is a wise career move. A rung up on the ladder of stardom. But for an elderly person such as yourself it isn't exactly—"

"Forty-two isn't elderly."

"True. And were you actually only forty-two, I'd agree that you weren't quite yet over the hill. But, love, you're forty-seven, remember? We had your birthday party, with all your dippy friends and associates, just three months ago. Surely you recall that."

"I'm not quite dotty yet, Danni. But in this town age is a handicap, and so I shave a little off—"

"If you had a ballsy agent, you could pass yourself off as forty."

"Why's the house smell like sulfur and brimstone, by the way?"

"It doesn't." Standing up, she stretched.

He sniffed. "So what's that foul odor, then?"

She shrugged her left shoulder. "Probably Ambrose misbehaved just before he went off to die." Smiling, fleetingly, Danni moved toward the doorway. "I'm fixing scrambled tofu for dinner. That okay?"

"We had tofu last night."

"That was tofu curry. This is entirely different."

"Okay," he said, "I guess I can tolerate it, then."

After she left, he took out the sheet of paper, unfolded it, and stared at the lines of Latin for several minutes.

Granny's in Santa Monica was one of a chain of restaurants that dotted Greater Los Angeles and catered to an elderly clientele. Even the waitresses were old and grey.

"I don't much like this place," confided Roy as he slid into the booth opposite his friend. "For one thing, it's right on the beach but they keep all the windows shuttered."

"Sunlight is bad for the skin." Dud Woodson was a tall, bald man of fifty-two and the author of such best-selling horror novels as *Temple of the Vampires* and *Temple of the Vampires Revisited.* "And my doctor says I ought to eat at places like this."

"He's got you on a high-grease diet?"

"The food here is healthful," Woodson assured him. "Tell me about your prob—hello, Irma. How goes it, dear?"

"Can't complain, Mr. Woodson, and my new hip is working just wonderfully." Irma was frail and white-haired. Her starched pale green uniform was several sizes too large. "The sea bass is good today."

"I'll try that."

"You always have that," said Roy, fidgeting in his seat. "Every time we come to this hole you order sea bass."

"It's a specialty of the house," he explained.

"And you, sir?" asked the ancient Irma.

"Just coffee."

"You ought to eat a wholesome meal, like your friend Mr. Woodson."

"I intend to, but not here."

Sighing, the waitress went shuffling away.

Leaning an elbow on the tabletop, Woodson asked, "Is this grouchiness of yours part of the problem?"

"I'm always grouchy. It's hereditary," he said. "The reason I called you is because of this." He took the folded sheet of paper from his coat pocket and handed it across.

Not immediately accepting it, the author said, "Do you suspect Danni's fooling around again? If so, I'm not sure I want to get involved in another long and—"

"This is, I'm pretty sure, an occult matter, Dud. Which is why I want to consult you." He thrust the paper closer to his friend. "Odd things have been going on."

"Where?"

"At my cottage."

"Such as." He accepted the paper, but left it folded in his hand.

"Ambrose disappeared three days ago."

"Cats do that. Especially old ones."

"When I started thinking about it, I realized there was a pattern. Other things have been vanishing. Such as my favorite running shoes and—"

"You don't run."

"I walk. I liked to wear them when I walked along the beach at sunset." He leaned forward. "That award statuette I won for the *I Married a Fat Girl Summer Reunion Special* in 1987 has also vanished."

"You were only a coauthor. One of six as I recall."

"Seven actually, but it's the only damn writing award I ever won, and it's gone."

"You suspect Danni's swiping the stuff and—what?—pawning it?"

"Yesterday an RPS driver disappeared."

"Rapid Package Service? Disappeared from your house, you mean?"

"The neighborhood. I noticed the empty truck parked in front of the cottage when I got back from a meeting with Pontius Gaffney. Those dimwits want to change all the campus scenes to a cathedral, but how are you going to put computers in a cathedral or—"

"The missing driver?"

"Nobody knows where he got to. A man from RPS came around last night, late, to ask after him. We were one of the houses he was supposed to have a package for."

"Did you get it?"

"Danni says no. But it isn't on his truck."

"What was it?"

"A rush delivery from the Occult Book Shoppe in Long Beach."

"For Danni?"

"She denies it, but I sure as hell didn't order anything from them."

Leaning back, Woodson gazed at the shuttered windows. "You suspect that Ambrose the cat and your shoes and the trophy and probably this driver have all been whisked off to the same place, huh?"

"It occurred to me, after I got a Latin dictionary and tried to translate that page there—words like *demon* and *summon* show up. I'm wondering, Dud, if something supernatural is going on here."

Unfolding the page, Woodson spread it out in front of him. "How'd you come by this?"

"Found it on my den floor, same day Ambrose vanished. I think Danni downloaded it off the Internet someplace. She denies that."

"You'll have to move your work, Mr. Woodson. So I can set down your split pea soup," said the returned Irma.

"Just put it on the edge of the table, dear."

"Be sure you eat it while it's warm."

After she'd gone tottering away, Woodson shook his head. "I don't suppose you've ever heard of a book called *The Compleat & Thoroughly Evil Account of How to Summon Up Foul Demons from the Bowels of the Infernal Regions & How To Cause*

Them To Do Thy Bidding & At The Same Time Avoid Eternal Damnation & Other Helpful Magikal Hints?"

"Have to change the title if they make a movie out of it. What the hell is it, Dud?"

"An infamous book by the notorious Count Monstrodamus."

Roy sat up. "Him I've heard of. I used him in a script I almost sold to *Tales From The Abattoir* three seasons ago," he said. "He was a powerful black magician and sorcerer in the Eighteenth Century, rumored to have made deals with the Devil himself."

"Among others of low repute, yeah." The bald author tapped the sheet with his stubby forefinger. "This happens to be a page from that odious book. Stuff like this shouldn't be floating around on the Internet. Very dangerous."

"You think Danni's been fooling around with demons?"

"Notice at the bottom of this page it says *three of fifteen*. That means she got hold of, at the very least, fifteen pages from the Count's book."

"Talk about irony. This is practically the plot of my movie. Except it's—"

"Get your butt home right now and confront the lady," advised his friend. "Explain to her that if she's messing around with spells and incantations that she's getting from the infamous works of Count Monstrodamus, she is in very deep trouble and has to quit *at once.*"

"I'm going." Roy jumped up, nearly collided with Irma, and hurried out into the hazy afternoon.

Danni was growing increasingly tearful. "It got all out of control," she said, commencing to sob into her palms as she sat hunched in the black armchair.

From the sofa he accused, "You're just acting. You're not really contrite at all."

The red-haired actress stiffened, sitting upright and lowering her hands. "You know damned well that I've never been any good at faking tears," she reminded, sniffling. "I lost that part in *Serial Killer's Serenade* because I couldn't cry."

"I thought that was because you couldn't scream."

"That, too, but chiefly it was because I couldn't bawl on cue." She sniffed, wiped at her pretty nose with the back of her hand.

"Okay, explain the rest of this to me," urged Roy.

"I did it all for you," she told him, continuing to cry. Well, for *us*. I've been using the gold, after it was melted down and sold, to finance this dippy movie."

"Gold?"

"That's what's been going on, yes. So far I've invested sixty-three thousand dollars in *Satan's Home Page*."

"And where is this gold coming from?"

She looked away from him, turning to watch twilight closing in around the cottage. "Don't rant and rave when I explain. Okay?"

"I rarely rant and rave."

"No, actually you have a long history of ranting and raving. And over stuff far less serious than this."

"How does my cat fit in?"

"Don't rant and rave?"

"Tell me, Danni."

"Well—well, Ambrose sort of got turned to gold."

"Turned to gold?" He shot to his feet, fists clenching. "Ambrose?"

"It wasn't my fault. See, the demon isn't that easy to control, and so—"

"You let a demon into my house? He slaughtered Ambrose?"

"You're not really paying close enough attention here, Roy," she mentioned. "Nobody—technically—killed Ambrose. He simply got transmuted."

"He's still defunct."

"True, but he became several pounds of gold."

"You turned the poor little guy into gold and *sold* him?"

"Well, what the heck would you do with a golden cat? Keep him as a souvenir?" She shook her head. "If it wasn't for me, keep in mind, the whole *Satan's Home Page* project would've gone belly-up. Pontius Gaffney's already mortgaged his house and the houses of two of his former wives. Plus most of his dippy furniture."

Roy made a back-up motion with his right hand. "This demon can turn things into gold?"

"Certainly, why the heck do you think I summoned him up in the first place?"

Roy sat back down. "What's he look like?"

"Green."

"How about a few more specifics?"

"You, trust me, don't want to hear any further specifics."

"I thought demons could assume human form if they wanted to."

"Not this guy." She looked into her lap, sniffling again. "The point I am trying to make is that he picked out what he was going to turn into gold. That's what happened to your shoes and that dingus you got for that dumb TV script ages ago and—"

"What about the RPS driver?"

"Blame the demon, yes."

"We're talking about murder."

"I mentioned that to the demon, but it only seemed to annoy him, and so I let the matter drop. You don't want, believe me, to annoy a demon."

"Where's the driver now?"

"Well, we melted him into gold ingots and—"

"We? You and the demon?"

"I wasn't about to look up gold melters in the yellow pages."

"I appreciate your wanting to keep the movie going, Danni, but this isn't the way to—"

"I have a great role and it may be your last gasp as a screen-writer."

"Your motives were, I guess, okay. Thing is, summoning demons and transmuting delivery men isn't—"

"It's wrong, terribly wrong, I know." She shivered, holding onto herself. "And I've stopped the whole business. Right after we melted down Leonard, I informed—"

"Leonard? Is that the poor driver?"

"Leonard M. Dobbins. The M stands for Maxwell."

"You apparently got fairly chummy with the guy before you transmuted him."

"People find it easy to confide in me," she answered. "And I didn't suspect the demon was going to turn him into gold. Before I could stop him, though, he reached out and touched Lennie on the arm. That's all it took."

"Wait now. Leonard M. Dobbins allowed a huge green demon to touch him? Where was the demon while you and Leonard were chatting? Sitting where I am now?"

"A little to the right. By that burned spot." Danni lowered her head. "Actually—and I wasn't going to tell you this, because you tend to get so jealous—Dirk had assumed a human form. He's not so scary when he does that."

"Dirk? What kind of name is that for a demon?"

"Oh, that's not his true name, obviously. When he's in human form, however, he calls himself Dirk Snowden," she explained. "A sort of show-business name."

"I take it that when he's human he's not green and ugly."

"No," she admitted. "He's actually quite cute and handsome. He looks a lot like that sexy actor who was in *Covered Bridges of the Heart* and died of an overdose of drugs in the phone booth at the Granny's in Malibu last Christmas. What was his name? Drummond Rimbaud, I think. Yes."

"So you've been consorting with a demon who looks like a sexy drug fiend, huh?"

"Better than consorting with him in his demonic form, I assure you, love."

Roy, after taking a slow deep breath in and out, said, "Explain to me how you summoned up Dirk in the first place."

"That's very strange, actually." She leaned forward in her chair to look directly at him. "I was just net-surfing one night a few days ago—you and Dud were out at some dumb screening and I was restless. I came across this very odd chat group—and, no, I've never been able to find it again. They were talking about a way you could change stuff into gold and I said to myself, 'Hey, that's neat.' And the next thing I knew I had downloaded about thirty pages of this strange old manuscript allegedly written centuries ago by a guy who called himself Count Monstrodamus."

"Why'd you leave a page on the den floor?"

"I must've dropped it after I made a photocopy of the whole thing."

"You can read Latin?"

"Sure, I have a classic education. I told you that."

"I thought you were kidding."

"No, my father really was a professor at a prestigious midwestern university and my mother truly was a crackerjack anthropologist. And my IQ really is quite high."

"Fine, then you should be smart enough to realize we can't keep fooling around with demons from the netherworld."

"Only one demon." She held up her forefinger. "But you are absolutely right, Roy. You'll be happy to learn that I burned all my copies of the excerpts from the Count's awful book. And I sent Dirk packing and we're in the clear. Absolutely."

"He went back to the fiery pit without protesting?"

"There's a neat spell for that. Worked just fine." Danni stood, rubbing her hands together. "I was thinking of making tofu stroganoff for dinner."

"We'll go out to dinner."

Smiling, she came over, put her arms around him and kissed him tenderly on the cheek. "You can be very understanding and supportive if you really try," she told him softly. "And when we both take giant strides up the ladder of success because of *Satan's Home Page,* you'll thank me for all I've done."

"Maybe," he conceded. "But it's going to be a long time before I ship anything RPS again."

It was raining on the afternoon a week later when Roy met again with his friend Woodson. But from inside Granny's you got no hint of what things were like on the outside. The place seemed especially dim and gloomy as Roy hurried over to the booth.

He noticed that the bent and grey waitress who was, shakily, placing a cup of coffee in front of Dud Woodson was clad in a black uniform today.

"Why'd you want to see me, Dud?" he inquired, sitting.

"Hold it a minute, Roy." Woodson patted the waitress's freckled hand. "It happens to us all."

"I know, I know. And yet . . ." Sobbing quietly, she tottered away.

Woodson explained, "Everybody's in mourning."

"Aren't they always at this place?"

"This is because of Irma."

"Wasn't *that* Irma?"

"No, that's Lola. Irma, alas, passed away yesterday."

"Proving that the food here isn't all that beneficial."

"She was sideswiped by a motorcycle."

Roy glanced around the dim-lit restaurant. "So all this gloom is because of Irma the waitress?"

"Well, Irma and Ollie."

"Who the hell is Ollie?"

"He was the pastry chef. He also passed away. That's why they have those votive candles burning in the donut case."

"Why'd you phone me? It couldn't just be because Irma and Ollie."

Woodson sipped his coffee, winced and said, "I happened to find out something about your movie."

"What—not more goddamned delays?"

His friend frowned up at the ceiling for a few silent seconds. "What did you say the demon's name was?"

"His show biz name, you mean?"

"That one, yeah."

"Dirk Snowden it was. But why do—"

"Danni informed you, as I recall from what you told me over the phone last week, that he'd returned to the fiery regions. Correct?"

"Yeah." He frowned. "Didn't he?"

"Nope." Woodson shook his head. "According to my sources,

Dirk Snowden is now slated to play a major role in *Satan's Home Page*. He'll take the part of the Archbishop."

"There's no Archbishop in my script."

"Supposedly Dirk is also doing a polish on the script," continued his friend. "And now there is an Archbishop. Plus a Bishop and a twenty-four-member choir."

"Why the hell would Pontius Gaffney let this demon have a leading role in the movie and mess with my script?"

"Dirk Snowden, so I hear, Roy, has become the chief investor in the film." He drank a bit more coffee. "Of course, this might well be another Dirk Snowden. Since Danni swore to you that—"

"It's the same guy." He was on his feet. "Apparently she wasn't being completely truthful."

"Apparently."

"I thought he'd returned to the nether regions," said Roy, pointing at the handsome suntanned man sitting on his sofa.

"He likes L.A. better," explained Danni, who stood, somewhat uneasily, just to the right of the seated demon.

"It's the ocean breeze I missed most." Dirk's voice was deep, his diction flawless.

"So starring in my movie and butchering my script—those are just incidental?"

Dirk smiled, showing his perfect teeth. "It happens to be *our* film now, old man," he said. "As the major investor, I naturally insisted on a certain amount of control."

"That's standard in Hollywood," reminded Danni.

"He's not from Hollywood." Roy, who was still in the living room doorway, nodded toward the floor. "He's from some demonic other world."

"Business is business," Dirk pointed out, "no matter where you're from."

"You ought to be grateful to Dirk," said Danni. "He's really brightened up your dippy script."

"Put some zing into it," added the demon.

"Zing? What in the hell is zing? Who the fug needs zing? Why does a potential horror classic like *Satan's Home Page* require zing?"

"Pontius Gaffney thought it needed some zing," Danni informed him. "So did the Rasmussen Brothers."

"Who the devil are the Rasmussen Brothers?"

Dirk said, "They're our other investors, old man."

"You know," said Danni, "they run all those rug discount stores."

"Rug merchants and fiends. That's great." Roy took a few forlorn steps into his living room, scowling. "I try to turn out a literate, poignant script and I end up having it ravaged by rug merchants and fiends."

Dirk stood, smiling. "Listen, old man, I been talking to Pontius and he agrees that you ought to be brought back to do the final polish on our script."

"Can I take out the cathedral and put back the college campus?"

"No, you just burnish the dialogue—you don't make any drastic changes to the structure," explained the smiling demon. "However, Roy, we'd be willing, once the final bit of financing is in place, to pay you a substantial bonus for this little chore."

"How substantial?"

"Twenty-five thousand dollars."

Roy looked from Dirk to Danni and then back at the demon. "That's not bad," he conceded.

"What say we make it thirty-thousand," suggested Dirk. "Is that a deal?" He held out his hand.

"Yeah, it's a deal." Roy took hold of the hand and started to shake it.

That was when he turned to gold.

Dirk stepped back, then tapped the golden statue with his knuckles. "This ought to bring enough to finish the movie."

Danni nodded. "With enough left over to buy that Mercedes you've been wanting."

Marvin Kaye

Professor Lubermayer's Final Lecture

"Professor Lubermayer's Final Lecture," from The Possession of Immanuel Wolf and Other Improbable Tales *(Doubleday, 1981), is couched in the fussy pedantry of its peppery pedagogue and describes with an academician's strict logic a field trip to Hell.*

> Vita nostra brevis est,
> Breve finietur—

"GOOD GOD," Belford sighed, fingering the weapon in his pocket, "it lacked only *that!*"

> Post jocundum juventu-u-tem,
> Post molestam senectu-u-tem,
> Nos habebit hu-u-mus—

Three sharp cracks snipped the melodic line like a filament of surgical floss: Lubermayer shutting the conference-room window on the improvised freshman concert in the college quadrangle; Lubermayer slamming two formidable black-leather doctoral dissertations on the mahogany tabletop.

"Since this is my last lecture," he snapped, "I will dispense with tedious expostulation. Consider my career, gentlemen: forty years of philosophy—except for poetry, the most tenuous, inutile indulgence on this most puerile planet!" He eyed the two doctoral candidates with unconcealed dislike: Rosner, in neat tweed jacket, sucking his prop of protracted adolescence, an unlit pipe;

Belford, a mountain of ill-contained avoirdupois, surmounted by the shifting suets of a balding cranium.

Bestowing a frosty nod on each pupil, the professor continued. "Today I quit my ridiculous profession." (Rosner: doleful nod, sanctioning an unavoidable personal loss; Belford: sardonic lip-twist of unalloyed pleasure.) "I have yet to fathom the purpose of philosophy. If only, after four decades of Venn Diagrams, of Übermenschen and dialectical materialism, I could piece out a viable reason for the blather. Bah!"

Sunlight straggled through dusty windows. Belford impatiently shifted in his seat, rearranging bulges. Lubermayer paused, hovered like a serpent preparing to strike . . .

And struck.

"The worth of philosophy, if you will! That is the theme. Come, come, gentlemen, order your thoughts! *Rosner—!*"

The neat little scholar jerked, startled by the peremptory tone of command. Dimly aware he was on trial and not simply satisfying the whim of idle pedagogical curiosity, he tried to frame a suitable reply. "I suppose," he murmured, gesturing with his pipe-stem in unconscious mimesis of masculinity, "I suppose the safest answer would be that the proper pursuit of philosophy is the nature of man, the discovery of the Good, the seeking-out of an unshakable ethical underpinning to the tenets of comparative morality." He was pleased with his sonority.

"Precisely evaluated, Rosner," the professor rumbled, a sour grin on his pursed lips. "The *safest* answer—exactly so. And you, Belford?"

The mountain stirred, preparing to unroll the proclamation of his thoughts. During contradiction, he addressed Lubermayer without respect, and, with a fierce riposte in abeyance, his fingers brushed the opening of his jacket pocket, a gesture derived from viewing too many westerns.

"The purpose of the philosopher," he pontificated, "and the rationale of the philosophic function is to ferret out the springs and causes of the cosmos, and to determine the eventual destiny of humanity—" (Verbal rapier drawn, he poised himself for his old argument with the professor) "—but, Lubermayer, such a pursuit must be mounted in a pragmatic, rational frame of reference! Metaphysics and the study of the occult is twaddle of—"

"Sufficient, Belford!" the professor tartly interposed, wearily but not without relish. "You also fulfill my expectations. I am now in a position to recommend to the faculty committee with respect to the doctoral candidacies of both—"

"WHAT?!" Belford roared, thumping the table with his fist. "Do you mean to foist off this farce as our oral examinations?! A single random answer extracted impromptu—"

"Belford," the professor interrupted, "you are a braying ass. I have worked with the pair of you for months and know your many limitations quite thoroughly. Rosner is a conglomerate of shortcomings: shallow perceptions; unscholarly complacency . . . but with a single talent: precerebral performance of the lowest work standard commensurate with continued degree candidacy. He is a willing debate participant, though prolixity preserves him from frequency of invitation to indulge the same. His dissertation: sound. The content: exegesis of a particularly trivial Hegelian conclusion. Genuine scholarship, but of such inconsequential stamp that the tome will molder in the library stacks unread. However—" (Lubermayer indulged in the personal luxury of a deep sigh) "—Rosner, I have no alternative but to approve your candidacy for the doctorate." (Rosner: relaxed, daring his complacent smile once more; Belford: quaking mass of blubber, his hypothetical academic honor sullied by extension to an unworthy colleague, an attitude not altogether unjustified. He fingered the weapon again.)

Nos habebit hu-u-mus—

"Raggletaggle vagabonds," Belford murmured to himself, characterizing the undergraduates outside whose lung power was able to penetrate windowpanes with the force of their offkey caroling.

"As for you, Belford," the professor continued, "you possess much of the genius wanted in Rosner. But you severely lack discipline. Furthermore, your mind is closed. You are a self-styled realist, which is laughable, since you prefer constructing illusions of your own rather than countenancing the evidence of your senses—"

"I know precisely what you are getting at!" Belford rumbled, his ample chins trembling. "Those idiotic *séances* of yours that you forced me to attend!"

The pedagogue, ignoring the interruption, offered deliberate insult by explaining his position to the muddle-brained Rosner. "You see, Belford bases his dissertation upon metaphysics, or rather, upon the systematic attack and refutation of certain aspects of same. Entirely unacceptable. Doctoral petition: denied."

"You *dare* to turn me down?!" the fat man shouted, his inflamed veins throbbing in his forehead. "Simply because I will not pander to your preposterous belief in *ghosts?!*"

"They exist," said Lubermayer complacently. "A wealth of reliable observations from every clime—"

"Perfect rot! Those damned mediums you—"

"From Plato and the Bible," the professor told Rosner, "and even through Belford's beloved Nietzsche, all treat the spirit as distinct entity. The state of sentience, uncharted, shade apart, shape without form: mass beyond mortality."

Belford snorted, his hand deeper in his pocket. "And because I do not agree with this mumbo-jumbo, you refuse my dissertation?"

"*I do!*"

The antagonists faced one another across the narrow table, but Lubermayer's superior hostility icily quelled Belford, if only momentarily. Eyes downcast, he tried a new, wheedling tack.

"Professor," he murmured, "I am not in the habit of beseeching favors—" (He took a breath, marshalling his nerve to beg a boon) "—but I have recently learned that I do not command a lengthy life span. I am expected to die in a few months." Rosner made a sympathetic clucking noise. "Before I expire, I should like to know that I will be awarded my doctorate, even if it is posthumous."

Lubermayer wasted a long moment of Belford's dwindling time. At length, he spoke with renewed acerbity.

"It appears, then, Belford, that you will soon be in a position to test for yourself the accuracy of my metaphysical posture. When you find that you yourself have become a ghost—"

"*I have already considered that contingency!*"

Sudden silence.

Belford's hand, withdrawing from one pocket, delved into another . . .

"What *are* you talking about, Belford?"

"Sign this," said the fat man, producing a document from his inner jacket pocket and smoothing the official-looking paper on the tabletop. He pushed it towards Lubermayer.

"What is it?" the professor asked testily, unused to surprises from Belford.

"It is a contract to be entered into by you and me. Rosner may witness it."

"A contract? What does it specify?"

"That, upon the death of either one of us, whichever comes first, the deceased shall attempt to communicate with the survivor. If he fails to do so in a reasonable period of time, the college must then accord me my degree, even though it be posthumous."

—habebit hu-u-mus—

"You will lose, Belford," the professor growled, signing the paper and passing it to Rosner. "The human spirit survives death. When you are gone—"

"I am sorry to contradict you," said Belford, "but I will *not* lose, Professor Lubermayer!" His fidgeting hand withdrew from his outer jacket pocket and produced a revolver.

A shot rang out.

Rosner's signature upon the deed trailed off in a ragged path of ink, mixed with the professor's spattered blood. Lubermayer, with an admonitory finger thrust into the air, toppled over backward from the force of the bullet. Rosner jumped to one side, shouting.

Belford spread his hands wide and spoke in a voice that mimicked the late professor. "Lubermayer: dead."

"My God, Belford," screamed the other scholar, "what *have* you done?"

"Come, come, Rosner," said Belford, placing the pistol against his own temple, "a philosopher must be trained to observe the phenomena of the physical universe. You have just witnessed an event in space-time. What is the evidence of your senses as to what occurred? And have you seen the thing-in-itself, or a fragmentation of the Real in the turnings of subjectivity that your own mind shapes? Then, for that matter, Rosner, what *is* reality? What, illusion?"

Not choosing to debate, Rosner rushed pell-mell from the room, the voice of Belford bellowing after him to remember the contract.

Then there was another shot.

Rosner heard no more. Wrenching open the outer door of the building, he plunged into the quadrangle where the drunken freshmen tirelessly continued to caterwaul.

> Vita nostra brevis est,
> Breve finietur—

Returning soon with a quaking pair of campus policemen, Rosner saw Belford lying on the floor next to Lubermayer, a hole in his shattered skull, a triumphant smile on his bloodless lips, and the contract clutched tightly in his dead, fat fist.

"Come here, Belford!" Lubermayer snapped.

The obese scholar approached, averting his eyes from Lubermayer's angry glare. Belford stared morosely at the first ragged bullet-hole he had created.

"Before you so rudely interrupted me," snarled the professor, "I *was* maintaining that the spirit is immortal. Now pray observe:

Proposition A	Dead men who see, hear, and speak are ghosts.
Proposition B	The two of us are dead.
Proposition C	The two of us see, hear, and speak.
ERGO:	*We are ghosts.*
Q.E.D."	

The cold wind whipped the professor's long, unruly sideburns against his brow and spectacles. He glowered at Belford, then continued. "Therefore, sir, it must be at last obvious—even to you—that, thanks to this enforced field trip and practicum, I cannot possibly accept your dissertation."

The professor curled his lip in derision and Belford flinched.

"In other words, Belford," snapped Lubermayer, *"you flunk!"*

Turning smartly on his heel, the professor strode into the surrounding fog with an air of complete assurance. The strains of *Gaudeamus Igitur* tinged the edge of the wind like an echo's ghost. Belford glumly watched the other walk purposefully off into the mist.

He wondered where in hell Lubermayer was going.

Jean Paiva

Cinnabar

During her tragically brief career, JEAN PAIVA *(1944–1989) edited and cofounded* Crawdaddy *magazine, wrote two novels published under New American Library's Onyx Books imprint,* The Lilith Factor, *a nominee for the Horror Writers of America's Best First Novel Award, and* The Last Gamble. *A short story, "Just Idle Chatter," was published in Kathryn Ptacek's* Women of Darkness II; *a second, "A Dozen Roses," appeared posthumously last year in* Angels of Darkness. *"Cinnabar," printed here for the first time, was probably one of the last short stories she wrote.*

"THE PROBLEM IS, I *don't* understand," Scott said, exasperated with his friend-turned-recluse. He leaned further over the narrow breakfast-nook table to impress, as if by his sheer physical presence, what he had to say.

"Cheryl's been dead three months and you haven't been out with anyone else. In fact, you've barely gone out. It's not like you were engaged, or even had an understanding. You'd only been seeing her, what, two–three weeks? And besides—"

"Don't say any more," Michael interrupted. He pushed himself off the nook bench and walked out into the large kitchen. The size of the room had originally intimidated them with its domestic implications, but the kitchen soon became, to their masculine surprise, the center of activity.

"I know she wasn't well liked, but there was something special about her. A drive, a will, an *energy*. All the others can be lumped in a single . . . well, lump." Michael rinsed out his empty coffee cup and stored it in the dishwasher for future use or washing—whichever came first.

Considering their age, under thirty, and their status, unmarried upwardly mobile young professionals, also known by a derogatory acronym, their house at 50 Monroe Place was well tended. At the front, a short sweep of gently sloping lawn led to a trimmed hedge at the sidewalk. Inside, the cottage's maintenance decreased only slightly. The usual—sweatpants and aromatic socks—littered the rooms, but was at least limited to what could accumulate in a week's time.

Scott still sat in the kitchen booth, idly pushing the combination salt and pepper shaker in circles around the economy-size ketchup bottle, already half emptied and less than a week old.

"Just come to the party," he pleaded, pushing lank blond hair out of his watery blue eyes. "I'm not asking you to take anyone home. I won't introduce you to anyone 'special.' Just show up. We moved to Dunwoody for the singles scene," he added with a grin, "and you're ruining my reputation."

Michael had to crack a smile. "I remember the realtor's pitch. He recited the litany with all the fervor of a devout convert. 'The only suburban community with over 80% singles and the other 20% met here, married and are moving out as soon as they can. Parties every night, all night and every weekend, all weekend long. Door-to-door carousing. The only dry-docked singles cruise in existence in the United States of America.' I expected him to wave a banner with crossed wine glasses."

"He wasn't far from wrong."

"That's part of the problem," Michael said thoughtfully. "I'm tired of using the local phone directory for my personal little black book. Everyone's almost always available. Cheryl wasn't."

"That might be because she was strange," Scott shot back, annoyed at the turn this conversation, as all others of late, had taken.

Michael flushed. "If strange means knowing that life has more to offer than fucking around Dunwoody, then she was strange."

"Spare me," Scott sighed, his eyes planning an escape from the confines of the room and topic.

"Even after the accident, when she was on life support, she had more guts than anyone I've ever known. She told me she wasn't ready to die, not after finding me. I told her I felt the same way, and she'd better live for both of us." Michael paused, his throat tightening on the words. "She smiled then. At least she died with a smile."

Scott grabbed his jacket on the way to the back door. "Just come to the party. Tonight at Ellen's."

"If I don't have to work late," Michael said, but his excuse was cut short by the slam of the door.

The door reopened a crack and a shout echoed in the kitchen.

"Then come late. But be there."

"Better late than never," Michael thought as he walked through Ellen's open front door, "but personally, never has its advantages." He'd taken time to shower and change, dawdling away an hour so there would be that much less time to spend at the party. His carefully blow-dried sandy brown hair received, most mornings, a quick brush after showering. Narrowing his eyes against the party's pulsating, near-visible sounds, Michael stepped through the door.

The smoke-filled room reverberated with the driving rhythms of Emerson Lake and Powell. Decorator lightbulbs cast eerie green and blue tones on healthy faces glossy with the sheen of sweat from uninterrupted dancing.

Those resting from their exertions lounged on twin sofas or sprawled on stacked pillows. The coupling for the night was, thankfully, almost complete. Only a few bodies remained untangled, only a few faces showed any alertness. All but one face, Michael saw, was slack with the effects of sweet smoke and dry wine. Only one face, still alone and across the room, registered neither the green nor the blue light but held onto the owner's inner focus; one pale face with long dark hair gently pulled back and braided in a single tail that hung heavily over her shoulder. One face that shone with all the radiance of a lighthouse in a storm. One face that looked like Cheryl down to the single braid.

It wasn't, though. Her grey eyes were softer than the smoke that surrounded them, but they weren't the neon-green, LED flashing beacons that Cheryl could turn on at whim. Her hair was dark brown with red glimmers, not the endless black of Cheryl's, the pitch black of endless night that would cascade unbound into a silken tent when she leaned down to kiss him. Her slender body lacked Cheryl's generous curves that, unclothed, were lusher than fashion allowed.

But she is here . . . and Cheryl is buried and cold and a rotting feast for maggots.

Forcing the thought out of his mind, Michael walked to her. She smiled; a shy smile, but one open with invitation. She would, at least, hear him out.

If I don't talk about Cheryl.

Her perfume reached out with unseen hands and pulled him closer. Her scent was the same: a deep musky odor, carrying with it all the secrets of the earth. When he'd asked Cheryl about it, she'd laughed her wonderful laugh.

"Cinnabar," she answered. "From the orient, they say, packaged in dusty red bottles tied with black silk ribbons. Its most secret part is cinnabar, the red ore used to create elusive mercury."

So like her, Michael knew. All the substance of the earth, yet quicksilver evading his most tentative touch. Unless she chose to respond, and then the earth moved and the fever glass soared to bursting.

Michael said to the woman standing before him, "You must be new in Dunwoody." Standard party conversation. "Otherwise I would have seen you before."

"No, not new," she smiled, offering her hand. Her smile was open and honest, but not, Michael thought, warm and inviting. Her laugh was delightful, but lacked Cheryl's deep resonance.

This laugh was the tinkle of bells. "Not new. Just one of those rare birds who keep to the bush. My name's Maggie." She offered him her hand.

"I didn't realize we had such dense underbrush here," he said, responding naturally to party banter.

"I've just finished my doctorate and, believe me, it wasn't easy finding the will to do it," Maggie said, still smiling her little-girl smile. "The party noises were tempting, but I closed the window and turned up the lamp. All finished now, though, and time to see what I've been missing."

She leaned closer and the musky tang of Cinnabar teased his nostrils. He closed his eyes and imagined she was Cheryl. Michael breathed deeply, filled himself with her essence, willing Cheryl's neon-green, LED flashing eyes to be there when he opened his own.

Maggie's smoky grey eyes looked at him curiously.

"Are you all right?" she asked softly.

"Yes," he reassured her, although the dizziness had not passed. *At least,* he thought, picturing the well-thumbed community phone directory on its shelf at home, *Maggie hasn't been checked off yet in everyone's book.*

50 Monroe Place on Saturday A.M. was like every other house in Dunwoody: bodies occasionally stumbling into doors and walls, glass coffee pots cracking when sobering hands tried to fill them with water, aspirin bottles uncapping with a symphonic echo from house to house to house.

Scott's usual morning fumbling was compounded by his hangover. He started the coffee brewing, then trudged back to the living room to pick up the jacket and tie he'd thrown on the floor the night before. He noticed Michael's clothing scattered from the front door to his bedroom. That wasn't unusual, even after a non-party night, but this morning there was a single high-heeled shoe, pantyhose and shawl mingled comfortably with Michael's brown loafers and corduroy slacks.

A stale metallic odor and the reek of spoiled food green with mould warred for dominance with a deeper, rich earthy scent. Holding his breath, Scott turned back toward the kitchen when he heard his roommate's voice.

"I smell coffee." Michael stood, rumpled and pale, leaning against his bedroom door for support.

"It's on, give it two minutes to finish." Scott gestured to the strewn clothing. "It looks like you made the party. I didn't see you, though."

Michael shot his friend a disarming grin. "Some of us don't have to hang out until all hours just to connect. Those of us with charm and grace, that is."

"Excuse *me*, Prince Charming! Who'd you get lucky with?"

"I met a woman named Maggie at the party. You might have seen her—long red-brown hair, grey eyes, slim."

"I did notice her, but I thought I saw her leave with Frank."

"That's what you get for being first in and last out," said Michael, picking up the feminine attire and tossing it through the half-open bedroom door. "By the end of the night you can't see straight."

"Come on," Scott persisted, "you couldn't have been there more than a few minutes."

"I was there long enough to meet Maggie, wasn't I? Could you do me a favor and dig up an unchipped mug?" Michael turned to go back to his room. "Don't knock—just leave the coffee."

Mumbling under his breath, Scott returned to the kitchen cursing Michael's attitude. "Who the fuck does he think he is? Why shouldn't I knock?" They'd always let each other get a glimpse of the woman the morning after. Not quite sophomoric bravado, but pretty close. Only now Michael was pulling a privacy routine and ordering room service as well.

A deep, resonant female laugh followed Scott back to the kitchen.

Let him find his own party tonight.

It wasn't necessary. Michael didn't leave his room all day or all night. Nor did anyone else. The sounds of bedsprings and laughter and soft murmurs seeped through the door. Occasionally, Michael's snore thundercracked an eerie stillness, but more often the subtle sounds of joining flesh were quietly obvious. The unseen woman's musky, earthy scent pulsed through the house.

Sunday came and almost went before the door to Michael's bedroom opened again. The noise of the television overrode the creak of floorboards, but Scott glimpsed Michael dressed only in slacks and moccasins before returning his attention to a news exposé of interstate shippers.

"Some weekend," Scott commented, half-relieved, half-envious. "For a fellow in mourning, you're doing pretty well."

"Not all that well," Michael murmured.

His sprawled housemate turned away from the interview on television to comment on the acrid stench of Michael's breath, but when Scott saw his friend, he gasped.

Michael's sunken, blood-shot eyes were heavily lined with black circles and his shaggy hair was tinged with grey. He looked as if he'd lost twenty pounds off his already lean frame . . . as if he'd spent a week on an alcoholic, sleepless bender—not two days in bed.

A deep laugh came from Michael's open bedroom door. Fear clouded his eyes; a sudden spasm cramped him. Michael hunched forward, knees bent, and slowly sank to the floor.

Scott rushed to his side. "My god, Michael, what is it?"

"I don't think god has anything to do with it," he gasped.

Scott intuitively sensed something sucking out Michael's life and replacing it with grave rot. The vision passed. He held the suddenly brittle shell of skin and crumbling bones until Michael's spasms gradually subsided.

Pale and drawn, the sufferer feebly pushed Scott away and started back towards the bedroom. Scott tried to follow.

"What can I do?"

"Stay out, stay away, go away," Michael answered softly. "This doesn't concern you."

"Damn it, don't keep doing this to me!" Scott complained as Michael closed the door. "I don't understand."

Long moments passed. Scott stood there, shaking with anger and frustration. When Michael's door finally reopened, Scott pushed past him into the bedroom. The stench of sweat and that sour metallic musk that had been seeping through the house all weekend hit him full force. Gagging, Scott staggered back out into the hallway just as Michael, coat in hand, stepped through the front door and closed it behind him.

Scott took one more swift glance into the bedroom and rushed outside. "Where are you going, Michael? Who were you with for two nights?! *Where is she?*"

Michael stopped on the sidewalk and turned back to the house. The glow from the mercury-vapor streetlamp cast even deeper lines on his sunken face and tinged it a sickly yellow-grey.

"I'm going to meet her," he answered simply. "I was with her and she's waiting for me."

As Michael quitted the streetlight's circle of illumination, the gas-filled bulb suddenly flickered out. Scott stared; he could swear he saw the lamp's mercury vapor being drawn *into* his friend, its gas absorbed by the crumbling shell of the man as he moved away.

When Michael reached the next lamp, it, too, sputtered and dimmed. Again, Scott saw the same image. And again at the next lamp.

At the corner, now only two lamps away, stood a lean young woman, the fullness of her figure apparent despite the belted raincoat. Her head was lowered and a dark braid hung over her shoulder.

It must be Maggie, Scott thought. *She'll know what to do.*

The woman lifted her head. Even from this distance, Scott could see her neon-green, LED eyes flashing at Michael as he moved towards her.

Another lamp went out.

Robert Sheckley

Message from Hell

ROBERT SHECKLEY *is one of the giants of modern science-fiction. His many books include* Citizen in Space, Immortality, Inc.*, Notions: Unlimited, The People Trap, Pilgrimage to Earth, Shards of Space and* Untouched by Human Hands. *He is the former fiction editor of* Omni *magazine and the author of the story that was filmed as* The Tenth Victim. *Here is one of Sheckley's more unusual forays into fantasy from the pages of* Weird Tales *magazine.*

MY DEAD brother-in-law Howard came to me in a dream and said, "Hi, Tom, long time no see; I've missed you, buddy, how you been?"

I trusted him no more dead than when he was alive. He had always been against Tracy and me. The first time we met, when Tracy brought me to her home and introduced me as the young man she had met in the writing program at NYU, her parents weren't exactly ecstatic about me, but Howard's reaction had been somewhat colder than frigid. He made it clear that he didn't want a down-at-heels writer marrying his one, his only, his beloved kid sister, Tracy.

But to Hell with that, right? Tracy and I got married and took a little apartment in Coconut Grove. I can't prove it, but I know it was Howard who tipped the cops that I was a big dope dealer masquerading as a bohemian. They came in with guns drawn and that wild who-do-I-shoot-first look in their eyes, expecting to find a laboratory in my closet or under my bed, where I turned paste into top grade cocaine. Ironic that they should expect this of me—a man who had flunked elementary science in college and whose idea of a chemical reaction was dropping an Alka-Seltzer into a glass of water.

They didn't find a thing, and the half ounce of mediocre weed under my socks finally was ruled inadmissible evidence. But it put a strain on our relationship all the same.

Lots of people marry without the approval of their family. Tracy and I did. We figured Howard would cool off after a while.

That year I sold my fifth short story and got my first novel contract, despite Howard spreading it around that I was a no-talent plagiarist and that Tracy wrote all my stuff for me.

Steady waves of hatred emanated from his stucco house in Coral Gables, permeating our little jungle apartment in the Grove. Things weren't going so well for Tracy and me. I won't say it was his fault, but he sure didn't help.

She had a nervous breakdown, left me, went to Houston, lived with a girlfriend for a while, divorced me and married somebody else. This was during the time I was finishing my second novel. I'm pretty sure Howard paid off somebody at the Miami *Herald* to give my book the worst review in the history of southern Florida.

So, in light of all this, perhaps you can understand why I didn't exactly mourn when, two years later, a rusted-out '73 Buick coupe driven by a drunk skindiving instructor from Marathon Shores screeched over the curb on Oceanside Boulevard like a bumper-toothed monster seeking its prey, and sieved Howard through the iron mesh fence at the foot of South Beach.

It was unworthy of me to feel so good about his getting killed, but I did. I couldn't have planned it better myself. I liked it so much I wished I'd thought of it first. I must also confess that attending Howard's funeral was the best day I had all year. I'm not proud of this, but there it is. I was miserable and I was glad he was dead and I wondered where he came off now stepping into my dream like this.

"Look, Howard," I said, "just what in the Hell are you doing in my dream, anyhow?"

"Funny you should mention Hell," Howard said, with that quick nervous laugh of his. "That's where I live these days."

"I could have figured that out for myself," I said.

"Come on, lighten up, Tom," Howard said, with a flash of irritation. "I'm not in Hell because I was bad. *Everybody's* here— everybody I've ever known, and most of the people I've ever heard of. I mean this is the place people go to after they die. Nobody even calls it Hell. I call it that because nobody ever smiles around here and I figure this has got to be the place. But it's not bad. There's a guy who runs things. He tells us to just call him Mr. Smith. But I figure he's the Devil. He doesn't seem to be a bad fellow and he's very cultured."

"I always figured the Devil would be a businessman," I said. "Or possibly a scientist."

"There you go with that cynicism, Tom," Howard said. "As a matter of fact, the Devil is an art critic and an expert on contemporary culture."

"Did he tell you that himself?"

"It's the only way I can explain how all the best jobs down here go to artists, writers, sculptors, musicians, painters, dancers . . . And they get the best housing, too, and the new cars."

I was interested. As I have mentioned, I'm a writer, not wildly successful, but not entirely unknown, either. My mother had always told me that my reward would come in Heaven; or wherever I happened to land. And here was proof of sorts.

"Tell me more," I said.

"A person's status down here depends entirely on how well known he was on Earth. The Supreme Court is run by guys like Tolstoi, Melville, Nijinsky, Beethoven. Even a loser like Poe has been given the directorship of a large interlocking conglomerate and he gets paid whether he works or not."

"I really like the sound of this," I said. "Thanks for letting me know."

"Oh, it's fine for guys like you," Howard said, with some bitterness. "For the rest of us it's not so great."

My brother-in-law told me that he lived in a one-room semi-detached house in a small suburb on the outskirts of Hell. His work—the only work available—was sorting gravel according to size and number of facets. All the unknowns did that.

"Doesn't sound too tough," I said.

"It's not. The real punishment is boredom. They did give me a television, but the reception is lousy and the only program I can get is *I Love Lucy* reruns. We also get to see a baseball game once a week, but it's always the same one, Phillies and Red Sox, Fenway Park, 1982. I could recite it for you play by play."

"Well, Howard," I said, "it's all pretty dreary, but there's nothing I can do about it. So take care of yourself and lots of luck in your new home."

"Wait!" Howard said. "Don't go wake up yet. I used up ten years' worth of cigarette rations to get into your dream. You could help me, Tom, and it would help you, too."

"What are you talking about, Howard?"

"You could write up this story for a magazine. They'd pay you for it. Just mention my name in the story. Even being mentioned by a published writer is worth something in Hell. I think it would give me enough status to get out of this suburb, take the next step, move into a cottage in a place that looks like Cape May in the rain, and I'd get to sort semi-precious stones instead of gravel and get two channels on the television with an NFL football game every Sunday as well as the baseball game. It's not much, but from where I'm sitting it looks like Heaven. Tom, say you'll do it!"

He looked at me imploringly. His time in Hell hadn't done much for his looks. He was drawn, haggard, strained, nervous, apathetic, anxious, and tired. I suppose that's how people on the lowest social rungs of Hell always look.

"All right, Howard, I'll do it. Now, please go back to Hell and have a good trip."

His face lighted up. "You'll do it? May Satan smile upon your reviews!" he cried. And then he was gone.

And so I sat down and wrote this story. My original intention was to use it to complete my revenge against Howard. You see, I have written this whole thing without using my brother-in-law's real name. As far as I'm concerned he can sort gravel in his semi-detached house in Hell forever.

That was my first intention. But then I relented. It was a fine revenge, but I couldn't let myself take it. I think it's all right to pursue vengeance to the grave, but not beyond. And you may laugh at this, but it's also my conviction that we living have a duty to do whatever we can to help out the dead.

So this one's for you, Howard, whose real name is Paul W. Whitman, late of 2244 Seacactus Drive, Miami Beach, Florida. I forgive you for all the bad stuff about Tracy. Maybe she and I would have split up anyway, even without your help. May this mention get you safely to your hotel room and your football game once a week.

And if you happen to see my old high school buddies, Manny Klein, killed in Vietnam, 1969; Sam Taylor, heart attack, Manhattan, 1971; and Ed Moscowitz, mugged in Morningside Heights, 1978, tell them I was asking after them and thus ensuring, I hope, their move to more pleasing surroundings.

Jessica Amanda Salmonson

A Child of
Earth and Hell

JESSICA AMANDA SALMONSON *is one of America's most erudite fantasy scholars. She publishes* Fantasy Macabre, *has edited* Amazons!, *which won the World Fantasy Award, as well as* Heroic Visions *and* Tales By Moonlight. *Her fiction includes* The Golden Naginata, Tomoe Gozen, *and* A Silver Thread of Madness, *from which the following tragic tale is drawn.*

I HAD SPENT many years in search of my parents, whom I remembered without clear detail: my mother weeping and hugging me and telling me what to say to whomever found me, my impatient father pressing her to hurry, and his face now and then grimacing as from pain. It was a simple yet nightmarish recollection, and I suspected even then that they were gone upon a life and death mission to which they would not imperil my life with theirs. Her tears made me cry also; and the crowded concrete sidewalk was a frightening thing in itself, to a child accustomed to soil and woodlands verdant.

My father, who had stood almost dispassionately in the background whilst my mother bid her sad good-byes, suddenly staggered against the wall and began to groan. That was when my mother with agonizing effort forced me through the huge door of the railroad station and I saw neither of them again, save in my uneasiest dreams of where they might have gone.

After minor efforts on the part of the authorities to find my parents and learn my identity, I was declared a ward to the state of Washington and placed in a foster home outside the suburbs of Seattle, the city where I'd been abandoned. It seems that the state had no orphanages, which were deemed dehumanizing, and in many cases it was necessary to place children in less than amiable situations merely to provide them any home at all. I was treated abhorrently by my foster family, except on those days, often months apart, when the welfare caseworker dropped by to see my circumstances.

Once, as I recall, I did try to inform the caseworker, during her visit, that I had not been kindly treated. But she could see I was not unhealthy or beaten or dirty, and she surmised, I presume, that I was lying, perhaps out of jealousy of the two older boys, who were my foster parents' own by birth and but one cause of my various distresses. Surely the caseworker recognized my conditions were less than adequate, but she never seemed to grasp the true extremity of the non-physical violence I endured. And it was, after all, especially difficult to find homes for deformed children.

My foster mother, after the caseworker left, locked me in an emptied closet as punishment for trying to be a "tattletale," as she called it. I was fed, twice daily, mixed scraps from the family's table, which I suppose was ample feed; and my box-sized room was cleaned daily, so I was at least as well kept as any caged house pet. My false brothers would torment me outside the door by describing the taste and flavor of candies and ice creams they were eating, or by pounding on the door and yelling until I was cowered so far into the corner that I could only withdraw into myself for further escape.

I was not released until a month later, on the occasion of the welfare worker's return visit. I was the epitome of good manners and obedience, complaining naught, for I knew she would not believe anything so outrageous as my being locked away all that time since her last visit, and I did not wish to be so punished for another month as well.

My gratefully accepted reward for being good and silent was my usual run of the basement. I did not mind being kept there at all, for I was seldom bothered except when food was delivered or thrown down the wooden staircase; and I had a private toilet there, several makeshift toys scrounged from the debris and stored items, and even a mange-scarred rat for company, with which I shared my adequate if motley food supply. My one true friend, the rat would generally eat with me, but he was too high-strung ever to let me touch him; he was, after all, wild, and he never came closer than arm's length. His was the first moral lesson I ever learned: a friend, but at a distance.

I should not belabor the cruelties of my childhood, for they lend either an air of disbelief or bitterness to my tale, however true the case may be. And I confess a vile detestation for that family, which emotion is bound to corrupt my memory of early life. But the fact that I spent much of those six years in the dank cellar of a foster home is important to my tale, for certain barely tangible occurrences, I now believe, were early clues to my heritage.

It must be said here, to state it mildly, that I was no handsome child. No attractive child would have been subjected to my treatment. My appearance, I feel, is a large reason for my being placed in a home with people whose only concern was receiving the added monthly income provided by the state for the care of its wards.

No hair graced my pate, and I was regularly taunted by my enemy foster siblings for that baldness. My fingernails were blunt, black, hard things that had to be cut almost weekly lest they grow into useful weapons against my hateful and hated brothers. Beyond these two abnormalities, I was reasonably ordinary and was never accused of being more than merely overgrown and homely.

During these six years of cellar life, I came to appreciate the darkness, even to prefer it. I went so far as to make a willful attempt to seal off the metal grid which allowed fingers of sunlight to stray into my domain each morning. But more, my senses were driven to acuteness. Not only were my eyes grown keen and accustomed to the night, but my sense of touch and hearing were so finely attuned that I could detect underground sounds and movement with uncanny accuracy. I had, by ear and fingertips, learned where the rat's every tunnel weaved, and I envied his smallness, his ability to explore those dark passages.

One of his tunnels I judged to be made of metal, probably a fragment of buried pipe; and one chamber was large enough to cause a perceptible echo of the old rat's padding feet. I thought also that I had detected passages which the rat never used, and I was curious as to why he limited his territory. If it were me, I reasoned, I would methodically conquer every reach of my domain of minuscule caverns and crevices.

One night, as I lay with only the thin, coverless cot-mattress between me and the floor, I blocked from my mind the sound of the late television shows upstairs, and listened to the rat scramble underground, questingly. I wondered what had him so busy. Then I heard something extraordinary, a faint noise that might ill-fittingly be termed "slithering." Whatever it was, it seemed to have entered the chamber which was the rat's chief lair, only a few inches beneath the cement floor. My heart beat hard, for I feared some rodent-eating snake had found its way to my one friend's main nest. But in the next moment I knew it was no serpent, for I heard a beguiling purring sound, which began to accompany the abrasive slithering on the tunnel floor, and this was confounding when one considered that no ophidian could make more than a hiss.

I sensed and heard my mammalian friend approach his favored lair and stop, sniffing the rank sub-cellar air for signs or odors of the unwanted guest which had risen from deeper, more sinister passages. The rat squeaked uneasily, uncertainly, as though unsure of the alien presence. I envisioned its sensitive whiskers dancing quizzically, its nervous tail, hairless as my pate, twitching. I wondered why the mangy little beast didn't flee; could it sense less than I the presence of the other? I knew the rat to be a wily, crafty sort—but perhaps senility was upon him at last. Or maybe the thing that purred had no odor the rat could perceive, and echoes made him uncertain which way to escape. *Run*, my mind was thinking, but the rat stood fast, either of senility, enchantment, foolhardiness, or the territorial instinct to stand against an invader.

The thing, the purring slitherer, at last struck. I heard their underground tussle and knew the elongated slitherer was trying to loop itself around its biting prey. The rat squealed loudly, furiously, so I knew that he was in peril. In my own panic for his well-being, I began pounding on the cement floor and screaming at the slitherer to go away, leave my rat alone, when suddenly the key rattled in the basement door.

My foster father, a shadowy hulk against the blinding light from the kitchen, beer can in hand, descended the steps in his untied shoes and approached where I lay. He kicked me in the face and two of my teeth were broken out. Without our exchanging a word, and without my whimpering, he left the cellar and relocked the door. That was my first really physical attack, but somehow it was less detestable to me than was the day-to-day revilement and spite I suffered without physical contact of any kind.

As I spat blood and bits of my teeth, I listened for the rat. The slitherer had gone, scared off by my shouting or by the larger footsteps. And the rat had not been killed. It crawled out through the crack in the concrete floor, its manged fur matted with dark blood, its yellow incisors dripping with ichorous slime. It stood there on the ledge of that small crevice, badly shaken by its ordeal, and that night we shared our mutual pain.

Several days later I was called up from the peace of the cellar and cleaned and clothed afresh for the benefit of the woman from the department of social services. Of course the caseworker was curious about my shattered front teeth. She was told by my foster mother that I had fallen down the basement steps. The caseworker demanded that she see the basement, as it was part of her job to see that the homes of state wards were not unduly dangerous. My foster mother hedged, refused, but with her husband gone, she hadn't enough backbone of her own to resist the caseworker's insistence that she be given access.

I followed innocently, precociously, as the caseworker carefully took the darkened stairway one step at a time, appalled by the stench and disrepair of the place. On the floor, she spied my toys: pieces of blue and green glass from shattered Bromo-Seltzer and antique canning jars, rusty cans and tools, an old brass water-hose spray-nozzle.

My foster mother was fidgeting with her own fingers and explaining nervously that the basement was almost always locked and no such accident would ever happen again. But the caseworker was not a complete fool and could see the area had been played in with regularity. My rat had been getting a drink from the stained porcelain toilet when we intruded; the caseworker choked back a cry when she saw it dart toward the crack in the floor. Dumbfounded, she stood at the base of the steps. She saw my blue-striped, filthy cot-mattress in the corner, stained with blood not yet turned brown, where my mouth had bled off and on for two nights running.

"Oh, that," my foster mother tried to explain before the question could be posed. "That's just an old thing my husband threw down here."

Still being true to my act of innocence, I passed the caseworker at the foot of the steps and walked with an almost casual stride to my mattress, where I laid myself down as to take a nap, facing the wall so that my insuppressible smile would not be witnessed.

Shortly after, I was taken from that place, and when most of the facts were learned, I understood that my foster parents were to be prosecuted for various offenses. The caseworker discovered that I had not, in my six-year stay, been enrolled in any school, and that my ex-foster parents were guilty of welfare fraud as well as breaking out my teeth and keeping me like an animal. Yet, they never came to trial. I was by then an estimated eleven years of age, large for the age, yet in many physiological ways underdeveloped. Whatever my true age, I was old enough to have developed a keen and compelling need for revenge. I doubted that the sentences they might receive would equal my torturous six years, and I knew with a certainty my two pseudo-brothers would escape any kind of punishment, for they were young and would not be held responsible for their part in my cruel treatment.

I did nothing overtly. Even mentally, I did not willfully cause the thing to happen. It was merely a dream I'd had—a dreamland wish-fulfillment, which afterward proved to be the physical reality. Perhaps I inadvertently made the thing happen by some sinister ability unrecognized even by myself, or perhaps I was only an astral witness and not the cause. Or possibly it was coincidence. Yet so strange was the circumstance, I cannot but think it was somehow linked to me. It was too bizarre a happening to be dismissed.

The dream was this, and I had it the second week following my removal from that foster home: I was viewing the familiar cellar and it seemed my spectral self was located near the ceiling, judging by the angle of my panoramic vision. I was calling, spiritually, to the purring slitherer, which I had longed to see since that night less than a month earlier when I heard it beneath the floor. "Slitherer," I called. "Slitherer. Come." I think I heard my voice command aloud, an echo in the darkness, but I knew no one else could hear me. None but one.

The rat, dear, untouchable companion, scurried frantically out from the crack and ran madly toward the toilet. He jumped atop the back of it and stood there twitching his tail and squeaking wildly.

The slitherer was coming to my call! I was overjoyed by this newfound power. When I saw it ooze its abominable snakelike, sluglike flesh up from the small crevice, I was tempted to further test my power over it. "Up the stairs," my whispering voice echoed, chanted. "Up the stairs. Up the stairs."

It glided smoothly, leaving a trail of slime to mark its path. The length of it, when entirely distended from below, was several meters, perhaps as many as six. It reared its flattened head with the slow purpose of a snail, and under it I saw the circular razored maw of a lamprey. It seemed to be testing the air by whatever senses it possessed in the four eyes dancing on stalks. A single hole on the side of its long body, immediately behind the head and which I imagined to be a gill or other breathing apparatus, fluttered rapidly, producing the purring sound. It started obediently for the steps, veritably *flowing* upward, matching the contour of the staircase.

My dream continued on and I was experiencing a high degree of delight over the success of my orders. Its slimy flesh squeezed under the door, stretched itself across the length of the kitchen's linoleum floor, and at my mental insistence sped its way around a corner and down a narrow hall, then through an open doorway to where the two boys slept in twin beds. It slithered up one bedpost, its air-hole purring with excitement. Unfelt, it attached its razored suction disc to the sleeping youth's neck. With a barely perceptible sucking sound, the boy jerked once, and was instantly leeched to whiteness.

The sticky maw drew away from the punctured jugular and the insatiable, blood-dripping, hideous little head with waving eyes-talks looked toward the other bed.

"Hurry," my echoing voice commanded. "There are two more in the other bedroom."

I awoke then, witnessing no other nightmarish feasts, not suspecting until years later that my command had been obeyed even after I woke from my dream. The authorities evidently kept the strange slaying unpublicized, and of course I was never told of the occurrence by my new keepers.

At first I was presumed retarded, but I was not responsible for my lack of education. Their initial judgment was born of other factors as well, aside from my low level of general knowledge. An abnormal growth rate made me seem awkward, though I later became exceptionally coordinated when the speed of my growth subsided and my physiology caught up to my size. I had always had a speech impediment, worsened by the loss of two front teeth, which grew back at an unusually slow pace. My teeth and skull and even the length of my arms particularly intrigued the doctors who initially examined me. My increasing ugliness must have added measurably to the overall appearance of a mentally deficient child. I bore some resemblance, in fact, to a leering spastic with little command over facial muscles, though I venture to say I was actually facially coordinated in my own way.

Because of my presumed mental handicap, I was moved from the Seattle Orthopedic Hospital to a virtual children's sanitarium in the town of Buckley, a goodly distance away. My new home in Buckley was the nearest thing the state had akin to an orphanage. The defective, sickly sorts were kept there—children no one could be expected to adopt, children who needed specialized training or constant care. My playmates were the spawn of inbred minorities, unwanted children of decadent or poor families—some blind, deaf, or mute, or combinations thereof, with birth defects, or scars acquired after birth, and a great many mentally retarded cases. We all had in common the single fact that no one wanted us, though I think no one was as fully cognizant as I of our shared trait.

I did not enjoy their company, and I think I might have gone truly mad and thereby adapted to my situation, but for one saving grace. I was given the opportunity of an education, as it was of primary concern to the establishment that as many residents as had the capacity would be raised into self-sufficient members of society, to one degree or another.

I relished the education, and it was quickly evident to all that I was not, after all, in any way mentally handicapped, though I think they still considered me somewhat deranged, a condition they may have attributed to my traumatic childhood history.

Told a thing once, I remembered it, and I had reached sixth-grade level within a few months. I was recognized as exceptional, but a special tutor was beyond the resources of the ill-funded home, and my teachers remained the same people who were trained to aid the underdeveloped mind, not the overly intelligent. I was my own best instructor anyway, once the fundamentals were at my command. I read voraciously, everything and anything I could lay my hands on, until I was adjudged as being at the college level of education and still accelerating. The teachers and hospital staff were easily overawed, however, and something inside me always reminded me of my basic inferiority.

My studious efforts were not well organized, thus I went through phases. I had books of more advanced and variegated subjects delivered regularly from neighboring libraries to the sanitarium on loan. For a while, I was deeply interested in prehistoric mammals, especially of the ice age. The likes of the woolly mammoth and the saber-tooth awakened what might well have been racial memories, sparking in me an academic intensity that was not quenched until I exhausted all available information, much of it exceedingly technical. Eventually I moved on to another obsessive interest, then another. American Indian lore held great fascination for me for a long duration. And though it would be ludicrous to suggest this attraction was also born of some genetic link to the past (for I was obviously kin to no Indian), there was always something barely beyond my grasp that was definitely familiar about those cultures. There were other phases as well that rendered me superficially expert in archeology, world history, philosophy, mythology, and all manner of subjects that had intrigued me fleetingly.

Always there was a feeling of emptiness after I'd completed a study, for though I did not know what it was I was hoping to discover, it seemed certain that I had not found that for which I quested.

And these studies kindled my sleeping imagination—or perhaps awakened an array of memories locked by heredity into my DNA. I would see as vividly as life the glacial ice and the great hairy beasts that roamed there, and in one such dream I saw a gray-robed old man sitting dwarfed astride the neck of a mammoth with long, widely curved tusks. That man was somber of face, and in my dream I could not be sure if the man were an aged and wizened version of myself or of my father. In another dream, I watched savages in a forest gather around a great, tall totem pole, and all the faces of the totem looked like my father. The savages knelt all around it in wonder, and they chanted a weird song in a tongue that was not their own.

That song I remembered even after I awoke. I chanted the words in the manner I had dreamed them, for I liked it better than the nursery rhymes the younger children were obsessed with, though the words were meaningless to me. One doctor took an interest in my dreams for a while, and I think he recorded the sounds of the chant I learned in my sleep. But his time was sparse, and his interest in me was aborted. So my dreams, like my studies, were largely private things, and I largely a private person.

I lived in the sanitarium only two years, until I was thirteen or fourteen. I had grown to astonishing proportions for my age, and the doctors suspected a thyroid problem. I was too large to be kept with normal-sized children any longer, and too intelligent to be left there to waste away. But I was too young to legally be on my own or to start any job rehabilitation program. These sorts of things were talked over in my presence, and I was told one day that I would probably be placed once again into a foster home and allowed to enroll in a regular high school. That circumstance did not appeal to me, however, so I ran away. It was simpler than I had imagined it would be, leaving.

It was not totally without preparation or purpose that I left, for I had two small clues to help me discover my true parents' identities, and I intended to find them. Being tall and intelligent, and too ugly for anyone to guess my true age, I had little trouble adapting to the outside world. Labor jobs, though paying poorly, were not hard to find. Additionally, I stole. My needs were few, but my search made travel necessary, and I learned the crafted art of thievery to make up the difference in bus or train fare—though I honestly did prefer to work for my subsistence whenever possible.

One clue to my identity was acquired from sanitarium files, during my quest for reading material and out of conniving curiosity. The file contained not only medical and educational records, but also a résumé of my earlier life as seen by old caseworkers. Portions that interested me were the areas covering my earliest known history—vague or completely forgotten by my own memory. I was presumed between four and six years of age when found wandering in Seattle's King Street Station. At the time, I carried a wrinkled lunch bag prepared by my mother so that I would not go hungry during the time it took some official to realize I was lost and abandoned. On the old and oft-reused brown paper sack was written a fragment of an address, possibly scrawled by one of my parents. It had been the police department's only clue, but it led them nowhere, since it was a rural street address without the name of a town or county, and it might not even be a Washington State residence. Nowhere else in that file was there a tangible clue, though I found out in that one reading how many misconceptions persons had about me.

The second clue was dredged out of my own blocked memory, or from my dreams. Often I had awakened, frightened by some terrible horror, with the stifled cry of "Momma Lydia!" almost bursting from my lips. Possibly I cried out to a Momma Lydia rather than simply Mother because my father called her that; I could not be sure. But at least the name Lydia was one clue I had of which no one else had been aware.

Then, too, I had the potential of remembering more, of seeing something that would trigger recollections of tothood experiences or places. Not three months on my own, one such memory tugged faintly at my mind. My first job was as a berrypicker, and it brought back something of that childhood trainride to abandonment: we had passed farms of a huge-leafed vegetable, which I suspect was rhubarb, though on that point my memory cannot say for certain. And people were bent among the agricultured waist-high forest chopping the leaves at their bases. That was all: only a rhubarb field, and it wasn't of much help. But if more memories of the countryside returned, perhaps I'd be able to place myself on the map somewhere near where my parents came from, with me, on that train.

Early detective work consisted of learning from where every train had come, that day I was abandoned. The train schedules were available from the newspaper morgue. It was a futile gesture, I knew, for it was ground covered by authorities when the trail was fresh. And the number of stops at towns and cities was incredible, the additional number of potential transfers incalculable. But I was determined to visit every single burg. Traveling, at least, I had a chance of spying something that would bring back memories.

Several years passed while I lived the life of a road tramp—a singular life, lonely but for the occasional hobo who would befriend me temporarily. From one tramp, as ragged and unkempt as any, I learned that the life of a hobo had once been noble in its way. In his youth, such wayfarers as we, he told me, could find their way into a subculture and network of carefully hidden hobo villages, colorful ragtag communities with boisterous elected officials, proud rail-riders, and friends returned from, say, Chicago or New Orleans or San Francisco, all with grand stories to tell. But alas, I was told, that life had died, though there were yet half a dozen or so hobo villages strung up and down the West Coast. Melville, for instance, around the northern Cascade region of Washington, could still boast a fairly large community, completely unknown to the remaining inhabitants of Melville itself.

Bells rang when I first heard my fellow tramp mention Melville in connection with a hobo village. I remembered, so very faintly, the tramps my father used to hire a day at a time to chop wood or plow or tend the vegetable gardens. Why Melville should trigger that recollection, I could not be certain. But that one previous clue, that rural address minus town, was embedded in my mind.

For one reason and then another, I did not make Melville for several months. The cold season was upon the land when I slipped out of a boxcar as the train approached that commercial forestry town. Snow splotched the ground sparingly, the really heavy snows not expected for another month; but the biting cold rain was already generously available. Collar up and hands thrust deep in my pockets, I walked away from the tracks, along a narrow muddy road through the trees.

It proved a fruitful journey. Set back among the Douglas firs far along that little-used road, I found that rural address, and it filled my heart and lungs with nostalgia and yearning. Though it smelled no differently than any number of abandoned barns and houses I'd used as shelter over those years, it had a quality all its own when joined with a familiar vision. Hadn't I played near that very porch, now sagging and ready to fall with the rain pouring off and through it? Wasn't that rotted rope on that lone elm's branch the remnant of a rubber-tire swing my father had once made?

It was a painful vision and my eyes blurred. I began to weep, though the tears were not distinguishable from the freezing rain that numbed my high-boned cheeks. There came an urge to turn and flee, not as from unknown terror, but as from an unbearable emotion, a commodity so long pent up in me and threatening to burst forth all in a single flood.

There, in the now-crumbling house and barn, walked the ghost of a man who never lived—myself. My ghost: me, as I could have been if some mystery hadn't driven my family to abandon me in a far city and then go on to some other life or place.

I was shaking all around at the shoulders, and my weeping became whimpering as I tried unsuccessfully to control myself between the elm and the firs. Crying for no specific reason to determine: for the atrocity that had been made of my life, for the loving childhood which was the best part but least recalled of my youngest years, for my parents who must have deserted me only by their own sacrifice.

With a few deep breaths, I managed to contain myself, and even managed a methodic countenance as I searched through the rotting timbers. Vulturous persons had been there before me, salvaging anything of value. Thus I found little but rubble and familiarity. Nothing noteworthy awaited at the top of the dangerously creaking stairs, and all I found in the main floor room was a broken bed-frame and a few dry logs some hunter had left unused by the still-sturdy fireplace.

Miserably wet and cold from the subsided rains, which still dripped from the eaves and leaves outside, I shook out my long coat, built a fire, and sat on a bed-frame plank across two logs, watching the flames that glowed orange on my face and hairless pate, and I thought.

There were flashes of memories tugging at the back of my mind—impressions almost tangible, here in this place where, quite likely, I was born. But the memories were not useful, merely teasing visions of my father sawing boards laid over a wood-horse or pitching hay or milking the single cow, and my long-skirted mother bent over a steaming pot on a wood-burning stove, which now lay rusted and broken in the weed-grown back yard.

Then, suddenly, I jerked forward, staring into the flames, mes-merized by the memory I envisioned there:

I crouched in a nightshirt at the top of the stairs, unseen be-tween the rails of the banister, as my father answered the rap at the front door and my mother stood immediately inside the kitchen. My father bore a shotgun, but the man outside stepped in with a wicked, twisted smile, unafraid.

"Leave us alone," my father demanded.

"You know I can't do that," a deep voice said calmly. Like my father, like me, this man was bald, as I saw when he removed his brimmed hat. "It was not easy to find you. But you can't hide your mind from ours, especially as the Time draws near, as the Change alters your metabolism."

My father cocked one side of the two-barrel shotgun.

The other did not plead, but said, "There will be others after me. And if there were not, would you die here?"

"I would *live* here!" my father shouted angrily, raising the gun to fire and cocking the companion barrel. But his finger tensed and he lowered the weapon. "I have never before begged," he said, in a tone I had never heard from this seemingly callous but truly caring man. "I beg you."

"To what avail?" The mysterious stranger shrugged.

"I have, perhaps, another month. Give me that long. Then I will return."

"Or you will die," concluded the other flatly.

My mother gasped from her listening place and hurried from the kitchen to my father's side. She exclaimed, "Why are you threatening us?"

"Shh," my father said. "He did not mean it as a threat." Then to the tall man—tall as my father and enough like him to be his brother—he said, "Come for me in a month if I have not come of my own accord, and there will be no resistance. Let me live a true life while I can."

The eyes of the other were without evident emotion. But behind that mask of uncaring, compassion must have rested, or pity, or even envy—all these feelings and others, carefully hidden and unexercised. After a cold, glaring minute, he turned abruptly and left without a word, the door slowly swinging shut behind him.

My parents clutched one another in terror, her terror that of not comprehending, his of comprehending too well. His almost clawlike hands ran gently, lovingly, down her back, and he spoke so quietly I almost couldn't overhear, "At least he knows nothing of our son, Momma Lydia. It may be that your blood has made him different from me. In what time I have, I must find safety for him, away from their clutches."

And then, before his beloved Momma Lydia's wondering, frightened eyes could search his with questions, he turned to the crackling fireplace and wrestled loose an unmortared stone. There, in the hollow, he retrieved a parchment tied with string, and he faced his wife again, to tell her with dour expression, "Lydia, were I a poet, I would recite you a verse of love. But instead, I must read to you a grave horror and truth, that you might know me as I really am."

Though sore afraid, strength and dignity was in her, and she promised, "Even then—I will love you."

There my memory, my vision, ended. How much, I wondered, originated in my own locked thoughts, and how much was relayed mystically in the flames now dying before me, like tattling ghosts of a haunted ruin. The fire, or my own mind, had given up its secret, and my fingers fumbled expectantly at the unmortared stone, pulled it loose, let it thump to the floor.

Inside the hollow lay two pieces of paper—my heritage.

• • • •

The first paper, laid flat and face down, was a yellowed and faded photograph of my father, mother and myself. My mother was plain, but not unattractive, my father like a brute beside her, smiling fawningly at the baby in her arms. On the back were written all our names, and at last I knew my identity, or part of it. It read, quite simply, "Bennet, Bennet, Jr., and Lydia Strlpretner."

So, I am Bennet Strlpretner Junior. Strlpretner—German? Swiss? Or something more arcane? It was anyone's guess. I tucked the family photo in my ragged shirt. The other paper, rolled and tied, was of rare parchment, so dry and brittle it gave a crinkling complaint as I unbound it. It was in a strange script; serpentine letters crawled across the scroll, familiar somehow, but beyond my reckoning.

I stood staring at that paper held taut between my hands, wondering if I really wanted to know what it meant, what it said. Here were things my father meant to protect me from: horrors he deemed more dread than anything the mortal world could mete out to an abandoned child. Before the last embers of the fire I stood, unmoving, uncertain, and I fancied shadows darker than the shadows reading over my shoulder and whispering among themselves. I let the paper roll shut, and in a desperate pang of fear I held ready to fling the parchment onto the coals. But I did not. I had come too far and suffered too much to throw it away now. I smashed the sides of the scroll flat, folded it lengthwise, and tucked it in my pocket.

I could not sleep there, for my own ghost would haunt me. The hobo village was not far, for it was from there tramps would come for handouts or a few hours work when I was a toddler. There I went, and was welcomed half-heartedly, and begrudgingly spared some hot beans from a campfire. My coat was heavy and usually served as a mattress and blanket, but tonight I would sleep with a real blanket, tattered thing though it was, proffered with the same slow reluctance. I was a stranger, and a beggar of beggars, and these were hard times for their kind. Perhaps in other years, they were warmer people who lived like these. Or perhaps they were warmer now, to their own kind; much as my mien resembled theirs, I was yet an outsider.

Before turning in, I sat with a few others around their fire, exchanging pleasantries so that they might more easily accept me, for a few days if necessary, while I collected my thoughts and laid the most tentative of plans. When I removed my hat, the oldest among them gasped in apparent surprise, though he was nearly as bald and not much handsomer than I. His eyes then looked down at my hands, the nails of which I had not cut in some time and were long, black, sharp. For a moment I feared he recognized me as a monster—for such I feared myself to be. But he asked again what I'd said my name was. I had cast off former titles; now I called myself Bennet Strlpretner. His eyes seemed to glisten then, for he had known my father, and worked for him upon occasion. "A generous man," he said. I was thereby linked to their company, and accepted so fully that their propriety and good nature was embarrassing.

I stayed a week, and learned much of my father's personality from the codger. But more, I learned of a strange circumstance following what the man admirably termed, "the sudden disappearance of the Strlpretners." It seems a huge dark traveler came into their village of lean-tos shortly after my family's home was vacated. "Could have been kin to you and your daddy," said the tramp, "and he asked questions about Benedictus Strlpretner." When the group of bums kept mum (as it was their rule never to aid detectives in finding someone who wished not to be found), the great tall man became violent.

"We all ganged up on 'im, though," the old man said, laughing. "He swung those hands like ball-and-chains, nearly killed ol' Pipeline Henry, but he couldn't outmatch us all with our rusty knives and broken whiskey bottles. He turned and beat a track out of here, and I cut him up the arse with a busted wine jug as he went. He didn't bleed, though, so I figure I didn't get deep. Strange feller, that one, no offense now, I mean because I said he was a bit like you."

"Hairless like me, you mean?"

"Can't say; wore a hat. But those hands. Huge! And nails like claws, like yours, like your daddy's. What causes that anyway?" He passed a puzzled look over my fingers and I closed my fists self-consciously to hide the nails. "I don't know," I said.

Shortly after, I was gone—at once sad to leave that supportive atmosphere and pleased to be free of their constant closeness.

I had to have that parchment translated, but a tramp cannot simply walk up to a language professor or an eminent archeologist and ask a favor. It was months before the time was right. I finagled my way into a gardener's job on a community college campus in Seattle. Did a right good job, too, and made certain I came to be on "howdy" terms with all the language teachers. With the meager wages, I rented a cramped room in the skid row district and slept in a bed for a pleasant change—a small bed, but with fewer lumps than the ground. Bought myself some new Salvation Army clothes. Then, one day after classes were done and I noticed one of my "howdying" professor friends had remained behind for whatever reasons, I walked into his empty classroom with my arcane scroll in hand.

He was immediately intrigued. I told him I did not know its origin, or what it said, but that it belonged to my father and I'd greatly appreciate it if I could find out what it said. He ventured that it might be Arabic, Turkish or some derivative, but he didn't know enough about it. If I'd let him keep it awhile, he said, he might be able to get one of his colleagues to look it over. I thanked him kindly, then spent the next few weeks quietly gardening about campus, betraying no impatience.

But I was impatient—for strange visions, waking dreams, were beginning to visit me; and I felt certain that the parchment would contain not only clues to my heritage, but lend purpose to the psychic phenomena I began to endure. At the same time as my occult experiences were beginning to unfold, my old affinity for darkness returned anew. Or perhaps that affinity had never left but, if anything, had only been suppressed.

Each afternoon, my gardening duties fulfilled on the campus grounds, I would escape to my cramped, windowless room, away from the dread sun, and sleep out the day. Come nightfall, I would roam the skid row streets, from the dark waterfront wharves to the decrepit and historic relics of First Avenue, preserved in their decay. From midnight to three A.M. the drunks and sexually disturbed and prostitutes were my unspeaking company; I would pass among them as a shadow, almost unnoticed. Once, a native American Indian, in the grip of sotted delirium, fled from the sight of me, bellowing in his tribal tongue. By four in the morning, the whores and homosexuals would be gone, the winos and alcoholics hidden into stairwells and abandoned buildings, and I would walk alone between the bleak exteriors of pioneer architecture a hundred years old.

But this architecture was young compared to what lay below the city streets. In another era, the whole of Seattle was gutted by fire. Instead of leveling the sturdy, burned out structures, iron girders were laid down and a new city built atop the old. Every year, new portions of that elder city are unearthed or rediscovered, for miles and miles of tunnels worm from one underground building to the next. Some of them are mapped, others are suspected to exist but have not yet been reached. Underground tours are conducted daily through the safest, tamest areas. In Pioneer Square itself, the underground buildings have been sandblasted clean, so that gift and novelty shops run amok, turning these confined areas into tourist ghettos. Few among the plebeian horde ever stop to realize that these obtainable areas are only the smallest fraction of the entire rat-infested complex beneath the shops and hotels of their mundane world.

I was attracted to that low and gloomy realm. A hound for the macabre, I sniffed out secret or forgotten entries and passages. My clawed hands had minimal trouble pulling up a manhole cover, and I walked beneath the nighted streets, an occasional police car or other vehicle the only sounds above, rumbling over my roof. I came to a section where the walls were interrupted by low archways, seldom visited but not unknown. I entered each building I found, scrutinizing worthless artifacts. The roofs were so low I had to stoop, as none of that early generation was so tall as me. I needed no light, though the eyes of another would be blind in such darkness. Soon, I had discovered places doubtlessly unseen by human eyes since the days they were paved over and forgotten.

Each night I would widen the outskirts of my territory, until dawn arrived and I'd perforce return to my rooming house, bathe at the end of the hall, and go to work, hoping each day for word on the translation of the script. Hearing nothing yet, I would grovel in the gardens beneath the horrid light of day, then bus to my room once more to sleep out the sun, and complete this cycle when returning to my explorations.

I had discovered a place on one of the lower side streets where the boards far behind a tall wooden staircase could be pulled loose and I could enter underground Seattle, then replace the board behind me. I disappeared into that corner, to the consternation of a night patrolman cruising the streets, who shone his spotlight my way an instant too late to see who'd been there.

I made my way along paths known to no other—I, and a few giant wharf-rats. But even they were not common in the specific area I had grown fondest of, and that was odd in itself. The stone-walled, rat-shunned building had once been a drugstore. Among the antiques I found in the strewn mess were many outdated pharmacy utensils, and in one area a pile of pill bottles fused together by the heat of that historic blaze. A blackened porcelain syrup fountain lay crashed on the floor. There was nothing overtly special about the place, but it attracted me, and I knew by psychic intuition that this would come to mean something.

Near a wall was a perfectly round hole that may have been where a sewage or water pipe once led. One night, I heard noises from that hole, which at first I took to be mere rats. But rats do not speak.

Out of the jumble of many voices, I picked the word "Benedictus" many times. It grew louder, but no easier to understand with so many blending undertones. And then I had my vision, not unlike the vision I'd seen in the flames of a fireplace many months before. Like a genie from a lamp, a ghostly vapor rose from that opening, and it took on the transparent, tenuous shape of a woman in ordinary dress, her arms held out to me as her form wavered into solidity. Her forward-held arms did not invite me, however. The way she held herself, I knew that she was warning me away.

"Go back!" I read her lips saying, though I could not pick her voice out of the other ghostly sounds. "Go back" was the message her mouth was forming.

"Momma Lydia," I called quietly, and walked forward, hoping to touch her, longing for the embrace of her loving arms. I begged to know: "How can I come to you?"

She shook her head, and warned me back vehemently. And then she vanished, like a popped bubble, rejecting me and abandoning me once again. And with her went the haunting sounds. I was left dumbfounded, empty, but not afraid. I was determined to carry on. Her very warning was proof of my nearness!

All morning as I tended the flowers, though the bright colors had come to offend me, though I affected a show of loving my endeavor, I reflected on the specter of the night before.

When first I began venturing into the eerie catacomblike hollows of old Seattle, it was merely the longing for darkness, I had thought, which drew me on. Only the instinct of a burrowing, nocturnal beast—for surely I was that, or made myself that, or had been made into that. But now I suspected premonitory, psychic ability, untrained, unrealized, native to my being, which had brought me to the depths below the city *on my quest.*

I remembered, or it struck me, suddenly, like a flash of lightning, a thing that had never before dawned on me, though it seemed so obvious in that instance of enlightenment. My true parents had abandoned me in the Seattle train depot, but *they themselves had never entered.* The train station was on the southern verge of underground Seattle. Indeed, the tracks leaving Seattle were themselves underground railways, buried beneath city traffic.

I had searched in Washington, Idaho, Oregon and Canada, when all the while they had been here. They had never left the city. And my instincts, my sixth sense, or some subconscious logician, had at last led me to their self-imposed burial place.

In my glee of realization, my strong hands broke the handle from the trowel I'd been using to lay rows of marigolds. I stood anxious from the chore, and would have fled downtown to reenter the maze of buried buildings and dark passages, never to return until I'd found where my parents had gone, or died in the trying. But I did not rush back then, for Professor Bunting was in my path, and the sight of him brought my fitful thinking back from plans of a sub-city existence, subsisting on rats captured by swift bare hands, drinking what seeped down from the gutters above.

What expression was on my visage, I could not know, but it must have frightened poor Bunting, for he stepped away from my hulking height as though I might be dangerous. But after composing my manic thoughts, I smiled amiably, and he reddened as though embarrassed by his moment of foolish terror. He said he had good news.

"The translation?" I asked.

"I imagine so," he told me with a nod. Young men and women hurried down the campus sidewalks to their next classes. "Professor Fennerson of the University of Washington has suggested I have you come by his office. Here—I have the directions written down. I expect he wants to know more of your parchment's origin. He's a noted archeologist, and when he says he's got something slightly phenomenal, you can bet the word 'slightly' is his modesty creeping in."

After minor pleasantries, we parted company, and I left knowing with a passion that I'd not return to that miserable daylight job. I had what I needed now. Or, rather, it awaited at the end of the bus connections to the opposite boundaries of Seattle.

Late that afternoon, I walked into Professor Fennerson's office. Skulls lined a shelf behind his desk, ranging from some tiny primitive primate's to a modern man's. Indian artifacts were hung in random attractiveness all about the room, with an unmatched pair of African masks glowering from among its Northwest cousins. After greeting me with a warm handshake and cordial manner, Fennerson, who was gray with years flesh-wise and hairwise, tottered to a cabinet from which he removed my parchment inheritance. He set it on his desk, using two ancient-looking pieces of carved stone to hold it flat, then opened his notebook beside it.

"Have a seat! Have a seat!" He waved in a direction and I pulled up a chair to one side of the desk he sat behind.

"I'd never seen a script like it," he was saying. "It's not that I was too busy to get to your request sooner, my friend. In fact, I set other matters aside to work on this every night. It simply took this long!" He was most apologetic as to the length of time I'd waited, as though his time had been worth nothing. But now all I cared about was the meat of the matter, and I craned my neck in an effort to read his notebook while he talked not of the work involved, but of the extremely interesting nature that made the work worthwhile.

"I worked with Leonard Styles on an expedition, oh, back before the war, in an area still considered Palestine. Styles, rest him, would have known more of this, I think, and would have delighted in it as well. He was always dabbling in arcane matters, forever trying to make some ancient spell or magic work. Poor fellow! He was a genius of archeology, but ignored by his peers for his eccentricities." Fennerson smiled then, mischief in that look. "And he *was* eccentric, I suppose. Never did get any of those spells to work—used to blame it on inadequate phonetics. Said he thought he had the right words, but the pronunciations were wrong."

Fennerson chuckled, and I was growing secretly impatient with his almost senile fondness for relating the past. Then his humor waned a moment and he added, "But no one ever knew exactly what became of Styles. Vanished utterly from his home in England after retirement. I often wonder if he finally got his pronunciations right." The humor that marked Fennerson's brow returned again and he completed his recollection: "I'd like to fancy he did, at last, herald some doom upon himself; he'd have liked that, I think—knowing in his last moment, after a long life, that he was right."

"Please, Professor. I don't mean to be reticent, but I'm dying of suspense. What precisely does the parchment relate?"

"Oh, yes!" he said, as though suddenly realizing the present. He fingered a pair of round spectacles from the pocket of his vest and wrapped one wire stem around each ear. Then he focused on the parchment, his lips pursed, and looked to be reading the Sunday paper spread out before him. Then, bursting into recital, he seemed to be reading directly from the text:

"We came before the French came down from Quebec, before the Spaniards from California. We were first to witness the Straits of Juan de Fuca. First missionaries to the shores of Puget Sound. Before Cook, before Lewis and Clark, before all others of Europe, we came.

"Constantinople was still a power then, from whence we fled. We sailed from that adopted homeland, ostracized, our numbers much reduced by attempted genocide, avowed to settle nowhere near the likes of civilization, nor where it soon might come.

"No martyrs had we been—only sources of heroism for Turks and sometimes Moors, who would prove their bravery by the slaying of a wizard. We sailed. By the sorcery of lost Mu, we crossed the wide Pacific, across seas that covered our once-proud nations. Our numbers dwindled further on the journey. But the strong survived, by tooth and claw and necromancy.

"There were cannibals on Puget Sound then. But it was ritual cannibalism, and the natives would not foul their honored heritage by adding the flesh of outsiders to their own. So we were unmolested. The tribes were peaceable, and always preoccupied with bizarre customs of greed and prestige: who owned the most baskets, who caught the most fish, who held the biggest feasts, who built the tallest totems. These were important among them; and they were, for their needs, a rich people. And we were, for the first time since our land was destroyed by angered gods, free of persecution."

The professor stopped here, took up a tissue to dry watery eyes. He smiled at me and said, "Imaginative, yes? A queer history, or a well-spun yarn? There's more."

He returned to the long page of tiny, snakelike marks.

"One day a young brave spied us fishing without nets. He carried this tale to his people. The story spread, and when it came back to us, we were already legend. Monstrous salmon, said the tale, threw themselves on the shores at our feet, in multitudes unequalled. By their custom, our prestige was unrivaled.

"We feared we might soon become objects of superstitious terror. Instead, the innocent people revered us. The natives made pests of themselves. They built their longhouses on the outskirts of our small community. They came to us begging and praying. We craved solitude, and could not stand their incessant curiosity, interest, reverence. But we could not smite them when they were as children or affectionate dogs.

"Three chiefs we took into our confidence, or made them think as much. We taught them small magicks: how to control a bear or sasquatch and make it do their bidding. How to conjure a ghost, though we were guarded enough that they could not also learn to summon demons. And how to leap uninjured from high places. Several medicine men we taught to heal wounds or cure certain common diseases by reciting incantations more powerful than their own. And we taught them to raise small rocks without touching them, which useless sport pleased them more than any. We were this generous, and more, but only for our own good.

"We knew the medicine men would want the workings of their new abilities kept their own secrets. And the chiefs would want no others to learn the same magicks that would equal them in prestige and power. So it was the medicine men and chiefs came to ensure our solitude, keeping their people from coming to our region and learning the same things they had learned.

"A cult sprung up around us. The sons of chiefs and medicine men, and the daughters of priestesses whose line had been more powerful in earlier generations, came to us each autumn with payment of gifts, to be our students. A mystic aura was given us, cultivated by the leaders of the tribes, so that we were no longer bothered save by the few young and honored students.

"Years passed. A century. Our numbers were still not great, but our survival seemed secure. And then one night we were attacked by an army of black bears, and we knew the magicks we had taught, though minor in themselves, had been turned into a weapon of some might by the combined efforts of all the chiefs. We were reduced to the border of extinction, and we were angered. For the first time, we proved our mightiness.

"We set upon one tribe a gigantic spectral raven whose wings produced hurricanes against their villages. This was a dread horror for them, for Raven was their greatest benefactor, creator and uncreator of the world, and they thought certainly they had incurred the wrath of their most honored god. On another village, whose chief and medicine man had betrayed us, we sent a likeness of their honored Thunderbird, who burned and ravaged their community beyond repair. Into another tribe ambled a grizzly bear that dwarfed the black bears beset us, and it killed every brave before it was completely subdued and died of its many wounds taken. Their nights were harried by the presence of soaring white owls, their symbol of eternal darkness and death. We caused crops to wither and fishing nets to come untied at every knot and our temper was so beyond our own control that we did not stop these evil sendings for three days.

"And then we mourned our own sins as much as our dead. We had gained nothing. Vengeance is so hollow. And so we saw that our past history of oppression was not all undeserved, and we deemed our kind unfit to walk with other races of humankind. Thus we cast repentant and repulsive spells upon ourselves that would last unto the hundredth generation. We condemned ourselves to a self-made hell in the depths of the earth, there to live in our so-precious solitude for all our lives, and our children's children's lives, accursed to the sun, accursed to all who might summon us from our living death."

The professor finished the script with a wry smile, and when he looked up to the chair I'd been sitting in, I was not in it. He glanced over his shoulder in time to know his fate. He slumped forward without a grunt, the top of his skull caved in by the carved rock I'd taken from a shelf behind him. I then left with his notebook and my parchment, and threw both into an incinerator before leaving the university. I made my way to downtown Seattle on foot, shunning the proximity even of transit passengers. The shops were closed by the time I attained the downtown area, but it was not so late that the movie crowd had yet deserted the streets. I felt lost in a sea of oppressive flesh while I made my way to the secret place behind the steps. All the crosswalk lights had seemed to work against me.

With the strength of my inhuman hands, I madly ripped away a large portion of the bricked and boarded section leading underground. I did not regret leaving my entryway more easily discovered, for none would follow so far as I intended to go. A ferret in the night, I found my way through areas none but I knew. There was a chamber, I knew by sense of hearing and touch, existing where I had been unable to find passage, deeper in the earth. I came to the stench of a long-buried, fire-gutted brick structure, and I cried out in despair: "Show me the way!"

My voice echoed with a commanding power and I felt a slight tremor, an earthquake that few would notice though the Richter scale at the university would tell of its passing. A section of the floor gave way beneath me, and I fell, screaming, and fell, screaming, and fell, screaming.

And from the depths of the earth resounded my cry . . . the name of my mother.

Read
at Your
Own Risk

David Madden

The Master's Thesis

DAVID MADDEN *sold only one story to* The Magazine of Fantasy and Science Fiction, *but it was a memorable one. "The Master's Thesis" seems deceptively low-key at first, perhaps even droll, but gradually takes on an aura of undefinable menace. Madden was an actor, radio announcer, assistant editor of* Kenyon Review, *associate editor of* Film Heritage *and a drama and English teacher at Ohio University.*

A SOUND like the crackling of a fire intruded upon Professor Swinnard's nap. He opened his eyes on a black sweater in full sunlight across the room. Faded and fuzzy, it had a white band just under the V of the neck where red reindeer lifted their feet.

Swinnard became aware that his finger still pointed at the place in *Current History* where he had begun an article by a former student, that his foot, turned inward in the unbuckled galosh, prickled and throbbed, and that a student, without knocking, had entered his office, had taken a chair, and was now peeling the wrapper from a Baby Ruth.

The professor started to speak but closed his mouth when he felt saliva slip down his chin, tremble at his dimple. He swallowed and wiped and settled his glasses in place. "My—office hours—"

"Yes, sir."

"—are posted on the—"

"Yes."

"Are you in my freshman survey course? Veteran students generally know better than to—"

"Sir," said the young man, uncrossing his long legs, tapping one of the reindeer with the exposed nub of his candy bar, "I am your advisee. I am a Master's candidate."

"What courses have you had with me?" Swinnard relaxed, depending upon the effect of his reputation to bring balance to the situation.

"None, sir. I earned my B.A. elsewhere."

The professor blinked. "You expect to *earn* your Master's here?" He closed *Current History* with a slow flourish.

"I can't miss, sir."

Professor Swinnard swiveled in his chair. "I beg your pardon?"

"Can't miss, sir," said the boy, rearranging the wrapper out of which the brown nub of his Baby Ruth protruded.

"Young man, you have already missed a great deal. You will never again invade the privacy of my office. You will knock, you will be granted permission to enter, you *may* be offered a chair. And you will not, if you please, rattle candy wrappers in my face."

The young man shoved the partially nude candy bar up under his sweater, agitating the reindeer. His eyes pale, his mouth soft, his ears flushed from the late September chill, he looked suddenly under sixteen. "My supper, sir."

"Suppose we—start all over again. Or rather, simply start."

"I'll buy that."

"Your name?"

"Philip Hockaday Fonville, so help me God."

"I—I am Professor Swinnard, as you know. Let's see. Ah, yes, here you are—on the list, I see—opposite my name."

"Oh, there's no mistake, sir."

"Did you . . . did you ask for me?"

"Frankly, sir, I had another preference. No reflection—since I hardly know you. But I *had*—"

"What? Whom did you want?"

"Professor Korpmann."

"But he died last summer."

"So, I said, if that's the way the ball bounces, anyone will do."

"I—see. Well, I haven't time this afternoon to engage in a long conference with you. Tomorrow perhaps we can outline your course of study, and once I have had an opportunity to review your work—somewhere near Christmas, I imagine—we may sit down and go over a list of possible thesis projects. I have a good list which has produced a number of—"

"We won't have to sweat that one, sir."

"Mr. Fonville, let me suggest that you—"

"No question about the thesis. Square that away right now. Put your mind at ease, sir."

"I'm sure none of us is without his pet topic, Mr. Fonville. We won't be bothered by that. Countless theses have been written. One must review the possibilities—"

"No, sir, I'm certain, this is virgin territory. Never been touched, sir. Mine will be an entirely new contribution."

"Your presumptuousness is colossal, Fonville. Perhaps we had best meet tomorrow, when you have had time to—"

"Time? For what, sir? I've chosen the subject of my thesis."

"In my forty years of teaching, I've often stumbled on your sort. Burning with a project that will transform—"

"I realize it will take hard work, sir, and I shall require your assistance at unusual hours of the day and night owing to its nature."

Swinnard was about to say, "My office hours are posted," when the telephone rang. His sister. Calling from her home forty miles away. Wanting to know whether he knew it was raining. He told her he did. Could see it on the window. Good. Just don't forget the galoshes. No. Then goodbye.

Fonville was almost to the door, but turned and pulled out his sweater, dropping the Baby Ruth into his open hand. "Only wanted to let you know I'm around, sir." He nodded, did an obsequious shuffle just beyond the cracked threshold, wandered away.

"Listen, young man, you—" He had to get it settled. But just as he leaned out the door, the red that streaked across the boy's sweater blinked around the corner. Swinnard put his hand over his heart and remembered a hot summer twilight when the ferris wheel jammed and his father kept rocking their chair. Later, as he was approaching the faculty parking lot, Swinnard discovered that he had forgotten to pull on the other galosh.

That night Swinnard got out his notes, yellowed and buffed, to review his first lecture. Somewhere in the late Bronze Age, he fell asleep. The telephone startled him awake. When he rose and took the phone in his hand, his notes slid to the carpet.

"You get the news about old Sanford?"

"Who?"

"Sanford, the music teacher. They found him on the bathroom floor."

"Who did?"

"I didn't get you out of bed, did I?" Now Swinnard recognized the voice of the department chairman. "Sanford—they found him dead—"

"No, I hadn't heard. Look—do you know a boy named—?" Swinnard began to ask, but the department chairman had hung up.

The next morning, the rain had turned to thick fog. In the dark basement hallway, Professor Swinnard almost stepped on the boy. Fonville looked up in the dim light and got to his feet. Close up, his eyes were red.

Swinnard would let the boy begin and at the first opportunity squash him. Not that Mr. Fonville had any kind of upper hand.

"Have a good night's rest, sir?"

"Now look here, young man, once and for all, you will kindly observe a little decorum."

"Sir, I was only inquiring into the state of your health." It sounded to Swinnard like parody.

"Sit down," he ordered. Then he realized he was late for a class and that he had quite forgotten his nine o'clock office hour.

But the boy sat down before he could explain. Swinnard noticed that the boy carried no books. He wore the same sweater, the reindeer crossing the snow to the gentle pace of his breathing.

Swinnard took his notes from the briefcase and tapped them sharply on the desk until they were precisely even. He sought a phrase that would work, but the insultingly eager look on Fonville's face persuaded Swinnard to deal with the boy more roughly. He simply went to class, leaving Fonville to sit in the shadows.

When Swinnard returned from his class to his office, Fonville was there, standing in front of Swinnard's desk with the telephone to his ear. He held it out to Swinnard. Furious, Swinnard jerked it out of the boy's hand and sat down.

It was the president, asking how he was. Fine. How was the president? The president was fine, never felt better, got in some golf before the rain set in last evening. Fine, sir. He had heard some fine things about Professor Swinnard from one of his students there in the office. Said everything was working out just fine. Well, fine. They would see each other soon, of course, and have a nice chat. It had been too long since the last one. In the men's john at a community concert, Swinnard remembered as he hung up.

It felt good to Swinnard to talk to the president without having to play up to him, or feeling as if one had, knowing that one never really had. With one more year, one didn't have to . . . There the boy sat, his slender legs crossed, his palms cupped under his elbows, his chest hairy with the sweater where those reindeer lifted their feet.

"He's a nice guy," said the boy.

Swinnard did not comment. After all, the boy had said something nice about him to the president.

"Now, young man," he said, turning *Current History* right side

up and looking for something, anything that he might have mis-
placed, "suppose we get this whole affair in perspective."

"I'm having it typed up now, sir."

"What's that?"

"The first chapter."

"Come now," Swinnard said, grinning, trying to find some way
to attack the problem. "We must be serious."

"Sir, how much seriouser can I get? Up all night gnawing on
candy bars to keep up my strength while I struggle with this
thing."

"You are actually in the writing phase of—"

"Oh, it's going to be ready before the deadline—way before.
Typed up in three neat copies, bound and everything. Neat and
crisp."

"I refuse to sit here," said Swinnard, rising, "and listen to you
rant in this manner."

"But, sir, as my advisor . . ."

Swinnard walked over to the boy and stood above him. "You
will please leave and not pester me again."

The boy looked up at Swinnard and pointed toward the desk.
"I'm *on* the list, sir."

"Confound the list!"

"Think," said the boy, standing now, "of the thousands who
died building the pyramids, sir."

"To what end?"

"The victims of the plague."

"What has the plague to do with—?"

"Men die."

"Assuredly, but I fail to see what this has to do with our graduate program in history." Swinnard moved away from an odor
that seemed to emanate from the boy.

"I know how to work in all the footnotes you want, sir.
Charts. Tables. Maps. Diagrams." He ticked them off on his long
skinny fingers. "Graphs. Indices. Appendices. You name it. I'll
whip it up for you in a shake, sir."

"Do you think that makes a thesis?"

"No."

"Then get out."

"I'll see you around, sir. I'll pick up those first pages and shoot them over to you personally."

"You will please not bother me."

"I can see you're upset just now, sir."

"Not in the least."

"You need to get off your feet, sir."

"I need to be left alone."

"Of course, you're right, sir."

The boy left. In the sudden emptiness of the room, Swinnard realized that he had forgotten something. Yes. The reason for the president's call. Surely not just to ask how he was. Worrying now, imagining, ready to apologize for having cut him off, he rang the president's office.

"No, no, Swinnard, I didn't call *you*. The young man in your office called *me.*"

At noon he crossed the campus to the bookstore. He had promised his sister he would bring *Flower Arranging Made Easy* when he came for dinner.

As he was starting up the steps to the bookstore, Swinnard saw Philip Hockaday Fonville running toward him, waving some white sheets, but not calling to him, the faded black sweater with the white band and the red reindeer circling his chest and back as though he were a Greek vase. Swinnard escaped, trying not to run.

The next morning, Professor Swinnard came out of the classroom at the end of the hall, and there was the boy, sitting on the sooty concrete floor, his back against the blighted chestnut office door, his head resting on his crossed arms. Swinnard wedged himself between two students, fell in behind three others, and left the building by another entrance.

Swinnard strolled into the administration building, glanced at some out-dated bulletins, then ambled back to his office. A student leaned against the wall. Fonville was gone.

"Did he say he would be back tomorrow?"

"Who?"

"The boy who was here," Swinnard said.

"Nobody was here."

Then he saw the note.

Dear Prof:

Waited two hours, through your office hours. I hope you realize that I am not an impatient sort, but after all, I *am* a graduate student, am I not, and should be granted periodic interviews???

Please inform me by student mail as to when you will be available.

Yours truly,

Philip Hockaday Fonville

The three-by-five note card was fastened firmly to his door with a white thumbtack, streaked with red, as though the boy had stuck himself.

Swinnard rose before dawn and went down to the kitchen and leaned against the sink. He drank a glass of water. The moon was a silver bow. There was one glint of light on the clothesline on the lawn. He imagined the bow he once made with a limb from a hedgeberry tree. It had been years since anything had disturbed him. As a child he would stand in his back yard and look up at the sun, upside-down through his legs. He remembered the odd thrill the view gave him. He realized that what he wanted most of all was peace, so, leaning against the front of the refrigerator, he wrote a note that put him face-to-face with the young man.

To Philip Hockaday Fonville:

Apparently you have been unsuccessful in trying to locate me for an interview. With school only a few days underway, I can't imagine what we would talk about, except a *possible* subject for your master's thesis. Should this be the case, please be advised that my office hours for today are 2 to 5.

Yours sincerely,
Professor Swinnard

Then he slept the sleep of the unburdened.

The Master's candidate hadn't come at two. At four, Swinnard admitted two other students to his office. They would take up the time. He closed the door and sat down with the first student. Something about never being able to remember dates, and Swinnard gave up listening. He thought of Fonville, and then he tried to remember something out of his own childhood. It was when Swinnard heard himself asking the student at his side where he was from that he also heard a light knock on the door.

"Did someone knock?" he asked the student.

"I believe someone did, sir."

Swinnard had half-risen to leave the desk when the door creaked open and Fonville stuck in his head and saluted with a slim white hand that protruded from the sleeve of his fuzzy black sweater.

"Don't get up, sir. Stay right where you are. Won't take but a minute." Shoving the door open, he swooped, making no noise with either door or feet, only a rattle with the papers in his hand. Swinnard remained half-squatting at his desk. "There we are, sir. Neat as the veritable pin. Chapter One. I'll just place it here and bother you not a second longer." Pivoting, he returned to the door, where he turned, suddenly, and raised his arm, like a child asking permission to speak: "Oh, yes. A report on that tomorrow morning at ten would be of immense help to me, sir. In the midst of things at the moment." He was gone before Swinnard could speak.

The professor dismissed the other student and glanced at the stack of white sheets. The cover page was blank. He locked up for the day. Later, sitting in his car, Swinnard couldn't move. He went back, got the pages, and rammed them into his briefcase.

It was as though he were afraid to let it into his house. At a Chinese restaurant where he occasionally celebrated a birthday, he sat down with orange tea and decided that he would read the piece and find in it such factual inaccuracy and inadequate documentation as could be used against the boy.

But he put it off until he had eaten, and then he opened the evening paper.

That night he realized he had forgotten to read the chapter, that he had, in fact, left it on the table in the Chinese restaurant. He telephoned, and the dishwasher answered. Yes, he had. It was in the garbage, and the garbage was on the truck. Yes, he could read a little English. One word on the second page, "Death," followed by a name in three parts. Swinnard thanked him and tried to sleep.

The telephone woke him. The blinds were still dark.

"Yes?"

"Sir?"

"Who is this?"

"Just called to see how you liked it so far. I'm going full speed on the second chapter."

Swinnard hung up. He turned on the bedside lamp. His wife used to say, "How can you see to talk in the dark?" He looked at the twin bed where she had died, and all of her unborn children with her.

He went downstairs and made some coffee. He opened the back door and stood behind the screen in the chill air, watching the rain clouds go over the moon.

At ten o'clock that morning he left his basement classroom with the students. Without even glancing down the hall at his office door, he walked briskly out the same way he had used to evade the boy before. But he heard someone call his name. He quickened his stride, his heart pounding hard in the soles of his feet. The touch of fingers turned him. A short, stocky boy, wearing a letter-man's sweater and carrying a load of books under his arm, handed him a note and galloped off.

> Dear Professor Swinnard:
>   Regrettably, I am unable to make our appointment at nine (or was it ten?). Like everyone else, I have my problems. The dentist insists on extracting three of my teeth.
>
> Yours cordially,
Philip Hockaday Fonville

Swinnard crumpled the note and dropped it where he stood. His hand empty, he put it to his head.

Professor Swinnard was rolling up the maps after Survey of European History when Fonville walked in, grinning to show where a front tooth was missing. Swinnard, up on his tiptoes to reach the map case, thought he was going to faint. He sat down at the desk.

"Well, sir, everything is now fine. Couldn't be better. Teeth out, pain gone, and here I am for that consultation."

Swinnard began to talk. When he realized he was stuttering, he stood up and looked the boy in the face. "Mr. Fonville," he said, "I have lost your first chapter," and then he turned away to put his notes in his briefcase.

"Sir, this is unforgivable."

"I'm sorry. It couldn't be helped. Now if you'll excuse me."

"But, sir. Think. Think. Where? Where?"

"I—don't recall."

"This means I'll have to write it over, sir. Interrupt my work at its present juncture."

"Don't you see how utterly impossible this whole thing is?" Swinnard blurted out.

"Sir, if you don't mind my saying so, this is a hell of an attitude to take. I come to you with a unique thesis. A little variety. What's impossible about it?"

"Don't raise your voice, young man!"

"Raise my voice? I'm entitled to raise my voice. You've just *lost,* and for no good reason, a thing into which I've put, you might say, sweat, sir! Blood, sir!"

"You will stop haranguing me in this melodramatic way!" Swinnard felt heavy. He backed toward the door. Inside his coat, he was hot. His skull felt numb. The boy kept talking, turning around and around talking, following him, and the reindeer reared up on the white band and the black quivered in the light coming through the tall windows. He reached out to touch the boy, to get him to stand still.

And Fonville was saying, "I am very quiet, sir. I am very quiet now, sir. It's all right. I've forgiven you." Swinnard was in the desk chair, his coat flung back, his shirt undone, his tie dangling between his legs.

Days passed with no sign of the boy. In Fonville's absence, Professor Swinnard tried to relax. Dozing off in his office, he would jerk up, anticipating the sound of a candy bar wrapper. He asked around. None of the students knew the boy. Yes, they'd noticed the sweater. He checked the boy's schedule in the registrar's office, but he was down for thesis credit only. That was a technicality Swinnard could use. One had to take certain required courses before even beginning to discuss a thesis.

But as the weeks passed Swinnard forgot that. The boy wasn't registered in the dormitories. The address in the files turned out to be on the other side of town, in a neighborhood with many misleading house numbers. He didn't want to see where Fonville lived. Somehow, the idea of the boy's room frightened him.

Maybe Fonville was ill. The hospitals said no. Or dead. The morgue had never heard of Philip Hockaday Fonville. At night, he would remember fainting in that classroom. He worried about his heart.

One night, he came home to find a note the cleaning woman had propped against the bread box. Philip Hockaday Fonville had called and left a number.

Swinnard couldn't eat supper. When he had started upstairs, he remembered the note and decided to make the call from his bed. Instead, he lay down in the dark and tried to sleep. Three hours later, he pulled himself up, went downstairs, and walked out onto the lawn. He looked up at the moon and wondered how the earth, that seemed to curve there in the yard, would look upside-down.

The next morning, Professor Swinnard called the university from a booth on the highway. He said he was sick. He spent the day driving in the country. Toward three o'clock, he felt guilty. He had never lied like that before. He was proud of his perfect attendance record. He would put in an appearance.

Crossing the campus, he saw the boy coming toward him, a huge bundle of papers in his skinny arms. Swinnard ducked behind a massive shrub and cut across the grass, glancing back. The boy was going toward the administration building.

At his office, Swinnard found a slip of paper on the floor instructing him to call the dean immediately.

The dean wanted to know what the problem was with this Fonville youngster. Swinnard's grip on the receiver relaxed. At last they were finding the boy out. But the dean went on to say that the boy had complained that he, Swinnard, was being stand-offish. What about that? The president, the dean said, had met with the boy. The president wanted to see that everything was done right by the young man. The boy was right there in the dean's office, very upset, and to tell the truth, hurt. Would Swinnard see him now? Yes, Swinnard would. He hung up.

He wouldn't try to explain. No student was going to do to him what this boy had done to him for almost a month. He would play along. In the end, he would be vindicated.

He sat, waited. After a while, it occurred to him that the boy might be making him wait. Resentment gave way to sleep, as he sat there in his galoshes, the gray light falling through the dusty windows. A light knock brought Swinnard awake with a start. The boy edged into the room quietly.

"I hate to disturb you, sir," he said very softly, "but as this seemed a good opportunity to have our long-awaited buzz session, I thought I'd come ahead."

"I have less than an hour. I must . . ."

"Oh, I understand, sir. Of course."

Fonville pulled a chair close to the desk until their knees almost touched. Swinnard noticed what tremendous feet the boy had. His galoshes made his own feet look large, but they were small alongside the boy's. Fonville settled himself, but first, Swinnard wanted to know what that odor was.

"Smell, sir?" The boy got up and looked all around the room, sniffing in each corner, sticking his head out the door into the hall, and peeping over the window sill into the yard under the bushes. When the boy sat down, Swinnard realized that the odor was stronger.

They faced each other, ready again for the conference. But the boy didn't speak. He only looked at Swinnard. Then he reached under his sweater and pulled out a Butterfinger and started to split the wrapper with the long, sharp nail of his little finger. "May I, sir? My supper."

Swinnard waited, but still the boy didn't speak. Then he reached under his sweater again and brought out what looked like a transistor radio. The little mechanism glinted like silver. The boy's thumb flicked a tiny switch and Swinnard heard a faint whirr.

"What in the devil is that vicious little object?"

"And I thought we knew each other well enough so you wouldn't shy from it. The quality on the other tapes has been rather substandard. My sweater seems to muffle your voice."

"Other tapes?" asked Swinnard, unable to look away from the gadget.

"I've recorded all our exchanges, sir. I believe in getting the full value of—"

"Please go on, young man. What is it you want to talk about?"

"My thesis, of course."

"Then go ahead."

"*Me*, sir?" Fonville pointed at one of the reindeer with the

Butterfinger. "Aren't *you*," he said, pointing the Butterfinger at Swinnard but then lowering it, "going to ask *me* questions?"

"I have no questions."

"Aren't you supposed to quiz me, to suggest, to comment, to analyze and evaluate?"

"I haven't the faintest idea what you've been writing."

"Well, now, sir, is that *my* fault?"

"I've heard quite enough of that, young man. I imagine you have written further on your project."

"That's it exactly, sir, sick as I was. Diarrhea. Inflammation of the gums. I'm sorry I didn't keep you informed."

"Quite all right. Turn what you have over to me. In a week or so, we'll meet again."

"You're being remarkably nice about it, sir. Thank you."

"Good, then. I'll take whatever you have."

"Oh, I don't have it with me. It's over at the Ad Building, being run off."

"Run off?"

"Yes, sir. Copies. In case of loss, fire, or something like that. If there's one thing you've taught me, sir, it's to take precautions."

"A very silly idea, Mr. Fonville. An unnecessary expenditure."

"That's okay, sir. I charged it to the department, in your name."

Later, Swinnard could not remember what he had said to the boy. No doubt the machine had recorded it.

The professor suffered that night. He could not sleep. His body trembled. He was certain he had a heart murmur. At dawn, the telephone rang.

"Sir?"

He hung up.

An hour later, it rang again. He answered, swaying, his knee braced on the bed that had been his wife's. "Yes?"

"I'll deliver it to your office, sir. You won't even have to speak to me. Goodbye, sir, thank you, sir."

Swinnard held the phone a long time before he hung up.

The turning of the key in his office door set him to trembling. He shut the door. When he heard the light knock, he ran across the room and bolted the door. The knob turned several times. Swinnard waited, knowing that the boy's feet, large as they were, never made noise. He thought he smelled them.

He stayed in the office through his class and heard the students leave his classroom down the corridor, talking loudly, laughing, glad he had not shown up. He tried to busy himself, but the sight of his notes made him dizzy. When he opened a bottom drawer and saw nothing but dust, a few rubber bands, and a rusty paper clip, he wept.

At ten-thirty, he went to the door, listened again. The odor was gone. He slipped the latch and looked out. A piece of cardboard was thumb-tacked to the door.

> Sir: I am looking for you. I must get the finished thesis to you before something happens to it. I'm in the mimeograph room in the Ad Bldg. ! ! !
>
> Respectfully,
> P.H.F.

Swinnard returned quickly to his desk and got his briefcase ready to go. His sense of hearing had become so extremely acute that he heard, very faintly, the outside door down the hall open. He rushed to the office door, slammed it, locked it, pressed his back against it. His throat was dry, his eyes burned, his legs were weak, and his heart beat heavily. A light knock. He waited for the knob to turn. A sound like a guillotine, and he looked down.

Between his feet lay a sheet of paper. He picked it up. A brief message informed him that his contribution to the United Faculty Flower Fund had not been received as pledged. Swinnard laughed, sat down at his desk, and wrote out a check. He put it in an envelope and mailed it in the campus box on the way to the parking lot.

He felt utterly calm at supper. Later, he watched television. He even watched a puppet show and smiled. Then he went to bed.

Like a large pimple, a stack of white paper lay on the bed-spread.

Fighting an impulse to run, he caught himself, clenched his fists as though arming against some wild creature. The stack was tied with frayed red cord. On top was a note from the cleaning woman.

Dear Prof. Swinnard,

A nice young man delivered this stuff this morning just after you left for the office. He begged me to make you read it tonight because he's leaving town tomorrow. I told him you couldn't possibly finish so much tonight, but he said he'd call you tonight to see what you think of the first part.

Yours truly,
Mildred.

Swinnard stepped back and the white bulk bounced slightly where his knee had pressed against the mattress.

He removed the receiver from its cradle, turned off the light, and softly closed the door. Moving through the living room, he lifted the receiver on the downstairs telephone and let it drop into the chair he had warmed watching television. The sound of the kitchen screen opening comforted him.

Standing on the peaceful lawn under the full moon, he knew that, despite the chill in the air, this was what he wanted to do. He ducked under the clothesline. The summer sound of the screen door was still in his ears. He bent over toward the curving grass and reached to grip the backs of his legs. Strands of his thin grey hair brushed the grass. His glasses slid down over the bridge of his nose and dangled from one ear as he peered between his legs, upside-down. The earth turned black, the moon melted, making the sky one white radiance, and in the soles of his feet, Swinnard felt the distant beat of hoofs.

Jack Vance

DP!

"DP!" is a forgotten masterpiece from the pages of The Avon Science Fiction and Fantasy Reader *published in 1953. Its author,* JACK VANCE, *has won virtually every important genre literary award in America, including the Hugo, the Nebula and even the Mystery Writers of America's Edgar. Vance's acclaimed fiction includes* The Dragon Masters, The Dying Earth, Galactic Effectuator, The Languages of Pao *and* To Live Forever. *His wonderful short story, "Green Magic," earned the closing spot in my 1993 anthology,* Masterpieces of Terror and the Unknown.

AN OLD woodcutter woman, hunting mushrooms up the north fork of the Kreuzberg, raised her eyes and saw the strangers. They came step by step through the ferns, arms extended, milk-blue eyes blank as clam shells. When they chanced into patches of sunlight, they cried out in hurt voices and clutched at their naked scalps, which were white as ivory, and netted with pale blue veins.

The old woman stood like a stump, the breath scraping in her throat. She stumbled back, almost falling at each step, her legs moving back to support her at the last critical instant. The strange people came to a wavering halt, peering through sunlight and dark-green shadow. The woman took an hysterical breath, turned, and put her gnarled old legs to flight.

A hundred yards downhill she broke out on a trail; here she

found her voice. She ran, uttering cracked screams and hoarse cries, lurching from side to side. She ran till she came to a wayside shrine, where she flung herself into a heap to gasp out prayer and frantic supplication.

Two woodsmen, in leather breeches and rusty black coats, coming up the path from Tedratz, stared at her in curiosity and amusement. She struggled to her knees, pointed up the trail. "Fiends from the pit! Walking in all their evil; with my two eyes I've seen them!"

"Come now," the older woodsman said indulgently. "You've had a drop or two, and it's not reverent to talk so at a holy place."

"I saw them," bellowed the old woman. "Naked as eggs and white as lard; they came running at me waving their arms, crying out for my very soul!"

"They had horns and tails?" the younger man asked jocularly. "They prodded you with their forks, switched you with their whips?"

"Ach, you blackguards! You laugh, you mock; go up the slope, and see for yourself . . . Only five hundred meters, and then perhaps you'll mock!"

"Come along," said the first. "Perhaps someone's been plaguing the old woman; if so, we'll put him right."

They sauntered on, disappeared through the firs. The old woman rose to her feet, hobbled as rapidly as she could toward the village.

Five quiet minutes passed. She heard a clatter; the two woodsmen came running at breakneck speed down the path. "What now?" she quavered, but they pushed past her and ran shouting into Tedratz.

Half an hour later fifty men armed with rifles and shotguns stalked cautiously back up the trail, their dogs on leash. They passed the shrine; the dogs began to strain and growl.

"Up through here," whispered the older of the two woodsmen. They climbed the bank, threaded the firs, crossed sun-flooded meadows and balsam-scented shade.

From a rocky ravine, tinkling and chiming with a stream of glacier water, came the strange, sad voices.

The dogs snarled and moaned; the men edged forward, peered into the meadow. The strangers were clustered under an over-hanging ledge, clawing feebly into the dirt.

"Horrible things!" hissed the foremost man. "Like great po-tato-bugs!" He aimed his gun, but another struck up the barrel. "Not yet! Don't waste good powder; let the dogs hunt them down. If fiends they be, their spite will find none of us!"

The idea had merit; the dogs were loosed. They bounded for-ward, full of hate. The shadows boiled with fur and fangs and jerking white flesh.

One of the men jumped forward, his voice thick with rage. "Look, they've killed Tupp, my good old Tupp!" He raised his gun and fired, an act which became the signal for further shoot-ing. And presently, all the strangers had been done to death, by one means or another.

Breathing hard, the men pulled off the dogs and stood looking down at the bodies. "A good job, whatever they are, man, beast, or fiend," said Johann Kirchner, the innkeeper. "But there's the point! What are they? When have such creatures been seen be-fore?"

"Strange happenings for this earth; strange events for Austria!"

The men stared at the white tangle of bodies, none pushing too close, and now with the waning of urgency their mood became uneasy. Old Alois, the baker, crossed himself and, furtively exam-ining the sky, muttered about the Apocalypse. Franz, the village atheist, had his reputation to maintain. "Demons," he asserted, "presumably would not succumb so easily to dog-bite and bullet; these must be refugees from the Russian zone, victims of torture and experimentation." Heinrich, the village Communist, angrily pointed out how much closer lay the big American lager near Innsbruck; this was the effect of Coca-Cola and comic books upon decent Austrians.

"Nonsense," snapped another. "Never an Austrian born of woman had such heads, such eyes, such skin. These things are something else. Salamanders!"

"Zombies," muttered another. "Corpses, raised from the dead."

Alois held up his hand. "Hist!"

Into the ravine came the pad and rustle of aimless steps, the forlorn cries of the troglodytes.

The men crouched back into the shadows; along the ridge appeared silhouettes, crooked, lumpy shapes feeling their way forward, recoiling from the shafts of sunlight.

Guns cracked and spat; once more the dogs were loosed. They bounded up the side of the ravine and disappeared.

Panting up the slope, the men came to the base of a great overhanging cliff, and here they stopped short. The base of the cliff was broken open. Vague, pale-eyed shapes wadded the gap, swaying, shuddering, resisting, moving forward inch by inch, step by step.

"Dynamite!" cried the men. "Dynamite, gasoline, fire!"

These measures were never put into effect. The commandant of the French occupation garrison arrived with three platoons. He contemplated the fissure, the oyster-pale faces, the oyster-shell eyes, and threw up his hands. He dictated a rapid message for the Innsbruck headquarters, then required the villagers to put away their guns and depart the scene.

The villagers sullenly retired; the French soldiers, brave in their sky-blue shorts, gingerly took up positions; and with a hasty enclosure of barbed wire and rails restrained the troglodytes to an area immediately in front of the fissure.

The April 18 edition of the *Innsbruck Kurier* included a skeptical paragraph: "A strange tribe of mountainside hermits, living in a Kreuzberg cave near Tedratz, was reported today. Local inhabitants profess the deepest mystification. The Tedratz constabulary, assisted by units of the French garrison, is investigating."

A rather less cautious account found its way into the channels of the wire services: "Innsbruck, April 19. A strange tribe has appeared from the recesses of the Kreuzberg near Innsbruck in the Tyrol. They are said to be hairless, blind, and to speak an incomprehensible language.

"According to unconfirmed reports, the troglodytes were attacked by terrified inhabitants of nearby Tedratz, and after bitter resistance were driven back into their caves.

"French occupation troops have sealed off the entire Kreuzertal. A spokesman for Colonel Courtin refuses either to confirm or deny that the troglodytes have appeared."

Bureau chiefs at the wire services looked long and carefully at the story. Why should French occupation troops interfere in what appeared on the face a purely civil disturbance? A secret colony of war criminals? Unlikely. What then? Mysterious race of troglodytes? Clearly hokum. What then? The story might develop, or it might go limp. In any case, on the late afternoon of April 19, a convoy of four cars started up the Kreuzertal, carrying reporters, photographers, and a member of the U.N. Minorities Commission, who by chance happened to be in Innsbruck.

The road to Tedratz wound among grassy meadows, storybook forests, in and out of little Alpine villages, with the massive snow-capped knob of the Kreuzberg gradually pushing higher into the sky.

At Tedratz, the party alighted and started up the now notorious trail, to be brought short almost at once at a barricade manned by French soldiers. Upon display of credentials the reporters and photographers were allowed to pass; the U.N. commissioner had nothing to show, and the NCO in charge of the barricade politely turned him back.

"But I am an official of the United Nations!" cried the outraged commissioner.

"That may well be," assented the NCO. "However, you are not a journalist, and my orders are uncompromising." And the angry commissioner was asked to wait in Tedratz until word would be taken to Colonel Courtin at the camp.

The commissioner seized on the word. " 'Camp'? How is this? I thought there was only a cave, a hole in the mountainside?"

The NCO shrugged. "Monsieur le Commissionaire is free to conjecture as he sees best."

A private was told off as a guide; the reporters and photographers started up the trail, with the long, yellow afternoon light slanting down through the firs.

It was a jocular group; repartee and wise cracks were freely exchanged. Presently the party became winded, as the trail was steep and they were all out of condition. They stopped by the wayside shrine to rest. "How much farther?" asked a photographer.

The soldier pointed through the firs toward a tall buttress of granite. "Only a little bit; then you shall see."

Once more they set out and almost immediately passed a platoon of soldiers stringing barbed wire from tree to tree.

"This will be the third extension," remarked their guide over his shoulder. "Every day they come pushing up out of the rock. It is"—he selected a word—*"formidable."*

The jocularity and wisecracks died; the journalists peered through the firs, aware of the sudden coolness of the evening.

They came to the camp, and were taken to Colonel Courtin, a small man full of excitable motion. He swung his arm. "There, my friends, is what you came to see; look your fill, since it is through your eyes that the world must see."

For three minutes they stared, muttering to one another, while Courtin teetered on his toes.

"How many are there?" came an awed question.

"Twenty thousand by latest estimate, and they issue ever faster. All from that little hole." He jumped up on tiptoe, and pointed. "It is incredible; where do they fit? And still they come, like the objects a magician removes from his hat."

"But—do they eat?"

Courtin held out his hands. "Is it for me to ask? I furnish no food; I have none; my budget will not allow it. I am a man of compassion. If you will observe, I have hung the tarpaulins to prevent the sunlight."

"With that skin, they'd be pretty sensitive, eh?"

"Sensitive!" Courtin rolled up his eyes. "The sunlight burns them like fire."

"Funny that they're not more interested in what goes on."

"They are dazed, my friend. Dazed and blinded and completely confused."

"But—what *are* they?"

"That, my friend, is a question I am without resource to answer."

The journalists regained a measure of composure, and swept the enclosure with studiously impassive glances calculated to suggest, *we have seen so many strange sights that now nothing can surprise us.* "I suppose they're men," said one.

"But of course. What else?"

"What else indeed? But where do they come from? Lost Atlantis? The land of Oz?"

"Now then," said Colonel Courtin, "you make jokes. It is a serious business, my friends; where will it end?"

"That's the big question, Colonel. Whose baby is it?"

"I do not understand."

"Who takes responsibility for them? France?"

"No, no," cried Colonel Courtin. "You must not credit me with such a statement."

"Austria, then?"

Colonel Courtin shrugged. "The Austrians are a poor people. Perhaps—of course I speculate—your great country will once again share of its plenitude."

"Perhaps, perhaps not. The one man of the crowd who might have had something to say is down in Tedratz—the chap from the Minorities Commission."

The story pushed everything from the front pages, and grew bigger day by day.

From the UP wire:

Innsbruck, April 23 (UP): The Kreuzberg miracle continues to confound the world. Today a record number of troglodytes pushed through the gap, bringing the total surface population up to forty-six thousand . . .

From the syndicated column, "Science Today" by Ralph Dunstaple, for April 28:

The scientific world seethes with the troglodyte controversy. According to the theory most frequently voiced, the trogs are descended from cavemen of the glacial eras, driven underground by the advancing wall of ice. Other conjectures, more or less scientific, refer to the lost tribes of Israel, the fourth dimension, Armageddon, and Nazi experiments.

Linguistic experts meanwhile report progress in their efforts to understand the language of the trogs. Dr. Allen K. Mendelson of the Princeton Institute of Advanced Research, spokesman for the group, classifies the trog speech as "one of the agglutinatives, with the slightest possible kinship to the Basque tongue—so faint as to be highly speculative, and it is only fair to say that there is considerable disagreement among us on this point. The trogs, incidentally, have no words for 'sun,' 'moon,' 'fight,' 'bird,' 'animal,' and a host of other concepts we take for granted. 'Food' and 'fungus,' however, are the same word."

From *The New York Herald Tribune:*
TROGS HUMAN, CLAIM SAVANTS; INTERBREEDING POSSIBLE
by Mollie Lemmon

Milan, April 30: Trogs are physiologically identical with surface humanity, and sexual intercourse between man and trog might well be fertile. Such was the opinion of a group of doctors and geneticists at an informal poll I conducted yesterday at the Milan Genetical Clinic, where a group of trogs are undergoing examination.

From "The Trog Story," a daily syndicated feature by Harlan B. Temple, April 31:

Today I saw the hundred thousandth trog push his way up out of the bowels of the Alps; everywhere in the world people are asking, where will it stop? I certainly have no answer.

This tremendous migration, unparalleled since the days of Alaric the Goth, seems only just now shifting into high gear. Two new rifts have opened into the Kreuzberg; the trogs come shoving out in close ranks, faces blank as custard, and only God knows what is in their minds.

The camps—there are now six, interconnected like knots on a rope—extend down the hillside and into the Kreuzertal. Tarpaulins over the treetops give the mountainside, seen from a distance, the look of a lawn with handkerchiefs spread out to dry.

The food situation has improved considerably over the past three days, thanks to the efforts of the Red Cross, CARE, and FAO. The basic ration is a mush of rice, wheat, millet or other cereal, mixed with carrots, greens, dried eggs, and reinforced with vitamins; the trogs appear to thrive on it.

I cannot say that the trogs are a noble, enlightened, or even ingratiating race. Their cultural level is abysmally low; they possess no tools, they wear neither clothing nor ornaments. To their credit, it must be said that they are utterly inoffensive and mild; I have never witnessed a quarrel or indeed seen a trog exhibit anything but passive obedience.

Still they rise in the hundreds and thousands. What brings them forth? Do they flee a subterranean Attila, some pandemonic Stalin? The linguists who have been studying the trog speech are closemouthed, but I have it from a highly informed source that a report will be published within the next day or so . . .

Report to the Assembly of the U.N., May 4, by V. G. Hendlemann. Coordinator for the Committee of Associated Anthropologists:

I will state the tentative conclusions to which this committee has arrived. The processes and inductions which have led to these conclusions are outlined in the appendix to this report.

Our preliminary survey of the troglodyte language has

convinced a majority of us that the trogs are probably the descendants of a group of European cave-dwellers who either by choice or by necessity took up underground residence at least fifty thousand, at most two hundred thousand, years ago.

The trog which we see today is a result of evolution and mutation, and represents adaptation to the special conditions under which the trogs have existed. He is quite definitely of the species *homo sapiens,* with a cranial capacity roughly identical to that of surface man.

In our conversations with the trogs we have endeavored to ascertain the cause of the migration. Not one of the trogs makes himself completely clear on the subject, but we have been given to understand that the great caves which the race inhabited have been stricken by a volcanic convulsion and are being gradually filled with lava. If this be the case the trogs are seen to become literally "displaced persons."

In their former home the trogs subsisted on fungus grown in shallow "paddies," fertilized by their own wastes, finely pulverized coal, and warmed by volcanic heat.

They have no grasp of "time" as we understand the word. They have only the sparsest traditions of the past and are unable to conceive of a future further removed than two minutes. Since they exist in the present, they neither expect, hope, dread, nor otherwise take cognizance of what possibly may befall them.

In spite of their deficiencies of cultural background, the trogs appear to have a not discreditable native intelligence. The committee agrees that a troglodyte child reared in ordinary surface surroundings, and given a typical education, might well become a valuable citizen, indistinguishable from any other human being except by his appearance.

Excerpt from a speech by Porfirio Hernandez, Mexican delegate to the U.N. Assembly, on May 17:

". . . We have ignored this matter too long. Far from being a scientific curiosity or a freak, this is a very human problem, one of the biggest problems of our day, and we must handle it as such. The trogs are pressing from the ground at an ever-increasing rate; the Kreuzertal, or Kreuzer Valley, is inundated with trogs as if by a flood. We have heard reports, we have deliberated, we have made solemn noises, but the fact remains that every one of us is sitting on his hands. These people—we must call them people—must be settled somewhere permanently; they must be made self-supporting. This hot iron must be grasped; we fail in our responsibilities otherwise . . . ."

Excerpt from a speech, May 19, by Sir Lyandras Chandryasam, delegate from India:
". . . My esteemed colleague from Mexico has used brave words; he exhibits a humanitarianism that is unquestionably praiseworthy. But he puts forward no positive program. May I ask how many trogs have come to the surface, thus to be cared for? Is not the latest figure somewhere short of a million? I would like to point out that in India alone five million people yearly die of malnutrition or preventable disease; but no one jumps up here in the assembly to cry for a crusade to help these unfortunate victims of nature. No, it is this strange race, with no claim upon anyone, which has contributed nothing to the civilization of the world, which now we feel has first call upon our hearts and purse-strings. I say, is not this a paradoxical circumstance . . . ."

From a speech, May 20, by Dr. Karl Byrnisted, delegate from Iceland:
". . . Sir Lyandras Chandryasam's emotion is understandable, but I would like to remind him that the streets of India swarm with millions upon millions of so-called sacred cattle and apes, who eat what and where they wish, very possibly the food to keep five million persons alive. The recurrent famines in India could be relieved, I believe, by a rationalistic dealing with these parasites, and by steps to

make the new birth-control clinics popular, such as a tax on babies. In this way, the Indian government, by vigorous methods, has it within its power to cope with its terrible problem. These trogs, on the other hand, are completely unable to help themselves; they are like babies flung fresh into a world where even the genial sunlight kills them . . ."

From a speech, May 21, by Porfirio Hernandez, delegate from Mexico:

"I have been challenged to propose a positive program for dealing with the trogs . . . I feel that as an activating principle, each member of the U.N. agree to accept a number of trogs proportionate to its national wealth, resources, and density of population . . . Obviously the exact percentages will have to be thrashed out elsewhere . . . I hereby move the President of the Assembly appoint such a committee, and instruct them to prepare such a recommendation, said committee to report within two weeks."

(Motion defeated, 20 to 35)

From "The Trog Story," June 2, by Harlan B. Temple:

No matter how many times I walk through Trog Valley, the former Kreuzertal, I never escape a feeling of the profoundest bewilderment and awe. The trogs number now well over a million; yesterday they chiseled open four new openings into the outside world, and they are pouring out at the rate of thousands every hour. And everywhere is heard the question, where will it stop? Suppose the earth is a honeycomb, a hive, with more trogs than surface men?

Sooner or later our organization will break down; more trogs will come up than it is within our power to feed. Organization already has failed to some extent. All the trogs are getting at least one meal a day, but not enough clothes, not enough shelter is being provided. Every day hundreds die from sunburn. I understand that the Old-Clothes-for-Trogs drive has nowhere hit its quota; I find it hard to comprehend.

Is there no feeling of concern or sympathy for these people merely because they do not look like so many chorus boys and screen starlets?

From *The Christian Science Monitor:*

CONTROVERSIAL TROG BILL
PASSES U.N. ASSEMBLY

New York, June 4: By a 35 to 20 vote—exactly reversing its first tally on the measure—the U.N. Assembly yesterday accepted the motion of Mexico's Hernandez to set up a committee for the purpose of recommending a percentage-wise distribution of trogs among member states.

Tabulation of voting on the measure found the Soviet bloc lined up with the United States and the British Commonwealth in opposition to the measure—presumably the countries which would be awarded large numbers of the trogs.

Handbill passed out at rally of the Socialist Reich (Neo-Nazi) party at Bremen, West Germany, June 10:

A NEW THREAT

COMRADES! It took a war to clean Germany of the Jews; must we now submit to an invasion of troglodyte filth? All Germany cries *no!* All Germany cries, hold our borders firm against these cretin moles! Send them to Russia; send them to the Arctic wastes! Let them return to their burrows; let them perish! But guard the Fatherland; guard the sacred German Soil!

(Rally broken up by police, handbills seized.)

Letter to the London *Times,* June 18:
To the Editor:

I speak for a large number of my acquaintances when I say that the prospect of taking to ourselves a large colony of "troglodytes" awakens in me no feeling of enthusiasm. Surely England has troubles more than enough of its own, without the added imposition of an unassimilable and nonproductive minority to eat our already meager rations and raise our already sky-high taxes.

> Yours, etc.,
> Sir Clayman Winifred, Bart.
> Lower Ditchley, Hants.

Letter to the London *Times,* June 21:
To the Editor:

Noting Sir Clayman Winifred's letter of June 18, I took a quick check-up of my friends and was dumbfounded to find how closely they hew to Sir Clayman's line. Surely this isn't our tradition, not to get under the load and help lift with everything we've got? The troglodytes are human beings, victims of a disaster we have no means of appreciating. They must be cared for, and if a qualified committee of experts sets us a quota, I say, let's bite the bullet and do our part.

The Ameriphobe section of our press takes great delight in baiting our cousins across the sea for the alleged denial of civil rights to the Negroes—which, may I add, is present in its most violent and virulent form in a country of the British Commonwealth: the Union of South Africa. What do these journalists say to evidences of the same unworthy emotion here in England?

> Yours, etc.,
> J.C.T. Harrodsmere
> Tisley-on-Thames, Sussex.

Headline in *The New York Herald Tribune,* June 22:
FOUR NEW TROG CAMPS OPENED; POPULATION AT TWO MILLION

Letter to the London *Times,* June 24:
To the Editor:

I read the letter of J.C.T. Harrodsmere in connection with the trog controversy with great interest. I think that in his praiseworthy efforts to have England do its bit, he is overlooking a very important fact: namely, we of England are a close-knit people, of clear clean vigorous blood, and admixture of any nature could only be for the worse. I know Mr. Harrodsmere will be quick to say, no admixture is intended. But mistakes occur, and as I understand a man-trog union to be theoretically fertile, in due course there would be a number of little half-breeds scampering like rats around our gutters, a bad show all around. There are countries where this type of mongrelization is accepted: the United States, for instance, boasts that it is the "melting pot." Why not send the trogs to the wide open spaces of the U.S., where there is room and to spare, and where they can "melt" to their heart's content?

Yours, etc.,
Col. G. P. Barstaple (Ret.), Queens Own Hussars.
Mide Hill, Warwickshire.

Letter to the London *Times,* June 28:
To the Editor:

Contrasting the bank accounts, the general air of aliveness of mongrel U.S.A. and non-mongrel England, I say maybe it might do us good to trade off a few retired colonels for a few trogs extra to our quota. Here's to more and better mongrelization!

Yours, etc.,
(Miss) Elizabeth Darrow Brown
London, S. W.

From "The Trog Story," June 30, by Harlan B. Temple:

Will it come as a surprise to my readers if I say the trog situation is getting out of hand? They are coming not slower but faster; every day we have more trogs and every day we have more at a greater rate than the day before. If the sentence sounds confused, it only reflects my state of mind.

Something has got to be done.

Nothing is being done.

The wrangling that is going on is a matter of public record. Each country is liberal with advice but with little else. Sweden says, send them to the center of Australia; Australia points to Greenland; Denmark would prefer the Ethiopian uplands; Ethiopia politely indicates Mexico; Mexico says, much more room in Arizona; and at Washington senators from below the Mason-Dixon Line threaten to filibuster from now till Kingdom Come rather than admit a single trog to the continental limits of the U.S. Thank the Lord for an efficient food administration! The U.N. and the world at large can be proud of the organization by which the trogs are being fed.

Incidental Notes: trog babies are being born—over fifty yesterday.

From the *San Francisco Chronicle:*
REDS OFFER HAVEN TO TROGS
PROPOSAL STIRS WORLD
New York, July 3: Ivan Pudestov, the USSR's chief delegate to the U.N. Assembly, today blew the trog question wide open with a proposal to take complete responsibility for the trogs.

The offer startled the U.N. and took the world completely by surprise, since heretofore the Soviet delegation has held itself aloof from the bitter trog controversy, apparently in hopes that the free world would split itself apart on the problem . . .

Editorial in the *Milwaukee Journal,* July 5, headed "A Question of Integrity":
At first blush the Russian offer to take the trogs appears to ease our shoulders of a great weight. Here is exactly what we have been grasping for, a solution without sacrifice, a sop to our consciences, a convenient carpet to sweep our dirt under. The man in the street, and the responsible official, suddenly are telling each other that perhaps the Russians aren't so bad

after all, that there's a great deal of room in Siberia, that the Russians and the trogs are both barbarians and really not so much different, that the trogs were probably Russians to begin with, etc.

Let's break the bubble of illusion, once and for all. We can't go on forever holding our Christian integrity in one hand and our inclinations in the other . . . Doesn't it seem an odd coincidence that while the Russians are desperately short of uranium miners at the murderous East German and Ural pits, the trogs, accustomed to life underground, might be expected to make a good labor force? . . . In effect, we would be turning over to Russia millions of slaves to be worked to death. We have rejected forced repatriation in West Europe and Korea, let's reject forced patriation and enslavement of the trogs.

Headline in *The New York Times,* July 20:
REDS BAN U.N. SUPERVISION OF
TROG COMMUNITIES
SOVEREIGNTY ENDANGERED, SAYS PUDESTOV
ANGRILY WITHDRAWS TROG OFFER

Headline in the New York *Daily News,* July 26:
BELGIUM OFFERS CONGO FOR TROG HABITATION
ASKS FUNDS TO RECLAIM JUNGLE
U.N. GIVES QUALIFIED NOD

From "The Trog Story," July 28, by Harlan B. Temple:
Four million (give or take a hundred thousand) trogs now breathe surface air. The Kreuzertal camps now constitute one of the world's largest cities, ranking under New York, London, Tokyo. The formerly peaceful Tyrolean valley is now a vast array of tarpaulins, circus tents, Quonset huts, water tanks, and general disorder. Trog City doesn't smell too good, either.

Today might well mark the high tide in what the Austrians are calling "the invasion from hell." Trogs still push through a dozen gaps ten abreast, but the pressure doesn't seem so intense. Every once in a while a space appears in the ranks, where formerly they came packed like asparagus in crates. Another difference: the first trogs were meaty and fairly well nourished. These late arrivals are thin and ravenous. Whatever strange subterranean economy they practiced, it seems to have broken down completely . . .

From "The Trog Story," August 1, by Harlan B. Temple:
Something horrible is going on under the surface of the earth. Trogs are staggering forth with raw stumps for arms, with great wounds . . .

From "The Trog Story," August 8, by Harlan B. Temple:
Operation Exodus got underway today. One thousand trogs departed the Kreuzertal bound for their new home near Cabinda, at the mouth of the Congo River. Trucks and buses took them to Innsbruck, where they will board special trains to Venice and Trieste. Here ships supplied by the U.S. Maritime Commission will take them to their new home.

As one thousand trogs departed Trog City, twenty thousand pushed up from their underground homeland, and camp officials are privately expressing concern over conditions. Trog City has expanded double, triple, ten times over the original estimates. The machinery of supply, sanitation and housing is breaking down. From now on, any attempts to remedy the situation are at best stopgaps, like adhesive tape on a rotten hose, when what is needed is a new hose or, rather, a four-inch pipe.

Even to maintain equilibrium, thirty thousand trogs per day will have to be siphoned out of the Kreuzertal camps, an obvious impossibility under present budgets and efforts . . .

From *Newsweek,* August 14:

Camp Hope, in the bush near Cabinda, last week took on the semblance of the Guadalcanal army base during World War II. There was the old familiar sense of massive confusion, the grind of bulldozers, sweating white, beet-red, brown and black skins, the raw earth dumped against primeval vegetation, bugs, salt tablets, Atabrine . . .

From the UP wire:

Cabinda, Belgian Congo, August 20 (UP): The first contingent of trogs landed last night under shelter of dark, and marched to temporary quarters, under the command of specially trained group captains.

Liaison officers state that the trogs are overjoyed at the prospect of a permanent home, and show an eagerness to get to work. According to present plans, they will till collective farms, and continuously clear the jungle for additional settlers.

On the other side of the ledger, it is rumored that the native tribesmen are showing unrest. Agitators, said to be Communist-inspired, are preying on the superstitious fears of a people themselves not far removed from savagery . . .

Headline in *The New York Times,* August 22:

CONGO WARRIORS RUN AMOK AT CAMP HOPE
KILL 800 TROG SETTLERS IN SINGLE HOUR
Military Law Established
Belgian Governor Protests
Says Congo Unsuitable

From the UP wire:

Trieste, August 23 (UP): Three shiploads of trogs bound for Trogland in the Congo today marked a record number of embarkations. The total number of trogs to sail from European ports now stands at 24,965 . . .

Cabinda, August 23 (UP): The warlike Matemba Confederation is practically in a stage of revolt against further trog immigration while Resident-General Bernard Cassou professes grave pessimism over eventualities.

Mont Blanc, August 24 (UP): Ten trogs today took up experimental residence in a ski-hut to see how well trogs can cope with the rigors of cold weather.

Announcement of this experiment goes to confirm a rumor that Denmark has offered Greenland to the trogs if it is found that they are able to survive Arctic conditions.

Cabinda, August 28 (UP): The Congo, home of witch-doctors, tribal dances, cannibalism and Tarzan, seethes with native unrest. Sullen anger smolders in the villages, riots are frequent and dozens of native workmen at Camp Hope have been killed or hospitalized.

Needless to say, the trogs, whose advent precipitated the crisis, are segregated far apart from contact with the natives, to avoid a repetition of the bloodbath of August 22 . . .

Cabinda, August 29 (UP): Resident-General Bernard Cassou today refused to allow debarkation of trogs from four ships standing off Cabina roadstead.

Mont Blanc, September 2 (UP): The veil of secrecy at the experimental trog home was lifted a significant crack this morning, when the bodies of two trogs were taken down to Chamonix via the ski-lift . . .

From "The Trog Story," September 10, by Harlan B. Temple:

It is one A.M.; I've just come down from Camp No. 4. The trog columns have dwindled to a straggle of old, crippled, diseased. The stench is frightful . . . But why go on? Frankly, I'm heartsick. I wish I had never taken on this assignment. It's doing something terrible to my soul; my hair is literally turning gray. I pause a moment, the noise of my typewriter stops, I listen to the vast murmur through the Kreuzertal; despondency, futility, despair come at me in a wave. Most of us here at Trog City, I think, feel the same.

There are now five or six million trogs in the camp; no one

knows the exact count; no one even cares. The situation has passed that point. The flow has dwindled, one merciful dispensation—in fact, at Camp No. 4 you can hear the rumble of the lava rising into the trog caverns.

Morale is going from bad to worse here at Trog City. Every day a dozen of the unpaid volunteers throw up their hands, and go home. I can't say as I blame them. Lord knows they've given the best they have, and no one backs them up. Everywhere in the world it's the same story, with everyone pointing at someone else. It's enough to make a man sick. In fact it has. I'm sick—desperately sick.

But you don't read "The Trog Story" to hear me gripe. You want factual reporting. Very well, here it is. Big news today was that movement of trogs out of the camp to Trieste has been held up pending clarification of the Congo situation. Otherwise, everything's the same here—hunger, smell, careless trogs dying of sunburn . . .

Headline in *The New York Times,* September 20:

TROG QUOTA PROBLEM RETURNED TO STUDY GROUP FOR ADJUSTMENT

From the UP wire:

Cabinda, September 25 (UP): Eight ships, loaded with 9,462 trog refugees, still wait at anchor, as native chieftains reiterated their opposition to trog immigration . . .

Trog City, October 8 (UP): The trog migration is at its end. Yesterday for the first time no new trogs came up from below, leaving the estimated population of Trog City at six million.

New York, October 13 (UP): Deadlock still grips the Trog Resettlement Committee, with the original positions, for the most part, unchanged. Densely populated countries claim they have no room and no jobs; the underdeveloped states insist that they have not enough money to feed their own mouths. The U.S., with both room and money, already has serious minority headaches and doesn't want new ones . . .

Chamonix, France, October 18 (UP): The Trog Experimental Station closed its doors yesterday, with one survivor of the original ten trogs riding the ski-lift back down the slopes of Mont Blanc.

Dr. Sven Emeldson, director of the station, released the following statement: "Our work proves that the trogs, even if provided shelter adequate for a European, cannot stand the rigors of the North; they seem especially sensitive to pulmonary ailments . . ."

New York, October 26 (UP): After weeks of acrimony, a revised set of trog immigration quotas was released for action by the U.N. Assembly. Typical figures are: USA 31%, USSR 16%, Canada 8%, Australia 8%, France 6%, Mexico 6%.

New York, October 30 (UP): The USSR adamantly rejects the principle of U.N. checking of the trog resettlement areas inside the USSR . . .

New York, October 31 (UP): Senator Bullrod of Mississippi today promised to talk till his "lungs came out at the elbows" before he would allow the Trog Resettlement Bill to come to a vote before the Senate. An informal check revealed insufficient strength to impose cloture . . .

St. Arlberg, Austria, November 5 (UP): First snow of the season fell last night . . .

Trog City, November 10 (UP): Last night, frost lay a sparkling sheath across the valley . . .

Trog City, November 15 (UP): Trog sufferers from influenza have been isolated in a special section . . .

Buenos Aires, November 23 (UP): Dictator Peron today flatly refused to meet the Argentine quota of relief supplies to Trog City until some definite commitment has been made by the U.N. . . .

Trog City, December 2 (UP): Influenza following the snow and rain of the last week has made a new onslaught on the trogs; camp authorities are desperately trying to cope with the epidemic . . .

Trog City, December 8 (UP): Two crematoriums, fired by fuel oil, are roaring full-time in an effort to keep ahead of the mounting influenza casualties . . .

From "The Trog Story," December 13, by Harlan B. Temple:
This is it . . .

From the UP wire:

Los Angeles, December 14 (UP): The Christmas buying rush got under way early this year, in spite of unseasonably bad weather . . .

Trog City, December 15 (UP): A desperate appeal for penicillin, sulfa, blankets, kerosene heaters, and trained personnel was sounded today by Camp Commandant Howard Kerkovits. He admitted that disease among the trogs was completely out of control, beyond all human power to cope with . . .

From "The Trog Story," December 23, by Harlan B. Temple:
I don't know why I should be sitting here writing this, because—since there are no more trogs—there is no more trog story. But I am seized by an irresistible urge to "tell-off" a rotten, inhumane world . . .

J. Timothy Hunt

Repeating Echo

A nightmare, mirror-imaged and seemingly endless, torments the narrator of this remarkable new fantasy by J. TIMOTHY HUNT, *author of the unforgettable "Moonflower" in* Lovers and Other Monsters *(GuildAmerica Books, 1992). Mr. Hunt is an ex-Montanan living in Manhattan, where he works as an emergency medical technician. He has held professional writing residencies in Greenwich Village and at the Helene Wurlitzer Foundation in Taos, New Mexico. His play,* Angel Fire, *was produced off-off-Broadway, and Mr. Hunt recently completed his first mystery novel,* Killing Time in Taos.

The Circle

I HAVE to get out of this church. I can't stand to be in here another moment. The organ, the coffins, the flowers; it's too much. I have to get out. Outside in the warm Montana air where things aren't different. Where life still looks the same.

I stumble down the narrow aisle and burst through the front doors. It's hard to see where I'm running, my eyes are all blurry with tears. It's hard to breathe and cry and run. It's hard.

There are wheat fields all around our church. It's right before the harvest and the shafts of wheat are higher than my waist. As I lurch through the dirt parking lot and run into the golden waves, it feels like I'm diving into an ocean. The wind is blowing the undulating, crackly stalks of grain brushing their heavy heads against one another with a hiss that even sounds like sea spray.

I plunge headlong into the wheat-field ocean and run, gasping for air, choking on crying, racing blindly away from that church. Although I don't look back, I can feel the white wooden spire receding away from me, hear the moaning organ fade, and feel the Montana sky, so wide and clear you'd think you might fall up into it, engulf the whole tragic mess and obliterate it.

The wheat field is about a hundred acres wide. I see a rimrock mesa on the horizon. I'm going to run toward it because it's in front of me. I'll run to those rimrocks, then I'll see another even further away and I'll run to them, too. I'll run until I reach the Rocky Mountain timberline. I'll run until I can't remember why I'm running.

I only get about a mile into the field when suddenly the wheat drops away. I stop and look about me. There in that vast expanse of grain is a large circular depression where the wheat is all matted down as if crushed from above by a giant round object. A crop circle. People in Billings laugh about them and joke about aliens but none of us ever really believes the crop circles are caused by anything other than something perfectly explainable— although we can't really say what that might be.

I pant and pant, my lungs are ravenous for air. The running has knocked the crying right out of me and I stop and look around the crop circle as I calm myself and breathe. I had no idea a crop circle would be this large. I'm wondering if I should look for radiation burns or other such nonsense when I come to the center of the circle and see them. The three green stones, big as a fist and placed in a triangle a foot apart from each other. A triangle in a circle . . .

I fall to my knees and immediately begin the chant. "Lincus, Memnon, Myrmidons, Pelion. A wish! Just one wish! I want to go back and do it all over. I want to go back, then they will be alive again and will never, ever die . . . No, wait!" I realize what I said and start to panic. By mistake I wished them immortality. I didn't mean to do it! I just blurted it out, so I quickly add a little stipulation. "But I don't want any of us to get a minute older."

The First Round

I am no longer in the wheat field. I'm in our first apartment on Broadwater Avenue. And there's Lydia! Standing right in front of me! But her hair is different, it's . . . it's just like it was when we were still in college. In fact, the whole room is just like it was our senior year.

There are party decorations all over the place, black and white balloons with big bar codes and the word "balloon" written across them in Magic Marker. It's my birthday three years ago. I have gone back three years! I am at the "generic" birthday party Lydia had so cleverly thrown for me. There are the birthday cards in white envelopes that simply say "card," the white cake with a black icing bar code and black block letters spelling "cake." She even made white T-shirts for the guests to wear that had a big bar code across their chests and the word "guest" across their bellies. Everyone is eating generic salted nuts out of white cans, generic potato chips out of crinkly white bags and drinking generic beer out of white Styrofoam cups. Lydia was a genius.

I want to rush over and grab Lydia, hold her tight and tell her how wonderful it is that she is back again, but I can't move.

I'm too overwhelmed. That must be it.

The doorbell rings. "Can you get that?" Lydia asks as she gathers up an armful of paper plates and dirty glasses. But I don't want to answer the door. I want to tell her about the miracle. She needs to know about the wish.

I start to rush to her, yet find myself walking in the opposite direction. "I'm coming!" I yell out and trip a little over a bump in the carpet as I head for the front door. Why did I say that? Why am I doing this?

I answer the door and let a group of five of my college friends into the room. Lydia has been as efficient and strict as usual for each one of the newcomers is dressed head to toe in white and carries a white parcel that says "gift" on it. I'm engulfed in hugs and birthday wishes by people I haven't seen in years. One fellow, tall, with sideburns and dark wavy hair that cascades past the collar of his white turtleneck, hands me a small white package and claps me on the shoulder with congratulations. For the life of me, I can't remember his name.

"How'd you do on the final, Tom?" I hear myself ask him.

"Eighty-six," he says. "Solid B. Blew Professor Dickens away. I mean, I only showed up for three goddamn classes the whole quarter."

Tom. That's right, his name was Tom. And professor Dickens taught Intro to Neuroanatomy. God, I'd forgotten about that stupid course. And about Tom. I continue to observe myself hold an intelligent conversation about a topic I cannot recall with a person whom I've forgotten—and a cold chill runs through me.

I know what has happened to me. Time had been shifted back three years and Lydia is restored to life. I have a chance to do everything over again with full knowledge of my future mistakes. No, that's wrong. I can't do everything over again. I can only watch it happen.

And I cannot control a single thing. Not even me.

My body is moving but I'm not moving it. I'm talking, but I'm not speaking my thoughts. I'm in a straitjacket of my own bones, gagged with my own speaking tongue. My thoughts are new, my words and actions old. With growing horror I realize, like someone seeing a film for the second time, I know full well what is going to happen at the end of the story. To Lydia. To the child to be.

I scream, or try to. I will to twist and flail my arms. I strain to kick my legs. I remember the two coffins in the church and the flames against the night sky and I'm overcome with a powerful wave of nausea.

A fat girl in the corner lights up a joint and Tom, enticed by the smoke, makes a shameless beeline for her. I follow along and laugh at Trent Holloway doing an impression of Ronald Reagan. President Reagan is going to be shot soon because of Jodie Foster. Trent Holloway is a hemophiliac who is going to come down with a new plague called AIDS no one has even heard of yet. The apartment building we are in is going to be torn down to make way for a six-plex movie house. I'm going to break the lamp next to me by accident on the day Lydia and I move to a bigger place. There's going to be a . . .

I cannot bear it. And I cannot stop it.

The Third Round

The doorbell rings. "Can you get that?"

I trip over a bump in the rug.

"How'd you do on the final, Tom?"

"Eighty-six. Solid B. Blew Professor Dickens away. I mean, I only showed up for three goddam classes the whole quarter."

The party again. My fourth time to see that generic birthday party: once for real and three times a visitor. In my travel down the river of time, I seem to be stuck in a whirlpool. I only get to see the same three years over and over. As awful as this is, it does have the distinct advantage of leaving me a little wiser with each cycle. For although I have seen a piece of the future and have traveled a bit in time, I've learned that there is no such thing as fortune-telling and no use to Man for time travel.

I know now that while the future does not exist at all, the past exists too well. It is chiseled in stone. The past is immutable, implacable. Those unfortunate as I am to travel to its shores will find they can only go to places they themselves have been. They can only do and say what was previously done and said. To change one grain of salt spilled on a tabletop would be to knock the world off its axis. The temple of the present only stands because of the foundation of the past. And the future? Like a fetus, it cannot be born until it is conceived. To conceive the future, you need to have a present moment. Being robbed of one, I have lost them both.

Curiously, I am getting accustomed to this new "life" of mine. The first time around was scary but exciting, for I didn't really know how or where it was going to end. I hoped somehow that when the three years were up, the outcome would be different and we could continue on with our lives as usual. I hoped I would be free. However, that was not to be the case.

At the end of the first cycle, I ended up standing on the dark highway, just as before, watching the car speed off in the distance—just as before—but right before the impact, I ended up back at the birthday party, three years younger. Lydia never died, and none of us got even a minute older.

It was during the second cycle that I learned to relax a bit. The past was still young enough to be interesting, yet familiar enough to be comforting. Familiarity, though, also proves to be disquieting.

Once more I observe how Tom gives me the small white package tied with black ribbon. Of course I knew instantly the first time it was a hardback book, now that I've seen the future twice, I also know that it's going to be a vintage copy of Ovid's *Metamorphosis*. I unwrap the gift and look at the stained and tattered cover. I gingerly open it up to look at the date on the flyleaf: 1759, London. The pages are very brown and very brittle. Tom says he found it in an alley in back of Moss Mansion in a box of discarded papers. Old lady Moss must have been doing some spring cleaning. I guess she didn't realize she is going to die next month and her house is going to be turned into a museum.

Jesus, this must have been what Cassandra felt like.

I watch again as I carefully turn back to the index of the book and see the note in the margin. The florid calligraphy of a prerevolutionary hand. "A wish. Triangle in a circle. Repeat the names." Four names are underlined: Lincus, Memnon, Myrmidons, Pelion.

The Seventh Round

There are no other cars on the dark highway. The baby is crying in her car seat in the back of the Datsun. Lydia pulls the car over to the side of the road slamming on the brakes so hard we skid and spin completely around on the shoulder.

"Get out! Get out!" she screams at me.

I am so furious I yell some obscenities at her and tell her to turn the car around and take us home. She starts slapping me and pushing me out of the car. I try to defend myself from her blows until I get so mad I haul off and slap her back. Hard. It knocks the breath out of her. I see a little bit of blood on the corner of her mouth. I open my door and jump out of the car. I kick the door shut so violently the whole chassis rocks side to side on its suspension.

Lydia puts the car into reverse and knocks a yield sign down. She throws the car into first and speeds off down the highway leaving me in a shower of gravel. I stand in the round pool of the streetlamp and watch as she fails to yield to an oncoming gasoline truck.

The Tenth Round

The doorbell rings. "Can you get that?"

I trip over a bump in the rug.

"How'd you do on the final, Tom?"

Oh god, oh god, I don't think I can take this any more. I can't live through that final night again. The generic birthday party is always like awakening from a horrible nightmare, but it's not. I know that in three years I will make the mistake again that will lead to the same fight again that will cost all three of us our lives.

I've got to think of a way out of this. How did this happen to me? That book. Those underlines in the index. I have to read the book again more carefully next time. And there will be a next time. I'm scheduled to read *Metamorphosis* cover to cover while we're on our honeymoon in two months. I'll read it again two years later, right before the accident, but I'll only skip through it. The answers are in there. I'll find them.

I need to wait and endure the ride for two months until the honeymoon. It's not difficult, it was a pleasant two months in my life, and it's actually enjoyable to relive. Sometimes, though, it gets boring watching the same TV shows and speaking the same conversations. I've learned that I can sleep while my body carries on its work of recreating the past. Of course the downside to this is that I'm wide awake while my body lies in bed with its eyes closed.

It. I now call my body "it." I suppose it's accurate. The way my life is now, my body is no more "me" than a honey jar is the honey or a lightbulb is the light.

I'm tired of this. I want to bust the honey jar wide open.

I patiently wait and endure for two months. I have my birthday party. Lydia and I graduate from college. I get my B.S. in economics, she gets her B.A. in music. We piss off all our relatives and friends by running off to Las Vegas to wed, then I relax to read a book.

By now I'm beginning to know *Metamorphosis* by heart. My favorite vignette in Ovid's epic poem is about the nymph Echo. Echo was very beautiful and very talkative. She was so chatty and engaging that she distracted Juno, who was trying to catch her husband, Jupiter, fooling around. When Juno realized that Echo's clever talk allowed Jupiter to sneak off with a couple of young nymphs, she became so enraged that she put a curse on Echo. Echo was no longer allowed to say anything except the last words of any phrase she heard.

Jupiter later took pity on the poor, beautiful girl, and although he could not undo Juno's curse, he offered her one wish. Echo took a stick and scratched into the sand the word "immortality." Jupiter, who was very wise, was saddened, but he granted her the wish. Being immortal himself, he knew the foolish girl should have wished for eternal youth also. Echo did live forever, but she eventually grew older and older and crumbled away in hideous decomposition until there was nothing left of her but her voice repeating the last words she hears.

That, of course, is why I added that stupid addendum to my wish in the crop circle. I didn't want to repeat Echo's mistake, but I managed to do it anyhow.

The Fourteenth Round

The doorbell rings. "Can you get that?"

I trip over a bump in the rug.

"How'd you do on the final, Tom?"

Yes, happy twenty-second birthday to me. I'm forever twenty-two it seems, or at least it's the fifteenth time I've been twenty-two. Technically, though, I've been conscious for sixty-four years and I think I look pretty good for sixty-four.

That's a joke. I've almost forgotten how to laugh at a joke, they're so stale now. It would be nice to hear a new joke just once. To read a new book. Hear a new song. See an invention made after 1984. I've combed every detail of my cyclical life looking for perhaps a previously unnoticed sunset, eavesdrop on every unremarkable conversation around me. A hungry search for something new to think about. It should be the year 2022 by now. I wonder what's happened in the world.

What I'd really love to see is a different movie. I never was much for going to the movies when I was twenty-two. However, when I was twenty-three (next year again) I happened to see *E.T. The Extra-terrestrial* three times. After thirteen cycles, I've seen that film thirty-nine times by now. I hate it. In fifteen months and seven days I'm going to see it again, and I'll celebrate it as a fortieth anniversary screening.

I do things like that now. Since everything happens more than once to me, everything is an occasion for an anniversary. Of course I celebrate the normal things like our wedding, our first anniversary, the birth of our child, and our second anniversary. We never quite get to make it to our third anniversary.

Reliving the wedding is always nice. Lydia and I will drive down to Las Vegas a month after we graduate and get married quickly and privately at the Little Chapel of the West in the parking lot of the Hacienda Hotel. We'll both cry when they play "Endless Love" on the cassette deck, then we'll go to an all-you-can-eat Casino buffet and steal knapsack-loads of food.

We will come home to Montana, get jobs, have a child and I will have one short-lived affair with Lydia's best friend. Lydia and I will fight, then I will be propelled back to my twenty-second birthday right before the car hits the truck head-on and bursts into flames.

This is what I have to look forward to, starting today. Happy birthday to me.

The Nineteenth Round

Our baby daughter is crying in the back seat.

"Get out! Get out!" my wife screams at me.

"Jesus, Lydia, what are you trying to do, kill us?"

"Get out!"

"Shut the fuck up and turn the car around!" Lydia starts slapping me and pushing me out of the car. I try to defend myself from her blows. "Stop it, stop it!" I yell at her. She continues to swing at me until I grab both her hands and force them together. I clamp them at the wrists with my left hand and use my right fist to bust her squarely in the jaw. She is stunned and starts to cry. A line of blood seeps from the corner of her mouth.

I am furious, embarrassed and just plain frightened that I have done such a horrible thing. I open my door and jump out of the car. She made me do it. She brought this upon herself. I kick the door shut so violently the whole chassis rocks side to side on its suspension.

Lydia puts the car into reverse and knocks a yield sign down. She throws the car into first and speeds off down the highway leaving me in a shower of gravel. I stand in the round pool of the streetlamp . . .

The triangular yield sign is at my feet.

A triangle in a circle.

My eyes watch as Lydia's tail lights recede into the distance and the headlights of the gasoline truck appear out of nowhere. My brain feverishly begins the chant.

"Lincus, Memnon, Myrmidons, Pelion. A wish . . ."

Twenty

"Grandpa?"

The room is done up in white paint and stainless steel. A young woman, about twenty-five or thirty years old looks down at me. I have no idea who she is. She is holding my hand. I just stare at her.

"Grandpa? It's me. How are you feeling today?"

"Who are you?" I ask. I ask! I had a thought and I willed my mouth to speak!

"Who am I?" The woman looks distressed and glances over at someone standing by the door. "He doesn't know who I am."

"That's not surprising," says the person by the door.

I turn my head. I do it. I tell my head to turn and it turns. My neck turns stiffly, though. I'm very tired. Why am I tired? The person by the door is a man in a blue jump suit, a cut of clothing I've never seen before.

"Where am I?" I ask him.

"It's very typical of the disease, complete loss of memory," he says, "especially in patients as old as your grandfather."

The young woman looks down on me, pityingly. "Will he ever get any better?"

"Where's Lydia?" I ask. "Lydia. What happened to Lydia and the baby?"

The man by the door looks questioningly at the young woman. "His first wife," she explains. "Killed in a car wreck. Grandpa, look at me. Do you know who I am?"

"It's a shame," I hear the man say, "to see these people who have lived long, happy, successful lives, end up like this: as if they missed the last sixty years. Like they weren't even around when it happened."

Jean Ray

The Shadowy Street

No biographical facts are available for JEAN RAY *other than the fact that a group of his superb horror stories was translated by Lowell Bair and published in 1965 by Berkley Books as* Ghouls in My Grave. *"The Shadowy Street" is told through the agency of not one, but two, mysterious manuscripts. You might think you know where the story is going, but the eerie second half may surprise you as it did me.*

ON A ROTTERDAM DOCK, winches were fishing bales of old paper from the hold of a freighter. The wind was fluttering the multicolored streamers that hung from the bales when one of them burst open like a cask in a roaring fire. The longshoremen hastily scooped up some of the rustling mass, but a large part of it was abandoned to the joy of the little children who gleaned in the eternal autumn of the waterfront.

There were beautiful Pearsons engravings, cut in half by order of Customs; green and pink bundles of stocks and bonds, the last echoes of resounding bankruptcies; pitiful books whose pages were still joined like desperate hands. My cane explored that vast residue of thought, in which neither shame nor hope was now alive.

Amid all that English and German prose I found a few pages of France: copies of *Le Magasin Pittoresque,* solidly bound and somewhat scorched by fire.

It was in looking through those magazines, so adorably illustrated and so dismally written, that I found the two manuscripts, one in German, the other in French. Their authors had apparently been unaware of each other, and yet the French manuscript seemed to cast a little light on the black anguish that rose from the German one like a noxious vapor—insofar as any light can be shed on that story which appears to be haunted by such sinister and hostile forces!

The cover bore the name Alphonse Archipetre, followed by the word *Lehrer*. I shall translate the German pages:

The German Manuscript

I am writing this for Hermann, when he comes back from sea.

If he does not find me here, if I, along with my poor friends, have been swallowed up by the savage mystery that surrounds us, I want him to know our days of horror through this little notebook. It will be the best proof of my affection that I can give him, because it takes real courage for a woman to keep a journal in such hours of madness. I am also writing so that he will pray for me, if he believes my soul to be in peril . . .

After the death of my Aunt Hedwige, I did not want to go on living in our sad Holzdamm house. The Rückhardt sisters offered to let me stay with them. They lived in a big apartment on the Deichstrasse, in the spacious house of Councillor Hühnebein, an old bachelor who never left the first floor, which was littered with books, paintings, and engravings.

Lotte, Eleonore, and Meta Rückhardt were adorable old maids who used all their ingenuity in trying to make life pleasant for me. Frida, our maid, came with me; she found favor in the eyes of the ancient Frau Pilz, the Rückhardts' inspired cook, who was said to have turned down ducal offers in order to remain in the humble service of her mistresses.

That evening . . .

On that evening, which was to bring unspeakable terror into our calm lives, we had decided against going to a celebration in

Tempelhof, because it was raining in torrents. Frau Pilz, who liked to have us stay home, had made us an outstanding supper: grilled trout and a guinea-hen pie. Lotte had searched the cellar and come up with a bottle of Cape brandy that had been aging there for over twenty years. When the table had been cleared, the beautiful dark liquor was poured into glasses of Bohemian crystal. Eleonore served the Lapsang Souchong tea that an old Bremen sailor brought back to us from his voyages.

Through the sound of the rain we heard the clock of Saint Peter's strike eight. Frida was sitting beside the fire. Her head drooped over her illustrated Bible; she was unable to read it, but she liked to look at the pictures. She asked for permission to go to bed. The four of us who remained went on sorting colored silks for Meta's embroidery.

Downstairs, the councillor noisily locked his bedroom door. Frau Pilz went up to her room, bade us good night through the door, and added that the bad weather would no doubt prevent us from having fresh fish for dinner the next day. A small cascade was splattering loudly on the pavement from a broken rain gutter on the house next door. A strong wind came thundering down the street; the cascade was dispersed into a silvery mist, and a window slammed shut on one of the upper stories.

"That's the attic window," said Lotte. "It won't stay closed." She raised the garnet-red curtain and looked down at the street. "I've never seen it so dark before. I'm not sleepy, and I certainly have no desire to go to bed. I feel as though the darkness of the street would follow me, along with the wind and the rain."

"You're talking like a fool," said Eleonore, who was not very gentle. "Well, since no one is going to bed, let's do as men do and fill our glasses again."

She went off to get three of those beautiful Sieme candles that burn with a pink flame and give off a delightful smell of flowers and incense.

I felt that we all wanted to give a festive tone to that bleak evening, and that for some reason we were unsuccessful. I saw Eleonore's energetic face darkened by a sudden shadow of ill-humor. Lotte seemed to be having difficulty in breathing. Only Meta was leaning placidly over her embroidery, and yet I sensed that she was attentive, as though she were trying to detect a sound in the depths of the silence.

Just then the door opened and Frida came in. She staggered over to the armchair beside the fire and sank into it, staring wild-eyed at each of us in turn.

"Frida!" I cried. "What's the matter?"

She sighed deeply, then murmured a few indistinct words.

"She's still asleep," said Eleonore.

Frida shook her head forcefully and made violent efforts to speak. I handed her my glass of brandy and she emptied it in one gulp, like a coachman or a porter. Under other circumstances we would have been offended by this vulgarity, but she seemed so unhappy, and the atmosphere in the room had been so depressing for the past few minutes, that it passed unnoticed.

"Fräulein," said Frida, "there's . . ." Her eyes, which softened for a moment, resumed their wild expression. "I don't know . . ."

Eleonore uttered an impatient exclamation.

"What have you seen or heard? What's wrong with you, Frida?"

"Fräulein, there's . . ." Frida seemed to reflect deeply. "I don't know how to say it . . . There's a great fear in my room."

"Oh!" said all three of us, reassured and apprehensive at the same time.

"You've had a nightmare," said Meta. "I know how it is: you hide your head under the covers when you wake up."

"No, that's not it," said Frida. "I hadn't been dreaming. I just woke up, that's all, and then . . . How can I make you understand? There's a great fear in my room . . ."

"Good heavens, that doesn't explain anything!" I said.

Frida shook her head in despair:

"I'd rather sit outside in the rain all night than go back to that room. No, I won't go back!"

"I'm going to see what's happening up there, you fool!" said Eleonore, throwing a shawl over her shoulders.

She hesitated for a moment before her father's old rapier, hanging among some university insignia. Then she shrugged, picked up the candlestick with its pink candles, and walked out, leaving a perfumed wake behind her.

"Oh, don't let her go there alone!" cried Frida, alarmed.

We slowly went to the staircase. The flickering glow of Eleonore's candlestick was already vanishing on the attic landing.

We stood in the semidarkness at the foot of the stairs. We heard Eleonore open a door. There was a minute of oppressive silence. I felt Frida's hand tighten on my waist.

"Don't leave her alone," she moaned.

Just then there was a loud laugh, so horrible that I would rather die than hear it again. Almost at the same time, Meta raised her hand and cried out, "There! . . . There! . . . A face . . . There . . ."

The house became filled with sounds. The councillor and Frau Pilz appeared in the yellow haloes of the candles they were holding.

"Fräulein Eleonore!" sobbed Frida. "Dear God, how are we going to find her?"

It was a frightening question, and I can now answer it: *We never found her.*

Frida's room was empty. The candlestick was standing on the floor and its candles were still burning peacefully, with their delicate pink flames.

We searched the whole house and even went out on the roof. We never saw Eleonore again.

We could not count on the help of the police, as will soon be seen. When we went to the police station, we found that it had been invaded by a frenzied crowd; some of the furniture had been overturned, the windows were covered with dust, and the clerks were being pushed around like puppets. Eighty people had vanished that night, some from their homes, others while they were on their way home!

The world of ordinary conjectures was closed to us; only supernatural apprehensions remained.

Several days went by. We led a bleak life of tears and terror.

Councillor Hühnebein had the attic sealed off from the rest of the house by a thick oak partition.

One day I went in search of Meta. We were beginning to fear another tragedy when we found her squatting in front of the partition with her eyes dry and an expression of anger on her usually gentle face. She was holding her father's rapier in her hand, and seemed annoyed at having been disturbed.

We tried to question her about the face she had glimpsed, but she looked at us as though she did not understand. She remained completely silent. She did not answer us, and even seemed unaware of our presence.

All sorts of wild stories were being repeated in the town. There was talk of a secret criminal league; the police were accused of negligence, and worse; public officials had been dismissed. All this, of course, was useless.

Strange crimes had been committed: savagely mutilated corpses were found at dawn. Wild animals could not have shown more ardent lust for carnage than the mysterious attackers. Some of the victims had been robbed, but most of them had not, and this surprised everyone.

But I do not want to dwell on what was happening in the town; it will be easy to find enough people to tell about it. I will limit myself to the framework of our house and our life, which, though narrow, still enclosed enough fear and despair.

The days passed and April came, colder and windier than the worst month of winter. We remained huddled beside the fire. Sometimes Councillor Hühnebein came to keep us company and give us what he called courage. This consisted in trembling in all his limbs, holding his hands out toward the fire, drinking big mugs of punch, starting at every sound, and crying out five or six times an hour, "Did you hear that? Did you hear? . . ."

Frida tore some of the pages out of her Bible, and we found them pinned or pasted on every door and curtain, in every nook and cranny. She hoped that this would ward off the spirits of evil. We did not interfere, and since we spent several days in peace we were far from thinking it a bad idea.

We soon saw how terribly mistaken we were. The day had been so dark, and the clouds so low, that evening had come early. I was walking out of the living room to put a lamp on the broad landing—for ever since the terrifying night we had placed lights all over the house, and even the halls and stairs remained lighted till dawn—when I heard voices murmuring on the top floor.

It was not yet completely dark. I bravely climbed the stairs and found myself before the frightened faces of Frida and Frau Pilz, who motioned me to be silent and pointed to the newly-built partition.

I stood beside them, adopting their silence and attention. It was then that I heard an indefinable sound from behind the wooden wall, something like the faint roar of giant conch shells, or the tumult of a faraway crowd.

"Fräulein Eleonore . . ." moaned Frida.

The answer came immediately and hurled us screaming down the stairs: a long shriek of terror rang out, not from the partition above us, but from downstairs, from the councillor's apartment. Then he called for help at the top of his lungs. Lotte and Meta had hurried out onto the landing.

"We must go there," I said courageously.

We had not taken three steps when there was another cry of distress, this time from above us.

"Help! Help!"

We recognized Frau Pilz's voice. We heard her call again, feebly.

Meta picked up the lamp I had placed on the landing. Halfway up the stairs we found Frida alone. Frau Pilz had disappeared.

At this point I must express my admiration of Meta Rückhardt's calm courage.

"There's nothing more we can do here," she said, breaking the silence she had stubbornly maintained for several days. "Let's go downstairs . . ."

She was holding her father's rapier, and she did not look at all ridiculous, for we sensed that she would use it as effectively as a man.

We followed her, subjugated by her cold strength.

The councillor's study was as brightly lighted as a traveling carnival. The poor man had given the darkness no chance to get in. Two enormous lamps with white porcelain globes stood at either end of the mantelpiece, looking like two placid moons. A small Louis XV chandelier hung from the ceiling, its prisms flashing like handfuls of precious stones. Copper and stone candlesticks stood on the floor in every corner of the room. On the table, a row of tall candles seemed to be illuminating an invisible catafalque.

We stopped, dazzled, and looked around for the councillor.

"Oh!" Frida exclaimed suddenly. "Look, there he is! He's hiding behind the window curtain."

Lotte abruptly pulled back the heavy curtain. Herr Hühnebein was there, leaning out the open window, motionless.

Lotte went over to him, then leapt back with a cry of horror.

"Don't look! For the love of heaven, don't look! He . . . he . . . his head is gone!"

I saw Frida stagger, ready to faint. Meta's voice called us back to reason:

"Be careful! There's danger here!"

We pressed up close to her, feeling protected by her presence of mind. Suddenly something blinked on the ceiling, and we saw with alarm that darkness had invaded two opposite corners of the room, where the lights had just been extinguished.

"Hurry, protect the lights!" panted Meta. "Oh! . . . There! . . . There he is!"

At that moment the white moons on the mantelpiece burst, spat out streaks of smoky flame, and vanished.

Meta stood motionless, but she looked all around the room with a cold rage that I had never seen in her before.

The candles on the table were blown out. Only the little chandelier continued to shed its calm light. I saw that Meta was keeping her eyes on it. Suddenly her rapier flashed and she lunged forward into empty space.

"Protect the light!" she cried. "I see him! I've got him! . . . Ah! . . ."

We saw the rapier make strange, violent movements in her hand, as though an invisible force were trying to take it away from her.

It was Frida who had the odd but fortunate inspiration that saved us that evening. She uttered a fierce cry, picked up one of the heavy copper candlesticks, leapt to Meta's side, and began striking the air with her gleaming club. The rapier stopped moving; something very light seemed to brush against the floor, then the door opened by itself, and a heartrending clamor arose.

"That takes care of one of them," said Meta.

One might wonder why we stubbornly went on living in that murderously haunted house.

At least a hundred other houses were in the same situation. People had stopped counting the murders and disappearances, and had become almost indifferent to them. The town was gloomy. There were dozens of suicides, for some people preferred to die by their own hands rather than be killed by the phantom executioners. And then, too, Meta wanted to take vengeance. She was now waiting for the invisible beings to return.

She had relapsed into her grim silence; she spoke to us only to order us to lock the doors and shutters at nightfall. As soon as darkness fell, the four of us went into the living room, which was now a dormitory and dining room as well. We did not leave it until morning.

I questioned Frida about her strange armed intervention. She was able to give me only a confused answer.

"I don't know," she said. "It seemed to me I saw something

. . . A face . . . I don't know how to say what it was . . . Yes, it was the great fear that was in my room the first night."

That was all I could get out of her.

One evening toward the middle of April, Lotte and Frida were lingering in the kitchen. Meta opened the living-room door and told them to hurry. I saw that the shadows of night had already invaded the landings and the hall.

"We're coming," they replied in unison.

Meta came back into the living room and closed the door. She was horribly pale. No sound came from downstairs. I waited vainly to hear the footsteps of the two women. The silence was like a threatening flood rising on the other side of the wall.

Meta locked the door.

"What are you doing?" I asked. "What about Lotte and Frida?"

"It's no use," she said dully.

Her eyes, motionless and terrible, stared at the rapier. The sinister darkness arrived.

It was thus that Lotte and Frida vanished into mystery.

Dear God, what was it? There was a presence in the house, a suffering, wounded presence that was seeking help. I did not know whether Meta was aware of it or not. She was more taciturn than ever, but she barricaded the doors and windows in a way that seemed designed more to prevent an escape than an intrusion. My life had become a fearful solitude. Meta herself was like a sneering specter.

During the day, I sometimes came upon her unexpectedly in one of the halls; in one hand she held the rapier, and in the other she held a powerful lantern with a reflector and a lens that she shone into all the dark corners.

During one of these encounters, she told me rather impolitely that I had better go back to the living room, and when I obeyed her too slowly she shouted furiously at me that I must never interfere with her plans.

Her face no longer had the placid look it had worn as she leaned over her embroidery only a few days before. It was now a savage face, and she sometimes glared at me with a flame of hatred in her eyes. For I had a secret . . .

Was it curiosity, perversity, or pity that made me act as I did? I pray to God that I was moved by nothing more than pity and kindness.

I had just drawn some fresh water from the fountain in the wash-house, when I heard a muffled moan: "Moh . . . Moh . . ."

I thought of our vanished friends and looked around me. I saw a well-concealed door that led into a storeroom in which poor Hühnebein had kept stacks of books and paintings, amid dust and cobwebs.

"Moh . . . Moh . . ."

It was coming from inside the storeroom. I opened the door and looked into the gray semidarkness. Everything seemed normal. The lamentation had stopped. I stepped inside. Suddenly I felt something seize my dress. I cried out. I immediately heard the moaning very close to me, plaintive, supplicating, and something tapped on my pitcher.

I put it down. There was a slight splashing sound, like that of a dog lapping, and the level of the water in my pitcher began to sink. The thing, the being, was drinking!

"Moh! . . . Moh! . . ."

Something caressed my hair more softly than a breath.

"Moh . . . Moh . . ."

Then the moaning changed to a sound of human weeping, almost like the sobbing of a child, and I felt pity for the suffering invisible monster. But there were footsteps in the hall; I put my hands over my lips and the being fell silent.

Without a sound, I closed the door of the secret storeroom. Meta was coming toward me in the hall.

"Did I hear your voice just now?" she asked.

"Yes. My foot slipped and I was startled . . ."

I was an accomplice of the phantoms.

• • • •

I brought milk, wine, and apples. Nothing manifested itself. When I returned, the milk had been drunk to the last drop, but the wine and the apples were intact. Then a kind of breeze surrounded me and passed over my hair for a long time . . .

I went back, bringing more fresh milk. The soft voice was no longer weeping, but the caress of the breeze was longer and seemed to be more ardent.

Meta began looking at me suspiciously and prowling around the storeroom.

I found a safer refuge for my mysterious protégé. I explained it to him by signs. How strange it was to make gestures to empty space! But he understood me. He was following me along the hall like a breath of air, when I suddenly had to hide in a corner.

A pale light slid across the floor. I saw Meta coming down the spiral staircase at the end of the hall. She was walking quietly, partially hiding the glow of her lantern. The rapier glittered. I sensed that the being beside me was afraid. The breeze stirred around me, feverishly, abruptly, and I heard that plaintive "Moh! . . . Moh! . . ."

Meta's footsteps faded away in the distance. I made a reassuring gesture and went to the new refuge: a large closet that was never opened.

The breeze touched my lips and remained there a moment. I felt a strange shame.

May came.

The twenty square feet of the miniature garden, which poor, dear Hühnebein had spattered with his blood, were dotted with little white flowers.

Under a magnificent blue sky, the town was almost silent. The cries of the swallows were answered only by the peevish sounds of closing doors, sliding bolts, and turning keys.

The being had become imprudent. He sought me out. All at once I would feel him around me. I cannot describe the feeling; it was like a great tenderness surrounding me. I would make him understand that I was afraid of Meta, and then I would feel him vanish like a dying wind.

I could not bear the look in Meta's fiery eyes.

On May 4, the end came abruptly.

We were in the living room, with all the lamps lighted. I was closing the shutters. Suddenly I sensed his presence. I made a desperate gesture, turned around, and met Meta's terrible gaze in a mirror.

"Traitress!" she cried.

She quickly closed the door. He was imprisoned with us.

"I knew it!" she said vehemently. "I've seen you carrying pitchers of milk, daughter of the devil! You gave him strength when he was dying from the wound I gave him on the night of Hühnebein's death. Yes, your phantom is vulnerable! He's going to die now, and I think that dying is much more horrible for him than it is for us. Then your turn will come, you wretch! Do you hear me?"

She had shrieked this in short phrases. She uncovered her lantern. A beam of white light shot across the room, and I saw it strike something like thin, gray smoke. She plunged her rapier into it.

"Moh! . . . Moh! . . ." cried the heartrending voice, and then suddenly, awkwardly, but in a loving tone, my name was spoken. I leapt forward and knocked over the lantern with my fist. It went out.

"Meta, listen to me," I begged, "have pity . . ."

Her face was contorted into a mask of demoniac fury.

"Traitress!" she screamed.

The rapier flashed before my eyes. It struck me below the left breast and I fell to my knees.

Someone was weeping violently beside me, strangely beseeching Meta. She raised her rapier again. I tried to find the words of supreme contrition that reconcile us with God forever, but then I saw Meta's face freeze and the sword fell from her hand.

Something murmured near us. I saw a thin flame stretch out like a ribbon and greedily attack the curtains.

"We're burning!" cried Meta. "All of us together!"

At that moment, when everything was about to sink into death, the door opened. An immensely tall old woman came in. I saw only her terrible green eyes glowing in her unimaginable face.

A flame licked my left hand. I stepped back as much as my strength allowed. I saw Meta still standing motionless with a strange grimace on her face, and I realized that her soul, too, had flown away. Then the monstrous old woman's eyes, without pupils, slowly looked around the flame-filled room and came to rest on me.

I am writing this in a strange little house. Where am I? Alone. And yet all this is full of tumult, an invisible but unrestrained presence is everywhere. He has come back. I have again heard my name spoken in that awkward, gentle way . . .

Here ends the German manuscript, as though cut off with a knife.

The French Manuscript

The town's oldest coachman was pointed out to me in the smoky inn where he was drinking heady, fragrant October beer.

I bought him a drink and gave him some tobacco. He swore I was a prince. I pointed to his droshky outside the inn and said, "And now, take me to Saint Beregonne's Lane."

He gave me a bewildered look, then laughed.

"Ah, you're very clever!"

"Why?"

"You're testing me. I know every street in this town—I can almost say I know every paving-stone! There's no Saint Bere . . . What did you say?"

"Beregonne. Are you sure? Isn't it near the Mohlenstrasse?"

"No," he said decisively. "There's no such street here, no more than Mount Vesuvius is in Saint Petersburg."

No one knew the town, in all its twisting byways, better than that splendid beer-drinker.

A student sitting at a nearby table looked up from the love letter he had been writing and said to me, "There's no saint by that name, either."

And the innkeeper's wife added, with a touch of anger, "You can't manufacture saints like sausages!"

I calmed everyone with wine and beer. There was great joy in my heart.

The policeman who paced up and down the Mohlenstrasse from dawn till dark had a face like a bulldog, but he was obviously a man who knew his job.

"No," he said slowly, coming back from a long journey among his thoughts and memories, "there's no such street here or anywhere else in town."

Over his shoulder I saw the beginning of Saint Beregonne's Lane, between the Klingbom distillery and the shop of an anonymous seed merchant.

I had to turn away with impolite abruptness in order not to show my elation. Saint Beregonne's Lane did not exist for the coachman, the student, the policeman, or anyone else: it existed only for me!

How did I make that amazing discovery? By an almost scientific observation, as some of my pompous fellow-teachers would have said. My colleague Seifert, who taught natural science by bursting balloons filled with strange gases in his pupils' faces, would not have been able to find any fault with my procedure.

When I walked along the Mohlenstrasse, it took me two or three seconds to cover the distance between the distillery and the seed merchant's shop. I noticed, however, that when other people passed by the same place they went immediately from the distillery to the shop, without visibly crossing the entrance of Saint Beregonne's Lane.

By adroitly questioning various people, and by consulting the town's cadastral map, I learned that only a wall separated the distillery from the shop.

I concluded that, for everyone in the world except myself, that street existed outside of time and space.

I knew that mysterious street for several years without ever venturing into it, and I think that even a more courageous man would have hesitated. What laws governed that unknown space? Once it had drawn me into its mystery, would it ever return me to my own world?

I finally invented various reasons to convince myself that that world was inhospitable to human beings, and my curiosity surrendered to my fear. And yet what I could see of that opening into the incomprehensible was so ordinary, so commonplace! I must admit, however, that the view was cut off after ten paces by a sharp bend in the street. All I could see was two high, badly whitewashed walls with the name of the street painted on one of them in black letters, and a stretch of worn, greenish pavement with a gap in which a viburnum bush was growing. That sickly bush seemed to live in accordance with our seasons, for I sometimes saw a little tender green and a few lumps of snow among its twigs.

I might have made some curious observations concerning the insertion of that slice of an alien cosmos into ours, but to do so I would have had to spend a considerable amount of time standing on the Mohlenstrasse; and Klingbom, who often saw me staring at some of his windows, became suspicious of his wife and gave me hostile looks.

I wondered why, of all the people in the world, I was the only one to whom that strange privilege had been given. This led me to think of my maternal grandmother. She was a tall, somber woman, and her big green eyes seemed to be following the happenings of another life on the wall in front of her.

Her background was obscure. My grandfather, a sailor, was

supposed to have rescued her from some Algerian pirates. She sometimes stroked my hair with her long, white hands and murmured, "Maybe he . . . Why not? After all . . ." She repeated it on the night of her death, and while the pale fire of her gaze wandered among the shadows she added, "Maybe he'll go where I wasn't able to return . . ."

A black storm was blowing that night. Just after my grandmother died, while the candles were being lit, a big stormy petrel shattered the window and lay dying, bloody and threatening, on her bed.

That was the only odd thing I remembered in my life; but did it have any connection with Saint Beregonne's Lane?

It was a sprig of the viburnum bush that set off the adventure.

But am I sincere in looking there for the initial tap that set events in motion? Perhaps I should speak of Anita.

Several years ago, in the Hanseatic ports one could see the arrival of little lateen-rigged ships creeping out of the mist like crestfallen animals.

Colossal laughter would immediately shake the port, down to the deepest beer cellars.

"Aha! Here come the dream ships!"

I always felt heartbroken at the sight of those heroic dreams dying in formidable Germanic laughter.

It was said that the sad crews of those ships lived on the golden shores of the Adriatic and the Tyrrhenian Sea in a mad dream, for they believed in a fantastic land of plenty, related to the Thule of the ancients, lying somewhere in our cruel North. Not having much more knowledge than their forefathers of a thousand years ago, they had carefully nurtured a heritage of legends about islands of diamonds and emeralds, legends that had been born when their forefathers encountered the glittering vanguard of an ice floe.

The compass was one of the few items of progress that their minds had seized upon in the course of the centuries. Its enigmatic needle, always pointing in the same direction, was for them a final proof of the mysteries of the North.

One day when a dream was walking like a new Messiah on the choppy waters of the Mediterranean, when the nets had brought up only fish poisoned by the coral on the bottom, and when Lombardy had sent neither grain nor flour to the poverty-stricken lands of the South, they had hoisted their sails in the offshore wind.

Their flotilla had dotted the sea with its hard wings; then, one by one, their ships had melted into the storms of the Atlantic. The Bay of Biscay had nibbled the flotilla and passed the remainder on to the granite teeth of Brittany. Some of the hulls were sold to firewood merchants in Germany and Denmark; one of the ships died in its dream, killed by an iceberg blazing in the sun off the Lofoten Islands.

But the North adorned the grave of that flotilla with a sweet name: "the dream ships." Although it made coarse sailors laugh, I was deeply moved by it, and I might well have been willing to set sail with those dreamers.

Anita was their daughter.

She came from the Mediterranean when she was still a baby in her mother's arms, aboard a tartan. The ship was sold. Her mother died, and so did her little sisters. Her father set out for America on a sailing ship that never returned. Anita was left all alone, but the dream that had brought the tartan to those moldering wooden docks never left her: she still believed in the fortune of the North, and she wanted it fiercely, almost with hatred.

In Tempelhof, with its clusters of white lights, she sang, danced, and threw red flowers that either fell on her like a rain of blood or were burned in the short flames of the Argand lamps. She would then pass among the crowd, holding out a pink conch shell. Silver was dropped into it, or sometimes gold, and only then did her eyes smile as they rested for a second, like a caress, on the generous man.

I gave gold—I, a humble teacher of French grammar in the Gymnasium, gave gold for one look from Anita.

. . . .

Brief notes:

I sold my Voltaire. I had sometimes read my pupils extracts from his correspondence with the King of Prussia; it pleased the principal.

I owed two months' room and board to Frau Holz, my landlady. She told me she was poor . . .

I asked the bursar of the school for another advance on my salary. He told me with embarrassment that it was difficult, that it was against regulations . . . I did not listen any longer. My colleague Seifert curtly refused to lend me a few thalers.

I dropped a heavy gold coin into the conch shell. Anita's eyes burned my soul. Then I heard someone laughing in the laurel thickets of Tempelhof. I recognized two servants of the Gymnasium. They ran away into the darkness.

It was my last gold coin. I had no more money, none at all . . .

As I was walking past the distillery on the Mohlenstrasse, I was nearly run over by a carriage. I made a frightened leap into Saint Beregonne's Lane. My hand clutched the viburnum bush and broke off a sprig of it.

I took the sprig home with me and laid it on my table. It had opened up an immense new world to me, like a magician's wand.

Let us reason, as my stingy colleague Seifert would say.

First of all, my leap into Saint Beregonne's Lane and my subsequent return to the Mohlenstrasse had shown that the mysterious street was as easy to enter and leave as any ordinary thoroughfare.

But the viburnum sprig had enormous philosophical significance. It was "in excess" in our world. If I had taken a branch from any forest in America and brought it here, I would not have changed the number of branches on earth. But in bringing that sprig of viburnum from Saint Beregonne's Lane I had made an intrinsic addition that could not have been made by all the tropical growths in the world, because I had taken it from a plane of existence that was real only for me.

I was therefore able to take an object from that plane and bring it into the world of men, where no one could contest my ownership of it. Ownership could never be more absolute, in fact, because the object would owe nothing to any industry, and it would augment the normally immutable patrimony of the earth . . .

My reasoning flowed on, wide as a river carrying fleets of words, encircling islands of appeals to philosophy; it was swollen by a vast system of logical tributaries until it reached a conclusive demonstration that a theft committed in Saint Beregonne's Lane was not a theft in the Mohlenstrasse.

Fortified by this nonsense, I judged that the matter was settled. My only concern would be to avoid the reprisals of the mysterious inhabitants of the street, or of the world to which it led.

When the Spanish conquistadores spent the gold they had brought back from the new India, I think they cared very little about the anger of the faraway peoples they had despoiled.

I decided to enter the unknown the following day.

Klingbom made me waste some time. I think he had been waiting for me in the little square vestibule that opened into his shop on one side and his office on the other. As I walked past, clenching my teeth, ready to plunge into my adventure, he grabbed me by my coat.

"Ah, professor," he said, "how I misjudged you! It wasn't you! I must have been blind to suspect you! She's left me, professor, but not with you. Oh, no, you're a man of honor! She's gone off with a postmaster, a man who's half coachman and half scribe. What a disgrace for the House of Klingbom!"

He had dragged me into the shadowy back room of his shop. He poured me a glass of orange-flavored brandy.

"And to think that I mistrusted you, professor! I always saw you looking at my wife's windows, but I know now that it was the seed merchant's wife you had your eye on."

I masked my embarrassment by raising my glass.

"To tell you the truth," said Klingbom, pouring me out some more of the reddish liquid, "I'd be glad to see you put one over on that malicious seed merchant: he's delighted by my misfortune."

He added, with a smile, "I'll do you a favor: the lady of your dreams is in her garden right now. Why don't you go and see her?"

He led me up a spiral staircase to a window. I saw the poisonous sheds of the Klingbom distillery smoking among a tangled array of little courtyards, miniature gardens, and muddy streams narrow enough to step across. It was through that landscape that the secret street ought to run, but I saw nothing except the smoky activity of the Klingbom buildings and the seed merchant's nearby garden, where a thin form was leaning over some arid flower beds.

One last swallow of brandy gave me a great deal of courage. After leaving Klingbom, I walked straight into Saint Beregonne's Lane.

Three little yellow doors in the white wall . . .

Beyond the bend in the street, the viburnum bushes continued to place spots of green and black among the paving stones; then the three little doors appeared, almost touching each other. They gave the aspect of a Flemish Beguine convent to what should have been singular and terrible.

My footsteps resounded clearly in the silence.

I knocked on the first of the doors. Only the futile life of an echo was stirred behind it.

Fifty paces away, the street made another bend.

I was discovering the unknown parsimoniously. So far I had found only two thinly whitewashed walls and those three doors. But is not any closed door a powerful mystery in itself?

I knocked on all three doors, more violently this time. The echoes departed loudly and shattered the silence lurking in the depths of prodigious corridors. Sometimes their dying murmurs seemed to imitate the sound of light footsteps, but that was the only reply from the enclosed world.

The doors had locks on them, the same as all the other doors I was used to seeing. Two nights before, I had spent an hour picking the lock on my bedroom door with a piece of bent wire, and it had been as easy as a game.

There was a little sweat on my temples, a little shame in my heart. I took the same piece of wire from my pocket and slipped it into the lock of the first little door. And very simply, just like my bedroom door, it opened.

Later, when I was back in my bedroom among my books, in front of the table on which lay a red ribbon that had fallen from Anita's dress, I sat clutching three silver thalers in my hand.

Three thalers!

I had destroyed my finest destiny with my own hand. That new world had opened for me alone. What had it expected of me, that universe more mysterious than those that gravitate toward the bottom of Infinity? Mystery had made advances to me, had smiled at me like a pretty girl, and I had entered it as a thief. I had been petty, vile, absurd.

Three thalers!

My adventure should have been so prodigious, and it had become so paltry!

Three thalers reluctantly given to me by Gockel, the antiques dealer, for that engraved metal dish. Three thalers . . . But they would buy one of Anita's smiles.

I abruptly threw them into a drawer: someone was knocking on my door.

It was Gockel. It was difficult for me to believe that this was the same malevolent man who had contemptuously put down the metal dish on his counter cluttered with barbarous and shabby trinkets. He was smiling now, and he constantly mingled my name—which he mispronounced—with the title of "Herr Doktor" or "Herr Lehrer."

"I think I did you a great injustice, Herr Doktor," he said. "That dish is certainly worth more."

He took out a leather purse and I saw the bright yellow smile of gold.

"It may be," he went on, "that you have other objects from the same source . . . or rather, of the same kind."

The distinction did not escape me. Beneath the urbanity of the antiques dealer was the spirit of a receiver of stolen goods.

"The fact is," I said, "that a friend of mine, an erudite collector, is in a difficult situation and needs to pay off certain debts, so he wants to sell part of his collection. He prefers to remain unknown: he's a shy scholar. He's already unhappy enough over having to part with some of the treasures in his showcases. I want to spare him any further sadness, so I'm helping him to sell them."

Gockel nodded enthusiastically. He seemed overwhelmed with admiration for me.

"That's my idea of true friendship!" he said. "Ach, Herr Doktor, I'll reread Cicero's *De Amicitia* this evening with renewed pleasure. How I wish that I had a friend like your unfortunate scholar has found in you! But I'll contribute a little to your good deed by buying everything your friend is willing to part with, and by paying very good prices . . ."

I had a slight stirring of curiosity:

"I didn't look at the dish very closely," I said loftily. "It didn't concern me, and besides, I don't know anything about such things. What kind of work is it? Byzantine?"

Gockel scratched his chin in embarrassment.

"Uh . . . I couldn't say for sure. Byzantine, yes, maybe . . . I'll have to study it more carefully . . . But," he went on, suddenly recovering his serenity, "in any case, it's sure to find a buyer." Then, in a tone that cut short all further discussion: "That's the most important thing to us . . . and to your friend, too, of course."

Late that night I accompanied Anita in the moonlight to the street where her house stood half-hidden in a clump of tall lilacs.

But I must go back in my story to the tray I sold for thalers and gold, which gave me for one evening the friendship of the most beautiful girl in the world.

· · · ·

The door opened onto a long hall with a blue stone floor. A frosted window pane cast light into it and broke up the shadows. My first impression of being in a Flemish Beguine convent became stronger, especially when an open door at the end of the hall led me into a broad kitchen with a vaulted ceiling and rustic furniture, gleaming with wax and polish.

This innocuous scene was so reassuring that I called aloud: "Hello! Is there anyone upstairs?"

A powerful resonance rumbled, but no presence cared to manifest itself.

I must admit that at no time did the silence and absence of life surprise me; it was as though I had expected it. In fact, from the time when I first perceived the existence of the enigmatic street, I had not thought for one moment of any possible inhabitants. And yet I had just entered it like a nocturnal thief.

I took no precautions when I ransacked the drawers containing silverware and table linen. My footsteps clattered freely in the adjoining rooms furnished like convent visiting-rooms, and on a magnificent oak staircase that . . . Ah, there *was* something surprising in my visit! That staircase led nowhere! It ran into the drab wall as though it continued on the other side of it.

All this was bathed in the whitish glow of the frosted glass that formed the ceiling. I saw, or thought I saw, a vaguely hideous shape on the rough plaster wall, but when I looked at it attentively I realized that it was composed of thin cracks and was of the same order as those monsters that we distinguish in clouds and the lace of curtains. Furthermore, it did not trouble me, because when I looked a second time I no longer saw it in the network of cracks in the plaster.

I went back to the kitchen. Through a barred window, I saw a shadowy little courtyard that was like a pit surrounded by four big, mossy walls.

On a sideboard there was a heavy tray that looked as though it ought to have some value. I slipped it under my coat. I was deeply disappointed: I felt as though I had just stolen a few coins from a child's piggy bank, or from an old-maid aunt's shabby woolen stocking.

I went to Gockel, the antiques dealer.

The three little houses were identical. In all of them, I found the same clean, tidy kitchen, the same sparse, gleaming furniture, the same dim, unreal light, the same serene quietness, the same senseless wall that ended the staircase. And in all three houses, I found identical candlesticks and the same heavy tray.

I took them away, and . . . and the next day I always found them in their places again. I took them to Gockel, who smiled broadly as he paid me for them.

It was enough to drive me mad; I felt my soul becoming monotonous, like that of a whirling dervish. Over and over again, I stole the same objects from the same house, under the same circumstances. I wondered whether this might not be the first vengeance of that unknown without mystery. Might not damnation be the unvarying repetition of sin for all eternity?

One day I did not go. I had resolved to space out my wretched incursions. I had a reserve of gold; Anita was happy and was showing wonderful tenderness toward me.

That same evening, Gockel came to see me, asked me if I had anything to sell, and, to my surprise, offered to pay me even more than he had been paying. He scowled when I told him of my decision.

"You've found a regular buyer, haven't you?" I said to him as he was leaving.

He slowly turned around and looked me straight in the eyes.

"Yes, Herr Doktor. I won't tell you anything about him, just as you never speak to me of . . . your friend, the seller." His voice became lower: "Bring me objects every day; tell me how much gold you want for them, and I'll give it to you, without bargaining. We're both tied to the same wheel, Herr Doktor. Perhaps we'll have to pay later. In the meantime, let's live the kind of life we like: you with a pretty girl, I with a fortune."

We never broached the subject again. But Anita suddenly became very demanding, and Gockel's gold slipped between her little fingers like water.

Then the atmosphere of the street changed, if I may express it that way. I heard melodies. At least it seemed to me that it was marvelous, faraway music. Summoning up my courage again, I decided to explore the street beyond the bend and go on toward the song that vibrated in the distance.

When I passed the third door and entered a part of the street where I had never gone before, I felt a terrible tightening in my heart. I took only three or four hesitant steps.

I turned around. I could still see the first part of the street, but it looked much smaller. It seemed to me that I had moved dangerously far away from my world. Nevertheless, in a surge of irrational temerity, I ran a short distance, then knelt, and, like a boy peering over a hedge, ventured to look down the unknown part of the street.

Disappointment struck me like a slap. The street continued its winding way, but again I saw nothing except three little doors in a white wall, and some viburnum bushes.

I would surely have gone back then if the wind of song had not passed by, like a distant tide of billowing sound . . . I surmounted an inexplicable terror and listened to it, hoping to analyze it if possible.

I have called it a tide: it was a sound that came from a considerable distance, but it was enormous, like the sound of the sea.

As I listened to it, I no longer heard the harmonies I had thought I discerned in it at first; instead, I heard a harsh dissonance, a furious clamor of wails and hatred.

Have you ever noticed that the first whiffs of a repulsive smell are sometimes soft and even pleasant? I remember that when I left my house one day I was greeted in the street by an appetizing aroma of roast beef. "Someone's doing some good cooking early in the morning," I thought. But when I had walked a hundred paces, this aroma changed into the sharp, sickening smell of burning cloth: a draper's shop was on fire, filling the air with sparks and smoky flames. In the same way, I may have been deceived by my first perception of the melodious clamor.

"Why don't I go beyond the next bend?" I said to myself. My apprehensive inertia had almost disappeared. Walking calmly now, I covered the space before me in a few seconds—and once again I found exactly the same scene that I had left behind.

I was overwhelmed by a kind of bitter fury that engulfed my broken curiosity. Three identical houses, then three more identical houses. I had plumbed the mystery merely by opening the first door.

Gloomy courage took possession of me. I walked forward along the street, and my disappointment grew at an incredible rate.

A bend, three little yellow doors, a clump of viburnum bushes, then another bend, the same three little doors in the white wall, and the shadow of spindle trees. This repetition continued obsessively while I walked furiously, with loud footsteps.

Suddenly, when I had turned one more bend in the street, this terrible symmetry was broken. There were again three little doors and some viburnum bushes, but there was also a big wooden portal, darkened and worn smooth by time. I was afraid of it.

I now heard the clamor from much closer, hostile and threatening. I began walking back toward the Mohlenstrasse. The scenes went by like the quatrains of a ballad: three little doors and viburnum bushes, three little doors and viburnum bushes . . .

Finally I saw the first lights of the real world twinkling before me. But the clamor had pursued me to the edge of the Mohlenstrasse. There it stopped abruptly, adapting itself to the joyous evening sounds of the populous streets, so that the mysterious and terrible shouting ended in a chorus of children's voices singing a roundelay.

The whole town is in the grip of an unspeakable terror.

I would not have spoken of it in these brief memoirs, which concern only myself, if I had not found a link between the shadowy street and the crimes that steep the town in blood every night.

Over a hundred people have suddenly disappeared, a hundred others have been savagely murdered.

I recently took a map of the town and drew on it the winding line that must represent Saint Beregonne's Lane, that incomprehensible street that overlaps our terrestrial world. I was horrified to see that *all the crimes have been committed along that line.*

Thus poor Klingbom was one of the first to disappear. According to his clerk, he vanished like a puff of smoke just as he was entering the room containing his stills. The seed merchant's wife was next, snatched away while she was in her sad garden. Her husband was found in his drying-room with his skull smashed.

As I traced the fateful line on the map, my idea became a certainty. I can explain the victims' disappearance only by their passage into an unknown plane; as for the murders, they are easy for invisible beings.

All the inhabitants of a house on Old Purse Street have disappeared. On Church Street, six corpses have been found. On Post Street, there have been five disappearances and four deaths. This goes on and on, apparently limited by the Deichstrasse, where more murders and disappearances are taking place.

I now realize that to talk about what I know would be to place myself in the Kirchhaus insane asylum, a tomb from which no Lazarus ever arises; or else it would give free rein to a superstitious crowd that is exasperated enough to tear me to pieces as a sorcerer.

And yet, ever since the beginning of my monotonous daily thefts, anger has been welling up inside me, driving me to vague plans of vengeance.

"Gockel knows more about this than I do," I thought. "I'm going to tell him what I know: that will make him more inclined to confide in me."

But that evening, while Gockel was emptying his heavy purse into my hands, I said nothing, and he left as usual with polite words that made no allusion to the strange bargain that had attached us to the same chain.

I had a feeling that events were about to leap forward and rush like a torrent through my tranquil life. I was becoming more and more aware that Saint Beregonne's Lane and its little houses were only a mask concealing some sort of horrible face.

So far, fortunately for me, I had gone there only in broad daylight, because for some reason I dreaded to encounter the shadows of evening there. But one day I lingered later than usual, stubbornly pushing furniture around, turning drawers inside out, determined to discover something new. And the "new" came of itself, in the form of a dull rumble, like that of heavy doors moving on rollers. I looked up and saw that the opalescent light had changed into an ashy semidarkness. The panes of glass above the staircase were livid; the little courtyards were already filled with shadow.

My heart tightened, but when the rumbling continued, reinforced by the powerful resonance of the house, my curiosity became stronger than my fear, and I began climbing the stairs to see where the noise was coming from.

It was growing darker and darker, but before leaping back down the stairs like a madman and running out of the house, I was able to see . . . There was no more wall! The staircase ended at the edge of an abyss dug out of the night, from which vague monstrosities were rising.

I reached the door; behind me, something was furiously knocked over.

The Mohlenstrasse gleamed before me like a haven. I ran faster. Something suddenly seized me with extreme savagery.

"What's the matter with you? Can't you see where you're going?"

I found myself sitting on the pavement of the Mohlenstrasse, before a sailor who was rubbing his sore skull and looking at me in bewilderment. My coat was torn, my neck was bleeding.

I immediately hurried away without wasting any time on apologies, to the supreme indignation of the sailor, who shouted after me that after colliding with him so brutally I should at least buy him a drink.

Anita is gone, vanished!

My heart is broken; I collapse, sobbing, on my useless gold.

And yet her house is far from the zone of danger. Good God! I failed through an excess of prudence and love! One day, without mentioning the street, I showed her the line I had drawn on the map and told her that all the danger seemed to be concentrated along that sinuous trail. Her eyes glowed strangely at that moment. I should have known that the great spirit of adventure that animated her ancestors was not dead in her.

Perhaps, in a flash of feminine intuition, she made a connection between that line and my sudden fortune . . . Oh, how my life is disintegrating!

There have been more murders and disappearances. And my Anita has been carried off in the bloody, inexplicable whirlwind!

The case of Hans Mendell has given me a mad idea: those vaporous beings, as he described them, may not be invulnerable.

Although Hans Mendell was not a distinguished man, I see no reason not to believe his story. He was a scoundrel who made his living as a mountebank and a cutthroat. When he was found, he had in his pocket the purses and watches of two unfortunate men whose corpses lay bleeding on the ground a few paces away from him.

It would have been assumed that he was guilty of murder if he himself had not been found moaning with both arms torn from his body.

Being a man with a powerful constitution, he was able to live long enough to answer the feverish questions of the magistrates and priests.

He confessed that for several days he had followed a shadow, a kind of black mist, and robbed the bodies of the people it killed. On the night of his misfortune, he saw the black mist waiting in the middle of Post Street in the moonlight. He hid in an empty sentry-box and watched it. He saw other dark, vaporous, awkward forms that bounced like rubber balls, then disappeared.

Soon he heard voices and saw two young men coming up the street. The black mist was no longer in sight, but he suddenly saw the two men writhe on their backs, then lie still.

Mendell added that he had already observed the same sequence in those nocturnal murders on seven other occasions. He had always waited for the shadow to leave, then robbed the bodies. This shows that he had remarkable self-control, worthy of being put to a better use.

As he was robbing the two bodies, he saw with alarm that the shadow had not left, but had only risen off the ground, interposing itself between him and the moon. He then saw that it had a roughly human shape. He tried to go back to the sentry-box but did not have time: the figure pounced on him.

Mendell was an extraordinarily strong man. He struck an enormous blow and encountered a slight resistance, as though he were pushing his hand through a strong current of air.

That was all he was able to say. His horrible wound allowed him to live only another hour after telling his story.

The idea of avenging Anita has now taken root in my brain. I said to Gockel, "Don't come anymore. I need revenge and hatred, and your gold can no longer do anything for me."

He looked at me with that profound expression that was familiar to me by now.

"Gockel," I said, "I'm going to take vengeance."

His face suddenly brightened, as though with great joy:

"And . . . do you believe . . . Herr Doktor, that they will disappear?"

I harshly ordered him to have a cart filled with faggots and casks of oil, raw alcohol and gunpowder, and to leave it without a driver early in the morning on the Mohlenstrasse. He bowed low like a servant, and as he was leaving he said to me, "May the Lord help you! May the Lord come to your aid!"

• • • •

I feel that these are the last lines I shall write in this journal.

I piled up the faggots, streaming with oil and alcohol, against the big door. I laid down trails of gunpowder connecting the nearby small doors with other oil-soaked faggots. I placed charges of powder in all the cracks in the walls.

The mysterious clamor continued all around me. This time I discerned in it abominable lamentations, human wails, echoes of horrible torments of the flesh. But my heart was agitated by tumultuous joy, because I felt around me a wild apprehension that came from *them*. They saw my terrible preparations and were unable to prevent them, for, as I had come to realize, only night released their frightful power.

I calmly struck a light with my tinderbox. A moan passed, and the viburnum bushes quivered as though blown by a sudden stiff breeze. A long blue flame rose into the air, the faggots began crackling, fire crept along the trails of gunpowder . . .

I ran down the winding street, from bend to bend, feeling a little dizzy, as though I were going too fast down a spiral staircase that descended deep into the earth.

The Deichstrasse and the whole surrounding neighborhood were in flames. From my window, I could see the sky turning yellow above the rooftops. The weather was dry and the town's water supply was nearly exhausted. A red band of sparks and flames hovered high above the street.

The fire had been burning for a day and a night, but it was still far from the Mohlenstrasse. Saint Beregonne's Lane was there, calm with its quivering viburnum bushes. Explosions rumbled in the distance.

Another cart was there, loaded and left by Gockel. Not a soul was in sight: everyone had been drawn toward the formidable spectacle of the fire. *It was not expected here.*

I walked from bend to bend to bend, sowing faggots, pools of oil and alcohol, and the dark frost of gunpowder. Suddenly, just as I had turned another bend, I stopped and stared. Three little houses, the everlasting three little houses, were burning calmly with pretty yellow flames in the peaceful air. It was as though even the fire respected their serenity, for it was doing its work without noise or ferocity. I realized that I was at the red edge of the conflagration that was destroying the town.

With anguish in my soul, I moved back from that mystery that was about to die.

I was near the Mohlenstrasse. I stopped in front of the first of the little doors, the one I had opened, trembling, a few weeks earlier. It was there that I would start the new fire.

For the last time, I saw the kitchen, the austere parlor, and the staircase, which now ended at the wall, as before; and I felt that all this had become familiar, almost dear to me.

On the big tray, the one I had stolen so many times before only to find it waiting for me again the next day, I saw some sheets of paper covered with elegant feminine handwriting.

I picked them up. This was going to be my last theft on the shadowy street.

Vampires! Vampires! Vampires!

So ends the French manuscript. The last words, evoking the impure spirits of the night, are written across the page in sharp letters that cry out terror and despair. Thus must write those who, on a sinking ship, want to convey a last farewell to the families they hope will survive them.

It was last year in Hamburg. I was strolling through the old city, with its good smell of fresh beer. It was dear to my heart, because it reminded me of the cities I had loved in my youth. And there, on an empty, echoing street, I saw a name on the front of an antique shop: Lockmann Gockel.

I bought an old Bavarian pipe with truculent decorations. The shopkeeper seemed friendly. I asked him if the name of Archipetre meant anything to him. His face had been the color of gray earth; in the twilight it now turned so white that it stood out from the shadows as though illuminated by an inner flame.

"Archipetre," he murmured slowly. "Oh! What are you saying? What do you know?"

I had no reason to conceal the story I had found on the dock. I told it to him.

He lit an archaic gaslight. Its flame danced and hissed foolishly. I saw that his eyes were weary.

"He was my grandfather," he said when I mentioned Gockel the antiques dealer.

When I had finished my story I heard a great sigh from a dark corner.

"That's my sister," he said.

I nodded to her. She was young and pretty, but very pale. She had been listening to me, motionless among grotesque shadows.

"Our grandfather talked to our father about it nearly every evening," he said in a faltering voice, "and our father used to discuss it with us. Now that he's dead too, we talk about it with each other."

"And now," I said nervously, "thanks to you, we're going to be able to do some research on the subject of that mysterious street, aren't we?"

He slowly raised his hand.

"Alphonse Archipetre taught French in the Gymnasium until 1842."

"Oh!" I said, disappointed. "That's a long time ago!"

"It was the year of the great fire that nearly destroyed Hamburg. The Mohlenstrasse and the vast section of the city between it and the Deichstrasse were a sea of flames."

"And Archipetre?"

"He lived rather far from there, toward Bleichen. The fire didn't reach his street, but in the middle of the second night, on May 6—a terrible night, dry and without water—his house burned down, all alone among the others that were miraculously spared. He died in the flames; or at least he was never found."

"The story . . ." I began.

Lockmann Gockel did not let me finish. He was so happy to

have found an outlet that he seized upon the subject greedily. Fortunately he told me more or less what I wanted to hear.

"The story compressed time, just as space was compressed at the fateful location of Saint Beregonne's Lane. In the Hamburg archives, there are accounts of atrocities committed *during the fire* by a band of mysterious evildoers. Fantastic crimes, looting, riots, red hallucinations on the part of whole crowds—all those things are precisely described, and yet they took place *before the fire*. Do you understand my reference to the contraction of space and time?"

His face became a little calmer.

"Isn't modern science driven back to Euclidean weakness by the theory of that admirable Einstein for whom the whole world envies us? And isn't it forced to accept, with horror and despair, that fantastic Fitzgerald-Lorentz law of contraction? Contraction! Ah, there's a word that's heavy with meaning!"

The conversation seemed to be going off on an insidious tangent.

The young woman silently brought tall glasses filled with yellow wine. Gockel raised his toward the flame and marvelous colors flowed onto his frail hand like a silver river of gems.

He abandoned his scientific dissertation and returned to the story of the conflagration:

"My grandfather, and other people of the time, reported that enormous green flames shot up from the debris. There were hallucinated people who claimed to see figures of indescribably ferocious women in them."

The wine had a soul. I emptied the glass and smiled at Gockel's terrified words.

"Those same green flames," he went on, "rose from Archipetre's house and roared so horribly that people were said to have died of fear in the street."

"Mr. Gockel," I said, "did your grandfather ever speak of the mysterious purchaser who came every evening to buy the same trays and the same candlesticks?"

A weary voice replied for him, in words that were almost identical with those that ended the German manuscript:

"A tall old woman, an immense old woman with fishy eyes in an incredible face. She brought bags of gold so heavy that our grandfather had to divide them into four parts to carry them to his coffers."

The young woman continued:

"When Professor Archipetre came to my grandfather, the Gockel firm was about to go bankrupt. It became rich, and we're still enormously rich, from the gold of the . . . yes, from the gold of those beings of the night!"

"They're gone now," murmured her brother, refilling our glasses.

"Don't say that! They can't have forgotten us. Remember our nights, our horrible nights! All I can hope for now is that there is, or was, a human presence with them that they cherish and that may intercede for us."

Her lovely eyes opened wide before the black abyss of her thoughts.

"Kathie!" exclaimed Gockel. "Have you again seen . . . ?"

"You know the things are here every night," she said in a voice as low as a moan. "They assail our thoughts as soon as sleep comes over us. Ah, to sleep no more! . . ."

"To sleep no more," repeated her brother in an echo of terror.

"They come out of their gold, which we keep, and which we love in spite of everything; they rise from everything we've acquired with that infernal fortune . . . They'll always come back, as long as we exist, and as long as this wretched earth endures!"

Aline Myette-Volsky

The Bear Garden

ALINE MYETTE-VOLSKY *is a resident of Fanwood, New Jersey, and mother of the esteemed fantasy novelist, Paula Volsky.* A chilly *little piece that proves there are risks even when one reads an "advert" (as they say in England), "The Bear Garden" is Ms. Myette-Volsky's first published story, but not her last. Her romantic pastiche, "The Woman," will appear in* The Confidential Casebook of Sherlock Holmes, *soon to be published by St. Martin's Press.*

DAMARIS HILL, fresh from Devonshire, had been for some weeks intrigued by the handbills posted along the narrow London streets she strolled with Robert, and on the day she came upon a folder of them in his rooms, a folder bulging with bold prints and drawings, it did seem to her to be a providential find. Her hand darted out to snatch it.

"Please don't touch that," Rob said, also reaching for the folder, but he was too late: the posters had already slid into her eager hands.

"But only look, Rob! Taverns with entertainment, mimes and puppets and fortune-telling Gypsies . . . I must see them all. Surely you understand! I want to taste of everything London has to offer. And you will take me?"

He was amused but reluctant as he tried gently to pry the posters from her grip. "Let me put these things away, Damaris.

Haven't you seen enough of the sights of London? Do you tell me you're feeling deprived of excitement?"

She waved one protesting hand, maintaining her hold on the posters with the other. "But they are very different excitements, Rob. Can you not see that?"

"Most of them are well enough, I suppose. But the bear gardens are not for you. I say no."

"So you say 'yes' to the jugglers, 'yes' to the puppets and the mimes and the stilt-walkers, but 'no' to the bear gardens. Well, I won't have it, Rob. Everyone, *everyone* I know is going to the bear gardens these nights, so why should we not go, too?"

"Because, Sweetheart, you are still a country girl at heart, and you're far too soft for some of these spectacles. And most especially for the bear gardens. Take my word for it."

She put her free hand on her hip and frowned at him. "Take your word for it? I vow and declare, Rob Archer, you do take too much upon yourself when you decide for me what I'd like and what I wouldn't like. I've seen the street posters and I'm convinced that I'd enjoy the bear gardens as much as any Londoner would!"

Rob was looking at her with that smile in his eyes which she usually loved to find in them but today it only irritated her, and when he began to whistle between his teeth, that irritated her still more.

"I'm out of humor with you," she told him crossly. "You're being unreasonable and unfair besides."

"Now, Damaris! Give me credit, girl. I have my reasons and I know whereof I speak. Remember, I've been to the bear garden and you haven't."

"Oh yes, to be sure you've been—and I notice it hasn't done you any great harm, has it?"

He made an impatient gesture. "I'm a man."

"Oh, man be—be—*damned!* I'm a grown woman, and what you can watch, I can watch."

"You'd puke," he warned her, grinning.

Damaris shook her head. "I never puke."

"But—"

"And if you refuse to take me I'll ask Maybelle if I may go with her and her young man. Because one way or another I'm set upon seeing for myself what all of London goes to see. All of London except for me, if you have *your* way!"

"Spitfire."

"Spoilsport!"

He smiled. "Very well. But I've warned you."

Damaris sniffed. "I know. I won't forget. I've been warned. Hah!"

They went to a bear garden that same evening.

Bearbaiting had been a popular sport for centuries and it was very popular indeed in London. Damaris had not exaggerated when she claimed everyone went. Everyone did, rich and poor, nobles and merchants and servants and soldiers and costers. The very beggar to whom you had tossed a coin that morning might be seen waving his crutch wildly at ringside that same evening, having perhaps paid his admission with that same coin.

Damaris, staring around at the crowd, was struck again by the mix of humanity in this great city. She caught Robert's eye and flashed him a smile. It was meant to thank him for bringing her and to reassure him of her determination not to puke. He smiled back at her, but with the smile went a shrug, and she took the shrug amiss. So he was not yet convinced of her sophistication? He still thought she was too soft for the spectacle? Was she indeed? Well, she would show him. He must have it proved to him how much of a Londoner she had become by now, and then he must admit it aloud, too, to cancel out those previous insulting doubts of her.

But that was for later. For now it was time to look around, to try to absorb the whole scene, which was so new to her and so exciting to all her senses at once.

The arena was lighted by dozens of smoking cressets mounted on poles like torches and placed in a circle surrounding what was to be the center of action later when the baiting would begin. The focus of that action to come was a large brown bear already staked out by a chain attached to one leg. He stood quietly, snuffling occasionally and swaying from side to side like an old hulk broadside to the tide. Damaris noticed a group of boys pelting him with apple cores and pebbles. She pointed them out to Robert. "Teasing him, as boys will," he told her. "They try to annoy him to make him roar."

But the bear did not oblige them by roaring. Indeed, he seemed to be almost asleep, and that worried her a little, for a sleepy bear might provide but a dull entertainment, and since she had a feeling that Robert might never again be induced to take her here, she wanted tonight's performance to be the ultimate in beargarden excitement. If one could be certain of going only once, then every moment should be one to treasure.

The gathering crowd, however, was wide awake and stimulated more than enough to make up for the bear's sluggishness. The uproar was deafening, and there was something going on in every direction in which she looked: good-natured shoving for seats, loud greetings between acquaintances, urchins squirming over and under benches, wooden whistles shrilling on every hand, and vendors pushing their way through the packed audience selling fairings at the top of their lungs: ribbons, clay dolls, the ubiquitous wooden whistles and cheap glass bangles, and even dubious little cakes wrapped in paper. It was all holiday noise and sights and smells, all one could ask of any evening's enjoyment, and Damaris was delighted. "Gemini! It's like a fair in the country, only better! You didn't tell me how much fun it would be!" Her eyes shone as she tried to take in everything at once. "It's small wonder everyone loves the bear gardens! And you would have had me miss all this? Oh, shame, Rob! I should never have forgiven you for it."

"You haven't seen all of it yet," was all he said, and then, "Are you hungry, love? Would you like a cheese bun? I think I see a vendor coming this way . . ."

She was standing, looking all around, wanting to miss nothing, balancing herself in the crush by one hand on his shoulder. "No, not now, thank you. I don't want to waste my time on cheese buns. I want to watch people, look at everything—I'm far too happy to eat—as *yet!*" she added warningly, and grinned down at him.

"... and won't be hungry later, I'll warrant at a guess," he muttered, but she didn't hear him and wouldn't have paid much attention if she had. She was far too fascinated by all that was going on around her.

At that moment there came the sound of a trumpet fanfare played very loud and very flat by some prankster in the arena, and the crowd laughed good-naturedly, and then a real roar went up as two handlers entered the ring. Now the real business of the evening would begin. Each handler was leading two giant mastiff dogs. The dogs' tails hung straight down their rumps as they were marched forward, but as they sighted and scented the bear their tails formed an upward curve, sign of a mastiff's excitement. Three of the four were white, and the fourth was piebald, but all four were alike in the breadth of their deep-chested frames. Dogs like these had been bred for fighting to the death even before Caesar's legions had conquered Britain, and they had undertaken their own wars against bulls and bears and even lions and tigers ever since. Few creatures could withstand a fighting mastiff.

Now the roar of the crowd reached a wild pitch, and in response the two handlers loosed their dogs. There was no signal needed: without a second's pause the four mastiffs rushed simultaneously upon the tethered bear, their heads thrust forward, the jaws agape, and at the rush the crowd went quiet. Then a sort of heavy sigh swept over the arena as the bear set itself to meet the dogs. His great form braced against them like a wall, and as the dogs hurled themselves against him, a swipe from each of his front paws sent two of the attackers rolling in the dirt, one howling from a long red wound along its back while the other lay belly-down where it had fallen, its neck broken from the force of the blow.

The remaining two dogs, joined now by two fresh ones released by another handler, went for the bear's flanks, slashing at them with murderous fangs while the chained animal tried to reach them with its huge paws to punish them as it had already punished their kennelmates. One of the dogs, darting in and out, worried away at the bear's chained leg.

"Oh, but this is unfair!" Damaris exclaimed. "Why doesn't the bear use his own teeth to fight them off?"

"He tries—see how he snaps at them? But his own teeth have been filed down so they can't do any damage. He must depend on his paws alone."

Her eyes flashed. "His teeth have been *filed down?*" she cried indignantly. "But they—those dogs—they are four to one against him!"

"I know. But only look at his size," Robert consoled her. "He has a chance. Consider his height and strength. Just look around you: there's a good deal of betting on him as well as on the dogs, you'll notice."

"Oh yes! Certainly! Betting as to how long he'll survive, most likely," she guessed bitterly. "And the pitiful creature all tied down as he is! Do you call that fair, Robert? Do you?"

"I knew you'd— Don't get into such a pelter about it. Sometimes the bear survives . . ."

Perhaps it was a fairer match than she thought, because at that moment two of the mastiffs gave identical howls as they were hurled across the ring to lie smashed and bloody and motionless. Damaris moaned and covered her eyes to avoid the sight while the cursing ring attendants removed the dead and wounded dogs.

"Oh, thank God that's over at last!" she said faintly, but she had spoken too soon. The audience was roaring again and she looked up, startled. It was not over. The crowd was on its feet and handlers were loosing two more mastiffs at the beleaguered bear. This time he lumbered to an upright position on his hind legs to receive the attack, his great flanks heaving and his mouth open in a grimace which disclosed his useless teeth. The moment he stood, one of the mastiffs went straight for his exposed genitals and hung there, chewing and snarling at the suffering beast's vulnerable member. The bear screamed like a human in its agony and came down again on all fours, slamming the dog to the ground with such force that the brains exploded from its skull.

The first wounded dog and the dead one were now dragged from the ring, and another fresh dog was set onto the visibly tiring bear to maintain the ratio of four to one.

But Damaris could no longer watch. She felt too sick. She fixed her eyes on her own hands, which were tensed in her lap, the stiff fingers quivering on her thighs. An occasional slow tear rolled down her cheeks and she tried to steady her mouth when she became aware of its trembling.

Around her the noise doubled and redoubled as the betting grew wilder. "Five pounds on the bear to last another five minutes! That's a pound a minute, you sporting gentry! What do you say to that? Can you afford to shit or spit on a pound a minute?"

"I'll take odds on the piebald bitch drawing next blood! Come, now! Speak fast or the bet's off! Move, all you sluggards with a few farthings to risk! Move your arses this way! This way, this way!"

"Move your silver, move your brass/Move your gold and move your arse!" (*This* way, if you please, *this* way!")

The cressets, flaring or subsiding with every gust of breeze, lighted the faces around the arena, emphasizing the blackness of cavernous screaming mouths and the gleam of half a thousand eyes. Sweat shone, highlighting cheekbones and jawbones to the likeness of polished skulls. The shorter members of the crowd jumped up and down in place trying to see over the heads of taller ones. Arms and fists waved overhead while bets were bellowed and accepted, and money was passed from hand to hand as wagers were made and paid.

Down on the battleground the dogs were barking in frenzy and the bear roared his pain and rage, but the animals could not even be heard over the human pandemonium. The noise had reached a pitch when betting calls could not be identified more than five or six feet away.

By this time Damaris could feel nausea clamping a grip on her middle and beginning to work up toward her throat, and she knew with certainty that Robert's prediction was on its way to coming true. She tried closing her eyes for a moment in the hope that that might help, but when she reopened them her head swam so that the stars swung wildly overhead and there was a dizzying impression of the scene around her as being all in red and black and surrounded by a ring of smoke and fire like an artist's concept of Hell, a devil's dance of death. Her head drooped, and Robert, watching her closely, saw her eyelids begin to flutter. He stood up swiftly, put an arm about her, and half led, half supported her stumblingly past the knees and feet of the watchers who shared their bench.

Feeling sicker by the moment, she could still be conscious of relief as he walked her out of the bear garden and the outcries and wildness began to die away behind them: her mind began to clear. He was guiding her toward the little wooded park nearby. She tried to speak but he hushed her. "Not now. Not yet. Sit here, Damaris. Sit here . . ." He urged her gently to the ground as they reached the first line of trees and sat down beside her. "Rest your back against this tree trunk. That's the girl, Sweetheart. There, now. Close your eyes—try to breathe deep . . ."

Obediently she did lean back and she did try to breathe deep, but after a moment or two she sat up again sharply. "Oh, you warned me! Yes! You did warn me, Rob!" She wailed it out like a child. Until that moment she had not uttered a sound, but now all at once she turned to him, shaking, clutching at his coat, her face streaming with moonlit tears.

Robert held her, steadying her, trying his best to comfort her with physical closeness. "It's all over, love," he kept telling her. "It's all over now," and he stroked her hair, hoping to soothe her, but she was too deeply distressed to notice.

"No, it isn't over!" By now she was crying so hard she was gasping, almost hysterical, and he watched her unhappily. "It will never be truly over! How can people—why do they—how can they watch those great sad beasts? And call it amusement? Oh, Rob! It was horrible! I've never seen anything so cruel and ugly— in all of my life! And they'll fight again tomorrow night, won't they? And the next night—and all those people will laugh at the pain—and the b-blood—soaking into the dirt—and . . . It will never be over!"

She collapsed into his arms, shivering, and he was silent, holding her, his cheek against her hair, not sure of what to do or say but waiting for her to grow calmer.

It took a while, but at last her crying began to subside and the shaking lessened. Little by little she found herself relaxing, and the tight coil of nausea in her stomach beginning to loosen its hold on her.

Robert seized her hand, covered it strongly with his own, and she looked up at him and gave him her blue-eyed smile, the upcurved fringe of dark lashes still wet with tears.

"Ay, my girl," he muttered huskily, "my sweet girl—"

It was then that he noticed for the first time the odd, unnatural look in her eyes, and since she was now reviving more rapidly he decided to return her to her rooms without further delay. What she needed now, he thought, was rest, rest above all else.

He could not foresee that all during the night she would be drowning in horror-filled dreams of attackers pursuing her with hungry howls for blood as she ran screaming through endless forests with no hope of escape.

At dawn she awoke to a feeling of terror she could not put aside, and rose to confront her own staring eyes in her mirror. She bathed her face with cool water while trying her best to avoid those eyes and the strange little smile that played about her mouth. Then she threw herself back upon her bed, where she remained for the greater part of the day with clenched hands and shaking limbs which would not or could not remain quiet.

When darkness finally refilled her chamber she arose, mechanically shrugged her shoulders into her cloak, and then, letting herself quietly out of the door, she set out alone for the bear garden.

Aleister Crowley

The Testament of Magdalen Blair

ALEISTER CROWLEY *(1875–1947) was an Englishman who culti-vated a reputation as the Beast from the Book of Revelation.* His *infamous exploits as a diabolist, drug addict and participant in orgies and black masses led to writers using Crowley as a model for various sinister characters, most notably* The Magician *by W. Somerset Maugham.* Crowley *wrote a handful of occult stories and novels, including* The Diary of a Drug Fiend, Moonchild *and the following tale, which for years was available only in a pri-vately printed edition.*

WARNING: *"The Testament of Magdalen Blair," which the author claimed to be based on his own personal experience, is monumentally harrowing. If you are extremely nervous, very sen-sitive and/or in poor health,* please do not read this story. *This is* not *reverse psychology to reel you in. I have been reading horror stories for over forty years, but never before encountered any-thing half as chilling or depressing as "The Testament of Magda-len Blair." I hope I never do again.*

PART ONE

[1]

In my third term at Newnham I was already Professor Blair's favourite pupil. Later, he wasted a great deal of time praising my slight figure and my piquant face, with its big round grey eyes and their long black lashes; but the first attraction was my singular gift. Few men, and, I believe, no other women, could approach me on one of the most priceless qualifications for scientific study, the faculty of apprehending minute differences. My memory was poor, extraordinarily so; I had the utmost trouble to enter Cambridge at all. But I could adjust a micrometer better than either students or professor, and read a vernier with an accuracy to which none of them could even aspire. To this I added a faculty of subconscious calculation which was really uncanny. If I were engaged in keeping a solution between (say) 70° and 80° I had no need to watch the thermometer. Automatically I became aware that the mercury was close to the limit, and would go over from my other work and adjust the Bunsen without a thought.

More remarkable still, if any object were placed on my bench without my knowledge and then removed, I could, if asked within a few minutes, describe the object roughly, especially distinguishing the shape of its base and the degree of its opacity to heat and light. From these data I could make a pretty good guess at what the object was.

This faculty of mine was repeatedly tested, and always with success. Extreme sensitiveness to minute degrees of heat was its obvious cause.

I was also a singularly good thought-reader, even at this time. The other girls feared me absolutely. They need not have done so; I had neither ambition nor energy to make use of any of my powers. Even now, when I bring to mankind this message of a doom so appalling that at the age of twenty-four I am a shrivelled, blasted, withered wreck, I am supremely weary, supremely indifferent.

I have the heart of a child and the consciousness of Satan, the lethargy of I know not what disease; and yet, thank—oh! there can be no God!—the resolution to warn mankind to follow my example, and then to explode a dynamite cartridge in my mouth.

[2]

In my third year at Newnham I spent four hours of every day at Professor Blair's house. All other work was neglected, gone through mechanically, if at all. This came about gradually, as the result of an accident.

The chemical laboratory has two rooms, one small and capable of being darkened. On this occasion (the May term of my second year) this room was in use. It was the first week of June, and extremely fine. The door was shut. Within was a girl, alone, experimenting with the galvanometer.

I was absorbed in my own work. Quite without warning I looked up. 'Quick,' said I, 'Gladys is going to faint.' Everyone in the room stared at me. I took a dozen steps towards the door, when the fall of a heavy body sent the laboratory into hysterics.

It was only the heat and confined atmosphere, and Gladys should not have come to work that day at all, but she was easily revived, and then the demonstrator acquiesced in the anarchy that followed. 'How did she know?' was the universal query; for that I knew was evident. Ada Brown *(Athanasia contra mundum)* pooh-poohed the whole affair; Margaret Letchmere thought I must have heard something; perhaps a cry inaudible to the others, owing to their occupied attention; Doris Leslie spoke of second sight, and Amy Gore of 'sympathy.' All the theories, taken together, went round the clock of conjecture. Professor Blair came in at the most excited part of the discussion, calmed the room in two minutes, elicited the facts in five, and took me off to dine with him. 'I believe it's this human thermopile affair of yours,' he said. 'Do you mind if we try a few parlour tricks after dinner?' His aunt, who kept house for him, protested in vain, and was appointed Grand Superintendent in Ordinary of my five senses.

My hearing was first tested, and found normal, or thereabouts. I was then blindfolded, and the aunt (by excess of precaution) stationed between me and the Professor. I found that I could describe even small movements that he made, so long as he was between me and the western window, not at all when he moved round to other quarters. This is in conformity with the 'thermopile' theory; it was contradicted completely on other occasions. The results (in short) were very remarkable and very puzzling; we wasted two precious hours in futile theorizing. In the event, the aunt (cowed by a formidable frown) invited me to spend the Long Vacation in Cornwall.

During these months the Professor and I assiduously worked to discover exactly the nature and limit of my powers. The result, in a sense, was nil.

For one thing, these powers kept on 'breaking out in a new place.' I seemed to do all I did by perception of minute differences; but then it seemed as if I had all sorts of different apparatus. 'One down, t'other come on,' said Professor Blair.

Those who have never made scientific experiments cannot conceive how numerous and subtle are the sources of error, even in the simplest matters. In so obscure and novel a field of research no result is trustworthy until it has been verified a thousand times. In our field we discovered no constants, all variables.

Although we had hundreds of facts any one of which seemed capable of overthrowing all accepted theories of the means of communication between mind and mind, we had nothing, absolutely nothing, which we could use as the basis of a new theory.

It is naturally impossible to give even an outline of the course of our research. Twenty-eight closely written note books referring to the first period are at the disposal of my executors.

[3]

In the middle of the day, in my third year, my father was dangerously ill. I bicycled over to Peterborough at once, never thinking of my work. (My father is a canon of Peterborough Cathedral.) On the third day I received a telegram from Professor Blair, 'Will you be my wife?' I had never realized myself as a woman, or him as a man, till that moment, and in that moment I knew that I loved him and had always loved him. It was a case of what one might call 'love at first absence.' My father recovered rapidly; I returned to Cambridge; we were married during the May week, and went immediately to Switzerland. I beg to be spared any recital of so sacred a period of my life; but I must record one fact.

We were sitting in a garden by Lago Maggiore after a delightful tramp from Chamonix over the Col du Géant to Courmayeur, and thence to Aosta, and so by degrees to Pallanza. Arthur rose, apparently struck by some idea, and began to walk up and down the terrace. I was quite suddenly impelled to turn my head to assure myself of his presence.

This may seem nothing to you who read, unless you have true imagination. But think of yourself talking to a friend in full light, and suddenly leaning forward to touch him. 'Arthur!' I cried, 'Arthur!'

The distress in my tone brought him running to my side. 'What is it, Magdalen?' he cried, anxiety in every word.

I closed my eyes. 'Make gestures!' said I. (He was directly between me and the sun.)

He obeyed, wondering.

'You are—you are—' I stammered—'no! I don't know what you are doing. I am blind!'

He sawed his arm up and down. Useless; I had become absolutely insensitive. We repeated a dozen experiments that night. All failed.

We concealed our disappointment, and it did not cloud our love. The sympathy between us grew even subtler and stronger, but only as it grows between all men and women who love with their whole hearts, and love unselfishly.

[4]

We returned to Cambridge in October, and Arthur threw himself vigorously into the new year's work. Then I fell ill, and the hope we had indulged was disappointed. Worse, the course of the illness revealed a condition which demanded the most complete series of operations which a woman can endure. Not only the past hope, but all future hope, was annihilated.

It was during my convalescence that the most remarkable incident of my life took place.

I was in great pain one afternoon, and wished to see the doctor. The nurse went to the study to telephone for him.

'Nurse!' I said, as she returned, 'don't lie to me. He's not gone to Royston; he's got cancer, and is too upset to come.'

'Whatever next?' said the nurse. 'It's right he can't come, and I was going to tell you he had gone to Royston; but I never heard nothing about no cancer.'

This was true; she had not been told. But the next morning we heard that my 'intuition' was correct.

As soon as I was well enough, we began our experiments again. My powers had returned, and in triple force.

Arthur explained my 'intuition' as follows: 'The doctor (when you last saw him) did not know consciously that he had cancer; but subconsciously Nature gave warning. You read this subconsciously, and it sprang into your consciousness when you read on the nurse's face that he was ill.'

This, far-fetched as it may seem, at least avoids the shallow theories about 'telepathy.'

From this time my powers constantly increased. I could read my husband's thoughts from imperceptible movements of his face as easily as a trained deaf mute can sometimes read the speech of a distant man from the movements of his lips.

Gradually as we worked, day by day, I found my grasp of detail ever fuller. It is not only that I could read emotions; I could tell whether he was thinking 3465822 or 3456822. In the year following my illness, we made 436 experiments of this kind, each extending over several hours; in all 9363, with only 122 failures, and these all, without exception, partial.

The year following, our experiments were extended to a reading of his dreams. In this I proved equally successful. My practice was to leave the room before he woke, write down the dream that he had dreamt, and await him at the breakfast table, where he would compare his record with mine.

Invariably they were identical, with this exception, that my record was always much fuller than his. He would nearly always, however, purport to remember the details supplied by me; but this detail has (I think) no real scientific value.

But what does it all matter, when I think of the horror impending?

[5]

That my only means of discovering Arthur's thought was by muscle-reading became more than doubtful during the third year of our marriage. We practised 'telepathy' unashamedly. We excluded the 'muscle-reader' and the 'super-auditor' and the 'human thermopile' by elaborate precautions; yet still I was able to read every thought of his mind. On our holiday in North Wales at Easter one year we separated for a week, at the end of that week he to be on the leeward, I on the windward side of Tryfan, at the appointed hour, he there to open and read to himself a sealed packet given him by 'some stranger met at Pen-y-Pass during the week.' The experiment was entirely successful; I reproduced every word of the document. If the 'telepathy' is to be vitiated, it is on the theory that I had previously met the 'stranger' and read from him what he would write in such circumstances! Surely direct communication of mind with mind is an easier theory!

Had I known in what all this was to culminate, I suppose I should have gone mad. Thrice fortunate that I can warn humanity of what awaits each one. The greatest benefactor of his race will be he who discovers an explosive indefinitely swifter and more devastating than dynamite. If I could only trust myself to prepare chloride of nitrogen in sufficient quantity . . .

[6]

Arthur became listless and indifferent. The perfection of love that had been our marriage failed without warning, and yet by imperceptible gradations. My awakening to the fact was, however, altogether sudden. It was one summer evening; we were paddling on the Cam. One of Arthur's pupils, also in a Canadian canoe, challenged us to a race. At Magdalen Bridge we were a length ahead—suddenly I heard my husband's thought. It was the most hideous and horrible laugh that it is possible to conceive. No devil could laugh so. I screamed, and dropped my paddle. Both the men thought me ill. I assured myself that it was not the laugh of some townee on the bridge, distorted by my over-sensitive organization. I said no more; Arthur looked grave. At night he asked abruptly after a long period of brooding. 'Was that my thought?' I could only stammer that I did not know.

Incidentally he complained of fatigue, and the listlessness, which before had seemed nothing to me, assumed a ghastly shape. There was something in him that was not he! The indifference had appeared transitory; I now became aware of it as constant and increasing. I was at this time twenty-three years old. You wonder that I write with such serious attitude of mind. I sometimes think that I have never had any thoughts of my own; that I have always been reading the thoughts of another, or perhaps of Nature. I seem only to have been a woman in those first few months of marriage.

[7]

The six months following held for me nothing out of the ordinary, save that six or seven times I had dreams, vivid and terrible. Arthur had no share in these. Yet I knew, I cannot say how, that they were his dreams and not mine; or rather that they were in his subconscious waking self, for one occurred in the afternoon, when he was out shooting, and not in the least asleep.

The last of them occurred towards the end of the October term. He was lecturing as usual, I was at home, lethargic after a too heavy breakfast following a wakeful night. I saw suddenly a picture of the lecture-room, enormously greater than in reality, so that it filled all space; and in the rostrum, bulging over it in all directions, was a vast, deadly pale devil with a face which was a blasphemy on Arthur's. The evil joy of it was indescribable. So wan and bloated, its lips so loose and bloodless; fold after fold of its belly flopping over the rostrum and pushing the students out of the hall, it leered unspeakably. Then dribbled from its mouth these words: 'Ladies and gentlemen, the course is finished. You may go home.' I cannot hope even to suggest the wickedness and filth of these simple expressions. Then, raising its voice to a grating scream, it yelled: 'White of egg! White of egg! White of egg!' again and again for twenty minutes.

The effect on me was shocking. It was as if I had a vision of Hell.

Arthur found me in a very hysterical condition, but soon soothed me. 'Do you know,' he said at dinner, 'I believe I have got a devilish bad chill?'

It was the first time I had known him to complain of his health. In six years he had not had as much as a headache.

I told him my 'dream' when we were in bed, and he seemed unusually grave, as if he understood where I had failed in its interpretation. In the morning he was feverish; I made him stay in bed and sent for the doctor. The same afternoon I learnt that Arthur was seriously ill, had been ill, indeed, for months. The doctor called it Bright's disease.

[8]

I said 'the last of the dreams.' For the next year we travelled, and tried various treatments. My powers remained excellent, but I received none of the subconscious horrors. With few fluctuations, he grew steadily worse; daily he became more listless, more indifferent, more depressed. Our experiments were necessarily curtailed. Only one problem exercised him, the problem of his personality. He began to wonder who he was. I do not mean that he suffered from delusions, I mean that the problem of the true Ego took hold of his imagination. One perfect summer night at Contrexéville he was feeling much better; the symptoms had (temporarily) disappeared almost entirely under the treatment of a very skilful doctor at that Spa, a Dr. Barbézieux, a most kind and thoughtful man.

'I am going to try,' said Arthur, 'to penetrate myself. Am I an animal, and is the world without a purpose? Or am I a soul in a body? Or am I, one and indivisible in some incredible sense, a spark of the infinite light of God? I am going to think inwards; I shall possibly go into some form of trance, unintelligible to myself. You may be able to interpret it.'

The experiment had lasted about half an hour when he sat up gasping with effort.

'I have seen nothing, heard nothing,' I said. 'Not one thought has passed from you to me.'

But at that very moment what had been in his mind flashed into mine.

'It is a blind abyss,' I told him, 'and there hangs in it a vulture vaster than the whole starry system.'

'Yes,' he said, 'that was it. But that was not all. I could not get beyond it. I shall try again.'

He tried. Again I was cut off from his thought, although his face was twitching so that one might have said that anyone might read his mind.

'I have been looking in the wrong place,' said he suddenly, but very quietly and without moving. 'The thing I want lies at the base of the spine.'

This time I saw. In a blue heaven was coiled an infinite snake of gold and green, with four eyes of fire, black fire and red, that darted rays in every direction; held within its coils was a great multitude of laughing children. And even as I looked, all this was blotted out. Crawling rivers of blood spread over the heaven, of blood purulent with nameless forms—mangy dogs with their bowels dragging behind them; creatures half elephant, half beetle; things that were but a ghastly bloodshot eye, set about with leathery tentacles; women whose skins heaved and bubbled like boiling sulphur, giving off clouds that condensed into a thousand other shapes, more hideous than their mother; these were the least of the denizens of these hateful rivers. The most were things impossible to name or to describe.

I was brought back from the vision by the stertorous and strangling breath of Arthur, who had been seized with a convulsion.

From this he never really rallied. The dim sight grew dimmer, the speech slower and thicker, the headaches more persistent and acute.

Torpor succeeded to his old splendid energy and activity; his days became continual lethargy ever deepening towards coma. Convulsions now and then alarmed me for his immediate danger.

Sometimes his breath came hard and hissing like a snake in anger; towards the end it assumed the Cheyne-Stokes type in bursts of ever increasing duration and severity.

In all this, however, he was still himself; the horror that was and yet was not himself did not peer from behind the veil.

'So long as I am consciously myself,' he said in one of his rare fits of brightness, 'I can communicate to you what I am consciously thinking; as soon as this conscious ego is absorbed, you get the subconscious thought which I fear—oh how I fear!—is the greater and truer part of me. You have brought unguessed explanations from the world of sleep; you are the one woman in the world—perhaps there may never be another—who has such an opportunity to study the phenomena of death.'

He charged me earnestly to suppress my grief, to concentrate wholly on the thoughts that passed through his mind when he could no longer express them, and also on those of his subconsciousness when coma inhibited consciousness.

It is this experiment that I now force myself to narrate. The prologue has been long; it has been necessary to put the facts before mankind in a simple way so that they may seize the opportunity of the proper kind of suicide. I beg my readers most earnestly not to doubt my statements; the notes, of our experiments, left in my will to the greatest thinker now living, Professor von Buehle, will make clear the truth of my relation, and the great and terrible necessity of immediate, drastic action.

PART TWO

[1]

The stunning physical fact of my husband's illness was the immense prostration. So strong a body, as too often the convulsions gave proof; such inertia with it! He would lie all day like a log; then without warning or apparent cause the convulsions would begin. Arthur's steady scientific brain stood it well; it was only two days before his death that delirium began. I was not with him, worn out as I was, and yet utterly unable to sleep, the doctor had insisted on my taking a long motor drive. In the fresh air I slumbered. I awoke to hear an unfamiliar voice saying in my ear, 'Now for the fun of the fair!' There was no one there. Quick on its heels followed my husband's voice as I had long since known and loved it, clear, strong, resonant, measured: 'Get this down right; it is very important. I am passing into the power of the subconsciousness. I may not be able to speak to you again. But I am here; I am not to be touched by all that I may suffer; I can always think; you can always read my—' The voice broke off sharply to inquire, 'But will it ever end?' as if someone had spoken to it. And then I heard the laugh. The laugh that I had heard by Magdalen Bridge was heavenly music beside that! The face of Calvin (even) as he gloated over the burning of Servetus would have turned pitiful had he heard it, so perfectly did it express the quintessence of damnation.

Now then my husband's thought seemed to have changed places with the other. It was below, within, withdrawn. I said to myself, 'He is dead!'

Then came Arthur's thought, 'I had better pretend to be mad. It will save her, perhaps; and it will be a change. I shall pretend I have killed her with an axe. Damn it! I hope she is not listening.' I was now thoroughly awake, and told the driver to get home quickly. 'I hope she is killed in the motor; I hope she is smashed into a million pieces. O God! hear my one prayer! Let an anarchist throw a bomb and smash Magdalen into a million pieces! Especially the brain! And the brain first. O God! my first and last prayer; smash Magdalen into a million pieces!'

The horror of this thought was my conviction—then and now—that it represented perfect sanity and coherence of thought. For I dreaded utterly to think what such words might imply.

At the door of the sick-room I was met by the male nurse, who asked me not to enter. Uncontrollably, I asked, 'Is he dead?' and though Arthur lay absolutely senseless on the bed I read the answering thought 'Dead!' silently pronounced in such tones of mockery, horror, cynicism and despair as I never thought to hear. There was a something or somebody who suffered infinitely, and yet who gloated infinitely upon that very suffering. And that something was a veil between me and Arthur.

The hissing breath recommenced; Arthur seemed to be trying to express himself—the self I knew. He managed to articulate feebly, 'Is that the police? Let me get out of the house! The police are coming for me. I killed Magdalen with an axe.' The symptoms of delirium began to appear. 'I killed Magdalen' he muttered a dozen times, then changing to 'Magdalen with' again and again; the voice low, slow, thick, yet reiterated. Then suddenly, quite clear and loud, attempting to rise in the bed: 'I smashed Magdalen into a million pieces with an axe.' After a moment's pause: 'a million is not very many nowadays.' From this—which I now see to have been the speech of a sane Arthur—he dropped again into delirium. 'A million pieces,' 'a cool million,' 'a million million million million million million' and so on; then abruptly: 'Fanny's dog's dead.'

I cannot explain the last sentence to my readers; I may, however, remark that it meant everything to me. I burst into tears. At that moment I caught Arthur's thought, 'You ought to be busy with the notebook, not crying.' I resolutely dried my eyes, took courage, and began to write.

[2]

The doctor came in at this moment and begged me to go and rest. 'You are only distressing yourself, Mrs. Blair,' he said, 'and needlessly, for he is absolutely unconscious and suffers nothing.' A pause. 'My God! why do you look at me like that?' he exclaimed, frightened out of his wits. I think my face had caught something of that devil's, something of that sneer, that loathing, that mire of contempt and stark despair.

I sank back into myself, ashamed already that mere knowledge—and such mean vile knowledge—should so puff one up with hideous pride. No wonder Satan fell! I began to understand all the old legends, and far more—

I told Doctor Kershaw that I was carrying out Arthur's last

wishes. He raised no further opposition; but I saw him sign to the male nurse to keep an eye on me.

The sick man's finger beckoned us. He could not speak; he traced circles on the counterpane. The doctor (with characteristic intelligence) having counted the circles, nodded, and said: 'Yes, it is nearly seven o'clock. Time for your medicine, eh?'

'No,' I explained, 'he means that he is in the seventh circle of Dante's Hell.'

At that instant he entered on a period of noisy delirium. Wild and prolonged howls burst from his throat; he was being chewed unceasingly by 'Dis'; each howl signalled the meeting of the monster's teeth. I explained this to the doctor. 'No,' said he, 'he is perfectly unconscious.'

'Well,' said I, 'he will howl about eighty times more.'

Doctor Kershaw looked at me curiously, but began to count. My calculation was correct.

He turned to me, 'Are you a woman?'

'No,' said I. 'I am my husband's colleague.'

'I think it is suggestion. You have hypnotized him?'

'Never; but I can read his thoughts.'

'Yes, I remember now; I read a very remarkable paper on Mind, two years ago.'

'That was child's play. But let me go on with my work.'

He gave some final instructions to the nurse, and went out.

The suffering of Arthur was at this time unspeakable. Chewed as he was into a mere pulp that passed over the tongue of 'Dis,' each bleeding fragment kept its own identity and his.

The papillae of the tongue were serpents, and each one gnashed its poisoned teeth upon that fodder.

And yet, though the sensorium of Arthur was absolutely unimpaired, indeed hyperaesthetic, his consciousness of pain seemed to depend upon the opening of the mouth. As it closed in mastication, oblivion fell upon him like a thunderbolt. A merciful oblivion? Oh! what a master stroke of cruelty! Again and again he woke from nothing to a hell of agony, of pure ecstasy of agony, until he understood that this would continue for all his life, the alternation was but systole and diastole; the throb of his envenomed pulse, the reflection in consciousness of his blood-beat. I became conscious of his intense longing for death to end the torture.

The blood circulated ever slower and more painfully; I could feel him hoping for the end.

This dreadful rose-dawn suddenly greyed and sickened with doubt. Hope sank to its nadir; fear rose like a dragon, with leaden wings. Suppose, thought he, that after all death does not end me!

I cannot express this conception. It is not that the heart sank, it had no whither to sink; it knew itself immortal, and immortal in a realm of unimagined pain and terror, unlighted by one glimpse of any other light than that pale glare of hate and of pestilence. This thought took shape in these words:

I AM THAT I AM

One cannot say that the blasphemy added to the horror; rather it was the essence of the horror. It was the gnashing of the teeth of a damned soul.

[3]

The demon-shape, which I now clearly recognize as that which had figured in my last 'dream' at Cambridge, seemed to gulp. At that instant a convulsion shook the dying man and a coughing eructation took the 'demon.' Instantly the whole theory dawned on me, that this 'demon' was an imaginary personification of the disease. Now at once I understood demonology, from Bodin and Weirus to the moderns, without a flaw. But was it imaginary or was it real? Real enough to swallow up the 'sane' thought!

At that instant the old Arthur reappeared. 'I am not the monster! I am Arthur Blair, of Fettes and Trinity. I have passed through a paroxysm.'

The sick man stirred feebly. A portion of his brain had shaken off the poison for the moment, and was working furiously against time.

'I am going to die.

'The consolation of death is Religion.

'There is no use for Religion in life.

'How many atheists have I not known sign the articles for the sake of fellowships and livings! Religion in life is either an amusement and a soporific, or a sham and a swindle.

'I was brought up a Presbyterian.

'How easily I drifted into the English Church!

'And now where is God?

'Where is the Lamb of God?

'Where is the Saviour?

'Where is the Comforter?

'Why was I not saved from that devil?

'Is he going to eat me again? To absorb me into him? O fate inconceivably hideous! It is quite clear to me—I hope you've got it down, Magdalen—that the demon is made of all those that have died of Bright's disease. There must be different ones for each disease. I thought I once caught sight of a coughing bog of bloody slime.

'Let me pray.'

A frenzied appeal to the Creator followed. Sincere as it was, it would read like irreverence in print.

And then there came the cold-drawn horror of stark blasphemy against this God—who would not answer.

Followed the bleak black agony of the conviction—the absolute certitude—'There is no God!' combined with a wave of frenzied wrath against the people who had so glibly assured him that there was, an almost maniac hope that they would suffer more than he, if it were possible.

(Poor Arthur! He had not yet brushed the bloom off Suffering's grape; he was to drink its fiercest distillation to the dregs.)

'No!' thought he, 'perhaps I lack their "faith."

'Perhaps if I could really persuade myself of God and Christ—perhaps if I could deceive myself, could make believe—'

Such a thought is to surrender one's honesty, to abdicate one's reason. It marked the final futile struggle of his will.

The demon caught and crunched him, and the noisy delirium began anew.

My flesh and blood rebelled. Taken with a deathly vomit, I rushed from the room, and resolutely, for a whole hour, diverted my sensorium from thought. I had always found that the slightest trace of tobacco smoke in a room greatly disturbed my power. On this occasion I puffed cigarette after cigarette with excellent effect. I knew nothing of what had been going on.

[4]

Arthur, stung by the venomous chyle, was tossing in that vast arched belly, which resembled the dome of Hell, churned in its bubbling slime. I felt that he was not only disintegrated mechanically, but chemically, that his being was loosened more and more into parts, that these were being absorbed into new and hateful things, but that (worst of all) Arthur stood immune from all, behind it, unimpaired, memory and reason ever more acute as ever new and ghastlier experience informed them. It seemed to me as if some mystic state were super-added to the torment; for while he was not, emphatically not, this tortured mass of consciousness, yet that was he. There are always at least two of us! The one who feels and the one who knows are not radically one person. This double personality is enormously accentuated at death.

Another point was that the time-sense, which with men is usually so reliable—especially in my own case—was decidedly deranged, if not abrogated altogether.

We all judged of the lapse of time in relation to our daily habits or some similar standard. The conviction of immortality must naturally destroy all values for this sense. If I am immortal, what is the difference between a long time and a short time? A thousand years and a day are obviously the same thing from the point of view of 'for ever.'

There is a subconscious clock in us, a clock wound up by the experience of the race to go for seventy years or so. Five minutes is a very long time to us if we are waiting for an omnibus, an age if we are waiting for a lover, nothing at all if we are pleasantly engaged or sleeping.*

We think of seven years as a long time in connection with penal servitude; as a negligibly small period in dealing with geology.

But, given immortality, the age of the stellar system itself is nothing.

This conviction had not fully impregnated the consciousness of Arthur; it hung over him like a threat, while the intensification of that consciousness, its liberation from the sense of time natural to life, caused each act of the demon to appear of vast duration, although the intervals between the howls of the body on the bed were very short. Each pang of torture or suspense was born, rose to its crest, and died to be reborn again through what seemed countless aeons.

Still more was this the case in the process of his assimilation by the 'demon.' The coma of the dying man was a phenomenon altogether out of time. The conditions of 'digestion' were new to Arthur, he had no reason to suppose, no data from which to calculate the distance of, an end. It is impossible to do more than sketch this process; as he was absorbed, so did his consciousness expand into that of the 'demon'; he became one with all its hunger and corruption. Yet always did he suffer as himself in his own person the tearing asunder of his finest molecules; and this was confirmed by a most filthy humiliation of that part of him that was rejected.

I shall not attempt to describe the final process; suffice it that the demoniac consciousness drew away; he was but the excrement of the demon, and as that excrement he was flung filthily

---

* It is one of the greatest cruelties of nature that all painful or depressing emotions seem to lengthen time; pleasant thoughts and exalted moods make time fly. Thus, in summing up a life from an outside standpoint, it would seem that, supposing pleasure and pain to have occupied equal periods, the impression would be that pain was enormously greater than pleasure. This may be controverted. Virgil writes: 'Forsitan haec olim meminisse juvabit,' and there is at least one modern writer thoroughly conversant with pessimism who is very optimistic. But the new facts which I here submit overthrow the whole argument; they cast a sword of infinite weight on that petty trembling scale.

further into the abyss of blackness and of night whose name is death.

I rose with ashen cheeks. I stammered: 'He is dead.' The male nurse bent over the body. 'Yes!' he echoed, 'he is dead.' And it seemed as if the whole Universe gathered itself into one ghastly laugh of hate and horror. 'Dead!'

[5]

I resumed my seat. I felt that I must know that all was well, that death had ended all. Woe to humanity! The consciousness of Arthur was more alive than ever. It was the black fear of falling, a dumb ecstasy of changeless fear. There were no waves upon that sea of shame, no troubling of those accursed waters by any thought. There was no hope of any ground to that abyss, no thought that it might stop. So tireless was that fall that even acceleration was absent; it was constant and level as the fall of a star. There was not even a feeling of pace; infinitely fast as it must be, judging from the peculiar dread which it inspired, it was yet infinitely slow, having regard to the infinitude of the abyss.

I took measures not to be disturbed by the duties that men—how foolishly!—pay to the dead; and I took refuge in a cigarette.

It was now for the first time, strangely enough, that I began to consider the possibility of helping him.

I analysed the position. It must be his thought, or I could not read it. I had no reason to conjecture that any other thoughts could reach me. He must be alive in the true sense of the word; it was he and not another that was the prey of this fear ineffable. Of this fear it was evident that there must be a physical basis in the constitution of his brain and body. All the other phenomena had been shown to correspond exactly with a physical condition; it was the reflection in a consciousness from which human limitation had fallen away, of things actually taking place in the body.

It was a false interpretation perhaps; but it was his interpretation; and it was that which caused suffering so beyond all that poets have ever dreamt of the infernal.

I am ashamed to say that my first thought was of the Catholic

Church and its masses for the repose of the dead. I went to the Cathedral, revolving as I went all that had ever been said—the superstitions of a hundred savage tribes. At bottom I could find no difference between their barbarous rites and those of Christianity.

However that might be, I was baffled. The priests refused to pray for the soul of a heretic.

I hurried back to the house, resumed my vigil. There was no change, except a deepening of the fear, an intensification of the loneliness, a more utter absorption in the shame. I could but hope that in the ultimate stagnation of all vital forces, death would become final, hell merged into annihilation.

This started a train of thought which ended in a determination to hasten the process. I thought of blowing out the brains, remembered that I had no means of doing so. I thought of freezing the body, imagined a story for the nurse, reflected that no cold could excite in his soul aught icier than that illimitable void of black.

I thought of telling the doctor that he had wished to bequeath his body to the surgeons, that he had been afraid of being buried alive, anything that might induce him to remove the brain. At that moment I looked into the mirror. I saw that I must not speak. My hair was white, my face drawn, my eyes wild and bloodshot.

In utter helplessness and misery, I flung myself on the couch in the study, and puffed greedily at cigarettes. The relief was so immense that my sense of loyalty and duty had a hard fight to get me to resume the task. The mingling of horror, curiosity, and excitement must have aided.

I threw away my fifth cigarette, and returned to the death chamber.

[6]

Before I had sat at the table ten minutes a change burst out with startling suddenness. At one point in the void the blackness gathered, concentrated, sprang into an evil flame that gushed aimlessly forth from nowhere into nowhere.

This was accompanied by the most noxious stench.

It was gone before I could realize it. As lightning precedes thunder, it was followed by a hideous clamour that I can only describe as the cry of a machine in pain.

This recurred constantly for an hour and five minutes, then ceased as suddenly as it began. Arthur still fell.

It was succeeded after the lapse of five hours by another paroxysm of the same kind, but fiercer and more continuous. Another silence followed, age upon age of fear and loneliness and shame.

About midnight there appeared a grey ocean of bowels below the falling soul. This ocean seemed to be limitless. It fell headlong into it, and the splash awakened it to a new consciousness of things.

This sea, though infinitely cold, was boiling like tubercles. Itself a more or less homogeneous slime, the stench of which is beyond all human conception (human language is singularly deficient in words that describe smell and taste; we always refer our sensations to things generally known)* it constantly budded into greenish boils with angry red craters, whose jagged edges were of a livid white; and from these issued pus formed of all things known of man—each one distorted, degraded, blasphemed.

Things innocent, things happy, things holy! Every one unspeakably defiled, loathsome, sickening! During the vigil of the day following I recognized one group. I saw Italy. First the Italy

---

* This is my general complaint, and that of all research students on the one hand and imaginative writers on the other. We can only express a new idea by combining two or more old ideas, or by the use of metaphor; just so any number can be formed from two others. James Hinton had undoubtedly a perfectly crisp, simple, and concise idea of the 'fourth dimension of space,' he found the utmost difficulty in conveying it to others, even when they were advanced mathematicians. It is (I believe) the greatest factor that militates against human progress that great men assume that they will be understood by others.

Even such a master of lucid English as the late Professor Huxley has been so vitally misunderstood that he has been attacked repeatedly for affirming propositions which he specifically denied in the clearest language.

of the map, a booted leg. But this leg changed rapidly through myriad phases. It was in turn the leg of every beast and bird, and in every case each leg was suffering with all diseases from leprosy and elephantiasis to scrofula and syphilis. There was also the consciousness that this was inalienably and for ever part of Arthur.

Then Italy itself, in every detail foul. Then I myself, seen as every woman that has ever been, each one with every disease and torture that Nature and man have plotted in their hellish brains, each ended with a death, a death like Arthur's, whose infinite pangs were added to his own, recognized and accepted as his own.

The same with our child that never was. All children of all nations, incredibly aborted, deformed, tortured, torn in pieces, abused by every foulness that the imagination of an arch-devil could devise.

And so for every thought. I realized that the putrefactive changes in the dead man's brain were setting in motion every memory of his, and smearing them with hell's own paint.

I timed one thought, despite its myriad million details, each one clear, vivid and prolonged, it occupied but three seconds of earthly time. I considered the incalculable array of the thoughts in his well-furnished mind; I saw that thousands of years would not exhaust them.

But, perhaps, when the brain was destroyed beyond recognition of its component parts—

We have always casually assumed that consciousness depends upon a proper flow of blood in the vessels of the brain; we have never stopped to think whether the records might not be excited in some other manner. And yet we know how tumour of the brain begets hallucinations. Consciousness works strangely; the least disturbance of the blood supply, and it goes out like a candle, or else takes monstrous forms.

Here was the overwhelming truth; in death man lives again, and lives for ever. Yet we might have thought of it; the phantasmagoria of life which throng the mind of a drowning man might have suggested something of the sort to any man with a sympathetic and active imagination.

Worse even than the thoughts themselves was the apprehension of the thoughts ere they arose. Carbuncles, boils, ulcers, cancers, there is no equivalent for these pustules of the bowels of hell, into whose seething convulsions Arthur sank, deeper, ever deeper.

The magnitude of this experience is not to be apprehended by the human mind as we know it. I was convinced that an end must come, for me, with the cremation of the body. I was infinitely glad that he had directed this to be done. But for him, end and beginning seemed to have no meaning. Through it all I seemed to hear the real Arthur's thought. 'Though all this is I, yet it is only an accident of me; I stand behind it all, immune, eternal.'

It must not be supposed that this in any way detracted from the intensity of the suffering. Rather it added to it. To be loathsome is less than to be linked to loathsomeness. To plunge into impurity is to become deadened to disgust. But to do so and yet remain pure—every vileness adds a pang. Think of Madonna imprisoned in a body of a prostitute, and compelled to acknowledge 'This is I,' while never losing her abhorrence. Not only immured in hell, but compelled to partake of its sacraments; not only high priest at its agapae, but begetter and manifestor of its cult; a Christ nauseated at the kiss of Judas, and yet aware that the treachery was his own.

[7]

As the putrefaction of the brain advanced, the bursting of the pustules occasionally overlapped, with the result that the confusion and exaggeration of madness with all its poignancy was super-added to the simpler hell. One might have thought that any confusion would have been a welcome relief to a lucidity so appalling; but this was not so. The torture was infused with a shattering sense of alarm.

The images rose up threatening, disappeared only by blasting themselves into pultaceous coprolite which was, as it were, the main body of the army which composed Arthur. Deeper and deeper as he dropped the phenomena grew constantly in every sense. Now they were a jungle in which the obscurity and terror of the whole gradually overshadowed even the abhorrence due to every part.

The madness of the living is a thing so abominable and fearful as to chill every human heart with horror; it is less than nothing in comparison with the madness of the dead!

A further complication now arose, in the destruction irrevocable and complete of that compensating mechanism of the brain, which is the basis of the sense of time. Hideously distorted and deformed as it had been in the derangement of the brain like a shapeless jelly shooting out, of a sudden, vast, unsuspected tentacles, the destruction of it cut a thousandfold deeper. The sense of consecution itself was destroyed; things sequent appeared as things superposed or concurrent spatially; a new dimension unfolded; a new destruction of all limitation exposed a new and unfathomable abyss.

To all the rest was added the bewilderment and fear which earthly agoraphobia faintly shadows forth; and at the same time the close immurement weighted upon him, since from infinitude there can be no escape.

Add to this the hopelessness of the monotony of the situation. Infinitely as the phenomena were varied, they were yet recognized as essentially the same. All human tasks are lightened by the certainty that they must end. Even our joys would be intolerable were we convinced that they must endure, through irksomeness and disgust, through weariness and satiety, even for ever and for evermore. In this inhuman, this praeterdiabolic inferno was a wearisome repetition, a harping on the same hateful discord, a continuous nagging whose intervals afforded no relief, only a suspense brimming with the anticipation of some fresh terror.

For hours which were to him eternities this stage continued as each cell that held the record of a memory underwent the degenerative changes which awoke it into hyperbromic purulence.

[8]

The minute bacterial corruption now assumed a gross chemistry. The gases of putrefaction forming in the brain and interpenetrating it were represented in his consciousness by the denizens of the pustules becoming formless and impersonal—Arthur had not yet fathomed the abyss.

Creeping, winding, embracing, the Universe enfolded him, violated him with a nameless and intimate contamination, involved his being in a more suffocating terror.

Now and again it drowned that consciousness in a gulf which his thought could not express to me; and indeed the first and least of his torments is utterly beyond human expression.

It was a woe ever expanded, ever intensified, by each vial of wrath. Memory increased, and understanding grew; the imagination had equally got rid of limit.

What this means who can tell? The human mind cannot really appreciate numbers beyond a score or so; it can deal with numbers by ratiocination, it cannot apprehend them by direct impression. It requires a highly trained intelligence to distinguish between fifteen and sixteen matches on a plate without counting them. In death this limitation is entirely removed. Of the infinite content of the Universe every item was separately realized. The brain of Arthur had become equal in power to that attributed by theologians to the Creator; yet of executive power there was no seed. The impotence of man before circumstance was in him magnified indefinitely, yet without loss of detail or of mass. He understood that The Many was The One without losing or fusing the conception of either. He was God, but a God irretrievably damned; a being infinite, yet limited by the nature of things, and that nature solely compact of loathliness.

[9]

I have little doubt that the cremation of my husband's body cut short a process which in the normally buried man continues until no trace of organic substance remains.

The first kiss of the furnace awoke an activity so violent and so vivid that all the past paled in its lurid light.

The quenchless agony of the pang is not to be described; if alleviation there were, it was but the exultation of feeling that this was final.

Not only time, but all expansions of time, all monsters of time's womb were to be annihilated; even the ego might hope some end.

The ego is the 'worm that dieth not,' and existence the 'fire that is not quenched.' Yet in this universal pyre, in this barathrum of liquid lava, jetted from the volcanoes of the infinite, this 'lake of fire that is reserved for the devil and his angels,' might not one at last touch bottom? Ah! but time was no more, neither any eidolon thereof!

The shell was consumed; the gases of the body, combined and recombined, flamed off, free from organic form.

Where was Arthur?

His brain, his individuality, his life, were utterly destroyed. As separate things, yes: Arthur had entered the universal consciousness.

And I heard this utterance; or rather this is my translation into English of a single thought whose synthesis is 'Woe.'

Substance is called spirit or matter.

Spirit and matter are one, indivisible, eternal, indestructible.

Infinite and eternal change!

Infinite and eternal pain!

No absolute; no truth, no beauty, no idea, nothing but the whirlwinds of form, unresting, unappeasable.

Eternal hunger! Eternal war! Change and pain infinite and increasing.

There is no individuality but in illusion. And the illusion is change and pain, and its destruction is change and pain, and its new segregation from the infinite and eternal is change and pain; and substance infinite and eternal is change and pain unspeakable.

Beyond thought, which is change and pain, lies being, which is change and pain.

These were the last words intelligible; they lapsed into the eternal moan, Woe! Woe! Woe! Woe! Woe! Woe! Woe! in unceasing monotony that rings always in my ears if I let my thought fall from the height of activity, listen to the voice of my sensorium.

In my sleep I am partially protected, and I keep a lamp constantly alight to burn tobacco in the room; yet too often my dreams throb with that reiterated Woe! Woe! Woe! Woe! Woe! Woe! Woe!

[10]

The final stage is clearly enough inevitable, unless we believe the Buddhist theories, which I am somewhat inclined to do, as their theory of the Universe is precisely confirmed in every detail by the facts here set down. But it is one thing to recognize a disease, another to discover a remedy. Frankly my whole being revolts from their methods, and I had rather acquiesce in the ultimate destiny and achieve it as quickly as may be. My earnest preoccupation is to avoid the preliminary tortures, and I am convinced that the explosion of a dynamite cartridge in the mouth is the most practicable method of effecting this. There is just the possibility that if all thinking minds, all 'spiritual beings,' were thus destroyed, and especially if all organic life could be annihilated, the Universe might cease to be, since (as Bishop Berkeley has shown) it can only exist in some thinking mind. And there is really no evidence (in spite of Berkeley) for the existence of any extra-human consciousness. Matter in itself may think, in a sense, but its monotony of woe is less awful than its abomination, the building up of high and holy things only to drag them through infamy and terror to the old abyss.

I shall consequently cause this record to be widely distributed. The notebooks of my work with Arthur (Vols. I–CCXIV) will be edited by Professor von Buehle, whose marvellous mind may perhaps discover some escape from the destiny which menaces mankind. Everything is in order in these notebooks; and I am free to die, for I can endure no more, and above all things I dread the onset of illness, and the possibility of natural or accidental death.

NOTES

I am glad to have the opportunity of publishing, in a medium so widely read by the medical profession, the MS. of the widow of the late Professor Blair.

Her mind undoubtedly became unhinged through grief at her husband's death; the medical man who attended him in his last illness grew alarmed at her condition, and had her watched. She tried (fruitlessly) to purchase dynamite at several shops, but on her going to the laboratory of her late husband, and attempting to manufacture chloride of nitrogen, obviously for the purpose of suicide, she was seized, certified insane, and placed in my care. The case is most unusual in several respects.

1. I have never known her inaccurate in any statement of verifiable fact.

2. She can undoubtedly read thoughts in an astonishing manner. In particular, she is actually useful to me by her ability to foretell attacks of acute insanity in my patients. Some hours before they occur she can predict them to a minute. On an early occasion my disbelief in her power led to the dangerous wounding of one of my attendants.

3. She combines a fixed determination of suicide (in the extraordinary manner described by her) with an intense fear of death. She smokes uninterruptedly, and I am obliged to allow her to fumigate her room at night with the same drug.

4. She is certainly only twenty-four years old, and any competent judge would with equal certainty declare her sixty.

5. Professor von Buehle, to whom the notebooks were sent, addressed to me a long and urgent telegram, begging her release on condition that she would promise not to commit suicide, but go to work with him in Bonn. I have yet to learn, however, that German professors, however eminent, have any voice in the management of a private asylum in England, and I am certain that the

Lunacy Commissioners will uphold me in my refusal to consider the question.

It will then be clearly understood that this document is published with all reserve as the lucubration of a very peculiar, perhaps unique, type of insanity.

V. ENGLISH, M.D.

Note

"Revised Expectations" (pp. 74–82)

Great Expectations is the first-person narrative of Pip, a humble, sweet-natured English boy raised by his shrewish sister and her husband, Joe, the village blacksmith. An escaped convict, Abel Magwitch, terrifies Pip into stealing food for him from his sister's larder. Though Magwitch is caught, the boy does not complain of the way he was treated. Later, he is introduced into the household of the wealthy eccentric, Miss Havisham, as a playmate for her young ward, Estella. Because she was jilted on her bridal night, Miss Havisham vengefully encourages Estella to use her beauty as a means of snaring and tormenting men. In spite of her disdain, Pip falls deeply in love with her. When a mysterious sponsor offers Pip the means of going to London to learn how to be a gentleman, the youth promptly resigns his intention to be his blacksmith brother-in-law's partner and leaves his hometown, believing that Miss Havisham is bankrolling his education in order for him to become "good enough" to wed Estella. His great expectations crumble when, years later, he discovers his benefactor is really Magwitch. Estella marries an unworthy boor, and Pip resigns himself to a humbler life than he'd hoped for.

In "Revised Expectations," Kathleen C. Szaj voices the romantic frustration of many readers (including me) when she attempts to "matchmake" Pip and Estella. Dickens himself had second thoughts on the subject. The novel's original ending had Pip and Estella meet by chance some years later. Her abusive first husband has died; she has remarried a worthier man, and Pip's final words are "I was very glad afterwards to have had the interview; for, in her face and in her voice, and in her touch, she gave me the assurance, that suffering had been stronger than Miss Havisham's teaching, and had given her a heart to understand what my heart used to be."

According to *The Oxford Companion to English Literature*, Dickens listened to the advice of fellow writer Edward Bulwer-Lytton when he revised the novel's conclusion and had a sadder, wiser Pip and Estella meet in the ruins of Miss Havisham's house, presumably to live semihappily ever after. But as editor-scholar Angus Calder points out in the Penguin Books edition of *Great Expectations*, a careful reading of the more familiar revised ending closes with masterful ambiguity: "I saw no shadow of another parting from her." Does that mean they will never again part . . . or never meet again?

Dickens himself might have endorsed the satisfyingly romantic solution to Pip's problem that director David Lean employed at the climax of his excellent 1946 film version of *Great Expectations*.

Acknowledgments

Special thanks to my mother-in-law, Rose Bransdorf, for suggesting the theme of this collection. Regrettably, she died before its publication.

"The Problem of the Country Mailbox" copyright © 1994 by Edward D. Hoch, first published in *Ellery Queen's Mystery Magazine*. Reprinted by permission of the author.

"The Sins of the Father" copyright © 1997 by Carole Buggé. All rights reserved. Permission granted by the author.

"The Moving Finger Types" copyright © 1968 by Mercury Press, Inc. Reprinted by permission of the author.

"The Story of Obbok" copyright © 1973 by Stuart David Schiff. Originally published December 1973 in *Whispers* #2. Reprinted by permission of the author.

"Revised Expectations" copyright © 1997 by Kathleen C. Szaj. All rights reserved. Permission granted by the author.

"The Pandora Heart" copyright © 1997 by Tanith Lee. All rights reserved. Permission granted by the author.

"Don't Open That Book!" copyright © 1997 by Patricia Mullen. All rights reserved. Permission granted by the author.

"Genesis for Dummies" copyright © 1997 by Patrick LoBrutto. All rights reserved. Permission granted by the author.

"Message from Hell" copyright © 1989 by Terminus Publishing Company, Inc. Permission granted by The Pimlico Agency.

"Turn the Page" copyright © 1957, 1985 by the Estate of Zenna

Henderson; first appeared in *The Magazine of Fantasy and Science Fiction*. Reprinted by permission of the author's Estate and the Estate's agent, Virginia Kidd.

"Become So Shining That We Cease to Be" copyright © 1991 by Chelsea Quinn Yarbro; first publication in *The World Horror Convention Program Book*. Reprinted by permission of the author.

"The Resurrection" copyright © 1997 by Christine Jacobsen. All rights reserved. Permission granted by the author.

"The Confession of Brother Blaise" copyright © 1986 by Jane Yolen; originally appeared in *Merlin's Booke* (Ace Fantasy Books). Reprinted by permission of Curtis Brown, Ltd.

"Never Again the Same" copyright © 1997 by L. Jagi Lamplighter. All rights reserved. Permission granted by the author.

"The Temple" copyright © 1925 Popular Fiction Publishing Co., first published in the September 1925 issue of *Weird Tales*. Reprinted by permission of Arkham House Publishers, Inc.

"The Green Thumb" copyright © 1997 by John Betancourt. All rights reserved. Permission granted by the author.

"Famous First Words" copyright © 1964 by Mercury Press, Inc.; first published in the January 1965 issue of *The Magazine of Fantasy and Science Fiction*. Reprinted by permission of the author's agent, Nat Sobel.

"I Am a Fine Musician . . ." copyright © 1997 by Roberta Rogow. All rights reserved. Permission granted by the author.

"Obituary" copyright © 1959 by Mercury Press, Inc.; first appeared in the August 1959 issue of *The Magazine of Fantasy and Science Fiction*. Reprinted by permission of The Estate of Isaac Asimov c/o Ralph M. Vicinanza, Ltd.

"One-Shot Beamish and His Wonderful Feminals" copyright © 1981 by Jay Rothbell (Sheckley); first appeared in the May 1981 issue of "Gallery." Reprinted by permission of the author.

"Patent Pending" copyright © 1957 by Arthur C. Clarke; from *Tales of the White Hart* (Ballantine Books). Reprinted by per-